Samuel Richardson (1689–1761) was born in Derbyshire to a joiner and received little formal education; in 1706 he was apprenticed to a printer in London. Thirteen years later, he set himself up as a stationer and printer and became one of the leading figures in the trade. At the age of fifty, he turned his hand to writing. His epistolary novels—including his masterpiece, *Clarissa, or The History of a Young Lady* (1747–48)—brought him great success and a bevy of admirers.

Sheila Ortiz-Taylor is Francis G. Townsend Professor of English at Florida State University, where she has taught the British and American novel, as well as creative writing and women's literature, since receiving her Ph.D. from UCLA in 1973. A former Fulbright Fellow, she is author of four novels, including *Faultline* and *Coachella*.

SAMUEL RICHARDSON

CLARISSA

or
The History of a Young Lady

NEWLY ABRIDGED AND WITH A
NEW INTRODUCTION BY
SHEILA ORTIZ-TAYLOR

SIGNET CLASSICS

SIGNET CLASSICS
Published by New American Library, a division of
Penguin Group (USA) Inc., 375 Hudson Street,
New York, New York 10014, USA
Penguin Group (Canada), 90 Eglinton Avenue East, Suite 700, Toronto,
Ontario M4P 2Y3, Canada (a division of Pearson Penguin Canada Inc.)
Penguin Books Ltd., 80 Strand, London WC2R 0RL, England
Penguin Ireland, 25 St. Stephen's Green, Dublin 2,
Ireland (a division of Penguin Books Ltd.)
Penguin Group (Australia), 250 Camberwell Road, Camberwell, Victoria 3124,
Australia (a division of Pearson Australia Group Pty. Ltd.)
Penguin Books India Pvt. Ltd., 11 Community Centre, Panchsheel Park,
New Delhi - 110 017, India
Penguin Group (NZ), cnr Airborne and Rosedale Roads, Albany,
Auckland 1310, New Zealand (a division of Pearson New Zealand Ltd.)
Penguin Books (South Africa) (Pty.) Ltd., 24 Sturdee Avenue,
Rosebank, Johannesburg 2196, South Africa

Penguin Books Ltd., Registered Offices:
80 Strand, London WC2R 0RL, England

Published by Signet Classics, an imprint of New American Library,
a division of Penguin Group (USA) Inc.

First Signet Classics Printing, October 2005
10 9 8 7 6 5 4 3 2

Introduction

I

Novels fascinate us because they mirror back to us our own lives, which we perceive as hurried and unintelligible, yet somehow strangely significant. Characters in novels stand in for real people, so we watch them with interest as they struggle within a stream of events marked in the beginning by the phrase *Once upon a time* and rounded at the end with the phrase *And they all lived happily ever after*. We may learn something vicariously by attending to their dilemmas and even experience a kind of consolation, a sense of solidarity, as Joseph Conrad envisioned it, with humankind.* Among the many preoccupations shared by people and characters is time.

Characters, like real people, are preoccupied with time. Each of us has a personal relationship with time, and each of us experiences the trajectory of a life determined by time, though that understanding may flicker within us uncertainly and only on occasion. Reading a novel permits us to carefully observe this compelling phenomenon through a distancing lens. Novels throw illuminating light on temporal dimensions because time works both as subject matter and as form.

This is particularly true of *Clarissa*, which though it records the events of a single year, does so with such density, such attention to detail, that we feel we have lived a whole year of real time in reading it. And in fact, because the novel was published over the space of a year, none of Richardson's contemporaries could possibly read Clarissa's experience faster than she could live it.

Richardson once characterized his technique as "this

---

*See Joseph Conrad, Preface to *The Nigger of the "Narcissus"* (1897; New York: Oxford University Press, 1985).

way of writing, to the moment."* The effect is an almost
cinematic focus on the present, yet with a curious preoc-
cupation with the perpetually reconstructed past and an
anxiety about the unknowable future. Something could
happen at any minute. Anything. Teetering on the present, reaching backward for support, eyes on the future,
the characters reel from moment to moment. This reel-
ing is the emotional atmosphere of *Clarissa*, but it is also
its intellectual content.

The language of the letters is tentative, speculative,
and wondering. The characters formulate and revise
their wishes, but they may be blocked by the wishes and
particularly by the strategies of others. Everyone wants
his or her own way.

The struggle for power rages over a reality that is
disputed territory. The world of *Clarissa* is presented
subjectively, with subjectivity itself becoming part of
our wondering inquiry—for in epistolary novels the
reader can never directly experience what actually happened. Instead, what happened must be reconstructed
for us, after the fact, by witnesses at various removes
from the action itself, witnesses with convoluted motives and varying degrees of credibility. Consequently,
our attention is not on what happened but instead on
what the different characters *believe* happened, or even
what they believe from one moment to the next. Evidence, after all, is perpetually trickling in, filtered
through mood and different perceptual biases. Characters may misrepresent their own feelings or actions;
Lovelace frequently lies. It is important to notice,
though, that each of the two main characters, Clarissa
and Lovelace, promise to their correspondents, Anna
Howe and John Belford, that they will tell them the
truth as far as they know it.

Both Lovelace and Clarissa return obsessively to re-
constructions of a past that can never be laid to rest

*From a letter to Lady Bradshaigh, 1756, unpublished correspon-
dence in the Forster Collection, vol. II.f.80, Victoria and Albert
Museum, London. Available on microfilm in the Research Publica-
tions series, Primary Source Microfilm, Gale Group, Woodbridge,
CT.

because it can never be objectively known or described. The letters function—for each—as a kind of history, a possible basis for interpreting the course of events leading up to the fictional present. They inhabit a world where reality resides only in text, in letters, and in the various ways they can be read and reread. When Clarissa turns over to Belford the collection of letters that constitutes her part of the novel, it is for the purpose of establishing the truth for her community and by implication for all readers, now and forever. Her correspondence functions as evidence. For Clarissa, "the pen is a witness on record" (L183).

Much of what Richardson himself considered to be the excessive length of his novel arises thematically out of this uncertainty over what actually happened and why. Notice that the novel begins with Anna Howe asking what passed between Lovelace and her brother that caused the domestic crisis that propels the novel. The opening duel is visited and revisited by all the characters until the concluding duel puts an end to all speculation. The time bracketed by the two duels represents a temporal nexus where future and past cross and recross.

Length arises too out of Clarissa and Lovelace's shared belief in the efficacy of delay. Once one commits to a particular course, then the number of available options necessarily diminishes. But delay offers opportunity to investigate alternative courses, to gather advice, to reexamine evidence, and most important, to change one's mind.

As in soap opera, the characters in this novel live suspended in thought and supposition, having no employment beyond accounting for the past and speculating on the future. They talk, they write, they feel, they plan, and above all, they manipulate one another and the facts of their shared existences.

For Clarissa and Lovelace the prime manipulations involve time and love or, if not love, then attraction. Clarissa admits to Anna Howe that she feels for Lovelace a "conditional kind of liking" (L28). The condition in question involves Lovelace's reformation. His values, those of the rake, conflict violently with her own, those of the pure maiden. If he is to have her, he must reform.

Re-form. Rather than loving the man he is, she loves the man he must become in the future in order to justify that love.

Meanwhile, Lovelace sets up his own conditions for Clarissa. Her virtue must be tested, not once but twice. If "ruined," he predicts, she will behave like all the other women whose virtue he has tried: She will accommodate herself to her situation and will grow to love him. Like Clarissa's, his "love" is based on a mistaken concept of the person the beloved might become rather than who that beloved is at the present moment.

Their conflicting values necessarily pull them in opposing directions, an oppositional dynamic that is underscored by their radically different conceptions of time. For Lovelace, time is an open-ended stream and can therefore be carefully navigated to his own advantage. His repeated phrase "a wife at any time" (L99) illustrates that for him marriage is *always* an option, though one that he hopes he will not be forced into. Whatever happens, with this one stroke he will always be able to "mend" his transgression against Clarissa. In this essentially comic view of existence, bad actions in the present are not necessarily visited by bad consequences in the future.

For Clarissa time is a closed-ended narration, even a tragedy. She underscores the irrevocability of time's linear trajectory when she asks Lovelace, "Canst thou call back time?" (L266). The question is rhetorical; she knows he cannot call time back, although he never agrees this is so.

This fundamental disagreement concerning the nature of time, taking place *over* time, deepens the widening abyss between them and fuels the dramatic tension that ultimately consumes them both. The ferocity of Clarissa and Lovelace's conditional love leaves behind an afterglow that no reader can ever quite forget.

II

> *"And I have run into such a length!—And am such*
> *a sorry pruner, though greatly luxuriant, that I am*
> *apt to add three pages for one I take away!"*
> —Samuel Richardson*

An abridgment necessarily reduces or all but elimi-
nates the important fact of the characters' mental and
psychological restlessness concerning the nature of reality. Their iteration and reiteration of the past, after all,
is their life's blood.

Certainly too what the abridger removes from the text
depends on her/his sensibilities, preconceptions, and assumptions. In effect the text in the reader's hands represents the abridger's interpretation of the text, much as
the orchestral performance heard by a music lover represents not so much what the composer wrote as how the
orchestra leader interprets that work.

My own abridgment was inspired by that of Philip
Stevick, now out of print;† both his edition and mine
use Richardson's first edition as source and approach the
text not just as an historical artifact but as a work of
art. Our view is that the second and third editions are
not only longer than the first, but suffer aesthetically
from the incessant advice of Richardson's friends and
readers, not all of which he was able to ignore. My
method was to approach the full version of the first edition, using Angus Ross's excellent 1985 Penguin edition,
and to do so with a mind as open as possible, gradually
pruning away what I found extraneous and preserving
what seemed essential.

To some extent the essential had to do with practical
matters, the most obvious of these being continuity. I
wanted the abridgment to read smoothly, as if nothing
had been excised. But I also worked to include the passages most often discussed in the critical discourse that
surrounds *Clarissa*.

---

*T. C. Duncan Eaves and Ben D. Kimpel, *Samuel Richardson: A
Biography* (Oxford: Clarendon Press, 1971) 206.
†Samuel Richardson, *Clarissa or the History of a Young Lady*, ed.
Philip Stevick (New York: Rinehart, 1971).

I removed sentences, paragraphs, and entire letters while preserving the language, as well as the sequence of paragraphs, the placement of paragraph breaks, and the order of significant events. In rare cases I deleted words within a sentence; these omissions are indicated with ellipses. I pruned whatever seemed repetitious without effect or moralistic without thought. I likewise removed many minor characters, though probably the sense of a fictional community suffers by such trimming. The Tomlinson plotline I removed entirely.

All this clearing away of shrubbery, of course, risks subverting Richardson's intention and accomplishment. The well-intentioned gardener, therefore, approaches her task with both humility and hubris: humility at laying violent hands on a classic, and hubris at the possibility that all this clearing away of overgrowth and undergrowth may actually reveal more clearly the design and shape of the original garden.

III

My own most memorable realization was the important role Anna Howe plays in the novel. Previous abridgments without exception reduced the significance of Anna Howe, instead casting a bright light on the struggles of the two principals, Lovelace and Clarissa.* This binary reading, I believe, fails to recognize that the central power struggle is actually a three-way conflict, an unstable dynamic providing more psychological complexity and dramatic tension. Richardson himself once confessed, "I love Miss Howe next to Clarissa."†

Anna Howe plays an active role in the fiction by observing the action, listening to Clarissa, and offering advice. Repeatedly she urges Clarissa to assume the estate her grandfather left her and so cut her ties of dependence with both her family and Lovelace. Anna is really urging revolution, though she and the other characters

---

*See the Stevick edition and also that of George Sherburn (Boston: Houghton Mifflin, 1962).
†William Beatty Warner, *Reading Clarissa: The Struggle of Interpretation* (New Haven, CT: Yale, 1979) viii.

recognize independence is an inappropriate goal for a young lady of family and fortune. At the beginning of the novel and repeatedly throughout it, Clarissa expresses a deep longing for independence and the single life. Yet she understands that setting up housekeeping would be a bold and potentially dangerous step. Her conventional side cannot resolve on angering or even litigating with her father over assumption of her estate.

Anna, who, as she confesses, risks nothing, can easily imagine herself in Clarissa's place, embracing independence:

> I'd be in my own mansion, pursuing my charming schemes and making all around me happy. I'd set up my own chariot. I'd visit them when they deserved it. But when my brother and sister gave themselves airs, I'd let them know that I was their sister, and not their servant; and if that did not do, I would shut my gates against them; and bid them be company for each other. (L27)

Lovelace recognizes that Clarissa's moods and decisions are shaped by the stream of correspondence from Anna Howe, and he acknowledges to Belford Miss Howe's importance and power. Having intercepted several letters from her to Clarissa, he complains that they are "of a treasonable nature" (L175). In his view, they justify violence. A recurring fantasy is that he will rape both women, suggesting perhaps that he cannot subdue one without subduing both. Possibly he sees them as two aspects of the same person, or as the two together composing the single "*double*-armed beauty" (L199) known as Miss Clarissa Harlowe.

Other times Lovelace imagines similarities between himself and Anna Howe, who has "too much fire and spirit in her eye indeed, for a girl" (L252). He notes how she loves to tease and bedevil her suitor, Hickman. He even imagines "that that vixen of a girl, who certainly likes not Hickman, was in love with *me*" (L201). And in fact, Anna does acknowledge to Clarissa more than once that Lovelace's spirit is more attractive than Hickman's torpor and timidity.

When Lovelace examines the relationship between Clarissa and Anna, he is provoked into denying women are capable of friendship. He explains to Belford, "truly, a single woman who thinks she has a soul, and knows that she wants something, would be thought to have found a fellow-soul for it in her own sex . . . ; when a *man* comes in between the pretended *inseparables*, [friendship] is given up like their music and other maidenly amusements" (L252).

In this complex, unstable triangle, we have both Clarissa and Lovelace equated with Anna, and each of the three principals expressing passion for the other two. This glimpse into the transgressive potential of relationship delays but cannot quite subvert the conventional direction of domestic fiction. Anna Howe, former spokesperson for women's independence, must eventually marry the sweet-tempered Mr. Hickman, thus restoring social coherence to the disrupted neighborhood.

And yet neither Clarissa nor Lovelace will so compromise. In Lovelace's words, "I must soon blow up the lady, or be blown up myself" (L255).

—Sheila Ortiz-Taylor

CLARISSA

Letter 1: MISS ANNA HOWE TO MISS CLARISSA HARLOWE

Jan. 10

I am extremely concerned, my dearest friend, for the disturbances that have happened in your family. I know how it must hurt you to become the subject of the public talk; and yet upon an occasion so generally known it is impossible but that whatever relates to a young lady, whose distinguished merits have made her the public care, should engage everybody's attention. I long to have the particulars from yourself, and of the usage I am told you receive upon an accident you could not help and in which, as far as I can learn, the sufferer was the aggressor.

Mr Diggs, whom I sent for at the first hearing of the rencounter to inquire for *your* sake how your brother was, told me that there was no danger from the wound, if there were none from the fever, which it seems has been increased by the perturbation of his spirits.

Mr Wyerley drank tea with us yesterday; and though he is far from being partial to Mr Lovelace, as it may be well supposed, yet both he and Mr Symmes blame your family for the treatment they gave him when he went in person to inquire after your brother's health, and to express his concern for what had happened.

They say that Mr Lovelace could not avoid drawing his sword: and that either your brother's unskilfulness or violence left him from the very first pass entirely in his power. This, I am told, was what Mr Lovelace said upon it, retreating as he spoke: 'Have a care, Mr Harlowe. Your violence puts you out of your defence. You give me too much advantage! For your sister's sake I will pass by everything if—'

But this the more provoked his rashness to lay himself open to the advantage of his adversary, who, after a slight wound in the arm, took away his sword.

There are people who love not your brother, because of his natural imperiousness and fierce and uncontrollable temper: these say that the young gentleman's passion was abated on seeing his blood gush plentifully down his arm; and that he received the generous offices of his adversary (who helped him off with his coat and waistcoat and bound up his arm, till the surgeon could come) with such patience as was far from making a visit afterwards from that adversary to inquire after his health appear either insulting or improper.

Be this as it may, everybody pities you. So steady, so uniform in your conduct; so desirous, as you always said, of sliding through life to the end of it unnoted; and, as I may add, not wishing to be observed even for your silent benevolence; sufficiently happy in the noble consciousness which rewards it: *Rather useful than glaring,* your deserved motto; though now pushed into blaze, as we see, to your regret; and yet blamed at home for the faults of others. How must such a virtue suffer on every hand! Yet it must be allowed that your present trial is but proportioned to your prudence! As all your friends without doors are apprehensive that some other unhappy event may result from so violent a contention, in which it seems the families on both sides are now engaged, I must desire you to enable me, on the authority of your own information, to do you occasional justice.

My mamma, and all of us, like the rest of the world, talk of nobody but you on this occasion, and of the consequences which may follow from the resentments of a man of Mr Lovelace's spirit; who, as he gives out, has been treated with high indignity by your uncles. My mamma will have it that you cannot now, with any decency, either see him or correspond with him. She is a good deal prepossessed by your uncle Antony, who occasionally calls upon us, as you know; and, on this rencounter, has represented to her the crime which it would be in a sister to encourage a man, who is to *wade* into her favour (this was his expression) through the blood of her brother.

Write to me therefore, my dear, the whole of your story from the time that Mr Lovelace was first introduced into your family; and particularly an account of all that passed between him and your sister, about which there are different reports; some people supposing that the younger sister (at least by her uncommon merit) has stolen a lover from the elder. And pray write in so full a manner as may gratify those who know not so much of your affairs as I do. If anything unhappy should fall out from the violence of such spirits as you have to deal with, your account of all things previous to it will be your justification.

You see what you draw upon yourself by excelling all your sex. Every individual of it who knows you, or has heard of you, seems to think you answerable to *her* for your conduct in points so very delicate and concerning.

Every eye, in short, is upon you with the expectation of an example. I wish to heaven you were at liberty to pursue your own methods; all would then, I dare say, be easy and honourably ended. But I dread your directors and directresses; for your mamma, admirably well qualified as she is to lead, must submit to be led. Your sister and brother will certainly put you out of your course.

But this is a point you will not permit me to expatiate upon: pardon me therefore, and I have done. Yet, why should I say, Pardon me? When your concerns are my concerns? When your honour is my honour? When I love you, as never woman loved another? And when you have allowed of that concern and of that love, and have for years, which in persons so young may be called many, ranked in the first class of your friends.

> Your ever-grateful and affectionate
> ANNA HOWE?

Letter 2: MISS CLARISSA HARLOWE TO MISS HOWE

Harlowe Place, Jan. 13

How you oppress me, my dearest friend, with your politeness! I cannot doubt your sincerity; but you should take care that you give me not reason from your *kind* partiality to call in question your judgement. You do not distinguish that I take many admirable hints from you, and have the art to pass them upon you for my own. For in all you do, in all you say, nay, in your very looks (so animated!) you give lessons, to one who loves you and observes you as I love and observe you, without knowing that you do. So, pray, my dear, be more sparing of your praise for the future, lest after this confession we should suspect that you secretly intend to praise yourself, while you would be thought only to commend another.

Our family has indeed been strangely discomposed. *Discomposed!* It has been in *tumults*, ever since the unhappy transaction; and I have borne all the blame; yet should have had too much concern from myself had I been more justly spared by everyone else.

For, whether it be owing to a faulty impatience, having been too indulgently treated to be *inured* to blame, or to the regret I have to hear those censured on my account whom it is my duty to vindicate; I have sometimes wished that it had pleased God to have taken me in my last fever, when I had everybody's love and good opinion; but oftener, that I had never been distinguished by my grandpapa as I was: which has estranged me, I doubt, my brother's and sister's affections; at least, has raised a jealousy, with regard to the apprehended favour of my two uncles, that now and then overshadows their love.

My brother being happily recovered of his fever and his wound in a hopeful way, although he has not yet ventured abroad, I will be as particular as you desire in the little history you demand of me. But heaven forbid that anything should ever happen which may require it to be produced for the purpose you so kindly mention!

I will begin as you command, with Mr Lovelace's address to my sister, and be as brief as possible. I will recite facts only, and leave you to judge of the truth of the report raised that the younger sister has robbed the elder.

It was in pursuance of a conference between Lord M. and my uncle Antony, that Mr Lovelace (my papa and mamma not forbidding) paid his respects to my sister Arabella. My brother was then in Scotland, busying himself in viewing the condition of the considerable estate which was left him there by his generous godmother, together with one as considerable in Yorkshire. I was also absent at my *dairy-house*, as it is called, busied in the accounts relating to the estate which my grandfather had the goodness to bequeath me, and which once a year are left to my inspection, although I have given the whole into my papa's power.

My sister made me a visit there the day after Mr Lovelace had been introduced, and seemed highly pleased with the gentleman. His birth, his fortune in possession a clear 2000 [£ per year] as Lord M. had assured my uncle; presumptive heir to that nobleman's large estate; his great expectations from Lady Sarah Sadleir and Lady Betty Lawrance who, with his uncle, interested themselves very warmly (he being the last of his line) to see him married.

'So handsome a man! Oh her beloved Clary!' (for then she was ready to love me dearly, from the overflowings of her good humour on his account!) 'He was but *too* handsome a man for *her*! Were she but as amiable as *somebody*, there would be a probability of *holding* his affections! For he was wild, she heard; *very* wild, very gay; loved intrigue. But he was young; a man of sense: would see his error, could she but have patience with his faults, if his faults were not cured by marriage.'

Thus she ran on; and then wanted me 'to see the charming man,' as she called him. Again concerned 'that she was not handsome enough for him'; with 'a sad thing, that the man should have the advantage of the woman in that particular.' But then, stepping to the glass she complimented herself, 'That she was very *well*: that there were many women deemed passable who were inferior to herself: that she was always thought comely; and, let her tell me, that comeliness having not so much to lose as beauty had would hold, when that would evaporate and fly off. Nay, for that matter' (and again she turned to the glass), 'her features were not irregular, her eyes not at all amiss.' And I remember they were more than usually brilliant at that time. 'Nothing, in short, to be found fault with, though nothing very engaging, she doubted—was there, Clary?'

Excuse me, my dear, I never was thus particular before; no, not to you. Nor would I now have written thus freely of a sister, but that she makes a merit to my brother of disowning that she ever liked him [Lovelace], as I shall mention hereafter: and then you will always have me give you minute descriptions, nor suffer me to

pass by the air and manner in which things are spoken
that are to be taken notice of; rightly observing that air
and manner often express more than the accompanying
words.

I congratulated her upon her prospects. She received
my compliments with a great deal of self-complacency.

She liked the gentleman still more at his next visit;
and yet he made no particular address to her, although
an opportunity was given him for it. This was wondered
at, as my uncle had introduced him into our family declaredly as a visitor to my sister. But as we are ever
ready to make excuses, when in good humour with ourselves, for the supposed slights of those whose approbation we wish to engage, so my sister found out a reason,
much to Mr Lovelace's advantage, for his not improving
the opportunity that was given him. It was bashfulness,
truly, in him. (Bashfulness in Mr Lovelace, my dear!)
But I fancy it is many, many years ago, since he was
bashful.

Thus, however, could my sister make it out. 'Upon
her word, she believed Mr Lovelace deserved not the
bad character he had as to women. He was really, to *her*
thinking, a *modest* man. He *would* have spoken out, she
believed; but once or twice, as he seemed to intend to
do so, he was under so *agree*-able a confusion! Such a
profound respect he seemed to show her; a perfect *reverence*, she thought. She loved dearly that a gentleman in
courtship should show a reverence to his mistress.' So
indeed we all do, I believe; and with reason, since, if I
may judge from what I have seen in many families, there
is little enough of it shown afterwards. And she told my
aunt Hervey that she would be a little less upon the
reserve next time he came: 'She was not one of those
flirts, not she, who would give pain to a person that
deserved to be well treated; and the more for the greatness of his value for her.'

In this third visit, Bella governed herself by this kind
and considerate principle; so that, according to her own
account of the matter, the man *might* have spoken but—
but he was still *bashful*; he was not able to overcome
this *unseasonable reverence*. So this visit went off as
the former.

But now she began to be dissatisfied with him. She compared his general character with this particular behaviour to her; and having never been courted before, owned herself puzzled how to deal with so odd a lover. 'What did the man mean! Had not her uncle brought him *declaredly* as a suitor to her? It could not be bashfulness (now she thought of it), since he might have opened his mind to her *uncle*, if he wanted courage to speak directly to *her.* Not that she cared much for the man neither; but it was right, surely, that a woman should be put out of doubt, early, as to a man's intentions in such a case as this, from his own mouth. But, truly, she had begun to think that he was more solicitous to cultivate her *mamma's* good opinion than *hers!* Everybody, she owned, admired her mamma's conversation. But he was mistaken if he thought that would do with *her.* And then, for his own sake, surely he should put it into her power to be complaisant to him, if he gave her cause of approbation. This distant behaviour, she must take upon her to say, was the more extraordinary, as he continued his visits and declared himself extremely desirous to cultivate a friendship with the whole family; and as he could have no doubt about her sense, if she might take upon her to join her own with the general opinion, he having taken great notice of, and admired many of her *good things* as they fell from her lips. Reserves were painful, she must needs say, to open and free spirits like hers; and yet she must tell my aunt' (to whom all this was directed) 'that she should never forget what she owed to her sex, and to herself, were Mr Lovelace as unexceptionable in his morals as in his figure, and were he to urge his suit ever so warmly.'

I was not of her council. I was still absent. And it was agreed between my aunt Hervey and her that she was to be quite solemn and shy in his next visit, if there were not a peculiarity in his address to her.

But my sister, it seems, had not considered the matter well. This was not the way, as it proved, to be taken with a man of Mr Lovelace's penetration, for matters of *mere omission*—nor with *any* man; since if love has not taken root deep enough to cause it to shoot out into declaration, if an opportunity be fairly given for it, there

is little room to expect that the blighting winds of anger
or resentment will bring it forward. Then my poor sister
is not naturally good-humoured. This is too well-known
a truth for me to endeavour to conceal it, especially from
you. She must therefore, I doubt, have appeared to great
disadvantage when she aimed to be worse-tempered
than ordinary.

How they managed it in this conversation I know not.
One would be tempted to think by the issue that Mr Lovelace was ungenerous enough to seek the occasion given
and to improve it. Yet he thought fit to put the question
too. But, she says, it was not till by some means or other
(she knew not how) he had wrought her up to such a
pitch of displeasure with him that it was impossible for
her to recover herself at the instant. Nevertheless he re-
urged his question, as expecting a definitive answer, without waiting for the return of her temper, or endeavouring
to mollify her; so that she was under a necessity of persisting in her denial; yet gave him reason to think that she
did not dislike his address, only the *manner* of it; his court
being rather made to her mamma than to herself, as if he
were sure of *her* consent at any time.

A good encouraging denial, I must own—as was the
rest of her plea, to wit, 'a disinclination to change her
state. Exceedingly happy as she was, she never could
be happier!'

Here I am obliged to lay down my pen. I will soon
resume it.

Letter 3: MISS CLARISSA HARLOWE TO MISS HOWE

Jan. 13, 14

And thus, as Mr Lovelace thought fit to *take it*, had he
his answer from my sister. It was with very great regret,
as he pretended (I doubt the man is a hypocrite, my
dear!), that he acquiesced in it. 'So much determined-
ness; such a noble firmness in my sister; that there was
no hope of prevailing upon her to alter sentiments she
had adopted on full consideration.' He sighed, as Bella
told us, when he took his leave of her: 'Profoundly

sighed: grasped her hand and kissed it with *such* an ardour—withdrew with *such* an air of solemn respect—she had him then before her. She could almost find in her heart, although he had vexed her, to pity him.'

He waited on my mamma after he had taken leave of Bella, and reported his ill success in so respectful a manner, both with regard to my sister and to the whole family, and with so much concern that he was not accepted as a relation to it, that it left upon them all (my brother being then, as I have said, in Scotland) impressions in his favour, and a belief that this matter would certainly be brought on again. But Mr Lovelace going up directly to town, where he stayed a whole fortnight, and meeting there with my uncle Antony, to whom he regretted his niece's unhappy resolution not to change her state, it was seen that there was a total end put to the affair.

My sister was not wanting to herself on this occasion, but made a virtue of necessity; and the man was quite another man with her. 'A vain creature! Too well knowing his advantages; yet those not what she had conceived them to be! Cool and warm by fits and starts; an ague-like lover. A steady man, a man of virtue, a man of morals was worth a thousand of such gay flutterers. Her sister Clary might think it worth her while perhaps to try to engage such a man; she had patience; she was mistress of persuasion; and indeed, to do the girl justice, had *something* of a person. But as for *her*, she would not have a man of whose heart she could not be sure for one moment; no, not for the world; and most sincerely glad was she that she had rejected him.'

But when Mr Lovelace returned into the country, he thought fit to visit my papa and mamma, hoping, as he told them, that however unhappy he had been in the rejection of the wished-for alliance, he might be allowed to keep up an acquaintance and friendship with a family which he should always respect. And then, unhappily, as I may say, was I at home, and present.

It was immediately observed that his attention was fixed on me. My sister, as soon as he was gone, in a spirit of bravery, seemed desirous to promote his address, should it be tendered.

My aunt Hervey was there, and was pleased to say we

should make the finest couple in England, if my sister
had no objection. No, indeed! with a haughty toss, was
my sister's reply. It would be strange if she had, after
the denial she had given him upon full deliberation.

My mamma declared that her only dislike of his alliance with either daughter was on account of his faulty
morals.

My uncle Harlowe, that his *daughter* Clary, as he delighted to call me from childhood, would reform him if
any woman in the world could.

My uncle Antony gave his approbation in high terms;
but referred, as my aunt had done, to my sister.

She repeated her contempt of him, and declared that
were there not another man in England she would not
have him. She was ready, on the contrary, she could
assure them, to resign her pretensions under hand and
seal, if Miss Clary were taken with his tinsel, and if everyone else approved of his address to the girl.

My papa, indeed, after a long silence, being urged to
speak his mind by my uncle Antony, said that he had a
letter from his son James, on his hearing of Mr Lovelace's visits to his daughter Arabella, which he had not
shown to anybody but my mamma, that treaty being at
an end when he received it; that in this letter he expressed great dislikes to an alliance with Mr Lovelace
on the score of his immoralities; that he knew, indeed,
there was an old grudge between them; that, being desirous to prevent all occasions of disunion and animosity
in his family, he would suspend the declaration of his
own mind, till his son arrived and till he had heard his
further objections; that he was the more inclined to
make his son this compliment, as Mr Lovelace's general
character gave but too much ground for his son's dislike
of him, adding, that he had heard (so he supposed had
everyone) that he was a very extravagant man; that he
had contracted debts in his travels; and, indeed, he was
pleased to say, he had the air of a spendthrift.

These particulars I had partly from my aunt Hervey,
and partly from my sister; for I was called out as soon
as the subject was entered upon. And when I returned,
my uncle Antony asked me how *I* should like Mr Love-

lace? Everybody saw, he was pleased to say, that I had made a conquest.

I immediately answered, Not at all: he seemed to have too good an opinion both of his person and parts to have any great regard to his wife, let him marry whom he would.

My sister particularly was pleased with this answer, and confirmed it to be just; with a compliment to my judgement—for it was *hers*.

But the very next day Lord M. came to Harlowe Place: I was then absent: and in his nephew's name, made a proposal in form, declaring that it was the ambition of all his family to be related to ours; and he hoped his kinsman would not have such an answer on the part of the younger sister as he had had on that of the elder.

In short, Mr Lovelace's visits were admitted as those of a man who had not deserved disrespect from our family; but, as to his address to me, with a reservation as above on my papa's part, that he would determine nothing without his son. My discretion, as to the rest, was confided in; for still I had the same objections as to the man: nor would I when we were better acquainted hear anything but general talk from him, giving him no opportunity of conversing with me in private.

He bore this with a resignation little expected from his natural temper, which is generally reported to be quick and hasty, unused it seems from childhood to check or control: a case too common in considerable families where there is an only son; and *his* mother never had any other child. But, as I have heretofore told you, I could perceive notwithstanding this resignation that he had so good an opinion of himself, as not to doubt that his person and accomplishments would insensibly engage me; and could that be once done, he told my aunt Hervey, he should hope from so steady a temper that his hold in my affections would be durable. While my sister accounted for his patience in another manner, which would perhaps have had more force if it had come from a person less prejudiced: 'That the man was not fond of marrying at all; that he might perhaps have half-a-score mistresses; and that delay might be as convenient for his *roving*, as for my *well-acted* indifference.' That was her kind expression.

And thus was he admitted to converse with our family almost upon his own terms; for while my friends saw nothing in his behaviour but what was extremely respectful and observed in him no violent importunity, they seemed to have taken a great liking to his conversation; while I considered him only as a common guest when he came, and thought myself no more concerned in his visits, nor at his entrance or departure, than any other of the family.

But this indifference of my side was the means of procuring him one very great advantage; for upon it was grounded that correspondence by letters which succeeded—and which, had it been to be begun when the family animosity broke out, would never have been entered into on my part. The occasion was this:

My uncle Hervey has a young gentleman entrusted to his care, whom he has thoughts of sending abroad a year or two hence, to make the Grand Tour, as it is called; and finding Mr Lovelace could give a good account of everything necessary for a young traveller to observe upon such an occasion, he desired him to write down a description of the courts and countries he had visited, and what was most worthy of curiosity in them.

He consented, on condition that I would *direct* his subjects, as he called it: and as everyone had heard his manner of writing commended, and thought his relations might be agreeable amusements in winter evenings; and that he could have no opportunity particularly to address me in them, since they were to be read in full assembly before they were to be given to the young gentleman, I made the less scruple to write, and to make observations and put questions for our further information. Still the less, perhaps, as I love writing; and those who do are fond, you know, of occasions to use the pen: and then, having everyone's consent, and my uncle Hervey's desire that I would, I thought that if I had been the only scrupulous person, it would have shown a particularity that a vain man would construe to his advantage, and which my sister would not fail to animadvert upon.

Thus was a kind of correspondence begun between

him and me with general approbation; while everyone wondered at, and was pleased with, his patient veneration of me, for so they called it. However, it was not doubted that he would soon be more importunate, since his visits were more frequent and he acknowledged to my aunt Hervey a passion for me, accompanied with an awe that he had never known before; to which he attributed what he called his but *seeming* acquiescence with my papa's pleasure and the distance I kept him at. And yet, my dear, this may be his usual manner of behaviour to our sex; for had not my sister, at first, all his reverences?

Meantime, my father, expecting this importunity, kept in readiness the reports he had heard in his disfavour, to charge them upon him then, as so many objections to his address. And it was highly agreeable to me, that he did so: it would have been strange, if it were not, since the person who could reject Mr Wyerley's address for the sake of his *free opinions* must have been inexcusable had she not rejected another's for his *freer practices*.

But I should own that in the letters he sent me upon the general subject, he more than once enclosed a particular one declaring his passionate regards for me, and complaining with fervour enough of my reserves: but of these I took not the least notice; for as I had not written to him at all, but upon a subject so general, I thought it was but right to let what he wrote upon one so particular pass off as if I never had seen it; and the rather as I was not then at liberty, from the approbation his letters met with, to break off the correspondence without assigning the true reason for doing so. Besides, with all his respectful assiduities, it was easy to observe (if it had not been his general character) that his temper is naturally haughty and violent; and I had seen of that untractable spirit in my brother to like it in one who hoped to be still nearer related to me.

I had a little specimen of this temper of his upon the very occasion I have mentioned; for after he had sent me a third particular letter with the general one, he asked me the next time he came to Harlowe Place if I had not received such a one from him? I told him I

should never answer one so sent, and that I had waited
for such an occasion as he had now given me to tell him
so. I desired him therefore not to write again on the
subject, assuring him that if he did, I would return both,
and never write another line to him.

You cannot imagine how saucily the man looked; as
if, in short, he was disappointed that he had not made
a more sensible impression upon me; and when he recollected himself (as he did immediately), what a visible
struggle it cost him to change his haughty airs for more
placid ones! But I took no notice of either, for I thought
it best to convince him by the coolness and indifference
with which I repulsed his forward hopes (at the same
time intending to avoid the affection of pride or vanity)
that he was not considerable enough in my eyes to make
me take over-ready offence at what he said, or how he
looked: in other words, that I had not value enough for
him to treat him with peculiarity either by smiles or
frowns. Indeed, he had cunning enough to give me, un-
designedly, a piece of instruction which taught me this
caution; for he had said in conversation once, 'That if a
man could not make a lady in courtship own herself
pleased with him, it was as *much* and oftentimes more
to his purpose to make her *angry* with him.'

I must break off here. But will continue the subject
the very first opportunity. Meantime, I am,

> Your most affectionate friend and servant,
> CL. HARLOWE

Letter 4: MISS CLARISSA HARLOWE TO MISS HOWE

> Jan. 15

This, my dear, was the situation Mr Lovelace and I were
in when my brother arrived from Scotland.

The moment Mr Lovelace's visits were mentioned to
him, he, without either hesitation or apology, expressed
his disapprobation of them. He found great flaws in his
character, and took the liberty to say in so many words
that he wondered how it came into the hearts of his
uncles to encourage such a man for *either* of his sisters;
at the same time returning his thanks to my father for

declining his consent till *he* arrived, in such a manner, I thought, as a superior would do when he commended an inferior for having well performed his duty in his absence.

He justified his avowed inveteracy by common fame, and by what he had known of him at college; declaring that he had ever hated him; ever should hate him; and would never own him for a brother, or me for a sister, if I married him.

That college-begun antipathy I have heard accounted for in this manner:

Mr Lovelace was always noted for his vivacity and courage; and no less, it seems, for the swift and surprising progress he made in all parts of literature; for diligence in his studies, in the hours of study, he had hardly his equal. This, it seems, was his general character at the university, and it gained him many friends among the more learned youth; while those who did not love him feared him by reason of the offence his vivacity made him too ready to give, and of the courage he showed in supporting the offence when given, which procured him as many followers as he pleased among the mischievous sort. No very amiable character, you'll say, upon the whole.

But my brother's temper was not happier. His native haughtiness could not bear a superiority so visible; and whom we fear more than love, we are not far from hating: and having less command of his passions than the other, was evermore the subject of his, perhaps *indecent*, ridicule: so that they never met without quarrelling. And everybody, either from love or fear, siding with his antagonist, he had a most uneasy time of it, while both continued in the same college. It was the less wonder, therefore, that a young man who is not noted for the gentleness of his temper should resume an antipathy early begun, and so deeply-rooted.

He found my sister, who waited but for the occasion, ready to join him in his resentments against the man he hated. She utterly disclaimed all manner of regard for him: 'Never liked him at all. His estate was certainly much encumbered: it was impossible it should be otherwise, so entirely devoted as he was to his pleasures. He

kept no house; had no equipage: nobody pretended that
he wanted pride: the reason therefore was easy to be
guessed at': And then did she boast of, and my brother
praise her for, refusing him; and both joined on all occasions to depreciate him, and not seldom *made* the occasions; their displeasure against him causing every subject
to run into this, if it began not with it.

Now and then, indeed, when I observed that their vehemence carried them beyond all bounds of probability,
I thought it but justice to put in a word for him. But
this only subjected me to reproach, as having a prepossession in his favour that I would not own. So that when
I could not change the subject, I used to retire either to
my music or to my closet [small study].

Their behaviour to him when they could not help
seeing him was very cold and disobliging; but as yet not
directly affrontive; for they were in hopes of prevailing
upon my papa to forbid his visits. But as there was nothing in his behaviour that might warrant such a treatment
of a man of his birth and fortune, they succeeded not;
and then they were very earnest with *me* to forbid them.
I asked what authority I had to take such a step in my
father's house; and when my behaviour to him was so
distant, that he seemed to be as much the guest of any
other person of the family, themselves excepted, as
mine? In revenge, they told me that it was cunning management between us; and that we both understood one
another better than we pretended to do. And at last they
gave such a loose to their passions all of a sudden, as I
may say, that instead of withdrawing as they used to do
when he came, they threw themselves in his way pur-
posely to affront him.

Mr Lovelace, you may believe, very ill brooked this;
but nevertheless contented himself to complain of it to
me, in high terms, however, telling me that but for my
sake my brother's treatment of him was not to be borne.

I was sorry for the merit this gave him, in his own
opinion, with me; and the more as some of the affronts
he received were too flagrant to be excused. But I told
him that I was determined not to fall out with my
brother, if I could help it, whatever were his faults; and
since they could not see one another with temper, should

be glad that he would not throw himself in my brother's way, and I was sure my brother would not seek *him*.

He was very much nettled at this answer; but said he must bear his affronts if I would have it so. He had been accused himself of violence in his temper, but he hoped to show on this occasion that he had a command of his passions which few young men, so provoked, would be *able* to show; and doubted not but it would be attributed to a *proper motive* by a person of my generosity and penetration.

I am obliged to break off. But I believe I have written enough to answer very fully all that you have commanded from me. It is not for a child to seek to clear her own character, or to justify her actions, at the expense of the most revered ones; yet, as I know that the account of all those further proceedings by which I may be affected will be interesting to so dear a friend (who will communicate to others no more than what is fitting), I will continue to write as I have opportunity, as minutely as we are used to write to each other. Indeed I have no delight, as I have often told you, equal to that which I take in conversing with you—by *letter*, when I cannot in *person*.

Meantime, I can't help saying that I am exceedingly concerned to find, that I am become so much the public talk, as you tell me, and as *everybody* tells me, I am. Your kind, your *precautionary* regard for my fame, and the opportunity you have given me to tell my own story, previous to any new accident (which heaven avert!), is so like the warm friend I have ever found my dear Miss Howe, that with redoubled obligation you bind me to be

Your ever-grateful and affectionate
CLARISSA HARLOWE

Letter 5: MISS CLARISSA HARLOWE TO MISS HOWE

Jan. 20

I have been hindered from prosecuting my intention. Neither nights nor mornings have been my own. My mamma has been very ill and would have no other nurse but me. I have not stirred from her bedside, for she kept

her bed, and two nights I had the honour of sharing it
with her.

Her disorder was a very violent colic. The contentions
of these fierce, these masculine spirits, and the apprehension of mischiefs that may arise from the increasing animosity which all *here* have against Mr Lovelace, and his
too-well-known resentful and intrepid character, she cannot bear. Then the foundations laid, as she dreads, for
jealousy and heart-burnings in her own family, late so
happy and so united, afflict exceedingly a gentle and
sensible mind, which has from the beginning on all occasions sacrificed its own inward satisfaction to outward
peace. My brother and sister, who used very often to
jar, are now so much one and are so much together
(*caballing* was the word that dropped from her, as if at
unawares) that she is full of fears of consequences that
may follow—to my prejudice, perhaps, is her kind concern, since she sees that they behave to me every hour
with more and more shyness and reserve; yet would she
but exert that authority which the superiority of her fine
talents gives her, all these family feuds might perhaps
be crushed in their but yet beginnings; especially as she
may be assured that all fitting concessions shall be made
by me, not only as they are my elders, but for the sake
of so excellent and so indulgent a mother.

For, if I may say to you my dear, what I would not
to any other person living, it is my opinion that had she
been of a temper that would have borne less, she would
have had ten times less to bear than she has had.

But whither may these reflections lead me? I know
you do not love any of us, but my mamma and me; and,
being above all disguises, make me sensible that you do
not, oftener than I wish you did. Ought I then to add
force to your *dislikes* of those whom I wish you more to
like—my father, especially; for he, poor gentleman! has
some excuse for his impatience of contradiction. He is
not naturally an ill-tempered man; and in his person and
air and in his conversation too, when not under the torture of a gouty paroxysm, everybody distinguishes the
gentleman born and educated.

But my brother! what excuse can be made for his
haughty and morose temper? He is really, my dear, I

am sorry to have occasion to say it, an ill-tempered
young man, and treats my mamma sometimes—indeed
he is not dutiful. But possessing everything, he has the
vice of age mingled with the ambition of youth, and en-
joys nothing—but his own haughtiness and ill-temper, I
was going to say. Yet again am I adding force to your
dislikes of some of us. Once, my dear, it was perhaps in
your power to have moulded him as you pleased. Could
you have been my sister [sister-in-law]! Then had I had
a friend in a sister.

But no more of this. I will prosecute my former intention in my next, which I will sit down to as soon as
breakfast is over, dispatching this by the messenger
whom you have so kindly sent to inquire after us, on
my silence. Meantime, I am

Your most affectionate and obliged
friend and servant,
CL. HARLOWE

Letter 6: MISS CLARISSA HARLOWE TO MISS HOWE

Harlowe Place, Jan. 20

I will now resume my narrative of proceedings here. My
brother being in a good way, although you may be sure
that his resentments are rather heightened than abated
by the galling disgrace he has received, my friends (my
papa and uncles, however, if not my brother and sister)
begin to think that I have been treated unkindly. My
mamma has been so good as to tell me this since I sent
away my last.

Nevertheless I believe they all think that I receive letters from Mr Lovelace. But Lord M. being inclined
rather to support than to blame his nephew, they seem
to be so much afraid of him that they do not put it to
me whether I do or not, conniving on the contrary, as
it should seem, at the only method left to allay the vehemence of a spirit which they have so much provoked,
for he still insists upon satisfaction from my uncles, and
this possibly (for he wants not art) as the best way to
be introduced again with some advantage into our family. And indeed my aunt Hervey has put it to my

mamma, whether it were not best to prevail upon my
brother to take a turn to his Yorkshire estate, which he
was intending to do before, and to tarry there till all is
blown over.

But this is very far from being his intention, for he
has already begun to hint again that he shall never be
easy or satisfied till I am married, and finding neither
Mr Symmes nor Mr Mullins will be accepted, has proposed Mr Wyerley once more on the score of his great
passion for me. This I have again rejected, and but yesterday he mentioned one who has applied to him by
letter, making high offers. This is Mr Solmes; *rich*
Solmes, you know they call him. But this has not met
with the attention of one single soul.

If none of his schemes of marrying me take effect, he
has thoughts, I am told, of proposing to me to go to
Scotland in order, as the compliment is, to put his house
there in such order as our own is in. But this my mamma
intends to oppose for her own sake; because, having relieved her, as she is pleased to say, of the household
cares (for which my sister, you know, has no turn) they
must again devolve upon her if I go. And if *she* did not
oppose it, *I* should; for, believe me, I have no mind to
be his housekeeper; and I am sure, were I to go with
him, I should be treated rather as a servant than a
sister—perhaps not the better because I *am* his sister.
And if Mr Lovelace should follow me, things might be
worse than they are now.

But I have besought my mamma, who is apprehensive
of Mr Lovelace's visits, and for fear of whom my uncles
never stir out without arms and armed servants (my
brother also being near well enough to go abroad again)
to procure me permission to be your guest for a fortnight, or so. Will your mamma, think you, my dear, give
me leave?

I dare not ask to go to my dairy-house, as my good
grandfather would call it; for I am now afraid of being
thought to have a wish to enjoy that independence to
which his will has entitled me: and as matters are situated, such a wish would be imputed to my favour to the
man whom they have now so great an antipathy to. And,
indeed, could I be as easy and happy here as I used to

be, I would defy that man, and all his sex, and never repent that I have given the power of my fortune into my papa's hands.

Just now, my mamma has rejoiced me with the news that my requested permission is granted. Everyone thinks it best that I should go to you, except my brother. But he was told that he must not expect to rule in everything. I am to be sent for into the great parlour, where are my two uncles and my aunt Hervey, and to be acquainted with this concession in form.

I will acquaint you with what passed at the general leave given me to be your guest. And yet I know that you will not love my brother the better for my communication. But I am angry with him myself, and cannot help it. And, besides, it is proper to let you know the terms I go upon, and their motives for permitting me to go.

Clary, said my mamma, as soon as I entered the great parlour, your request, to go to Miss Howe's for a few days has been taken into consideration and granted.

Much against my liking, I assure you, said my brother, rudely interrupting her.

Son James! said my father, and knit his brows.

He was not daunted. His arm is in a sling. He often has the mean art to look upon *that*, when anything is hinted that may be supposed to lead towards the least favour to, or reconciliation with, Mr Lovelace. Let the *girl* then (I am often *the girl* with him!) be prohibited seeing that vile libertine.

Nobody spoke.

Do you hear, sister Clary? taking their silence for approbation of what *he* had dictated; you are not to receive visits from Lord M.'s nephew.

Everyone still remained silent.

Do you so understand the licence you have, miss? interrogated he.

I would be glad, sir, said I, to understand that you are my *brother*—and that *you* would understand, that you are *only* my brother.

Oh the fond, fond heart! with a sneer of insult, lifting up his hands.

Sir, said I to my papa, to your justice I appeal. If I
have deserved reflection, let me not be spared. But if I
am to be answerable for the rashness—

No more! No more, of either side, said my papa. You
are not to receive the visits of that Lovelace, though.

I will not, sir, in any way of encouragement, I do assure you; nor at all, if I can decently avoid it.

Thus ended this conference.

Will you engage, my dear, that the hated man shall
not come near your house? but what an inconsistence is
this, when they consent to my going, thinking his visits
here no otherwise to be avoided! But if he does come I
charge you never leave us alone together.

As I have no reason to doubt a welcome from your
mamma, I will put everything in order here and be with
you in two or three days.

Meantime, I am

> Your most affectionate and obliged
> CLARISSA HARLOWE

Letter 7: MISS CLARISSA HARLOWE TO MISS HOWE

Harlowe Place, Feb. 20

I beg your excuse for not writing sooner. Alas, my dear,
I have sad prospects before me! My brother and sister
have succeeded in all their views. They have found out
another lover for me; a hideous one! yet he is encouraged by everybody. No wonder that I was ordered home
so suddenly! at an hour's warning! No other notice, you
know, than what was brought with the chariot that was
to carry me back. It was for fear, as I have been informed (an unworthy fear!), that I should have entered
into any concert with Mr Lovelace had I known their
motive for commanding me home; apprehending, 'tis evident, that I should dislike the man.

And well might they apprehend so. For who do you
think he is? No other than that *Solmes!* Could you have
believed it? And they are all determined too; my
mamma with the rest! Dear, dear excellence! how could
she be thus brought over! when I am assured that, on
his first being proposed, she was pleased to say that had

Mr Solmes the *Indies* in possession, and would endow me with them, she should not think him deserving of her Clarissa Harlowe.

The reception I met with at my return, so different from what I used to meet with on every little absence (and now I had been from them three weeks), convinced me that I was to suffer for the happiness I had had in your company and conversation for that most agreeable period. I will give you an account of it.

My brother met me at the door, and gave me his hand when I stepped out of the chariot. He bowed very low. 'Pray, miss, favour me.' I thought it in good humour, but found it afterwards mock respect; and so he led me in great form, I prattling all the way, inquiring of everybody's health (although I was so soon to see them, and there was hardly time for answers), into the great parlour, where were my father, mother, my two uncles and my sister.

I was struck all of a heap as soon as I entered to see a solemnity which I had been so little used to on the like occasions in the countenance of every dear relation. They all kept their seats. I ran to my papa, and kneeled; then to my mamma; and met from both a cold salute; from my papa a blessing but half-pronounced; my mamma, indeed, called me, child, but embraced me not with her usual indulgent ardour.

After I had paid my duty to my uncles and my compliments to my sister, which she received with solemn and stiff form, I was bid to sit down. But my heart was full: and I said it became me to stand, if I *could* stand a reception so awful and unusual. I was forced to turn my face from them and pull out my handkerchief.

My unbrotherly accuser hereupon stood forth and charged me with having received no less than *five or six visits* at Miss Howe's from the man they had all so much reason to hate (that was the expression) notwithstanding the commands I had received to the contrary. And he bid me deny it if I could.

I had never been used, I said, to deny the truth; nor would I now. I owned I had, in the past three weeks, seen the person I presumed he meant *oftener* than five or six times. (Pray hear me out, brother, said I; for he was going to flame.) But he always came and asked for Mrs or Miss Howe.

I proceeded that I had reason to believe that both Mrs Howe and Miss, as matters stood, would much rather have excused his visits; but they had more than once apologized that, having not the same reason my papa had to forbid him their house, his rank and fortune entitled him to civility.

You see, my dear, I made not the pleas I might have made.

My brother seemed ready to give a loose to his passion; my papa put on the countenance which always portends a gathering storm; my uncles mutteringly whispered; and my sister aggravatingly held up her hands. While I begged to be heard out—and my mamma said, let the *child*, that was her kind word, be heard.

I hoped, I said, there was no harm done; that it became not me to prescribe to Mrs or Miss Howe who should be their visitors; that Mrs Howe was always diverted with the raillery that passed between Miss and him; that I had no reason to challenge *her* guest for *my* visitor, as I should seem to have done had I refused to go into their company when he was with them; that I had never seen him out of the presence of one or both of those ladies, and had signified to him once, on his urging for a few moments' private conversation with me, that unless a reconciliation were effected between my family and his he must not expect that I would countenance his visits, much less give him an opportunity of that sort.

I told them further that Miss Howe so well understood my mind that she never left me a moment while he was there; that when he came, if I was not below in the parlour, I would not suffer myself to be called to him; although I thought it would be an affectation which would give him advantage rather than the contrary if I had left company when he came in, or refused to enter into it when I found he would stay any time.

My brother heard me out with such a kind of impatience as showed he was resolved to be dissatisfied with me, say what I would. The rest, as the event has proved, behaved as if they *would* have been satisfied had they not further points to carry by intimidating me. All this made it evident, as I mentioned above, that they themselves expected not my voluntary compliance, and was a tacit confession of the disagreeableness of the person they had to propose.

I was no sooner silent than my *brother* swore, although in my papa's presence (swore, unchecked either by eye or countenance), that, for his part, he would *never* be reconciled to that libertine; and that he would renounce me for a sister if I encouraged the addresses of a man so obnoxious to them all.

A man who had like to have been my brother's murderer, my *sister* said, with a face even bursting with restraint of passion.

The poor Bella has, you know, a plump, high-fed face, if I may be allowed the expression—you, I know, will forgive me for this liberty of speech sooner than I can myself; yet how can one be such a reptile as not to turn when trampled upon!

My *papa*, with vehemence both of action and voice (my father has, you know, a terrible voice, when he is angry!), told me that I had met with too much indulgence in being allowed to refuse *this* gentleman and the *other* gentleman, and it was now *his* turn to be obeyed.

Very true, my *mamma* said—and hoped his will would not now be disputed by a child so favoured.

To show they were all of a sentiment, my uncle *Harlowe* said he hoped his beloved niece only wanted to know her papa's will to obey it.

And my uncle *Antony*, in his rougher manner, that I would not give them reason to apprehend that I thought my grandfather's favour to me had made me independent of them all. If I did, he could tell me, the will *could* be set aside, and *should*.

I did not know, I said, that I had given occasion for this harshness; I hoped I should always have a just sense of their favour to me, superadded to the duty I owed as a daughter and a niece; but that I was so much surprised at a reception so unusual and unexpected that I hoped my papa and mamma would give me leave to retire in order to recollect myself.

No one gainsaying, I made my silent compliments and

withdrew—leaving my brother and sister, as I thought,
pleased, and as if they wanted to congratulate each other
on having occasioned so severe a beginning to be made
with me.

But I will at present only add my humble thanks and
duty to your honoured mamma (to whom I will particularly write to express the grateful sense I have of her
goodness to me) and that I am,

Your ever-obliged
CL. HARLOWE

Letter 8: MISS CLARISSA HARLOWE TO MISS HOWE

Feb. 24

They drive on here at a furious rate. The man [Solmes]
lives here, I think. He courts them and is more and more
a favourite. Such terms, such settlements! That's the cry!

I have already stood the shock of three of this man's
particular visits, besides my share in his more general
ones, and find it is impossible I should ever endure him.
He has but a very ordinary share of understanding, is
very illiterate, knows nothing but the value of estates
and how to improve them, and what belongs to land-
jobbing, and husbandry. Yet am I as one stupid, I think.
They have begun so cruelly with me that I have not
spirit enough to assert my own negative.

Help me, dear Miss Howe, to a little of your charming
spirit; I never more wanted it.

The man, you may suppose, has no reason to boast of
his progress with me. He has not the sense to say anything to the purpose. His courtship, indeed, is to *them*;
and my brother pretends to court me as his proxy, truly!

February 25

I hate him more than before. One great estate is already obtained at the expense of the relations to it,
though distant relations, my brother's, I mean, by his
godmother; and this has given the hope, however chime-
rical that hope, of procuring others, and that my own at
least may revert to the family. And yet, in my opinion,
the world is but one great family; originally it was so;

what then is this narrow selfishness that reigns in us, but relationship remembered against relationship forgot?

But here, upon my absolute refusal of him upon *any* terms, have I had a signification made me that wounds me to the heart. How can I tell it you? Yet I must. It is, my dear, that I must not for a month to come or till licence obtained correspond with *anybody* out of the house.

How have I deserved this?

Feb. 25 in the evening

What my brother and sister have said against me I cannot tell. But I am in heavy disgrace with my papa.

I was sent for down to tea. I went with a very cheerful aspect, but had occasion soon to change it.

Such a solemnity in everybody's countenance! My mamma's eyes were fixed upon the tea-cups; and when she looked up it was heavily, as if her eyelids had weights upon them, and then not to me. My papa sat half-aside in his elbow-chair, that his head might be turned from me; his hands folded, and waving, as it were, up and down; his fingers, poor dear gentleman! in motion, as if angry to the very ends of them.

I took my seat. Shall I make tea, madam, to my mamma? I always used, you know, my dear, to make tea.

No! a very short sentence in one very short word was the expressive answer; and she was pleased to take the canister in her own hand.

My heart was up at my mouth. I did not know what to do with myself. What is to follow? thought I.

Just after the second dish out stepped my mamma. So I was left alone with my papa.

He looked so very sternly that my heart failed me, as twice or thrice I would have addressed myself to him; nothing but solemn silence on all hands having passed before.

At last, I asked, if it were his pleasure that I should pour him out another dish?

He answered me with the same angry monosyllable which I had received from my mamma before, and then arose and walked about the room. I arose too, with intent to throw myself at his feet, but was too much over-awed by his sternness even to make such an expression of my duty to him as my heart overflowed with.

At last, as he supported himself because of his gout on the back of a chair, I took a little more courage, and approaching him, besought him to acquaint me in what I had offended him?

He turned from me and, in a strong voice, Clarissa Harlowe, said he, know that I will be obeyed.

God forbid, sir, that you should not! I have never yet opposed your will—

Nor I your whimsies, Clarissa Harlowe, interrupted he. Don't let me run the fate of all who show indulgence to your sex, to be the more contradicted for mine to you.

My papa, you know, my dear, has not (any more than my brother) a kind opinion of our sex, although there is not a more condescending wife in the world than my mamma.

I was going to make protestations of duty. No protestations, girl! No words. I will not be prated to! I will be obeyed! I have no child—I will have no child, but an obedient one.

Sir, you never had reason, I hope—

Tell me not what I never *had*, but what I *have*, and what I *shall* have.

And I hope, sir—

Hope nothing. Tell me not of *hopes*, but of facts. I ask nothing of you but what is in your power to comply with, and what it is your duty to comply with.

Then, sir, I will comply with it. But yet I hope from your goodness—

No expostulations! No *but's*, girl! No qualifyings! I will be obeyed, I tell you! and cheerfully too! or you are no child of mine!

I wept.

Let me beseech you, my dear and ever-honoured papa (and I dropped down on my knees), that I may have only yours and my mamma's will, and not my brother's, to obey. I was going on, but he was pleased to withdraw, leaving me on the floor, saying that he would not hear me thus by subtlety and cunning aiming to distinguish away my duty, repeating that he would be obeyed.

My heart is too full—so full that it may endanger my duty were I to unburden it to you on this occasion; so I will lay down my pen. But can—Yet, positively, I will lay down my pen!

Letter 9: MISS CLARISSA HARLOWE TO MISS HOWE

Feb. 26, in the morning

My aunt who stayed here last night made me a visit this morning as soon as it was light.

I find by a few words which dropped from her unawares, that they have all an absolute dependence upon what they suppose to be a meekness in my temper. But in this they may be mistaken, for I verily think upon a strict examination of myself that I have almost as much in me of my father's as of my mother's family.

My aunt advises me to submit for the present to the interdicts they have laid me under; and indeed to encourage Mr Solmes's address. I have absolutely refused the latter, let what will as I have told her be the consequence. The visiting prohibition I will conform to. But as to that of not corresponding with you, nothing but the menace that our letters shall be intercepted can engage my observation of it.

I cannot bear the thought of being deprived of the principal pleasure of my life, for such is your conversation by person and by letter.

But can you, my dear Miss Howe, condescend to carry on a private correspondence with me? If you can, there is one way I have thought of by which it may be done.

You must remember the Green Lane, as we call it, that runs by the side of the wood-house and poultry-yard where I keep my bantams, pheasants and pea-hens, which generally engage my notice twice a day, the more my favourites because they were my grandfather's, and recommended to my care by him, and therefore brought hither from my dairy-house, since his death.

The lane is lower than the floor of the wood-house, and in the side of the wood-house the boards are rotted away down to the floor for half an ell together in several places. Hannah can step into the lane and make a mark with chalk where a letter or parcel may be pushed in under some sticks, which may be so managed as to be an unsuspected cover for the written deposits from either.

I have been just now to look at the place and find it will answer. So your faithful Robert may, without coming near the house, and as only passing through the green lane which leads to two or three farmhouses (out of livery, if you please), very easily take from thence my letters and deposit yours.

This place is the more convenient because it is seldom resorted to but by myself or Hannah on the above-mentioned account, for it is the general store-house for firing, the wood for constant use being nearer the house.

One corner of this being separated off for the roosting-place of my little poultry, either she or I shall never want a pretence to go thither.

Try, my dear, the success of a letter this way, and give me your opinion and advice what to do in this disgraceful situation, as I cannot but call it, and what you think of my prospects, and what you would do in my case.

But beforehand I must tell you that your advice must not run in favour of this Solmes; and yet it is very likely they will endeavour to engage your mamma in order to induce you, who have such an influence over me, to favour him.

Yet, on second thoughts, if you incline to that side of the question I would have you write your whole mind. Determined as I think I am, and cannot help it, I would at least give a patient hearing to what may be said on the other side. For my regards are not so much engaged (upon my word they are not; I know not myself if they be) to another person, as some of my friends suppose; and as you, giving way to your lively vein, upon his last visits affected to suppose. What preferable favour I may have for him to any other person is owing more to the usage he has received, and for my sake borne, than to any personal consideration.

I write a few lines of grateful acknowledgement to your mamma for her favours to me in the late happy period. I fear I shall never know such another! I hope she will forgive me that I did not write sooner.

Your affectionate
CLARISSA HARLOWE

Letter 10: MISS HOWE TO MISS CLARISSA HARLOWE

Feb. 27

What odd heads some people have! Miss Clarissa Harlowe to be sacrificed in marriage to Mr Roger Solmes! Astonishing!

I must not, you say, *give my advice in favour of this man!* You now half convince me, my dear, that you are allied to the family that could think of so preposterous a match, or you could never have had the least notion of my advising in his favour.

Ask me for his picture. You know I have a good hand at drawing an ugly likeness. But I'll see a little farther first; for who knows what may happen since matters are in such a train, and since you have not the *courage* to oppose so overwhelming a torrent?

You ask me to help you to a little of my spirit. Are you in earnest? But it will not now, I doubt, do you service. It will not sit naturally upon you. You are your mamma's girl, think what you will, and have violent spirits to contend with. Alas! my dear, you should have borrowed some of mine a little sooner—that is to say, before you had given the management of your estate into the hands of those who think they have a prior claim to it. What though a *father's?* Has not that father two elder children? And do they not both bear his stamp and image more than you do?

But you are so tender of some people who have no tenderness for anybody but themselves, that I must conjure you to speak out. Remember that a friendship like ours admits of no reserves. You may trust my impartiality. It would be an affront to your own judgement if you did not; for do you not *ask* my advice? And have you not taught me that friendship should never give a bias against justice?

You are all too rich to be happy, child. For must not each of you by the constitutions of your family marry to be *still* richer? Is true happiness any part of your family-view? So far from it, that none of your family but yourself could be happy were they not rich. So let them fret on, grumble and grudge, and accumulate; and wondering what ails them that they have not happiness when they have riches, think the cause is want of more; and so go on heaping up till Death, as greedy an accumulator as themselves, gathers them into his garner!

That they prohibit your corresponding with *me* is a wisdom I neither wonder at, nor blame them for, since it is an evidence to me that they know their own folly; and if they do, is it strange that they should be afraid to trust another's judgement upon it?

You are pleased to say, and *upon your word too!*— that your *regards* (a mighty quaint word for *affections*) *are not so much engaged, as some of your friends suppose, to another person.* What need you give one to imagine, my dear, that the last month or two has been a period extremely favourable to that *other* person!— whom it has made an obliger of the niece for his patience with the uncles.

But, to pass that by. *So much* engaged! *How much*, my dear? Shall I infer? *Some of your friends* suppose *a great deal*. You seem to own *a little*.

Don't be angry. It is all fair, because you have not acknowledged to me that *little*. People, I have heard you say, who affect secrets always excite curiosity.

But you proceed with a kind of drawback upon your averment, as if recollection had given you a doubt. *You know not yourself, if they be* (so much engaged). Was it necessary to say this to me?—and to say it *upon your word* too? But you know best. Yet you don't neither, I believe. For a beginning love is acted by a subtle spirit; and oftentimes discovers itself to a bystander when the person possessed (why should I not call it *possessed?*) knows not it has such a demon.

But further you say, what PREFERABLE *favour you may have for him to any other person is owing more to the usage he has received, and for your sake borne, than to any personal consideration.*

This is generously said. It is in character. But, oh my friend, depend upon it you are in danger. Depend upon it, whether you know it or not, you are a little in for't. Your native generosity and greatness of mind endanger you; all your friends by fighting *against* him with impolitic violence fight *for him*. And Lovelace, my life for yours, notwithstanding all his veneration and assiduities has seen further than that veneration and those assiduities (so well calculated to your meridian) will let him own he has seen—has seen, in short, that his work is doing for him more effectually than he could do it for himself. And have you not before now said that nothing is so penetrating as the vanity of a lover, since it makes the person who has it frequently see in his own favour what is *not*, and hardly ever fail of observing what *is*. And who says Lovelace wants vanity?

In short, my dear, it is my opinion, and that from the easiness of his heart and behaviour that he has seen more than *I* have seen; more than you think *could* be seen—more than I believe you *yourself* know, or else you would have let *me* know it.

Already, in order to restrain him from resenting the indignities he has received and which are daily offered him, he has prevailed upon you to correspond with him privately. I know he has nothing to boast of from *what* you have written. But is not his inducing you to receive his letters, and to answer them, a great point gained? By your insisting that he should keep this correspondence private, it appears that there is *one secret* that you do not wish the world should know; and *he* is master of that secret. He is indeed *himself*, as I may say, that secret! What an intimacy does this beget for the lover! How is it distancing the parent!

Yet who, as things are situated, can blame you? Your condescension has no doubt hitherto prevented great mischiefs. It must be continued for the same reasons while the cause remains. You are drawn in by a perverse fate against inclination; but custom, with such laudable purposes, will reconcile the inconveniency and *make* an inclination. And I would advise you (as you would wish to manage on an occasion so critical with that prudence which governs all your actions) not to be afraid of enter-

ing upon a close examination into the true springs and
grounds of this your *generosity* to that happy man.

It is my humble opinion, I tell you frankly, that on
inquiry it will come out to be LOVE. Don't start, my dear!

To be sure Lovelace is a charming fellow. And were
he only—But I will not make you *glow* as you read!
Upon *my word, I* won't. Yet, my dear, don't you find at
your heart somewhat unusual make it go throb, throb,
throb, as you read just here? If you do, don't be
ashamed to own it. It is your *generosity*, my love! that's
all. But, as the Roman augur said, Caesar, beware of the
ides of March!

Adieu, my dearest friend, and forgive; and very speedily by the new-found expedient tell me that you forgive

Your ever-affectionate
ANNA HOWE

Letter 11: MISS CLARISSA HARLOWE TO MISS HOWE

Wednesday, March 1

You both nettled and alarmed me, my dearest Miss
Howe, by the concluding part of your last. At first reading it I did not think it necessary, said I to myself, to
guard against a critic when I was writing to so dear a
friend. But then recollecting myself, is there not more
in it, said I, than the result of a vein so naturally lively?
Surely I must have been guilty of an inadvertence. Let
me enter into the close examination of myself which my
beloved friend advises.

I did so, and cannot own any of the *glow*, any of the
throbs you mention. *Upon my word,* I will repeat, I cannot. And yet the passages in my letter upon which you
are so humorously severe lay me fairly open to your
agreeable raillery. I own they do. And I cannot tell what
turn my mind had taken to dictate so oddly to my pen.

But pray now, is it saying so much, when one who has
no very particular regard to *any* man says, there are
some who are preferable to *others*? And is it blameable
to say, *those* are the preferable who are not well used
by one's relations, yet dispense with that usage out of
regard to one's self, which they would otherwise resent?

Mr Lovelace, for instance, I may be allowed to say, is a man to be preferred to Mr Solmes; and that I *do* prefer him to that man. But surely this may be said, without its being a necessary consequence that one must be in love with him.

Indeed I would not be *in love* with him, as it is called, for the world: first, because I have no opinion of his morals, and think it a fault in which our whole family, my brother excepted, has had a share, that he was permitted to visit us with a hope, which however being distant did not, as I have observed heretofore, entitle any of us to call him to account for such of his immoralities as came to our ears. Next, because I think him to be a vain man, capable of triumphing, secretly at least, over a person whose heart he thinks he has engaged. And, thirdly, because the assiduities and veneration which you impute to him seem to carry a haughtiness in them, as if his address had a merit in it that would be an equivalent for a lady's favour. In short, he seems to me so to behave when most unguarded as if he thought himself above the very politeness which his birth and education (perhaps therefore more than his choice) oblige him to show. In other words, his very politeness appears to me to be constrained; and, with the most remarkably easy and genteel *person*, something seems to be behind in his *manner* that is too studiously kept in.

Indeed, my dear, THIS man is not THE man. I have great objections to him. My heart *throbs* not after him; I *glow* not, but with indignation against myself for having given room for such an imputation. But you must not, my dearest friend, construe common gratitude into love. I cannot bear that you should. But if ever I should have the misfortune to think it love, I promise you, *upon my word*, which is the same as *upon my honour*, that I will acquaint you with it.

You bid me to tell you very speedily and by the new-found expedient that I am not displeased with you for your agreeable raillery. I dispatch this therefore immediately, postponing to my next the account of the inducements which my friends have to promote with so much earnestness the address of Mr Solmes.

Be satisfied, my dear, meantime, that I am *not* displeased with you; indeed I am not. On the contrary, I give you my hearty thanks for your friendly premonitions. And I charge you, as I have often done, that if you observe anything in me so very faulty, as would require from you to others in my behalf the palliation of friendly and partial love, you acquaint me with it; for, methinks, I would so conduct myself as not to give reason even for an *adversary* to censure me; and how shall so weak and so young a creature avoid the censure of such, if my *friend* will not hold a looking-glass before me to let me see my imperfections?

Judge me then, my dear, as any indifferent person (knowing what you know of me) would do. I may at first be a little pained; may *glow* a little, perhaps, to be found less worthy of your friendship than I wish to be; but assure yourself that your kind correction will give me reflection that shall *amend* me. If it do not, you will have a fault to accuse me of that will be utterly *in*-excusable; a fault, let me add, that should you *not* accuse me of it, if in your opinion I am guilty, you will not be so much, so *warmly* my friend, as I am yours, who have never spared you, you know, my dear, on the like occasions.

Here I break off to begin another letter to you, with the assurance, meantime, that I am, and ever will be,

Your equally affectionate and grateful
Cl. Harlowe

Letter 12: MISS HOWE TO MISS CLARISSA HARLOWE

Thursday morn. March 2
Indeed you would not be in love with him for the world! Your servant, my dear. But let me congratulate you, however, on your being the first of our sex that ever I heard of who has been able to turn that lion, Love, at her own pleasure, into a lap-dog.

Well but, if you have not the throbs and the glows, you have not; and are not in love; good reason why—because you would not be in love, and there's no more to be said. Only, my dear, I shall keep a good look out upon you; and so I hope you will upon yourself, for it is no manner of argument that because you would not

be in love, you are not. But before I part entirely with
this subject, a word in your ear, my charming friend. 'Tis
only by way of caution, and in pursuance of the general
observation that a stander-by is often a better judge of
the game than those that play. May it not be, that you
have had, and have, such cross creatures and such odd
heads to deal with as have not allowed you to attend to
the throbs? Or, if you had them a little now and then,
whether, having had two accounts to place them to, you
have not by mistake put them to the wrong one?

Talk of the devil is an old saying. The lively wretch
has made me a visit, and is but just gone away. He is
all impatience and resentment at the treatment you meet
with, and full of apprehensions too, that they will carry
their point with you.

I told him my opinion, that you will never be brought
to think of such a man as Solmes, but that it will probably end in a composition never to have either.

No man, he said, whose fortunes and alliances are so
considerable ever had so little favour from a lady, for
whose sake he had borne so much.

I told him my mind, as freely as I used to do. But
who ever was in fault, self being judge? He complained
of spies set upon his conduct, and to pry into his life
and morals; and this by your brother and uncles.

I told him that this was very hard upon him, and the
more so as neither the one nor the other, perhaps, would
stand a fair inquiry.

He smiled, and called himself *my servant*. The occasion was too fair, he said, for Miss Howe, who never
spared him, to let it pass. But, Lord help their shallow
souls, would I believe it? they were for turning plotters
upon *him*. They had best take care he did not pay them
in their own coin. Their *hearts* were better turned for
such works than their *heads*.

I asked him if he valued himself upon having a head
better turned than theirs for *such works*, as he called
them?

He drew off; and then ran into the highest professions
of reverence and affection for you. The object so meritorious, who can doubt the reality of his professions?

Adieu, my dearest, my noble friend! I love and admire you for the generous conclusion of your last more than I can express. Though I began this letter with impertinent raillery, knowing that you always loved to indulge my mad vein, yet never was there a heart that more glowed with friendly love than that of

Your own
ANNA HOWE

Letter 15: MISS HOWE TO MISS CLARISSA HARLOWE

Friday, March 3

I have both your letters at once. It is very unhappy, my dear, since your friends will have you marry, that such a merit as yours should be addressed by a succession of worthless creatures, who have nothing but their presumption for their excuse.

Yet I am afraid all opposition will be in vain. You must, you will, I doubt, be sacrificed to this odious man [Solmes]! I know your family! There will be no resisting such baits as he has thrown out.

And now I am more than ever convinced of the propriety of the advice I formerly gave you, to keep in your own hands the estate bequeathed to you by your grandfather. Had you done so, it would have procured you at least an *outward* respect from your brother and sister, which would have made them conceal the envy and ill-will that now is bursting upon you from hearts so narrow.

I know your dutiful, your laudable motives, and one would have thought that you might have trusted to a father who so dearly loved you. But had you been actually in possession of that estate, and living up to it and upon it (your youth protected from blighting tongues by the company of your prudent [nurse] Norton, as you had purposed), do you think that your brother, grudging it to you at the time as he did, and looking upon it as his right as an only son, would have been practising about it and aiming at it? I told you some time ago that I thought your trials but proportioned to your prudence. But you will be more than woman if you can extricate yourself with honour, having such violent spirits and sordid minds as in some, and such tyrannical and despotic wills as in others, to deal with. Indeed, all *may* be done, and the world be taught further to admire you, for your blind duty and will-less resignation, if you can persuade yourself to be Mrs Solmes!

I long for your next letter. Continue to be as particular as possible. I can think of no other subject but what relates to you and to your affairs; for I am, and ever will be, most affectionately,

All your own
ANNA HOWE

Letter 16: MISS CLARISSA HARLOWE TO MISS HOWE

Friday, March 3

Oh my dear friend, I have had a sad conflict! trial upon trial; conference upon conference! But what law, what ceremony, can give a man a right to a heart which abhors him more than it does any of God Almighty's creatures?

I hope my mamma will be able to prevail for me. But I will recount all, though I sit up the whole night to do it, for I have a vast deal to write and will be as minute as you wish me to be.

I went down this morning when breakfast was ready with a very uneasy heart, from what Hannah had told me yesterday afternoon; wishing for an opportunity, however, to appeal to my mamma in hopes to engage her interest in my behalf, and purposing to try to find one, when she retired to her own apartment after breakfast. But, unluckily, there was the odious Solmes sitting asquat between my mamma and sister, with *so much* assurance in his looks! But you know, my dear, that those we love not cannot do anything to please us.

Had the wretch kept his seat, it might have been well enough, but the bent and broad-shouldered creature must needs rise and stalk towards a chair, which was just by that which was set for me.

I removed it at a distance, as if to make way to my

own; and down I sat, abruptly I believe; what I had heard all in my head.

But this was not enough to daunt him. The man is a very confident, he is a very bold, staring man!

He took the removed chair and drew it so near mine, squatting in it with his ugly weight, that he pressed upon my hoop. I was so offended (all I had heard, as I said, in my head) that I removed to another chair. I own I had too little command of myself. It gave my brother and sister too much advantage. I dare say they took it—but I did it involuntarily, I think; I could not help it. I knew not what I did.

I saw my papa was excessively displeased. When angry, no man's countenance ever showed it so much as my papa's. Clarissa Harlowe! said he with a big voice, and there he stopped. Sir! said I, and curtsied. I trembled and put my chair nearer the wretch, and sat down; my face I could feel all in a glow.

Make tea, child, said my kind mamma. Sit by me, love, and make tea.

I removed with pleasure to the seat the man had quitted, and being thus indulgently put into employment, soon recovered myself; and in the course of the breakfasting officiously asked two or three questions of Mr Solmes, which I would not have done, but to make up with my papa. *Proud spirits may be brought to,* whispering spoke my sister to me over her shoulder, with an air of triumph and scorn; but I did not mind her.

My mamma was all kindness and condescension. I asked her once if she were pleased with the tea? She said softly, and again called me *dear*, she was pleased with all I did. I was very proud of this encouraging goodness; and all blew over, as I hoped, between my papa and me, for he also spoke kindly to me two or three times.

Small incidents these, my dear, to trouble you with; only as they lead to greater, as you shall hear.

Before the usual breakfast-time was over my papa withdrew with my mamma, telling her he wanted to speak to her. My sister and my aunt, who was with us, next dropped away.

I saw what all this was for. I curtsied. Your servant,

sir. The man cried, Madam, Madam, twice, and looked like a fool. But away I went.

I had but just got into my own apartment and began to think of sending Hannah to beg an audience of my mamma (the more encouraged by her condescending goodness at breakfast), when Shorey, her woman, brought me her commands to attend her in her closet.

My papa, Hannah told me, had just gone out of it with a positive, angry countenance. Then I as much dreaded the audience as I had wished for it before.

I went down, however; but, apprehending the subject, approached her trembling and my heart in visible palpitations.

She saw my concern. Holding out her kind arms as she sat, Come kiss me, my dear, said she with a smile like a sunbeam breaking through the cloud that over-shadowed her naturally benign aspect. Why flutters my jewel so?

This preparative sweetness, with her goodness just before, confirmed my apprehensions. My mamma saw the bitter pill wanted gilding.

Oh my mamma! was all I could say, and I clasped my arms round her neck and my face sunk into her bosom.

My child! my child! restrain, said she, your powers of moving! I dare not else trust myself with you.

Lift up your sweet face, my best child, my own Clarissa Harlowe. Why these sobs? Is an apprehended duty so affecting a thing that before I can speak—But I am glad, my love, you can guess at what I have to say to you. I am spared the pains of breaking to you what was a task upon me reluctantly enough undertaken to break to you.

And drawing her chair still nearer to mine, she put her arms round my neck and my glowing cheek, wet with my tears, close to her own. Let me talk to you, my child, since silence is your choice; hearken to me, and *be* silent.

You know, my dear, what I every day forgo and undergo, for the sake of peace. Your papa is a very good man and means well; but he will not be controlled, nor yet persuaded. You have seemed to pity *me* sometimes, that I am obliged to give up every point. Poor man! *his*

reputation the less for it; *mine* the greater; yet would I
not have this credit, if I could help it, at so dear a rate
to *him* and to *myself*. You are a dutiful, a prudent and
a *wise* child, she was pleased to say (in hope, no doubt,
to make me so); you would not add, I am sure, to my
trouble. You would not wilfully break that peace which
costs your mamma so much to preserve. Obedience is
better than sacrifice.

You have had your own way six or seven times. We
want to secure you against a man so vile [Lovelace]. Tell
me; I have a right to know; whether you prefer this man
to all others? Yet God forbid that I should know you
do! for such a declaration would make us all miserable.
Yet, tell me, are your affections engaged to this man?

I knew what the inference would be, if I had said they
were not.

You hesitate; you answer me not; you cannot answer
me. Never more will I look upon you with an eye of
favour.

Oh madam, madam! Kill me not with your displea-
sure. I would not, I *need* not, hesitate one moment, did
I not dread the inference if I answer you as you wish.
Yet be that inference what it will, your threatened dis-
pleasure will make me speak. And I declare to you that
I know not my own heart if it be not absolutely free.

Well then, Clary (passing over the force of my plea),
if your heart be free—

Oh my beloved mamma, let the usual generosity of
your dear heart operate in my favour. Urge not upon
me the inference that made me hesitate.

Am I to be questioned and argued with? You know
this won't do somewhere else. You know it won't. What
reason then, ungenerous girl, can you have for arguing
with me thus, but because you think from my indulgence
to you, you may?

Dearest madam, forgive me. It was always my pride
and my pleasure to obey you. But look upon that man—
see but the disagreeableness of his person.

Condition thus with your papa. Will *he* bear, do you
think, to be thus dialogued with? And will *you* give up
nothing? Have you not refused as many as have been
offered to you?

And saying this, she arose and went from me.

I will deposit thus far; and as I know you will not think me too minute in my relation of particulars so very interesting to one you honour with your love, proceed in the same way. As matters stand, I don't care to have papers so freely written about me.

Pray let Robert call every day, if you can spare him, whether I have anything ready or not.

What a generosity in you to write as frequently from friendship as I am forced to do from misfortune! The letters being taken away will be an assurance that you have them. As I shall write and deposit as I have opportunity, the formality of *super-* and *sub*-scription will be excused. For I need not say how much I am,

Your sincere and ever-affectionate,
CL. HARLOWE

Letter 17: MISS CLARISSA HARLOWE TO MISS HOWE

Determined and perverse, my dear mamma called me; and after walking twice or thrice in anger about the room, she turned to me. Your heart *free!* Clarissa! How can you tell me your heart is free? Such extraordinary antipathies to a particular person must be owing to extraordinary prepossessions in another's favour! Tell me, Clary, and tell me truly—Do you not continue to correspond with Mr Lovelace?

Dearest madam, replied I, you know my motives; to prevent mischief, I answered his letters. The reason for our apprehensions of this sort are not over.

I see not, that the continuance of your correspondence with him either can, or ought to be permitted. I therefore now forbid it to you, as you value my favour.

Be pleased, madam, only to advise me how to break it off with safety to my brother and uncles; and it is all I wish for. But, madam, as my uncles and my brother will keep no measures—as he has heard what the view is; and as I have reason to think that he is only restrained by his regard for me from resenting their violent treatment of him and his family; what can I do? Would you have me, madam, make him desperate?

The law will protect us, child!

But, madam, may not some dreadful mischief first happen? The law asserts not itself till it is offended.

You have made offers, Clary. Are you really in earnest to break off all correspondence with Mr Lovelace? Let me know this.

Indeed, I am; and I will. You, madam, shall see every letter that has passed between us. You shall see I have given him no encouragement, independent of my duty. And when you have seen them you will be better able to direct me how, on that condition, to break entirely with him.

I take you at your word, Clarissa. Give me *his* letters; and the copies of *yours*.

I am sure, madam, you will keep the knowledge that I write, and what I write—

No conditions with your mamma. Surely my prudence may be trusted to.

I begged her pardon, and besought her to take the key of the private drawer in my escritoire where they lay, that she herself might see that I had no reserves to my mamma.

She did; and took all his letters, and the copies of mine, *un*-conditioned with; she was pleased to say, they shall be yours again, unseen by anybody else.

I thanked her; and she withdrew to read them, saying she would return them when she had.

In about an hour my mamma returned. Take your letters, Clary: I have nothing to task your discretion with, as to the wording of yours to him. You have even kept up a proper dignity, as well as decorum; and you have resented, as you ought to resent, his menacing invectives. But *can* you think from the avowed hatred of one side, and the avowed defiance of the other, that this can be a suitable match? *Can* you think it becomes you to encourage an address from a man who has fought a duel with your brother, let his fortune and professions be what they will?

By no means it can, madam; you will be pleased to observe that I have said as much to him. But now, madam, the whole correspondence is before you; and I beg your commands what to do in a situation so very disagreeable.

One thing I will tell you, Clary Harlowe: but I charge you, as you would not have me question the generosity of your spirit, to take no advantage of it, either *mentally* or *verbally* were the words: that I am so much pleased with the offer of your keys to me, in so cheerful and unreserved a manner, and in the prudence you have shown in your letters, that were it practicable to bring everyone, or your father only, into my opinion, I should readily leave all the rest to your discretion, reserving only to myself the direction or approbation of your future letters; and to see that you broke off the correspondence as soon as possible. But as it is not, and as I know your papa would have no patience with you, should it be acknowledged that you correspond with Mr Lovelace, or that you *have* corresponded with him since the time he prohibited you so to do, I forbid you continuing such a liberty. Yet, as the case is difficult, let me ask you, what you yourself can propose? Your heart, you *say, is free.* You own that you cannot think, as matters are circumstanced, that a match with a man so obnoxious as he now is to us all is proper to be thought of. What do you propose to do? What, Clary, are your own thoughts of the matter?

Without hesitation (for I saw I was upon a new trial) thus I answered. What I humbly propose is this: 'That I will write to Mr Lovelace (for I have not answered his last) that he has nothing to do between my father and me: that I neither *ask* his advice, nor *need* it: but that since he thinks he has some pretence for interfering, because of my brother's avowal of the interest of Mr Solmes in malice to him, I will assure him, without giving him any reason to impute the assurance to be in the least favourable to himself, that I never will be that man's.' And if, proceeded I, I may be permitted to give him this assurance; and Mr Solmes, in consequence of it, be discouraged from prosecuting his address; let Mr Lovelace be satisfied or dissatisfied, I will go no farther; nor write another line to him; nor ever see him more, if I can avoid it: and shall have a good excuse for it, without bringing in any of my family.

Ah! my love! But what shall we do about the *terms* Mr Solmes offers. Your brother, in short, has given in a plan that captivates us all; and a family so rich in all its branches that has its views to honour must be pleased to see a very great probability of being on a footing with the principal in the kingdom.

And for the sake of these views, for the sake of this plan of my brother's, am I, madam, to be given in marriage to a man I never can endure! Oh my dear mamma, save me, save me, if you can, from this heavy evil! I had rather be buried alive, indeed I had, than have that man!

She chid me for my vehemence, but was so good as to tell me that she would venture to talk with my uncle Harlowe, and, if he encouraged her (or would engage to second her), with my papa; and I should hear further in the morning.

She went down to tea and kindly undertook to excuse my attendance at supper; and I immediately had recourse to my pen, to give you these particulars.

Letter 19: MISS CLARISSA HARLOWE TO MISS HOWE

Sat. March 4, 12 o'clock

Hannah has just now brought me from the usual place your favour of yesterday. The contents of it have made me very thoughtful, and you will have an answer in my gravest style.

As to the article of giving up to my papa's control the estate bequeathed me, my motives at the time, as you acknowledge, were not blameable. Your advice to me on the subject was grounded, as I remember, on your good opinion of me; believing that I should not make a bad use of the power willed me.

It is true, thought I, that I have formed agreeable schemes of making others as happy as myself by the proper discharge of the stewardship entrusted to me (are not all estates stewardships, my dear?). But let me examine myself: is not vanity or secret love of praise a principal motive with me at the bottom? Ought I not to suspect my own heart? If I set up for myself, puffed up with everyone's good opinion, may I not be *left* to myself? Everyone's eyes are upon the conduct, upon the visits, upon the visit-*ors* of a young creature of our sex made independent. And then, left to myself, should I take a wrong step though with ever so good an intention, how many should I have to triumph over me, how few to pity?—the more of the one, and the fewer of the other, for having aimed at excelling.

These were some of my reflections at the time: and I have no doubt but that in the same situation I should do the very same thing; and that upon the maturest deliberation. Who can command or foresee events? To act up to our best judgements at the time is all we can do. If I have erred, 'tis to worldly wisdom only that I have erred. If we suffer by an act of duty, or even by an act of generosity, is it not pleasurable on reflection that the fault is in others, rather than in ourselves? I had rather, a vast deal, have reason to think others unkind, than that they should have any to think me undutiful. And so, my dear, I am sure had you.

And now for the *most* concerning part of your letter.

You think I must of necessity be Mr Solmes's wife, as matters are circumstanced. I will not be very rash, my dear, in protesting to the contrary. But I think it never, never can, nor *ought* to be! My temper, I know, is depended upon; but I have heretofore said that I have something in me of my father's family, as well as of my mother's. And have I any encouragement to follow too implicitly the example which my mamma sets of meekness and resignedness to the wills of others? Is she not for ever obliged to be, as she was pleased to hint to me, of the *forbearing* side? In my mamma's case, your observation is verified, that those who will bear much shall have much to bear. What is it, as she says, that *she* has not sacrificed to peace? Yet, has *she* by her sacrifices always found the peace she has deserved to find? Indeed No! I am afraid the very contrary.

I have said that I never can be, that I never ought to be, Mrs Solmes. I repeat, that I *ought* not; for surely, my dear, I should not give up to my brother's ambition the happiness of my future life. Surely I ought not to be the instrument to deprive Mr Solmes's relations of their natural rights and reversionary prospects, for the sake of further aggrandizing a family (although *that* I am of) which already lives in great affluence and splendour; and who might be as justly dissatisfied were what some of them aim at to be obtained, that they were not princes, as now they are that they are not peers (for when ever was an ambitious mind, as you observe in the case of avarice, satisfied by acquisition?). The less, surely, ought I to give into these grasping views of my brother, as I myself heartily despise the end aimed at; as I wish not either to change my state, or better my fortunes; and as I am fully persuaded that happiness and riches are *two* things, and very seldom meet together.

So, my dear, were we perfect, which no one can be, we could not be happy in this life, unless those with whom we have to deal (those, more especially, who have any control upon us) were governed by the same principles. What have we then to do but, as I have hinted above, to choose right, and pursue it steadily, and leave the issue to Providence?

I am stopped. Hannah shall deposit this. She was ordered by my mamma, who asked where I was, to tell me that she would come up and talk with me in my own closet. She is coming! Adieu, my dear.

Letter 20: MISS CLARISSA HARLOWE TO MISS HOWE

Sat. p.m.

The expected conference is over; but my difficulties are increased. This, as my mamma was pleased to tell me, being the last *persuasory* effort that will be attempted, I will be as particular in the account of it as my head and my heart will allow me to be.

I have made, said she, as she entered my room, a short as well as early dinner, on purpose to confer with you. And I do assure you, that it will be the last conference I shall either be permitted or *inclined* to hold with you on the subject, if you should prove as refractory as some, whom I hope you'll disappoint, imagine you will; and thereby demonstrate that I have not the weight with you that my indulgence to you deserves.

Who at the long run *must* submit—*all* of us to *you*; or *you* to *all* of us?

I wept. I knew not what to say; or rather how to express what I had to say.

Take notice that there are flaws in your grandfather's will; not a shilling of that estate will be yours, if you do not yield. Your grandfather left it to you as a reward of your duty to *him* and to *us*. You will *justly* forfeit it, if—

Permit me, good madam, to say that, if it were *unjustly* bequeathed me, I ought not to wish to have it. But I hope Mr Solmes will be apprised of these flaws.

This was very pertly said, she was pleased to tell me; but bid me reflect, that the forfeiture of that estate, through my opposition, would be attended with the total loss of my papa's favour; and then how destitute I must be; how unable to support myself; and how many benevolent designs and good actions must I give up!

I must accommodate myself, I said, in the latter case, to my circumstances.

What perverseness! said my mamma. But if you depend upon the favour of either or both your uncles, vain will be that dependence. *They* will give you up, I do assure you, if your *papa* does, and absolutely renounce you.

I told her, I was sorry that I had had so little merit as to have made no deeper impressions of favour for me in their hearts; but that I would love and honour them as long as I lived.

All this, she was pleased to say, made my prepossession in a certain man's favour the more evident. Indeed my brother and sister could not go anywhither, but they heard of these prepossessions.

I received her rebukes in silence.

You are sullen, Clarissa! I see you are sullen! And she walked about the room in anger. Then turning to me. You can *bear* the imputation, I see! You have no concern to clear yourself of it. I was afraid of telling you all I was enjoined to tell you in case you were to be unpersuadeable. But I find that I had a greater opinion of your delicacy and gentleness than I needed to have. It cannot discompose so steady, so inflexible a young creature, to be told that the [marriage] settlements are actually drawn; and that you will be called down, in a very few days, to hear them read, and to sign them; for it is impossible, if your heart be free, that you can make the least objection to them, except that they are so much in your favour and in all our favour be one.

I was speechless, absolutely speechless; although my heart was ready to burst, yet could I neither weep nor speak.

She folded the *warm statue*, as she was pleased to call me, in her arms; and entreated me, for God's sake, and for her sake, to comply.

I would, madam, said I, folding my hands with an earnestness that my whole heart was engaged in, bear the cruellest tortures, bear loss of limb, and even of life, to give *you* peace. But this man, every moment I would at your command think of him with favour, is the more my aversion. You cannot, indeed you cannot, think, how my whole soul resists him!

I then, half-frantically I believe, laid hold of her gown. Have patience with me, dearest madam! said I. Do not *you* renounce me totally!

Permit me, dearest madam, to say, that *your* goodness to me, *your* patience, *your* peace, weigh more with me, than all the rest put together: for although I am to be treated by my brother and, through his instigations, by my papa, as a slave in this point, and not as a daughter, yet my mind is not that of a slave. You have not brought me up to be mean.

So, Clary, you are already at defiance with your papa! I have had too much cause before to *apprehend* as much. What will this come to?

You may guess what your father's first question on his return will be. He must know that I can do nothing with you. I have done my part. Seek *me*, if your mind change before he comes back. You have yet a little more time, as he stays supper: I will no more seek *you*, nor *to* you. And away she flung.

What could I do but weep?

I had rather all the world should be angry with me, than my mamma!

Meantime, to clear my hands from papers of such a nature, Hannah shall deposit this. If two or three letters reach you together, they will but express, from one period to another, the anxieties and difficulties which the mind of your unhappy, but ever affectionate friend labours under.

CL. H.

Letter 21: MISS CLARISSA HARLOWE TO MISS HOWE

Sat. night

I have been down. I *am* to be unlucky in all I do, I think, be my intention ever so good. I have made matters worse instead of better—as I shall now tell you.

I found my mamma and sister together in my sister's parlour. My mamma, I fear, by the glow in her fine face (and as the browner, sullener glow in my sister's confirmed) had been expressing herself with warmth against her *unhappier* child; perhaps giving such an account of what had passed, as should clear herself and convince Bella, and through *her,* my brother and uncles, of the sincere pains she had taken with me!

I entered like a dejected criminal, I believe—and besought the favour of a private audience.

I came down, I said, to beg of her to forgive me for anything she might have taken amiss in what had passed above respecting herself, and to use her interest to soften my papa's displeasure when she made the report she was to make to him.

Such aggravating looks, such lifting-up of hands and eyes, such a furrowed forehead in my sister!

My mamma was angry enough without all that; and asked me, to what purpose I came down if I were still so untractable?

She had hardly spoke the words, when Shorey came in to tell her that Mr Solmes was in the hall, and desired admittance.

Ugly creature! What, at the close of day, quite dark, brought him hither? But, on second thoughts, I believe it was contrived that he should be here at supper, to know the result of the conference between my mamma and me; and that my papa on his return might find us together.

I was hurrying away; but my mamma commanded me, since I had come down only, as she said, to mock her, not to stir; and at the same time see if I could behave so to him, as might encourage her to make the report to my papa which I had so earnestly besought her to make.

The man stalked in. His usual walk is by pauses, as if . . . he was telling [counting] his steps: and first paid his clumsy respects to my mamma, then to my sister; next to me, as if I were already his wife and therefore to be last in his notice; and sitting down by me, told us in general what weather it was. Very cold he made it; but I was warm [i.e., angry] enough. Then addressing himself to me: And how do *you* find it, miss, was his question; and would have took my hand.

I withdrew it, I believe with disdain enough: my mamma frowned; my sister bit her lip.

My sister rose with a face all over scarlet, and stepping to the table where lay a fan, she took it up and, although Mr Solmes had observed that the weather was cold, fanned herself very violently.

My mamma came to me, and angrily taking my hand led me out of that parlour into my own, which, you know, is next to it. Is not this behaviour very bold, very provoking, think you, Clary?

I beg your pardon, madam, if it has that appearance to you. But indeed, my dear mamma, there seem to be snares laying for me. Too well I know my brother's drift. With a good word he shall have my consent for all he wishes to worm me out of. Neither he, nor my sister, shall need to take half this pains.

My mamma was about to leave me in high displeasure.

I besought her to stay. One favour, but one favour, dearest madam, said I, give me leave to beg of you—

What would the girl?

I see how everything is working about. I never, never can think of Mr Solmes.

I was ready to sink. She was so good as to lend me her arm to support me.

But, Clary, this one further opportunity I give you. Go in again to Mr Solmes, and behave discreetly to him; and let your papa find you together, upon *civil* terms at least.

What, madam, to give *him* hope? To give hope to Mr Solmes?

Obstinate, perverse, undutiful Clarissa Harlowe!

She flung from me with high indignation: and I went up with a very heavy heart, and feet as slow as my heart was heavy.

Twelve o'clock

This moment the keys of everything are taken from me. It was proposed to send for me down; but my papa said he could not bear to look upon me. Strange alteration in a few weeks! Shorey was the messenger. The tears stood in her eyes when she delivered her message.

You, my dear, are happy! May you always be so! And then I can never be wholly miserable. Adieu, my beloved friend!

CL. HARLOWE

Letter 22: MISS CLARISSA HARLOWE TO MISS HOWE

Sunday morning, March 5

Hannah has just brought me, from the private place in the garden-wall, a letter from Mr Lovelace, deposited last night, signed also by Lord M.

He tells me in it, 'That Mr Solmes makes it his boast that he is to be married in a few days to one of the shyest women in England; that my brother explains his meaning to be me, assuring everyone that his youngest sister is very soon to be Mr Solmes's wife. He tells me of the patterns bespoke, which my mamma mentioned to me.'

Not one thing escapes him that is done or said in this house!

'He knows not what my relations' inducements can be, to prefer such a man as Solmes to him.

'As to his estate or family, the first cannot be excepted against; and for the second, he will not disgrace himself by a comparison so odious. He appeals to Lord M. for the regularity of his life and manners, ever since he has made his addresses to me, or had hope of my favour.'

I suppose he would have his Lordship's signing to this letter to be taken as a voucher for him.

'He desires my leave, in company with my Lord, in a pacific manner to attend my father or uncles, in order to make proposals that must be accepted, if they will but see him and hear what they are; and tells me that he will submit to any measures that I shall prescribe, in order to bring about a reconciliation.'

He presumes to be very earnest with me 'to give him a private meeting some night in my father's garden, attended by whom I please.'

Really, my dear, were you to see his letter, you would think I had given him great encouragement and were in direct treaty with him; or that he were sure that my friends would drive me into a foreign protection; for he has the boldness to offer, in my Lord's name, an asylum to me should I be tyrannically treated in Solmes's behalf.

I suppose it is the way of this sex to endeavour to entangle the thoughtless of ours by bold supposals and offers, in hopes that we shall be too complaisant or bashful to quarrel with them; and, if not checked, to reckon upon our silence as assents voluntarily given, or concessions made in their favour.

There are other particulars in this letter which I ought to mention to you; but I will take an opportunity to send you the letter itself, or a copy of it.

For my own part, I am very uneasy to think how I have been *drawn* on one hand, and *driven* on the other, into a clandestine, in short, into a mere lover-like correspondence, which my heart condemns.

It is easy to see that if I do not break it off, Mr Lovelace's advantages by reason of my unhappy situation will every day increase, and I shall be more and more entangled; yet if I do put an end to it, without making it a condition of being freed from Mr Solmes's address— May I, my dear—is it best to continue it a little longer, in hopes, by giving him up, to extricate myself out of the other difficulty? Whose advice can I now ask but yours?

All my relations are met. They are at breakfast together. Solmes is expected. I am excessively uneasy. I must lay down my pen.

Letter 23: MISS CLARISSA HARLOWE TO MISS HOWE

Mon. morning, Mar. 6

They are resolved to break my heart. My poor Hannah
is discharged—disgracefully discharged! Thus it was.

Half an hour after I had sent the poor girl down for
my breakfast, that bold creature Betty Barnes, my sister's confidant and servant (if a favourite maid and confidant can be deemed a *servant*), came up.

What, miss, will you please to have for breakfast?

I was surprised. What will I have for breakfast, Betty!
How! what!—how comes it! Then I named Hannah. I
could not tell what to say.

Don't be surprised, miss. But you'll see Hannah no
more in this house!

God forbid! Is any harm come to Hannah! What!
What is the matter with Hannah?

Why, miss, the short and the long is this: your papa
and mamma think Hannah has stayed long enough in
the house to do mischief; and so she is ordered to *troop*
(that was the confident creature's word); and I am directed to wait upon you.

I burst into tears. I have no service for you, Betty
Barnes, none at all. But where is Hannah? Cannot I
speak with the poor girl. I owe her half a year's wages.
May I not see the honest creature and pay her her
wages? I may never see her again perhaps, for they are
resolved to break my heart.

And they think, you are resolved to break theirs: so
tit for tat, miss.

Impertinent I called her; and asked her if it were upon
such confident terms that her service was to commence.

I was so very earnest to see the poor maid that, to
oblige me, as she said, she went down with my request.

The worthy creature was as earnest to see me; and
the favour was granted in presence of Shorey and Betty.

I thanked her, when she came up, for her past service
to me.

Her heart was ready to break. And she fell a-
vindicating her fidelity and love, and disclaiming any
mischief she had ever made.

I told her that those who occasioned her being turned
out of my service made no question of her integrity: that
it was an indignity levelled at me: that I was very sorry
for it, and hoped she would meet with as good a service.

Never, never, wringing her hands, a mistress she loved
so well. And the poor creature ran on in my praises, and
in professions of love to me.

I gave her a little linen, some laces and other odd
things; and, instead of four pounds which were due to
her, ten guineas: and said, if ever I were again allowed
to be my own mistress, I would think of *her* in the first
place.

Hannah told me, before their faces, having no other
opportunity, that she had been examined about letters
to me, and *from* me: and that she had given her pockets
to Miss Harlowe, who looked into them and put her
fingers in her stays, to satisfy herself that she had not
any.

She gave me an account of the number of my pheasants and bantams; and I said they should be my own
care twice or thrice a day.

We wept over each other at parting. The girl prayed
for all the family.

To have so good a servant so disgracefully dismissed
is a cutting thing: and I could not help saying, that these
methods might break my heart, but not any other way
answer the end of the authors of my disgraces.

Thus have I been forced to part with my faithful Hannah. If you can commend the good creature to a place
worthy of her, pray do, for my sake.

Letter 25: MISS CLARISSA HARLOWE TO MISS HOWE

Tues. March 7

By my last deposit, you'll see how I am driven, and what
a poor prisoner I am; no regard had to my reputation.
The whole matter is now before you. Can *such* measures
be supposed to soften? But surely they can only mean
to try to frighten me into my brother's views. All my
hope is to be able to weather this point till my cousin
Morden comes from Florence; and he is expected soon.

Yet, if they are determined upon a short day, I doubt he will not be here time enough to save me.

They think they have done everything by turning away my poor Hannah: but as long as the liberty of the garden, and my poultry-visits are allowed me, they will be mistaken.

I asked *Mrs Betty* if she had any orders to watch or attend me? or, whether I were to ask *her* leave, whenever I should be disposed to walk in the garden, or to go to feed my bantams?

Lord bless her! what could I mean by such a question! Yet she owned that she had heard that I was not to walk in the garden when my papa, mamma, or uncles were there.

However, as it behoved me to be assured on this head, I went down directly, and stayed an hour, without question or impediment: and yet a good part of the time, I walked under, and in *sight* (as I may say) of my brother's study window, where both he and my sister happened to be. And I am sure they saw me, by the loud mirth they affected by way of insult, as I suppose.

So this part of my restraint was doubtless a stretch of the authority given him. The enforcing of that may perhaps come next. But I hope not.

Tuesday night

Since I wrote the above, I have ventured to send a letter by Shorey to my mamma. I directed her to give it into her own hand when nobody was by.

I shall enclose the copy of it. You'll see that I would have it thought, that now Hannah is gone I have no way to correspond out of the house. I am far from thinking all I do, right. I am afraid this is a little piece of art, that is *not* so. But this is an afterthought: the letter went first.

Clarissa to Mrs Harlowe

Honoured madam,

Having acknowledged to you that I had received letters from Mr Lovelace full of resentment, and that I answered them purely to prevent further mischief; and having showed you copies of my answers, which you did not disapprove of, although you thought fit, after you had read them, to forbid me any further correspondence with him; I think it my duty to acquaint you that another letter from him has since come to my hand, in which he is very earnest with me to permit him to wait on my papa, or you, or my two uncles, in a pacific way, accompanied by Lord M. on which I beg your commands.

I own to you, madam, that had not the prohibition been renewed, and had not Hannah been so suddenly dismissed my service, I should have made the less scruple to have written an answer and to have commanded her to convey it to him with all speed, in order to dissuade him from these visits, lest anything should happen on the occasion that my heart aches but to think of.

This communication being as voluntarily made as dutifully intended, I humbly presume to hope that I shall not be required to produce the letter itself. I cannot either in honour or prudence do that, because of the vehemence of his style; for having heard (not, I assure you, by my means, or through Hannah's) of some part of the harsh treatment I have met with, he thinks himself entitled to place it to his own account by reason of speeches thrown out by some of my relations equally vehement.

If I do *not* answer him, he will be made desperate, and think himself justified (though I shall not think him so) in resenting the treatment he complains of. If I *do*, and if in compliment to me he forbears to resent what he thinks himself entitled to resent, be pleased, madam, to consider the obligation he will suppose he lays me under.

If I were as strongly prepossessed in his favour as is supposed, I should not have wished this to be considered by you. And permit me, as a still further proof that I am not prepossessed, to beg of you to consider, whether, upon the whole, the proposal I made of declaring for the single life (which I will religiously adhere to) is not the best way to get rid of his pretensions with honour. To renounce him, and not to be allowed to aver that I will never be the other man's will make him conclude (driven as I am driven) that I am determined in that other man's favour.

And so leaving the whole to your own wisdom, and

whether you choose to consult my papa and uncles upon
this humble application, or not; or whether I shall be
allowed to write an answer to Mr Lovelace, or not (and
if allowed so to do, I beg your direction by whom to
send it); I remain,

Honoured madam,
Your unhappy, but ever-dutiful daughter,
CL. HARLOWE

Wednesday morning
I have just received an answer to the enclosed letter.
My mamma, you'll observe, has ordered me to burn it:
but as you will have it in your safe keeping and nobody
else will see it, her end will be equally answered. It has
neither date nor superscription.

Mrs Harlowe to Clarissa

Clarissa,
Say not all the blame and all the punishment is yours.
I am as much blamed and as much punished as you are;
yet am more innocent. When your obstinacy is equal to
any other person's passion, blame not your brother. We
judged right that Hannah carried on your correspondencies. Now she is gone, and you cannot write (we
think you cannot) to Miss Howe, nor she to you, without
our knowledge, one cause of uneasiness and jealousy
is over.

I had no dislike to Hannah. I did not tell her so, because Somebody was within hearing when she desired
to pay her duty to me at going. I gave her a caution, in
a raised voice, to take care wherever she went to live
next, if there were any young ladies, how she made parties, and assisted in clandestine correspondencies: but I
slid two guineas into her hand. Nor was I angry to hear
you were *more* bountiful to her. So much for Hannah.

I don't know what to write about your answering that
man of violence. What can you think of it, that such a
family as ours should have such a rod held over it? You
was once all my comfort: you made all my hardships
tolerable. But now! However, nothing, it is plain, can
move you; and I will say no more on that head: for you

are under your papa's discipline now; and he will neither
be prescribed to, nor entreated.

I should have been glad to see the letter you tell me
of, as I saw the rest. You say both honour and prudence
forbid you to show it me! Oh Clarissa! what think you
of receiving letters that honour and prudence forbid you
to show to a mother! But it is not for me to see it, if
you would *choose* to show it me. I will not be in your
secret. I will not know that you did correspond. And, as
to an answer, take your own methods. But let him know
it will be the last you will write. And if you do write, I
won't see it: so seal it up, if you do, and give it to Shorey
and she—Yet do not think I give you licence to write!

As to the rest, you have by your obstinacy put it out
of my power to do anything for you. Your papa takes
upon himself to be answerable for all consequences. You
must not therefore apply to me for any favour. I shall
endeavour to be only an observer; happy, if I could be
an unconcerned one! While I had power, you would not
let me use it as I *would* have used it.

I charge you, let not this letter be found. Burn it.
There is too much of the *mother* in it, to a daughter so
unaccountably obstinate.

Write not another letter to me. I can do nothing for
you. But you can do everything for yourself.

Letter 26: MISS CLARISSA HARLOWE TO MISS HOWE

Thursd. morn. Mar. 9

I have another letter from Mr Lovelace, although I had
not answered his former.

This man, somehow or other, knows everything that
passes in our family: my confinement; Hannah's dismission; and more of the resentments and resolutions of
my father, uncles, and brother, than I can possibly know,
and almost as soon as things happen. He cannot come
at these intelligences fairly.

He is excessively uneasy upon what he hears; and his
expressions both of love to me and resentment to them
are very fervent. He solicits me much 'To engage my

honour to him, never to have Mr Solmes.' I think I may fairly promise him that I will not.

He begs, 'That I will not think he is endeavouring to make to himself a *merit* at any man's expense, since he hopes to obtain my favour on the foot of his *own*; nor that he seeks to *intimidate* me into a consideration for him. But declares that the treatment he meets with from my family is so intolerable that he is perpetually reproached for not resenting it; and that as well by Lord M. and his two aunts, as by all his other friends: and if he must have no hope from me, he cannot answer for what his despair will make him do.'

Indeed, he says, his relations, the ladies particularly, advise him to have recourse to a *legal* remedy: 'But how, he asks, can a man of honour go to law for verbal abuses, given by people entitled to wear swords?'

You see, my dear, that my mamma seems as apprehensive of mischief as I, and has indirectly offered to let Shorey carry my answer to the letter he sent me before.

He is full of the favour of the ladies of his family to me: to whom, nevertheless, I am personally a stranger.

It is natural, I believe, for a person to be the more desirous of making new friends in proportion as she loses the favour of old ones, yet had I rather appear amiable in the eyes of my own relations and in your eyes than in those of all the world besides: but these four ladies of his family have such excellent characters that one cannot but wish to be thought well of by them. I cannot, for my own part, think so well of myself as to imagine that they can wish him to persevere in his views with regard to me, through such contempts and discouragements.

Curiosity at present is all my motive: nor will there ever, I hope, be a stronger, notwithstanding your questionable *throbs*; even were Mr Lovelace to be less exceptionable than he is.

I have answered his letters. This is the substance of my letter:

'I express my surprise at his knowing (and so early) all that passes here. I assure him, that were there not such a man in the world as himself, I would not have Mr Solmes.'

I tell him, 'That to return, as I understand he does, defiances for defiances, to my relations, is far from being a proof with me, either of his politeness or of the consideration he pretends to have for me.

'On all these accounts, I desire that the one more letter which I will allow him to deposit in the usual place may be the very *last*; and that only to acquaint me with his acquiescence that it shall be so; at least till happier times!'

This last I put in, that he may not be quite desperate. But if he take me at my word, I shall be rid of one of my tormentors.

I have promised to lay before you all his letters and my answers. I repeat that promise; and am the less solicitous for that reason to amplify upon the contents of either. But I cannot too often express my vexation to be driven to such straits and difficulties, here at home, as oblige me to answer letters (from a man I had not absolutely intended to encourage and had really great objections to) filled as *his* are with such warm protestations, and written to me with a spirit of expectation.

For, my dear, you never knew so bold a supposer. In short, my dear, like a restive horse he pains one's hands, and half disjoints one's arms to rein him in. And when you see his letters, you must form no judgement upon them, till you have read my answers: if you do, you will indeed think you have cause to attribute *self-deceit*, and *throbs,* and *glows* to your friend. If he has a design by this conduct (sometimes complaining of my shyness, at others exulting in my imaginary favours) to induce me at one time to acquiesce with his compliments, at another to be more complaisant for his complaints; and if the contradiction be not the effect of his inattention and giddiness; I shall think him as deep and as artful (too probably, as *practised*) a creature as ever lived; and were I to be sure of it, should hate him, if possible, worse than I do Solmes.

But enough for the present of a creature so very various!

Letter 27: MISS HOWE TO MISS CLARISSA HARLOWE

Thursday night, March 9

I have no patience with any of the people you are with. I know not what to advise you to do. How do you know that you are not punishable for being the cause, though to your own loss, that the will of your grandfather is not complied with? Wills are sacred things, child. You see that they, even *they*, think so, who imagine they suffer by a will through the distinction paid you in it.

Your grandfather knew the family-failing: he knew what a noble spirit you had to do good. He himself, perhaps (excuse me, my dear), had done too little in his lifetime; and therefore he put it in your power to make up for the defects of the whole family. Were it to me, I would resume it [the estate bequeathed her]. Indeed I would.

You will say, you cannot do it, while you are with them. I don't know that. Do you think they can use you worse than they do? And is it not your *right*? And do they not make use of your own generosity to oppress you? Your uncle Harlowe is one trustee, your cousin Morden is the other. Insist upon your right to your uncle, and write to your cousin Morden about it. This, I dare say, will make them alter their behaviour to you.

Your insolent brother, what has *he* to do to control you? Were it me (I wish it were for one month, and no more), I'd show him the difference. I'd be in my own mansion, pursuing my charming schemes and making all around me happy. I'd set up my own chariot. I'd visit them when they deserved it. But when my brother and sister gave themselves airs, I'd let them know that I was their sister, and not their servant; and if that did not do, I would shut my gates against them; and bid them be company for each other.

It must be confessed, however, that this brother and sister of yours, judging as such narrow spirits will ever judge, have some reason for treating you as they do. It must have long been a mortifying consideration to them (set disappointed love on her side, and avarice on his, out of the question) to be so much eclipsed by a younger sister. Such a sun in a family where there are none but faint twinklers, how could they bear it! Can you wonder then, that they should embrace the first opportunity that offered to endeavour to bring you down to their level?

Depend upon it, my dear, you will have more of it, and more still, as you bear it.

As to this odious Solmes, I wonder not at your aversion to him. It is needless to say anything to you, who have so sincere an antipathy to him, to strengthen your dislike: yet who can resist her own talents? One of mine, as I have heretofore said, is to give an ugly likeness. Shall I indulge it? I will. And the rather as, in doing so, you will have my opinion in justification of your aversion to him, and in approbation of a steadiness that I ever admired, and must for ever approve in your temper.

I was twice in this wretch's company. At one of the times your Lovelace was there. I need not mention to you, who have such a *pretty curiosity*, though at present, *only* a curiosity, you know! the unspeakable difference!

Lovelace entertained the company in his lively gay way, and made everybody laugh at one of his stories. It was before this creature was thought of for you. Solmes laughed too. It was, however, *his* laugh; for his first three years, at least, I imagine, must have been one continual fit of crying; and his muscles have never yet been able to recover a risible tone. His very smile (you never saw him smile, I believe; never at least gave him cause to smile) is so little natural to his features, that it appears in him as hideous as the *grin* of a man in malice.

I took great notice of him, as I do of all the noble lords of the creation in their peculiarities, and was disgusted, nay, shocked at him even then. I was glad, I remember, on that particular occasion, to see his strange features recovering their natural gloominess, though they did this but slowly, as if the muscles which contributed to his distortions had turned upon rusty springs.

What a dreadful thing must even the love of such a husband be! For my part, were I his wife! (but what have I done to myself to make but such a supposition?) I should never have comfort but in his absence, or when I was quarrelling with him.

Yet this is the man they have found out, for the sake

of considerations as sordid as those he is governed by, for a husband (that is to say, for a lord and master) for Miss Clarissa Harlowe!

You must not have him, my dear—that I am clear in—though not so clear how you will be able to avoid it, except you assert the independence which your estate gives you.

Mr Hickman is expected from London this evening. I have desired him to enquire after Lovelace's life and conversation in town. If he has not, I shall be very angry with him. Don't expect a very good account of either. He is certainly an intriguing wretch, and full of inventions.

Upon my word, I most heartily despise that sex! I wish they would let our fathers and mothers alone; teasing *them* to tease *us* with their golden promises, and protestations, and settlements, and the rest of their ostentatious nonsense. How charmingly might you and I live together and despite them all! But to be cajoled, wire-drawn, and ensnared, like silly birds, into a state of bondage or vile subordination: to be courted as princesses for a few weeks, in order to be treated as slaves for the rest of our lives. Indeed, my dear, as you say of Solmes, I cannot endure them!

Mr Hickman shall sound Lord M. upon the subject you recommend. But beforehand, I can tell you what he and what his sisters will say when they *are* sounded. Who would not be proud of such a relation as Miss Clarissa Harlowe?

If I have not been clear enough in my advice about what you shall do, let me say that I can give it in one word: it is only by re-urging you to RESUME. If you do, all the rest will follow.

Your mamma tells you, 'That you will have great trials: that you are under your papa's discipline.' But can it be, that such a lady, such a sister, such a wife, such a mother, has no influence in her own family? Who indeed, as you say, would marry, that can live single? My choler is again beginning to rise. RESUME, my dear. And that's all I will give myself time to say further, lest I offend you when I cannot serve you. Only this, that I am

Your truly affectionate friend and servant

ANNA HOWE

Letter 28: MISS CLARISSA HARLOWE TO MISS HOWE

Friday, Mar. 10

You will permit me, my dear, to touch upon a few passages in your last favour, that affect me sensibly.

In the first place, you must allow me to say, low as I am in spirits, that I am very angry with you for your reflections on my relations, particularly on my father, and on the memory of my grandfather. Nor, my dear, does your own mamma always escape the keen edge of vivacity.

As to the advice you give, to resume my estate, I am determined not to litigate with my papa, let what will be the consequence to myself. I may give you, at another time, a more particular answer to your reasonings on this subject: but at present will only observe, that it is my opinion that Lovelace himself would hardly think me worth addressing, were he to know *this* to be my resolution.

You very ingeniously account for the love we bear to one another, from the *difference* in our tempers. I own, I should not have thought of that. There may possibly be something in it: but whether there be, or not, whenever I am cool, and give myself time to reflect, I will love you the better for the correction you give me, be as severe as you will upon me. Spare me not therefore, my dear friend, whenever you think me in the least faulty. I love your agreeable raillery: you know I always did: nor, however *over*-serious you think me, did I ever think you *flippant*, as you harshly call it. One of the first conditions of our mutual friendship was that each should say or write to the other whatever was upon her mind, without any offence to be taken; a condition that is indeed an indispensable in all friendship.

I should be very blameable to endeavour to hide any the least bias upon my mind from you: and I cannot but say—that this man—this Lovelace—is a person that might be liked well enough if he bore such a character as Mr Hickman bears; and even if there were hopes of reclaiming him: but LOVE, methinks, as short a word as it is, has a *broad* sound with it. Yet do I find that one may be driven by violent measures step by step, as it

were, into something that may be called—I don't know
what to call it—a *conditional kind of liking*, or so. But
as to the word LOVE—justifiable and charming as it is in
some cases (that is to say, in all the *relative*, in all the
social and, what is still beyond both, in all our *superior*
duties, in which it may be properly called *divine*), it has,
methinks, in this narrow, circumscribed, selfish, peculiar
sense, no very pretty sound with it. Treat me as freely
as you will in all other respects, I will love you, as I
have said, the better for your friendly freedom: but, methinks, I could be glad, for SEX'S sake, that you would
not let this imputation pass so glibly from *your* pen, or
your lips, as attributable to one of your own sex, whether
I be the person or not: since the *other* must have a *double* triumph, when a person of your delicacy (armed with
such contempts of them all, as you would have one
think) can give up a friend, with an exultation over her
weakness, as a silly, love-sick creature!

I will not acquaint you with all proceedings here; but
these shall be the subject of another letter.

Letter 30: MISS CLARISSA HARLOWE TO MISS HOWE

                                    Sunday night, March 12

This man, this Lovelace, gives me great uneasiness. He
is extremely bold and rash. He was this afternoon at our
church: in hopes to see me, I suppose: and yet, if he had
such hopes, his usual intelligence must have failed him.

Shorey was at church; and a principal part of her observation was upon his haughty and proud behaviour
when he turned round in the pew where he sat to our
family pew. My papa and both my uncles were there; so
were my mamma and sister. My brother happily was not!
They all came home in disorder. Nor did the congrega-
tion mind anybody but him; it being his first appearance
there since the unhappy rencounter.

What did the man come for, if he intended to look
challenge and defiance, as Shorey says he did, and as
others observed it seems as well as she? Did he come
for *my* sake; and, by behaving in such a manner to those
present of my family, imagine he was doing me either

service or pleasure? He knows how they hate him: nor
will he take pains, would pains do, to obviate their
hatred.

You and I, my dear, have often taken notice of his
pride, and you have rallied him upon it; and instead of
exculpating himself, he has owned it; and, by owning it,
has thought he has done enough.

He has talents, indeed: but those talents, and his personal advantages, have been snares to him. It is plain
they have. And this shows that, weighed in an equal
balance, he would be found greatly wanting.

Had my friends confided, as they did at first, in that
discretion which they do not accuse me of being defective in, I dare say I should have found him out: and then
should have been as resolute to dismiss *him* as I was to
dismiss others, and as I *am* never to have Mr Solmes.
Oh that they did but know my heart! It shall sooner
burst, than voluntarily, uncompelled, undriven, dictate a
measure that shall cast a slur either upon them, my sex,
or myself.

Excuse me, my dear friend, for these grave *soliloquies*,
as I may call them. How have I run from reflection to
reflection! But the occasion is recent! They are all in
commotion below upon it!

Shorey says that he watched my mamma's eye, and
bowed to her: and she returned the compliment. He always admired my mamma. She would not, I believe,
have hated *him* had she not been *bid* to hate him; and
had it not been for the rencounter between him and her
only son.

My father it seems is more and more incensed against
me. And so are my uncles.

They are angry, it seems, at my mamma, for returning
his compliment. What an enemy is hatred, even to the
common forms of civility!

I am extremely apprehensive that this worse than
ghost-like appearance of his bodes some still bolder step.
If he come hither (and very desirous he is of my leave
to come), I am afraid there will be murder. To avoid
that, if there were no other way, I would most willingly
be buried alive.

CL. H.

Letter 31: MR LOVELACE TO JOHN BELFORD, ESQ.

Monday, March 13

In vain dost thou and thy compeers press me to go to town, while I am in such an uncertainty as I am at present with this proud beauty. All the ground I have hitherto gained with her is entirely owing to her concern for the safety of people whom I have reason to hate.

Write then, thou biddest me, if I will not come. That, indeed, I can do; and as well without a subject, as with one. And what follows shall be a proof of it.

But is it not a confounded thing to be in love with one who is the daughter, the sister, the niece, of a family I must eternally despise? And the devil of it, that love increasing, with her—what shall I call it? 'tis not scorn—'tis not pride—'tis not the insolence of an adored beauty—but 'tis to *virtue*, it seems, that my difficulties are owing. And I pay for not being a sly sinner, a hypocrite: for being regardless of my reputation; for permitting slander to open its mouth against me. But is it necessary for such a one as I, who have been used to carry all before me upon my own terms—I, who never inspired a fear that had not a discernibly-predominant mixture of love in it, to be a hypocrite?

Well, but it seems I must *practise* for this art, if I would succeed with this truly admirable creature! But why *practise* for it? Cannot I *indeed* reform? I have but *one* vice—have I, Jack? Thou knowest my heart, if any man living does. As far as I know it myself, thou knowest it. But 'tis a cursed deceiver. For it has many and many a time imposed upon its master. *Master*, did I say? That am I not now: nor have I been from the moment I beheld this angel of a woman.

I have boasted that I was once in love before: and indeed I thought I was. It was in my early manhood—with that quality-jilt, whose infidelity I have vowed to revenge upon as many of the sex as shall come into my power. I believe, in different climes, I have already sacrificed a hecatomb to my Nemesis in pursuance of this vow. But upon recollecting what I was *then*, and comparing it with what I find in myself *now*, I cannot say that I was ever in love before.

What was it then, dost thou ask me, since the disappointment had such effects upon me, when I found myself jilted, that I was hardly kept in my senses? Why I'll tell thee what, as near as I can remember; for it was a great while ago. It was—egad, Jack, I can hardly tell what it was—but a vehement aspiration after a novelty, I think.

Then I had a vanity of *another* sort in my passion: I found myself well received among the women in general; and I thought it a pretty *lady-like* tyranny (I was very young then, and very vain) to single out some *one* of the sex to make *half a score* jealous. And I can tell thee, it had its effect: for many an eye have I made to sparkle with rival indignation: many a cheek glow; and even many a fan have I caused to be snapped at a sister-beauty, accompanied with a reflection, perhaps, at being seen alone with a wild young fellow who could not be in private with both at once.

In short, Jack, it was more pride than love, as I now find it, that put me upon making such a confounded rout about losing this noble varletess. I thought she loved me at least as well as I believed I loved her: nay, I had the vanity to suppose she could not help it. My friends were pleased with my choice. They wanted me to be shackled, for early did they doubt my morals as to the sex. They saw that the dancing, the singing, the musical ladies were all fond of my company: for who (I am in a humour to be vain, I think! for who) danced, who sung, who touched the string, whatever the instrument, with a better grace than thy friend?

But to return to my fair jilt. I could not bear that a woman, who was the first that had bound me in silken fetters (they were not iron ones, like those I now wear) should prefer a coronet to me: and when the bird was flown, I set more value upon it than when I had it safe in my cage and could visit it when I would.

But now am I in-*deed* in love. I can think of nothing, of nobody else, but the divine Clarissa Harlowe. *Harlowe!* How that hated word sticks in my throat, but I shall give her for it, the name of Love [Lovelace].

For, dost thou think that if it were not from the hope that this stupid family are all combined to do my work

for me, I would bear their insults? Is it possible to imagine that I would be braved as I am braved, threatened
as I am threatened, by those who are afraid to see me;
and by this brutal brother too, to whom I gave a life (a
life, indeed, not worth my taking!), had I not a greater
pride in knowing that by means of his very spy upon me
I am playing him off as I please; cooling, or inflaming,
his violent passions, as may best suit my purposes; permitting so much to be revealed of my life and actions,
and intentions, as may give him such a confidence in his
double-faced agent [Joseph Leman], as shall enable me
to dance his employer upon my own wires?

This it is that makes my pride mount above my resentment. By this engine, whose springs I am continually
oiling, I play them all off.

And what my motive, dost thou ask? No less than
this, that my beloved shall find no protection out of my
family—for, if I know *hers*, fly she must, or have the
man she hates. This, therefore, if I take my measures
right, and my familiar fail me not, will secure her mine,
in spite of them all; in spite of her own inflexible heart:
mine, without condition; without reformation promises;
without the necessity of a siege of years, perhaps; and to
be even then, after wearing the guise of a merit-doubting
hypocrisy, at an uncertainty, upon a probation unap-
proved of. Then shall I have all the rascals, and rasca-
lesses of the family come creeping to me: I prescribing
to them; and bringing that sordidly-imperious brother to
kneel at the foot-stool of my throne.

All my fear arises from the little hold I have in the
heart of this charming frostpiece: such a constant glow
upon her lovely features; eyes so sparkling; limbs so di-
vinely turned; health so florid; youth so blooming; air so
animated: to have a heart so impenetrable. And *I*, the
hitherto successful Lovelace, the addresser. How can it
be? Yet there are people, and I have talked with some
of them, who remember that she was *born*. Her nurse
Norton boasts of her maternal offices in her earliest infancy; and in her education *gradatim*. So that there is
full proof that she came not from above, all at once an
angel! How then can she be so impenetrable?

But here's her mistake; nor will she be cured of it—

she takes the man she calls her father (her mother had been faultless, had she not been her father's wife); she takes the men she calls her uncles; the fellow she calls her brother; and the poor contemptible she calls her sister; to *be* her father, to *be* her uncles, her brother, her sister; and that as such, she owes to some of them reverence, to others respect, let them treat her ever so cruelly! sordid ties! mere cradle-prejudices! For had they not been imposed upon her by nature, when she was in a perverse humour, or could she have chosen her relations, would any of these have been among them?

How my heart rises at her preference of them to me, when she is convinced of their injustice to me! Convinced that the alliance would do honour to them all— herself excepted; to whom everyone owes honour; and from whom the most princely family might receive it. But how much more will my heart rise with indignation against her, if I find she hesitates but one moment (however persecuted) about preferring me to the man she avowedly hates! But she cannot surely be so mean as to purchase her peace with them at so dear a rate. She cannot give a sanction to projects formed in malice and founded in a selfishness (and that at her own expense) which she has spirit enough to despise in others; and ought to disavow, that we may not think her a Harlowe.

By this incoherent ramble thou wilt gather that I am not likely to come up in haste, since I must endeavour first to obtain some assurance from the beloved of my soul that I shall not be sacrificed to such a wretch as Solmes!

That her indifference to me is not owing to the superior liking she has for any other man is what rivets my chains: but take care, fair one; take care, oh thou most exalted of female minds, and loveliest of persons, how thou debasest thyself by encouraging such a competition as thy sordid relations have set on foot in mere malice to me! Thou wilt say I rave. And so I do!

Thou art curious to know, if I have not started a new game? If it be possible for so universal a lover to be confined so long to one object? Thou knowest nothing of this charming creature, that thou canst put such questions to me; or thinkest thou knowest me better than

thou dost. All that's excellent in her sex is this lady!
Until by *matrimonial* or *equal* intimacies I have found
her less than angel, it is impossible to think of any other.
Then there are so many stimulatives to such a spirit as
mine in this affair, besides love: such a field for stratagem and contrivance, which thou knowest to be the delight of my heart. Then the rewarding end of all—to
carry off such a girl as this, in spite of all her watchful
and implacable friends; and in spite of a prudence and
reserve that I never met with in any of the sex. What a
triumph! What a triumph over the whole sex! And then
such a revenge to gratify, which is only at present politi-
cally reined in, eventually to break forth with the greater
fury. Is it possible, thinkest thou, that there can be room
for a thought that is not *of* her, and devoted *to* her?

But be this as it may, there is a present likelihood of
room for glorious mischief. A confederacy had been for
some time formed against me; but the uncles and the
nephew are *now* to be *double*-servanted (*single*-
servanted they were before), and those servants are to
be *double*-armed when they attend their masters abroad.
This indicates their resolute enmity to me, and as resolute favour to Solmes.

The reinforced orders for this hostile apparatus are
owing, it seems, to a visit I made yesterday to their
church; a good place to begin a reconciliation in, were
the heads of the family christians, and did they mean
anything by their prayers. My hopes were to have an
invitation (or, at least, to gain a pretence) to accompany
home the gloomy sire; and so get an opportunity to see
my goddess: for I believed they durst not but be *civil* to
me, at least. But they were filled with terror, it seems,
at my entrance; a terror they could not get over. I saw it
indeed in their countenances; and that they all expected
something extraordinary to follow. And so it *should*
have done, had I been more sure than I am of their
daughter's favour. Yet not a hair of any of their stupid
heads do I intend to hurt.

Thus, Jack, as thou desirest, have I written: written
upon something; upon nothing; upon revenge, which I
love; upon love, which I hate, *heartily* hate, because 'tis
my master: and upon the devil knows what besides: for,

looking back, I'm amazed at the length of it. *Thou* mayest read it: *I* would not for a king's ransom—but so as
I do *but* write, thou sayest thou wilt be pleased.

Be pleased then. I *command* thee to be pleased: if not
for the writer's, or written's sake, for thy word's sake.
And so in the royal style (for am I not likely to be thy
king and thy emperor, in the great affair before us?) I
bid thee very heartily

Farewell

Letter 34: MR LOVELACE TO JOHN BELFORD, ESQ.

Friday, March 17

I receive, with great pleasure, the early and cheerful assurances of your loyalty and love.

I would have thee, Jack, come down as soon as thou
canst.

Thou wilt find me at a little alehouse; they call it an
inn; the White Hart; most terribly wounded (but by the
weather only) the sign—in a sorry village, within five
miles from Harlowe Place. Everybody knows Harlowe
Place—for, like Versailles, it is sprung up from a dunghill within every elderly person's remembrance. Every
poor body, particularly, knows it: but that only for a few
years past, since a certain angel has appeared there
among the sons and daughters of men.

The people here at the Hart are poor but honest; and
have gotten it into their heads that I am a man of quality
in disguise, and there is no reining in their officious respect.
There is a pretty little smirking daughter, seventeen six
days ago: I call her my Rosebud. Her grandmother (for
there is no mother) a good neat old woman as ever filled
a wicker-chair in a chimney-corner has besought me to
be merciful to her.

This is the right way with me. Many and many a pretty
rogue had I spared, whom I did not spare, had my power
been acknowledged and my mercy been in time implored.

This simple chit (for there is a simplicity in her thou
wilt be highly pleased with: all humble; all officious; all
innocent. I love her for her humility, her officiousness
and even for her *innocence*) will be pretty amusement

to thee, while I combat with the weather, and dodge and creep about the walls and purlieus of Harlowe Place. Thou wilt see in her mind, all that her superiors have been taught to conceal in order to render themselves less natural, and more undelightful.

But I charge thee, that thou do not (what I would not permit myself to do, for the world—I charge thee, that thou do not) crop my Rosebud. She is the only flower of fragrance that has blown in this vicinage for ten years past, or will for ten years to come: for I have looked backward to the *have-been's*, and forward to the *will-be's*, having but too much leisure upon my hands in my present waiting.

I never was so honest for so long together since my matriculation. It behoves me so to be. Some way or other, my recess may be found out; and it will then be thought that my Rosebud has attracted me. A report in my favour from simplicities so amiable may establish me; for the grandmother's relation to my Rosebud may be sworn to: and the father is an honest poor man: has no joy but in his Rosebud.

The gentle heart is touched by Love! Her soft bosom heaves with a passion she has not yet found a name for. I once caught her eye following a young carpenter, a widow neighbour's son, living (to speak in her dialect) *at the little white house over the way.* A gentle youth he also seems to be, about three years older than herself: playmates from infancy till his eighteenth and her fifteenth year furnished a reason for a greater distance in show, while their hearts gave a better for their being nearer than ever: for I soon perceived the love reciprocal: a scrape and a bow at first seeing his pretty mistress; turning often to salute her following eye; and when a winding lane was to deprive him of her sight his whole body turned round, his hat more reverently doffed, than before. This answered (for, unseen, I was behind her) by a low curtsy, and a sigh that Johnny was too far off to hear!

I have examined the little heart: she has made me her confidant. She owns she could love Johnny Barton very well: and Johnny Barton has told her he could love her better than any maiden he ever saw. But, alas! it must

not be thought of. Why not be thought of? She don't
know! And then she sighed: but Johnny has an aunt who
will give him a hundred pounds when his time is out;
and her father cannot give her but a few things, or so,
to set her out with. And though Johnny's mother says
she knows not where Johnny would have a prettier, or
notabler wife, yet—And then she sighed again—What
signifies talking? I would not have Johnny be unhappy
and poor for me! For what good would that do *me*, you
know, sir!

What would I give (by my soul, my angel will indeed
reform me if her friends' implacable folly ruin us not
both!—what would I give) to have so innocent and so
good a heart as either my Rosebud's, or Johnny's!

I have a confounded mischievous one—by *nature* too,
I think! A good motion now and then rises from it: but
it dies away presently—a love of intrigue!—an invention
for mischief!—a triumph in subduing!—fortune encouraging and supporting!—and a constitution—What signifies palliating? But I believe I had been a rogue had I
been a plough-boy.

But the devil's in this sex! Eternal misguiders! Who
that has once trespassed ever recovered his integrity?
And yet where there is not virtue, which nevertheless
we free-livers are continually plotting to destroy, what
is there even in the ultimate of our wishes with them?
Preparation and *expectation* are, in a manner, everything:
reflection, indeed, may be something, if the mind be
hardened above feeling the guilt of a past *trespass*: but
the *fruition*, what is there in that? And yet, that being
the end, nature will not be satisfied without it.

See what grave reflections an innocent subject will
produce! It gives me some pleasure to think that it is
not out of my *power* to reform: but then, Jack, I am
afraid I must keep better company than I do at
present—for we certainly harden one another. But be
not cast down, my boy; there will be time enough to
give thee, and all thy brethren, warning to choose another leader: and I fancy thou wilt be the man.

Meantime, as I make it my rule whenever I have committed a very capital enormity to do some good by way
of atonement, and as I believe I am a pretty deal in-

debted on that score, I intend before I leave these parts (successfully shall I leave them, I hope, or I shall be tempted to do double the mischief by way of revenge, though not to my Rosebud any) to join a hundred pounds to Johnny's aunt's hundred pounds, to make one innocent couple happy. I repeat, therefore, and for half a dozen more *therefores*, spare thou my Rosebud.

An interruption—another letter anon; and both shall go together.

Letter 35: MR LOVELACE TO JOHN BELFORD, ESQ.

I have found out by my watchful spy almost as many of my charmer's motions as those of the rest of her relations. It delights me to think how the rascal is caressed by the uncles and nephew; and let into *their* secrets; yet proceeds all the time by *my* line of direction. I have charged him, however, on forfeiture of his present weekly stipend, and my future favour, to take care that neither my beloved or any of the family suspect him: I have told him, that he may indeed watch her egresses and regresses; but that only to keep off other servants from her paths; yet not to be seen by her himself.

The dear creature has tempted him, he told *them*, with a bribe (*which she never offered*), to convey a letter (*which she never wrote*) to Miss Howe; he believes, with one enclosed (*perhaps to me*): but he declined it: and he begged they would take no notice of it to *her*. This brought him a stingy shilling; great applause; and an injunction followed it to all the servants for the strictest look-out lest she should contrive some way to send it. And, about an hour after, an order was given him to throw himself in her way; and (expressing his concern for denying her request) to tender his service to her and to bring them her letter: which it will be *proper for him to report* that she has refused to give him.

Now seest thou not, how many good ends this contrivance answers?

In the first place, the lady is secured by it against her own knowledge, in the liberty allowed her of taking her private walks in the garden: for this attempt has con-

firmed them in their belief that now they have turned
off her maid she has no way to send a letter out of the
house: if she had, she would not have run the risk of
tempting a fellow who had not been in her secret so that
she can prosecute unsuspectedly her correspondence
with me and Miss Howe.

In the next place, it will afford me an opportunity,
perhaps, of a private interview with her, which I am
meditating, let her take it as she will; having found out
by my spy (who can keep off everybody else), that she
goes every morning and evening to a wood-house remote from the dwelling-house, under pretence of visiting
and feeding a set of bantam poultry, which were produced from a breed that was her grandfather's, and
which for that reason she is very fond of; as also of some
other curious fowls brought from the same place. I have
an account of all her motions here. And as she has
owned to me in one of her letters that she corresponds
privately with Miss Howe, I presume it is by this way.

The interview I am meditating will produce her consent, I hope, to other favours of the like kind: for, should
she not choose the place I am expecting to see her in, I
can attend her anywhere in the rambling, Dutch-taste
garden, whenever she will permit me that honour: for
my implement, hight [named] Joseph Leman, has given
me the opportunity of procuring two keys (one of which
I have given him, for reasons good) to the garden door,
which opens to the haunted coppice, as tradition has
made the servants think it; a man having been found
hanging in it about twenty years ago: and Joseph, upon
the least notice, will leave it unbolted.

But I was obliged to give him previously my honour,
that no mischief shall happen to any of my adversaries,
from this liberty: for the fellow tells me, that he loves
all his masters; and, only that he knows I am a man of
honour; and that my alliance will do credit to the family;
and after prejudices are overcome everybody will think
so; or he would not for the world act the part he does.

There never was a rogue, who had not a salvo to himself for being so. What a praise to *honesty*, that every
man pretends to it even at the instant that he knows he
is pursuing the methods that will perhaps prove him a

knave to the whole world, as well as to his own conscience!

But what this stupid family can mean, to make all this
necessary, I cannot imagine. My REVENGE and my LOVE
are uppermost by turns. If the latter succeed not, the
gratifying of the former will be my only consolation: and,
by all that's good, they shall feel it; although, for it, I
become an exile from my native country for ever.

I will throw myself into my charmer's presence: I have
twice already attempted it in vain. I shall then see what
I may depend upon from her favour. If I thought I had
no prospect of that, I should be tempted to carry her
off. That would be a rape worthy of a Jupiter!

But all gentle shall be my movements: all respectful,
even to reverence, my address to her! Her hand shall be
the only witness to the pressure of my lip—my trembling
lip: I *know* it will tremble, if I do not *bid* it tremble. As
soft my sighs as the sighs of my gentle Rosebud. By *my*
humility will I invite *her* confidence: the loneliness of the
place shall give me no advantage: to dissipate her fears,
and engage her reliance upon my honour for the future,
shall be my whole endeavour: but little will I complain
of, not at all will I threaten those who are continually
threatening me.

Letter 36: MISS CLARISSA HARLOWE TO MISS HOWE

Sat. night, Mar. 18

I have been frighted out of my wits—still am in a manner out of breath—thus occasioned. I went down under
the usual pretence in hopes to find something from you.
Concerned at my disappointment I was returning from
the wood-house, when I heard a rustling, as of somebody
behind a stack of wood. I was extremely surprised: but
still more, to behold a man coming from behind the
furthermost stack. Oh thought I, at that moment, the sin
of a prohibited correspondence!

In the same point of time that I saw him, he besought
me not to be frighted: and still nearer approaching me,
threw open a horseman's coat: and who should it be but
Mr Lovelace! I could not scream out (yet attempted to

scream, the moment I saw a man; and again when I saw
who it was) for I had no voice: and had I not caught
hold of a prop, which supported the old roof, I should
have sunk.

I had hitherto, as you know, kept him at distance: and
now, as I recovered myself, judge of my first emotions
when I recollected his character from every mouth of
my family; his enterprising temper; and found myself
alone with him in a place so near a by-lane and so remote from the house.

But his respectful behaviour soon dissipated these
fears, and gave me others lest we should be seen together, and information of it given to my brother: the
consequences of which, I could readily think, would be,
if not further mischief, an imputed assignation, a stricter
confinement, a forfeited correspondence with you, my
beloved friend, and a pretence for the most violent compulsion: and neither the one set of reflections, nor the
other, acquitted him to me for his bold intrusion.

As soon therefore as I could speak, I expressed with
the greatest warmth my displeasure; and told him that
he cared not how much he exposed me to the resentments of all my friends, provided he could gratify his
own impetuous humour; and I commanded him to leave
the place that moment: and was hurrying from him;
when he threw himself in the way at my feet, beseeching
my stay for one moment; declaring that he suffered himself to be guilty of this rashness, as I thought it, to avoid
one much greater—for in short, he could not bear the
hourly insults he received from my family with the
thoughts of having so little interest in my favour, that
he could not promise himself, that his patience and forbearance would be attended with any other issue than
to lose me for ever, and be triumphed over and insulted
upon it.

This man, you know, has very ready knees. You have
said that he ought in small points frequently to offend,
on purpose to show what an address he is master of.

I told him he might be assured that the severity and
ill-usage I met with would be far from effecting the intended end: that although I could with great sincerity
declare for a single life, which had always been my

choice; and particularly, that if ever I married, if they would not insist upon the man I had an aversion to, it should not be with the man they disliked—

He interrupted me here: he hoped I would forgive him for it; but he could not help expressing his great concern that, after so many instances of his passionate and obsequious devotion—

And pray, sir, said I, let me interrupt you in my turn. Why don't you assert, in still plainer words, the obligation you have laid me under by this your boasted devotion? Why don't you let me know, in terms as high as your implication, that a perseverance I have not wished for, which has set all my relations at variance with me, is a merit that throws upon me the guilt of ingratitude for not answering it as you seem to expect?

As to the perseverance I mentioned, it was impossible for him *not* to persevere: but I must needs know, that were he not in being, the terms Solmes had proposed were such as would have involved me in the same difficulties with my relations that I now laboured under. He therefore took the liberty to say, that my favour to him, far from increasing those difficulties, would be the readiest way to extricate me from them. They had made it impossible (he told me, with too much truth) to oblige them any way but by sacrificing myself to Solmes. They were well apprised besides of the difference between the two; one whom they hoped to manage as they pleased; the other who could and would protect me from every insult; and who had *natural* prospects much superior to my brother's *foolish* views, of a title.

How comes this man to know so well all our foibles? But I more wonder, how he came to have a notion of meeting me in this place!

I was very uneasy to be gone; and the more as the night came on apace. But there was no getting from him, till I had heard a great deal more of what he had to say.

As he hoped that I would one day make him the happiest man in the world, he assured me that he had so much regard for my fame that he would be as far from advising any step that were likely to cast a shade upon my reputation (although that step were to be ever so much in his own favour) as I would be to follow such

advice. But since I was not to be permitted to live single,
he would submit it to my consideration whether I had
any way but *one* to avoid the intended violence to my
inclinations.

To be sure, my dear, there is a great deal in what the
man said. I may be allowed to say this without an imputed *glow* or *throb*.

He appealed to me whether ever I knew my papa
recede from any resolution he had once fixed, especially
if he thought either his prerogative, or his authority concerned in the question. His acquaintance with our family,
he said, enabled him to give several instances (but they
would be too grating to me) of an arbitrariness that had
few examples even in the families of princes: an arbitrariness which the most excellent of women, my mamma,
too severely experienced.

He was proceeding, as I thought, with reflections of
this sort; and I angrily told him I would not permit my
father to be reflected upon; adding, that his severity to
me, however unmerited, was not a warrant for me to
dispense with my duty to him.

How unhappy, my dear, that there is but too much
reason for these observations, and for this inference;
made, likewise, with more coolness and respect to my
family than one would have apprehended from a man so
much provoked, and of passions so high, and generally
thought uncontrollable!

Will you not question me about *throbs* and *glows*, if
from such instances of a command over his fiery temper
for my sake, I am ready to infer that were my friends
capable of a reconciliation with him he might be affected
by arguments apparently calculated for his present and
future good?

I should easily, I think, detect a hypocrite: and *this*
man particularly, who is said to have allowed himself in
great liberties, were he to pretend to instantaneous lights
and convictions—at his time of life too: habits, I am
sensible, are not so easily changed. You have always
joined with me in remarking that he will speak his mind
with freedom, even to a degree of unpoliteness sometimes; and that his very treatment of my family is a proof
that he cannot make a mean court to anybody for

interest-sake. What pity, where there are such laudable traces, that they should have been so mired, and choked up, as I may say! We have heard that the man's head is better than his heart: but do you really think Mr Lovelace can have a *very* bad heart?

He then again pressed that I would receive a letter from his aunt Lawrance of offered protection.

I told him that, however greatly I thought myself obliged to Lady Betty Lawrance, if this offer came from herself, yet it was easy to see to what it led.

I then assured him that it was with infinite concern, that I had found myself drawn into an epistolary correspondence with him; especially since that correspondence had been prohibited. And the only agreeable use I could think of making of this unexpected and undesired interview was to let him know that I should from henceforth think myself obliged to discontinue it. And I hoped that he would not have the *thought* of engaging me to carry it on, by menacing my relations.

There was light enough to distinguish that he looked very grave upon this. He so much valued my *free* choice, he said, and my *unbiased* favour (scorning to set himself upon a foot with Solmes in the compulsory methods used in that man's behalf), that he should hate himself were he capable of a view in intimidating me by so very poor a method. Nor was there a necessity, he said, if I were actually in Lady Betty's protection, that I should be his, if I should see anything objectible in his conduct, afterwards.

But what would the world conclude would be the end, I asked him, were I to throw myself into the protection of *his* friends, but that it was with such a view?

And what less did the world think *now*, he asked, than that I was confined that I *might not*? You are to consider, madam, you have not now an option; and to whom it is owing that you have not; and that you are in the power of those (parents why should I call them?) who are determined that you shall *not* have an option. All I propose is, that you will embrace such a protection—but not till you have tried every way to avoid the necessity for it.

And give me leave to say, that if a correspondence on

which I have founded all my hopes is at this critical conjuncture to be broken off; and if you are resolved not to be provided against the worst; it must be plain to me that you will at last yield to that worst—worst to *me* only—It cannot be to *you*—And *then!* (and he put his hand clenched to his forehead) how shall I bear the supposition? *Then* you be that Solmes's!

The man's vehemence frightened me: yet, in resentment, I would have left him; but, throwing himself at my feet again, Leave me not thus, I beseech you, dearest madam, leave me not thus, in despair.

I told him that he talked to me in very high language; but he might assure himself that I never would have Mr Solmes (yet that this I said not in favour to him): and I had declared as much to my relations, were there not such a man as himself in the world.

Would I declare that I would still honour him with my correspondence? He could not bear that, hoping to obtain *greater* instances of my favour, he should forfeit the *only one* he had to boast of.

I bid him forbear rashness or resentment to any of my family, and I would, for some time at least, till I saw what issue my present trials were likely to have, proceed with a correspondence which nevertheless my heart condemned.

I made many efforts to go; and now it was so dark that I began to have great apprehensions—I cannot say from his behaviour: indeed, he has a good deal raised himself in my opinion by the personal respect, even to reverence, which he paid me during the whole conference.

He recommended himself to my favour at parting, with great earnestness, yet with as great submission; not offering to condition any thing with me; although he hinted his wishes for another meeting: which I forbid him ever attempting again in the same place. And I'll own to you, from whom I should be really blameable to conceal anything, that his arguments (drawn from the disgraceful treatment I meet with) of what I *am* to expect make me begin to apprehend, that I shall be under an obligation to be either the one man's or the other's. And if so, I fancy I shall not incur your blame were I

to say *which* of the two it must be. You have said, which
it must *not* be. But, Oh my dear, the single life is by far
the most eligible to me: *indeed* it is. And I yet hope to
obtain the blessing of making that option.

I got back without observation: but the apprehension
that I should not, gave me great uneasiness; and made
me begin my letter in a greater flutter than he gave me
cause to be in, except at the first seeing him; for then,
indeed, my spirits failed me; and it was a particular felicity that, in such a place, in such a fright, and alone with
him, I fainted not away.

I have written a very long letter. To be so particular
as you require in subjects of conversation, it is impossible to be short. I will add to it only the assurance, that
I am, and ever will be,

> Your affectionate and faithful
> friend and servant,
> CL. HARLOWE

Letter 40: MISS CLARISSA HARLOWE TO MISS HOWE

In order to acquit myself of so heavy a charge as that
of having reserves to so dear a friend, I will acknowledge
(and I thought I had over and over) that it is owing to
my particular situation, if Mr Lovelace appears to me in
a tolerable light: and I take upon me to say, that had
they opposed to him a man of sense, of virtue, of generosity; one who enjoyed his fortune with credit; who had
a tenderness in his nature for the calamities of others,
which would have given a moral assurance that he would
have been still less wanting in grateful returns to an
obliging spirit: had they opposed such a man as this to
Mr Lovelace, and been as earnest to have me married,
as now they are, I do not know myself if they would
have had reason to tax me with that invincible obstinacy
which they lay to my charge: and this, whatever had
been the *figure* of the man: since the *heart* is what we
women should judge by in the choice we make, as the
best security for the party's good behaviour in every relation of life.

But, situated as I am, thus persecuted and driven; I

own to you that I have now and then had a little more difficulty than I wished for in passing by Mr Lovelace's tolerable qualities, to keep up my dislike to him for his others.

You say I must have argued with myself in his favour, and in his disfavour, on a supposition that I might possibly be one day his. I own that I have.

A great deal of the treatment a wife may expect from him will possibly depend upon herself. Perhaps she must *practise*, as well as *promise*, obedience to a man so little used to control; and must be careful to oblige. And what husband expects not this? The *more*, perhaps, if he has not reason to assure himself of the preferable love of his wife, before she became such. And how much easier and pleasanter to obey the man of her choice, if he should be even unreasonable sometimes, than one she would not have had, could she have avoided it? Then, I think, as the men were the framers of the matrimonial office, and made *obedience* a part of the woman's vow, she ought not, even in *policy*, to show him that she can break through *her* part of the contract, however lightly she may think of the instance; lest *he* should take it into his head (himself is judge) to think as lightly of other points, which *she* may hold more important. But indeed no point, so solemnly vowed, can be slight.

Thus principled, and *acting* accordingly, what a wretch must that husband be, who could treat such a wife brutally! Will Lovelace's *wife* be the only person to whom he will not pay the grateful debt of civility and good manners?

At worst, will he confine me prisoner to my chamber? Will he deny me the visits of my dearest friend, and forbid me to correspond with her? Will he take from me the mistressly management, which I had not faultily discharged? Will he set a servant over me, with licence to insult me? It cannot be. Why then, think I often, do you tempt me, oh my cruel friends, to try the difference?

And then has the secret pleasure intruded itself, to be able to reclaim such a man to the paths of virtue and honour: to be a *secondary* means, if I were to be his, of saving him, and preventing the mischiefs so enterprising a creature might otherwise be guilty of, if he be such a one.

In these lights when I have thought of him (and that
as a man of sense he will sooner see his errors than
another), I own to you, that I have had some difficulty
to avoid taking the path they so violently endeavour to
make me shun: and all that command of my passions,
which has been attributed to me as my greatest praise,
and in so young a creature, as my distinction, has hardly
been sufficient for me.

Reflecting upon these things, I cannot help conjuring
you, my dear, to pray *with* me, and to pray *for* me, that
I may not be pushed upon such indiscreet measures as
will render me inexcusable *to* myself: for that is the test,
after all; the world's opinion ought to be but a secondary consideration.

Sometimes we have both thought him one of the most
undesigning *merely* witty men we ever knew; at other
times one of the deepest creatures we ever conversed
with. So that, when in one visit we have imagined we
fathomed him, in the next he has made us ready to give
him up as impenetrable.

But I used then to say, and I still am of opinion, that
he wants a *heart*: and if he does, he wants everything. A
wrong *head* may be convinced, may have a right turn
given it: but who is able to give a *heart*, if a heart be
wanting? Divine grace, working miracle, or next to a
miracle, can only change a bad heart. Should not one fly
the man who is but *suspected* of such a one?

From these considerations; from these *over-balances*;
it was, that I said in a former [letter], that I would not
be in love with this man for the world: and it was going
further than prudence would warrant, when I was for
compounding with you by the words *conditional liking*;
which you so humorously rally.

Well but, methinks you say, what is all this to the
purpose? This is still but reasoning: but, if you *are* in
love, you *are*: and love, like the vapours, is the deeper
rooted for having no sufficient cause assignable for its
hold. And so you call upon me again to have no reserves, and so forth.

Why then, my dear, if you will have it, I think that,
with all his preponderating faults, I like him better than

I ever thought I should like him; and, those faults considered, better perhaps than I *ought* to like him. And, I
believe, it is possible for the persecution I labour under
to induce me to like him still more; especially while I
can recollect to his advantage our last interview, and as
every day produces stronger instances of *tyranny*, I will
call it, on the other side. In a word, I will frankly own
(since you cannot think anything I say too explicit), that
were he *now* but a moral man, I would prefer him to
all the men I ever saw.

So that this is but *conditional liking* still, you'll say.
Nor, I hope, is it more. I never was in *love*; and whether
this be *it*, or not, I must submit to *you*—But will venture
to think it, if it be, no such *mighty* monarch, no such
unconquerable power, as I have heard it represented;
and it must have met with greater encouragements than
I think I have given it, to be so *irresistible*—Since I am
persuaded, that I could yet, without a *throb*, most willingly give up the *one* man [Lovelace] to get rid of the
other [Solmes].

I lay down my pen, here, that you may consider of it
a little, if you please.

                                                CL. HARLOWE

Letter 47: MISS HOWE TO MISS CLARISSA HARLOWE

                                      Thursday morn. 7 o'clock
I must begin with blaming you, my dear, for your resolution not to litigate for your right, if occasion were to be
given you. Justice is due to one's self, as well as to everybody else. Still more must I blame you for declaring to
your aunt and sister that you will *not*: since (as they will
tell it to your father and brother) the declaration must
needs give advantages to spirits who have so little of
that generosity for which you yourself are so much
distinguished.

I know how much you despise riches in the main: but
yet it behoves you to remember that in one instance you
yourself have judged them valuable: 'In that they put it
into one's power to *lay* obligations; while the want of

them puts a person under a necessity of *receiving* favours; receiving them, perhaps, from grudging and narrow spirits, who know not how to confer them with that grace, which gives the principal merit to a beneficent action.' Reflect upon this, my dear, and see how it agrees with the declaration you have made to your aunt and sister, that you would not resume your estate, were you to be turned out of doors, and reduced to indigence and want. Their very fears that you will resume, point out to you the *necessity* of resuming, upon the treatment you meet with.

You have chidden me, and again will, I doubt not, for the liberties I take with some of your relations. But, my dear, need I tell *you*, that pride in *ourselves* must, and forever will, provoke contempt, and bring down upon us abasement from *others*? I am very loath to offend you, yet I cannot help speaking of *them*, as well as of *others*, as I think they deserve. I despise them all, but your mamma: indeed I do—and as for her—But I will spare the good lady for your sake. And one argument, indeed, I think may be pleaded in her favour, in the present contention. She who has for so many years, and with such absolute resignation, borne what she has borne, to the sacrifice of her own will, may think it an easier task, than another person can imagine it, for her daughter to give up *hers*. But to think to whose instigation all this is originally owing. God forgive me; but with such usage I should have been with Lovelace before now. Yet remember, my dear, that the step which would not be wondered at from such an hasty-tempered creature as me, would be inexcusable in such a considerate person as you.

Did I think you would have any manner of doubt, from the style or contents of this letter, whose saucy pen it is that has run on at this rate, I would write my name at length; since it comes too much from my heart to disavow it—but at present the initials shall serve; and I will go on again directly.

A.H.

Letter 49: MISS HOWE TO MISS CLARISSA HARLOWE

Thursday afternoon, March 23

An unexpected visitor has turned the course of my
thoughts, and changed the subject I had intended to pursue. The only one for whom I would have dispensed
with my resolution not to see anybody all the dedicated
day: a visitor, whom, according to Mr Hickman's report
from the expectations of his libertine friends, I supposed
to be in town. Now, my dear, have I saved myself the
trouble of telling you, that it was your too-agreeable
rake. Our sex is said to love to trade in surprises: yet
have I, by my over-promptitude, surprised myself out of
mine. I had intended, you must know, to run twice the
length, before I had suffered you so much as to guess
who, and of which sex, my visitor was: but since you
have the discovery at so cheap a rate, you are welcome
to it.

The end [purpose] of his coming was, to engage my
interest with my *charming friend*; and as he was sure
that I knew all your mind, to acquaint him what he had
to trust to. He mentioned what had passed in the interview between you: but could not be satisfied with the
result of it, and with the little satisfaction he had obtained from you; the malice of your family to him increasing, and their cruelty to you not abating—his heart,
he told me, was in tumults, for fear you should be prevailed upon in favour of a man despised by everybody.

He proposed several schemes for you to choose some
one of them, in order to enable you to avoid the persecutions you labour under. One I will mention; that you
will resume your estate; and if you find difficulties that
can be no otherwise surmounted, that you will, either
avowedly or privately, as he had proposed to you, accept
of his aunt Lawrance's or Lord M.'s assistance to instate
you in it. He declared that, if you did, he would leave
it absolutely to your own pleasure afterwards, and to the
advice which your cousin Morden on his arrival should
give you, whether to encourage his address or not, as
you shall be convinced of the sincerity of the reformation which his enemies make him so much want.

I told him, as you yourself I knew had done, that you

were extremely averse to Mr Solmes; and that might you be left to your own choice, it would be the single life. As to himself, I plainly said that you had great and just objections to him on the score of his careless morals: that it was surprising that young gentlemen, who gave themselves the liberties he was said to take, should presume to think that, whenever they took it into their heads to marry, the most virtuous and worthy of the sex were to fall to their lot: that as to the resumption, it had been very strongly urged by myself, and would be more, though you had been averse to it hitherto.

I told him, that with regard to the mischief he threatened, neither the act nor the menace could serve any end but theirs who persecuted you; as it would give them a pretence for carrying into effect their compulsatory projects; and that with the approbation of all the world, since he must not think the public would give its voice in favour of a violent young man, of no extraordinary character as to morals, who should seek to rob a family of eminence of a child so valuable; and who threatened, if he could not obtain her in preference to a man chosen by themselves, that he would avenge himself upon them all by acts of violence.

I added that he was very much mistaken, if he thought to intimidate *you* by such menaces: for that, though your disposition was all sweetness, yet I knew not a steadier temper in the world than yours; nor one more inflexible (as your friends had found, and would still farther find if they continued to give occasion for its exertion) whenever you thought yourself in the right; and that you were dealt ungenerously with in matters of too much moment to be indifferent about. Miss Clarissa Harlowe, Mr Lovelace, let me tell you, said I, timid as her foresight and prudence may make her in some cases, where she apprehends dangers to those she loves, is above fear in points where her honour and the true dignity of her sex are concerned. In short, sir, you must not think to frighten Miss Clarissa Harlowe into such a mean or unworthy conduct as only a weak or unsteady mind can be guilty of.

He was so very far from intending to intimidate you, he said, that he besought me not to mention one word

to you of what had passed between us: that what he had
hinted at, that carried the air of a menace, was owing to
the fervour of his spirits, raised by his apprehensions of
losing all hope of you for ever; and on a supposition that
you were to be actually forced into the arms of a man
you hated: that were this to be the case, he must own that
he should pay very little regard to the world or its censures: especially as the menaces of some of your family
now, and their triumph over him afterwards, would both
provoke and warrant all the vengeance he could take.

I did not like the determined air he spoke this with.
He is certainly, my dear, capable of great rashness.

This man is a violent man. I should wish, methinks,
that you should not have either him or Solmes. You will
find, if you get out of your brother's and sister's way,
what you *can* or can-*not* do with regard to either.

I am, my dearest friend, and will be ever,

Your most affectionate and faithful
ANNA HOWE

Letter 50: MISS CLARISSA HARLOWE TO MISS HOWE

Wed. night, March 22

On my aunt's and sister's report of my obstinacy, my
assembled relations have taken an *unanimous* resolution
(as Betty tells me it is) against me. This resolution you
will find signified to me in the enclosed letter from my
brother, just now brought me. Be pleased to return it,
when perused. I may have occasion for it in the alterca-
tions between my relations and me.

James Harlowe, Jun. to Clarissa Harlowe

I am commanded to let you know that my father and
uncles having heard your aunt Hervey's account of all
that has passed between her and you; having heard from
your sister what sort of treatment she has had from you;
having recollected all that has passed between your
mamma and you; having weighed all your pleas and proposals; having taken into consideration their engagements with Mr Solmes, that gentleman's patience and

great affection for you, and the little opportunity you have given yourself to be acquainted either with his merit, or his proposals; having considered two points more; to wit, the wounded authority of a father; and Mr Solmes's continual entreaties (little as you have deserved regard from him) that you may be freed from a confinement to which he is desirous to attribute your perverseness to him (*averseness* I should have said, but let it go), he being unable to account otherwise for so strong a one, supposing you told truth to your mamma when you asserted that your heart was *free*; and which Mr Solmes is willing to believe, though nobody else does. For all these reasons, it is resolved that you shall go to your uncle Antony's: and you must accordingly prepare yourself so to do. You will have but short notice of the day for obvious reasons.

I will honestly tell you the motive for your going: it is a double one; first, that they may be sure that you shall not correspond with anybody they do not like, for they find from Mrs Howe, that by some means or other you *do* correspond with her daughter; and through her, perhaps with somebody else: and next, that you may receive the visits of Mr Solmes, which you have thought fit to refuse to do here; by which means you have deprived yourself of the opportunity of knowing *whom* and *what* you have hitherto refused.

It is hoped that, as you *must* go, you will go cheerfully. Your uncle Antony will make everything at his house agreeable to you. But indeed he won't promise that he will not, at *proper times*, draw up the bridge.

Your answer is required, whether you *cheerfully* consent to go? And your indulgent mamma bids me remind you from her, that a fortnight's visits from Mr Solmes are all that is meant at present.

I am, as you shall be pleased to deserve,

Yours, etc.
JAMES HARLOWE, JUN.

So here is the master-stroke of my brother's policy! Called upon to consent to go to my uncle Antony's, *avowedly* to receive Mr Solmes's visits! A chapel!—a moated house! Deprived of the opportunity of corresponding with you!—or of any possibility of escape, should violence be used to compel me to be that odious man's!

Late as it was when I received this insolent letter, I wrote an answer to it directly, that it might be ready for the writer's time of rising. I enclose the rough draught of it.

Clarissa Harlowe to James Harlowe, Jun.

Give me leave to tell you, sir, that if *humanity* were a branch of your studies at the university, it has not found a genius in you for mastering it. Nor is either my sex or myself, though a sister, I see, entitled to the least decency from a brother who has studied, as it seems, rather to cultivate the malevolence of his natural temper, than any tendency which one would have hoped his parentage, if not his education, might have given him to a tolerable politeness.

The time is indeed come that I can no longer bear those contempts and reflections which a brother, least of all men, is entitled to give. And let me beg of you one favour, officious sir—it is *this*, that you will not give yourself any concern about a husband for *me*, till I shall have the forwardness to propose a wife to *you*.

One word more, provoked as I am, I will add: that had I been thought as really obstinate and perverse as of late I am said to be, I should not have been so disgracefully treated as I have been. Lay your hand upon your heart, brother, and say by whose instigations. And examine what I have done to deserve to be made thus unhappy, and to be obliged to style myself,

Your injured sister,
CL. HARLOWE

When, my dear, you have read my answer to this letter, tell me what you think of me? It *shall go*!

Letter 53: MISS CLARISSA HARLOWE TO MISS HOWE

Friday morning, six o'clock

Mrs Betty tells me there is now nothing talked of but of my going to my uncle Antony's. She has been ordered, she says, to get ready to attend me thither. And, upon my expressing my averseness to go, had the confidence to say that having heard me often praise the *romantic-ness* of the place, she was *astonished* (her hands and eyes lifted up) that I should set myself against going to a house so much in *my taste*.

I asked if this was her own insolence, or her young mistress's observation?

to Mr James Harlowe, Jun.

SIR,   Friday morning
If, notwithstanding your prohibition, I should be silent on occasion of your last, you would perhaps conclude that I was consenting to go to my uncle Antony's upon the condition you mention. My father must do as he pleases with his child. He may turn me out of his doors, if he thinks fit, or give *you* leave to do it; but (loath as I am to say it) I should think it very hard to be carried by force to anybody's house when I have one of *my own* to go to.

Far be it from me, notwithstanding yours and my sister's provocations, to think of taking my estate into my own hands without my papa's leave: but why, if I must not stay any longer here, may I not be permitted to go thither? I will engage to see nobody they would not have me see, if this favour be permitted. *Favour* I call it, and am ready to receive and acknowledge it as such, although my grandfather's will has made it matter of right.

And now, sir, if I have seemed to show some spirit not quite foreign to the relation I have the honour to bear to *you* and to my *sister*; and which may be deemed not altogether of a piece with that part of my character which once, it seems, gained me everyone's love; be pleased to consider to *whom*, and to *what* it is owing; and that this part of that character was not dispensed with till it subjected me to that scorn and those insults which a brother, who has been *so tenacious of an independence* that I *voluntarily* gave up, and who has appeared *so exalted* upon it, ought not to have shown to *anybody*, much less to a *weak* and *defenceless* sister: who is notwithstanding an affectionate and respectful one, and would be glad to show herself to be so upon all future occasions; as she has in every action of her past life, although of late she has met with such unkind returns.

CL. HARLOWE

See the force and volubility, as I may say, of passion; for the letter I send you is my first draught, struck off without a blot or erasure.

Friday, three o'clock

As soon as I had transcribed it, I sent it down to my brother by Mrs Betty.

The wench came up soon after, all aghast with her *Lord, Miss!* What *have* you done? What *have* you written? For you have set them all in a *joyful* uproar!

My sister is but this moment gone from me: she came up all in a flame, which obliged me abruptly to lay down my pen: she run to me—

Oh spirit! said she; tapping my neck a little *too* hard. And is it come to this at last!

Do you beat me, Bella?

Do you call this beating you? Only tapping your shoulder *thus*, said she; tapping again more gently. This is what we expected it would come to. You want to be independent. My papa has lived too long for you!

I was going to speak with vehemence; but she put her handkerchief before my mouth, very rudely. Take your course, perverse one; call in your rake to help you to an *in*-dependence upon your parents and a dependence upon him! Do so! Prepare this moment. Resolve what you will take with you! Tomorrow you go! Depend upon it, tomorrow you go! No longer shall you tarry here, watching and creeping about to hearken to what people say! 'Tis determined, child! You go tomorrow!

Thus she ran on, almost foaming with passion, till, quite out of patience, I said: No more of your violence, Bella. Had I known in what a way you would come up, you should not have found my chamber door open! Talk to your servant in this manner: unlike *you*, as I bless God I am, I am nevertheless your sister. And let me tell you that I won't go tomorrow, nor next day, nor next day to that—except I am dragged away by violence.

Is not this usage enough to provoke one to a rashness one had never thought of committing?

As it is but too probable that I may be hurried away to my uncle's without being able to give you previous notice of it, I beg that as soon as you shall hear of such a violence, you will send to the usual place to take back such of your letters as may not have reached my hands, or to fetch any of mine that may be there. May you, my dear, be always happy, prays your

CL. HARLOWE

Letter 55: MISS CLARISSA HARLOWE TO MISS HOWE

Friday midnight

I have now a calmer moment. Envy, ambition, high and selfish resentment and all the violent passions are now, most probably, asleep all around me; and shall not my own angry ones give way to the silent hour, and subside likewise? They *have* given way to it; and I have made use of the gentler space to re-peruse your last letters. I will touch upon some passages in them: and that I may the less endanger the but just-recovered calm, I will begin with what you write about Mr Hickman.

Give me leave to say, that I am sorry you cannot yet persuade yourself to think better, that is to say, *more justly*, of that gentleman than your whimsical picture of him shows you do; or at least than the humorousness of your natural vein would make one *think* you do.

I do not imagine that you yourself will say he sat for the picture you have drawn. And yet, upon the whole, it is not greatly to his disadvantage. Were I at ease in my mind, I would venture to draw a much more amiable and just likeness.

If Mr Hickman has not that assurance which some men have, he has that humanity and gentleness which many want: and which, with the infinite value he has for you, will make him one of the properest husbands in the world for a person of your vivacity and spirit.

I am glad you own that you like no one better than

Mr Hickman. In a little while, I make no doubt you will
be able, if you challenge your heart upon it, to acknowledge that you like not any man so well: especially when
you come to consider that the very faults you find in Mr
Hickman admirably fit him to make you happy: that is
to say, if it be necessary to your happiness that you
should have your own will in everything.

But let me add one thing: and that is this—you have
such a spritely turn that with your admirable talents you
would make any man in the world, who loved you, look
like a fool, except he were such a one as Lovelace.

Forgive me, my dear, for my frankness: and forgive
me also for so soon returning to subjects so immediately
relative to myself as those I now must touch upon.

You again insist, strengthened by Mr Lovelace's opinion, upon my assuming my own estate: and I have given
you room to expect that I will consider this subject more
closely than I had done before.

The will and the deeds have flaws in them, they say:
my brother sometimes talks of going to reside at *The
Grove*: I suppose with a design to make ejectments necessary, were I to offer at assuming; or should I marry
Lovelace, in order to give him all the opposition and
difficulty the law would help him to give.

And to go to law with my *father*, what a sound has
that? You will see that I have mentioned my wish (as
an alternative, and as a favour) to be permitted, if I *must*
be put out of his house, to go thither: but not one step
further can I go. And you see how this is resented.

As to Mr Lovelace's approbation of your assumption-
scheme, I wonder not at it. He, very probably, penetrates
the difficulties I should have to bring it to effect without
his assistance. Were I to find myself as free as I would
wish myself to be, perhaps that man would stand a worse
chance with me than his vanity may permit him to imagine; notwithstanding the pleasure you take in rallying me
on his account.

To threaten as he threatens—yet to pretend that it is
not to intimidate me; and to beg of you not to tell me,
when he must know you *would*, and no doubt must *intend* that you *should*, is so meanly artful! The man must
think he has a frighted fool to deal with.

I shall deposit this the first thing: when you have it, lose no time, I pray you, to advise (lest it be too late)

Your ever-obliged,
CL. HARLOWE

Letter 56: MISS HOWE TO MISS CLARISSA HARLOWE

Sat. March 25

What *can* I advise you, my noble creature? Your merit is your crime. You can no more change *your* nature, than your persecutors can *theirs*. Your distress is owing to the vast disparity between you and them. What would you have of them? Do they not act in character? And to whom? To an alien. You are not one of them. They have two dependencies—upon their own *impenetrableness*, one (I'd give it a properer name, if I dared); the other, on the regard you have always had for your *character* (have they not heretofore owned as much?) and upon your apprehensions from *that* of Lovelace, which would discredit you, should you take any step by his means to extricate yourself. Then they know that resentment and unpersuadableness are not natural to you; and that the anger they have wrought you up to will subside, as all *extraordinaries* soon do; and that once married, you'll make the best of it.

As to that wretch's perseverance, those only who know not the man [Solmes] will wonder at it. He has not the least delicacy. When-*ever* he shall marry, his view will not be for mind. How should it? He has *not* a mind: and does not *like seek its like*? And if it finds something beyond itself, how shall that be valued which cannot be comprehended? Were you to be his and show a visible want of tenderness to him, it is my opinion he would not be much concerned at it; since that would leave him the more at liberty to pursue those sordid attachments which are predominant in him.

While I was in hope that the asserting of your own independence would have helped you, I was pleased that you had *one* resource, as I thought: but now that you have so well proved that such a step would not avail you, I am entirely at a loss what to say. I will lay down my pen, and think.

I have considered, and considered again; but, I protest, I know no more what to say, than before. Only this: that I am young, like yourself; and have a much weaker judgement and stronger passions than you have.

One thing you must consider, that, if you leave your parents, your duty and love to them will not suffer you to appeal against them to justify yourself for so doing; and so you'll have the world against you. And should Lovelace continue his wild life, and behave ungratefully to you, how will that justify their conduct to *you* (which nothing *else* can), as well as their resentments against *him*?

You must, if possible, avoid being carried to that uncle's. The man, the parson, the chapel, your brother and sister present! They'll certainly there marry you to Solmes. Nor will your newly-raised spirit support you in your resistance on such an occasion. Your meekness will return; and you will have nothing for it but tears (tears despised by them all), and ineffectual appeals and lamentations—and *these*, when the ceremony is *profaned*, as I may say, you must suddenly put a stop to, and dry up: and endeavour to dispose yourself to such an humble frame of mind as may induce your new-made lord to forgive all your past declarations of aversion.

I will add nothing, though I could an hundred things, on occasion of your latest communications, but that I am,

Your ever-affectionate and faithful,
ANNA HOWE

Letter 62: MISS CLARISSA HARLOWE TO MISS HOWE

Tuesday morning, 7 o'clock

To be carried away on Thursday—to the moated house—to the chapel—to Solmes! How can I think of this! They will make me desperate!

Tuesday morn, eight o'clock

I have another letter from Mr Lovelace. I opened it, with the expectation of its being filled with bold and free complaints, on my not writing to prevent his two nights watching, in weather not extremely agreeable. But, instead of complaints, he is 'full of tender concern lest I may have been prevented by indisposition, or by the closer confinement which he has frequently cautioned me that I may expect.'

He says, 'he had been in different disguises loitering about our garden and park wall all the day on Sunday last; and all Sunday night was wandering about the coppice, and near the back door. It rained; and he has got a great cold, attended with feverishness, and so hoarse, that he has almost lost his voice.'

Why did he not flame out in his letter? Treated, as I am treated by my friends, it is dangerous for me to lie under the sense of an obligation to anyone's patience, when that person suffers in health for my sake.

'He had no shelter, he says, but under the great overgrown ivy, which spreads wildly round the heads of two or three oaklings; and that was soon wet through.'

You and I, my dear, once thought ourselves obliged to the natural shade they afforded us in a sultry day.

I can't help saying, I am sorry he has suffered for my sake—but 'tis his own seeking!

His letter is dated last night at eight: 'And indisposed as he is, he tells me that he will watch till ten, in hopes of my giving him the meeting he so earnestly requests. And after that, he has a mile to walk to his horse and servant; and four miles then to ride to his inn.'

He owns, 'that he has an intelligencer in our family; who has failed him for a day or two past: and not knowing how I do, or how I may be treated, his anxiety is the greater.'

This circumstance gives me to guess who this treacherous man is: one Joseph Leman: the very creature employed and confided in, more than any other, by my brother.

This is not an honourable way of proceeding in Mr Lovelace. Did he learn this infamous practice of corrupting the servants of other families at the French Court, where he resided a good while?

I have been often jealous of this Leman in my little airings and poultry-visits: I have thought him (doubly obsequious as he was always to me) my brother's spy upon me; and although he obliged me by his hastening out of the garden and poultry-yard, whenever I came into either, have wondered that from his reports my liberties of those kinds have not been abridged. So, possibly this man may take a bribe of both, and yet betray both.

'He presses with the utmost earnestness for an interview. He would not offer, he says, to disobey my last personal commands that he should not endeavour to attend me again in the wood-house. But says he can give me such reasons for my permitting him to wait upon my father or uncles, as he hopes will be approved by me: for he cannot help observing that it is no more suitable to my own spirit than to his, that he, a man of fortune and family, should be obliged to pursue such a clandestine address, as would only become a vile fortune-hunter. But if I will give my consent for his visiting me like a man, and a gentleman, no treatment shall provoke him to forfeit his temper.

'His uncle will accompany him, if I please: or his aunt Lawrance will first make the visit to my mamma, or to my aunt Hervey, or even to my uncles, if I choose it. And such terms shall be offered, as *shall* have weight upon them.

'He begs that I will not deny him making a visit to Mr Solmes. By all that's good, he vows that it shall not be with the least intention either to hurt or affront him; but only to set before him calmly and rationally, the consequences that may possibly flow from so fruitless a perseverance; as well as the ungenerous folly of it, to a mind so noble as mine. He repeats his own resolution to attend my pleasure, and Mr Morden's arrival and advice, for the reward of his own patience.

'It is impossible, he says, but one of these methods *must* do. He therefore most earnestly repeats his importunities for the supplicated interview.' Says, 'he has business of consequence in London: but cannot stir from the inconvenient spot where he has for some time resided in disguises unworthy of himself, until he can be absolutely certain that I shall not be prevailed upon, either by force or otherwise; and until he find me delivered from the insults of my brother.

'He renews his professions of reformation: he is convinced, he says, that he has already run a long and dangerous course; and that it is high time to think of returning. It must be from proper convictions, he says, that a person who has lived too gay a life resolves to reclaim before age or sufferings come upon him.'

I am afraid to ask you, my dear, what *you* would have done, thus situated. But what I *have* done, I *have* done. In a word, I wrote, 'that I would, if possible, give him a meeting tomorrow night, between the hours of nine and twelve, by the ivy summer-house, or in it, or near the great cascade at the bottom of the garden; and would unbolt the door that he might come in by his own key. But that, if I found the meeting impracticable, or should change my mind, I would signify as much by another line; which he must wait for until it were dark.'

Tuesday, eleven o'clock

I am just returned from depositing my billet. How diligent is this man! It is plain he was in waiting: for I had walked but a few paces after I had deposited it, when, my heart misgiving me, I returned, to have taken it back, in order to reconsider it as I walked, and whether I should, or should not, let it go: but I found it gone.

In all probability there was but a brick wall of a few inches thick between Mr Lovelace and me at the very time I put the letter under the brick.

I am come back dissatisfied with myself. But I think, my dear, there can be no harm in meeting him: if I do *not*, he may take some violent measures: what he knows of the treatment I meet with in malice to him, and with a view to frustrate all his hopes, may make him desperate. His behaviour last time I saw him, under the disadvantages of time and place, and surprised as I was, gives me no apprehension of anything but discovery. What he requires is not unreasonable, and cannot affect my future choice and determination: it is only to assure him from my own lips that I will never be the wife of a man I hate.

If I have not an opportunity to meet without hazard or detection, he must once more bear the disappointment. All his trouble, and mine too, is owing to his faulty character. This, although I hate tyranny and arrogance in all shapes, makes me think less of the risks he runs and the fatigues he undergoes, than otherwise I should do; and still less, as my sufferings (derived from the same source) are greater than his.

Betty confirms the intimation that I must go to my uncle's on Thursday. She was sent on purpose to direct me to prepare myself for going, and to help me to get up everything in order to it.

Letter 64: MISS CLARISSA HARLOWE TO MISS HOWE

　　　　　　　　　Wednesday morning, nine o'clock
I am just returned from my morning walk, and already have received a letter from Mr Lovelace in answer to mine deposited last night. He must have had pen, ink, and paper, with him, for it was written in the coppice with this circumstance; on one knee, kneeling with the other. Not from reverence to the written-to, however, as you'll find.

This man has vexed me heartily. I see his gentleness was *art*; fierceness, and a temper like what I have been too much used to at home, are *nature* in him. In the mind I am in, nothing shall ever make me forgive him, since there can be no good reason for his impatience on an expectation given with reserve, and absolutely revocable. *I* so much to suffer through him; yet, to be treated as if I were obliged to bear insults *from* him!

But here you will be pleased to read his letter; which I shall enclose.

to Miss Clarissa Harlowe

Good God!
What is now to become of me! How shall I support this disappointment! No new cause! On one knee, kneeling with the other, I write! My feet benumbed with midnight wanderings through the heaviest dews that ever fell: my wig and my linen dripping with the hoar frost

dissolving on them! Day but just breaking—sun not risen to exhale. May it never rise again!—unless it bring healing and comfort to a benighted soul!

In proportion to the joy you had inspired (ever lovely promiser!), in such proportion is my anguish!

And *are things drawing towards a crisis between your friends and you?* Is not this a reason for me to expect, the *rather* to expect, the promised interview?

Oh the wavering, the changeable sex! But can Miss Clarissa Harlowe—

Forgive me, madam! I know not what I write! Yet, I must, I do, insist upon your promise—or that you will condescend to find better excuses for the failure or convince me that stronger reasons are imposed upon *you*, than those you offer. A promise *once* given; upon *deliberation* given!—the promise-*ed* only can dispense with; or some very apparent necessity imposed upon the promise-*er*, which leaves no power to perform it.

The first promise you ever made me! Life and death, perhaps, depending upon it. My heart desponding from the barbarous methods resolved to be taken with you, in malice to me!

You would sooner choose death than Solmes. (How my soul spurns the competition!) Oh my beloved creature, what are these but *words! Whose* words?—sweet and ever-adorable. What?—promise-breaker must I call you? How shall I believe the asseveration (your supposed duty in the question! persecution so flaming! hatred to me so strongly avowed!) after this instance of your so lightly dispensing with your promise!

If, my dearest life! you would prevent my distraction, or at least distracted consequences, renew the promised hope! My *fate* is indeed upon its crisis.

Forgive me; dearest creature, forgive me! I know I have written in too much anguish of mind! Writing this, in the same moment that the just-dawning light has imparted to me the heavy disappointment!

I dare not re-peruse what I have written. I *must* deposit it. It may serve to show you my distracted apprehensions that this disappointment is but a prelude to the greatest of all. Nor having here any other paper, am I able to write again if I would, on this gloomy spot.

Gloomy is my soul; and all nature round me partakes of my gloom! I trust it, therefore, to your goodness! If its fervour excites your displeasure, rather than your pity, you wrong my passion; and I shall be ready to apprehend that I am intended to be the sacrifice of more miscreants than one! Have patience with me, dearest creature! I mean Solmes, and your brother only. But if, exerting your usual generosity, you will excuse and *re*-appoint, may that God, whom you profess to serve, and who is the God of *truth* and of *promises*, protect and bless you, for both; and for restoring to Himself, and to hope,

Ivy-Cavern in the Coppice—day but just breaking.	Your ever-adoring, yet almost desponding LOVELACE!

This is the answer I shall return.

Wednesday morning

I am amazed, sir, at the freedom of your reproaches. Pressed and teased against convenience and inclination to give you a private meeting, am I to be thus challenged and upbraided, and my sex reflected upon, because I thought it prudent to change my mind? A liberty I had reserved to myself when I made the *appointment*, as you call it. I wanted not instances of your impatient spirit to other people: yet may it be happy for me, that I have this new one; which shows that you can as little spare *me,* when I pursue the dictates of my own reason, as you do *others* for acting up to theirs. Two motives you must be governed by in this excess. The one *my easiness*; the other *your own presumption*. Since you think you have found out the *first*; and have shown so much of the *last* upon it, I am too much alarmed not to wish and desire, that your letter of this day may conclude all the trouble you have had from, or for,

Your humble servant,
CL. HARLOWE

I believe, my dear, I may promise myself your approbation, whenever I write or speak with spirit, be it to whom it will. Indeed, I find but too much reason to exert it, since I have to deal with people who measure their conduct to me, not by what is fit or decent, right or wrong, but by what they think my temper will bear. I have, till very lately, been praised for mine; but it has always been by those who never gave me opportunity to return the compliment to themselves. Some people have acted as if they thought forbearance on *one side* absolutely necessary for them and me to be upon good terms together; and in this case have ever taken care rather to *owe* that obligation than to *lay* it. You have hinted to me that resentment is not natural to my temper, and that therefore it must soon subside. It may be so, with respect to my relations: but not to Mr Lovelace, I assure you.

Wednesday noon, March 29

We cannot always answer for what we *can* do: but to convince you that I can keep my above resolution, with regard to this Lovelace, angry as my letter is, and three hours as it is since it was written, I assure you that I repent it not, nor will soften it, although I find it is not taken away. And yet I hardly ever before did anything in anger and that I did not repent in half an hour; and question myself in *less* than that time, whether I was right or wrong.

In this respite till Tuesday, I have a little time to look about me, as I may say, and consider of what I *have* to do, and *can* do. And Mr Lovelace's insolence will make me go very home with myself.

But, with all my courage, I am exceedingly apprehensive about Tuesday next, and about what may result from my steadfastness; for steadfast I am sure I shall be. They are resolved, I am told, to try every means to induce me to comply with what they are determined upon. I am resolved to do the like, to avoid what they would force me to do.

What can I do? Advise me, my dear!

Be pleased to remember, my dear, that your last favour was dated on Saturday. This is Wednesday: and none of mine have been taken away since. My situation is extremely difficult. But I am sure you love me still:

and not the less on *that* account. Adieu, my beloved friend.

CL. HARLOWE

Letter 70: MISS HOWE TO MISS CLARISSA HARLOWE

Thursday night, March 30

The fruits of my inquiry after your abominable wretch's behaviour and baseness at the paltry alehouse, which he calls an inn; prepare to hear.

Wrens and sparrows are not too ignoble a quarry for this villainous goshawk! His assiduities; his watchings; his nightly risks; the inclement weather he travels in; must not be all placed to *your* account. He has opportunities of making everything light to him of that sort. A sweet pretty girl, I am told—innocent till he went thither. Now! Ah! poor girl!—who knows what?

But just turned of seventeen! His friend and brother rake [Belford]; a man of humour and intrigue, as I am told, to share the social bottle with. And sometimes another disguised rake or two. No sorrow comes near their hearts. Be not disturbed, my dear, at his *hoarsenesses*. His pretty Betsy, his Rosebud, as the vile wretch calls her, can *hear* all he says.

He is very fond of her. They say she is innocent even yet! Her father, her grandmother, believe her to be so. He is to fortune her out to a young lover! Ah! the poor young lover! Ah! the poor simple girl!

Yet I wish I may be able to snatch the poor young creature out of his villainous paws. I have laid a scheme to do so; if *indeed* she is hitherto innocent and heart-free.

He appears to the people as a military man, in disguise, secreting himself on account of a duel fought in town; the adversary's life in suspense. They believe he is a great man. His friend passes for an inferior officer; upon a foot of freedom with him. He, accompanied by a third man, who is a sort of subordinate companion to the second. The wretch himself but with one servant. Oh my dear! How pleasantly can these devils, as I must call them, pass their time, while our gentle bosoms heave with pity for their supposed sufferings for us!

I am just now informed that, at my desire, I shall see this girl and her father: I will sift them thoroughly. I shall soon find out such a simple thing as this, if he has not corrupted her already. And if he has, I shall soon find that out too. But, depend upon it, the girl's undone.

He is said to be fond of her. He places her at the upper end of his table. He sets her a-prattling. He keeps his friend at a distance from her. She prates away. He admires for nature all she says. Anybody but Solmes and Lovelace be yours! So advises

Your
ANNA HOWE

Letter 71: MISS CLARISSA HARLOWE TO MISS HOWE

Friday, three o'clock

You incense, alarm and terrify me, at the same time! Hasten, my dearest friend, hasten to me, what further intelligence you can gather about this vilest of men!

But never talk of innocence, of simplicity, and this unhappy girl together! Must she not know, that such a man as that, dignified in his very aspect; and no disguise able to conceal his being of condition—must mean too much, when he places her at the upper end of his table, and calls her by such tender names? Would a girl, modest as simple, above seventeen, be set a singing at the pleasure of such a man as that? A stranger, and professedly in disguise! Would her father and grandmother, if honest people, and careful of their simple girl, permit such freedoms?

Keeps his friend at a distance from her! To be sure his *designs* are villainous, if they have not been already effected.

Warn, my dear, if not too late, the unthinking father, of his child's danger. There cannot be a father in the world, who would sell his child's virtue. No mother!— the poor thing!

Fine hopes of such a wretch's reformation! I would

not, my dear, for the world, have anything to say—but
I need not make resolutions. I have not opened, nor will
I open, his letter.

To be already on a foot!—in his esteem, I mean, my
dear. For myself, I despise him. I hate myself almost for
writing so much about *him*, and of such a simpleton as
this sweet pretty girl: but nothing can be either *sweet* or
pretty, that is not modest, that is not virtuous.

I think I hate him worse than I do Solmes himself.
But I will not add one other word about him; after I
have wished to know, as soon as possible, what further
occurs from your inquiry; because I shall not open his
letter till then; and because then, if it comes out, as I
dare say it will, I'll directly put the letter unopened into
the place I took it from, and never trouble myself more
about him. Adieu, my dearest friend.

CL. HARLOWE

Letter 72: MISS HOWE TO MISS CLARISSA HARLOWE

Friday noon, March 31

Justice obliges me to forward this after my last, on the
wings of the wind, as I may say. I really believe the man
is innocent. Of this *one* accusation, I think, he must be
acquitted; and I am sorry I was so forward in dispatching
away my intelligence by halves.

I have seen the girl. She is really a very pretty, a very
neat, and what is still a greater beauty, a very innocent
young creature. He who could have ruined such an undesigning home-bred must have been indeed infernally
wicked. Her father is an honest simple man; entirely
satisfied with his child, and with her new acquaintance.

I am almost afraid for your heart, when I tell you that
I find, now I have got to the bottom of this inquiry,
something noble come out in this Lovelace's favour.

The girl is to be married next week; and this promoted
and brought about by him. He is resolved, her father
says, to make one couple happy, and wishes he could
make more so. (There's for you, my dear!) And having
taken a liking also to the young fellow whom she pro-
fesses to love, he has given her a hundred pounds: the

grandmother actually has it in her hands, to answer to the like sum given to the youth by one of his own relations: while Mr Lovelace's companion, attracted by the example, has presented twenty-five guineas to the father, who is poor, towards clothes to equip the pretty rustic.

But what, my dear, will become of us now? Why, my sweet friend, your generosity is now engaged in his favour! Fie, upon this *generosity*! I think in my heart that it does as much mischief to the noble-minded, as *love* to the ignobler. What before was only a *conditional liking*, I am now afraid will turn to *liking unconditional*.

I could not endure to turn my invective into panegyric all at once, and so soon. We, or such as I, at least, love to keep ourselves in countenance for a rash judgement, even when we know it to be rash. Everybody has not your generosity in confessing a mistake. It requires a greatness of soul to do it. So I made still farther inquiry after his life and manners, and behaviour there, in hopes to find something bad: but all uniform!

Upon the whole, Mr Lovelace comes out with so much advantage from this inquiry, that were there the least room for it, I should suspect the whole to be a plot set on foot to wash a blackamoor white. Adieu, my dear.

ANNA HOWE

Letter 73: MISS CLARISSA HARLOWE TO MISS HOWE

Saturday, April 1

Hasty censurers do indeed subject themselves to the charge of variableness and inconsistency in judgement: and so they ought; for, if you, even you, were really so loath to own a mistake, as, in the instance before us, you pretend to say you were, I believe I should not have loved you so well as I really do love you. Nor could you, my dear, have so frankly thrown the reflection I hint at, upon yourself, had you not had one of the most ingenuous minds that ever woman boasted.

Then the real generosity of the act—I protest, my beloved friend, if he would be good for the rest of his life from this time, I would forgive him a great many of his past errors, were it only for the demonstration he has given in this, that he is *capable* of so good and bountiful a manner of thinking.

You may believe I made no scruple to open his letter, after the receipt of your second on this subject: nor shall I of answering it, as I have no reason to find fault with it. An article in his favour procured him, however, so much the easier (as I must own) by way of amends for the undue displeasure I took against him; though he knows it not.

It is lucky enough that this matter was cleared up to me by your friendly diligence so soon: for had I wrote at all before that, it would have been to reinforce my dismission of him; and perhaps the very motive mentioned; for it had affected me more than I think it ought: and then, what an advantage would that have given him, when he could have cleared up the matter so happily for himself?

When I send you this letter of his, you will see how very humble he is: what acknowledgements of natural impatience: what confession of faults, as you prognosticated.

Saturday, April 1

I have written; and to this effect: 'That I had never intended to write another line to a man who could take upon himself to reflect upon my sex and myself, for having thought fit to make use of my own judgement.

'That I have submitted to this interview with Mr Solmes, purely as an act of duty, to show my friends that I will comply with their commands as far as I can; and that I hope, when Mr Solmes himself shall see how determined I am, he will no longer prosecute a suit, in which it is impossible he should succeed with my consent.

'That my aversion to him is too sincere to permit me to doubt myself on this occasion. But, nevertheless, he, Mr Lovelace, must not imagine that my rejecting of Mr Solmes is in favour to him. That I value my freedom and independency too much, if my friends will but leave me to my own judgement, to give them up to a man so uncontrollable, and who shows me beforehand, what I have to expect from him were I in his power.'

I see not any of my family, nor hear from them in any way of kindness.

My uncle Antony's intended presence I do not much like: but that is preferable to my brother's or sister's. My uncle is very impetuous in his anger. I can't think Mr Lovelace can be much more so; at least, he cannot *look it*, as my uncle, with his harder features can.

I believe both Mr Solmes and I shall look like a couple of fools, if it be true, as my uncle Harlowe writes, and Betty often tells me, that he is as much afraid of seeing me as I am of seeing him.

Adieu, my happy, thrice happy, Miss Howe, who have no hard terms affixed to your duty!

To *know* your own happiness; and that it is *now*, nor to leave it to *after*-reflection to look back upon the *preferable past* with a heavy and self-accusing heart, that you did not choose it when you might have chosen it, is all that is necessary to complete your felicity! And this power is wished you by

Your
CL. HARLOWE

Letter 80: MISS CLARISSA HARLOWE TO MISS HOWE

Wednesday, four o'clock in the afternoon
I am just returned from depositing the letter I so lately finished, and such of Mr Lovelace's letters as I had not sent you. My long letter I found remaining there—so you'll have both together.

I am concerned, methinks, it is not with you—but your servant cannot always be at leisure. However, I'll deposit as fast as I write: I must keep nothing by me now; and when I write, lock myself in, that I may not be surprised, now they think I have no pen and ink.

I found in the usual place another letter from this diligent man: and by its contents a confirmation that nothing passes in this house, but he knows it; and that, as soon as it passes. For this letter must have been written before he could have received my billet; and deposited, I suppose, when that was taken away; yet he compliments me in it upon asserting myself, as he calls it, on that occasion, to my uncle and to Mr Solmes.

'He assures me, however, that they are more and more determined to subdue me.

'He sends me the compliments of his family; and acquaints me with their earnest desire to see me amongst them. Most vehemently does he press for my quitting this house while it is in my power to get away: and again craves leave to order his uncle's chariot and six to attend my orders at the stile leading to the coppice adjoining to the paddock.

'Settlements to my own will, he again offers. Lord M. and both his aunts to be guaranties of his honour and justice. But, if I choose not to go to either of his aunts, nor yet to make him the happiest of men so soon as it is nevertheless his hope that I will, he urges me to withdraw to my own house; and to accept of my Lord M. for my guardian and protector till my cousin Morden arrives. There can be no pretence for litigation, he says, when I am once in it. Nor, if I choose to have it so, will he appear to visit me; nor presume to mention marriage to me till all is quiet and easy; till every method I shall prescribe for a reconciliation with my friends is tried; till my cousin comes; till such settlements are drawn as he shall approve of for me; and that I have unexceptionable proofs of his own good behaviour.'

As to the disgrace a person of my character may be apprehensive of upon quitting my father's house, he observes, too truly I doubt, 'That the treatment I meet with is in everyone's mouth: yet, he says, that the public voice is in my favour: My friends themselves, he says, *expect* that I will do myself what he calls this justice; why else do they confine me? He urges that, thus treated, the independence I have a right to will be my sufficient excuse, going but from their house to my own, if I choose that measure; or, in order to take possession of my own, if I do not: that all the disgrace I *can* receive, they have already given me: that his concern, and his family's concern *in* my honour will be equal to my own, if he may be so happy ever to call me his: and he presumes to aver that no family can better supply the loss of my own friends to me than his, in whatever way I do them the honour to accept of his and their protection.

Something, however, I must speedily resolve upon, or it will be out of my power to help myself.

Now I think of it, I will enclose his letter (so might have spared the abstract of it), that you may the better judge of all his proposals and intelligence; and lest it should fall into other hands. I cannot forget the contents, although I am at a loss what answer to return.

Wednesday night

All is in a hurry below-stairs. Betty is in and out like a spy. Something is working, I know not what. I am really a good deal disordered in body as well as mind. Indeed I am quite heart-sick!

I will go down, though 'tis almost dark, on pretence of getting a little air and composure. Robert has my two former, I hope, before now: and I will deposit this with Lovelace's enclosed, if I can, for fear of another search.

How am I driven to and fro, like a feather in the wind, at the pleasure of the rash, the selfish and the headstrong! and when I am as averse to the proceedings of the one as I am to those of the other! But being forced into a clandestine correspondence, indiscreet measures are fallen upon by the rash man before I can be consulted: and between them, I have not an option, although my ruin (for is not the loss of reputation a ruin?) may be the dreadful consequence of the steps taken. What a perverse fate is mine!

If I am prevented depositing this and the enclosed, as I intend to try to do, late as it is, I will add to it, as occasion shall offer. Meantime, believe me to be

Your ever affectionate and grateful
CL. HARLOWE

Letter 81: MISS HOWE TO MISS CLARISSA HARLOWE

Thursday morning, April 6

I have your three letters.

I know not what to say to Lovelace; nor what to think of his promises, nor of his proposals to you. 'Tis certain that you are highly esteemed by all his family. The ladies are persons of unblemished honour. My Lord M. is also, as men and peers go, a man of honour. I could tell what to advise any other person in the world to do but you. So much expected from you! Such a shining light! Your quitting your father's house, and throwing yourself into the protection of a family, however honourable, that has a man in it whose person, parts, declarations and pretensions will be thought to have engaged your warmest esteem! Methinks I am rather for advising that you should get privately to London; and not to let either him, or anybody else but me, know where you are, till your cousin Morden comes.

As to going to your uncle's, that you must not do, if you can help it. Nor must you have Solmes, that's certain: not only because of his unworthiness in every respect, but because of the aversion you have so openly avowed to him; which everybody knows and talks of; as they do of your approbation of the other. For your reputation-sake, therefore, as well as to prevent mischief, you must either live single or have Lovelace.

If you think of going to London, let me know; and I hope you will have *time* to allow me a farther concert as to the manner of your getting away and thither, and how to procure proper lodgings for you.

To obtain this *time*, *you* must palliate a little, and come into some seeming compromise if you cannot do otherwise. Driven as you are driven, it will be strange if you are not obliged to part with a few of your admirable punctilios.

London, I am told, is the best hiding-place in the world. I have written nothing but what I will stand to at the word of command. Women love to engage in knight-errantry, now and then, as well as to encourage it in the men. But in your case, what I propose will have nothing in it of what can be deemed *that*. It will enable me to perform what is no more than a duty in serving and comforting a dear and worthy friend, labouring under undeserved oppression: and you will *ennoble*, as I may say, your Anna Howe, if you will allow her to be your companion in affliction.

I'll engage, my dear, we shall not be in town together one month, before we surmount all difficulties; and this without being beholden to any men-fellows for their protection.

I must repeat what I have often said, that the authors of your persecutions would not have presumed to set on foot their selfish schemes against you, had they not depended upon the gentleness of your spirit: though now, having gone so far and having engaged *Old* AU-THORITY in it (chide me if you will!), neither *he* nor *they* know how to recede.

When they find you out of their reach, and know that I am with you, you'll see how they'll pull in their odious horns.

Adieu, my dear! Happier times must come!—and that quickly too. The strings cannot long continue thus over-strained. They must break, or be relaxed. In either way, the certainty must be preferable to the suspense.

One word more.

I think in my conscience you must take one of these two alternatives: [firstly] to consent to let us go to London together privately: in which case, I will procure a vehicle and meet you at your appointment at the stile Lovelace proposes to bring his uncle's chariot to: or, secondly, to put yourself into the protection of Lord M. and the ladies of his family.

You have another, indeed; and that is, if you are absolutely resolved against Solmes, to meet and marry Lovelace directly.

Whichsoever of those you make choice of, you'll have this plea, both to yourself and to the world, that you are concluded by the same uniform principle that has governed your whole conduct ever since the contention between Lovelace and your brother has been on foot: that is to say, that you have chosen a lesser evil in hope to prevent a greater.

Adieu! and Heaven direct for the best my beloved creature, prays

Her
ANNA HOWE

Letter 82: MISS CLARISSA HARLOWE TO MISS HOWE

Thursday, April 6

I thank you, my dearest friend, for the kind pains you have taken in accounting so affectionately for my papers [letters] not being taken away yesterday [by Robert]; and for the kind protection you would have procured for me, if you could.

Indeed, my dearest love (permit me to be *very* serious), I am afraid I am singled out, either for my own faults or for the faults of my family, or for the faults of both, to be a very unhappy creature!—*signally* unhappy! For see you not how irresistibly the waves of affliction come tumbling down upon me?

We have been till within these few weeks, everyone of us, too happy. No crosses, no vexations, but what we gave ourselves from the *pamperedness*, as I may call it, of our own wills. Surrounded by our heaps and stores, hoarded up as fast as acquired, we have seemed to think ourselves out of the reach of the bolts of adverse fate. I was the pride of all my friends, proud *myself* of *their* pride, and glorying in my standing. Who knows what the justice of Heaven may inflict in order to convince us that we are not out of the reach of misfortune; and to reduce us to a better reliance than that we have hitherto presumptuously made?

Your partial love will be ready to acquit me of capital and intentional faults but oh, my dear! my calamities have humbled me enough to make me turn my gaudy eye inward; to make me look into myself! And what have I discovered there? Why, my dear friend, more *secret* pride and vanity than I could have thought had lain in my unexamined heart.

If *I* am to be singled out to be the *punisher* of myself, and family, who so lately was the *pride* of it, pray for me, my dear, that I may not be left wholly to myself; and that I may be enabled to support my character, so as to be *justly* acquitted of wilful and premeditated faults. The will of Providence be resigned to in the rest: as *that* leads, let me patiently and unrepiningly follow! I shall not live always! May but my *closing* scene be happy!

But I will not oppress you, my dearest friend, with further reflections of this sort. I will take them all into myself. Surely I have a mind that has room for them. My afflictions are too sharp to last long. The crisis is at hand. Happier times you bid me hope for. I *will* hope!

But yet I cannot but be impatient at times to find myself thus driven, and my character so depreciated and sunk, that were all the *future* to be happy I should be ashamed to show my face in public, or to look up. And all by the instigation of a selfish brother, and envious sister!

But let me stop: let me reflect! Are not these suggestions the suggestions of the *secret* pride I have been censuring? Then, *already* so impatient! But this moment so resigned! so much better disposed for reflection! Yet 'tis hard, 'tis very hard, to subdue an embittered spirit!—in the instant of its trial too! Oh my cruel brother! But now it rises again! I will lay down a pen I am so little able to govern—and I will try to subdue an impatience, which (if my afflictions are sent me for corrective ends) may otherwise lead me into still more punishable errors!

What appears to me, upon the fullest deliberation, the most eligible if I *must* be thus driven, is the escaping to London. But I would forfeit all my hopes of happiness in this life, rather than you should go off with me, as you rashly propose.

If, my dear, you can procure a conveyance for us *both*, you can perhaps procure one for me *singly*; but can it be done without embroiling *yourself* with your mamma, or *her* with our family? Be it coach, chariot, chaise, waggon, or horse, I matter not, provided you appear not in it.

Had you, my dear friend, been married, then should I have had no doubt but you and Mr Hickman would have afforded an asylum to a poor creature, more than half lost, in her own apprehension, for want of one kind, protecting friend!

But you tell me that in order to gain time, I must *palliate*; that I must seem to compromise with my friends. But how *palliate*? how *seem* to compromise?

You would not have me endeavour to make them believe that I will consent to what I never intend to consent
to! You would not have me try to gain time with a view
to *deceive*!

And is there, after all, no way to escape one great
evil, but by plunging myself into another? What an ill-
fated creature am I? Pray for me, my dearest Nancy!
My mind is at present so much disturbed that I hardly
can for myself!

Letter 83: MISS CLARISSA HARLOWE TO MISS HOWE

Thursday night

The rash man has indeed so far gained his point, as to
intimidate them from attempting to carry me away: but
he has put them upon a surer and a more desperate
measure: and this has put me also upon one *as* desperate, the consequence of which, although he could not
foresee it, may perhaps too well answer his great end,
little as he deserves to have it answered.

In short, I have done as far as I know the rashest
thing that ever I did in my life!

But let me give you the motive, and then the action
will follow of course.

About six o'clock this evening, my aunt (who stays
here all night; on my account, no doubt) came up and
tapped at my door; for I was writing, and had locked
myself in. I opened it; and she entering, thus delivered
herself:

I come once more to visit you, my dear; but sorely
against my will; because it is to impart to you matters
of the utmost concern to you, and to the whole family.

What, madam, is now to be done with me? said I;
wholly attentive.

You will not be hurried away to your uncle's, child;
let that comfort you. They see your aversion to go. You
will not be obliged to go to your uncle Antony's.

How you revive me, madam! (I little thought what
was to follow this supposed condescension). This is a
cordial to my heart!

And then I ran over with blessings for this good news

(and she permitted me so to do, by her silence); congrat-
ulating myself that I *thought* my papa could not resolve
to carry things to the last extremity—

Hold, niece, said she, at last. You must not give yourself too much joy upon the occasion neither. Don't be
surprised, my dear. Why look you upon me, child, with
so affecting an earnestness! But you must be Mrs
Solmes, for all that.

I was dumb.

She then told me that they had had undoubted information that a certain desperate *ruffian* (I must excuse
her that word, she said) had prepared armed men to
waylay my brother and uncles, and seize me and carry
me off. Surely, she said, I was not consenting to a violence that might be followed by murder on one side or
the other; perhaps on both.

I was still silent.

That therefore my father (still more exasperated than
before) had changed his resolution as to my going to my
uncle's; and was determined next Tuesday to set out
thither *himself* with my mamma; and that (for it was to
no purpose to conceal a resolution so soon to be put in
execution)—I must not dispute it any longer—on Wednesday I must give my hand—as they would have me.

She proceeded: That orders were already given for a
licence: that the ceremony was to be performed in my
own chamber, in presence of all my friends, except of
my father and mother; who would not return, nor see
me, till all was over, and till they had a good account of
my behaviour.

I was still dumb—only sighing as if my heart would
break.

My dear, you must have Mr Solmes: indeed you must.

Well, madam, then nothing remains for me to say. I
am made desperate. I care not what becomes of me!

Your piety, and your prudence, my dear, and Mr
Lovelace's immoral character, together with his daring
insults and threatenings, which ought to incense you as
much as anybody, are everyone's dependence. We are
sure the time will come, when you'll think very differently of the steps your friends take to disappoint a man
who has made himself so justly obnoxious to them all.

I put it to her, in the most earnest manner, to tell me whether I might not obtain the favour of a fortnight's respite?

She assured me it would not be granted.

Would a week? Surely a week would?

She believed a week might, if I would promise two things: the first, upon my honour, not to write a line out of the house, in that week: for it was still suspected, she said, that I found means to write to *somebody*. And, secondly, to marry Mr Solmes, at the expiration of it.

Impossible! Impossible! I said with passion. What! might I not be obliged with one week, without such a horrid condition at the last?

I even stamped with impatience! I called upon her to witness, that I was guiltless of the consequence of this compulsion; this barbarous compulsion, I called it; let that consequence be what it would.

My aunt chid me in an higher strain than ever she did before.

While I, in a half frenzy, insisted upon seeing my papa: such usage, I said, set me above fear. I would rejoice to owe my death to him, as I did my life.

She owned that she feared for my head.

I did go down half way of the stairs, resolved to throw myself at his feet, wherever he was. My aunt was frighted. Indeed I was quite frenzical for a few minutes. But hearing my brother's voice, as talking to somebody in my sister's apartment just by, I stopped; and heard the barbarous designer say, speaking to my sister: This works charmingly, my dear sister!

It does! It does! said she, in an exulting accent.

Let us keep it up, said my brother. The villain is caught in his own trap! Now she must be what we'd have her be.

Do you keep my father to it; I'll take care of my mamma, said Bella.

Never fear, said he!—and a laugh of congratulation to each other, and derision of me (as I made it out) quite turned my frenzical humour into a vindictive one.

My aunt, just then coming down to me, and taking my hand, led me up; and tried to soothe me.

*　　　*　　　*

I revolved, after she was gone, all that my brother and sister had said: I dwelt upon their triumphings over me: and found rise in my mind a rancour that I think I may say was new to me; and which I could not withstand. And putting every thing together, dreading the near day, what could I do? Am I in any manner excusable for what I *did* do? If I am condemned by the world, who know not my provocations, may I be acquitted by you? If *not*, I am unhappy indeed—for this I did.

Having shook off Betty as soon as I could, I wrote to Mr Lovelace to let him know, 'That all that was threatened at my uncle Antony's was intended to be executed *here*. That I had come to a resolution to throw myself upon the protection of either of his two aunts, who would afford it me: in short, that by endeavouring to obtain leave on Monday to dine in the ivy summerhouse, I would, if possible, meet him without the garden door at two, three, four, or five o'clock on Monday afternoon, as I should be able. That in the meantime he should acquaint me, whether I might hope for either of those ladies' protection. And if so, I absolutely insisted that he should leave me with either, and go to London himself or remain at his uncle's; nor offer to visit me till I were satisfied that nothing could be done with my friends in an amicable way; and that I could not obtain possession of my own estate, and leave to live upon it: and particularly, that he should not hint marriage to me, till I consented to hear him upon that subject.

This was the purport of what I wrote; and down into the garden I slid with it in the dark, which at another time I should not have had the courage to do, and deposited it, and came up again, unknown to anybody.

My mind so dreadfully misgave me when I returned, that to divert in some measure my increasing uneasiness, I had recourse to my private pen; and in a very short time ran this length.

And now that I am come to this part, my uneasy reflections begin again to pour in upon me. Yet what can I do? I believe I shall take it back again the first thing I do in the morning—yet what *can* I do?

For fear they should have an earlier day in their intention than that which will too soon come, I will begin to

be very ill. Nor need I feign much; for indeed I am
extremely low, weak and faint.

I hope to deposit this early in the morning for you, as
I shall return from resuming my letter, if I do resume
it, as my *inwardest* mind bids me.

Although it is now near two o'clock, I have a good
mind to slide down once more, in order to take back
my letter. Our doors are always locked and barred up
at eleven; but the seats of the lesser hall windows being
almost even with the ground without, and the shutters
not difficult to open, I could easily get out.

Yet why should I be thus uneasy?—since, should the
letter go, I can but hear what Mr Lovelace says to it.
His aunts live at too great a distance for him to have an
immediate answer from them; so I can scruple going off
till I have invitation. Twenty things may happen to afford me a suspension at least: why should I be so very
uneasy?—when, too, I can resume it early, before it is
probable he will have the thought of finding it there.

But these strange forebodings! Yet I can, if you advise, cause the chariot he shall bring with him, to carry
me directly for town, whither in my London scheme, if
you were to approve it, I had proposed to go: and this
will save you the trouble of procuring for me a vehicle;
as well as the suspicion from your mamma of contribut-
ing to my escape.

But, solicitous for your advice and approbation too, if
I *can* have it, I will put an end to this letter.

Adieu, my dearest friend, adieu!

Letter 84: MISS CLARISSA HARLOWE TO MISS HOWE

         Friday morning, seven o'clock, April 7
My aunt Hervey, who is a very early riser, was walking
in the garden (Betty attending her, as I saw from my
window this morning), when I arose; for, after such a
train of fatigue and restless nights, I had unhappily over-
slept myself: so all I durst venture upon was to step
down to my poultry-yard, and deposit mine of yesterday
and last night. And I am just come up; for she is still in
the garden: this prevents me from going to resume my

letter, as I think still to do; and hope it will not be too late.

Eight o'clock

The man, my dear, has got the letter! What a strange diligence! What an advantage have I given him over me!

Now the letter is out of my power, I have more uneasiness and regret than I had before. For, till now, I had a doubt whether it should, or should not go: and now I think it ought *not* to have gone. And yet is there any other way than to do as I have done, if I would avoid Solmes? But what a giddy creature shall I be thought if I pursue the course to which this letter must lead me?

My dearest friend, tell me, have I done wrong? Yet do not *say* I have, if you *think* it; for should all the world besides condemn me, I shall have some comfort, if *you* do not. The first time I ever besought you to flatter me. That, of itself, is an indication that I have done wrong, and am afraid of hearing the truth. Oh tell me (but yet do not tell me) if I have done wrong!

Friday, eleven o'clock

I will go down and deposit this; for Betty has seen I have been writing. The saucy creature took a napkin, and dipped it in water, and with a fleering air: Here, miss; holding the wet corner to me.

What's that for, said I?

Only, miss, one of the fingers of your right hand, if you please to look at it.

It was inky.

I gave her a look: but said nothing.

But lest I should have another search, I will close here.

CL. HARLOWE

Letter 85: MISS CLARISSA HARLOWE TO MISS HOWE

Friday, one o'clock

I have a letter from Mr Lovelace, full of transports, vows, and promises. I will send it to you enclosed. You'll see how he engages in it for his aunt Lawrance's protection, and for Miss Charlotte Montague's accompanying me. 'I have nothing to do, but to persevere, he says, and prepare to receive the personal congratulations of his whole family.'

But you'll see, how he presumes upon my being *his*, as the consequence of throwing myself into that lady's protection.

The chariot and six is to be ready at the place he mentions. You'll see, as to the slur upon my reputation which I am so apprehensive about, how boldly he argues. Generously enough, indeed, were I to be *his*; and had given him reason to believe that I would!—but that I have not done.

How one step brings on another with this encroaching sex! How soon may a young creature who gives a man the least encouragement be carried beyond her intentions, and out of her own power! You would imagine, by what he writes, that I have given him reason to think that my aversion to Mr Solmes is all owing to my favour for him!

However, I have replied to the following effect: 'That although I had given him room to expect that I would put myself into his aunt's protection; yet, as I have three days to come, between this and Monday, and as I hope that my friends will still relent or that Mr Solmes will give up a point they will both find it impossible to carry; I shall not look upon myself as absolutely bound by the appointment: and expect therefore, if I recede, that I shall not be called to account for it by him.'

This I will deposit as soon as I can. And as he thinks things are near their crisis, I dare say it will not be long before I have an answer to it.

Letter 87: MISS HOWE TO MISS CLARISSA HARLOWE

Sat. afternoon

A time, I hope, will come, that I shall be able to read your affecting narratives without that impatience and bitterness which now boils over in my heart, and would flow to my pen were I to enter into the particulars of what you write. And, indeed, I am afraid of giving you my advice at all, or of telling you what I should do in your case (supposing you will still refuse my offer); finding too, what you have been brought, or rather driven, to, without it; lest any evil should follow it: in which case, I should never forgive myself. And this consideration has added to my difficulties in writing to you, now you are upon such a crisis, and yet refuse the only method—But I said I would not for the present touch any more that string. Yet, one word more, chide me if you please: if any harm betide you, I shall for ever blame my mamma—indeed I shall—and perhaps yourself, if you do not accept of my offer.

But one thing, in your present situation and prospects, let me advise: it is this, that if you *do* go away with Mr Lovelace, you take the first opportunity to permit the ceremony to pass. Why should you *not*, when everybody will know by *whose* assistance, and in *whose* company, you leave your father's house, go whithersoever you will? You may, indeed, keep him at distance, until settlements are drawn and such-like matters are adjusted to your mind.

Give this matter your most serious consideration. Punctilio is out of doors the moment you are out of your father's house. I know how justly severe you have been upon those inexcusable creatures, whose giddiness and even want of decency have made them, in the same hour, as I may say, leap from a parent's window to a husband's bed. But, considering Lovelace's character, I repeat my opinion that your reputation in the eye of the world requires that no delay be made in this point, when once you are in his power.

I need not, I am sure, make a stronger plea to *you*.

From this critical and distressful situation, it shall be my hourly prayers that you may be delivered without blemish to that fair fame, which has hitherto, like your heart, been unspotted.

With this prayer, twenty times repeated, concludes

Your ever affectionate
ANNA HOWE

I hurried myself in writing this; and I hurry Robert away with it, that in a situation so very critical, you may have all the time possible to consider what I have writ-

ten, upon two points so very important. I will repeat
them in a very few words:

'Whether you choose not rather to go off with one of
your own sex; with your Anna Howe—than with one of
the *other*; with Mr Lovelace?'

And if not,

'Whether you should not marry him as soon as
possible?'

Letter 88: MISS CLARISSA HARLOWE TO MISS HOWE

                                        Saturday afternoon
Already have I an ecstatic answer, as I may call it, to
my letter.

'He promises compliance in every article with my will:
approves of all I propose; particularly of the private
lodging: and thinks it a happy expedient to obviate the
censures of the busy and the unreflecting: and yet he
hopes, that the putting myself into the protection of either of his aunts, treated as I am treated, would be far
from being looked upon by any in a disreputable light.

'He flatters himself now (my last letter *confirming* my
resolution) that he can be in no apprehension of my
changing my mind, unless my friends change their manner of acting by me; which he is too sure they will not.
And now will all his relations, who take such a kind and
generous share in his interests, glory and pride themselves in the prospects he has before him.'

Thus artfully does he hold me to it!

'As to fortune, he begs of me not to be solicitous on
that score: that his own estate is sufficient for us both;
not a *nominal*, but a *real*, two thousand pounds *per
annum*, equivalent to some estates reputed a third more:
that it never was encumbered: that he is clear of the
world, both as to book and bond-debts; thanks, perhaps,
to his pride more than to his virtue. That his uncle moreover resolves to settle upon him a thousand pounds *per
annum* on his nuptials. All which it will be in my power
to see done, and proper settlements drawn, *before* I
enter into any farther engagements with him; if I *will*
have it so.

'He is afraid that the time will hardly allow of his procuring Miss Charlotte Montague's attendance upon me at St Albans, as he had proposed she should; because, he understands, she keeps her chamber, with a violent cold and sore throat. But both she and her sister, the first moment she is able to go abroad, shall visit me at my private lodgings; and introduce me to their aunts, or their aunts to me, as I shall choose; and accompany me to town if I please; and stay as long in it with me, as I shall think fit to stay there.'

So, my dear, the enterprise requires courage and high spirits, you see! And indeed it does! What am I about to do!

Lord bless me!—what am I about to do!

After all, far as I have gone, I know not but I may still recede: and if I do, a mortal quarrel, I suppose, will ensue. And what if it does? Could there be any way to escape this Solmes, a breach with Lovelace might make way for the single life (so much my preferable wish!) to take place: and then I would defy the sex. For I see nothing but trouble and vexation that they bring upon ours: and when once entered, one is obliged to go on with them, treading with tender feet upon thorns and sharper thorns, to the end of a painful journey.

What to do, I know not. The more I think, the more I am embarrassed!—and the stronger will be my doubts, as the appointed time draw nearer.

But I will go down, and take a little turn in the garden; and deposit this, and his letters, all but the two last; which I will enclose in my next, if I have opportunity to write another.

Meantime, my dear friend—But what can I desire you to pray for? Adieu then!—let me only say—adieu!

Letter 90: MISS CLARISSA HARLOWE TO MISS HOWE

Sunday morning, April 9

Nobody, it seems, will go to church this day. No blessing to be expected perhaps upon views so worldly, and in some so cruel.

They have a mistrust that I have some device in my head. Betty has been looking among my clothes. I found her, on coming up from depositing my letter to Lovelace (for I *have* written!), peering among them, the key being in the lock. She coloured, and was confounded to be caught. But I only said I should be accustomed to *any* sort of treatment in time!

This is the substance of my letter to Mr Lovelace:

'That I have reasons, of the greatest consequence to *myself*, and which when known must satisfy *him*, to suspend, for the present, my intention of leaving my father's house: that I have hopes that matters may be brought to an happy conclusion, without taking a step which nothing but the last necessity could justify: and that he may depend upon my promise, that I will die, rather than consent to marry Mr Solmes.'

Sunday, four o'clock, p.m.

My letter is not yet taken away! If he should not send for it, or take it, and come hither on my not meeting him tomorrow, in doubt of what may have befallen me, what shall I do? Why had I any concerns with this sex! I, that was so happy till I knew this man!

Sunday evening, seven o'clock

There remains my letter still! He is busied, I suppose, in his preparations for tomorrow. But then he has servants. Does the man think he is so *secure* of me, that having appointed he need not give himself any further concern about me, till the very moment! He knows how I am beset. He knows not what may happen. I *might* be ill, or still more closely watched or confined than before. The correspondence *might* be discovered. It *might* be necessary to vary the scheme. I *might* be forced into measures, which might entirely frustrate my purpose. I *might* have new doubts: I *might* suggest something more convenient, for anything he knew. What can the man mean, I wonder! Yet it shall lie; for if he has it any time before the appointed hour, it will save me declaring to him personally my changed purpose, and the trouble of contending with him on that score. If he send for it at all, he will see by the date that he might have had it in

time; and if he be put to any inconvenience from short-
ness of notice, let him take it for his pains.

Mon. morn. April 10, seven o'clock
Oh my dear! There yet lies the letter, just as I left it!
Does he think he is so sure of me! Perhaps he imagines
that I *dare not* alter my purpose. I wish I had never known
him! I begin now to see this rashness in the light everyone
else would have seen it in, had I been guilty of it.

Yet, short as the time is, he may still perhaps send,
and get the letter. Something may have happened to
prevent him, which, when known, will excuse him.

After I have disappointed him more than once before,
on a requested *interview* only, it is impossible he should
not have *curiosity*, at least, to know if something has not
happened; and if my mind hold in this more *important
case*.

CL. HARLOWE

Letter 91: MISS CLARISSA HARLOWE TO MISS HOWE

Ivy summer-house, eleven o'clock
But I now can think of nothing but this man!—this
interview!—would to Heaven it were over! To meet to
quarrel—but I will not stay a moment with him, let him
take what measures he will upon it, if he be not quite
calm and resigned.

Don't you see how crooked some of my lines are?
Don't you see how some of the letters stagger more
than others!

But, after all, should I, *ought* I, to meet him? How I
have taken it for granted that I should! I wish there were
time to take your advice. Yet you are so loath to speak
quite out! But that I owe, as you own, to the difficulty
of my situation.

Will you doubt, my dear, that my next trial will be
the most affecting that I have yet had?

The time of meeting is at hand. Oh that he may not
come! But should I, or should I not, meet him? How I
question, without possibility of a timely answer!

I know that this wretch will, if he *can,* be his own judge, and *mine* too. But the latter he shall *not* be.

I dare say we shall be all to pieces. But I don't care for that. It would be hard if I, who have held it out so sturdily to my father and uncles, should not—But he is at the garden-door—

I was mistaken! How may noises *un*-like, be made *like* what one fears! Why flutters the fool so!

I will hasten to deposit this. Then I will for the last time go to the usual place, in hopes to find that he has got my letter. If he *has,* I will not meet him. If he has *not,* I will take it back and show him what I have written.

Perhaps I shall not be able to write again one while. Perhaps not till I am the miserable property of that Solmes! But that shall never, never be, while I have my senses.

If your servant find nothing from me by Wednesday morning, you may conclude that I can then neither write to you, nor receive your favours.

In that case, pity and pray for me, my beloved friend, and continue to me that place in your affection, which is the pride of my life, and the only comfort left to

Your
CLARISSA HARLOWE

Letter 92: MISS CLARISSA HARLOWE TO MISS HOWE

St Albans, Tuesday morn., past one

Oh my dearest friend!

After what I had resolved upon, as by my former, what shall I write? What *can* I? With what consciousness, even by *letter,* do I approach you! You will soon hear (if already you have not heard from the mouth of common fame) that your Clarissa Harlowe is gone off with a man!

I am busying myself to give you the particulars at large. The whole twenty-four hours of each day (to begin the moment I can fix) shall be employed in it till it is finished: Every one of the hours, I mean, that will be spared me by this interrupting man, to whom I have

made myself so foolishly accountable for too many of
them. Rest is departed from me. I have no call for that:
and that has no balm for the wounds of my mind. So
you'll have all those hours without interruption till the
account is ended.

But will you receive, shall you be *permitted* to receive,
my letters, after what I have done?

Oh, my dearest friend! But I must make the best of
it. I hope that will not be very bad! Yet am I convinced
that I did a rash, an inexcusable thing, in meeting him;
and all his tenderness, all his vows, cannot pacify my
inward reproaches on that account.

Adieu, my dearest friend! I beseech you to love me
still! But, alas! what will your mamma say?—what will
mine!—what my other relations?—and how will my
brother and sister triumph?

I cannot at present tell you how, or where, you can
direct to me. For very early shall I leave this place; ha-
rassed and fatigued to death! But, when I can do nothing
else, constant use has made me able to write. Long, very
long, has that been all my amusement and pleasure: yet
could not that have been such to me, had I not had you,
my best-beloved friend, to write to. Once more adieu.
Pity, and pray for,

Your
CL. HARLOWE

Letter 93: MISS HOWE TO MISS CLARISSA HARLOWE

Tuesday, nine o'clock

I write, because you enjoin me to do so. Love you still!—
how can I help it, if I would? You may believe how I
stand aghast, your letter communicating the first news—
Good God of heaven and earth!—but what shall I say?
I shall be all impatience for particulars.

Lord have mercy upon me!—but can it be?

My mamma will, *indeed*, be astonished! How can I tell
it to her?

But, once more, can it be? What woman, at this
rate!—but, God preserve you!

Let nothing escape you in your letters. Direct them for me, however, to Mrs Knollys's, till further notice.

Observe, my dear, that I don't blame you by all this—your relations only are in fault! Yet how you came to change your mind is the surprising thing!

How to break it to my mamma, I know not. Yet, if she hear it first from any other, and find I knew it before, she will believe it is by my connivance! Yet, as I hope to live, I know not how to break it to her!

But this is teasing you! I am sure without intention.

Let me now repeat my former advice. If you are *not* married by this time, be sure delay not the ceremony. Since things are as they are, I wish it were thought that you were privately married before you went away.

I send what you write for [a "parcel of linen"]. If there be anything else you want that is in my power, command without reserve,

> Your ever affectionate
> ANNA HOWE

Letter 94: MISS CLARISSA HARLOWE TO MISS HOWE

Tuesday night

I think myself obliged to thank you, my dear Miss Howe, for your condescension, in taking notice of a creature who has occasioned you so much scandal.

I am grieved on this account, as much, I verily think, as for the evil itself.

Tell me—but yet I am afraid to know—what your mamma said.

I long, and yet I dread to be told, what the young ladies my companions, now never more, perhaps, to be so, say of me.

They cannot, however, say worse of me than I will of myself. Self-accusation shall flow in every line of my narrative, where I think I am justly censurable. If any thing can arise from the account I am going to give you, for extenuation of my fault (for that is all a person can hope for, who cannot excuse herself), I know I may expect it from your friendship, though not from the charity

of any other: since by this time I doubt not every mouth
is opened against me; and all that know Clarissa Harlowe, condemn the fugitive daughter.

After I had deposited my letter to you, written down
to the last hour, as I may say, I returned to the ivy
summer-house; first taking back my letter from the loose
bricks: and there I endeavoured, as coolly as my situation would permit, to recollect and lay together several
incidents that had passed between my aunt and me; and
I began to hope, that I need not be so very apprehensive
as I had been of the next Wednesday. And thus I argued
with myself.

I expected a contention with him, 'tis true, as he had
not my letter: but I thought it would be very strange, as
I mentioned in one of my former, if I, who had so steadily held out against characters so venerable, against au-
thorities so sacred, as I may say, when I thought them
unreasonably exerted, should not find myself more equal
to such a trial as this; especially as I had so much reason
to be displeased with him for not having taken away
my letter.

When the bell rang to call the servants to dinner,
Betty came to me and asked if I had any commands
before she went to hers.

She could hardly have got into the house, when I
heard the first signal. Oh, how my heart fluttered! But
no time was to be lost. I stepped to the garden door;
and seeing a clear coast, unbolted the ready-unlocked
door—and there was he, all impatience, waiting for me!

A panic next to fainting seized me when I saw him.
My heart seemed convulsed; and I trembled so, that I
should hardly have kept my feet had he not supported
me.

Fear nothing, dearest creature, said he! Let us hasten
away! The chariot is at hand! And by this sweet condescension, you have obliged me beyond expression, or
return!

Recovering my spirits a little, as he kept drawing me
after him, Oh Mr Lovelace, said I, I cannot go with you!
Indeed I cannot! I wrote you word so! Let go my hand
and you shall see my letter. It has lain there from yester-

day morning till within this half-hour. I bid you watch to the last for a letter from me, lest I should be obliged to revoke the appointment; and had you followed the direction, you would have found it.

I have been watched, my dearest life, said he, half out of breath—I have been watched in every step I took: and my trusty servant has been watched too, ever since Saturday; and dared not to come near your wall. And here we shall be discovered in a moment! Speed away, my charmer!—this is the moment of your deliverance! If you neglect this opportunity, you *never* can have such another!

What is it you mean, sir! Let go my hand: for I tell you (struggling vehemently) that I will sooner die than go with you!

Good God, said he! with a look of wildness and surprise, what is it I hear!—but (still drawing me after him as he retreated farther from the door) it is no time to argue. By all that's good you must go!—surely you cannot doubt my honour, nor give me cause to question your own.

As you value me, Mr Lovelace, urge me no farther. I come fixed and resolved. Let me give you the letter I had written. My further reasons shall follow; and they will convince you that I ought not to go.

Nothing, madam, can convince me. By all that's sacred, I will not leave you! To leave you now is to lose you for ever!

Am I to be thus compelled? interrupted I, with equal indignation and vehemence. Let go my hands. I am resolved not to go with you—and I will convince you that I *ought* not.

All my friends expect you, madam!—all your own are determined against you! Wednesday next is the day! the important, perhaps the fatal day! Would you stay to be Solmes's wife? Can this be your determination at last?

No, never, never will I be that man's!—but I will not go with you! Draw me not thus! How dare you, sir? I would not have seen you, but to tell you so! I had not met you, but for fear you would have been guilty of some rashness!—and, once more, I will *not* go! What mean you!—striving with all my force to get from him—

Unhand me this moment or I will cry out for help.

I will obey you, my dearest creature!—and quitted my hand with a look full of tender despondency that, knowing the violence of his temper, half-concerned me for him. Yet I was hastening from him when, with a solemn air, looking upon his sword but catching as it were his hand from it, he folded both his arms as if a sudden thought had recovered him from an intended rashness.

Stay one moment!—but one moment stay, oh best beloved of my soul! Your retreat is secure, if you *will* go: the key lies down at the door—but, oh madam, next Wednesday, and you are Mr Solmes's. Fly me not so eagerly!—hear me but a few words.

When near the garden door I stopped; and was the more satisfied, as I saw the key there, by which I could let myself in again at pleasure. But, being uneasy lest I should be missed, I told him I could stay no longer: I had already stayed too long: that I would write to him all my reasons. And depend upon it, Mr Lovelace, said I, just upon the point of stooping for the key, in order to return, I will die rather than have that man. You know what I have promised if I find myself in danger.

One word, madam, however, one word more, approaching me, his arms still folded as if (as I thought) he would not be tempted to mischief. Remember only that I come at your appointment, to redeem you at the hazard of my life from your gaolers and persecutors, with a resolution, God is my witness, or may He for ever blast me! (that was his shocking imprecation), to be a father, uncle, brother, and as I humbly hoped, in your own good time, a *husband* to you, all in one. But since I find you are so ready to cry out for *help* against me, which must bring down upon me the vengeance of all your family, I am contented to run all risks. I will not ask you to retreat with *me*; I will attend you into the garden, and into the *house*, if I am not intercepted.

Had he offered to draw his sword upon himself, I was prepared to have despised him for supposing me such a poor novice as to be intimidated by an artifice so common. But this resolution, uttered with so serious an air, of accompanying me in to my friends, made me gasp almost with terror.

What can you mean, Mr Lovelace, said I? Would you thus expose yourself? Would you thus expose me? Is this your generosity? Is everybody to take advantage thus of the weakness of my temper?

And I wept. I could not help it.

He threw himself upon his knees at my feet.

I bid him rise: he rose and I told him that were I not thus unaccountably hurried by his impatience, I doubted not to convince him that both he and I had looked upon next Wednesday with greater apprehension than was necessary: and was proceeding to give him my reasons; but he broke in upon me—

Had I, madam, but the shadow of a probability to hope what *you* hope, I would be all obedience and resignation. But the licence is actually got: the parson is provided. Oh my dearest creature, do these preparations mean only a trial?

I was sure, I said, of procuring a delay at least. Many ways I had to procure delay. Nothing could be so fatal to us both, as for me now to be found with him. My apprehensions on this score, I told him, grew too strong for my heart. I should think very hardly of him if he sought to detain me longer. But his acquiescence should engage my gratitude.

And then stooping to take up the key to let myself into the garden, he started and looked as if he had heard somebody near the door, on the inside, clapping his hand on his sword.

This frighted me so, that I thought I should have sunk down at his feet. But he instantly reassured me: he thought, he said, he had heard a rustling against the door: but *had* it been so, the noise would have been stronger. It was only the effect of his apprehension for my mind's sake.

And then taking up the key, he presented it to me. If you *will* go, madam—yet I cannot, cannot leave you! I must enter the garden with you—forgive me, but I *must* enter the garden with you.

And will you, will you, thus ungenerously, sir, take advantage of my fears!—of my wishes to prevent mischief? I, vain fool, to be concerned for everyone; nobody for me!

I was offering the key to the lock, when, starting from his knees, with a voice of affrightment loudly whispering, and as if out of breath, *They are at the door, my beloved creature!* And taking the key from me, he flew to it, and fluttered with it as if he would double-lock it. And instantly a voice from within cried out, bursting against the door, as if to break it open, and, repeating its violent pushes: *Are you there? Come up this moment!—this moment! Here they are—Here they are both together! Your pistol this moment! your gun!* Then another push, and another. He at the same moment drew his sword, and clapping it naked under his arm, took both my trembling hands in his; and, drawing me swiftly after him: Fly, my charmer; this moment is all you have for it! said he. Your brother!—your uncles! or this Solmes!—they will instantly burst the door! Fly, my dearest life! if you would not be more cruelly used than ever!—if you would not see two or three murders committed at your feet, fly, fly, I beseech you!

Now behind me, now before me, now on this side, now on that, turned I my affrighted face in the same moment; expecting a furious brother here, armed servants there, an enraged sister screaming and a father armed with terror in his countenance, more dreadful than even the drawn sword which I saw or those I apprehended. I ran as fast as he, yet knew not that I ran; my fears at the same time that they took all power of thinking from me adding wings to my feet: my fears, which probably would not have suffered me to know what course to take, had I not had him to urge and draw me after him: especially as I beheld a man, who must have come out of the garden door, keeping us in his eye, running backward and forward, beckoning and calling out to others, whom I supposed *he* saw, although the turning of the wall hindered *me* from seeing them; and whom I imagined to be my brother, my father and their servants.

Thus terrified, I was got out of sight of the door in a very few minutes: and then, although quite breathless between running and apprehension, he put my arm under his, his drawn sword in the other hand, and hurried me on still faster: my voice, however, contradicting my action; crying, No, no, no, all the while, straining my neck to look back as long as the walls of the garden and park were within sight, and till he brought me to his uncle's chariot: where attending were two armed servants of his own, and two of Lord M.'s on horseback.

Here I must suspend my relation for a while: for now I am come to this sad period of it, my indiscretion stares me in the face: and my shame and my grief give me a compunction that is more poignant, methinks, than if I had a dagger in my heart. To have it to reflect, that I should so inconsiderately give in to an interview which, had I known either myself or him, or in the least considered the circumstances of the case, I might have supposed would put me into the power of his resolution and out of that of my own reason.

For, might I not have believed that *he*, who thought he had cause to apprehend that he was on the point of losing a person who had cost him so much pains and trouble, would not hinder her, if possible, from returning? That he, who knew I had promised to give him up for ever, if insisted on as a condition of reconciliation, would not endeavour to put it out of my power to do so? In short, that he, who had artfully forborne to send for my letter (for he could not be watched, my dear) lest he should find in it a countermand to my appointment (as I myself could apprehend, although I profited not by the apprehension), would want a device to keep me with him till the danger of having our meeting discovered might throw me absolutely into his power to avoid my own worse usage, and the mischiefs which might have ensued, perhaps in my very sight, had my friends and he met?

But if it shall come out that the person within the garden was his corrupted implement, employed to frighten me away with him, do you think, my dear, that I shall not have reason to hate him and myself still more? I hope his heart cannot be so deep and so vile a one: I hope not: but how came it to pass, that one man could get out at the garden door, and no more? How, that that man kept aloof, as it were, and pursued us not; nor run back to alarm the house? My fright and my distance would not let me be certain; but really this single man had the air of that vile Joseph Leman, as I recollect.

You know, my dear, that your Clarissa's mind was ever above justifying her own failings by those of others. God forgive those of my friends who have acted cruelly by me! but their faults *are* their own, and not excuses for mine. And mine began early: for I ought not to have corresponded with him.

You don't know, nor can you imagine, my dear, how I am mortified! how much I am sunk in my own opinion! I, that was proposed for an example, truly, to others! Oh that I were again in my father's house, stealing down with a letter to you; my heart beating with expectation of finding one from you!

This is the Wednesday morning I dreaded so much that I once thought of it as my doomsday: but of the Monday, it is plain, I ought to have been most apprehensive. Had I stayed, and had the worst I dreaded happened, my friends would then have been answerable, if any bad consequences had followed—but, now, I have this *one* consolation left me (a very sad one, you'll say), that I have cleared *them* of blame, and taken it all upon *myself*!

You will not wonder to see this narrative so dismally scrawled. It is owing to different pens and ink, all bad, and written by snatches of time, my hand trembling too with fatigue and grief.

I will not add to the length of it, by the particulars of his behaviour to me, and of our conversation at St Albans and since; because those will come in course, in the continuation of my story; which no doubt you will expect from me.

Only thus much I will say, that he is extremely respectful, even obsequiously so, at present, though I am so much dissatisfied with him, and myself; that he has hitherto had no great cause to praise my complaisance to him. Indeed I can hardly at times bear the seducer in my sight.

The lodgings I am in are inconvenient. I shall not stay in them: so it signifies nothing to tell you how to direct to me hither. And where my next may be, as yet I know not.

He knows that I am writing to you; and has offered to send my letter, when finished, by a servant of his. But I thought I could not be too cautious, as I am now situated, in having a letter of this importance conveyed to you. Who knows what such a man may do? So very wicked a contriver! The contrivance, if a contrivance, so insolently mean! But I hope it is not a contrivance neither! Yet, be that as it will, I must say that the *best* of him, and of my prospects with him, are bad: and yet, having enrolled myself among the too-late repenters, who shall pity me?

Nevertheless, I will dare to hope for a continued interest in your affections (I shall be miserable indeed, if I may not!), and to be remembered in your daily prayers. I am, my dearest friend,

> Your ever affectionate
> CL. HARLOWE

Letter 95: MR LOVELACE TO JOSEPH LEMAN

Sat. April 8

Honest Joseph,

At length your beloved young lady has consented to free herself from the cruel treatment she has so long borne. She is to meet me without the garden door, at about four o'clock on Monday afternoon; as I told you she had promised. She has confirmed her promise. Thank God, she has confirmed her promise!

I shall have a chariot and six ready in the by-road fronting the private path to Harlowe Paddock; and several of my friends and servants not far off, armed to protect her, if there be occasion: but everyone charged to avoid mischief. That, you know, has always been my principal care.

All my fear is that when she comes to the point, the over-niceness of her principles will make her waver, and want to go back: although *her* honour is *my* honour, you know, and *mine* is *hers*. If she should, and I should be unable to prevail upon her, all your past services will avail nothing and she will be lost to me for ever: the prey, then, of that cursed Solmes, whose vile stinginess will never permit him to do good to any of the servants of the family.

I have no doubt of your fidelity, honest Joseph; nor of your zeal to serve an injured gentleman and an oppressed young lady. You see by the confidence I repose in you that I have *not*; more particularly, on this very important occasion, in which your assistance may crown the work: for if she wavers, a little innocent contrivance will be necessary.

Be very mindful, therefore, of the following directions: take them into your heart. This will probably be your last trouble, until my beloved and I are joined in holy wedlock: and then we will be sure to take care of you. You know what I have promised. No man ever reproached me for breach of word.

These, then, honest Joseph, are they:

Contrive to be in the garden in disguise, if possible, and unseen by your young lady. If you find the garden door unbolted, you'll know that she and I are together although you should not see her go out at it. It will be locked, but my key shall be on the ground at the bottom of the door, without, that you may open it with yours as it may be needful.

If you hear our voices parleying, keep at the door, till I cry Hem, hem, twice: but be watchful for this signal, for I must not hem very loud, lest she should take it for a signal: perhaps in struggling to prevail upon the dear creature, I may have an opportunity to strike the door hard with my elbow, or heel, to confirm you. Then you are to make a violent burst against the door, as if you'd break it open, drawing backward and forward the bolt in a hurry: then, with another push, but with more noise than strength, lest the lock give way, cry out (as if you saw some of the family): Come up, come up, instantly!—Here they are! Here they are! hasten!—this instant hasten! And mention swords, pistols, guns, with as terrible a voice, as you can cry out with. Then shall I prevail upon her, no doubt, if loath before, to fly: if I cannot, I will enter the garden with her, and the house too, be the consequence what it will. But so 'frighted, there is no question but she will fly.

When you think us at a sufficient distance (and I shall raise my voice, urging her swifter flight, that you may guess at *that*), then open the door with your key: but you must be sure to open it very cautiously, lest we should not be far enough off. I would not have her know you have a hand in this matter, out of my great regard to you.

When you have opened the door, take your key out of the lock, and put it in your pocket: then, stooping for mine, put it in the lock on the *inside*, that it may appear as if the door was opened by herself, with a key they'll suppose of my procuring (it being new), and left open by us.

They should conclude she is gone off by her own consent, that they may not pursue us: that they may see no hopes of tempting her back again.

Tell the family that you saw me enter a chariot with her: a dozen, or more, men on horseback, attending us; all armed; some with blunderbusses, as you believe; and that we took the quite contrary way to that we shall take.

You must tell them that your young lady seemed to run as fast off with me, as I with her. This will also confirm to them that all pursuit is in vain. An end will be hereby put to Solmes's hopes: and her friends, after a while, will be more studious to be reconciled to her, than to get her back. So you will be an happy instrument of great good to all round. And this will one day be acknowledged by both families. You will then be every one's favourite: and every good servant, for the future, will be proud to be likened to honest Joseph Leman.

Your assured friend,
R. LOVELACE

Letter 97: MR LOVELACE TO JOHN BELFORD, ESQ.

St Albans, Monday night

I snatch a few moments, while my beloved is retired (as I hope, to rest), to perform my promise. No pursuit!—

nor have I apprehensions of any; though I must make my charmer dread that there will be one.

And now, let me tell thee that never was joy so complete as mine! But let me inquire! is not the angel flown away?

Oh no! she is in the next apartment!—securely mine!—mine for ever!

I knew that the whole stupid family were in a combination to do my business for me. I told thee that they were all working for me, like so many underground moles; and still more blind than the moles are said to be, unknowing that they did so. I myself, the director of their principal motions; which falling in with the malice of their little hearts, they took to be all their own.

But did I say my joy was perfect? Oh no! It receives some abatement from my disgusted pride. For how can I endure to think that I owe more to her relations' persecutions than to her favour for me? Or even, as far as I know, to her preference of me to another man?

But let me not indulge this thought. Were I to do so, it might cost my charmer dear. Let me rejoice that she has passed the Rubicon: that she cannot return: that, as I have ordered it, the flight will appear to the implacables to be altogether with her own consent: and that, if I doubt her love, I can put her to trials as mortifying to her niceness, as glorious to my pride. For, let me tell thee, dearly as I love her, if I thought there was but the shadow of a doubt in her mind whether she preferred me to any man living, I would show her no mercy.

Letter 98: MISS CLARISSA HARLOWE TO MISS HOWE

Wednesday, April 12

I will pursue my melancholy story.

Being thus hurried to the chariot, it would have been to no purpose to have refused entering into it, had he not, in my fright, lifted me in as he did: and it instantly drove away a full gallop, and stopped not till it brought us to St Albans; which was just as the day shut in.

I thought I should have fainted several times by the way. With lifted-up hands and eyes, God protect me,

said I often to myself! Can it be I that am here!—my
eyes running over and my heart ready to burst with sighs
as involuntary as my flight.

How different, how inexpressibly different, the gay
wretch; visibly triumphing (as I could not but construe
his almost rapturous joy) in the success of his arts! But
overflowing with complimental flourishes, yet respectfully distant his address, all the way we *flew*; for that,
rather than *galloping*, was the motion of the horses;
which took, as I believe, a roundabout way, to prevent
being traced.

I have reason to think there were other horsemen at
his devotion; three or four different persons above the
rank of servants galloping by us now and then, on each
side of the chariot: but he took no notice of them; and
I had too much grief, mingled with indignation, notwithstanding all his blandishments, to ask any questions
about them, or anything else.

Think, my dear, what were my thoughts on alighting
from the chariot; having no attendant of my own sex;
no clothes but what I had on, and those little suited for
such a journey as I had *already* taken, and was still *further* to take: neither hood nor hat, nor anything but a
handkerchief about my neck and shoulders: fatigued to
death: my mind still more fatigued than my body: and
in such a foam the horses, that everyone in the inn we
put up at guessed (they could not do otherwise) that I
was a young giddy creature who had run away from
her friends.

The gentlewoman of the inn, whom he sent into me,
showed me another apartment; and seeing me ready to
faint, brought me hartshorn and water; and then, upon
my desiring to be left alone for half an hour, retired: for
I found my heart ready to burst, on revolving everything
in my thoughts: and the moment she was gone, fastening
the door, I threw myself into an old great chair, and gave
way to a violent flood of tears; which a little relieved me.

Mr Lovelace, sooner than I wished, sent up the gentlewoman, who pressed me in his name to admit my
brother, or to come down to him: for he had told her I
was his sister; and that he had brought me, against my
will and without warning, from a friend's house where I

had been all the winter, in order to prevent my marrying against the consent of my friends; to whom he was now conducting me; and that, having given me no time for a travelling-dress, I was greatly offended at him.

The room I was in being a bedchamber, I chose to go down, at his repeated message, attended by the gentlewoman of the inn, to that in which he was. He approached me with great respect, yet not exceeding a brotherly politeness, where a brother is polite; and, calling me his dearest sister, asked after the state of my mind; and hoped I would forgive him; for never brother half so well loved a sister, as he me.

When we were alone, he besought me (I cannot say but with all the tokens of a passionate and respectful tenderness) to be better reconciled to myself, and to him. He repeated all the vows of honour and inviolable affection that he ever made me: he promised to be wholly governed by me in every future step: he asked me to give him leave to propose, whether I chose to set out next day to either of his aunts?

I was silent. I knew not what to say, nor what to do.

Whether I chose to have private lodgings procured me, in either of those ladies' neighbourhood, as were once my thoughts?

In lodgings, I said, anywhere, where he was not to be.

He had promised this, he owned; and he would religiously keep to his word, as soon as he found all danger of pursuit over; and that I was settled to my mind. But if the place were indifferent to me, London was the safest and the most private: and his relations should all visit me there, the moment I thought fit to admit them.

I told him I wished not to go (immediately, however, and in the frame I was in, and likely not to be out of) to any of his relations: that my reputation was concerned to have *him* absent from me: that, if I were in some private lodging (the meaner the less to be suspected, as it would be known that I went away by his means; and he would be supposed to have provided me handsome accommodations), it would be most suitable both to my mind and my situation: that this might be best, I should think, in the country for *me*; in town for *him*.

If he might deliver his opinion, he said, since I declined going to any of his relations, London was the only place in the world to be private in. Every newcomer in a country town or village excited a curiosity: a person of my figure (and many compliments he made me) would excite more. Even messages and letters, where none used to be brought, would occasion inquiry.

I thought myself, I said, extremely unhappy. I knew not what to determine upon: my reputation now, no doubt, utterly ruined: destitute of clothes fit to be seen by anybody: my very indigence, as I might call it, proclaiming my folly to everyone who saw me: who would suppose that I had been taken at advantage, or had given an undue one; and had no power over either my will, or my actions: that I could not but think I had been dealt artfully with: that he had seemed to have taken what he might suppose the just measure of my weakness, founded on my youth and inexperience: that I could not forgive myself for meeting him: that my heart bled for the distresses of my father and mother on this occasion: that I would give the world, and all my hopes in it, to have been still in my father's house, whatever had been my usage: that, let him protest and vow what he would, I saw something low and selfish in his love, that he could study to put a young creature upon making such a sacrifice of her duty and conscience: when a person actuated by a generous love must seek to oblige the object of it in everything essential to her honour, and to her peace of mind.

Forgive me, madam. . . . Have I not, in your own opinion, hazarded my life to redeem you from oppression?

You may glory in your fancied merits, in getting me away; but the cause of *your* glory, I tell you plainly, is *my* shame.

No more shall you need to tell me of your *sufferings*, and your *merits*!—your *all hours*, and *all weathers*! For I will bear them in memory as long as I live; and, if it be impossible for me to *reward* them, be ever ready to *own* the obligation. All that I desire of you now is to leave it to myself to seek for some private abode: to take the chariot with you to London or elsewhere: and, if I have any further occasion for your assistance and protection, I will signify it to you, and be still *further* obliged to you.

You are warm, my dearest life! But indeed there is no occasion for it.

Then he began again to vow the sincerity of his intentions.

But I took him up short. I am willing to *believe* you, sir. It would be unsupportable but to suppose there were a *necessity* for such solemn declarations (at this he seemed to collect himself, as I may say, into a little more circumspection). If I thought there *were*, I would not sit with you here, in a public inn, I assure you, although *cheated* hither, as far as I know, by methods (you must excuse me, sir!) that the very suspicion that it may be so gives me too much vexation for me to have patience with you or with myself.

I broke from him to write to you my preceding letter; but refused to send it by his servant, as I told you. The gentlewoman of the inn helped me to a messenger, who was to carry what you should give him to Lord M.'s seat in Hertfordshire, directed for Mrs Greme the house-keeper there. And early in the morning, for fear of pursuit, we were to set out that way: and there he proposed to exchange the chariot and six for a chaise and pair of his own, which happened to be at that seat, as it would be a less-noticed conveyance.

I looked over my little stock of money; and found it to be no more than seven guineas and some silver. The rest of my stock was but fifty guineas, and that five more than I thought it was, when my sister challenged me as to the sum I had by me: and those I left in my escritoire, little thinking to be prevailed upon to go away with him.

Indeed my case abounds with a shocking variety of indelicate circumstances. Among the rest, I was forced to account to *him*, who knew I could have no clothes but what I had on, how I came to have linen with me (for he could not but know I sent for it); lest he should imagine I had an early design to go away with him, and made that a part of the preparation.

Mrs Greme came to pay her duty to me, as Mr Lovelace called it; and was very urgent with me to go to her lord's house; letting me know what handsome things she had heard her lord, and his two nieces, and all the family, say of me; and what wishes, for several months past, they had put up for the honour she now hoped soon would be done them all.

This gave me some satisfaction, as it confirmed from the mouth of a very good sort of woman all that Mr Lovelace had told me.

Upon inquiry about a private lodging, she recommended me to a sister-in-law of hers, eight miles from thence—where I now am.

I should have mentioned that, before I set out for this place, I received your kind letter. Everything is kind from so dear a friend. I own you might well be surprised (I *was* myself; as by this time you will have seen)—after I had determined, too, so strongly against going away.

I have not the better opinion of Mr Lovelace for his extravagant volubility. He is too full of professions: he says too many fine things *of* me, and *to* me.

The man, to be sure, is, at times, all upon the *ecstatic*, one of his phrases; but, to my shame and confusion, I know too well what to attribute it to, in a great measure—To his *triumph*, my dear, in one word; it needs no further explanation; and, to give it *that* word, perhaps, equally exposes my vanity and condemns my folly.

We have been alarmed with notions of a pursuit, founded upon a letter from his intelligencer.

Most heavily, he says, they take it; but show not so much grief as rage—and he can hardly have patience to hear of the virulence and menaces of my brother against himself. Then a merit is made to me of his forbearance.

What a satisfaction am I robbed of, my dearest friend, by this rash action? I can now, too late, judge of the difference there is in being an *offended* rather than an *offending* person! What would I give to have it once more in my power to say I *suffered* wrong, rather than *did* wrong? That others were more wanting in their kindness to me, than I in duty (where duty is owing) to them?

What more concerns me is that every time I see this man, I am still at a greater loss than before what to make of him. I watch every turn of his countenance: and I think I see very deep lines in it. He looks with more meaning, I verily think, than he used to look; yet not more serious; not less gay. I don't know how he looks. But with more confidence a great deal than formerly; and yet he never wanted that.

I shall send this, as my former, by a poor man who travels every day with pedlary matters, who will leave it at Mrs Knollys's, as you direct.

If you hear anything of my father and mother, and of their health, and how my friends were affected by my unhappy step, pray be so good as to write me a few lines by the messenger, if his waiting for them can be known to you.

I am afraid to ask you whether, upon reading that part of my narrative already in your hands, you think any sort of extenuation lies for

Your unhappy
CLARISSA HARLOWE

Letter 99: MR LOVELACE TO JOHN BELFORD, ESQ.

Tuesday, Wed. Apr. 11, 12
Thou claimest my promise that I will be as particular as possible in all that passes between me and my goddess. Indeed, I never had a more illustrious subject to exercise my pen upon: and, moreover, I have leisure; for by her good will my access would be as difficult to her as that of the humblest slave to an eastern monarch.

I told thee my reasons for not going in search of a letter of countermand. I was right; for, if I had, I should have found such a one; and had I received it, she would not have met me. Did she think that after I had been more than once disappointed, I would not keep her to her promise; that I would not hold her to it, when I had got her in so deeply?

The moment I heard the door unbolt, I was sure of her. That motion made my heart bound to my throat. But when that was followed with the presence of my charmer, flashing upon me all at once in a flood of brightness, sweetly dressed, though all unprepared for a journey, I trod air, and hardly thought myself a mortal.

Her wax-like flesh (for, after all, flesh and blood I

think she is!) by its delicacy and firmness, answers for the soundness of her health. Thou hast often heard me launch out in praise of her complexion. But this lady is all alive, all glowing, all charming flesh and blood, yet so clear, that every meandering vein is to be seen in all the lovely parts of her which custom permits to be visible.

Her morning gown was a pale primrose-coloured paduasoy: the cuffs and robings curiously embroidered by the fingers of this ever charming Arachne in a running pattern of violets and their leaves; the light in the flowers silver; gold in the leaves. A pair of diamond snaps in her ears. A white handkerchief, wrought by the same inimitable fingers, concealed. Oh Belford! what still more inimitable beauties did it not conceal! And I saw, all the way we rode, the bounding heart; by its throbbing motions I saw it! dancing beneath the charming umbrage.

I have told thee what were *my* transports, when the undrawn bolt presented to me my long-expected goddess. *Her* emotions were more sweetly feminine, after the first moments; for then the fire of her starry eyes began to sink into a less dazzling languor. She trembled: nor knew she how to support the agitations of a heart she had never found so ungovernable. She was even fainting, when I clasped her in my supporting arms. What a precious moment that! How near, how sweetly near, the throbbing partners!

I'll tell thee all, when I see thee: and thou shalt then judge of my difficulties, and of her perverseness. And thou wilt rejoice with me, at my conquest over such a watchful and open-eyed charmer.

But seest thou not now (as I think I do) the wind-outstripping fair one flying *from* her love *to* her love? Is there not such a game? Nay, flying from friends she was resolved not to abandon to the man she was determined not to go off with? The sex! the sex, all over!—charming contradiction! Hah, hah, hah, hah! I must here lay down my pen to hold my sides; for I must have my laugh out, now the fit is upon me!

*   *   *

Thou wilt not dare, methinks I hear thee say, to attempt to reduce such a goddess as this to a standard unworthy of her excellencies. It is impossible, Lovelace, that thou shouldst intend to break through oaths and protestations so solemn.

That I did *not* intend it, is certain. That I *do* intend it, I cannot (my heart, my reverence for her, will not let me) say. But knowest thou not my aversion to the state of shackles? And is she not IN MY POWER?

And wilt thou, Lovelace, abuse that power, which—

Which what, puppy?—which I obtained not by her own consent, but against it.

But which thou hadst never obtained, had she not esteemed thee above all men.

And which I had never taken so much pains to obtain, had I not loved her above all women. So far upon a par, Jack! And, if thou pleadest honour, ought not honour to be mutual? If mutual, does it not imply mutual trust, mutual confidence?—and what have I had of *that* from her to boast of? Thou knowest the whole progress of our warfare: for a warfare it has truly been; and far, very far, from an amorous warfare too.

Does she not deserve to pay for all this? To make an honest fellow look like an hypocrite; what a vile thing is that!

Then thou knowest what a false little rogue she has been! How little conscience she has made of disappointing me! Hast thou not been a witness of my ravings on this score? Have I not, in height of them, vowed revenge upon the faithless charmer?

Then, I fancy, by her circumspection, and her continual grief, that she expects some mischief from me. I don't care to disappoint anybody I have a value for.

How it swells my pride to have been able to outwit such a vigilant charmer! I am taller by half a yard, in my imagination, than I was! I look *down* upon everybody now! Last night I was still more extravagant. I took off my hat, as I walked, to see if the lace were not scorched, supposing it had brushed down a star; and, before I put it on again, in mere wantonness and heart's-ease, I was for buffeting the moon. In short, my whole soul is joy. When I go to bed, I laugh myself asleep: and I awake either laughing or singing. Yet nothing *nearly* in view, neither. For why? *I am not yet reformed enough!*

I told thee at the time, if thou remembrest, how capable this restriction was of being turned upon the over scrupulous dear creature, could I once get her out of her father's house; and were I disposed to punish her for her family's faults, and for the infinite trouble she herself had given me. Little thinks she that I have kept an account of both; and that when my heart is soft, and all her own, I can but turn to my *memoranda*, and harden myself at once.

But, ah! Jack, when I see my angel, when I am admitted to the presence of this radiant beauty, what will become of all this vapouring?

But, be my end what it may, I am obliged by thy penetration, fair one, to proceed by the sap. *Fair and softly*—a wife at any time! that will be always in my power.

But how I ramble! This it is to be in such a situation that I know not what to resolve upon.

I'll tell thee my *inclinings*, as I proceed. The *pro's* and the *con's*, I'll tell thee. But being got too far from the track I set out in, I will close here. But, perhaps, may write every day something, and send it as opportunity offers.

Letter 100: MISS HOWE TO MISS CLARISSA HARLOWE

Wednesday night, April 12

I have your narrative, my dear. You are the same noble creature you ever were. Above disguise, above art, above extenuating a failing.

The only family in the world, yours, surely, that could have driven such a daughter into such extremities.

But you must not be so very much too good for *them*, and for the *case*.

I am not surprised, now I have read your narrative, that so bold and so contriving a man—I am forced to break off—

* * *

You stood it out much better and longer—Here again comes my bustling, jealous mother!

Thursday, April 13

I have this moment your continuation letter, and a little absence of my Argus-eyed mamma.

Dear creature!—I can account for all your difficulties. A person of your delicacy!—and with such a man! I must be brief—

Sometimes I think you should go to Lady Betty's. I know not what to advise you to. I could, if you were not so intent upon reconciling yourself to your relations. But they are implacable, you can have no hopes from them.

You need not to have been afraid of asking me whether I thought upon reading your narrative, any extenuation could lie for what you have done. I have told you above my mind as to that. And I repeat that I think, your *provocations* and *inducements* considered, you are free from blame: at least, the freest, that ever young creature was who took such a step.

But you took it not. You were driven on one side, and possibly tricked on the other. If any young person on earth shall be circumstanced as you were, and shall hold out so long as you did against her persecutors on one hand, and her seducer on the other, I will forgive her for all the rest.

Your father is all rage and violence. He ought, I am sure, to turn his rage inward. All your family accuse you of acting with deep art; and are put upon supposing that you are actually every hour exulting over them, with your man, in the success of it.

They all pretend now, that your trial of Wednesday was to be the last.

How they took your flight, when they found it out, may be better supposed than described.

Plotting wretch as I doubt your man is, I wish to heaven that you were married, that you might brave them all; and not be forced to hide yourself, and be hurried from one inconvenient place to another. I charge you, omit not to lay hold on any handsome opportunity that may offer for that purpose.

Here again comes my mamma.

We look mighty glum upon each other, I can tell you. She had not best *Harlowe* me at this rate! I won't bear it!

I have a vast deal to write. I know not what to write first. Yet my mind is full, and seems to run over.

I am got into a private corner of the garden to be out of her way. Lord help these mothers! Do they think they can prevent a daughter's writing, or doing anything she has a mind to do, by suspicion, watchfulness and scolding?

You have a nice, a very nice part to act with this wretch—who yet has, I think, but one plain path before him. I pity you!—but you must make the best of the lot you have been forced to draw. Yet I see your difficulties—but if he do not offer to abuse your confidence, I would have you *seem*, at least, to place some in him.

If you think not of marrying soon, I approve of your resolution to fix somewhere out of his reach: and if he know not where to find you, so much the better. Yet I verily believe they would force you back, could they but come at you, if they were not afraid of *him.*

I think, by all means, you should demand of both your trustees to be put in possession of your own estate. Meantime I have sixty guineas at your service. I beg you will command them. Before they are gone I'll take care you shall be further supplied. I don't think you'll have a shilling or a shilling's worth of your own from your relations, unless you extort it from them.

As they believe you went off by your own consent, they are surprised, it seems, and glad that you have left your jewels and money behind you, and have contrived for clothes so ill. Very little likelihood, this shows, of their answering your requests.

And I will find a way to send you also any of my clothes and linen for present supply. I beg, my dearest Miss Harlowe, that you will not put your Anna Howe upon a foot with Lovelace, in refusing to accept of my offer. If you do not oblige me, I shall be apt to think that you rather incline to be obliged to him, than to favour me. And if I find this, I shall not know how to reconcile it with your delicacy in other respects.

Pray inform me of everything that passes between you and him. My cares for you (however needless, from your own prudence) make me wish you to continue to be very minute. A stander-by may see more of the game than one that plays. Great consequences, like great folks, are generally attended and even *made* great by small causes, and little incidents.

It is moonlight.

I hear, from where I sit, my mamma calling about her and putting everybody into motion. She will soon, I suppose, make *me* and *my* employment the subject of her inquiry.

Adieu, my dear. May heaven preserve you, and restore you with honour as unsullied as your mind, to

Your ever affectionate
ANNA HOWE

Letter 107: MISS CLARISSA HARLOWE TO MISS HOWE

Thursday night, April 13

I always loved writing, and my unhappy situation gives me now enough of it; and you, I fear, too much. I have had another very warm debate with Mr Lovelace. It brought on the subject which you advised me not to decline when it handsomely offered. And I want to have either your acquittal or blame, for having suffered it to go off without effect.

The impatient wretch sent up to me several times, while I was writing my last to you, to desire my company; yet his business nothing particular; only to hear him talk. The man seems pleased with his own volubility; and, whenever he has collected together abundance of smooth things, he wants me to find ears for them. Yet he need not: for I don't often gratify him either with giving him the praise, or showing the pleasure in his verboseness, that he would be fond of.

When I had dispatched the letter, and given it to Mr Hickman's friend [for delivery to Miss Howe], I was going up again: but he besought me to stop, and hear what he had to say.

We began presently our angry conference. He provoked me; and I repeated several of the plainest things I had said before; and particularly told him that I was every hour more and more dissatisfied with myself, and with him: that he was not a man who, in my opinion, improved upon acquaintance: and that I should not be easy till he had left me to myself.

He might be surprised at my warmth, perhaps. But really the man looked so like a simpleton; hesitating, and having nothing to say for himself, or that should excuse the peremptoriness of his demand upon me (when he knew I was writing a letter, which a gentleman waited for), that I flung from him, declaring that I would be mistress of my own time, and of my own actions, without being called to account for either.

He told me that he had, upon this occasion, been entering into himself, and had found a great deal of reason to blame himself for an impatiency and inconsideration which, although he meant nothing by it, must be very disagreeable to one of my delicacy. That having always aimed at a manly sincerity and openness of heart, he had not till now discovered that both were very consistent with that true politeness, which he feared he had too much disregarded while he sought to avoid the contrary extreme; knowing that in me he had to deal with a lady who despised a hypocrite, and who was above all flattery. But from this time forth, I should find such an alteration in his whole behaviour as might be expected from a man, who knew himself to be honoured with the presence and conversation of a person who had the most delicate mind in the world—that was his flourish.

He prefaced and paraded on; and then out came, with great diffidence and many apologies, and a bashfulness which sat very awkwardly upon him, a proposal of speedy solemnization: which, he said, would put all right: would make my first three or four months which otherwise must be passed in obscurity and apprehension, a round of visits and visitings to and from all his relations; to Miss Howe; to whom I pleased: and would pave the way to the reconciliation I had so much at heart.

Your advice had great weight with me just then, as well as his reasons, and the consideration of my unhappy situation. But what could I say? I wanted somebody to speak for me: I could not, all at once, act as if I thought that *all punctilio was at an end.* I was unwilling to suppose it *was* so soon.

The man saw I was not angry at his motion. I only blushed up to the ears; that I am sure I did: looked silly, and like a fool.

Would he have had me catch at his first, at his *very* first word? I was *silent* too! How was it possible I could encourage with very ready signs of approbation such an early proposal? especially so soon after the free treatment he had provoked from me. If I were to die, I could not.

He looked at me with great confidence; as if (notwithstanding his contradictory bashfulness) he would look me through, while my eye but now and then could glance at him. He begged my pardon with great obsequiousness: he was *afraid* I would think he deserved no other answer, but that of a contemptuous silence. True love was fearful of offending—(Take care, Lovelace, thought I, how yours is tried by that rule.) Indeed so sacred a regard (foolish man!) would he have to all my declarations made before I honoured him.

I would hear him no further; but withdrew in too visible confusion, and left him to make his nonsensical flourishes to himself.

I will only add that, if he really wishes for a speedy solemnization, he never could have had a luckier time to press for my consent to it. But he let it go off; and indignation has taken place of it; and now it shall be my point to get him at a distance from me.

I am, my dearest friend,

Your ever faithful and obliged servant,
CL. H.

Letter 108: MR LOVELACE TO JOHN BELFORD, ESQ.

What can be done with a woman who is above flattery, and despises all praise but that which flows from the approbation of her own heart?

But why will this admirable creature urge her destiny? Why will she defy the power she is absolutely dependent upon? Why will she still wish to my face that she had never left her father's house? Why will she deny me her company, till she makes me lose my patience, and lay myself open to her resentment? And why, when she is offended, does she carry her indignation to the utmost length that a scornful beauty in the very height of her power and pride can go?

Is it prudent, thinkst thou, in her circumstances, to tell me, *repeatedly* to tell me that she is every hour more and more dissatisfied with herself and me? That I am not one who improve upon her in my conversation and address? (Couldst thou, Jack, bear this from a captive!) That she shall not be easy while she is with me? That she was thrown upon me by a perverse fate? That she knew better than to value herself upon my volubility? That she would take care of herself; and since her friends thought it not worth while to pursue her, she would be left to that care? That I should make Mrs Sorlings's house more agreeable by my absence? and go to Berks, to town, or wherever I would (to the devil, I suppose), with all her heart?

But she took me down with a vengeance! She made me look about me. So much advantage had she over me; such severe turns upon me; by my soul, Jack, I had hardly a word to say for myself. I am ashamed to tell thee what a poor creature she made me look like! But I could have told her something that would have humbled her pretty pride at the instant, had she been in a proper place, and proper company about her.

To such a place then—and where she cannot fly me. And *then* to see how my will works, and what can be done by the *amorous see-saw*; now humble; now proud; now expecting, or demanding; now submitting, or acquiescing—till I have tired resistance. But these hints are at present enough.

Letter 109: MR LOVELACE TO JOHN BELFORD, ESQ.

(In continuation)

These angry commands to leave her. What shall we say, if all were to mean nothing but MATRIMONY? And what if my forbearing to enter upon that subject come out to be the true cause of her petulance and uneasiness?

I had once before played about the skirts of the irrevocable obligation; but thought myself obliged to speak in clouds, and to run away from the subject as soon as she took my meaning, lest she should imagine it to be ungenerously urged, now she was in some sort in my power, as she had forbid me, beforehand, to touch upon it, till I were in a state of visible reformation, and till a reconciliation with her friends were probable.

Charming creature, thought I (but I charge thee, that thou let not any of the sex know my exultation), is it so *soon* come to this? Am I *already* lord of the destiny of a Clarissa Harlowe! Am I already the reformed man thou resolvedst I *should* be, before I had the *least* encouragement given me? And can art and design enter into the breast so celestial; To banish me from thee, to insist so rigorously upon my absence, in order to bring me closer to thee, and make the blessing dear? Well do *thy* arts justify *mine*; and encourage me to let loose my plotting genius upon thee.

Letter 110: MR LOVELACE TO JOHN BELFORD, ESQ.

(In continuation)
And what! (methinks thou askest with surprise): dost thou question this most admirable of women? The virtue of a Clarissa dost thou question?

I do not, I dare not question it. My reverence for her will not let me, *directly*, question it. But let me, in my turn, ask thee—Is not, may not her virtue be founded rather in *pride* than *principle*? Whose daughter is she? And is she not a *daughter*? If impeccable, how came she by her impeccability? The pride of setting an example to her sex has run away with her hitherto, and may have made her till *now* invincible. But is not that pride abated? What may not both men and women be brought to do in a mortified state? What mind is superior to calamity? Pride is perhaps the principal bulwark of female virtue. Humble a woman, and may she not be *effectually* humbled?

Then who says Miss Clarissa Harlowe is the paragon of virtue? Is virtue itself?

Has her virtue ever been *proved*? Who has dared to try her virtue?

It was her character that drew me to her: and it was her beauty and good sense that rivetted my chains; and now, all together make me think her subject worthy of my attempts; worthy of my ambition.

But has she not, as above, already taken steps which she herself condemns? Steps which the world, and her own family, did not think her *capable* of taking? And for which her own family will not forgive her?

May not then the success of him who could carry her *thus far* be allowed to be an encouragement for him to try to carry her *farther*? 'Tis but to try, Jack. Who will be afraid of a trial for this divine lady? Thou knowest that I have more than once, twice or thrice been tempted to make this trial upon young ladies of name and character: but never yet found one of them to hold me out for a month; nor so long as could puzzle my invention. I have concluded against the whole sex upon it. And now, if I have not found a virtue that cannot be corrupted, I will swear that there is not one such in the whole sex. Is not then the whole sex concerned that this trial should be made?—and who is it that knows her, that would not stake upon her head the honour of the whole? Let her who would refuse it, come forth and desire to stand in her place.

What must that virtue be which will not stand a trial? What that woman, who would wish to shun it?

Well then, a trial seems necessary for the further establishment of the honour of so excellent a creature.

And who shall put her to this trial? Who but the man who has, as she thinks, already induced her in *lesser* points to swerve? And this for her *own sake*, in a double sense—not only as he has been able to make some impression, but as she regrets the impression made; and so may be presumed to be guarded against his further attempts.

The situation she is at present in, it must be confessed, is a disadvantageous one to her: but if she overcome, that will redound to her honour.

Nor is one effort, one trial, to be sufficient. Why? Because a woman's heart may be at one time *adamant*, at another *wax*—as I have often experienced. And so, no doubt, hast thou.

But what, methinks thou askest, is to become of the lady if she fail?

What? Why will she not *if once subdued* be *always subdued*? another of our libertine maxims. And what an immense pleasure to a marriage-hater, what rapture to thought, to be able to prevail upon such a lady as Miss Clarissa Harlowe to live with him without *real* change of name!

But if she resist—if nobly she stand her trial—

Why then I will marry her, to be sure; and bless my stars for such an angel of a wife.

But will she not hate thee? Will she not refuse—

No, no, Jack! Circumstanced and situated as we are, I am not afraid of that. And hate me! Why should she hate the man who loves her upon proof?

And then for a little hint at *reprisal*. Am I not justified in my resolutions of trying *her* virtue, who is resolved, as I may say, to try *mine*?—who has declared that she will not marry me till she has hopes of my reformation?

And now, to put an end to this sober argumentation, wilt thou not thyself (whom I have supposed an advocate for the lady, because I know that Lord M. has put thee upon using the interest he thinks thou hast in me to persuade me to enter the pale; *wilt thou not thyself*) allow me to try if I cannot awaken the *woman* in her?— to try if she, with all that glowing symmetry of parts and that full bloom of vernal graces, by which she attracts every eye, be really inflexible as to the grand article?

Let me begin then, as opportunity presents—I will— and watch her every step to find one sliding one; her every moment to find the moment critical. And the rather, as she spares not me but takes every advantage that offers to puzzle and plague me; nor expects, nor thinks me to be a good man.

Now, Belford, all is out. The lady is mine; shall be *more* mine. Marriage, I see, is in my power, now she is so (else perhaps it had not). If I can have her *without*, who can blame me for trying? If *not*, great will be her glory, and my future confidence—and well will she merit the sacrifice I shall make her of my liberty; and from all her sex honours next to divine, for giving a proof that there was once a woman whose virtue no trials, no stratagems, no temptations, even from the man she hated not, could overpower.

Now wilt thou see all my circulation: as in a glass wilt thou see it.

Letter 111: MISS HOWE TO MISS CLARISSA HARLOWE

Don't be so much concerned, my dearest friend, at the bickerings between my mamma and me. We love one another dearly notwithstanding. If my mamma had not me to find fault with, she must find fault with somebody else. And as to me, I am a very saucy girl; and were there not this occasion, there would be some other to show it.

You have heard me *say* that this was always the case between us. You could not *otherwise* have known it. For when *you* was with us, you harmonized us both; and indeed I was always more afraid of you than of my mamma. But then that awe is accompanied with love. Your reproofs (as I have always found) are so charmingly mild and instructive! so evidently calculated to improve, and not to provoke, that a generous temper must be amended by them.

Don't advise me, my dear, to obey my mamma in her prohibition of corresponding with you. She has no reason for it. Nor would she of her own judgement have prohibited me. If your talent is *scribbling,* as you call it; so is mine. And I will scribble on, at all opportunities; and to you; let 'em say what they will. Nor let your letters be filled with the self-accusations you mention: there is no cause for them. I wish that your Anna Howe, who continues in her mother's house, were but half so good as Miss Clarissa Harlowe, who has been driven out of her father's.

I cannot, however, but say that I am charmed with your spirit. So much sweetness, where sweetness is requisite; so much spirit, where spirit is called for—what a *true* magnanimity!

But I doubt, in your present circumstances, you must endeavour after a little more of the reserve, and palliate a little. That humility which he puts on when you rise upon him is not natural to him.

Methinks I see the man hesitating, and looking like the fool you paint him, under your corrective superiority! But he is not a fool. Don't put him upon mingling resentment with his love.

I have only to add (and yet that is needless to tell you) that I am, and will ever be,

Your affectionate friend and servant,
ANNA HOWE

Letter 116: MISS CLARISSA HARLOWE TO MISS HOWE

Friday, April 14

I will now give you the particulars of a conversation that has just passed between Mr Lovelace and me; which I must call agreeable.

It began with his telling me that he had just received intelligence, that my friends were of a sudden come to a resolution to lay aside all thoughts of pursuing me, or of getting me back: and that therefore, he attended me, to know my pleasure; and what *I* would do, or have *him* do?

I told him that I would have him leave me directly; and that, when it was known to everybody that I was absolutely independent of him, it would pass that I had left my father's house because of my brother's ill-usage of me: which was a plea that I might make with justice, and to the excuse of my father, as well as of myself.

He mildly replied that if he could be certain that my relations would *adhere* to this their new resolution, he could have no objection, since such was my pleasure: but that, as he was well assured that they had taken it only from apprehensions that a more *active* one might involve my brother (who had breathed nothing but revenge) in some fatal misfortune, there was too much reason to believe that they would resume their former purpose, the moment they should think they *safely* might.

This, madam, said he, is a risk I cannot run. You would think it strange, if I could.

Let me hear, said I, willing to try if he had any particular view, what *you* think most advisable?

I will only propose what I think will be most agreeable to *you*. Suppose, if you choose not to go to Lady Betty's, that you take a turn cross the country to Windsor?

Why to Windsor?

Because it is a pleasant place: because it lies in the way either to Berkshire, to Oxford, or to London. *Berkshire*, where Lord M. is at present: *Oxford*, in the neighbourhood of which lives Lady Betty: *London*, whither you may retire at your pleasure: or, if you will *have* it so, whither I may go, you staying at Windsor; and yet be within an easy distance of you, if anything should happen, or if your friends should change their pacific resolution.

This displeased me not. But I said my only objection was the distance from Miss Howe, of whom I should be glad to be always within two or three hours' reach by a messenger, if possible.

If I had thoughts of any other place than Windsor, or nearer to Miss Howe, he wanted but my commands and would seek for proper accommodations: but, fix as I pleased, farther or nearer, he had servants, and they had nothing else to do but to obey me.

A grateful thing then he named to me—to send for my Hannah as soon as I should be fixed; unless I would choose one of the young gentlewomen *here* to attend me, both of whom, as I had acknowledged, were very obliging; and he knew I had generosity enough to make it worth either of their whiles.

Not to be off of my caution: Have you any acquaintance at Windsor? said I. Know you of any convenient lodgings there?

Except with the forest, replied he, where I have often hunted, I know the least of Windsor of any place so noted and so pleasant. Indeed, I have not a single acquaintance there.

Upon the whole, I told him, that I thought his proposal of Windsor not amiss; and that I would remove thither if I could get a lodging only for myself, and an upper chamber for Hannah; for that my stock of money was but small, as was easy to be conceived; and I should be very loath to be obliged to anybody. I added that the sooner I removed the better; for that then he could have no objection to go to London or Berkshire, as he pleased: and I should let everybody know my independence.

He again proposed himself, in very polite terms, for my banker. But I, as civilly, declined his offers.

This conversation was to be, all of it, in the main, agreeable.

Adding, with a very serious air—I am but a young man, madam; but I have run a long course: let not your purity of mind incline you to despise me for the acknowledgement. It is high time to be weary of it, and to reform.

I was agreeably surprised. I looked at him, I believe, as if I doubted my ears and my eyes! His features and aspect, however, became his words.

I expressed my satisfaction in terms so agreeable to him, that he said he found a delight in this early dawning of a better day to him, and in *my* approbation, which he had never received from the success of the most favoured of his pursuits.

Surely, my dear, the man *must* be in earnest. He could not have said this; he could not have *thought* it, had he not.

Nevertheless, you may depend upon it, my dear, that these agreeable assurances and hopes of his begun reformation shall not make me forget my caution. Not that I think, at worst, any more than you, that he dare to harbour a thought injurious to my honour: but he is very various, and there is an *apparent*, and even an *acknowledged* unfixedness in his temper, which at times gives me some uneasiness. I am resolved therefore to keep him at distance from my person and my thoughts as much as I can: for whether *all* men are, or are not, encroachers, I am sure Mr Lovelace is one.

Mr Lovelace is gone to Windsor, having left two servants to attend me. He purposes to be back tomorrow.

Here I close for the present, with the assurance that
I am

> Your ever obliged and affectionate
> CLARISSA HARLOWE

Letter 121: MISS CLARISSA HARLOWE TO MISS HOWE

> Saturday evening

Mr Lovelace has seen divers apartments at Windsor; but
not one, he says, that he thought fit for me, or in any
manner answering my description.

He had been very solicitous to keep to the letter of
my instructions: which looks well: and the better I liked
him, as, although he proposed that town, he came back
dissuading me from it: for he said that, in his journey
from thence, he had thought Windsor, although of his
own proposal, a wrong choice; because I coveted privacy
and that was a place generally visited and admired.

I told him that if Mrs Sorlings thought me not an
encumbrance, I would be willing to stay there a little
longer; provided he would leave me, and go to Lord
M.'s or to London, which ever he thought best.

He hoped, he said, that he might suppose me absolutely safe from the insults or attempts of my brother;
and therefore, if it would make me easier, he would
obey, for a few days at least.

He hinted to me that he had received a letter from
Lady Betty, and another, as I understood him, from one
of the Miss Montagues. If they take notice of *me* in
them, I wonder that he did not acquaint me with the
contents. I am afraid, my dear, that his relations are
among those who think I have taken a rash and inexcusable step.

> Sunday morning

Why did not the man show them [the letters] to me
last night? Was he afraid of giving me too much
pleasure?

Lady Betty in hers, expresses herself in the most obliging manner, in relation to me. 'She wishes him so to
behave, as to encourage me to make him soon happy.

She desires her compliments to me; and expresses her impatience to see, as her niece, so *celebrated* a lady (those are her high words). She shall take it for an honour, she says, to be put into a way to oblige me. She hopes I will not too long delay the ceremony; because that performed, will be to her, and to Lord M. and Lady Sarah, a sure pledge of her nephew's merits and good behaviour.'

She says, 'She was always sorry to hear of the hardships I had met with on his account. That he will be the most ungrateful of men, if he make not *all up* to me: and that she thinks it incumbent upon all their family to supply to me the lost favour of my own: and, for her part, nothing of that kind, she bids him assure me, shall be wanting.'

But her ladyship gives me no direct invitation to attend her before marriage. Which I might have expected from what he had told me.

Letter 123: MISS CLARISSA HARLOWE TO MISS HOWE

(In continuation)
You may believe, my dear, that these letters put me in good humour with him. He saw it in my countenance, and congratulated himself upon it. But yet I wondered that I could not have the contents of them communicated to me last night.

He then urged me to go directly to Lady Betty's, on the strength of her letter.

But how, said I, can I do that, were I out of all hope of a reconciliation with my friends (which yet, however improbable to be brought about, is my duty to attempt), as her ladyship has given me no particular invitation.

That, he was sure, was owing to her doubt that it would be accepted: else she had done it with the greatest pleasure in the world.

That doubt itself, I said, was enough to deter me: since her ladyship, who knew so well the boundaries of the fit and the unfit, by her not expecting I would accept of an invitation, had she given it, would have reason to think me very forward if I *had* accepted it; and much more

forward to go without it. Then, said I, I thank *you*, sir,
I have no clothes fit to go anywhere, or to be seen by
anybody.

Would I choose to go to London, for a few days only,
in order to furnish myself with clothes?

Not at *his* expense. I was not prepared to wear his
livery yet.

He wished he knew but my mind—that should direct
him in his proposals, and it would be his delight to observe it, whatever it was.

My mind was, that he should leave me out of hand.
How often must I tell him so?

Upon his soul, the wretch swore, he did not think it
safe, for the reasons he had before given, to leave me
here. He hoped I would think of some place, to which
I should like to go. But he must take the liberty to say,
that he hoped his behaviour had not been so exceptionable as to make me so *very* earnest for his absence in
the interim: and the less, surely, as I was almost *eternally*
shutting up myself from him; although he presumed, he
said, to assure me that he never went from me, but with
a corrected heart and with strengthened resolutions of
improving by my example.

Eternally shutting myself up from you! repeated I. I
hope, sir, that you will not pretend to take it *amiss*, that
I expect to be uninvaded in my retirements. I hope you
do not think me so weak a creature (novice as you have
found me in a very capital instance) as to be fond of
occasions to hear your fine speeches, especially as no
differing circumstances require your over-frequent visits;
nor that I am to be addressed to as if I thought hourly
professions needful to assure me of your honour.

He seemed a little disconcerted.

You know, Mr Lovelace, proceeded I, why I am so
earnest for your absence. It is that I may appear to the
world independent of you; and in hopes, by that means,
to find it less difficult to set on foot a reconciliation with
my friends. They know that I have a power given me by
my grandfather's will, to bequeath the estate he left me,
together with my share of the effects, in a way that may
affect them, though not absolutely from them: this *consideration*, I hope, will procure me *some* from them,

when their passion subsides, and they know I am independent of you.

Charming reasoning! And let him tell me, that the assurance I had given him was all he wished for. It was more than he could ask. What a happiness to have a woman of honour and generosity to depend upon! Had he, on his first entrance into the world, met with such a one, he had never been other than a man of strict virtue.

I said I took it for granted that he assented to the reasoning he seemed to approve, and would leave me. And then I asked him what he really, and in his most deliberate mind, would advise me to, in my present situation? He must needs see, I said, that I was at a great loss what to resolve upon; entirely a stranger to London, having no adviser, no protector, at present—himself, he must give me leave to tell him, greatly deficient in *practice*, if not in the *knowledge*, of those decorums which, I had apprehended, were indispensable in the character of a man of birth, fortune and education.

Letter 125: MISS CLARISSA HARLOWE TO MISS HOWE

(In continuation)
We are both great watchers of each other's eyes; and indeed seem to be more than half afraid of each other.

He then made a grateful proposal to me; that I would send for my [nurse] Mrs Norton to attend me.

How could this man, with such powers of right thinking, be so far depraved by evil habits as to disgrace his talents by wrong acting?

Is there not room, after all, thought I at the time, for hope (as he so lately led me to hope) that the example it will behove me, for both our sakes, to endeavour to set him, may influence him to a change of manners in which both may find their account?

Give me leave, sir, said I, to tell you there is a strange mixture in your mind. You must have taken *pains* to suppress many good motions and reflections as they arose, or levity must have been surprisingly predominant in it.

Well, madam, I can only say I would find out some

expedient, if I could, that should be agreeable to you. But since I cannot, will you be so good as to tell me what you would *wish* to have done? Nothing in the world but I will comply with, excepting leaving you here, at such a distance from the place I shall be in, if anything should happen; and in a place where my gossiping rascals have made me in a manner public, for want of proper cautions at first.

I am quite at a loss, said I, what to do, or whither to go. Would you, Mr Lovelace, in earnest, advise me to think of going to London?

And I looked at him with steadfastness. But nothing could I gather from his looks.

At first, madam, said he, I was for proposing London, as I was then more apprehensive of pursuit. But as your relations seem cooler on that head, I am the more indifferent about the place you go to. So as *you* are pleased— So as *you* are easy, I shall be happy.

This indifference of his to London, I cannot but say, made me like going thither the better. I asked him (to hear what he would say) if he could recommend me to any *particular place* in London?

No, he said: none that was fit for me, or that I should like. His friend Belford indeed had very handsome lodgings near Soho Square, at a relation's, a lady of virtue and honour. These, as Mr Belford was generally in the country, he could borrow till I were better accommodated.

I was resolved to refuse these at the first mention, as I should any other he had named. Nevertheless, I will see, thought I, if he has really thoughts of these for me. If I break off the talk here, and he resume this proposal with earnestness in the morning, I shall apprehend that he is less indifferent than he seems to be about my going to London; and that he has already a lodging in his eye for me. And then I won't go at all.

But after such generous motions from him, I really think it a little barbarous to act and behave as if I thought him capable of the blackest and most ungrateful baseness. But his character, his principles, are so faulty! He is so light, so vain, so various, that there is no certainty that he will be next hour what he is this. Then, my dear, I have no guardian now; no father, no mother!

Nothing but God and my vigilance to depend upon. And
I have no reason to expect a miracle in my favour.

Well, sir, said I, rising to leave him, something must
be resolved upon: but I will postpone this subject till
tomorrow morning.

He would fain have engaged me longer; but I said I
would see him as early as he pleased in the morning.
He might think of any convenient place in London, or
near it, meantime.

And so I retired from him. As I do from my pen;
hoping for better rest for the few hours that will remain
for that desirable refreshment, than I have had of a
long time.

CL. HARLOWE

Letter 126: MISS CLARISSA HARLOWE TO MISS HOWE

(In continuation)

Monday morning, April 17
Late as I went to bed, I have had very little rest. Sleep
and I have quarrelled; and although I court it, it will not
be friends. I hope its fellow-irreconcilables at Harlowe
Place enjoy its balmy comforts. Else that will be an aggravation of my fault. My brother and sister, I dare say,
want it not.

Mr Lovelace, who is an early riser as well as I, joined
me in the garden about six; and after the usual salutations, asked me to resume our last night's subject. It was
upon lodgings at London, he said.

I think you mentioned one to me, sir—did you not?

Yes, madam, but (watching the turn of my countenance) rather as what you'd be welcome to, than perhaps approve of.

I believe so too. To go to town upon an *uncertainty*,
I own, is not agreeable; but to be obliged to any gentleman of your acquaintance, when I want to be thought
independent of you; and to a gentleman especially, to
whom my friends are to direct to me, if they vouchsafe
to take notice of me at all, is an absurd thing to
mention.

We had a good deal of discourse upon the same topic.

But, at last, the result of all was this—He wrote a letter to one Mr Doleman, a married man of fortune and character (I excepting to Mr Belford), desiring him to provide decent apartments ready furnished (for I had told him what they should be) for a single woman; consisting of a bedchamber; another for a maidservant, with the use of a dining-room or parlour. This he gave me to peruse; and then sealed it up and dispatched it away in my presence by one of his own servants, who having business in town is to bring back an answer.

I attend the issue of it; holding myself in readiness to set out for London, unless you advise the contrary. I will only add, that I am

Your ever-affectionate
CL. HARLOWE

Letter 127: MR LOVELACE TO JOHN BELFORD, ESQ.

Sat., Sunday, Monday

Thou seest, Belford, that my charmer has no notion that Miss Howe herself is but a puppet danced upon my wires, at second or third hand. To outwit and impel, as one pleases, two such girls as these, who think they know everything; and by taking advantage of the pride and ill-nature of the old ones of both families, to play them off likewise at the very time that they think they are doing me spiteful displeasure; what charming revenge!

But don't think me the *cause* neither of her family's malice and resentment. It is all in their hearts. I work but with their materials. They, if left to their own wicked direction, would perhaps express their revenge by fire and faggot; that is to say, by the private dagger, or by Lord Chief Justice's warrants, by law, and so forth: I only point the lightning and teach it where to dart, without the thunder: in other words, I only guide the effects: the cause is in their malignant hearts: and, while I am doing a little mischief, I prevent a great deal.

I wanted her to propose London herself. This made me again mention Windsor. If you would have a woman do one thing, you must always propose another! The sex! the very sex! as I hope to be saved! Why, they lay one under a necessity to deal doubly with them: and when they find themselves outwitted, they cry out upon an honest fellow who has been too hard for them at their own weapons.

I could hardly contain myself. My heart was at my throat. Down, down, said I to myself, exuberant exultation! A sudden cough befriended me: I again turned to her, all as *indifferenced over* as a girl at the first long-expected question who waits for two more. I heard out the rest of her speech: and when she had done, instead of saying anything of London, I proposed to her to send for her Mrs Norton.

As I knew she would be afraid of lying under obligations had she accepted of my offer, I could have proposed to do so much for the good woman and her son as would have made her resolve that I should do nothing. This, however, not merely to avoid expense: but there was no such thing as allowing of the presence of Mrs Norton. I might as well have had her mother or aunt Hervey with her.

How unequal is a modest woman to the adventure when she throws herself into the power of a rake! Punctilio will, at any time, stand for reasons with such a one. She cannot break through a well-tested modesty.

I am in the right train now. Every hour, I doubt not, will give me an increasing interest in the affections of this proud beauty! I have just carried *un*-politeness far enough to *make her afraid of me*; and to show her that I am *no whiner*. Every instance of politeness, *now*, will give me double credit with her! My next point will be to make her acknowledge a *lambent* flame, a preference of me to all other men at least: and then my happy hour is not far off. And *acknowledged* love sanctifies every freedom: and one freedom begets another. And if she call me *ungenerous*, I can call her *cruel*. The sex love to be called cruel. Many a time have I complained of cruelty, even in the act of yielding, because I knew it gratified their pride.

Letter 128: MISS HOWE TO MISS CLARISSA HARLOWE

Tuesday, April 18

But you ask me if I would treat Mr Lovelace, were he
to be in Mr Hickman's place, as I do Mr Hickman? Why
really, my dear, I believe I should not. I have been very
sagely considering this point of behaviour, in general, on
both sides in courtship; and I will very candidly tell you
the result. I have concluded that politeness, even to excess, is necessary on the men's part, to bring us to listen
to their first address, in order to induce us to bow our
necks to a yoke so unequal. But upon my conscience, I
very much doubt whether a little intermingled insolence
is not requisite from them, to keep up that interest, when
once it has got footing. Men must not let us see that we
can make fools of them. And I think that *smooth* love,
that is to say, a passion without rubs; in other words, a
passion without passion, is like a sleepy stream that is
hardly seen to give motion to a straw. So that, sometimes
to make us fear, and even, for a short space, to *hate* the
wretch, is productive of the *contrary* extreme.

If this be so, Lovelace, than whom no man was ever
more polite and obsequious at the *beginning*, has hit the
very point. For his turbulence *since*, his readiness to offend and his equal readiness to humble himself, as he is
known to be a man of sense, and of courage too, must
keep a woman's passion alive; and at last tire her into a
non-resistance that shall make her as passive as a tyrant
husband would wish her to be.

I verily think that the different behaviour of our two
heroes to their heroines makes out this doctrine to demonstration. I am so much accustomed, for my own part,
to Hickman's whining, creeping, submissive courtship
that I now expect nothing but whine and cringe from
him; and am so little moved with his nonsense that I am
frequently forced to go to my harpsichord to keep me
awake and to silence his humdrum. Whereas Lovelace
keeps up the ball with a witness, and all his address and
conversation is one continual game at racquet.

Your frequent quarrels and reconciliations verify this
observation: and I really believe that could Hickman
have kept my attention alive after the Lovelace manner,

only that he had preserved his morals, I should have married the man by this time. But then he must have *set out* accordingly. For now, he can never, never recover himself; that's certain: but must be a dangler to the end of the courtship chapter; and what is still worse for him, a passive to the end of his life.

Poor Hickman! perhaps you'll say. I have been called your echo. Poor Hickman! say I.

You wonder, my dear, that Mr Lovelace took not notice to you of his aunt's and cousin's letters to him, overnight. I don't like his keeping such a material and *relative* circumstance, as I may call it, one moment from you. By his communicating the contents of them to you next day, when you was angry with him, it looks as if he withheld them for occasional pacifiers; and if so, must he not have had a forethought that he might give you *cause* for anger? Of all the circumstances that have happened since you have been with him, I think I like this the least. This alone, my dear, small as it might look to an indifferent eye, in mine warrants all your cautions. Yet the foolish man, to let you know overnight that he *had* such letters! I can't tell what to make of him.

I am pleased with what these ladies write. And the more as I have caused them to be again sounded, and find that the whole family are as desirous as ever of your alliance.

I think there can be no objection to your going to London. There, as in the centre, you'll be in the way of hearing from everybody and sending to anybody. And then you will put all his sincerity to the test, as to his promised absence and such-like.

But really, my dear, I think you have nothing for it but marriage. You may try (that you may say you *have* tried) what your relations can be brought to. But the moment they refuse your proposals, submit to the yoke and make the best of it. He will be a savage indeed, if he makes you speak out. Yet it is my opinion that you *must* bend a little; for he cannot bear to be thought slightly of.

All the world, in short, expect you to have this man. They think that you left your father's house for this very purpose. The longer the ceremony is delayed, the worse appearance it will have in the world's eye. And it will not

be the fault of some of your relations if a slur be not
thrown upon your reputation while you continue unmarried.

I have written through many interruptions: and you'll
see the first sheet creased and rumpled, occasioned by
putting it into my bosom on my mamma's sudden coming upon me. We have had one very pretty debate, I'll
assure you; but it is not worth while to trouble you with
the particulars. But upon my word—no matter though—

Your Hannah cannot attend you. The poor girl left
her place about a fortnight ago on account of a rheu-
matic disorder which has confined her to her room ever
since. She burst into tears when Kitty carried to her your
desire of having her, and called herself doubly unhappy
that she could not wait upon a mistress whom she so
dearly loved.

You must take your own way: but if you suffer any
inconvenience either as to clothes or money, that is in
my power to supply, I will never forgive you. My
mamma (if *that* be your objection) need not know anything of the matter.

Your next letter, I suppose, will be from London. Pray
direct it, and your future letters till further notice, to Mr
Hickman at his own house. He is entirely devoted to
you. Don't take so heavily my mamma's partiality and
prejudices. I hope I am past a baby.

Heaven preserve you, and make you as happy as I
think you deserve to be, prays

Your ever affectionate
ANNA HOWE

Letter 129: MISS CLARISSA HARLOWE TO MISS HOWE

Wedn. morn. April 19

I am glad, my dear friend, that you approve of my removal to London.

The disagreement between your mamma and you
gives me inexpressible affliction. I hope I think you both
more unhappy than you are.

If I am to be obliged to anybody in England for
money, it shall be to you. Your mother need not know

of your kindness to me, you say. But she *must* know it, if it be done, and if she challenge my beloved friend upon it—for would you either falsify or prevaricate? I wish your mamma could be made easy on this head. Forgive me, my dear—but I know—yet once she had a better opinion of me. Oh my inconsiderate rashness! Excuse me once more, I pray you. Pride, when it is *native*, will show itself sometimes, in the midst of mortifications!— but my stomach is down already!

I am unhappy that I cannot have my worthy Hannah! I am as sorry for the poor creature's illness as for my own disappointment by it. Come, my dear Miss Howe, since you press me to be beholden to you; and would think me proud if I absolutely refused your favour, pray be so good as to send her two guineas in my name.

If I have nothing for it, as you say, but matrimony, it yields a little comfort that his relations do not despise the *fugitive*, as persons of their rank and quality-pride might be supposed to do, for having *been* a fugitive.

Your ever obliged and affectionate friend,
CL. H.

Letter 130: MISS CLARISSA HARLOWE TO MISS HOWE

Thursday, April 20

Mr Lovelace's servant is already returned with an answer from his friend Mr Doleman, who has taken pains in his inquiries, and is very particular. Mr Lovelace brought me the letter as soon as he had read it; and as he now knows that I acquaint you with everything that offers, I desired him to let me send it to you for your perusal. Be pleased to return it by the first opportunity. You will see by it that his friends in town have a notion that we are actually married.

to Robert Lovelace, Esq.

Tuesday night, April 18

Dear sir,

I am extremely rejoiced to hear that we shall so soon have you in town after so long an absence. You will be

the more welcome still, if what report says be true; which
is that you are actually married to the fair lady upon
whom we have heard you make such encomiums. Mrs
Doleman and my sister both wish you joy, if you are, and
joy upon your near prospect, if you are not. I have been
in town for this week past, to get help if I could, from my
paralytic complaints, and am in a course for them—
which nevertheless did not prevent me from making the
desired inquiries. This is the result.

You may have a first floor, well-furnished, at a mercer's in Bedford Street, Covent Garden, with what conveniencies you please for servants: and these either by
the quarter or month. The terms according to the conveniencies required.

Mrs Doleman has seen lodgings in Norfolk Street and
others in Cecil Street; but though the prospects to the
Thames and Surrey hills look inviting from both these
streets, yet I suppose they are too near the city.

The owner of those in Norfolk Street would have half
the house go together. It would be too much for your
description therefore: and I suppose that you will hardly,
when you think fit to declare your marriage, be in lodgings.

Those in Cecil Street are neat and convenient. The
owner is a widow of good character; but she insists, that
you take them for a twelvemonth certain.

You may have good accommodations in Dover Street,
at a widow's, the relict of an officer in the guards, who
dying soon after he had purchased his commission (to
which he had a good title by service, and which cost him
most part of what he had), she was obliged to let lodgings.

This may possibly be an objection. But she is very careful, she says, that she takes no lodgers but of figure and
reputation. She rents two good houses, distant from each
other, only joined by a large handsome passage. The inner
house is the genteelest, and is very elegantly furnished;
but you may have the use of a very handsome parlour in
the outer house, if you choose to look into the street.

A little garden belongs to the inner house, in which
the old gentlewoman has displayed a true female fancy,
and crammed it with vases, flower-pots and figures, without number.

As these lodgings seemed to me the most likely to

please you, I was more particular in my inquiries about them. The apartments she has to let are in the inner house: they are a dining-room, two neat parlours, a withdrawing-room, two or three handsome bedchambers (one with a pretty light closet in it, which looks into the little garden); all furnished in taste.

The widow consents that you should take them for a month only, and *what* of them you please. The terms, she says, she will not fall out upon when she knows what your lady expects, and what *her* servants are to do, or *yours* will undertake; for she observed that servants are generally worse to deal with than their masters or mistresses.

The lady may board or not, as she pleases.

As we suppose you married, but that you have reason from family differences to keep it private for the present, I thought it not amiss to hint as much to the widow (but as uncertainty, however), and asked her if she could in that case accommodate you and your servants, as well as the lady and hers? She said she could; and wished by all means it were to be so; since the circumstance of a person's being single, if not as well recommended as this lady, was one of her usual exceptions.

Let me add that the lodgings at the mercer's, those in Cecil Street, those at the widow's in Dover Street, any of them, may be entered upon at a day's warning.

I am, my dear sir,
> Your sincere and affectionate friend and servant,
> Tho. Doleman

You will easily guess, my dear, when you have read the letter, which lodgings I made choice of. But first, to try him, as in so material a point I thought I could not be too circumspect, I seemed to prefer those in Norfolk Street, for the very reason the writer gives why he thought I would *not*; that is to say, for its neighbourhood to a city so well governed as London is said to be. Nor should I have disliked a lodging in the heart of it, having heard but indifferent accounts of the liberties sometimes taken at the other end of the town—then seeming to incline to the lodgings in Cecil Street—then to the mercer's. But he made no visible preference: and when I asked his opinion of the widow gentlewoman's, he said, he thought these the most to my taste and convenience. But as he hoped that I would think lodgings necessary but for a very little while, he knew not which to give his vote for.

I then fixed upon the widow's; and he has written accordingly to Mr Doleman, making my compliments to his lady and sister for their kind offer.

I am to have the dining-room, the bedchamber with the light closet (of which, if I stay any time at the widow's, I shall make great use), and a servant's room; and we propose to set out on Saturday morning. As for a maidservant, poor Hannah's illness is a great disappointment to me: but, as he says, I can make the widow satisfaction for one of hers, till I can get one to my mind. And you know, I want not much attendance.

Mr Lovelace has just now, of his own accord, given me five guineas for poor Hannah. I send them enclosed. Be so good as to cause them to be conveyed to her; and to let her know from whom they came.

He has obliged me much by this little mark of his considerateness. Indeed I have the better opinion of him ever since he proposed her return to me.

And now, my dear, lest anything should happen, in so variable a situation as mine to overcloud my prospects (which at present are more promising than ever yet they have been since I quitted Harlowe Place), I will snatch the opportunity to subscribe myself

Your not unhoping
and ever obliged friend and servant,
CL. HARLOWE

Letter 131: MR LOVELACE TO JOHN BELFORD, ESQ.

Thursday, April 20

Thou knowest the widow; thou knowest her nieces; thou knowest the lodgings: and didst thou ever read a letter more artfully couched than this of Tom Doleman? Every

possible objection anticipated! Every accident provided
against! Every tittle of it plot-proof!

Who could forbear smiling to see my charmer, like a
farcical dean and chapter, choose what was before chosen for her; and sagaciously (as they go in form to prayers, that God would direct their choice) pondering upon
the different proposals, as if she would make me believe
she has a mind for some other? The dear sly rogue looking upon me, too, with a view to discover some emotion
in me: *that* I can tell her lay deeper than her eye could
reach, though it had been a sunbeam.

No confidence in me, fair one! None at all, 'tis plain.
And shall it be said, that I, a master of arts in love, shall
be overmatched by so unpractised a novice?

But to see the charmer so far satisfied with my contrivance as to borrow my friend's letter, in order to satisfy
Miss Howe likewise!

Silly little rogues! to walk out into by-paths on the
strength of their own judgements!—when nothing but
experience can teach them how to disappoint us, and
learn them grandmother-wisdom! When they have it indeed, then may they sit down, like so many Cassandras,
and preach caution to others; who will as little mind
them as they did *their* instructresses, whenever a fine
handsome confident fellow, such a one as thou knowest
who, comes cross them.

But, Belford, didst thou not mind that sly rogue Doleman's naming Dover Street for the widow's place of
abode! What dost think could be meant by that? 'Tis
impossible thou shouldst guess. So, not to puzzle thee
about it—suppose the widow Sinclair's in Dover Street
should be inquired after by some officious person in
order to come at characters (Miss Howe is as *sly* as the
devil, and as *busy* to the full); and neither such a name,
nor such a house can be found in that street, nor a house
to answer the description, then will not the keenest
hunter in England be at a fault?

But how wilt thou do, methinks thou askest, to hinder
the lady from resenting the fallacy, and mistrusting thee
the more on that account when she finds it out to be in
another street?

Pho! never mind that: either I shall have a way for it,

or we shall thoroughly understand one another by that time; or if we don't, she'll know enough of me not to wonder at *such* a peccadillo.

If thou further objectest that Tom Doleman is too great a dunce to write such a letter in answer to mine;—canst thou not imagine that, in order to save honest Tom all this trouble, I, who know the town so well, could send him a copy of what he should write, and leave him nothing to do but transcribe?

This it is to have leisure upon my hands! What a matchless plotter thy friend! Stand by and let me swell! I am already as big as an elephant; and ten times wiser! mightier too by far! Have I not reason to snuff the moon with my proboscis?

I shall make good use of the *Dolemanic* hint of being married. But I will not tell thee all at once. Nor, indeed, have I thoroughly digested that part of my plot. When a general must regulate himself by the motions of a watchful adversary, how can he say beforehand what he will, or what he will not do?

I never forget the *minutiae* in my contrivances. In all *doubtable* matters the *minutiae* closely attended to and provided for are of more service than a thousand oaths, vows and protestations made to supply the neglect of them, when jealousy has actually got into the working mind.

But I will not anticipate—besides, it looks as if I were afraid of leaving anything to my old friend CHANCE; which has many a time been an excellent second to me; and ought not to be affronted or despised; especially by one who has the art of making unpromising incidents turn out in his favour.

Letter 135: MISS CLARISSA HARLOWE TO MISS HOWE

(In continuation)

I must write on, although I were not to send it to anybody. You have often heard me own the advantages I have found from writing down everything of moment that befalls me; and of all I *think* and of all I *do* that may be of future use to me. For, besides that this helps to form one to a style, and opens and expands the duc-

tile mind, everyone will find that many a good thought
evaporates in thinking; many a good resolution goes off,
driven out of memory, perhaps, by some other not so
good. But when I set down what I *will* do, or what I
have done on this or that occasion; the resolution or
action is before me, either to be adhered to, withdrawn
or amended; and I have entered into *compact* with myself, as I may say; having given it under my own hand,
to *improve* rather than go *backward*, as I live longer.

I would willingly therefore write to *you*, if I *might*; the
rather as it would be more inspiriting to have some end
in view in what I write; some friend to please; besides
merely seeking to gratify my passion for scribbling.

But why, if your mamma will permit our correspondence on communicating to her all that passes in it, and
if she will condescend to one only condition, may it not
be complied with?

Would she not, do you think, my dear, be prevailed
upon to have the communication made to her *in
confidence*?

But if your mamma will receive the communications
in confidence, pray show her all that I have written, or
shall write. If my past conduct deserves not *heavy* blame,
I shall then perhaps have the benefit of her advice as
well as yours. And if I shall wilfully deserve blame for
the time to come, I will be contented to be denied yours
as well as hers for ever.

And all this upon the following consideration: 'That it
is much more eligible, as well as honourable, to be corrected with the gentleness of an undoubted friend, than
by continuing either blind or wilful, to expose ourselves
to the censures of an envious and perhaps malignant
world.'

But it is as needless, I dare say, to remind you of this,
as it is to repeat my request, that you will not, in your
turn, spare the follies and the faults of

Your ever affectionate
CL. HARLOWE

(Subjoined to the above)

I said that I would avoid writing anything of my own
particular affairs in the above address, if I could.

I will write one letter more to inform you how we stand.

I fear, I very much fear that my unhappy situation will draw me in to be guilty of evasion, of little affectations and of curvings from the plain simple truth which I was wont to value myself upon. But allow me to say, and this for your sake and in order to lessen your mother's fears of any ill consequences that she might apprehend from our correspondence, that if I am at any time guilty of a failure in these respects, I will not go on in it: but repent and seek to recover my lost ground, that I may not bring error into habit.

Letter 136: MISS HOWE TO MISS CLARISSA HARLOWE

Friday morn. April 21

My mamma will not comply with your condition, my dear. I hinted it to her, as from myself. But the *Harlowes* (excuse me) have got her entirely in with them. It is a scheme of mine, she told me, to draw her into your party against your parents—which, for her own sake, she is very careful about.

And let me tell you, my dear, that as long as I can satisfy my own mind that good is intended, and that it is hardly possible that evil should ensue from our correspondence; as long as I know that this prohibition proceeds originally from the same spiteful minds which have been the occasion of all these mischiefs; as long as I know that it is not your fault if your relations are not reconciled to you; and that upon conditions which no reasonable people would refuse—you must give me leave, with all deference to your judgement and to your excellent lessons (which would reach almost every other case of this kind but the present), to insist upon your writing to me, and that minutely, as if this prohibition had not been laid.

It is not from humour, from perverseness, that I insist upon this. I cannot express how much my heart is in your concerns. And you must, in short, allow me to think that if I can do you service by writing, I shall be better justified by *continuing* to write than my mamma is by her prohibition.

But yet, to satisfy you all I can, I will as seldom return answers while the interdict lasts as may be consistent with my notions of friendship, and the service I owe you and can do you.

As to your expedient of writing by Hickman (and now, my dear, your modest man comes in: and as you love modesty in that sex, I will do my endeavour by a proper distance to keep him in your favour), I know what you mean by it, my sweet friend. It is to make that man significant with me. As to the correspondence, THAT *shall* go on, I do assure you, be as scrupulous as you please—so that *that* will not suffer, if I do not close with your proposal as to him.

I think I must tell you that it will be honour enough for him to have his name made use of so frequently betwixt us. This, of itself, is placing a confidence in him that will make him walk bolt upright, and display his white hand and his fine diamond ring; and most mightily lay down his services, *and* his pride to oblige, *and* his diligence, *and* his fidelity, *and* his contrivances to keep our secret; *and* his excuses, *and* his evasions to my mamma when challenged by her; with fifty *and's* beside. And will it not moreover give him pretence and excuse oftener than ever to pad-nag it hither to good Mrs Howe's fair daughter?

But to admit him into my company *tête-à-tête,* and into my closet as often as I would wish to write to you; I only to dictate to *his* pen—my mamma all the time supposing that I was going to be heartily in love with him—to make him master of my sentiments, and of my *heart,* as I may say, when I write to you—indeed, my dear, I won't. Nor, were I married to the best HE in England, would I honour him with the communication of my correspondencies.

No, my dear, it is sufficient, surely, for him to parade it in the character of our letter-conveyer, and to be honoured in a cover [envelope]. And never fear but, modest as you think him, he will make enough of that.

You are always blaming me for want of generosity to this man, and for abuse of power. But I profess, my

dear, I cannot tell how to help it. Do, dear, now, let me
spread my plumes a little, and now and then make myself feared. This is my time, you know, since it will be
no more to *my* credit, than to *his*, to give myself those
airs when I am married. He has a joy when I am pleased
with him that he would not know but for the pain my
displeasure gives him.

This, I am satisfied, will be the consequence, if I do
not make him quake now and then, he will endeavour
to make me fear. All the animals in the creation are
more or less in a state of hostility with each other. The
wolf, that runs away from a lion, will devour a lamb the
next moment. I remember that I was once so enraged
at a game-chicken that was continually pecking at another (a poor humble one, as I thought him), that I had
the offender caught, and without more ado, in a pet of
humanity, wrung his neck off. What followed this execution? Why that other grew insolent, as soon as *his* in-
sulter was gone, and was continually pecking at one or
two under *him*. Peck and be hanged, said I. I might as
well have preserved the first; for I see it is the *nature of
the beast*.

Excuse my flippancies. I wish I were with you. I would
make you smile in the midst of your gravest airs, as I
used to do. Oh that you had accepted of my offer to
attend you! But nothing that I offer, will you accept.
Take care! you will make me very angry with you: and
when I am, you know I value nobody—for, dearly as I
love you, I must be, and cannot always help it,

Your saucy
ANNA HOWE

Letter 137: MISS CLARISSA HARLOWE TO MISS HOWE

Friday, April 21
Mr Lovelace communicated to me this morning early,
from his intelligencer, the news of my brother's [abduc-
tion] scheme. I like him the better for making very light
of it; and for his treating it with contempt. And indeed,
had I not had the hint of it from you, I should have
suspected it to be some contrivance of his, in order to

hasten me to town, where he has long wished to be himself.

I asked Mr Lovelace, seeing him so frank and cool, what he would advise me to do?

Shall I ask *you*, madam, what are your own thoughts? Why I return the question, said he, is because you have been so very earnest that I should leave you as soon as you are in London, that I know not what to propose without offending you.

My opinion is, said I, that I should studiously conceal myself from the knowledge of everybody but Miss Howe.

You condescended, dearest creature, said he, to ask my advice. It is very easy, give me leave to say, to advise you what to do. I hope I may, on this *new* occasion speak without offence, notwithstanding your former injunctions. You see that there can be no hope of reconciliation with your relations. Can you, madam, consent to honour with your hand a wretch whom you have never yet obliged with one *voluntary* favour?

What a recriminating, what a reproachful way, my dear, was this, of putting a question of this nature!

I expected not from him, at the time, either the question or the manner. I am ashamed to recollect the confusion I was thrown into—all your advice in my head at the moment: yet his words so prohibitory. He confidently seemed to enjoy my confusion (indeed, my dear, he knows not what respectful love is!); and gazed upon me as if he would have looked me through.

He was still more declarative afterwards indeed, as I shall mention by and by, but it was half-extorted from him.

My heart struggled violently between resentment and shame to be thus teased by one who seemed to have all *his* passions at command, at a time when I had very little over *mine*; till at last I burst into tears, and was going from him in high disgust; when, throwing his arms about me, with an air, however, the most tenderly respectful, he gave a *stupid* turn to the subject.

It was far from his heart, he said, to take so much advantage of the strait which the discovery of my brother's foolish project had brought me into, as to renew without my permission a proposal which I had hitherto discountenanced, and which for that reason—

And then he came with his half-sentences, apologizing for what he had hardly half proposed.

Surely he had not the insolence to *intend* to tease me, to see if I could be brought to speak what became me not to speak. But, whether he had or not, it *did* tease me, insomuch that my very heart was fretted and I broke out at last into fresh tears, and a declaration that I was very unhappy. And just then recollecting how like a tame fool I stood, with his arms about me, I flung from him with indignation. But he seized my hand, as I was going out of the room, and upon his knees besought me stay for one moment: and then tendered himself, in words the most clear and explicit, to my acceptance, as the most effectual means to disappoint my brother's [abduction] scheme and set all right.

But what could I say to this? Extorted from him, as it seemed to me, rather as the effect of his compassion, than of his love? What could I say? I paused, I looked silly! I am *sure* I looked very silly. He suffered me to pause and look silly; waiting for me to say something: and at last, ashamed of my confusion, and aiming to make an excuse for it, I told him that I desired he would avoid such measures as might add to an uneasiness which was so visible upon reflecting on the irreconcileableness of my friends, and what unhappy consequences might follow from this unaccountable project of my brother.

He promised to be governed by me in everything.

I told him I had hopes it would not be long before Mr Morden arrived; and doubted not that he would be the readier to engage in my favour, when he found that I made no other use of his, Mr Lovelace's, assistance than to free myself from the addresses of a man so disagreeable to me as Mr Solmes: I must therefore wish that everything might remain as it was, till I could hear from my cousin.

Good God! and you, madam, still resolve to show me that I am to hope for no share in your favour, while any the remotest prospect remains that you will be received

by my bitterest enemies at the price of my utter
rejection?

This was what I returned, with warmth, and with a
salving art *too*—You have seen, Mr Lovelace, how much
my brother's violence can affect me: but you will be
mistaken if you let loose yours upon me with a thought
of terrifying me into measures, the contrary of which
you have acquiesced with.

One word more he begged me to hear. He was determined studiously to avoid all mischief, and every step
that might lead to mischief, let my brother's proceedings,
short of a violence upon my person, be what they would:
but if any attempt that should extend to that were to be
made, would I have him to be a quiet spectator of my
being seized, or carried back, or aboard, by this [accom-
plice] Singleton; or in case of extremity, was he not permitted to stand up in my defence?

Stand up in my defence, Mr Lovelace! I should be very
miserable were there to be a call for that: but do you
think I might not be *safe* and *private* in London? By
your friend's description of the widow's house, I should
think I might be safe there.

The widow's house, he replied, as described by his
friend, being a back house within a front one, and
looking to a garden rather than a street, had the appearance of privacy: but if, when there, it was not approved, it would be easy to find another more to my
liking—though, as to his part, the method he would
advise should be to write to my uncle Harlowe as one
of my trustees, and wait the issue of it here at Mrs
Sorlings's, fearlessly directing it to be answered *hither.*
To be afraid of little spirits, was but to encourage insults, he said.

Inwardly vexed, I told him that he himself had proposed to leave me when I was in town: that I expected
he would: and that, when I was known to be absolutely
independent, I should consider what to write and what
to do: but that, while he was hanging about me, I neither
would nor could.

He would be very sincere with me, he said: this project
of my brother's had changed the face of things. He must,

before he left me, see how I liked the London widow and her family, if I chose to go thither: they might be people whom my brother might buy. But if he saw they were persons of integrity, he then might go for a day or two, or so. But he must needs say, he could not leave me longer.

Do you propose, sir, said I, to take up your lodgings in the same house?

He did not, he said; as he knew the use I intended to make of his absence, and my punctilio. And yet the house where he had lodgings was new-fronting: but he could go to his friend Belford's, in Soho; or perhaps, to the same gentleman's house at Edgware, and return on mornings, till he had reason to think this wild project of my brother's laid aside. But no farther till then would he venture.

The result of all was, to set out on Monday next for town. I hope it will be in a happy hour.

I cannot, my dear, say too often, how much I am

Your ever obliged
CL. HARLOWE

Letter 138: MR LOVELACE TO JOHN BELFORD, ESQ.

Friday, April 21

And now, Belford, what wilt thou say, if like the fly buzzing about the bright taper, I had like to have singed the silken wings of my liberty? Never was man in greater danger of being caught in his own snares—all his views anticipated: all his schemes untried; and not having brought the admirable creature to town nor made an effort to know if she be really angel or woman.

I offered myself to her acceptance, with a suddenness, 'tis true, that gave her no time to wrap herself in reserve; and in terms *less tender* than *fervent,* tending to upbraid her for her past indifference, and reminding her of her injunctions—for it was her brother's plot, not love of me, that had inclined her to dispense with them.

I gave way to her angry struggle; but, absolutely overcome by so charming a display of innocent confusion, I caught hold of her hand as she was flying from me; and kneeling at her feet, Oh my angel, said I (quite destitute of reserve, and hardly knowing the tenor of my own speech; and had a parson been there, I had certainly been a gone man), receive the vows of your faithful Lovelace. Make him yours, and only yours, for ever! This will answer every end! Who will dare to form plots and stratagems against my wife? That you are not so is the ground of all their foolish attempts and of their insolent hopes in Solmes's favour. Oh be mine! I beseech you (thus on my knee I *beseech* you) to be mine. We shall then have all the world with us: and everybody will applaud an event that everybody expects.

Was the devil in me! I no more intended all this ecstatic nonsense than I thought the same moment of flying in the air! All power is with this charming creature! It is I, not she, at this rate, that must fail in the arduous trial.

Well, but what was the result of this involuntary impulse on my part? Wouldst thou not think I was taken at my offer?—an offer so solemnly made, and on one knee too?

No such thing! The pretty trifler let me off as easily as I could have wished.

Her brother's project, and to find that there were no hopes of a reconciliation for her; and the apprehension she had of the mischiefs that might ensue—these, not *my offer* nor *love of me,* were the causes to which she ascribed all her sweet confusion. High treason the *ascription* against my sovereign pride—to make marriage with me but a second-place refuge!—and as good as to tell me that her confusion was owing to her concern that there were no hopes that my enemies would accept of her intended offer to renounce a man who had ventured his life for her, and was still ready to run the same risk in her behalf!

I re-urged her to make me happy. But I was to be postponed to her cousin Morden's arrival. On him are now placed all her hopes.

I raved; but to no purpose.

A confounded thing! The man to be so bashful; the lady to want so much courting! How shall two such come together, no kind mediatress in the way?

But I can't help it. I must be contented. 'Tis seldom, however, that a love so ardent meets with a spirit so resigned in the same person. But true love, I am now convinced, only wishes: nor has it any active will but that of the adorable object.

Letter 143: MR BELFORD TO ROBERT LOVELACE, ESQ.

Friday, April 21

Thou, Lovelace, hast been long the *entertainer*; I the *entertained*. Nor have I been solicitous to animadvert, as thou wentest along, upon thy inventions and their tendency. For I believed, that with all thy airs, the unequalled perfections and fine qualities of this lady would always be her protection and security. But now that I find thou hast so far succeeded as to induce her to come to town, and to choose her lodgings in a house, the people of which will too probably damp and suppress any honourable motions which may arise in thy mind in her favour, I cannot help writing: and that professedly in her behalf.

My inducements to this are not owing to virtue—but if they *were*, what hope could I have of affecting thee by pleas arising from it?

Nor would such a man as thou art be deterred, were I to remind thee of the vengeance which thou mayest one day expect if thou insultest a woman of her character, family and fortune.

Neither are gratitude and honour motives to be mentioned in a woman's favour, to men such as we are, who consider all those of the sex as fair prize, whom we can obtain a power over. For *our honour*, and *honour* in the *general acceptation* of the word, are two things.

What then is my motive? Why, the true friendship that I bear thee, Lovelace; which makes me plead *thy own sake* and *thy family's sake,* in the justice thou owest to this incomparable creature; who, however, so well deserves to have *her sake* to be mentioned as the principal consideration.

Last time I was at M. Hall, thy noble uncle so earnestly pressed me to use my interest to persuade thee to enter the pale, and gave me so many family reasons for it, that I could not help engaging myself heartily on his side of the question; and the rather as I knew that thy own intentions with regard to this fine woman were then worthy of *her*. And of this I assured his lordship; who was half-afraid of thee because of the ill usage thou receivedst from her family. But now that the case is altered, let me press the matter home to thee from other considerations.

By what I have heard of this lady's perfections from every mouth, as well as from thine, and from every letter thou hast written, where wilt thou find such another woman? And why shouldst thou tempt her virtue? Why shouldst thou be for trying, where there is no reason to doubt?

Were I in thy case, and designed to marry, and if I preferred a lady as I know thou dost this to all the women in the world, I should dread to make further trial, knowing what *we* know of the sex, for *fear* of succeeding; and especially if I doubted not that if there were a woman in the world virtuous at heart, it is she.

And let me tell thee, Lovelace, that in this lady's situation, the trial is not a fair trial. Considering the depth of thy plots and contrivances: considering the opportunities which I see thou must have with her, in spite of her own heart; all her relations' follies acting in concert, though unknown to themselves, with thy wicked scheming head: considering how destitute of protection she is: considering the house she is to be in, where she will be surrounded with thy implements; *specious, well-bred* and *genteel* creatures, not easily to be detected when they are disposed to preserve appearances, especially by a young, inexperienced lady wholly unacquainted with the town: considering all these things, I say—what glory, what cause of triumph wilt thou have, if she should be overcome?

May there not be other Lovelaces, thou askest, who, attracted by her beauty, may endeavour to prevail with her?

No; there cannot, I answer, be such another man, person, mind, fortune and thy character, as above given, taken in. If thou imaginedst there could, such is thy pride, that thou wouldst think the worse of thyself.

And let me, for the utter confusion of thy poor pleas of this nature, ask thee: Would she, in thy opinion, had she willingly gone off with thee, have been entitled to better quarter? For a *mistress* indeed she might: but wouldst thou for a *wife* have had cause to like her half so well as now?

That she loves thee, wicked as thou art, and cruel as a panther, there is no reason to doubt.

Thou wilt perhaps think that I have departed from my proposition, and pleaded the *lady's sake* more than *thine* in the above—but no such thing. All that I have written is more in thy behalf than in hers—since she may make *thee* happy. But it is next to impossible, I should think, if she preserves her delicacy that thou canst make *her* so. I need not give my reasons. Thou'lt have ingenuity enough, I dare say, were there occasion for it, to subscribe to my opinion.

I plead not for the [marriage] state from any great liking to it myself. Nor have I, at present, thoughts of entering into it. But as thou art the last of thy name; as thy family is of note and figure in thy country; and as thou thyself thinkest that thou shalt one day marry; is it possible, let me ask thee, that thou canst have such another opportunity as thou now hast, if thou lettest this slip?

And shall this admirable woman suffer for her generous endeavours to set on foot thy reformation; and for insisting upon proofs of the sincerity of thy professions before she will be thine?

Upon the whole matter let me wish thee to consider well what thou art about, before thou goest a step farther in the path which thou hast chalked out for thyself to tread, and art just going to enter into. Hitherto all is so far right, that if the lady mistrusts thy honour, she has no *proofs*. Be honest to her, then, in *her* sense of the word. None of thy companions, thou knowest, will offer to laugh at what *thou* dost. And if they *should* (on thy entering into a state which has been so much ridiculed by thee, and by all of us), thou hast one advantage: it is this; that thou canst not be ashamed.

I suppose you will soon be in town. Without the lady, I hope. Farewell.

Be honest, and be happy.
J. BELFORD

Letter 145: MISS CLARISSA HARLOWE TO MISS HOWE

Sat morn. April 22

I may go to London, I see, or where I will. No matter what becomes of me.

I was the willinger to suspend my journey thither, till I heard from Harlowe Place. I thought if I could be encouraged to hope for a reconciliation, I would let this man see that he should not have me in his power but upon my own terms, if at all.

But I find I must be *his*, whether I will or not; and perhaps through still greater mortifications than those great ones which I have already met with. And must I be so absolutely thrown upon a man with whom I am not at all satisfied!

Much did I consider, much did I apprehend, *before* my fault, supposing I *were* to be guilty of it: but I saw it not in all its shocking lights.

Although I never saw a man, whose *person* I could like, before this man; yet his faulty character allowed me but little merit from the indifference I pretended to on his account. But now I see him in nearer lights, I like him less than ever. Indeed, I never liked him so little as now. Upon my word, I think I could hate him (if I do not already hate him) sooner than any man I ever thought tolerably of—a good reason why: because I have been more disappointed in my expectations of him; although they never were so high as to have made him my choice in preference to the single life, had that been permitted me. Still, if the giving him up for ever will make my path to reconciliation easy, and if they will signify as much to me, they shall see that I never will be *his*: for I have the vanity to think my soul his soul's superior.

Oh this artful, this designing Lovelace! Yet I must repeat that most ought I to blame myself for meeting him.

But far, far be banished from me fruitless recrimination! Far banished, *because* fruitless! Let me wrap myself about in the mantle of my own integrity, and take comfort in my unfaulty intention! Since it is now too late to look back, let me collect all my fortitude and endeavour to stand those shafts of angry providence which it will not permit me to shun! That whatever the trials may be which I am destined to undergo, I may not behave unworthily in them; but come out amended by them.

Join with me in this prayer, my beloved friend; for your own honour's sake, as well as for love's sake, join with me in it: lest a deviation on my side should, with the censorious, cast a shade upon a friendship which has no *body*, no levity in it, and whose basis is improvement as well in the greater as lesser duties.

CL. HARLOWE

Letter 146: MISS CLARISSA HARLOWE TO MISS HOWE

Saturday, p.m. April 23

Oh my best, my only friend! Now indeed is my heart broken! It has received a blow it never will recover! Think not of corresponding with a wretch who now seems absolutely devoted! How can it be otherwise, if a parent's curses have the weight I always attributed to them and have heard so many instances of their being followed by! Yes, my dear Miss Howe, superadded to all my afflictions, I have the consequences of a father's curse to struggle with! How shall I support this reflection!—my past and my present situation so much authorizing my apprehensions!

I have at last a letter from my unrelenting sister. I enclose the letter itself. Transcribe it I cannot. There is no bearing the thoughts of it: for (shocking reflection!) the curse extends to the life beyond this.

I am in the depth of vapourish despondency. I can

only repeat: shun, fly, correspond not with a wretch so devoted as

Your CLARISSA HARLOWE

Letter 147: MISS ARABELLA HARLOWE TO MISS CLARISSA HARLOWE

To the most ungrateful and undutiful of daughters

Harlowe Place, Sat. April 15

Sister that was,

For I know not what name you are *permitted* or *choose* to go by.

You have filled us all with distraction. My father, in the first agitations of his mind on discovering your wicked, your shameful elopement, imprecated on his knees a fearful curse upon you. Tremble at the recital of it! No less, than 'that you may meet your punishment, both *here* and *hereafter*, by means of the very wretch in whom you have chosen to place your wicked confidence.'

Your clothes will not be sent you. You seem, by leaving them behind you, to have been secure of them whenever you demanded them. But perhaps you could think of nothing but meeting your fellow—nothing but how to get off your forward self!—for everything seems to have been forgot but what was to contribute to your wicked flight. Yet you judged right, perhaps, that you would have been detected, had you endeavoured to get off your clothes! Cunning creature! not to make *one* step that we could guess at you by! Cunning to effect your own ruin and the disgrace of all the family!

But does the wretch put you upon writing for your things for fear you should be too expensive to him? That's it, I suppose.

Was there ever a giddier creature? Yet this is the celebrated, the blazing Clarissa—Clarissa, *what? Harlowe,* no doubt!—and Harlowe it will be to the disgrace of us all!

Your drawings and your pieces are all taken down; as is also your own whole-length picture in the Vandyke taste, from your late parlour: they are taken down and thrown into your closet, which will be nailed up as if it were not a part of the house; there to perish together: for who can bear to see them?

My brother vows revenge upon your libertine—for the *family's* sake he vows it—not for *yours*! For he will treat you, he declares, like a common creature, if ever he sees you: and doubts not that this will be your fate.

My uncle Harlowe renounces you for ever.

So does my uncle Antony.

So does my aunt Hervey.

So do *I*, base unworthy creature!—the disgrace of a good family and the property of an infamous rake, as questionless you will soon find yourself, if you are not already!

Your books, since they have not taught you what belongs to your family, to your sex and to your education, will not be sent you. Your money neither. Nor yet the jewels so undeservedly made yours! For it is wished you may be seen a beggar along London streets!

If all this is heavy, lay your hand to your heart and ask yourself why you have deserved it?

Everybody, in short, is ashamed of you: but none more than

ARABELLA HARLOWE

Letter 148: MISS HOWE TO MISS CLARISSA HARLOWE

Tuesday, April 25

Be comforted; be not dejected; do not despond, my dearest and best-beloved friend. God Almighty is just and gracious, and gives not His assent to rash and inhuman curses. If He did, malice, envy and the blackest passions in the blackest hearts would triumph, and the best (blasted by the malignity of the worst) would be miserable in both worlds.

This malediction shows only what manner of spirit they are of, and how much their sordid views exceed their parental love. 'Tis all rage and disappointment, my dear; disappointment in designs proper to be frustrated; and all you have to grieve for is that their own rashness will turn upon their own hearts. God Almighty cannot

succeed a curse so presumptuous as to be carried into
His futurity!

My mother blames them for this wicked letter; and
she pities you; and of her own accord wished me to write
to comfort you, for this once. For she says, it is pity your
heart which was so noble (and when the sense of your
fault and the weight of a parent's curse are so strong
upon you) should be quite broken.

You will now see that you have nothing left but to
overcome all scrupulousness, and marry as soon as you
have opportunity. Determine upon this, my dear.

I will give you a motive for it, regarding myself. For
this I have resolved, and this I have vowed (Oh friend,
the best beloved of my heart, be not angry with me for
it!): 'That so long as your happiness is in suspense, I will
never think of marrying.' In justice to the man I shall
have, I have vowed this: for, my dear, must I not be
miserable if you are so? And what an unworthy wife
must I be to any man, who cannot have interest enough
in my heart to make his obligingness a balance for an
affliction he has not caused?

I would show Lovelace your sister's abominable letter,
were it to me. I enclose it. It shall not have a place in
this house.

I would not have you be too sure that their project to
seize you is over. So it will be best, when you are at
London, to be private and to let every direction be to a
third place, for fear of the worst; for I would not for the
world have you fall into the hands of such flaming and
malevolent spirits by surprise.

I will myself be content to direct to you at some *third*
place; and that I may have it to aver to my mother,
or to any other if occasion be, that I know not where
you are.

I would have you direct to Mr Hickman even your
answer to this.

Come, my dear, when things are at worst they must
mend. Good often comes when evil is expected. Happily
improved upon, this very curse may turn to a blessing.
But if you despond, there can be no hopes of cure. Don't
let them break your heart; for that, it is plain to me, is
now what some people have in view to do.

I send fifty guineas by the bearer, enclosed in single papers in my *Norris's Miscellanies.* I charge you, as you love me, return them not.

I have more at your service. So if you like not your lodging, or his behaviour, when you get to town, leave both out of hand.

I would advise you to write to Mr Morden without delay. If he intends for England, it may hasten him. And you'll do very well till he can come. But surely Lovelace is bewitched if he takes not his happiness from *your consent*, before that of Mr Morden's is made needful by his arrival.

Come, my dear, be comforted. All is hastening to be well. Nothing but words has passed, vehement and horrid as those are. The divine goodness will not let them be more. Manage with your usual prudence the stake before you, and all will be still happy.

This is the true light, as I humbly conceive, that this matter should appear to you in, and to everybody. If you let not despondency seize you, you will strengthen, you will add more day to this but glimmering light, from

Your ever affectionate and faithful
ANNA HOWE

Letter 149: MISS CLARISSA HARLOWE TO MISS HOWE

Wednesday morning, April 26

Your letter, my beloved Miss Howe, gives me great comfort.

Your messenger finds me just setting out for London: the chaise at the door. Already I have taken leave of the good widow, who has obliged me with the company of her eldest daughter, at Mr Lovelace's request, while he rides by us. The young gentlewoman is to return in two or three days with the chaise, in its way to my Lord M.'s Hertfordshire seat.

I received this dreadful letter on Sunday when Mr Lovelace was out. He saw, on his return, my extreme anguish and dejection; and he was told how much worse I had been: for I had fainted away twice.

I think it has touched my head as well as my heart.

He would fain have seen it. But I would not permit that because of the threatenings he would have found in it against himself. As it was, the effect it had upon me made him break out into execrations and menaces. I was so ill, that he himself advised me to delay going to town on Monday, as I proposed to do.

He is extremely regardful and tender of me. All that you supposed *would* follow this violent letter, from him, *has* followed it. He has offered himself to my acceptance in so unreserved a manner that I am concerned I have written so freely and so diffidently of him. Pray, my dearest friend, keep to yourself everything that may appear disreputable of him from me.

I must own to you that this kind behaviour and my low-spiritedness, cooperating with your former advice and my unhappy situation, made me that very Sunday evening receive unreservedly his declarations: And now, indeed, I am more in his power than ever.

He presses me every hour for fresh tokens of my esteem *for* him, and confidence *in* him. He owns that he doubted the one, and was ready to despair of the other. And as I have been brought to some verbal concessions, if he should prove unworthy, I am sure I shall have great reason to blame this violent letter: for I have no resolution at all. Abandoned thus of all my natural friends, and only you to pity me; and *you* restrained as I may say; I have been forced to turn my desolate heart to such protection as I could find.

All my comfort is that your advice repeatedly given to the same purpose, in your kind letter before me, warrants me. Upon the strength of that, I now set out the more cheerfully to London: for, before, a heavy weight hung upon my heart, and although I thought it best and safest to go, yet my spirit sunk, I know not why, at every motion I made towards a preparation for it.

I hope no mischief will happen on the road. I hope these violent spirits will not meet.

I must add one thing more, notwithstanding my hurry; and that is: Mr Lovelace offered to attend me to Lord M.'s, or to send for his chaplain, yesterday: he pressed me to consent to this proposal most earnestly; and even seemed more desirous to have the ceremony pass here than at London: for when there, I had told him, it was time enough to consider of so weighty and important a matter. Now, upon the receipt of your kind, your consolatory letter, methinks I could almost wish it *had been* in my power to comply with his earnest solicitations. But this dreadful letter has unhinged my whole frame. Then some little punctilio surely is necessary. No preparation made. No articles drawn. No licence ready. Grief so extreme: no pleasure in prospect, nor so much as in wish. Oh my dear, who could think of entering into so solemn an engagement! Who, *so* unprepared, could seem to be *so* ready!

If I could flatter myself that my indifference to all the joys of this life proceeded from *proper* motives, and not rather from the disappointments and mortifications my pride has met with, how much rather, I think, should I choose to be wedded to my shroud than to any man on earth!

Indeed I have at present no pleasure but in *your* friendship. Continue that to me, I beseech you. If my heart rises hereafter to more, it must be built on that foundation.

My spirits sink again on setting out. Excuse this depth of vapourish dejection which forbids me even *hope*, the cordial that keeps life from stagnating, and which never was denied me till within these eight-and-forty hours.

But 'tis time to relieve you.

Adieu, my best beloved and kindest friend! Pray for your

CL. HARLOWE

Letter 152: MR LOVELACE TO JOHN BELFORD, ESQ.

Monday, April 24

Fate is weaving a whimsical web for thy friend; and I see not but I shall be inevitably manacled.

Thou wilt be still the more surprised, when I tell thee that there seems to be a coalition going forward between the black angels and the white ones; for here has hers induced her in one hour, and by one retrograde accident, to *acknowledge* what the charming creature never before acknowledged, a preferable favour for me. She even owns an intention to be mine: mine, without reformation conditions. She permits me to talk of love to her: of the irrevocable ceremony: yet, another extraordinary! postpones that ceremony; chooses to set out for London; and even to go to the widow's in town.

Well, but how comes all this about, methinks thou askest? Thou, Lovelace, dealest in wonders, yet aimest not at the *marvellous*. How did all this come about?

I'll tell thee—I was in danger of losing my charmer for ever. She was soaring upward to her native skies. She was got above earth, by means, too, of the *earthborn*: and something extraordinary was to be done to keep her with us sublunaries. And what so effectually as the soothing voice of love, and the attracting offer of matrimony from a man not hated, can fix the attention of the maiden heart aching with uncertainty; and before impatient of the questionable question?

This, in short, was the case. While she was refusing all manner of obligation to me, keeping me at haughty distance; in hopes that her cousin Morden's arrival would soon fix her in a full and absolute independence of me: disgusted likewise at her adorer, for holding himself the reins of his own passions, instead of giving them up to her control—she writes a letter urging an answer to a letter before written, for her apparel, her jewels and some gold which she had left behind her; all which was to save her pride from obligation and to promote the independence her heart was set upon. And what followed but a shocking answer, made still more shocking by the communication of a paternal curse upon a daughter deserving only blessings?

Absent when it came, on my return I found her recovering from fits, again to fall into stronger fits; and nobody expecting her life; half a dozen messengers dispatched to find me out. Nor wonder at her being so affected; she, whose filial piety gave her dreadful faith in a father's curses; and the curse of this gloomy tyrant extending, to use her own words when she could speak, to *both worlds*. Oh that it had turned in the moment of its utterance to a mortal quinsy, and sticking in his gullet had choked the old execrator, as a warning to all such unnatural fathers.

What a miscreant had I been, not to have endeavoured to bring her back by all the endearments, by all the vows, by all the offers that I could make her?

I did bring her back. More than a father to her; for I have given her a life her unnatural father had well-nigh taken away; shall I not cherish the fruits of my own benefaction? I have been in earnest in my vows to marry, and my ardour to urge the present time was a *real* ardour. But extreme dejection, with a mingled delicacy that in her dying moments I doubt not she will preserve have caused her to refuse me the *time*, though not the solemnity; for she has told me that now she must be wholly in my protection, *being destitute of every other*! More indebted still, thou seest, to her cruel friends, than to herself for her favour!

She has written to Miss Howe an account of their barbarity; but has not acquainted her how very ill she was.

Low, very low, she remains; yet dreading her stupid brother's enterprise, she wants to be in London: where, but for *this* accident and (wouldst thou have believed it?) my persuasions, seeing her so very ill, she would have been this night; and we shall actually set out on Wednesday morning if she be not worse.

Mrs Sorlings's eldest daughter, at my motion, is to attend her in the chaise; while I ride by way of escort: for she is extremely apprehensive of the Singleton plot; and has engaged me to be all patience if anything should happen on the road. But nothing I am sure *will* happen: for, by a letter received just now from Joseph, I understand that James Harlowe has already laid aside his stupid project: and this by the earnest desire of all his friends to whom he had communicated it; who were afraid of the consequences that might attend it. But it is not over with *me*, however; although I am not determined at present as to the uses I may make of it.

My beloved tells me she shall have her clothes sent her: she hopes also her jewels and some gold which she left behind her. But Joseph says clothes *only* will be sent.

I will not, however, tell her that. On the contrary, I say there is no doubt but they will send *all* she wrote for, of personals. The greater her disappointment from them, the greater must be her dependence on me.

Letter 153: MR LOVELACE TO JOHN BELFORD, ESQ.

Tuesday, April 25

All hands at work in preparation for London. What makes my heart beat so strong? Why rises it to my throat in such half-choking flutters, when I think of what this removal may do for me? I am hitherto resolved to be honest: and that increases my wonder at these involuntary commotions. 'Tis a plotting villain of a heart: it ever was; and ever will be, I doubt. Such a joy when any roguery is going forward! I so little its master!

The dear creature continues extremely low and dejected. Tender blossom! How unfit to contend with the rude and ruffling winds of passion, and haughty and insolent control! Never till now from under the wing (it is not enough to say of indulging, but) of *admiring* parents; the mother's bosom only fit to receive this charming flower!

And can I be a villain to such an angel! I hope not. But why once more, thou varlet, puttest thou me in mind that she *may be* overcome? And why is her own reliance on my honour so late and so reluctantly shown?

But after all, so low, so dejected continues she to be that I am terribly afraid I shall have a vapourish wife, if I *do* marry. I should then be doubly undone. Not that I shall be much at home with her, perhaps, after the first fortnight or so. But when a man has been ranging like the painful bee from flower to flower, perhaps for a month together, and the thoughts of home and a wife begin to have their charms with him, to be received by a Niobe who, like a wounded vine, weeps its vitals away while it but involuntarily curls about you; how shall I be able to bear that?

May heaven restore my charmer to health and spirits, I hourly pray, that a man may see whether she can love anybody but her father and mother! In *their* power, I am confident, it will be at any time, to make her husband joyless; and that, as I hate them so heartily, is a shocking thing to reflect upon. Something *more* than woman, an *angel,* in some things, but a *baby* in others: so father-sick! so family-fond! what a poor chance stands a husband with such a wife, unless, forsooth, they vouchsafe to be reconciled to her and *continue* reconciled?

It is infinitely better for her and for me that we should not marry! What a delightful manner of life (Oh that I could persuade her to it!) would that be with such a lady! The fears, the inquietudes, the uneasy days, the restless nights; all arising from doubts of having disobliged me! Every absence dreaded to be an absence for ever! And then, how amply rewarded, and rewarding, by the rapture-causing return! Such a passion as this keeps love in a continual fervour; makes it all alive. The happy pair, instead of sitting dozing and nodding at each other in two opposite chimney-corners in a winter-evening, and over a wintry love, always new to each other, and having always something to say.

Tuesday afternoon

If you are in London when I get thither, you will see me soon. My charmer is a little better than she was. Her eyes show it, and her harmonious voice, hardly audible last time I saw her, now begins to cheer my heart once more. But yet she has no love, no sensibility! There is no addressing her with those *meaning* yet *innocent* freedoms (innocent at first setting out they may be called) which soften others of her sex. The more strange this, as she now acknowledges preferable favour for me; and is highly susceptible of grief. Grief mollifies and enervates. The grieved mind looks round it, silently implores consolation, and loves the soother. Grief is ever an inmate with joy. Though they won't show themselves at the same window at *one* time; yet have they the whole house in common between them.

Letter 154: MR LOVELACE TO JOHN BELFORD, ESQ.

Wed. Apr. 26

At last my lucky star has directed us into the desired port, and we are safely landed.

But in the midst of my exultation, something, I know not what to call it, checks my joys, and glooms over my brighter prospects. If it be not conscience, it is wondrously like what I thought so, many, many years ago.

Surely, Lovelace, methinks thou sayest: Thy good motions are not gone off already! Surely thou wilt not now at last be a villain to this lady.

My beloved, who is charmingly amended, is retired to her constant employment, writing. I must content myself with the same amusement till she shall be pleased to admit me to her presence: having already given to every one her cue.

But here comes the widow, with Dorcas Wykes in her hand. Dorcas Wykes, Jack, is to be the maid-servant to my fair one; and I am to introduce them both to her. In so many ways will it be in my power to have the dear creature now, that I shall not know which of them to choose!

So! The honest girl [Dorcas] is accepted!—of good parentage: but, through a neglected education, plaguy illiterate—she can neither write, nor read writing. A kinswoman of Mrs Sinclair's: so could not well be refused, the widow in person recommending her; and the wench only taken till her Hannah can come. What an advantage has an imposing or forward nature over a courteous one! So here may something arise to lead into correspondencies, and so forth! To be sure, a person need not be so wary, so cautious of what she writes, or what she leaves upon her table or toilet, when her attendant cannot read.

Dorcas is a neat girl both in person and dress; a countenance not vulgar. But I saw she had a dislike to her at her very first appearance—yet I thought the girl behaved very modestly—overdid it a little perhaps!—shrunk back and looked shy upon her. The doctrine of sympathies and antipathies is a surprising doctrine. But

Dorcas will be excessively obliging, and win her lady's
favour soon, I doubt not—I am secure in her *incorrupt-
ibility*. A great point that! For a lady and her maid of
one party will be too hard for half a score devils.

She [Clarissa] will insist, I suppose, upon my leaving
her, and that I shall not take up my lodgings under the
same roof. But circumstances are changed since I first
made her that promise. I have taken all the vacant apartments; and must carry this point also.

I hope in a while to get her with me to the public
entertainments. She knows nothing of the town, and has
seen less of its diversions than ever woman of her taste,
her fortune, her endowments, did see. She has indeed a
natural politeness which transcends all acquirement. Indeed she took so much pleasure in her own chosen
amusements till persecuted out of them, that she had
neither leisure nor inclination for the town diversions.

These diversions will amuse. And the deuce is in it, if
a little susceptibility will not put forth, now she receives
my address, and if I can manage it so as to be allowed
to live under *one* roof with her. What though the appearance be at first no more than that of an early spring
flower in frosty weather, that seems afraid of being
nipped by an easterly blast; that will be enough for me.

Letter 155: MISS CLARISSA HARLOWE TO MISS HOWE

Wed. p.m. Apr. 26
At length, my dearest Miss Howe, I am in London, and
in my new lodgings. They are neatly furnished, and the
situation, for the town, is pleasant. But I think you must
not ask me how I like the old gentlewoman. Yet she
seems courteous and obliging. Her kinswomen just appeared to welcome me at my alighting. They seem to be
genteel young women.

And now give me leave to chide you, my dearest
friend, for your rash, and I hope revocable resolution,
not to make Mr Hickman the happiest man in the world
while my happiness is in suspense. Suppose I were to be
unhappy, what, my dear, would your resolution avail
me? Marriage is the highest state of friendship: if happy,

it lessens our cares by dividing them, at the same time that it doubles our pleasures by a mutual participation. Why, my dear, if you love me, will you not rather give another friend to one who has not two that she is sure of?

Here I was broken in upon by Mr Lovelace; introducing the widow leading in a kinswoman of hers to attend me, if I approved of her, till my Hannah should come, or till I had provided myself with some other servant. The widow gave her many good qualities; but said that she had one great defect; which was that she could not write, nor read writing; that part of her education having been neglected when she was young. But for discretion, fidelity, obligingness, she was not to be outdone by anybody.

As for her defect, I can easily forgive that. She is very likely and genteel; too genteel indeed, I think, for a servant. But what I like least of all in her, she has a strange sly eye. I never saw such an eye—half-confident, I think. But indeed Mrs Sinclair herself (for that is the widow's name) has an odd winking eye; and her respectfulness seems too much studied, methinks, for the London ease and freedom. But people can't help their looks, you know; and after all, she is extremely civil and obliging: and as for the young woman (Dorcas her name), she will not be long with me.

I accepted her: how could I do otherwise (if I had a mind to make objections, which in my present situation I had not), her aunt present and the young woman also present; and Mr Lovelace officious in his introducing of them for my sake? But upon their leaving me, I told him, who seemed inclinable to begin a conversation with me that I desired that this apartment might be considered as my retirement: that when I saw him, it might be in the dining-room; and that I might be as little broke in upon as possible, when I am here. He withdrew very respectfully to the door; but there stopped; and asked for my company then in the dining-room. If he was about setting out for other lodgings, I would go with him now, I told him: but if he did not just then go, I would first finish my letter to Miss Howe.

I see he has no mind to leave me if he can help it. My brother's scheme may give him a pretence to try to engage me to dispense with his promise. But if I now do, I must acquit him of it entirely.

My approbation of his tender behaviour in the midst of my grief has given him a right, as he seems to think, of addressing me with all the freedom of an approved lover. He has been ever since Sunday last continually complaining of the distance I keep him at; and thinks himself entitled now, to call in question my value for him; strengthening his doubts by my declared readiness to give him up to a reconciliation with my friends—and yet has himself fallen off from that *obsequious tenderness*, if I may couple the words, which drew from me the concessions he builds upon.

While we were talking at the door, my new servant came up with an invitation to us both to tea. I said *he* might accept of it, if he pleased; but I must pursue my writing; and not choosing either tea or supper, I desired him to make my excuses below, as to both; and inform them of my choice to be retired as much as possible; yet to promise for me my attendance on the widow and her nieces at breakfast in the morning.

He objected particularity in the eye of strangers as to avoiding supper.

You know, said I, and can tell them that I seldom eat suppers. My spirits are low. You must never urge me against a declared choice. Pray, Mr Lovelace, inform them of all my particularities. If they are obliging, they will allow for them. I come not here to make new acquaintance.

I am exceedingly out of humour with Mr Lovelace: and have great reason to be so: as you will allow when you have read the conversation I am going to give you an account of; for he would not let me rest till I gave him my company in the dining-room.

He began with letting me know that he had been out to inquire after the character of the widow; which was the more necessary, he said, as he supposed that I would *expect* his frequent absence.

I did, I said; and that he would not think of taking up

his lodging in the same house with me. But what was the issue of his inquiry?

Why, indeed, it was in the main what he liked well enough. But as it was Miss Howe's opinion, as I had told him, that my brother had not given over his scheme; as the widow lived by letting lodgings; and had others to let in the same part of the house which might be taken by an enemy; he knew no better way than for him to take them all, as it could not be for a long time; unless I would think of removing to others.

So far was well enough: but as it was easy for me to see that he spoke the slighter of the widow, in order to have a pretence to lodge here himself, I asked him his intention in that respect. And he frankly owned that if I chose to stay here, he could not, as matters stood, think of leaving me for six hours together; and he had prepared the widow to expect that we should be here but for a few days—only till we could fix ourselves in a house suitable to our condition; and this, that I might be under the less embarrass, if I pleased to remove.

Fix *our*selves in a house, and *we* and *our*, Mr Lovelace—pray, in what light—

He interrupted me. Why, my dearest life, if you will hear me with patience—yet I am half afraid that I have been too forward, as I have not consulted you upon it. But as my friends in town, according to what Mr Doleman has written in the letter you have seen conclude us to be married—

Surely, sir, you have not presumed—

I perfectly raved at him. I would have flung from him in resentment; but he would not let me. And what could I do? Whither go, the evening advanced?

I am astonished at you! said I. If you are a man of honour, what need of all this strange obliquity? You delight in crooked ways. Let me know, since I must stay in your company (for he held my hand), let me know all you have said. Indeed, indeed, Mr Lovelace, you are a very unaccountable man.

My dearest creature, need I to have mentioned anything of this; and could I not have taken up my lodgings in this house unknown to you, if I had not intended to make you the judge of all my proceedings? But this is what I have told the widow before her kinswomen, and before your new servant—That indeed we were privately married at Hertford; but that you had preliminarily bound me under a solemn vow, which I am most religiously resolved to keep, to be contented with separate apartments, and even not to lodge under the same roof, till a certain reconciliation shall take place which is of high consequence to both. And further, that I might convince you of the purity of my intentions, and that my whole view in this was to prevent mischief, I have acquainted them that I have solemnly promised to behave to you before everybody, as if we were only betrothed and not married; not even offering to take any of those innocent freedoms which are not refused in the most punctilious loves.

I told him that I was not by any means satisfied with the tale he had told, nor with the necessity he wanted to lay me under of appearing what I was not: that every step he took was a wry one, a needless wry one: and since he thought it necessary to tell the people below anything about me, I insisted that he should unsay all he had said, and tell them the truth.

'Tis true I should have consulted you first, and had your leave. But since you dislike what I have said, let me implore you, dearest madam, to give the only proper sanction to it, by naming an early day. Would to heaven that were to be tomorrow! For God's sake, let it be tomorrow!

What could I say? What could I do? I verily think that had he urged me again, in a proper manner, I should have consented (little satisfied as I am with him) to give him a meeting tomorrow morning at a more solemn place than in the parlour below.

But this I resolve, that he shall not have my consent to stay a night under this roof. He has now given me a stronger reason for this determination than I had before.

Alas! my dear, how vain a thing to say what we will or what we will not do, when we have put ourselves into the power of this sex! He went down to the people below, on my desiring to be left to myself; and stayed till their supper was just ready; and then, desiring a moment's *audience*, as he called it, he besought my leave to stay that one night, promising to set out either for Lord M.'s, or for Edgware to his friend Belford's, in the morning after breakfast. But if I were against it, he said, he would not stay supper; and would attend me about eight next day—yet he added, that my denial would have a very particular appearance to the people below, from what he had told them; and the more as he had actually agreed for all the vacant apartments (indeed only for a month), for the reason he had before hinted at. But I need not stay here two days if, upon conversing with the widow and her nieces in the morning, I should have any dislike to them.

I thought, notwithstanding my resolution above-mentioned, that it would seem too punctilious to deny him; under the circumstances he had mentioned—having, besides, no reason to think he would obey me; for he looked as if he were determined to debate the matter with me. And, as now I see no likelihood of a reconciliation with my friends, and had actually received his addresses with less reserve than ever; I thought I would not quarrel with him if I could help it, especially as he asked to stay but for one night, and could have done so without my knowing it; and you being of opinion that the proud wretch, distrusting his own merits with me, or at least my regard for him, will probably bring me to some concessions in his favour. For all these reasons, I thought proper to yield *this* point; yet I was so vexed with him on the *other*, that it was impossible for me to comply with that grace which a concession should be made with, or not made at all.

He withdrew in the most respectful manner, beseeching me only to favour him with such a meeting in the morning as might not make the widow and her nieces think he had given me reason to be offended with him.

I retired to my own apartment, and Dorcas came to me soon after to take my commands. I told her that I required very little attendance, and always dressed and undressed myself.

She seemed concerned, as if she thought I had repulsed her, and said it should be her whole study to oblige me.

I told her that I was not difficult to please. And should
let her know from time to time what assistances I should
expect from her. But for that night I had no occasion
for her further attendance.

She is not only genteel, but is well-bred, and well-
spoken. She must have had what is generally thought to
be the polite part of education: but it is strange that
fathers and mothers should make so light, as they generally do, of that preferable part in girls, which would improve their minds and give a grace to all the rest.

As soon as she was gone, I inspected the doors, the
windows, the wainscot, the dark closet as well as the
light one; and finding very good fastenings to the door
and to all the windows, I again had recourse to my pen.

If, my dear, you will write against prohibition, be
pleased to direct, *To Miss Laetitia Beaumont; to be left
till called for, at Mr Wilson's in Pall Mall.*

Mr Lovelace proposed this direction to me, not knowing of your desire that our letters should pass by a third
hand. As his motive for it was that my brother might
not trace out where we are, I am glad, as well from this
instance as from others, that he seems to think he has
done mischief enough already.

Mr Lovelace is so full of his contrivances and expedients that I think it may not be amiss to desire you to
look carefully to the seals of my letters, as I shall to
those of yours. If I find him base in this particular, I
shall think him capable of any evil; and will fly him as
my worst enemy.

Letter 159: MR LOVELACE TO JOHN BELFORD, ESQ.

Sunday

Have been at church, Jack—behaved admirably well too!
My charmer is pleased with me now: for I was exceedingly attentive to the discourse, and very ready in the
auditor's part of the service. Eyes did not much wander.
How could they? when the loveliest object, infinitely the
loveliest, in the whole church, was in my view.

Dear creature! how fervent, how amiable, in her devotions! I have got her to own that she prayed for me! I

hope a prayer from so excellent a mind will not be made in vain.

There is, after all, something beautifully solemn in devotion! The Sabbath is a charming institution to *keep* the heart right, when it *is* right. One day in seven, how reasonable! I think I'll go to church once a day often. I fancy it will go a great way towards making me a reformed man.

But let me tell thee what passed between us in my first visit of this morning; and then I will acquaint thee more largely with my good behaviour at church.

I could not be admitted till after eight. I found her ready prepared to go out. I pretended to be ignorant of her intention, having charged Dorcas not to own that she had told me of it.

Going abroad, madam?—with an air of indifference.

Yes, sir; I intend to go to church.

I hope, madam, I shall have the honour to attend you.

No: she designed to take a chair, and go to the next church.

This startled me: a chair to carry her to the next church from Mrs Sinclair's, her right name not Sinclair, and to bring her back thither, in the face of people who might not think well of the house! There was no permitting that—yet I was to appear indifferent.

I beg the favour of attending you, dear madam, said I. I have not been at church a great while: we shall sit in different stalls: and the next time I go, I hope it will be to give myself a title to the greatest blessing I can receive.

She made some further objections: but at last permitted me the honour of attending her.

Sunday evening

We all dined together in Mrs Sinclair's parlour! All ex-*cessive*-ly *right*! The two nieces have topped their parts: Mrs Sinclair hers. Never so easy yet as now! 'She really thought a little oddly of these people at first, she said: Mrs Sinclair seemed very forbidding! Her nieces were persons with whom she could not wish to be acquainted. But really we should not be too hasty in our

censures. Some people improve upon us. The widow
seems *tolerable*.' (She went no farther than *tolerable*.)

I have been letting her into thy character, and into
the characters of my other three esquires, in hopes to
excite her curiosity to see you tomorrow night. I have
told her some of the *worst*, as well as *best* parts of your
characters, in order to exalt myself, and to obviate any
sudden surprises, as well as to teach her what sort of
men she may expect to see, if she will oblige me.

By her observations upon each of you, I shall judge
what I may or may not do to *obtain* or *keep* her good
opinion: what she will *like*, what *not*; and so pursue the
one, or avoid the other, as I see proper. So, while she
is penetrating into your shallow heads, I shall enter her
heart and know what to bid my own hope for.

All will be over in three weeks, or bad will be my
luck! Who knows but in three days! Have I not carried
that great point of making her pass for my wife to the
people below? And that other great one of fixing myself
here night and day? What lady ever escaped me, that
lodged under one roof with me? The house too, THE
house; the people, people after my own heart: her servants Will and Dorcas both my servants. *Three days* did
I say! Pho! pho! *Three hours!*

Letter 163: MISS CLARISSA HARLOWE TO MISS HOWE

Tuesday, May 2

With infinite regret I am obliged to tell you that I can
no longer write to you, or receive letters from you. Your
mother has sent me a letter enclosed in a cover to Mr
Lovelace, directed for him at Lord M.'s (and which was
brought him just now), reproaching me on this subject
in very angry terms, and forbidding me, as I would not
be thought to intend to make her and you unhappy, to
write to you, without her leave.

This, therefore, is the last you must receive from me,
till happier times: and as my prospects are not very bad,
I presume we shall soon have leave to write again; and
even to see each other: since an alliance with a family
so honourable as Mr Lovelace's is, will not be a disgrace.

She is pleased to write that if I would wish to *inflame* you, I should let you know her written prohibition: but otherwise find some way of my own accord (without bringing *her* into the question) to decline a correspondence, which I must know she has for some time past forbidden. But all I can say is, to beg of you *not* to be inflamed—to beg of you, not to let her *know*, or even by your behaviour to her, on this occasion, *guess*, that I have acquainted you with my reason for declining to write to you. For how else, after the scruples I have heretofore made on this very subject, yet proceeding to correspond, can I honestly satisfy you about my motives for this sudden stop? So my dear, I choose, you see, rather to rely upon your discretion, than to feign reasons you would not be satisfied with, but with your usual active penetration sift to the bottom, and at last find me to be a mean and low qualifier; and that, with an implication injurious to you, that I supposed you had not prudence enough to be trusted with the naked truth.

I repeat, that my prospects are not bad. The house, I presume, will soon be taken. The widow has a less forbidding appearance than at first. Mr Lovelace, on my declared dislike of his four friends [Belford, Belton, Mowbray, Tourville], has assured me that neither they nor anybody else shall be introduced to me, without my leave.

These circumstances I mention, as you will suppose, that your kind heart may be at ease about me; that you may be induced by them to acquiesce with your mother's commands, *cheerfully* acquiesce, and that for *my* sake, lest I should be thought an *inflamer*; who am, with very contrary intentions, my dearest, and best-beloved friend,

Your ever obliged and affectionate
CLARISSA HARLOWE

Letter 164: MISS HOWE TO MISS CLARISSA HARLOWE

Wed. May 3

I am astonished that my mother should take such a step—purely to exercise an unreasonable act of authority; and to oblige the most remorseless hearts in the world. If I find that I can be of use to you either by advice or information, do you think I will not give it? Were it to any other person, *less* dear to me than you are, do you think, in such a case, I would forbear giving it?

This I will come into, if it will make you easy: I will forbear to write to you for a few days, if nothing extraordinary happen—and till the rigour of her prohibition is abated. But be assured that I will not dispense with your writing to me. My heart, my conscience, my honour, will not permit it.

But how will I help myself? How! Easy enough. For I do assure you that I want but very little further provocation to fly privately to London: and if I do, I will not leave you till I see you either honourably married, or absolutely quit of the wretch: and in this last case, I will take you down with me in defiance of the whole world: or, if you refuse to go with me, stay with you, and accompany you as your shadow whithersoever you go.

If anything happens to delay your nuptials, I would advise you to remove: but if you marry, you may, perhaps, think it no great matter to stay where you are, till you take possession of your own estate. The knot once tied, and with so resolute a man, it is my opinion your relations will soon resign what they cannot legally hold: and were even a litigation to follow, you will not be *able*, nor ought you to be *willing*, to help it: for your estate will then be his right; and it will be unjust to wish it to be withheld from him.

One thing I would advise you to think of; and that is, of proper settlements. It will be to the credit of your prudence, and of his justice (and the more as matters stand), that something of this should be done before you marry. Bad as he is, nobody accounts him a sordid man. And I wonder he has been hitherto silent on that subject.

I repeat—continue to write to me—I insist upon it; and that as minutely as possible: or, take the consequence. I send this by a particular hand. I am, and ever will be,

Your most affectionate
ANNA HOWE

Letter 165: MISS CLARISSA HARLOWE TO MISS HOWE

Thursday, May 4

I forgo every other engagement, I suspend every wish, I banish every other fear, to take up my pen to beg of you that you will not think of being *guilty* of such an act of love as I can never thank you for; but must for ever regret. If I *must* continue to write to you, I must. I know full well your impatience of control when you have the least imagination that your generosity or friendship is likely to be wounded by it.

My dearest, dearest creature, would you incur a maternal, as I have a paternal, malediction? Would not the world think there was an infection in my fault, if it were to be followed by Miss Howe? There are some points so flagrantly wrong that they will not bear to be argued upon. This is one of them. I need not give reasons against such a rashness. Heaven forbid that it should be known that you had it but once in your *thought,* be your motives ever so noble and generous, to follow so bad an example! The rather as that you would, in such a case, want the extenuations that might be pleaded in my favour; and particularly that one of being *surprised* into the unhappy step.

The restraint your mamma lays you under would not have appeared heavy but on my account.

Learn, my dear, I beseech you learn, to subdue your own passions. Be the motives what they will, excess is excess. Those passions in our sex, which we take no pains to subdue, may have one and the same source with those infinitely blacker passions which we used so often to condemn in the violent and headstrong of the other sex; and which may be heightened in them only by custom, and their freer education. Let us both, my dear, ponder well this thought; look into ourselves, and fear.

If I write, as I find I must, I insist upon *your* forbearance. Your silence to *this* shall be the sign to me that you will not think of the rashness you threaten me with; and that you will obey your mamma as to your *own* part of the correspondence, however: especially as you can inform or advise me in every weighty case, by Mr Hickman's pen.

My trembling writing will show you what a trembling heart you, my dear impetuous creature, have given to

Your ever obliged,
Or, if you take so rash a step,
Your forever disobliged,
CLARISSA HARLOWE

Letter 167: MR LOVELACE TO JOHN BELFORD, ESQ.

Tuesday May 2

I must never talk of reformation, she told me, having such companions and taking such delight as I seemed to take in their frothy conversation.

I, no more than you, imagined she could possibly like ye: but then, as *my* friends, I thought a person of her education would have been more sparing of her censures.

I defended ye all, as well as I could: but you know there was no attempting ought but a palliative defence, to one of her principles.

Plainly, she said, she neither liked my companions, nor the house she was in.

I liked not the house any more than she: though the people were very obliging, and she had owned they were less exceptionable to herself than at first: and were we not about another of our own?

For her own part, she had seen nothing of the London world: but thought she must tell me plainly, that she never was in such company in her life; nor ever again wished to be in it.

I thanked her heartily. But I must take the liberty to say that good folks were generally so uncharitable that, devil take me, if I would choose to be good, were the consequence to be that I must think hardly of the whole world besides.

She congratulated me upon my charity: but told me that, to enlarge her own, she hoped it would not be expected of her to approve of the low company I had brought her into last night.

I saw not, I said, begging her pardon, that she liked *anybody* (Plain dealing for plain dealing! Why then did she abuse my friends? *Love me, and love my dogs,* as Lord M. would say). However, let me but know whom and what she did or did not like; and, if possible, I would like and dislike the very same persons and things.

She bid me then, in a pet, *dislike myself.*

Cursed severe! Does she think she must not pay for it one day, or one night? And if *one, many*; that's my comfort!

I had like to have been blasted by two or three flashes of lightning from her indignant eyes; and she turned scornfully from me, and retired to her own apartment. She says I am not a polite man. But is she, in the instance before us, more polite for a lady?

Letter 169: MR BELFORD TO ROBERT LOVELACE, ESQ.

Edgware, Tuesday night, May 2

Without staying for the promised letter from you to inform us what the lady says of *us*, I write to tell you that we are all of *one* opinion with regard to *her*; which is, that there is not of her age a finer lady in the world, as to her understanding. As for her person, she is at the age of bloom, and an admirable creature; a perfect beauty: but this *poorer* praise a man can hardly descend to give, who has been honoured with her conversation; and yet she was brought amongst us against her will.

Permit me, dear Lovelace, to be a means of saving this excellent creature from the dangers she hourly runs from the most plotting heart in the world. In a former, I pleaded your own family, Lord M.'s wishes particularly; and then I had not seen her. But now, I join her sake, honour's sake, motives of justice, generosity, gratitude and humanity, which are all concerned in the preservation of so fine a creature.

She is, in my eye, all mind: and were she to meet with a man all mind likewise, why should the charming qualities she is mistress of be endangered? Why should such an angel be plunged so low as into the vulgar offices of domestic life? Were she mine, I should hardly wish to see her a mother unless there were a kind of moral certainty that minds like hers could be propagated. For why, in short, should not the work of bodies be left to *mere* bodies? I know that you yourself have an opinion of this lady little less exalted than mine. Belton, Mowbray, Tourville, are all of my mind; are full of her praises; and swear it would be a million of pities to ruin a lady in whose fall none but devils can rejoice.

And wouldst thou make her unhappy for her whole life, and thyself not happy for a single moment?

Be honest, and marry; and be thankful that she will condescend to have thee. If thou dost not, thou'lt be the worst of men; and will be condemned in this world and the next: as I am sure thou oughtest, and shouldst too, wert thou to be judged by one who never before was so much touched in a woman's favour, and whom thou knowest to be

Thy partial friend,
J. BELFORD

Letter 170: MR LOVELACE TO JOHN BELFORD, ESQ.

Wednesday, May 3

When I have already taken pains to acquaint thee in full with my views, designs and resolutions, with regard to this admirable creature, it is very extraordinary that thou shouldst vapour as thou dost in her behalf, when I have made no trial, no attempt: and yet givest it as thy opinion in a former letter, that advantage may be taken of the situation she is in; and that she may be overcome.

I own with thee, and with the poet, *that sweet are the joys that come with willingness*—but is it to be expected that a woman of education, and a lover of forms, will yield before she is attacked? And have I so much as summoned this to surrender? I doubt not but I shall meet with difficulty. I must therefore make my first effort by surprise. There may possibly be some cruelty necessary. But there may be consent in struggle; there may be yielding in resistance. But the first conflict over, whether the following may not be weaker and weaker, till *willingness* follow, is the point to be tried. I will illustrate what I have said by the simile of a bird new caught.

We begin with birds as boys, and as men go on to ladies; and both perhaps, in turns, experience our sportive cruelty.

Hast thou not observed the charming gradations by which the ensnared volatile has been brought to bear with its new condition? How at first, refusing all sustenance, it beats and bruises itself against its wires, till it makes its gay plumage fly about, and overspread its well-secured cage. Now it gets out its head; sticking only at its beautiful shoulders: then, with difficulty, drawing back its head, it gasps for breath, and erectedly perched, with meditating eyes, first surveys, and then attempts, its wired canopy. As it gets breath, with renewed rage it beats and bruises again its pretty head and sides, bites the wires, and pecks at the fingers of its delighted tamer. Till at last, finding its efforts ineffectual, quite tired and breathless, it lays itself down and pants at the bottom of the cage, seeming to bemoan its cruel fate and forfeited liberty. And after a few days, its struggles to escape still diminishing, as it finds it to no purpose to attempt it, its new habitation becomes familiar; and it hops about from perch to perch, resumes its wonted cheerfulness, and every day sings a song to amuse itself, and reward its keeper.

Now let me tell thee that I have known a bird actually starve itself, and die with grief, at its being caught and caged. But never did I meet with a lady who was so silly. Yet have I heard the dear souls most vehemently threaten their own lives on such an occasion. But it is saying nothing in a woman's favour, if we do not allow her to have more sense than a bird. And yet we must all own that it is more difficult to catch a bird than a lady.

And now, Belford, were I to go no further, how shall I know whether this sweet bird may not be brought to sing me a fine song, and in time to be as well contented with her condition as I have brought other birds to be; some of them very shy ones?

But another word or two, as to thy objection relating to my trouble and my reward.

Does not the keen foxhunter endanger his neck and his bones in pursuit of a vermin which, when killed, is neither fit food for men nor dogs?

Do not the hunters of the nobler game value the venison less than the sport?

Why then should I be reflected upon, and the sex affronted, for my patience and perseverance in the most noble of all chases; and for not being a poacher in love, as thy question may be made to imply?

Learn of thy master, for the future, to treat more respectfully a sex that yields us our principal diversions and delights.

Letter 175: MR LOVELACE TO JOHN BELFORD, ESQ.

Tuesday, May 9

I am a very unhappy fellow. This lady is said to be one of the sweetest-tempered creatures in the world: and so I thought her. But to me, she is one of the most perverse. I nevèr was supposed to be an ill-natured puppy neither. How can it be? I imagined for a long while that we were born to make each other happy: but, quite the contrary; we really seem to be sent to plague one another.

I will write a comedy, I think. I have a title ready; and that's half the work. *The Quarrelsome Lovers.* 'Twill do. There's something new and striking in it. Yet, more or less, all lovers quarrel. 'Tis natural that it should be so. But with us, we fall out so often, without falling in once; and a second quarrel so generally happens before a first is made up; that it is hard to guess what event our loves will be attended with. No man living bears crosses better than myself: but then they must be of *my own* making: and even this is a great merit, and a great excellence, think what thou wilt: since most of the troubles which fall to the lot of mortals are brought upon themselves, either by their *too large* desires, or *too little* deserts. But I shall make myself a common man by-and-by: which is what no one yet ever thought me. I will now lead to the occasion of this preamble.

I had been out. On my return, meeting Dorcas on the stairs—Your lady in her chamber, Dorcas? In the dining-room, sir: and if ever you hope for an opportunity to come at a letter, it must be now. For at her feet I saw one lie which, by its opened folds, she has been reading, with a little parcel of others she is now busied with. All pulled out of her pocket, as I believe: so, sir, you'll know where to find them another time.

I was ready to leap for joy, and instantly resolved to bring forward an expedient which I had held *in petto*; and entering into the dining-room with an air of transport, I boldly clasped my arms about her as she sat (she huddling up her papers in her handkerchief all the time, the dropped paper unseen).

And clasping her closer to me, I gave her a more fervent kiss than ever I had dared to give her before: but still let not my ardour overcome my discretion; for I took care to set my foot upon the letter and scraped it farther from her, as it were behind her chair.

She was in a passion at the liberty I took. Bowing low, I begged her pardon; and stooping still lower, in the same motion took it up and whipped it in my bosom.

Pox on me for a puppy, a fool, a blockhead, a clumsy varlet, and a mere Jack Belford! I thought myself a much cleverer fellow than I am! Why could I not have been followed in by Dorcas; who might have taken it up while I addressed her lady?

For here, the letter being unfolded, I could not put it into my bosom without alarming her ears, as my sudden motion did her eyes. Up she flew in a moment: Traitor! Judas! her eyes flashing lightning, and a perturbation in her eager countenance, so charming! What have you taken up? And then, what for both my ears I durst not to have done to her, she made no scruple to seize the stolen letter, though in my bosom.

Beg-pardon apologies were all that now remained for me on so palpable a detection. I clasped her hand, which had hold of the ravished paper, between mine: Oh my beloved creature! can you think I have not *some* curiosity? Is it possible you can be thus for ever employed; and I, loving narrative letter-writing above every other species of writing, and admiring your talent that way, should not (thus upon the dawn of my happiness, as I presume to hope) burn with a desire to be admitted into so sweet a correspondence?

Let go my hand!—stamping with her pretty foot. How dare you, sir! At this rate, I see—too plainly I see—and

more she could not say: but, gasping, was ready to faint
with passion and affright; the devil a bit of her accustomed gentleness to be seen in her charming face, or to
be heard in her musical voice.

Having gone thus far, loath, very loath was I to lose
my prize. Once more I got hold of the rumpled-up letter!
Impudent man! were her words: stamping again: for
God's sake, then it was! I let go my prize, lest she should
faint away: but had the pleasure first to find my hand
within both hers, she trying to open my reluctant fingers.
How near was my heart, at that moment, to my hand,
throbbing to my fingers' ends, to be thus familiarly, although angrily, treated by the charmer of my soul!

When she had got it in her possession, she flew to the
door. I threw myself in her way, shut it, and in the humblest manner besought her to forgive me: and yet do
you think the Harlowe-hearted charmer would; notwithstanding the agreeable annunciation I came in with? No,
truly! but pushing me rudely from the door, as if I had
been nothing (yet do I love to try, so innocently to try,
her strength too!); she gaining that force through passion, which I had lost through fear; and out she shot to
her own apartment (thank my stars she could fly no further!); and as soon as she entered it, in a passion still,
she double-locked and double-bolted herself in. This my
comfort, on reflection, that upon a greater offence it cannot be worse!

I retreated to my own apartment with my heart full.
And my man Will not being near me, gave myself a
plaguy knock on the forehead with my double fist.

And now is my charmer shut up from me: refusing to
see me; refusing her meals. Resolves *not* to see me,
that's more. Never again, if she can help it.

But thinkest thou that I will not make it the subject
of one of my first plots to inform myself of the reason
why all this commotion was necessary on so slight an
occasion as this would have been, were not the letters
that pass between these ladies of a treasonable nature?

Wednesday morning

No admission to breakfast, any more than to supper.
Repeated charges has she given for Wilson, by a par-

ticular messenger, to send any letter directed for her the
moment it comes.

I must keep a good look-out. She is not now afraid of
her brother's plot.

But to own the truth, I have overplotted myself. To
make my work secure, as I thought, I have frighted the
dear creature with my four Hottentots, and I shall be a
long time, I doubt, before I can recover my lost ground.
And then these cursed folks at Harlowe Place have
made her out of humour with me, with herself, and with
all the world but Miss Howe, who no doubt is continually adding difficulties to my other difficulties. And then
I am very unwilling to have recourse to measures which
these demons below are continually urging me to take.
And the rather, as I am sure that, at last, she must be
legally mine. One complete trial over, and I think I will
do her noble justice.

But now I hear the rusty hinges of my beloved's door
give me creaking invitation. My heart creaks and throbs
with respondent trepidations. Whimsical enough though!
For what relation has a lover's heart to a rusty pair of
hinges? But they are the hinges that open and shut the
door of my beloved's bed chamber! Relation enough
in that!

I hear not the door shut again. I shall have her commands I hope anon. What signifies her keeping me thus
at a distance? She must be mine, let me do or offer what
I will.

Should I even make the grand attempt, and fail, and
should she hate me for it, her hatred can be but tempo-
rary. She has already incurred the censure of the world.
She must therefore choose to be mine for the sake of
soldering up her reputation in the eye of that impudent
world. For who that knows me and knows that she has
been in my power, though but for twenty-four hours,
will think her spotless as to fact, let her inclination be
what it will? And then human nature is such a well-
known rogue, that every man and woman judges by what
each knows of themselves, that inclination is no more to
be trusted, where an opportunity is given, than I am;
especially where a woman young and blooming loves a

man well enough to go off with him; for such will be the
world's construction in the present case.

She calls her maid Dorcas. No doubt that I may hear
her harmonious voice, and to give me an opportunity to
pour out my soul at her feet; to renew all my vows; and
to receive her pardon for the past offence: and then,
with what pleasure shall I begin upon a new score; and
afterwards wipe out that; and begin another, and another; till the *last* offence passes; and there can be no
other. And once, after that, to be forgiven, will be to be
forgiven for ever.

The door is again shut. Dorcas tells me that she denies
to admit me to dine with her, as I had ordered her to
request for me next time she saw her. Not uncivilly, however, denies. Coming to by degrees! Nothing but the last
offence, the honest wench tells me in the language of
her principals below, will do with her. The last offence
is meditating.

Letter 177: MISS HOWE TO MISS CLARISSA HARLOWE

Wednesday, May 10

I much approve of your resolution to leave this man, if
you can have any encouragement from your uncle
[Harlowe].

I will have your uncle sounded, as you desire, and that
out of hand. But yet I am afraid of the success; and this
for several reasons. 'Tis hard to say what the sacrifice of
your estate would do with some people: and yet I must
not, when it comes to the test, permit you to make it.

As your Hannah continues ill, I would advise you to
try to attach Dorcas to your interest. Have you not been
impoliticly shy of her?

You have exceedingly alarmed me by what you hint
of his attempt to get one of my letters. I am assured by
my new informant that he is the head of a gang of
wretches (those he brought you among, no doubt, were
some of them), who join together to betray innocent
creatures, and to support one another, when they have
done, by violence. And were he to come at the knowl-

edge of the freedoms I take with him, I should be afraid to stir out without a guard.

I wonder not at the melancholy reflections you so often cast upon yourself in your letters, for the step you have been forced upon on one hand, and tricked into on the other. A strange fatality! As if it were designed to show the vanity of all human prudence.

But do not talk, as in one of your former, of being a warning only. You will be as excellent an example as ever you hoped to be, as well as a warning. And that will make your story, to all that shall come to know it, of double efficacy: for were it that such a merit as yours could not ensure to herself noble and generous usage from a libertine heart, who will expect any tolerable behaviour from men of his character?

So, upon the whole, there seems as I have often said a kind of fate in your error, if an error; and this, perhaps, admitted for the sake of a better example to be collected from your *sufferings* than could have been given had you *never erred*: for, my dear, ADVERSITY is your SHINING-TIME: I see evidently that it must call forth graces and beauties that could not have been seen in a run of that prosperous fortune which attended you from your cradle till now; admirably as you became, and as we all thought greatly as you deserved, that prosperity.

I will add no more at present, than that I am

Your ever-faithful and affectionate
ANNA HOWE

Letter 178: MISS CLARISSA HARLOWE TO MISS HOWE

Sunday, May 14

I have not been able to avoid a short debate with Mr Lovelace. I had ordered a coach to the door. When I had notice that it was come, I went out of my chamber to go to it; but met him dressed on the stairs head, with a book in his hand, but without his hat and sword. He asked with an air very solemn, yet respectful, if I were going abroad. I told him I was. He desired leave to attend me, if I were going to church. I refused him. And then he complained heavily of my treatment of him, and declared that he would not live such another week as the past, for the world.

I owned to him very frankly, that I had made an application to my friends; and that I was resolved to keep myself to myself till I knew the issue of it.

He coloured, and seemed surprised.

He called to Dorcas to bring him his sword and hat; and following me down into the passage, placed himself between me and the door; and again besought me to permit him to attend me.

Mrs Sinclair came out at that instant, and asked me if I did not choose a dish of chocolate?

I wish, Mrs Sinclair, said I, you would take this man in with you to your chocolate. I don't know whether I am at liberty to stir out without his leave or not. Then turning to him, I asked, if he kept me there his prisoner?

Dorcas just then bringing him his sword and hat, he opened the street door, and taking my resisting hand led me, in a very obsequious manner, to the coach. People passing by, stopped, stared, and whispered. But he is so graceful in his person and dress, that he generally takes every eye.

I was uneasy to be so gazed at; and he stepped in after me, and the coachman drove to St Paul's.

He was very full of assiduities all the way, while I was as reserved as possible: and when I returned, dined, as I had done the greatest part of the week, by myself.

He told me, upon my resolving to do so, that although he would continue his passive observance till I knew the issue of my application, yet I must expect that then I should never rest one moment till I had fixed his happy day: for that his very soul was fretted with my slights, resentments, and delays.

Adieu, my dearest friend! This shall lie ready for an exchange, as I hope for one tomorrow from you that will decide, as I may say, the destiny of

Your CLARISSA HARLOWE

Letter 181: MISS HOWE TO MRS JUDITH NORTON

Saturday evening, May 13

Dear good Woman,

Could I have had hope of a reconciliation, all my view was, that she should not have had this man! All that can be said now is, she must run the risk of a bad husband: she of whom no man living is worthy.

You pity her mother!—so don't *I*! I pity nobody that puts it out of their power to show maternal love and humanity, in order to patch up for themselves a precarious and sorry quiet, which every blast of wind shall disturb!

I hate tyrants in every form and shape. But paternal and maternal tyrants are the worst of all: for they can have no bowels.

I repeat, that I pity *none* of them! My beloved and your beloved *only* deserves pity. She had never been in the hands of this man, but for them. She is quite blameless. You don't know all her story. Were I to tell you she had no intention to go off with this man, it would avail her nothing. It would only condemn those who drove her to extremities; and him, who now must be her refuge. I am

Your sincere friend and servant,
ANNA HOWE

Letter 183: MISS HOWE TO MISS CLARISSA HARLOWE

Sunday, May 14

How it is now, my dear, between you and Mr Lovelace, I cannot tell. But wicked as the man is, I am afraid he must be your lord and master.

Upon the whole, it is now evident to me, and so it must be to you when you read this letter, that you have but one choice. And the sooner you make it the better. Shall we suppose that it is not in your power to make it? I cannot have patience to suppose that.

I am concerned, methinks, to know how you will do to condescend, now you see you must be his, after you have kept him at such a distance; and for the revenge his pride may put him upon taking for it. But let me tell you, that if my going up and sharing fortunes with you will prevent such a noble creature from stooping too low, much more were it likely to prevent your ruin, I would not hesitate a moment about it. What's the whole world to me, weighed against such a friendship as ours. Think you that any of the enjoyments of this life could be enjoyments to me, were such a friend as you to be involved in calamities which I could either relieve her from, or alleviate, by giving them up? And what in saying this, and acting up to it, do I offer you, but the fruits of a friendship your worth has created?

Excuse my warmth of expression. The warmth of my heart wants none. I am enraged at your relations. I am angry at my own mother's narrowness of mind and adherence to old notions indiscriminately. And I am exasperated against your foolish, your low-vanitied Lovelace! But let us stoop to take the wretch as he is, and make the best of him, since you are destined to stoop to keep grovellers and worldlings in countenance. He has not been guilty of direct indecency to you. Nor *dare* he. Not so much of a devil as that comes to neither! Had he such villainous intentions, so much in his power as you are, they would have shown themselves before now to such a penetrating and vigilant eye, and to such a pure heart as yours. Let us save the wretch then, if we can, though we soil our fingers in lifting him up from his dirt.

There is yet, to a person of your fortune and independence, a good deal to do, if you enter upon those terms which *ought* to be entered upon. I don't find that he has once talked of settlements; much less of the licence. It is hard! But as your evil destiny has thrown you out of all other protection and mediation, you must be father, mother, uncle to yourself; and enter upon the requisite points for yourself. Indeed you must. Your situation requires it. What room for delicacy now? Or would you have *me* write to the wretch? Yet that would be the same thing as if you were to write yourself. Yet write you should, I think, if you cannot speak. But speaking is certainly best: for words leave no traces; they pass as breath; and mingle with air, and may be explained with latitude. But the pen is a witness on record.

Twice already have you, my dear, if not oftener, *modestied* away such opportunities as you ought not to have slipped. As to settlements, if they come not in naturally, e'en leave them to his own justice, and to the justice of his family. And there's an end of the matter.

This is *my* advice. Mend it as circumstances offer, and follow *your own*. But indeed, my dear, this, or something like it, would I do. As witness

YOUR ANNA HOWE

Letter 184: MISS CLARISSA HARLOWE TO MISS HOWE

Monday, p.m. May 15

Now indeed is it evident, my best, my only friend, that I have but one choice to make. And now do I find that I have carried my resentment against this man too far; since now I am to appear as if under an obligation to his patience with me for conduct that perhaps he will think, if not humoursome and childish, plainly demonstrative of my little esteem of him; of but a secondary esteem at least, where before his pride rather than his merit had made him expect a *first*.

You give me, my dear, good advice as to the peremptory manner in which I ought to treat him: but do you consider to whom it is that you give that advice?

The occasion for it should never have been given by *me*, of all creatures; for I am unequal, utterly unequal to it! What, *I*, to challenge a man for a husband! *I*, to exert myself to quicken the delayer in his resolutions! And, having lost an opportunity, to begin to try to recall it, as *from myself*, and *for myself*!—to *threaten* him, as I may say, into the marriage-state! Oh my dear! if this be right to be done, how difficult is it, where modesty and self (or where pride, if you please) is concerned to do that right? Or, to express myself in your words, to be father, mother, uncle, to myself! Especially where one thinks a triumph over one is intended. Do, my dear, advise me, persuade me, to renounce the man for ever: and then I will for ever renounce him!

You say you have tried Mrs Norton's weight with my mamma. 'My uncle, you say, believes me ruined: he declares that he can believe everything bad of a creature who could run away with a man: and they have all made a resolution not to stir an inch in my favour; no, not to save my life.'

I was forced to quit my pen.

Well, but now to look forward: you are of opinion that I must be his; and that I cannot leave him with reputation to myself, whether with or without his consent. I must, if so, make the best of the bad matter.

He went out in the morning; intending not to return to dinner, unless (as he sent me word) I would admit him to dine with me.

I excused myself. The man whose anger is now to be of such high importance to me was, it seems, displeased.

As he, as well as I, expected that I should receive a letter from you this day by Collins, I suppose he will not be long before he returns; and then, possibly, he is to be mighty stately, mighty *mannish,* mighty *coy,* if you please! And then must I be very humble, very submissive, and try to whine myself into his good graces: with downcast eye, if not by speech, beg his forgiveness for the distance I have so perversely kept him at! Yes, I warrant you! But I'll see how this behaviour will sit upon me! You have always rallied me upon my meekness, I think! Well then, I'll try if I can be still meeker, shall I! Oh my dear!

But let me sit with my hands before me, all patience, all resignation; for I think I hear him coming up. Or shall I roundly accost him, in the words, in the form, you, my dear, have prescribed?

He is come in. He has sent to me, all impatience in his aspect, Dorcas says. But I cannot, cannot see him!

Monday night

The contents of your letter, and my own heavy reflections, rendered me incapable of seeing this expecting man! The first word he asked Dorcas was, If I had received a letter since he had been out? She told me this; and her answer, That I had; and was fasting, and had been in tears ever since.

He sent to desire an interview with me.

Indifference, worse than indifference! said he, in a passion—

Interrupting him—Indifference let it be.

Dearest, dearest creature! (snatching my hand with wildness), let me beseech you to be *uniformly* noble! *Civil regards*, madam! *Civil regards!* Can you so expect to narrow and confine such a passion as mine!

Such a passion as yours, Mr Lovelace, *deserves* to be narrowed and confined. It is either the passion *you* do not think it; or *I* do not. I question whether your mind is capable of being *so* narrowed and *so* widened, as is necessary to make it be what I wish it to be. Lift up your hands and your eyes, sir, in that emphatical silent wonder, as you please: But what does it express, what does it convince me of, but that we are not born for one another?

By his soul, he said, and grasped my hand with an eagerness that hurt it, we *were* born for one another. I *must* be his. I *should* be his (and put his other arm round me), although his damnation were to be the purchase!

Hope what you will, interrupted I; I must insist upon it that our minds are by no means suited to each other. You have brought me into difficulties. I am deserted of every friend but Miss Howe. My true sentiments I will not conceal . . . Yet I *will* owe to you this protection, if it be necessary, in the earnest hope that you will *shun* rather than *seek* mischief, if any further inquiry after me be made. But what hinders you from leaving me? If you leave me, I will take a civil leave of these people, and retire to some one of the neighbouring villages, and there, secreting myself, wait my cousin Morden's arrival with patience.

He presumed, he told me, from what I said, that my application to my relations was unsuccessful: that therefore he hoped I would give him leave now to mention the terms in the nature of settlements, which he had long intended to propose to me; and which having till now delayed to do, through accidents not proceeding from himself, he had thoughts of urging to me the moment I entered upon my new house; and upon finding myself as independent in *appearance* as I was in *fact*.

Permit me, madam, to propose these matters to you. Not with an expectation of your immediate answer; but for your consideration.

Were not hesitation, a self-felt glow, a downcast eye, more than enough? Your advice was too much in my head: I hesitated.

He urged on upon my silence: he would call God to witness to the justice, nay to the *generosity* of his intentions to me, if I would be so good as to hear what he had to propose to me, as to settlements.

Could not the man have fallen into the subject without this *parade?* Many a point, you know, *is* refused, and *ought to be* refused, if leave be asked to introduce it; and when once refused, the refusal must in honour be adhered to—whereas, had it been *slid* in upon one, as I may say, it might have merited further consideration. If such a man as he knows not this, who should?

I thought myself obliged, though not to depart from this subject entirely, yet to give it a more diffuse turn; in order, on the one hand, to save myself the mortification of appearing too ready in my compliance, after such a distance as had been between us; and on the other, to avoid (in pursuance of your advice) the necessity of giving him such a repulse as might again throw us out of the course.

A cruel alternative to be reduced to!

You talk of *generosity*, Mr Lovelace, said I; and you talk of *justice*; perhaps without having considered the force of the words, in the sense you use them on this occasion. Let me tell you what *generosity* is, in my sense of the word. TRUE GENEROSITY is not confined to pecuniary instances: it is *more* than politeness: it is *more* than good faith: it is *more* than honour: it is *more* than *justice*: since all these are but duties, and what a worthy mind cannot dispense with. But TRUE GENEROSITY is greatness of soul: it incites us to do more by a fellow-creature, than can be strictly required of us: it obliges us to hasten to the relief of an object that wants relief, anticipating even hope or expectation. Generosity, sir, will not surely permit a worthy mind to doubt of its honourable and beneficent intentions: much less will it allow itself to shock, to offend anyone; and, least of all, a person thrown by adversity, mishap, or accident, into its protection.

His divine monitress, he called me! He would endeavour to form his manners, as he had often promised, by my example. But he hoped I would now permit him to mention briefly the *justice* he proposed to do me, in the terms of the settlement.

I have no spirits just now, sir, to attend to such weighty points. What you have a mind to propose, write to me: and I shall know what answer to return.

He *looked* as if he would choose rather to speak than write: but had he *said so*, I had a severe return to have made upon him; as possibly he might see by *my* looks.

In this way are we now: a sort of calm, as I said, succeeding a storm. What may happen next, whether a storm or a calm, with such a spirit as I have to deal with, who can tell?

But be that as it will, I think, my dear, I am not *meanly* off: and that is a great point with me; and which I know you'll be glad to hear: if it were only that I can see this man without losing any of that dignity (what other word can I use, speaking of *myself,* that betokens *decency* and not *arrogance*?) which is so necessary to enable me to look *up*, or rather, with the *mind's* eye, I may say, to look *down* upon a man of this man's cast.

Be pleased then to allow me to think that my motives on this occasion arise not *altogether* from maidenly niceness; nor yet from the apprehension of what my present tormentor, and future husband, may think of a precipitate compliance, on such a disagreeable behaviour as his. But they arise principally from what offers to my own heart, respecting, as I may say, its own rectitude, its own judgement of the *fit* and the *unfit*; as I would without study answer *for* myself *to* myself, in the *first* place; to *him* and to the *world*, in the *second* only.

I hope, my dear, I do not deceive myself, and instead of setting about rectifying what is amiss in my heart, endeavour to find excuses for habits and peculiarities which I am unwilling to cast off or overcome. The heart is very deceitful: do you, my dear friend, lay mine open (but surely it is always open before you!) and spare me not, if you find or think it culpable.

I am, my dearest friend,

Your ever-obliged
CLARISSA HÀRLOWE

Letter 186: MISS CLARISSA HARLOWE TO MISS HOWE

Tuesday night, May 16

Mr Lovelace has sent me, by Dorcas, his proposals, as follow:

'To spare a delicacy so extreme, and to obey you, I write: and the rather that you may communicate this paper to Miss Howe, who may consult any of her friends you shall think proper to have entrusted on this occasion. I say *entrusted* because, as you know, I have given it out to several persons that we are actually married.

'In the first place, madam, I offer to settle upon you, by way of jointure, your whole estate. And moreover to vest in trustees such a part of mine in Lancashire as shall produce a clear four hundred pounds a year, to be paid to your sole and separate use, quarterly.

'My own estate is a clear £2000 *per annum*. Lord M. proposes to give me possession either of that which he has in Lancashire (to which, by the way, I think I have a better title than he has himself), or that we call *The Lawn* in Hertfordshire, upon my nuptials with a lady whom he so greatly admires; and to make that I shall choose a clear £1000 *per annum*.

'If, as your own estate is at present in your father's hands, you rather choose that I should make a jointure out of mine, tantamount to yours, be it what it will, it shall be done. I will engage Lord M. to write to *you*, what he proposes to do on the happy occasion: not as your desire or expectation, but to demonstrate that no advantage is intended to be taken of the situation you are in with your own family.

'To show the beloved daughter the consideration I have for her, I will consent that she shall prescribe the terms of agreement in relation to the large sums, which must be in her father's hands, arising from her grandfather's estate. I have no doubt but he will be put upon making large demands upon you. All those it shall be in your power to comply with, for the sake of your own peace. And the remainder shall be paid into your hands, and be entirely at your disposal, as a fund to support those charitable donations, which I have heard you so famed for *out* of your family; and for which you have been so greatly reflected upon *in* it.

'As to clothes, jewels, and the like, against the time you shall choose to make your appearance, it will be my pride that you shall not be beholden for such of these as shall be answerable to the rank of both, to those who have had the stupid folly to renounce a daughter they deserved not. You must excuse me, madam: you would mistrust my sincerity in the rest, could I speak of these people with less asperity, though so nearly related to you.

'These, madam, are my proposals. They are such as I always designed to make, whenever you would permit me to enter into the delightful subject.

'I will only add, that if I have omitted anything that would have given you further satisfaction; or if the above terms be short of what you would wish; you will be pleased to supply them as you think fit. And when I know your pleasure, I will instantly order articles to be drawn up conformably; that nothing in my power may be wanting to make you happy.

'You will now, dearest madam, judge how far all the rest depends upon yourself.'

You see, my dear, what he offers. You see it is all my fault that he has not made these offers before. I am a strange creature! To be to blame in everything, and to everybody! Yet neither intend the ill at the time, nor know it to *be* the ill till too late, or so nearly too late that I must give up all the delicacy he talks of to compound for my fault!

Would you not, as you read, have supposed that the paper would conclude with the most earnest demand of a day? I own I had that expectation so strong, resulting *naturally*, as I may say, from the premises, that without studying for dissatisfaction, I could not help being dissatisfied when I came to the conclusion.

I will consider this paper; and write to it, if I am able: for it seems *now, all the rest depends upon myself.*

Letter 187: MISS CLARISSA HARLOWE TO MISS HOWE

Wednesday morning, May 17

Mr Lovelace would fain have engaged me last night. But as I was not prepared to enter upon the subject of his proposals, intending to consider them maturely, and was not highly pleased with his conclusion (and then there is hardly any getting from him in tolerable time over-night), I desired to be excused seeing him till morning.

About seven o'clock we met in the dining-room. I find he was full of expectation that I should meet him with a very favourable, who knows but with *thankful* aspect? And I immediately found by his sullen countenance, that he was under no small disappointment that I did not.

My dearest love, are you well? Why look you so solemn upon me? Will your indifference never be over? If I have proposed terms in any respect *short* of your expectation—

I told him that he had very considerately mentioned my showing his proposals to Miss Howe, and consulting any of her friends upon them by her means; and I should have an opportunity to send them to her by Collins by-and-by, and so insisted to suspend any talk upon that subject till I had her opinion upon them.

Good God! If there were but the least loop-hole, the least room for delay! But he was writing a letter to his uncle, to give him an account of his situation with me, and could not finish it so satisfactorily, either to my lord or to himself, as if I would condescend to say whether the terms he had proposed were acceptable or not.

But by his soul, he knew not, so much was I upon the reserve, and so much latent meaning did my eye import, whether, when he most hoped to please me, he was not farthest from doing so. Would I vouchsafe to say, whether I approved of his compliment to Lord M. or not?

Miss Howe, thought I at that moment, says I must *not* run away from this man!

To be sure, Mr Lovelace, if this matter is *ever to be*, it must be agreeable to me to have the full approbation of *one* side, since I cannot have that of the *other*.

If this be ever to be! Good God! what words were those at this time of day! And full *approbation* of one side! Why that word *approbation*? when the greatest pride of all his family was that of having the honour of so dear a creature for their relation? Would to Heaven, my dearest life, added he, that, without complimenting *any*body, tomorrow might be the happiest day of my life! What say you, my angel? with a trembling impatience that *seemed* not affected. What say you for *tomorrow*?

No, no! you cannot think all of a sudden there should be reason for such a hurry. It will be most agreeable, to be sure, for my lord to be present.

I am all obedience and resignation, returned the wretch, with a self-pluming air, as if he had acquiesced to a proposal made by me, and had complimented me with a great piece of self-denial.

Modesty, I think, required it of me that it should pass so. Did it not? I think it did. Would to Heaven—but what signifies wishing?

But when he would have *rewarded himself*, as he had heretofore called it, for this self-supposed concession, with a kiss, I repulsed him with a just and very sincere disdain.

He seemed both vexed and surprised, as one who had made proposals that he had expected everything from. He plainly said that he thought our situation would entitle him to such an innocent freedom: and he was both amazed and grieved to be thus scornfully repulsed.

No reply could be made by me. I abruptly broke from him. I recollect, as I passed by one of the pier-glasses, that I saw in it his clenched hand offered in wrath to his forehead: the words, *indifference, by his soul, next to hatred*, I heard him speak: and something of *ice* he mentioned: I heard not what.

And so much at present for Mr Lovelace's proposals: of which I desire your opinion.

I am, my dearest friend,

Your ever-obliged
Cl. Harlowe

Letter 188: MISS HOWE TO MISS CLARISSA HARLOWE

Thursday, May 18

I have neither time nor patience, my dear friend, to answer to every material article in your last letters just now received. Mr Lovelace's proposals are all I like of him. And yet (as you do) I think that he concludes them not with that warmth and earnestness which we might naturally have expected from him. Never in my life did I hear or read of so patient a man, with such a blessing in his reach. But wretches of his cast, between you and me, my dear, have not, I fancy, the ardours that honest men have.

But, as matters now stand betwixt you, I am very unseasonable in expressing my resentments against him. Yet I don't know whether I am or not, neither; since it is the cruellest of states for a woman to be forced to have a man whom her heart despises. You must, at *least*, despise him; at times, however. His clenched fist offered to his forehead on your leaving him in just displeasure; I wish it had been a poleaxe, and in the hand of his worst enemy.

I will endeavour to think of some method, of some scheme, to get you from him, and to fix you safely somewhere till your cousin Morden arrives; a scheme to lie by you, and to be pursued as occasion may be given. You are sure that you can go abroad when you please; and that our correspondence is safe. I cannot, however, for the reasons heretofore mentioned respecting your own reputation, wish you to leave him while he gives you not cause to suspect his honour. But your heart, I know, would be the easier if you were sure of some asylum, in case of necessity.

Yet once more, I say, I can have no notion that he

can or dare to mean you dishonour. But then the man is a fool, my dear. That's all.

However, since you are thrown upon a fool, marry the fool at the first opportunity; and though I doubt that this man will be the most ungovernable of fools, as all witty and vain fools are, take him as a punishment, since you cannot as a reward. In short, as one given to convince you that there is nothing but imperfection in this life.

I shall be impatient till I have your next. I am, my dearest friend,

Your ever-affectionate and faithful
ANNA HOWE

Letter 194: MR LOVELACE TO JOHN BELFORD, ESQ.

Saturday, May 20

And what must necessarily be the consequence of all this, with regard to my beloved's behaviour to me? Canst thou doubt that it was all complaisance next time she admitted me into her presence?

Thursday we were very happy. All the morning *extremely* happy. I kissed her charming hand. I need not describe to thee her hand and arm. *Fifty* times kissed her hand, I believe. Once her cheek, intending her lip, but so rapturously, that she could not help seeming angry.

Had she not thus kept me at arms-length; had she not denied me those innocent liberties which our sex, from degree to degree, aspire to; could I but have gained access to her in her hours of heedlessness and dishabille (for full dress creates dignity, augments consciousness, and compels distance), we had been familiarized to each other long ago. But keep her up ever so late; meet her ever so early; by breakfast-time dressed for the day; and at her earliest hour, as nice as others dressed. All her forms thus kept up, wonder not that I have made so little progress in the proposed trial. But how must all this distance stimulate!

Thursday morning, I said, we were extremely happy. About *noon,* she numbered the hours she had been with me; all of them to me but as one minute; and desired to be left to herself. I was loth to comply: but observing the sunshine begin to shut in, I yielded.

I dined out. Returned; talked of the house. Had written to my uncle; expected an answer soon from him. I was admitted to sup with her. Urged for her approbation or correction of my written terms. She promised an answer as soon as she had heard from Miss Howe.

Friday passed as the day before.

Here were two happy days to both! Why cannot I make every day equally happy? It looks as if it were in my power to do so. Strange I should thus delight in teasing a woman I so dearly love! I must, I doubt, have something in my temper like Miss Howe, who loves to plague the man who puts himself in her power. But I could not do thus by such an angel as this, did I not believe that after her probation-time is expired, and if there is no bringing her to *cohabitation* (my darling view), I shall reward her as she wishes.

Letter 196: MISS HOWE TO MISS CLARISSA HARLOWE

Saturday, May 20

I did not know, my dear, that you deferred giving an answer to Mr Lovelace's proposals till you had my opinion of them. A particular hand occasionally going to town will leave this at Wilson's, that no delay may be made on that account.

I never had any doubt of the man's justice and generosity in matters of settlement; and all his relations are as noble in their spirits as in their descent: but *now*, it may not be amiss for you to wait to see what returns my lord makes to his letter of invitation.

The scheme I think of is this.

There is a person (I believe you have seen her with me), one Mrs Townsend, who is a great dealer in Indian silks, Brussels and French laces, cambrics, linen, and other valuable goods; which she has a way of coming at, duty-free; and has a great vend for them, and for other curiosities which she imports, in the private families of the gentry round us.

She has her days of being in town, and then is at a

chamber she rents in an inn in Southwark, where she has patterns of all her silks and much of her portable goods, for the conveniency of her London customers. But her place of residence, and where she has her principal warehouse, is at Deptford, for the opportunity of getting her goods on shore.

And having applied to me, to recommend her to you (as it is her view to be known to young ladies who are likely to change their condition), I am sure I can engage her to give you protection at her house at Deptford; which she says is a populous village; and one of the last, I should think, that you would be sought for in. She is not much there, you will believe, by the course of her dealings; but no doubt must have somebody on the spot in whom she can confide: and there perhaps you might be safe, till your cousin comes. And I should not think it amiss, that you write to him out of hand. I cannot suggest to you what you should write. That must be left to your own discretion. For you will be afraid, no doubt, of the consequence of a variance between the two men.

I will think further of this scheme of mine in relation to Mrs Townsend, if you find it necessary that I should. But I hope there will be no occasion to do so, since your prospects seem to be changed, and that you have had *twenty-four not unhappy hours together.* How my indignation rises for this poor consolation in the courtship (*courtship* must I call it?) of such a lady!

The wretch is no assassin, no night-murderer. He is an *open*, because a *fearless* enemy; and should he attempt anything that should make him obnoxious to the laws of society, you might have a fair riddance of him either by flight or the gallows; no matter which.

I showed Mr Lovelace's proposals to Mr Hickman, who had chambers once at Lincoln's Inn, being designed for the law had his elder brother lived. He looked so wise, so proud, and so important, upon the occasion; and wanted to take so much consideration about them— would take them home if I pleased—and weigh them well—and so forth—and the like—and all that—that I had no patience with him, and snatched them back with anger.

He begged my pardon. *Saw* no objection, indeed. But might he be allowed once more—

No matter—no matter—I would have shown them to my mother, I said, who, though of no Inn of Court, knew more of these things than half the lounging lubbers of them; and that at first sight.

But, my dear, let the articles be drawn up, and ingrossed; and solemnize upon them; and there's no more to be said.

I send this away directly. May your prospects be still more and more happy, prays

Your own
ANNA HOWE

Letter 198: MR LOVELACE TO JOHN BELFORD, ESQ.

Sunday, May 21

I am too much disturbed in my mind to think of any thing but revenge; or I had intended to give thee an account of Miss Harlowe's curious observations on the play. *Miss Harlowe's,* I say. Thou knowest that I hate the name of *Harlowe;* and I am exceedingly out of humour with her, and with her saucy friend.

What's the matter *now*, thou'lt ask? Matter enough; for while we were at the play, Dorcas, who had her orders and a key to her lady's chamber, as well as a master-key to her drawers and mahogany chest, closet-key and all, found means to come at some of Miss Howe's last-written letters. The vigilant wench was directed to them by seeing her lady take a letter out of her stays, and put it to the others, before she went out with me—afraid, as the women upbraidingly tell me, that I should find it there.

Dorcas no sooner found them, than she assembled three ready writers of the *non-apparents*, and Sally, and she and they employed themselves with the utmost diligence, in making extracts according to former directions, from these cursed letters, for my use. *Cursed*, I may well call them. Such abuses, such virulence! Oh this little fury Miss Howe! Well might her saucy friend (who has been equally free with me, or the occasion could not have been given) be so violent as she lately was at my endeavouring to come at one of these letters.

And here, just now, is another letter brought from the same little virulent devil. I hope to procure transcripts from that too, very speedily, if it be put to the rest; for the saucy lady is resolved to go to church this morning; not so much from a spirit of devotion, I have reason to think, as to try whether she can go out without check or control, or my attendance.

I have been denied breakfasting with her. Indeed she was a little displeased with me last night; because, on our return from the play, I obliged her to pass the rest of the night with the women and me, in their parlour, and to stay till near one. She told me at parting that she expected to have the whole next day to herself. I had not read the extracts then; so was all affectionate respect, awe, and distance; for I had resolved to begin a new course, and, if possible, to banish all jealousy and suspicion from her heart: and yet I had no reason to be much troubled at her past suspicions; since, if a woman will continue with a man whom she suspects, when she can get from him, or *thinks* she can, I am sure it is a very hopeful sign.

She is gone. Slipped down before I was aware. She had ordered a chair, on purpose to exclude my personal attendance.

But she would not be so careless of obliging me, if she knew what I have already come at, and how the women urge me on; for they are continually complaining of the restraint they lie under in their behaviour, in their attendance; neglecting all their concerns in the front house and keeping this elegant back one entirely free from company, that she may have no suspicion of them. They doubt not my generosity, they say: but *why* for my own sake, in Lord M.'s style, *should I make so long a harvest of so little corn?* Women, ye reason well. I think I will begin my operations the moment she comes in.

I have come at the letter brought her from Miss Howe today. Plot, conjuration, sorcery, witchcraft, all going forward! I shall not be able to see *Miss Harlowe* with patience. As the nymphs below say, why is *night* necessary? And Sally and Polly upbraidingly remind me of my first attempts upon themselves. Yet force answers not my end. And yet it may, if there be truth in that part of the libertine's creed, *that once subdued, is always subdued!* And what woman answers *affirmatively* to the question?

She is returned. But refuses to admit me. Desires to have the day to herself.

But since I must not see her (she will be mistress of her *own will*, and of her *time* truly!), let me fill up mine by telling thee what I have come at.

The first letter the women met with is dated April 27. Where can she have put the preceding ones? It mentions Mr Hickman as a busy fellow between them. Hickman had best take care of himself.

The next letter is dated May 3. In this the little termagant expresses her astonishment that her mother should write to Miss Harlowe to forbid her to correspond with her daughter. Mr Hickman, she says, is of opinion *that she ought not to obey her mother.* How the creeping fellow trims between both! I am afraid I must punish him as well as this virago. But observe the vixen, *'Tis well he is of her opinion; for her mother having set her up, she must have somebody to quarrel with.* Could a Lovelace have allowed himself a greater license? This girl's a devilish rake in her heart. Had she been a man, and one of us, she'd have outdone us all in enterprise and spirit.

Thou wilt say to thyself by this time: And can this proud and insolent girl be the same Miss Howe who sighed for honest Sir George Colmar; and who, but for this her beloved friend, would have followed him in all his broken fortunes, when he was obliged to quit the kingdom?

Yes, she is the very same. And I always found in others, as well as in myself, that a first passion thoroughly subdued, made the conqueror of it a rover; the conqueress a tyrant.

In another letter, *She approves of her design to leave me, if she can be received by her friends.*

In the next, wicked as I am, *she fears I must be her lord and master*. I hope so.

The fire of friendship then blazes out and crackles. I never before imagined that so fervent a friendship could subsist between two sister-beauties, both toasts. But even here it may be inflamed by opposition, and by that contradiction which gives spirit to female spirits of a warm and romantic turn.

She raves about *coming up, if by so doing she could prevent so noble a creature from stooping too low, or save her from ruin*. One reed to support another! These girls are frenzical in their friendship. They know not what a steady fire is.

How comes it to pass, that I cannot help being pleased with this virago's spirit, though I suffer by it? Had I her but here, I'd engage in a week's time to teach her submission without reserve. What pleasure should I have in breaking such a spirit! I should wish for her but for one month, in all, I think. She would be too tame and spiritless for me after that. How sweetly pretty to see the two lovely friends, when humbled and tame, both sitting in the darkest corner of a room, arm in arm, weeping and sobbing for each other! And I their emperor, their then *acknowledged* emperor, reclined on a sophee, in the same room, Grand Signor-like, uncertain to which I should first throw out my handkerchief?

Mind the girl: *she is enraged at the Harlowes: she is angry at her own mother; she is exasperated against her foolish and low-vanitied Lovelace.* FOOLISH, a little toad! (God forgive me for calling a virtuous girl a toad!) *Let us stoop to lift the wretch out of his dirt, though we soil our fingers in doing it! He has not been guilty of direct indecency to you.* It seems *extraordinary* to Miss Howe that I have not. *Nor dare he.* She should be sure of that. If women have such things in their heads, why should not I in my heart? *Not so much of a devil as that comes to, neither. Such villainous intentions would have shown themselves before now, if I had them.* Lord help them!

She then puts her friend upon urging for *settlements, licence,* and so forth. *No room for delicacy now*, she says. And tells her what she shall say, to *bring all forward from me.* Dost think, Jack, that I should not have carried my point long ago, but for this vixen? She *reproaches her for having* MODESTY'D *away*, as she calls it, *more than one opportunity that she ought not to have slipped.* Thus thou seest that the noblest of the sex mean nothing in the world by their shyness and distance, but to pound a poor fellow whom they dislike not, when he comes into their purlieus.

But I have still more unpardonable transcripts from other letters.

Letter 199: MR LOVELACE TO JOHN BELFORD, ESQ.

The next letter is of such a nature, that I dare say these proud varletesses would not have had it fall into my hands for the world.

I see by it to what her displeasure with me, in relation to my proposals, was owing. They were not summed up, it seems, with the warmth, with the *ardour,* which she had expected. This whole letter was transcribed by Dorcas, to whose lot it fell. Thou shalt have copies of them all at full length shortly.

Men of our cast, this little devil says, *she fancies, cannot have the ardours that honest men have.* Miss Howe has very pretty fancies, Jack. Charming girl! Would to heaven I knew whether my fair one answers her as freely as she writes! 'Twould vex a man's heart, that this virago should have come honestly by her *fancies.*

His clenched fist to his forehead on your leaving him in just displeasure—that is, when she was not satisfied with my ardours, and please ye! I remember the motion: but her back was toward me at the time. Are these watchful ladies all eye? But observe her wish, *I wish it had been a poleaxe, and in the hands of his worst enemy.* I *will* have patience, Jack; I *will* have patience! My day is at hand. Then will I steel my heart with these remembrances.

How passion drives a man on! Now my resentments are warm, I will see, and perhaps will punish, this proud, this *double*-armed beauty. I have sent to tell her that I must be admitted to sup with her. We have neither of us dined: she refused to drink tea in the afternoon. And

I believe neither of us will have much stomach to our supper.

Letter 200: MISS CLARISSA HARLOWE TO MISS HOWE

Sunday morning, May 21
Near nine o'clock

I have your kind letter of yesterday. He knows I have. And I shall expect that he will be inquisitive next time I see him after your opinion of his proposals. I doubted not your approbation of them, and had written an answer on that presumption; which is ready for him. He must study for occasions of procrastination, and to disoblige me, if now anything happens to set us at variance again.

He has just sent me word that he insists upon supping with me. As we had been in a good train for several days past, I thought it not prudent to break with him for little matters. Yet, to be in a manner threatened into his will, I know not how to bear that.

While I was considering, he came up and, tapping at my door, told me, in a very angry tone, he must see me this night. He could not rest, till he had been told what he had done to deserve this treatment.

I must go to him. Yet perhaps he has nothing new to say to me. I shall be very angry with him.

On my entering the dining-room, he took my hands in his, in such a humour as I saw plainly he was resolved to quarrel with me. *And for what?* I never in my life beheld in anybody such a wild, such an angry, such an impatient spirit. I was terrified; and instead of being as angry as I intended to be, I was forced to be all mildness. I can hardly remember what were his first words, I was so frighted. But, *You hate me, madam! You hate me, madam!* were some of them—with such a fierceness—I wished myself a thousand miles distant from him. I hate nobody, said I; I thank God I hate nobody. You terrify me, Mr Lovelace. Let me leave you. The man, my dear,

looked quite ugly. I never saw a man look so ugly, as
passion made him look. *And for what?* And he so
grasped my hands—fierce creature! In short, he seemed
by his looks, and by his words (once putting his arms
about me), to wish me to provoke him. So that I had
nothing to do but to beg of him, which I did repeatedly,
to permit me to withdraw; and to promise to meet him
at his own time in the morning.

It was with a very ill grace that he complied, on that
condition; and at parting he kissed my hand with such a
savageness, that a redness remains upon it still.

Perfect for me, my dearest Miss Howe, perfect for me,
I beseech you, your kind scheme with Mrs Townsend—
and I will then leave this man. See you not how from
step to step, he grows upon me? I tremble to look back
upon his encroachments. And now to give me cause to
apprehend more evil from him than indignation will permit me to express!

I was so disgusted with him, as well as frighted by
him, that on my return to my chamber, in a fit of passionate despair, I tore almost in two, the answer I had
written to his proposals.

I will see him in the morning, because I promised I
would. But I will go out, and that without him, or any
attendant.

Your CLARISSA HARLOWE

Letter 201: MR LOVELACE TO JOHN BELFORD, ESQ.

Monday morn. May 22
No generosity in this lady. None at all. Wouldst thou not
have thought that after I had permitted her to withdraw,
primed for mischief as I was, that she would meet me
next morning early; and that with a smile; making me
one of her best curtsies?

I was in the dining-room before six, expecting her. She
opened not her door. I went upstairs and down, and
hemmed, and called Will, called Dorcas: threw the doors
hard to; but still she opened not her door. Thus till half

an hour after eight, fooled I away my time; and then, breakfast ready, I sent Dorcas to request her company.

But I was astonished, when, following the wench at the first invitation, I saw her enter dressed, all but her gloves, and those and her fan in her hand; in the same moment, bidding Dorcas direct Will to get her a chair to the door.

Cruel creature, thought I, to expose me thus to the derision of the women below!

Going abroad, madam?

I am, sir.

I looked cursed silly, I am sure. You will breakfast first, I hope, madam, in a very humble strain: yet with an hundred tenter-hooks in my heart.

Had she given me more notice of her intention, I had perhaps wrought myself up to the frame I was in the day before, and begun my vengeance. And immediately came into my head all the virulence that had been transcribed for me from Miss Howe's letters, and in that I had transcribed myself.

Yes, she would drink one dish; and then laid her gloves and fan in the window just by.

I was perfectly disconcerted. I hemmed and hawed, and was going to speak several times; but knew not in what key. Who's modest now, thought I! Who's insolent now! How a tyrant of a woman confounds a bashful man! She was my Miss Howe, I thought; and I the Spiritless Hickman.

At last, I *will* begin, thought I.

She a dish—I a dish.

Sip, her eyes her own, she; like an haughty and imperious sovereign, conscious of dignity, every look a favour.

Sip, like her vassal, I; lips and hands trembling, and not knowing that I sipped or tasted.

Dorcas came in just then. Dorcas, said she, is a chair gone for?

Damned impertinence, thought I, putting me out of my speech! And I was forced to wait for the servant's answer to the insolent mistress's question.

William is gone for one, madam.

What weather is it, Dorcas? said she, as regardless of me, as if I had not been present.

A little lowering, madam. The sun is gone in. It was very fine half an hour ago.

I had no patience. Up I rose. Down went the tea-cup, saucer and all. Confound the weather, the sunshine, and the wench! Begone for a devil, when I am speaking to your lady, and have so little opportunity given me.

Up rose the lady, half frighted; and snatched from the window her gloves and fan.

You must not go, madam!—by my soul, you must not—taking her hand.

Must not, sir! But I must. You can curse your maid in my absence, as well as if I were present. Except—except—you intend for *me,* what you direct to *her.*

Do not make me desperate, madam. Had Miss Howe been my friend, I had not been thus treated. It is but too plain to whom my difficulties are owing. I have long observed that every letter you receive from her makes an alteration in your behaviour to me. She would have *you* treat *me,* as *she* treats Mr Hickman, I suppose: but neither does that treatment become your admirable temper to offer, nor me to receive.

This startled her. She did not care to have me think hardly of Miss Howe.

But recollecting herself, Miss Howe, said she, is a friend to virtue, and to good men. If she like not you, it is because you are not one of those.

Yes, madam; and therefore, to speak of Mr Hickman and myself, as you both, I suppose, think of each, she treats *him* as she would not treat a *Lovelace.*

She would have flung from me: I *will* go out, Mr Lovelace. I will *not* be detained.

Indeed you must not, madam, in this humour. And I placed myself between her and the door. And then she threw herself into a chair, fanning herself, her sweet face all crimsoned over with passion.

Monday evening

At my repeated request she condescended to meet me in the dining-room to afternoon tea, and not before.

She entered with bashfulness, as I thought; in a pretty confusion for having carried her apprehensions too far.

Sullen and slow moved she towards the tea-table. Dorcas present, busy in tea-cup preparations. I took her reluctant hand, and pressed it to my lips. Dearest, loveliest of creatures, why this distance? Why this displeasure? How can you thus torture the faithfullest heart in the world? She disengaged her hand.

Oh Mr Lovelace, we have been long enough together to be tired of each other's humours and ways; ways and humours so different, that perhaps you ought to dislike *me*, as much as I do *you*. I think, I think, that I cannot make an answerable return to the value you profess for me. My temper is utterly ruined. You have given me an ill opinion of all mankind; of yourself in particular: and withal so bad a one of myself that I shall never be able to look up, having utterly and for ever lost all that self-complacency and conscious pride, which are so necessary to carry a woman through this life with tolerable satisfaction to herself.

She paused. I was silent. By my soul, thought I, this sweet creature will at last undo me!

She proceeded. What now remains, but that you pronounce me free of all obligation to you? And that you will not hinder me from pursuing the destiny that shall be allotted me?

Again she paused. I was still silent; meditating whether to renounce all further designs upon her; whether I had not received sufficient evidence of a virtue, and of a greatness of soul, that could not be questioned or impeached.

She went on: Propitious to me be your silence, Mr Lovelace! Tell me that I am free of all obligation to you. You know I never made *you* promises. You know that you are not under any to *me*. My broken fortunes I matter not.

I had not a word to say for myself. Such a war in my mind had I never known. Gratitude, and admiration of the excellent creature before me, combating with villainous habit, with resolutions so premeditately made, and with views so much gloried in! An hundred new contrivances in my head, and in my heart, that, to be honest, as it is called, must all be given up by a heart delighting in intrigue and difficulty. Miss Howe's virulences endeavoured to be recollected—yet recollection refusing to bring them forward with the requisite efficacy.

One favour, dearest creature. Let me but know whether Miss Howe approves or disapproves of my proposals? I know her to be my enemy. Must not, madam, the sudden change in your conduct, the very next morning, astonish and distress me? And this persisted in with still stronger declarations, after you had received the impatiently-expected letter from Miss Howe; must I not conclude, that all was owing to her influence; and that some other application or project was meditating, that made it necessary to keep me again at distance till the result were known, and which was to deprive me of you for ever? for was not that your constantly proposed preliminary? Well, madam, might I be wrought up to a half-frenzy by this apprehension; and well might I charge you with hating me. And now, dearest creature, let me know, I once more ask you, what is Miss Howe's opinion of my proposals?

Were I disposed to debate with you, Mr Lovelace, I could very easily answer your fine harangue. But at present, I shall only say that your ways have been very unaccountable. Whether owing in you to the want of a clear head, or a sound heart, I cannot determine; but it is to the want of one of them, I verily think, that I am to ascribe the greatest part of your strange conduct.

Curse upon the heart of the little devil, said I, who instigates you to think so hardly of the faithfullest heart in the world!

How dare you, sir? And there she stopped; having almost overshot herself; as I designed she should.

How dare I *what*, madam? And I looked with meaning. How dare I *what*?

Vile man! And do you—and there again she stopped.

Do I *what*, madam? And why *vile man*?

How dare you to curse *anybody* in my presence?

Well, madam, it is just as I thought. And now I know how to account for a temper, that I hope is not *natural* to you.

Artful wretch! And is it thus you would entrap me? But know, sir, that I receive letters from nobody but

Miss Howe. Miss Howe likes some of your ways as little as I do; for I have set everything before her. Yet she is thus far *your* enemy, as she is *mine*—she thinks I should not refuse your offers; but endeavour to make the best of my lot. And now you have the truth. Would to Heaven you were capable of dealing with equal sincerity!

I *am*, madam. And here, on my knee, I renew my vows, and my supplication, that you will make me yours—yours for ever. And let me have cause to bless you and Miss Howe in the same breath.

To say the truth, Belford, I had before begun to think that that vixen of a girl, who certainly likes not Hickman, was in love with *me*.

Rise, sir, from your too-ready knees; and mock me not.

Mock you, madam! and I arose, and re-urged her for the [wedding] day.

My day, sir, said she, is never. But I will retire. I will see you again tomorrow. I cannot before. I think I hate you. You may look—Indeed I think I hate you. And if, upon a re-examination of my own heart, I find I do, I would not for the world that matters should go on farther between us.

I was too much vexed, disconcerted, mortified, to hinder her retiring.

Letter 207: MR LOVELACE TO JOHN BELFORD, ESQ.

Thursday, May 25

Now have I a foundation to go upon in my terms. My lord, in the exuberance of his generosity, mentions a thousand pounds a year penny-rents. *This* I know, that were I to marry this lady, he would rather settle upon her all he has a mind to settle, than upon me: and has even threatened that if I prove not a good husband to her, he will leave all he can at his death, from me, to her. Yet considers not that a woman so perfect can never be displeased with her husband but to *his* disgrace; for who will blame *her*? Another reason why a Lovelace should not wish to marry a Clarissa.

But what a pretty fellow of an uncle mine, to think of making a wife independent of her emperor, and a rebel of course—yet smarted himself for an error of this kind!

My beloved, in her torn paper, mentions but two hundred pounds a year for her separate use. I insisted upon her naming a larger sum. She said it might then be three; and I, for fear she should suspect very large offers, named five, and the entire disposal of all arrears in her father's hands, for the benefit of Mrs Norton, or whom she pleased.

But yet, what mortifies my pride is, that this exalted creature, if I were to marry her, would not be governed in her behaviour to me by love, but by generosity merely, or by blind duty; and had rather live single, than be mine.

I cannot bear this. I would have the woman whom I honour with my name, if ever I confer this honour upon any, forgo even her superior duties for me. I would have her look after me when I go out, as far as she can see me, as my Rosebud after her Johnny; and meet me at my return with rapture. I would be the subject of her dreams, as well as of her waking thoughts. I would have her look upon every moment lost, that is not passed with me: sing to me, read to me, play to me when I pleased; no joy so great as in obeying me. When I should be inclined to love, overwhelm me with it; when to be serious or solitary, if intrusive, awfully so; retiring at a nod; approaching me only if I smiled encouragement: steal into my presence with silence; out of it, if not noticed, on tiptoe. Be a *Lady Easy* to all my pleasures, and valuing those most, who most contributed to them; only sighing in private, that it was not *herself* at the time. Thus of old did the contending wives of the honest patriarchs; each recommending her handmaid to her lord, as she thought it would oblige him, and looking upon the genial product as her own.

Another agreeable conversation. The day of days the subject. As to fixing a particular one, that need not be done till the settlements are completed. As to marrying at my lord's chapel, the ladies of my family present, that would be making a public affair of it; and my charmer observed with regret, that it seemed to be my lord's intention to make it so.

The sex may say what they will, but a poor innocent fellow had need to take great care of himself, when he dances upon the edge of the matrimonial precipice. Many a faint-hearted man, when he began in jest, or only designed to ape gallantry, has been forced into earnest, by being over-prompt, and taken at his word, not knowing how to own that he meant less than the lady supposed he meant.

Then these little sly rogues, how they lie couchant, ready to spring upon us harmless fellows the moment we are in their reach! When the ice is once broken for them, how swiftly can they make to port! Meantime, the subject they can least *speak* to, they most *think* of. Nor can you talk of the ceremony before they have laid out in their minds how it is all to be. Little saucy-face designers! how first they draw themselves in, then us!

LOVELACE

Letter 209: MR LOVELACE TO JOHN BELFORD, ESQ.

Wilt thou believe me, when I tell thee that I have so many contrivances rising up and crowding upon me for preference, with regard to my Gloriana, that I hardly know which to choose? I could tell thee of no less than six princely ones, any of which *must* do. But as the dear creature has not grudged giving me trouble, I think I ought not, in gratitude, to spare combustibles for her; but, on the contrary, to make her stare and stand aghast, by springing three or four mines at once.

And now, Jack, what dost think?

That thou art a cursed fellow, if—

If! No if's. But I shall be very sick tomorrow. I shall, 'faith.

Sick! Why sick? What a devil shouldst thou be sick for?

Perhaps thou thinkest my view to be, to draw the lady to my bedside: that's a trick of three or four thousand years old; and I should find it much more to my purpose, if I could get to hers. However, I'll condescend to make thee as wise as myself.

I don't intend to be so very bad as Dorcas shall represent me to be. But yet I know I shall retch confoundedly, and bring up some clotted blood. To be sure, I shall break a vessel: there's no doubt of that; and a bottle of Eaton's styptic shall be sent for; but no doctor. If she has *humanity*, she will be concerned. But if she has *love*, let it have been pushed ever so far back, it will, on this occasion, come forward, and show itself; not only in her eye, but in every line of her sweet face.

I will be very intrepid. I will not fear death, or anything else. I will be sure of being well in an hour or two, having formerly found great benefit by this balsamic medicine, on occasion of an inward bruise by a fall from my horse in hunting, of which, perhaps, this malady may be the remains. And this will show her, that though those about me may make the most of it, I don't; and so can have no design in it.

Well, methinks thou sayest, I begin to think tolerably of this device.

I knew thou wouldst, when I explained myself.

Now, Belford, if she be not much concerned at the broken vessel, which, in one so fiery in his temper as I have the reputation to be thought, may be very dangerous; a malady that I shall calmly attribute to the harasses and doubts that I have laboured under for some time past; which will be a further proof of my love, and will demand a grateful return—

What then, thou egregious contriver?

Why then I shall have the less remorse, if I am to use a little violence: for can she deserve compassion, who shows none?

And what if she show a great deal of concern?

Then shall I be in hope of building on a good foundation. Love hides a multitude of faults, and diminishes those it cannot hide. Love, when found out or acknowledged, authorizes freedom; and freedom begets freedom; and I shall then see how far I can go.

Well but, Lovelace, how the deuce wilt thou, with that full health and vigour of constitution, and with that bloom in thy face, make anybody believe thou art sick?

How! Why take a few grains of ipecacuanha; enough to make me retch like a fury.

Good! But how wilt thou manage to bring up blood, and not hurt thyself?

Foolish fellow! Are there not pigeons and chickens in every poulterer's shop?

And now, Belford, wilt thou, or wilt thou not, allow that it is a right thing to be sick? Lord, Jack, so much delight do I take in my contrivances, that I shall be half sorry when the occasion for them is over; for never, never shall I again have such charming exercise for my invention.

Letter 211: MR LOVELACE TO JOHN BELFORD, ESQ.

Cocoa Tree [coffee house], Saturday, May 27

This ipecacuanha is a most disagreeable medicine! That these cursed physical folks can find out nothing to do us good, but what would poison the devil!

But now this was to take down my countenance. It has done it: for, with violent retchings, having taken enough to make me sick, and not enough water to carry it off, I presently looked as if I had kept my bed a fortnight.

Two hours it held me. I had forbid Dorcas to let my beloved know anything of the matter; out of tenderness to her; being willing, when she knew my prohibition, to let her see that I *expected* her to be concerned for me.

Well, but Dorcas nevertheless is a *woman*, and she can *whisper* to her lady the secret she is enjoined to keep!

What's the matter, Dorcas?

Nothing, madam.

My beloved wonders she has not seen me this morning, no doubt; but is too shy to say she wonders. Repeated What's the matter's, however, as Dorcas runs up and down stairs by her door, bring on, Oh! madam! my master!—my master!

What! How! When!—and all the monosyllables of surprise.

I must not tell you, madam. My master ordered me not to tell you. But he is in a worse way than he thinks for! But he would not have *you* frighted.

High concern took possession of every sweet feature. She pitied me! By my soul, she pitied me!

Out she darts. As how! as how, Dorcas!

Oh madam—a vomiting of blood! a vessel broke, to be sure!

Down she hastens; finds everyone as busy over my blood in the entry, as if it were that of the Neapolitan saint.

In steps my charmer! with a face of sweet concern.

How do you, Mr Lovelace!

Oh my best love! Very well! Very well! Nothing at all! Nothing of consequence! I shall be well in an instant!

In short, Belford, I have gained my end. I see the dear soul loves me. I see she forgives me all that's past. I see I have credit for a new score.

Nor will the choicest of my fair one's favours be long prohibited goods to me!

Everyone now is sure that she loves me. Tears were in her eyes more than once for me. She suffered me to take her hand, and kiss it as often as I pleased. On Mrs Sinclair's mentioning that I too much confined myself, she pressed me to take an airing, but obligingly desired me to be careful of myself. Wished I would advise with a physician.

I kissed her hand again! She was all goodness! Would to Heaven I better deserved it, I said! But all were golden days before us! Her presence and generous concern had done everything. I was well! Nothing ailed me. But since my beloved will have it so, I'll take a little airing! Let a chair be called! All the art of healing is in your smiles! Your late displeasure was the only malady!

And now, Belford, was it not worth while to be sick? And yet I must tell thee, that too many pleasanter expedients offer themselves, to make trial any more of this confounded ipecacuanha.

Letter 219: MR LOVELACE TO JOHN BELFORD, ESQ.

Friday, June 2

Notwithstanding my studied-for politeness and complaisance for some days past; and though I have wanted

courage to throw the mask quite aside; yet I have made
the dear creature more than once look about her by the
warm though decent expressions of my passion.

I endeavoured to justify my passion, by laying over-
delicacy at her door. That was *not*, she said, *my* fault, if
it were *hers*. She must plainly tell me that I appeared to
her incapable of distinguishing what were the requisites
of a pure mind.

I have just now been called to account for some innocent liberties which I thought myself entitled to take
before the women; as they suppose us married, and now
within view of consummation.

I took the lecture very hardly; and with impatience
wished for the happy day and hour when I might call
her all my own, and meet with no check from a niceness
that had no example.

She looked at me with a bashful kind of contempt. I
thought it *contempt*, and required the reason for it; not
being conscious of offence, as I told her.

This is not the first time, Mr Lovelace, said she, that
I have had cause to be displeased with you, when you,
perhaps, have not thought yourself exceptionable. But,
sir, let me tell you that the married state, in my eye, is
a state of purity, and (I think she told me) not of *licen-
tiousness*; so at least, I understood her.

Marriage purity, Jack! Very comical, 'faith. Yet, sweet
dears, half the female world ready to run away with a
rake, *because* he is a rake; and for no *other* reason; nay,
every other reason *against* their choice.

From the whole of the above, thou wilt gather that I
have not been a mere dangler, a Hickman, in the past
days, though not absolutely active and a Lovelace.

The dear creature now considers herself as my wife-
elect. The *unsaddened* heart, no longer prudish, will not
now, I hope, give the sable turn to every action of the
man she dislikes not. And yet she must keep up so
much reserve as will justify past inflexibilities. Many
and many a pretty soul would yield, were she not afraid
that the man she favoured would think the worse of
her for it.

Sat. June 3

Just returned from Doctors' Commons. I have been endeavouring to get a licence. Very true, Jack. I have the mortification to find a difficulty in obtaining this all-fettering instrument, as the lady is of rank and fortune, and as there is no consent of father or *next friend*.

I made report of this difficulty. It is very right, she says, that such difficulties should be made.

I asked if she approved of the settlements? She said she had compared them with my mother's, and had no objection. She had written to Miss Howe upon the subject, she owned; and to inform her of our present situation.

We have held that women have no souls. And if so, to whom shall I be accountable for what I do to them? Nay, if souls they have, as there is no sex in ethereals, nor need of any, what plea can a lady hold of injuries done her in her lady-*state*, when there is an end of her lady-*ship*?

Letter 220: MR LOVELACE TO JOHN BELFORD, ESQ.

Monday, June 5

I am now almost in despair of succeeding with this charming frost-piece by love or gentleness. I have been again at the Commons.

Twice indeed with rapture, which once she called rude, did I salute her; and each time, resenting the freedom, did she retire; though, to do her justice, she favoured me again with her presence at my first entreaty, and took no notice of the cause of her withdrawing.

Is it policy to show so open a resentment for innocent liberties which, in her situation, she must so soon forgive?

Yet the woman who resents not initiatory freedoms must be lost. For love is an encroacher. Love never goes backward. Love is always aspiring. Always must aspire. Nothing but the highest act of love can satisfy an indulged love. And what advantages has a lover who val-

ues not breaking the peace, over his mistress who is
solicitous to keep it!

I have now at this instant wrought myself up, for the
dozenth time, to a half-resolution. A thousand agreeable
things I have to say to her. She is in the dining-room.
Just gone up. She always expects me when there.

I sat down by her. I took both her hands in mine. I
would *have* it so. All gentle my voice. Her father mentioned with respect. Her mother with reverence. Even
her brother amicably spoken of. I never thought I could
have wished so ardently, as I told her I did wish, for a
reconciliation with her family.

A sweet and grateful flush then overspread her fair
face; a gentle sigh now and then heaved her
handkerchief.

I would hasten again to the Commons; and would not
return without the licence.

The Lawn I proposed to retire to, as soon as the
happy ceremony was over. This day and that day I
proposed.

It was time enough to name the day when the settlements were completed, and the licence obtained.

No new delays, for heaven's sake, I besought her; reproaching her gently for the past. Name but the day—
an early day, I hoped in the following week—that I
might hail its approach and number the tardy hours.

My cheek reclined on her shoulder—kissing her hands
by turns. Rather bashfully than angrily reluctant, her
hands sought to be withdrawn; her shoulder avoiding
my reclined cheek—apparently loath and more loath to
quarrel with me; her downcast eye confessing more than
her lips could utter. Now surely, thought I, it is my time
to try if she can forgive a still bolder freedom than I
had ever yet taken.

I then gave her struggling hands liberty. I put one arm
round her waist: I imprinted a kiss on her sweet lips,
with a *Be quiet* only, and an averted face, as if she
feared another.

Encouraged by so gentle a repulse, the tenderest
things I said; and then, with my other hand, drew aside
the handkerchief that concealed the beauty of beauties,

and pressed with my burning lips the charmingest breast
that ever my ravished eyes beheld.

A very contrary passion to that which gave her bosom
so delightful a swell immediately took place. She struggled out of my encircling arms with indignation. I detained her reluctant hand. Let me go, said she. I see
there is no keeping terms with you. Base encroacher! Is
this the design of your flattering speeches? Far as matters have gone, I will for ever renounce you. You have
an odious heart. Let me go, I tell you.

I was forced to obey, and she flung from me, repeating
base, and adding *flattering*, encroacher.

In vain have I urged by Dorcas for the promised favour of dining with her. She would not dine *at all*. She
could not.

But why makes she every inch of her person thus
sacred?—so near the time too, that she must suppose, that
all will be my own by deed of purchase and settlement?

And should not my beloved, for her own sake, descend by *degrees* from *goddess-hood* into *humanity*? If
it be *pride* that restrains her, ought not that pride to
be punished?

Let me perish, Belford, if I would not forgo the brightest diadem in the world for the pleasure of seeing a twin
Lovelace at each charming breast, drawing from it his
first sustenance; the pious task continued for one month,
and no more!

I now, methinks, behold this most charming of women
in this sweet office, pressing with her fine fingers the
generous flood into the purple mouths of each eager
hunter by turns: her conscious eye now dropped on one,
now on the other, with a sigh of maternal tenderness;
and then raised up to my delighted eye, full of wishes,
for the sake of the pretty varlets, and for her own sake,
that I would deign to legitimate; that I would condescend to put on the nuptial fetters.

Letter 224: MR LOVELACE TO JOHN BELFORD, ESQ.

Wednesday night, 11 o'clock

Faith, Jack, thou hadst half undone me with thy non-sense, though I would not own it in my yesterday's letter. But I think I am my own man again.

So near to execution my plot! So near springing my mine!

I have time for a few lines preparative to what is to happen in an hour or two; and I love to write to the moment.

We have been extremely happy. How many agreeable days have we known together! What may the next two hours produce!

When I parted with my charmer (which I did with infinite reluctance, half an hour ago), it was upon her promise that she would not sit up to write or read. For so engaging was the conversation to me (and indeed my behaviour throughout the whole of it was confessedly agreeable to her), that I insisted, if she did not directly retire to rest, that she should add another happy hour to the former.

To have sat up writing or reading half the night, as she sometimes does, would have frustrated my view, as thou wilt observe when my little plot unravels.

What—what—what now!—bounding villain! wouldst thou choke me!

I was speaking to my heart, Jack! It was then at my throat. And what is all this for? These shy ladies, how, when a man thinks himself near the mark, do they tempest him!

Is all ready, Dorcas? Has my beloved kept her word with me? Whether are these billowy heavings owing more to love or to fear? I cannot tell for the soul of me which I have most of. If I can but take her before her apprehension, before her eloquence, is awake.

Limbs, why thus convulsed! Knees, till now so firmly knit, why thus relaxed? Why beat ye thus together? Will not these trembling fingers, which twice have refused to direct the pen, and thus curvedly deform the paper, fail me in the arduous moment?

Why and for what all these convulsions? This project
is not to end in matrimony surely!

But the consequences must be greater than I had
thought of till this moment. My beloved's destiny or my
own may depend upon the issue of the two next hours!

I will recede, I think!

Soft, oh virgin saint, and safe as soft, be thy slumbers!

I will now once more turn to my friend Belford's letter. Thou shalt have fair play, my charmer. I'll re-peruse
what thy advocate has to say for thee. Weak arguments
will do, in the frame I am in!

But, what's the matter! What's the matter! But the
uproar abates! What a *double coward* am I? Or is it that
I am taken in a cowardly minute? for heroes have their
fits of *fear*; cowards their *brave* moments: and virtuous
ladies, all but my Clarissa, their moment *critical*—

But thus coolly enjoying thy reflections in a hurricane!
Again the confusion's renewed!

What! Where! How came it!

Is my beloved safe!

Oh wake not too roughly my beloved!

Letter 225: MR LOVELACE TO JOHN BELFORD, ESQ.

Thursday morning, five o'clock (June 8)

Now is my reformation secured; for I never shall love
any other woman! Oh she is all variety! She must be
ever new to me! *Imagination* cannot form; much less can
the pencil paint; nor can the soul of painting, *poetry*,
describe an angel so exquisitely, so elegantly lovely!

Thus then, connecting my last with the present, I lead
to it.

Didst thou not, by the conclusion of my former, perceive the consternation I was in, just as I was about to
re-peruse thy letter, in order to prevail upon myself to
recede from my purpose of awaking in terrors my slum-
bering charmer? And what dost thou think was the
matter?

I'll tell thee.

At a little after two, when the whole house was still,

or seemed to be so, and, as it proved, my Clarissa abed
and fast asleep; I also in a manner undressed for an hour
before, and in my gown and slippers though, to oblige
thee, writing on—I was alarmed by a trampling noise
overhead, and a confused buzz of mixed voices, some
louder than others, like scolding, and little short of
screaming, all raised to vocatives, as in a fright: and
while I was wondering what could be the matter, downstairs ran Dorcas, and at my door, in an accent rather
frightedly and hoarsely inward than shrilly clamorous,
cried out Fire! Fire! And this the more alarmed me, as
she seemed to endeavour to cry out louder, but could
not.

My pen (its last scrawl a benediction on my beloved)
dropped from my fingers; and up started I; and making
but three steps to the door, opened it, and cried Where!
Where! almost as much terrified as the wench. While
she, more than half-undressed, her petticoats in her
hand, unable to speak distinctly, pointed upstairs.

I was there in a moment, and found all owing to the
carelessness of Mrs Sinclair's cook-maid, who, having sat
up to read the simple history of Dorastus and Faunia
when she should have been in bed, had set fire to an
old pair of calico window-curtains.

She had had the presence of mind in her fright, to
tear down the half-burnt valance as well as curtains, and
had got them, though blazing, into the chimney, by the
time I came up; so that I had the satisfaction to find the
danger happily over.

Meantime Dorcas, after she had directed me upstairs,
not knowing the worst was over, and expecting every
minute the house would be in a blaze, out of tender
regard for her lady (I shall for ever love the wench for
it) ran to her door, and rapping loudly at it, in a recovered voice, cried out with a shrillness equal to her love,
Fire! Fire! The house is on fire! Rise, madam! This instant rise—if you would not be burnt in your bed!

No sooner had she made this dreadful outcry, but I
heard her lady's door with hasty violence unbar, unbolt,
unlock, and open, and my charmer's voice sounding like
that of one going into a fit.

You may believe how much I was affected. I trembled

with concern for her, and hastened down faster than the alarm of fire had made me run up, in order to satisfy her that all the danger was over.

When I had *flown down* to her chamber door, there I beheld the charmingest creature in the world, supporting herself on the arm of the gasping Dorcas, sighing, trembling, and ready to faint, with nothing on but an under-petticoat, her lovely bosom half-open, and her feet just slipped into her shoes. As soon as she saw me, she panted, and struggled to speak; but could only say, oh, Mr Lovelace! and down was ready to sink.

I clasped her in my arms with an ardour she never felt before: My dearest life! fear nothing: I have been up—the danger is over—the fire is got under. And how (foolish devil! to Dorcas) could you thus, by your hideous yell, alarm and frighten my angel!

Oh Jack! how her sweet bosom, as I clasped her to mine, heaved and panted! I could even distinguish her dear heart flutter, flutter, flutter, against mine; and for a few minutes, I feared she would go into fits.

Lest the half-lifeless charmer should catch cold in this undress, I lifted her to her bed, and sat down by her upon the side of it, endeavouring with the utmost tenderness, as well of action as expression, to dissipate her terrors.

But, far from being affected by an address so fervent (although from a man she had so lately owned a regard for, and with whom, but an hour or two before, she had parted with so much satisfaction), that I never saw a bitterer, or more moving grief, when she came fully to herself.

She appealed to Heaven against my *treachery*, as she called it; while I, by the most solemn vows, pleaded my own equal fright, and the reality of the danger that had alarmed us both.

She conjured me, in the most solemn and affecting manner, by turns threatening and soothing, to quit her apartment, and permit her to hide herself from the light, and from every human eye.

I besought her pardon, yet could not avoid offending; and repeatedly vowed that the next morning's sun should witness our espousals. But taking, I suppose, all my protestations of this kind, as an indication that I intended to proceed to the last extremity, she would hear nothing that I said; but, redoubling her struggles to get from me, in broken accents, and exclamations the most vehement, she protested that she would not survive what she called a treatment so disgraceful and villainous; and, looking all wildly round her as if for some instrument of mischief, she espied a pair of sharp-pointed scissors on a chair by the bedside, and endeavoured to catch them up, with design to make her words good on the spot.

Seeing her desperation, I begged her to be pacified; that she would hear me speak but one word, declaring that I intended no dishonour to her: and having seized the scissors, I threw them into the chimney; and she still insisting vehemently upon my distance, I permitted her to take the chair.

But, oh the sweet discomposure! Her bared shoulders and arms, so inimitably fair and lovely: her spread hands crossed over her charming neck; yet not half concealing its glossy beauties: the scanty coat, as she rose from me, giving the whole of her admirable shape and fine-turned limbs: her eyes running over, yet seeming to threaten future vengeance: and at last her lips uttering what every indignant look and glowing feature portended; exclaiming as if I had done the worst I could do, and vowing never to forgive me; wilt thou wonder that I could avoid resuming the incensed, the already too-much-provoked fair one?

I did; and clasped her once more to my bosom: but, considering the delicacy of her frame, her force was amazing, and showed how much in earnest she was in her resentment; for it was with the utmost difficulty that I was able to hold her: nor could I prevent her sliding through my arms, to fall upon her knees: which she did at my feet. And there, in the anguish of her soul, her streaming eyes lifted up to my face with supplicating softness, hands folded, dishevelled hair; for her night head-dress having fallen off in her struggling, her charming tresses fell down in naturally shining ringlets, as if officious to conceal the dazzling beauties of her neck and shoulders; her lovely bosom too heaving with sighs,

and broken sobs, as if to aid her quivering lips in pleading for her—in this manner, but when her grief gave way
to her speech, in words pronounced with that emphatical
propriety which distinguishes this admirable creature in
her elocution from all the women I ever heard speak;
did she implore my compassion, and my honour.

'Consider me, *dear* Lovelace,' were her charming
words! 'on my knees I beg you to consider me, as a
poor creature who has no protector but you; who has
no defence but your honour: by that honour! by your
humanity! by all you have vowed! I conjure you not
to make me abhor myself! Not to make me vile in my
own eyes!'

I mentioned the morrow as the happiest day of my
life.

Tell me not of tomorrow; if indeed you mean me honourably, *now*, this very instant NOW! you must show it,
and begone! You can never in a whole long life repair
the evils you may NOW make me suffer!

Wicked wretch!—insolent villain! Yes, she called me
insolent villain, although so much in my power! And
for what?—only for kissing (with passion indeed) her
inimitable neck, her lips, her cheeks, her forehead, and
her streaming eyes, as this assemblage of beauties offered itself at once to my ravished sight; she continuing
kneeling at my feet, as I sat.

If I *am* a villain, madam—And then my grasping but
trembling hand—I hope I did not hurt the tenderest and
loveliest of all her beauties. If I am a villain, madam—

She tore my ruffle, shrunk from my happy hand, with
amazing force and agility, as with my other arm I would
have encircled her waist.

Indeed you are! The worst of villains! Help! dear
blessed people! and screamed—No help for a poor
creature!

Am I then a villain, madam? *Am* I then a villain, say
you?—and clasped both my arms about her, offering to
raise her to my bounding heart.

Oh no! and yet you are! And again I was her *dear*
Lovelace! Her hands again clasped over her charming
bosom. Kill me! kill me!—if I am odious enough in your
eyes, to deserve this treatment; and I will thank you!

Too long, much too long, has my life been a burden to me!—or, wildly looking all around her, give me but the means, and I will instantly convince you that my honour is dearer to me than my life!

Then, with still folded hands, and fresh-streaming eyes, I was her *blessed* Lovelace; and she would thank me with her latest breath if I would permit her to make that preference, or free her from farther indignities.

I sat suspended for a moment. By my soul, thought I, thou art upon full proof an angel and no woman! Still, however, close clasping her to my bosom, as I had raised her from her knees, she again slid through my arms, and dropped upon them: 'See, Mr Lovelace! Good God! that I should live to see this hour, and to bear this treatment! see, at your feet a poor creature, imploring your pity, who for your sake is abandoned of all the world! Let not my father's curse thus dreadfully operate! Be not you the inflicter, who have been the *cause* of it! But spare me! I beseech you spare me!—for how have I deserved this treatment from you? For your own sake, if not for my sake, and as you would that God Almighty, in your last hour, should have mercy upon you, spare me!'

What heart but must have been penetrated?

I would again have raised the dear suppliant from her knees; but she would not be raised, till my softened mind, she said, had yielded to her prayer, and bid her rise to be innocent.

Rise then, my angel, rise, and be what you are, and all you wish to be! Only pronounce me pardoned for what has passed, and tell me you will continue to look upon me with that eye of favour and serenity, which I have been blessed with for some days past, and I will submit to my beloved conqueress, whose power never was at so great an height with me, as now; and retire to my apartment.

God Almighty, said she, hear your prayers in your most arduous moments, as you have heard mine! And now leave me, this moment leave me, to my own recollection: in *that* you will leave me to misery enough, and more than you ought to wish to your bitterest enemy.

Impute not everything, my best beloved, to design; for design it was not.

Oh Mr Lovelace!

Upon my soul, madam, the fire was real—(and so it was, Jack!). The house might have been consumed by it, as you will be convinced in the morning by ocular demonstration.

Oh Mr Lovelace!

Let my passion for you, madam, and the unexpected meeting of you at your chamber door, in an attitude so charming—

Leave me, leave me, this moment! I beseech you, leave me; looking wildly and in confusion, now about her, and now upon herself.

Excuse me, dearest creature, for those liberties which, innocent as they were, your too great delicacy may make you take amiss.

No more! no more! Leave me, I beseech you! Again looking upon herself, and around her, in a sweet confusion. Begone! Begone! Then weeping, she struggled vehemently to withdraw her hands, which all the while I held between mine. Her struggles! Oh what additional charms, as I now reflect, did her struggles give to every feature, every limb, of a person so sweetly elegant and lovely!

Impossible! my dearest life, till you pronounce my pardon! Say but you forgive me! Say you do!

I beseech you, begone! Leave me to myself, that I may think what I *can* do, and what I *ought* to do.

That, my dearest creature, is not enough. You must tell me that I am forgiven; that you will see me tomorrow, as if nothing had happened.

And then, clasping her again in my arms, hoping she would not forgive me—

I will—I do forgive you—wretch that you are!

And will you look upon me tomorrow, as if nothing had passed?

Yes, yes!

I cannot take these peevish affirmatives, so much like intentional negatives! Say you will, upon your honour!

Upon my honour, then. Oh now, begone! begone! and never—

What, never, my angel! Is this forgiveness?

Never, said she, let what has passed be remembered more!

I insisted upon one kiss to seal my pardon—and retired like a fool, a woman's fool, as I was! I sneakingly retired! Couldst thou have believed it?

But I had no sooner entered my own apartment, than, reflecting upon the opportunity I had lost, and that all I had gained was but an increase of my own difficulties; and upon the ridicule I should meet with below, upon a weakness so much out of my usual character; I repented, and hastened back, in hope that through the distress of mind which I left her in, she had not so soon fastened her door; and I was fully resolved to execute all my purposes, be the consequence what it would; for, thought I, I have already sinned beyond *cordial* forgiveness, I doubt; and if fits and desperation ensue, I can but marry at last, and then I shall make her amends.

But I was justly punished—for her door was fast: and hearing her sigh and sob, as if her heart would burst, My beloved creature, said I, rapping gently, and her sobbings ceasing, I want but to say three words to you, which must be the most acceptable you ever heard from me. Let me see you but for one moment.

I thought I heard her coming to open the door, and my heart leaped in that hope; but it was only to draw another bolt to make it still the faster, and she either could not, or would not, answer me, but retired to the further end of her apartment, to her closet, probably: and more like a fool than before, again I sneaked away.

This was my mine, my plot! And this was all I made of it!

I love her more than ever! And well I may! Never saw I such polished ivory as her arms and shoulders seemed to be; never touched I velvet so soft as her skin. Then such an elegance! Oh Belford, she is all perfection! Her pretty foot, in her struggling, losing her shoe but just slipped on, as I told thee, equally white and delicate as the hand of any other lady, or even as her own hand!

But if she can *now* forgive me—*Can*! She *must*. Has she not upon her honour already done it? But how will the dear creature keep that part of her promise, which

engages her to see me in the morning as if nothing
had happened?

As to thy apprehensions of her committing any rashness
upon herself, whatever she might have done in her passion,
if she could have seized upon her scissors, or found any
other weapon, I dare say there is no fear of that from her
deliberate mind. A man has trouble enough with these truly
pious, and truly virtuous girls (now I believe there are
such); he had need to have some benefit *from*, some security *in*, the rectitude of their minds.

In short, I fear nothing in this lady but grief; yet that's
a slow worker, you know; and gives time to pop in a
little joy between its sullen fits.

Letter 226: MR LOVELACE TO JOHN BELFORD, ESQ.

Thursday morning, eight o'clock

Her chamber door has not yet been opened. I must not
expect she will breakfast with me: nor dine with me, I
doubt. A little silly soul, what troubles does she make
to herself by her over-niceness! All I have done to her
would have been looked upon as a frolic only, a
romping-bout, and laughed off by nine parts in ten of
the sex accordingly. The more she makes of it, the more
painful to herself, as well as to me.

Past ten o'clock

I never longed in my life for anything with so much
impatience, as to see my charmer. She has been stirring,
it seems, these two hours.

Dorcas just now tapped at her door, to take her morning commands.

She had none for her, was the answer.

She desired to know if she would not breakfast?

A sullen and low-voiced *negative* she received.

I will go myself.

Three different times tapped I at the door, but had
no answer.

Permit me, dearest creature, to inquire after your

health. As you have not been seen today, I am impatient
to know how you do.

Not a word of answer; but a deep sigh, even to sobbing.

Let me beg of you, madam, to accompany me up another pair of stairs—you'll rejoice to see what a happy
escape we have all had.

A happy escape indeed, Jack!—for the fire had
scorched the window-board, singed the hangings, and
burned through the slit-deal lining of the window-jambs.

No answer, madam! Am I not worthy of one word?
Is it thus you keep your promise with me? Shall I not
have the favour of your company for two minutes, only
for two minutes, in the dining-room?

Then, in a faintish but angry voice, Begone from my
door!—wretch, inhuman, barbarous, and all that's base
and treacherous! Begone from my door! Nor tease thus
a poor creature, entitled to protection, not outrage.

Well, madam, I see how you keep your word with
me! *If* a sudden impulse, the effects of an unthought-of
accident, cannot be forgiven—

Oh the dreadful weight of a father's curse, thus in the
letter of it so likely to be fulfilled!

And then her voice dying away into inarticulate mur-
murs, I looked through the keyhole, and saw her on her
knees, her face, though not towards me, lifted up, as
well as hands, and these folded, deprecating I suppose
that gloomy tyrant's curse.

I could not help being moved.

My dearest life! When you see the reality of the danger that gave occasion for this your unhappy resentment,
you will think less hardly of me. And let me beseech
you to perform a promise, on which I made a reliance
not altogether ungenerous.

I cannot see you! Would to Heaven I never had! If I
write, that's all I can do.

Let your writing then, my dearest life, confirm your
promise. And I will withdraw in expectation of it.

Past eleven o'clock

Just now she rung her bell for Dorcas; and, with her
door in her hand, only half-opened, gave her a billet
for me.

These are the contents. No inscriptive Sir! No Mr Lovelace!

I CANNOT see you: nor will I, if I can help it. Words cannot express the anguish of my soul on your baseness and ingratitude.

Vilest of men! and most detestable of plotters! how have I deserved from you the shocking indignities—But no more—only for your own sake, wish not, at least for a week to come, to see

The undeservedly injured and insulted,
CLARISSA HARLOWE

But not to see her for a week! Dear pretty soul! how she anticipates me in everything! The counsellor will have finished the writings, ready to sign, today or tomorrow at furthest: the licence with the parson, or the parson without the licence, must be also procured within the next four-and-twenty hours. *Yet not to see her for a week!* Dear sweet soul! Her good angel is gone a journey: is truanting at least. But nevertheless, in thy week's time, and much less, my charmer, I doubt not to have completed my triumph!

Letter 228: MR LOVELACE TO JOHN BELFORD, ESQ.

Thursday evening, June 8

Oh for a curse to kill with! Ruined! Undone! Outwitted, tricked! Zounds, man, the lady is gone off! Absolutely gone off! Escaped!

And thou, too, who hast endeavoured to weaken my hands, wilt but clap thy dragon's wings at the tidings!

Yet I must write, or I shall go distracted. Little less have I been these two hours; dispatching messengers to every stage; to every inn; to every waggon or coach, whether flying or creeping, and to every house with a bill up, for five miles round.

The little hypocrite, who knows not a soul in this town *(I thought I was sure of her at any time)* such an inexperienced traitress; giving me hope too, in her first billet, that her expectation of the family reconciliation would

withhold her from taking such a step as this. Curse upon
her contrivances! I thought that it was owing to her
bashfulness; to her modesty, that after a few innocent
freedoms she could not look me in the face; when, all
the while, she was impudently (yes, I say *impudently*,
though she be Clarissa Harlowe) contriving to rob me
of the dearest property I had ever purchased—
Purchased by a painful servitude of many months; fighting through the wild beasts of her family for her, and
combating with a windmill virtue, that hath cost me millions of perjuries only to attempt; and which now, with
its damned air-fans, has tossed me a mile and a half
beyond hope! And this, just as I had arrived within view
of the consummation of all my wishes!

To what purpose brought I this angel (angel I must
yet call her!) to this hellish house! And was I not meditating to do her deserved honour? By my soul, Belford,
I was resolved—But thou knowest what I had *condition-
ally* resolved. And now, though I was determined so
much in her favour, who can tell what hands she may
have fallen into?

I am mad, stark mad, by Jupiter, at the thoughts of this!
Unprovided, destitute, unacquainted—some villain, worse
than myself, who adores her not as I adore her, may have
seized her, and taken advantage of her distress!

Coming home with resolutions so favourable to her,
judge thou of my distraction when her escape was first
hinted to me, although but in broken sentences. I knew
not what I said, nor what I did; I wanted to kill somebody. I charged bribery and corruption, in my first fury,
upon all; and threatened destruction to old and young,
as they should come in my way.

Dorcas continues *locked* up from me: Sally and Polly
have not yet dared to appear: the vile Sinclair—

But here comes the odious devil: she taps at the door,
though that's only ajar, whining and snuffling, to try, I
suppose, to coax me into temper.

But *is* she, *can* she, be gone! Oh how Miss Howe will
triumph! But if that little fury receive her, fate shall

make me rich amends; for then will I contrive to have them both.

I have been traversing her room, meditating, or taking up everything she but touched or used: the glass she dressed at I was ready to break, for not giving me the personal image it was wont to reflect, of *her*, whose idea is for ever present with me. I call for her, now in the tenderest, now in the most reproachful terms, as if within hearing: wanting *her*, I want my own soul, at least everything dear to it. What a void in my heart! what a chillness in my blood, as if its circulation were arrested! From her room to my own; in the dining-room, and in and out of every place where I have seen the beloved of my heart, do I hurry; in none can I tarry; her lovely image in every one, in some lively attitude, rushing cruelly upon me, in differently remembered conversations.

But when in my first fury, at my return, I went up two pair of stairs, resolved to find the locked-up Dorcas, and beheld the vainly-burnt window-board, and recollected my baffled contrivances, baffled by my own weak folly, I thought my distraction completed, and down I ran as one frighted at a spectre, ready to howl for vexation; my head and my temples shooting with a violence I had never felt before; and my back aching as if the vertebrae were disjointed, and falling in pieces.

But now that I have heard the mother's [Mrs Sinclair's] story, and contemplated the dawning hopes given by the chairman's information, I am a good deal easier, and can make cooler reflections. If I lose her, all my rage will return with redoubled fury. The disgrace to be thus outwitted by a novice, an infant, in stratagem and contrivance, added to the violence of my passion for her, will either break my heart or (what saves many a heart in evils insupportable) turn my brain.

I have collected, from the result of the inquiries made of the chairman, and from Dorcas's observations before the cruel creature escaped, a description of her dress; and am resolved, if I cannot otherwise hear of her, to advertise her in the Gazette as an eloped wife, both by her maiden and acknowledged name.

She had on a brown lustring nightgown, fresh, and looking like new, as everything she wears does, whether new or not, from an elegance natural to her. A beaver hat, a black riband about her neck, and blue knots on her breast. A quilted petticoat, of carnation-coloured satin; a rose-diamond ring supposed on her finger; and in her whole person and appearance, as I shall express it, a dignity, as well as beauty, that commands the repeated attention of everyone who sees her.

The description of her person I shall take a little more pains about. My mind must be more at ease before I can undertake that. And I shall threaten that if, after a certain period given for her voluntary return, she be not heard of, I will prosecute any person who presumes to entertain, harbour, abet, or encourage her, with all the vengeance that an injured gentleman and husband may be warranted to take by law, or otherwise.

Letter 229: MR LOVELACE TO JOHN BELFORD, ESQ.

A letter is put into my hands by Wilson himself.
  Such a letter!
  A letter from Miss Howe to her cruel friend!
  I made no scruple to open it.
  It is a miracle that I fell not into fits at the reading of it; and at the thought of what might have been the consequence had it come to the hands of *this Clarissa Harlowe*. Let my justly excited rage excuse my irreverence.
  Oh this devilish Miss Howe! Something must be resolved upon, and done with that little fury!

Read it here; and avoid trembling for me, if thou canst.

to Miss Laetitia Beaumont

Wednesday, June 7

My dearest friend,
  You will perhaps think that I have been too long silent. But I had begun two letters at different times since

my last, and written a great deal each time; and with spirit enough, I assure you; incensed as I was against the abominable wretch you are with; particularly on reading yours of the 21st of the past month.

But I must stop here, and take a little walk, to try to keep down that just indignation which rises to my pen, when I am about to relate to you what I must communicate.

I am not my own mistress enough—then my mother—always up and down—and watching as if I were writing to a fellow—but I will try if I can contain myself in tolerable bounds—

The women of the house where you are—oh my dear—the women of the house—but you never thought highly of them—so it cannot be so very surprising—nor would you have stayed so long with them, had not the notion of removing to one of your own made you less uneasy, and less curious about their characters, and behaviour. In short, my dear, you are certainly in a devilish house! Be assured that the woman is one of the vilest of women!—nor does she go to you by her right name. Very true—her name is *not* Sinclair—nor is the street she lives in, Dover Street.

The wretch might indeed have held out these false lights a little more excusably had the house been an honest house; and had his end only been to prevent mischief from your brother. But this contrivance was antecedent, as I think, to your brother's project: so that no excuse can be made for his intentions at the *time*—The man, whatever he may *now* intend, was certainly then, even *then*, a villain in his heart!

I write, perhaps, with too much violence to be clear. But I cannot help it. Yet I lay down my pen, and take it up every ten minutes, in order to write with some temper. My mother too in and out. What need I (she asks me) lock myself in, if I am only reading past correspondencies? for that is my pretence, when she comes poking in with her face sharpened to an edge, as I may say, by a curiosity that gives her more pain than pleasure. The Lord forgive me; but I believe I shall huff her next time she comes in.

Do *you* forgive me too, my dear. My mother *ought*; because she says I am my father's girl; and because I am sure I am *hers*. I don't know what to do—I don't know what to write next—I have so much to write, yet have so little patience, and so little opportunity.

Oh my dear, the man is a villain! the greatest of villains in every light!

But can I think (you will ask with indignant astonishment), that Lovelace can have designs upon your honour?

That such designs he *has had*, if he *still* hold them not, I can have no doubt, now that I know the house he has brought you to, to be a vile one. This is a clue that has led me to account for all his behaviour to you ever since you have been in his hands.

I knew by experience that love is a fire that is not to be played with without burning one's fingers.

But now, my dear, do I apprehend that you are in greater danger than ever yet you have been in; if you are not married in a week; and yet stay in this abominable house. For were you out of it, I own, I should not be much afraid for you.

What then have you to do, but to fly this house, this infernal house! Oh that your heart would let you fly *him*!

But if you meet with the least ground for suspicion; if he would detain you at the odious house, or wish you to stay, now you know what the people are, fly *him*, whatever your prospects are, as well as *them*.

If you do not fly the house upon reading of this, or some way or other get out of it, I shall judge of his power over you by the little you will have over either him or yourself.

I shall send this long letter by Collins, who changes his day to oblige me; and that he may try (now I know where you are), to get it into your own hands. If he cannot, he will leave it at Wilson's. As none of our letters by that conveyance have miscarried when you have

been in more *apparently* disagreeable situations than you
are in at present, I hope that this will go safe, if Collins
should be obliged to leave it there.

And now, I think, taking to your aid other circumstances as they *have* offered, or *may* offer, you will be
sufficiently armed to resist all his machinations, be they
what they will.

One word more. Command me up, if I can be of the
least service or pleasure to you. I value not fame: I value
not censure; nor even life itself, I verily think, as I do
your honour, and your friendship—for, is not your honour my honour? And is not your friendship the pride of
my life?

May heaven preserve you, my dearest creature, in
honour and safety, is the prayer, the hourly prayer, of
Your ever-faithful and affectionate
Anna Howe

Thursday morn. 5. I have
    written all night.

to Miss Howe

My dearest creature,

How you have shocked, confounded, surprised, astonished me, by your dreadful communication! My *heart is
too weak* to bear up against such a stroke as this! When
all hope was with me! When my prospects were so much
mended! But can there be such villainy in men, as in
this vile principal, and equally vile agent!

I am really ill—very ill—Grief and surprise, and now
I will say, despair, have overcome me! All, all, you have
laid down as conjecture, appears to me now to be *more*
than conjecture!

Oh that your mother would have the goodness to permit me the presence of the only comforter that my afflicted, my half-broken heart, could be raised by! But I
charge you, think not of coming up without her indulgent permission. I am too ill at present, my dear, to
think of combating with this dreadful man; and of flying
from this horrid house! My bad writing will show you

this. But my illness will be my present security, should he indeed have meditated villainy. Forgive, oh forgive me, my dearest friend, the trouble I have given you! All must soon—But why add I grief to grief, and trouble to trouble? But I charge you, my beloved creature, not to think of coming up without your mother's leave, to the truly desolate and broken-spirited

CLARISSA HARLOWE

Well, Jack! And what thinkest thou of this last letter? Miss Howe values not either *fame* or censure; and thinkest thou that this letter will not bring the little fury up, though she could procure no other conveyance than her higgler's panniers, one for herself, the other for her maid? She knows where to come now! Many a little villain have I punished for knowing more than I would have her know; and that by adding to her knowledge and experience. What thinkest thou, Belford, if by getting hither this virago, and giving *cause* for a lamentable letter from her to the fair fugitive, I should be able to recover *her?* Would she not visit that friend in *her* distress, thinkest thou, whose intended visit to her in *hers* brought her into the condition she herself had so perfidiously escaped from?

Let me enjoy the thought!

Shall I send this letter? Thou seest I have left room, if I fail in the exact imitation of so charming a hand, to avoid too strict a scrutiny. Do they not both deserve it of me? Seest thou not how the raving girl threatens her mother? Ought she not to be punished? And can I be a worse devil, or villain, or monster, than she calls me in this letter; and has called me in her former letters; were I to punish them both, as my vengeance urges me to punish them. And when I have executed that my vengeance, how charmingly satisfied may they both go down into the country, and keep house together, and have a much better reason than their pride could give them for living the single life they have both seemed so fond of?

I am on tiptoe, Jack, to enter upon this project. Is not one country as good to me as another, if I should be obliged to take another tour upon it?

*   *   *

But I will not venture. Mr Hickman is a good man, they tell me. I love a good man. I hope one of these days to be a good man myself.

But the principal reason that withholds me (for 'tis a tempting project!) is, for fear of being utterly blown up if I should not be quick enough with my letter, or if Miss Howe should deliberate on setting out, or try her mother's consent first; in which time, a letter from my frighted beauty might reach her; for I have do doubt, wherever she has refuged, but her first work was to write to her vixen friend. I will therefore go on patiently; and take my revenge upon the little fury at my leisure.

But, in spite of my compassion for Hickman, whose better character is sometimes my envy, and who is one of those mortals that bring clumsiness into credit with the *mothers*, to the disgrace of us clever fellows, and often to our disappointment with the *daughters*; and who has been very busy in assisting these double-armed beauties against me; I swear by all the *dii majores,* as well as *minores*, that I will have Miss Howe, if I cannot have her more exalted friend! And then, if there be so much flaming love between these girls as they pretend, what will my charmer profit by her escape?

And now that I shall permit Miss Howe to reign a little longer, let me ask thee if thou hast not, in the enclosed letter, a *fresh* instance that a great many of my difficulties with her sister-toast are owing to this flighty girl?

Letter 230: MISS CLARISSA HARLOWE TO MISS HOWE

Thursday evening, June 8

After my last, so full of other hopes, the contents of this will surprise you. Oh my dearest friend, the man has at last proved himself to be a villain! It was with the utmost difficulty last night, that I preserved myself from the vilest dishonour. He extorted from me a promise of forgiveness; and that I would see him next day, as if nothing had happened: but if it were possible to escape from a wretch who, as I have too much reason to believe, formed a plot to fire the house, to frighten me almost naked into his arms, how could I see him next day?

I have escaped, Heaven be praised, I have!

All my present hope is to find some reputable family, or person of my own sex, who is obliged to go beyond sea, or who lives abroad; I care not whither; but if I might choose, in some one of our American colonies— never to be heard of more by my relations, whom I have so grievously offended.

Neither is there need of the renewal of your so often tendered goodness to me: for I have with me rings and other valuables that were sent me with my clothes, which will turn into money, to answer all I can want till Providence shall be pleased to put me into some way to help myself, if, for my further punishment, my life is to be lengthened beyond my wishes.

I am at present at one Mrs Moore's at Hampstead. My heart misgave me at coming to this village, because I had been here with him more than once: but the coach hither was so ready a conveniency, that I knew not what to do better. Then I shall stay here no longer than till I can receive your answer to this: in which you will be pleased to let me know if I cannot be hid, according to your former contrivance (happy, had I given into it at the time!) by Mrs Townsend's assistance, till the heat of his search be over. The Deptford road, I imagine, will be the right direction to hear of a passage, and to get safely aboard.

I am sure you will approve of my escape—the rather, as the people of the house must be very vile: for they, and that Dorcas too, did hear me (I know they did) cry out for help. If the fire had been other than a villainous plot (although in the morning, to blind them, I pretended to think it otherwise), they would have been alarmed as much as I; and have run in, hearing me scream, to *comfort me*, supposing my terror was the fire; to *relieve me,* supposing it were anything else. But the vile Dorcas went away, as soon as she saw the wretch throw his arms about me! An evident contrivance of them all. God be praised, I am out of their house!

My terror is not yet over: I can hardly think myself

safe: every well-dressed man I see from my windows, whether on horseback or on foot, I think to be him.

I know you will expedite an answer. What a dreadful hand have I made of it!

You will direct for me, my dear, by the name of Mrs Harriot Lucas.

Had I not made escape when I did, I was resolved to attempt it again and again.

How hard, how next to impossible, my dear, to avoid many lesser deviations when we are betrayed into a capital one!

When I began, I thought to write but a few lines. But, be my subject what it will, I know not how to conclude when I write to you.

> Your unhappy, but ever-affectionate,
> CLARISSA HARLOWE

Letter 231: MR LOVELACE TO JOHN BELFORD, ESQ.

Friday morning, past two o'clock

Io Triumphe! Io Clarissa, sing! Once more, what a happy man thy friend! A silly dear novice, to be heard to tell the coachman whither to carry her! And to go to *Hampstead*, of all the villages about London! The place where we had been together more than once!

Methinks I am sorry she managed no better! I shall find the recovery of her too easy a task, I fear! Had she but known how much difficulty enhances the value of anything with me, and had she had the least notion of obliging me, she would never have stopped short at *Hampstead*, surely.

Well, but after all this exultation, thou wilt ask, If I have already got back my charmer? I have not. But knowing where she is, is almost the same thing as having her in my power: and it delights me to think how she will start and tremble, when I first pop upon her! How she will look with conscious guilt, that will more than wipe off my guilt of Wednesday night, when she sees her injured lover, and acknowledged husband, from whom, the greatest of felonies, she would have stolen herself.

*   *   *

Now, Jack, will not her *feints* justify mine? Does she not invade my province, thinkest thou? And is it not now fairly come to *Who shall most deceive and cheat the other?* So, I thank my stars, we are upon a par, at last, as to this point—which is a great ease to my conscience, thou must believe.

Letter 232: MR LOVELACE TO JOHN BELFORD, ESQ.

Upper Flask, Hampstead, Friday (June 9)
morn. 7 o'clock

I am now here, and here have been this hour and half. What an industrious spirit have I! Nobody can say that I eat the bread of idleness. I take true pains for all the pleasure I enjoy. I cannot choose but to admire myself strangely; for, certainly, with this active soul, I should have made a very great figure in whatever station I had filled.

And now I have so much leisure upon my hands, that, after having informed myself of all necessary particulars, I am set to my shorthand writing, in order to keep up with time as well as I can: for the subject is now become worthy of me; and it is yet too soon, I doubt, to pay my compliments to my charmer, after all her fatigues for two or three days past. And, moreover, I have abundance of matters preparative to my future proceedings to recount, in order to connect and render all intelligible.

And here, supposing my narrative of the dramatic kind, ends Act the First. And now begins

ACT II. Scene, Hampstead Heath continued
Enter my Rascal

Will told them, before I came, 'That his lady was but lately married to one of the finest gentlemen in the world. But that, he being very gay and lively, she was *mortal* jealous of him; and in a fit of that sort, had eloped from him. For although she loved him dearly, and he doted upon her (as well he might, since, as they had seen, she was the finest creature *that ever the sun shone upon*), yet she was apt to be very wilful and sullen, if he might take the liberty to say so—but truth was truth—and if she could not have her own way in everything, would be for leaving him. That she had three or four times played his master such tricks; but with all the virtue and innocence in the world; running away to an intimate friend of hers, who, though a young lady of honour, was but too indulgent to her in this her *only* failing: for which reason his master had brought her to London lodgings; their usual residence being in the country: and that, on his refusing to satisfy her about a lady he had been seen with in the park, she had, for the first time since she came to town, served his master thus: whom he had left half-distracted on that account.'

And truly well he might, poor gentleman! cried the honest folks, pitying me before they saw me.

When I came, my person and dress having answered Will's description, the people were ready to worship me. I now and then sighed, now and then put on a lighter air; which, however, I designed should show more of vexation ill-disguised, than of real cheerfulness. And they told Will it was a thousand pities so fine a lady should have such *skittish tricks*; adding, that she might expose herself to great dangers by them; for that there were rakes everywhere *(Lovelaces in every corner, Jack!),* and many about that town who would leave nothing unattempted to get into her company: and although they might not prevail upon her, yet might they nevertheless hurt her reputation; and, in time, estrange the affections of so fine a gentleman from her.

Good sensible people, these! Hey, Jack!

Here, landlord; one word with you. My servant, I find, has acquainted you with the reason of my coming this way. An unhappy affair, landlord! A very unhappy affair! But never was there a more virtuous woman.

So, sir, she seems to be. A thousand pities her ladyship has such ways. And to so good-humoured a gentleman as you seem to be, sir.

Mother-spoilt, landlord! Mother-spoilt! that's the thing! But, sighing, I must make the best of it. What I want *you* to do for me, is to lend me a great-coat. I care not what it is. If my spouse should see me at a distance, she would make it very difficult for me to get at her speech.

A great-coat with a cape, if you have one. I must come upon her before she is aware.

I am afraid, sir, I have none fit for such a gentleman as you.

Oh, anything will do! The worse the better.

Exit landlord. Re-enter with two great-coats

Ay, landlord, this will be best; for I can button the cape over the lower part of my face. Don't I look devilishly down and concerned, landlord?

I never saw a gentleman with a better-natured look. 'Tis pity you should have such trials, sir.

I must be very unhappy, no doubt of it, landlord.

The good woman, who was within hearing of all this, pitied me much.

Pray, your honour, said she, if I may be so bold, was madam ever a mamma?

No!—and I sighed. We have been but a little while married; and, as I may say to *you*, it is her own fault that she is not in that way.

She'll get over all these freaks if once she be a mamma, I warrant.

I can't be severe to her; she knows that. The moment I see her, all resentment is over with me if she give me but one kind look.

All this time, I was adjusting my horseman's coat, and Will was putting in the ties of my wig, and buttoning the cape over my chin.

I asked the gentlewoman for a little powder. She brought me a powder-box, and I lightly shook the puff over my hat, and flapped one side of it, though the lace looked a little too gay for my covering; and slouching it over my eyes, Shall I be known, think you, madam?

Your honour is so expert, sir! I wish, if I may be so bold, your lady has not some *cause* to be jealous.

The good woman, smiling, wished me success; and so did the landlord. And as thou knowest that I am not a bad mimic, I took a cane which I borrowed of the landlord, and stooped in the shoulders to a quarter of a foot of less height, and stumped away cross to the bowling-green, to practise a little the hobbling gait of a gouty man.

And now I am going to try if I can't agree with goody Moore for lodgings and other conveniencies for my sick wife.

Wife, Lovelace! methinks thou interrogatest.

Yes, *wife*; for who knows what cautions the dear fugitive may have given in apprehension of me?

But has goody Moore any other lodgings to let?

Yes, yes; I have taken care of that; and find that she has just such conveniencies as I want. And I know that my wife will like them. For, although married, I can do everything I please; and that's a bold word, you know.

Letter 233: MR LOVELACE TO JOHN BELFORD, ESQ.

Hampstead, Friday night, June 9

Now, Belford, for the narrative of narratives. I will continue it as I have opportunity; and that so dextrously, that if I break off twenty times, thou shalt not discern where I piece my thread.

Although grievously afflicted with the gout, I alighted out of my chariot (leaning very hard on my cane with one hand, and on my new servant's shoulder with the other) the same instant almost that he had knocked at the door, that I might be sure of admission into the house.

I took care to button my great-coat about me, and to cover with it even the pommel of my sword; it being a little too gay for my years. I stooped forward; blinked with my eyes to conceal their lustre (no vanity in saying that, Jack!); my chin wrapped up for the toothache; my slouched laced hat, and so much of my wig as was visible, giving me all together the appearance of an antiquated beau.

The maid came to the door. I asked for her mistress. She showed me into one of the parlours; and I sat down, with a gouty Oh!

Enter goody Moore

Your servant, madam—but you must excuse me; I cannot well stand. I find by the bill at the door that you have lodgings to let (mumbling my words as if, like my

man Will, I had lost some of my fore-teeth): be pleased
to inform me what they are; for I like your situation—
and I will tell you my family. I have a wife, a good old
woman—older than myself, by the way, a pretty deal.
She is in a bad state of health, and is advised into the
Hampstead air.

When, sir, shall you want to come in?

I will take them from this very day; and, if convenient,
will bring my wife in the afternoon.

We have a single lady, who will be gone in two or
three days. She has one of the best apartments: that will
then be at liberty.

You have one or two good ones meantime, I presume,
madam, just to receive my wife; for we have lost time.
These damned physicians. Excuse me, madam, I am not
used to curse; but it is owing to the love I have for my
wife. And, as I told you, we have lost time.

You shall see what accommodations I have, if you
please, sir. But I doubt you are too lame to walk
upstairs.

I can make shift to hobble up, now I have rested a little.
I'll just look upon the apartment my wife is to have.

There were three rooms on a floor; two of them handsome; and the third, she said, still handsomer; but the
lady was in it.

I saw! I saw, she was! for as I hobbled up, crying out
upon my weak ankles in the hoarse mumbling voice I
had assumed, I beheld a little piece of her, just casting
an eye, with the door ajar, as they call it, to observe
who was coming up; and, seeing such an old clumsy fellow great-coated in weather so warm, slouched and muffled up, she withdrew, shutting the door without any
emotion. But it was not so with me; for thou canst not
imagine how my heart danced to my mouth at the very
glimpse of her; so that I was afraid the thump, thump,
thumping villain, which had so lately thumped as much
to no purpose, would have choked me.

But, madam, cannot a body just peep into the other
apartment, that I may be more particular to my wife in
the furniture of it?

The lady desires to be private, sir—but—and was
going to ask her leave.

I caught hold of her hand. However, stay, stay, madam: it mayn't be proper, if the lady loves to be private. Don't let me intrude upon the lady.

I will go ask, if I may show a gentleman the apartment, sir; and, as you are a married gentleman, and not *over*-young, she'll perhaps make the less scruple.

I appeared, upon the whole, so indifferent about seeing the room, or the lady, that the good woman was the more eager I should see both.

To be brief, she went in; and after a little while came out again. The lady, sir, is retired to her closet, so you may go in and look at the room.

Then how my heart began again to play its pug's tricks!

I hobbled in, and stumped about, and liked it very much; and was sure my wife would. But we would not turn the lady out of her lodging for the world. The other two apartments will do for us at the present.

Then stumping towards the closet, over the door of which hung a picture—What picture is that? Oh! I see: A St Cecilia!

A common print, sir.

Pretty well, pretty well! It is after an Italian master. I would not for the world turn the lady out of her apartment. We can make shift with the other two, repeated I, louder still: but yet mumblingly hoarse; for I had as great regard to uniformity in accent, as to my words.

I was resolved to fetch her out, if possible: and pretending to be going—You can't agree as to any *time*, Mrs Moore, when we can have this third room, can you? Not that (whispered I, loud enough to be heard in the next room); not that I would incommode the lady: but I would tell my wife *when*abouts—and women, you know, Mrs Moore, love to have everything before them of this nature.

Mrs Moore, says my charmer (and never did her voice sound so harmonious to me. Oh how my heart bounded again! It even talked to me, in a manner; for I thought I *heard*, as well as *felt*, its unruly flutters; and every vein about me seemed a pulse): Mrs Moore, you may acquaint the gentleman that I shall stay here only for two or three days, at most, till I receive an answer to a letter

I have written into the country; and rather than be your hindrance, I will take up with any apartment a pair of stairs higher.

She opened not the door yet; and I said, But since you have so much goodness, madam, if I could but just look into the closet, as I stand, I could tell my wife whether it is large enough to hold a cabinet she much values, and will have with her wherever she goes.

Then my charmer opened the door, and blazed upon me, as it were in a flood of light, like what one might imagine would strike a man who, born blind, had by some propitious power been blessed with his sight, all at once, in a meridian sun.

Upon my soul, I never was so strangely affected before. I had much ado to forbear discovering myself that instant: but, hesitatingly, and in great disorder, I said, looking into the closet, and around it, There is room, I see, for my wife's cabinet; and it has many jewels in it of high price; but, upon my soul (for I could not forbear swearing, like a puppy: habit is a cursed thing, Jack)— nothing so valuable as the lady I see, can be brought into it!

She started, and looked at me with terror. The truth of the compliment, as far as I know, had taken dissimulation from my accent.

I saw it was impossible to conceal myself longer from her, any more than (from the violent impulses of my passion) to forbear manifesting myself. I unbuttoned therefore my cape, I pulled off my flapped, slouched hat; I threw open my great-coat and, like the devil in Milton (an odd comparison though!),

> I started up in my own form divine,
> Touched by the beam of her celestial eye,
> More potent than Ithuriel's spear!

Now, Belford, for a similitude—now for a likeness to illustrate the surprising scene, and the effect it had upon my charmer and the gentlewoman! But nothing *was* like it, or equal to it. The plain fact can only describe it, and set it off. Thus then take it.

She no sooner saw who it was, than she gave three

violent screams; and, before I could catch her in my arms (as I was about to do the moment I discovered myself), down she sunk at my feet in a fit; which made me curse my indiscretion for so suddenly, and with so much emotion, revealing myself.

The gentlewoman, seeing so strange an alteration in my person, and features, and voice, and dress, cried out, Murder, help! Murder, help! by turns, for half a dozen times running. This alarmed the house, and up ran two servant-maids, and *my* servant after them. I cried out for water and hartshorn, and everyone flew a different way, one of the maids as fast down as she came up; while the gentlewoman ran out of one room into another, and by turns up and down the apartment we were in, without meaning or end, wringing her foolish hands, and not knowing what she did.

For my part, I was so intent upon restoring my angel that I regarded nobody else. And at last, she slowly recovering motion, with bitter sighs and sobs (only the whites of her eyes however appearing for some moments), I called upon her in the tenderest accent, as I kneeled by her, my arm supporting her head; My angel! My charmer! My Clarissa! look upon me, my dearest life! I am not angry with you! I will forgive you, my best beloved!

I threw up the closet-sash for air, and then left her to the care of the young gentlewoman, the same notable Miss Rawlins, whom I had heard of at the Flask; and to that of Mrs Moore; who by this time had recovered herself; and then retiring to one corner of the room, I made my servant pull off my gouty stockings, brush my hat, and loop it up into the usual smart cock.

I then stepped to the closet to Mr Rawlins, whom, in the general confusion, I had not much minded before. Sir, said I, you have an uncommon scene before you. The lady is my wife, and no gentleman's presence is necessary here but my own.

I beg pardon, sir: *If* the lady is your wife, I have no business here. *But*, sir, by her concern at seeing you—

The ladies only are proper to be present on this occasion, added I; and I think myself obliged to them for their care and kind assistance.

'Tis well he made not another word: for I found my choler begin to rise. I could not bear that the finest neck, and arms, and foot, in the world, should be exposed to the eyes of any man living but mine.

I withdrew once more from the closet, finding her beginning to recover, lest the sight of me too soon should throw her back again.

The first words she said, looking round her with great emotion, were, Oh hide me! hide me! Is he gone! Oh hide me! Is he gone!

Sir, said Miss Rawlins, coming to me with an air somewhat peremptory and assured, this is some surprising case. The lady cannot bear the sight of you. What you have done is best known to yourself. But another such fit will probably be her last. It would be but kind, therefore, for you to retire.

The dear creature, said I, may *well* be concerned to see me. If *you*, madam, had a husband who loved you, as I love her, you would not, I am confident, fly from him and expose yourself to hazards, as she does whenever she has not all her way—and yet with a mind not capable of intentional evil. But, mother-spoilt!

You *speak* like a gentleman; you *look* like a gentleman, said Miss Rawlins. But, sir, this is a strange case; the lady seems to dread the sight of you.

No wonder, madam; taking her a little on one side, nearer to Mrs Moore. I have three times already forgiven the dear creature. But this *jealousy*—there is a spice of *that* in it—and of *frenzy* too (whispered I, that it might have the face of a secret, and of consequence the more engage their attention)—but our story is too long.

I then made a motion to go to the lady. But they desired that I would walk into the next room; and they would endeavour to prevail upon her to lie down.

I begged that they would not suffer her to talk; for that she was accustomed to fits and would, when in this way, talk of anything that came uppermost; and the more she was suffered to run on, the worse she was; and if not kept quiet would fall into ravings; which might possibly hold her a week.

They promised to keep her quiet; and I withdrew into

the next room; ordering everyone down but Mrs Moore and Miss Rawlins.

By this time, I hoped that she was enough recovered to bear a presence, that it behoved me to make her bear; and fearing she would throw out something in her exclamations that would still more disconcert me, I went into the room again.

Oh! there he is! said she, and threw her apron over her face. I cannot see him! I cannot look upon him! Begone! begone! touch me not!

For I took her struggling hand, beseeching her to be pacified; and assuring her that I would make all up with her, upon her own terms and wishes.

Base man! said the violent lady, I have no wishes, but never to behold you more! Why must I be thus pursued and haunted? Have you not made me miserable enough already? Despoiled of all succour and help, and of every friend, I am contented to be poor, low, and miserable, so I may be free from your persecutions!

Miss Rawlins stared at me (a confident slut this Miss Rawlins, thought I!): so did Mrs Moore. I told you so! whisperingly said I, turning to the women; shaking my head with a face of great concern and pity; and then to my charmer, My dear creature, how you rave! You will not easily recover from the effects of this violence! Have patience, my love! Be pacified! These ladies will certainly think you have fallen among robbers; and that I am the chief of them.

So you are! so you are! stamping, her face still covered (she thought of Wednesday night, no doubt); and, sighing as if her heart were breaking, she put her hand to her forehead. I shall be quite distracted!

And I would have pressed her hand, as I held it, with my lips; but she drew it from me with indignation.

Unhand me, sir, said she. I will not be touched by you. Leave me to my fate. What right, what title have you to persecute me thus?

I touched a delicate string, on purpose to set her in such a passion before the women as might confirm the intimation I had given of a frenzical disorder.

What a turn is here! Lately so happy! Nothing wanting but a reconciliation between you and your friends!—that reconciliation in such a happy train!—shall so *slight*, so *accidental* an occasion be suffered to overturn all our happiness?

Now, said she, that thou darest to call the occasion *slight* and *accidental*, and that I am happily out of thy vile hands, and out of a house I have reason to believe *as* vile, traitor and wretch that thou art, I will venture to cast an eye upon thee—and Oh that it were in my power, in mercy to my sex, to look thee first into shame and remorse, and then into death!

This violent tragedy speech, and the high manner in which she uttered it, had its desired effect. I looked upon the women, and upon her, by turns, with a pitying eye; and they shook their wise heads, and besought *me* to retire, and *her* to lie down to compose herself.

This hurricane, like other hurricanes, was presently allayed by a shower. She threw herself once more into her armed chair—and begged pardon of the women for her passionate excess; but not of me: yet I was in hopes that when compliments were stirring, I should have come in for a share.

Indeed, ladies, said I (with assurance enough, thou'lt say), this violence is not natural to my beloved's temper—misapprehension—

Begone! Begone! With a face so unblushing, how darest thou my presence?

I will only say, before these two gentlewomen, that since it *must* be so, and since your former esteem for me is turned into so riveted an aversion, I will soon, *very* soon, make you entirely easy. I *will* be gone. I *will* leave you to *your own fate*, as you call it; and may that be happy!

Ever since I knew you, said she, I have been in a wilderness of doubt and error. I bless God that I am out of your hands. I will transact for myself what relates to myself. I dismiss all your solicitude for me. Am I not my own mistress! Am I not—

It was high time to stop her here. I raised my voice to drown hers. You used, my dearest creature, to have a tender and apprehensive heart. You never had so much reason for such a one as now.

Let me judge for myself upon what I shall *see*, not upon what I shall *hear*. Do you think I shall ever—

I dreaded her going on—I *must* be heard, madam, raising my voice still higher.

Begone from me, man!

Still louder raised I my voice. She was overborne. Sweet soul! It would be hard, thought I (and yet I was very angry with her), if such a spirit as thine cannot be brought to yield to such a one as mine!

I lowered my voice on her silence. All gentle, all *in-treative,* my accent: my head bowed; one hand held out; the other on my honest heart. Lady Betty will be in town with my cousin Montague in a day or two. They will be your visitors. I beseech you do not carry this misunderstanding so far, as that Lord M. and Lady Betty, and Lady Sarah, may know it. *(How considerable this made me look to the women!)* Lady Betty will not let you rest till you consent to accompany her to her own seat—and to that lady may you safely entrust your cause.

Again, upon my pausing a moment, she was going to break out. I liked not the turn of her countenance, nor the tone of her voice. 'And thinkest thou, base wretch,' were the words she *did* utter. I again raised my voice, and drowned hers. *Base wretch*, madam! Words so op-probrious from a mind so gentle—but this treatment is from *you*, madam!—from *you*, whom I love more than my own soul. By that soul, I swear that I do. (The women looked upon each other. They seemed pleased with my ardour. Women, whether wives, maids, or wid-ows, love ardours. Even Miss Howe, thou knowest, speaks up for ardours.)

If we are to *separate for ever*, in a strong and solemn voice, proceeded I, this island shall not long be troubled with me. Anything will I come into (renounce me if you will), that shall make for *your* peace, and for the recon-ciliation your heart was so lately set upon.

I then . . . retired into the next apartment with a low bow, and a very solemn air.

I was soon followed by the two women.

I excused myself to Mrs Moore for the disguise I had appeared in at first, and for the story I had invented. I told her that I held myself obliged to satisfy her for the whole floor we were upon; and for an upper room for my servant; and that for a month certain.

She made many scruples, and begged she might not be urged on this head till she had consulted Miss Rawlins.

I consented; but told her that she had taken my earnest; and I hoped there was no room for dispute.

I said that ours was a very particular case: that were I to acquaint them with it, some part of it would hardly appear credible.

I told them the condition my spouse had made me swear to; and which she held me to, in order, I said, to induce me the sooner to be reconciled to her relations.

I owned that this restraint made me sometimes ready to fly out. And Mrs Moore was so good as to declare that she did not much wonder at it.

A foundation here, thought I, to procure these women's help to get back the fugitive, or their connivance at least at my doing so; as well as for anticipating any future information from Miss Howe.

I gave them a character of that virago: and intimated, 'that for a head to contrive mischief, and a heart to execute it, she had hardly her equal in her sex.'

To *this* Miss Howe it was, Mrs Moore said she supposed, that my spouse was so desirous to dispatch a man and horse, by day-dawn, with a letter she wrote before she went to bed last night; proposing to stay no longer than till she had received an answer to it.

The very same, said I. I *knew* she would have immediate recourse to her. I should have been but too happy, could I have prevented such a letter from passing, or so to have managed as to have it given into Mrs Howe's hands instead of her daughter's. Women who had lived some time in the world, knew *better* than to encourage such skittish pranks in young wives.

I told the women, 'That I despaired it would ever be better with us while Miss Howe had so strange a predominance over my spouse, and remained herself *unmarried*; and until the reconciliation with her friends could be effected; or a *still* happier event—as I should think it, who am the last male of my family; and which my foolish vow, and her rigour, had hitherto'—

Here I stopped, and looked modest, turning my diamond ring round my finger: while goody Moore looked mighty significant, calling it a very particular case; and the maiden lady fanned away, and primmed and pursed, to show that what I said needed no farther explanation.

I told them the occasion of our present difference: avowed the reality of the fire: but owned that I would have made no scruple of breaking the unnatural oath she had bound me in (having a husband's right of my side), when she was so accidentally frighted into my arms: and I blamed myself excessively that I did not; since she thought fit to carry her resentment so high, and had the injustice to suppose the fire to be a contrivance of mine.

Nay, for that matter, Mrs Moore said—as we were married, and *madam* was so odd—every gentleman would not—and there stopped Mrs Moore.

A most extraordinary case, truly! the maiden lady: fanning, yet coming in with her *Well but's*, and her sifting *Pray, sir's!* And her restraining *Enough, sir's!*—flying *from* the question *to* the question; her seat now and then uneasy, for fear my want of delicacy should hurt her abundant modesty; and yet it was difficult to satisfy her *super*-abundant curiosity.

Excuse me, ladies; traversing the room. And having rubbed my eyes till I supposed them red, I turned to the women; and pulling out my letter-case, I will show you one letter—here it is—read it, Miss Rawlins, if you please.

to Robert Lovelace, Esq.

M. Hall, Wed. June 7

Cousin Lovelace,

I think you might have found time to let us know of your nuptials being actually solemnized. I might have expected this piece of civility from you. But perhaps the ceremony was performed at the very time that you asked me to be your lady's father—but I shall be angry if I proceed in my guesses—and *little said is soon amended.*

But I can tell you that Lady Betty Lawrance, whatever Lady Sarah does, will not so soon forgive you as I have done. *Women resent slights longer than men.* You that know so much of the sex (I speak it not however to your praise) might have known *that.* But never was you before acquainted with a lady of such an amiable character. I hope there will be but one soul between you. I have before now said that I will disinherit you, and settle all I can upon her, if you prove not a good husband to her.

May this marriage be crowned with a great many fine boys (I desire no girls) to build up again a family so antient! The first boy shall take my surname by Act of Parliament. That is in my will.

Lady Betty and niece Charlotte will be in town about business *before you know where you are*. They long to pay their compliments to your fair bride. I suppose you will hardly be at The Lawn when they get to town; because Greme informs me you have sent no orders there for your lady's accommodation.

Pritchard has all things in readiness for signing. I will take no advantage of your slights. Indeed I am too much used to them—more praise to my patience than to your complaisance, however.

One reason for Lady Betty's going up, as I may tell you *under the rose*, is, to buy some suitable presents for Lady Sarah and all of us to make on this agreeable occasion.

We would have blazed it away, could we have had timely notice, and thought it would have been agreeable to all round. The *like occasions don't happen every day.*

My most affectionate compliments and congratulations to my new niece; conclude me, for the present, in violent pains that with all your heroicalness would make you mad,

Your truly affectionate uncle,
M.

Letter 234: MR LOVELACE TO JOHN BELFORD, ESQ.

I cannot but stop here for one minute to remark, though against myself, upon that security which innocence gives, that nevertheless had better have in it a greater mixture of the serpent with the dove. For here, heedless of all I could say behind her back, because she was satisfied with her own worthiness, she permitted me to go on with

my own story without interruption, to persons as great
strangers to her as to me; and who, as strangers to *both,*
might be supposed to lean to the side most injured: and
that, as I managed it, was to mine. A dear silly soul!
thought I, at the time, to depend upon the goodness of
her own heart, when the heart cannot be seen into but
by its actions; and she, to appearance, a runaway, an
eloper, from a tender, a most indulgent husband!—to
neglect to cultivate the opinion of individuals, when the
whole world is governed by appearance!

Yet, what can be expected of an angel under twenty?
She has a world of knowledge; knowledge *speculative,*
as I may say; but no *experience!* How should she?
Knowledge by theory only is a vague uncertain light: a
will o' the wisp, which as often misleads the doubting
mind as puts it right.

There are many things in the world, could a moraliser
say, that would afford inexpressible pleasure to a reflecting mind, were it not for the mixture they come to
us with. I am half sorry to say that I find a pleasure in
playing the tyrant over what I love. Call it an ungenerous pleasure, if thou wilt: softer hearts than mine know
it. The women to a woman know it, and *show* it too,
whenever they are trusted with power. And why should
it be thought strange that I, who love them so dearly,
and study them so much, should catch the infection of
them?

Letter 236: MR LOVELACE TO JOHN BELFORD, ESQ.

(In continuation)

We had at dinner, besides Miss Rawlins, a young
widow-niece of Mrs Moore, who is come to stay a
month with her aunt—*Bevis* her name; very forward,
very lively, and a great admirer of *me,* I assure you—
hanging smirkingly upon all I said; and prepared to
approve of every word before I spoke: and who, by
the time we had half-dined (by the help of what she
had collected before), was as much acquainted with
our story as either of the other two.

As it behoved me to prepare them in my favour

against whatever might come from Miss Howe, I improved upon the hint I had thrown out above-stairs against that mischief-making lady. I represented her to be an arrogant creature, revengeful, artful, enterprising, and one who, had she been a man, would have sworn and cursed, and committed rapes, and played the devil, as far as I knew (and I have no doubt of it, Jack): but who, nevertheless, by advantage of a female education, and pride, and insolence, I believed was *personally* virtuous.

However, I declared that Miss Howe was a subtle contriver of mischief; one who had always been *my* enemy: her motives I knew not: but despising the man whom her mother was desirous she should have, one Hickman; although I did not directly aver, that she would rather have had me; yet they all immediately imagined that *that* was the ground of her animosity to me, and of her envy to my beloved; and it was pity, they said, that so fine a young lady did not see through such a pretended friend.

And, truly, I must needs say they have almost persuaded even me myself, that Miss Howe is actually in love with me. I have often been willing to hope this. And who knows but she may? And what's thy opinion, Jack? She certainly hates Hickman: and girls who are *disengaged* seldom *hate*, though they may not *love*: and if she had rather have *another*, why not that *other* ME? For am I not a smart fellow, and a rake? And do not your sprightly ladies love your smart fellows, and your rakes? And where is the wonder that the man who could engage the affections of Miss Harlowe should engage those of a lady (with her *Alas's*) who would be honoured in being deemed her second?

But now I have appealed this matter to thee, let me use another argument in favour of my observation that the ladies generally prefer a rake to a sober man; and of my presumption upon it that Miss Howe is in love with me: It is this—Common fame says that Hickman is a very virtuous, a very innocent fellow—a *male-virgin*, I warrant! An odd dog I always thought him. Now women, Jack, like not novices. They are pleased

with a love of the sex that is founded in the knowledge
of it. Novices expect more than they can possibly find
in the commerce with them. The man who knows
them yet has *ardours* for them, to borrow a word from
Miss Howe, though those ardours are generally owing
more to the devil *within* him than to the witch *without*
him, is the man who makes them the highest and most
grateful compliment. He knows what to expect, and
with what to be satisfied.

Then the merit of a woman, in some cases, must be
ignorance, whether *real* or *pretended.* The man, in
these cases, must be an *adept.* Will it then be wondered
at that a woman prefers a libertine to a novice? While
she expects in the one the confidence *she* wants; she
considers the other and herself as two parallel lines;
which, though they run side by side, can never meet.

But to proceed with my narrative:

Having thus prepared everyone against any letter
should come from Miss Howe, and against my beloved's messenger returns, I thought it proper to conclude that subject with a hint that my spouse could
not bear to have anything said *that reflected upon Miss
Howe;* and, with a deep sigh, added that I had been
made very unhappy more than once by the ill-will of
ladies whom I had never offended.

The widow Bevis believed that might very easily be.

Letter 241: MR LOVELACE TO JOHN BELFORD, ESQ.

Eight o'clock, Sat. morn. June 10

I am come back from Mrs Moore's, whither I went in
order to attend my charmer's commands. But no admittance. A very bad night.

Doubtless she must be as much concerned, that she
has carried her resentments so very far, as I have reason
to be that I made such a poor use of the opportunity I
had on Wednesday night.

But now, Jack, for a brief review of my present situation; and a slight hint or two of my precautions.

I have seen the women this morning, and find them
half right, half doubting.

Mrs Moore can do nothing without Miss Rawlins.

Though not permitted to lodge there myself, I have engaged all the rooms she has to spare, to the very garrets; and *that* as I have told thee before, for a month certain, and at her own price, board included; my spouse's and all: but she must not, at present, know it. So I hope I have Mrs Moore fast *by the interest.*

This, devil-like, is suiting temptations to inclinations.

Miss Rawlins fluctuates as she hears the lady's story, or as she hears mine. Somewhat of an infidel, I doubt, is this Miss Rawlins. I have not yet considered *her* foible. The next time I see her, I will take particular notice of all the moles and freckles in her mind; and then *infer* and *apply.*

The Widow Bevis, as I have told thee, is all my own.

My man Will lies in the house. My other new fellow attends upon *me*; and cannot therefore be quite stupid.

Already is Will over head and ears in love with one of Mrs Moore's maids. He was struck with her the moment he set his eyes upon her. A raw country wench too. But all women, from the countess to the cookmaid, are put into high good humour with themselves, when a man is taken with them at first sight.

The post, general and penny, will be strictly watched likewise.

Miss Howe's Collins is remembered to be described. Miss Howe's and Hickman's liveries also.

I am to be acquainted with any inquiry that shall happen to be made after my spouse, whether by her married or maiden name, before *she* shall be told of it—and this that I may have it in my power to *prevent mischief.*

As to my spouse herself, has she not reason to be pleased with me for having permitted her to receive Miss Howe's letter from Wilson's? A plain case, either that I am no deep plotter, or that I have no further views but to make my peace with her for an offence so slight, and so *accidental.*

But I return to the scene of action. I must keep the women steady.

Letter 246: MR LOVELACE TO JOHN BELFORD, ESQ.

Sat. midnight

No rest, says a text that I once heard preached upon, *to the wicked*—and I cannot close my eyes; yet wanted only to compound for half an hour in an elbow-chair. So must scribble on.

And can I have taken all this pains for nothing? Or for a wife only, that, however excellent (and *any* woman, do I think, I could make good, because I could make any woman *fear* as well as *love* me), might have been obtained without the plague I have been at, and much more reputably than with it? And hast thou not seen that this haughty lady knows not how to forgive with graciousness? Indeed has not at all forgiven me? But holds my soul in a *suspense,* which has been so grievous to her own.

At this silent moment I think that if I were to pursue my former scheme, and resolve to try whether I cannot make a greater fault serve as a sponge to wipe out a less; and then be forgiven for that; I can justify myself to *myself*; and that, as the fair implacable would say, is all in all.

Well then, if this sweet creature must *fall,* as it is called, for the benefit of all the pretty fools of the sex, she *must*; and there's an end of the matter. And what would there have been in it of uncommon or rare, had I not been so long about it? And so I dismiss all further argumentation and debate upon the question: and I impose upon thee, when thou writest to me, an eternal silence on this head.

She [Conscience] had stolen my pen. While I was thus meditating, doubting as to my future measures, she stole it; and thus she wrote with it, in a hand exactly like my own; and would have faced me down, that it was really my own handwriting.

'But let me reflect, before it be too late. On the manifold perfections of this ever-admirable creature, let me reflect. The hand yet is only held up. The blow is not struck. Miss Howe's next letter may blow thee up. In policy thou shouldest be now at least honest. Thou canst

not live without her. Thou wouldst rather marry her than
lose her absolutely. Thou mayest undoubtedly prevail
upon her, inflexible as she seems to be, for marriage.
But if now she find thee a villain, thou mayest never
more engage her attention, and she perhaps will refuse
and abhor thee.

'Yet already have I not gone too far? Like a repentant
thief, afraid of his gang and obliged to go on in fear of
hanging till he comes to be hanged, I am afraid of the
gang of my cursed contrivances.

'As I hope to live, I am sorry at the present writing,
that I have been such a foolish plotter as to put it, as I
fear I have done, out of my *own power* to be honest. I
hate compulsion in all forms; and cannot bear, even to
be *compelled* to be the wretch my choice has made me!
So now, Belford, as thou hast said, I am a machine at
last, and no free agent.'

Thus far had my *conscience* written with my pen; and
see what a recreant she had made me! I seized her by
the throat. *There! There*, said I, thou vile impertinent!
Take *that*, and *that*!

How hard diest thou! Adieu! Adieu to thee for ever!

Letter 248: MR LOVELACE TO JOHN BELFORD, ESQ.

Sunday morning
I have had the honour of my charmer's company for two
complete hours. We met before six in Mrs Moore's garden: a walk on the heath refused me.

The sedateness of her aspect, and her kind compliance
in this meeting, gave me hopes.

But the utmost I could obtain was, that she would
take no resolution in my favour till she received Miss
Howe's next letter.

I will not repeat the arguments used by me: but I
will give thee the substance of what she said in answer
to them.

She had considered of everything, she told me. My
whole conduct was before her. The house I carried her
to must be a vile house. They heard her cries. My insult
was undoubtedly premeditated. By my whole recollected

behaviour to her, previous to it, it must be so. I had the vilest of views, no question. And my treatment of her put it out of all doubt.

Soul all over, Belford! She seems sensible of liberties that my passion made me insensible of having taken.

She besought me to give over all thoughts of her. Sometimes; she said, she thought herself cruelly treated by her nearest and dearest relations: at *such* times, a spirit of repining, and even of resentment, took place, and the reconciliation, at other times so desirable, was not then so much the favourite wish of her heart, as was the scheme she had formerly planned—of taking her good Norton for her directress and guide, and living upon her own estate in the manner her grandfather had intended she should live.

This scheme she doubted not that her cousin Morden, who was one of her trustees for that estate, would enable her (and that as she hoped, without litigation) to pursue. And if he can, and does, what, sir, let me ask you, said she, have I seen in your conduct that should make me prefer to it an union of interests, where there is such a disunion in minds?

So thou seest, Jack, there is *reason*, as well as *resentment*, in the preference she makes against me! Thou seest that she presumes to think that she can be happy *without* me; and that she must be unhappy *with* me!

I had besought her, in the conclusion of my re-urged arguments, to write to Miss Howe before Miss Howe's answer could come, in order to lay before her the present state of things.

Miss Howe, proceeded she, knows the full state of matters already, sir. The answer I expect from her respects *myself*, not *you*. Her heart is too warm in the cause of friendship, to leave me in suspense one moment longer than is necessary as to what I want to know. Nor does her answer depend absolutely upon herself. She must see a person first; and that person perhaps must see others.

The cursed smuggler-woman, Jack! Miss Howe's Townsend, I doubt not! Plot, contrivance, intrigue, stratagem! Underground moles these ladies. But let the earth cover me! let me be a mole too, thought I, if they carry their point!—and if this lady escape me now.

Oh Jack! I am sick to death, I pine, I die, for Miss Howe's next letter! I would bind, gag, strip, rob, and do anything but murder, to intercept it.

But, determined as she seems to be, it was evident to me, nevertheless, that she had still some tenderness for me.

She often wept as she talked, and much oftener sighed. She looked at me twice with an eye of *undoubted* gentleness, and three times with an eye *tending* to compassion and softness: but its benign rays were as often *snatched* back, as I may say, and her face averted, as if her sweet eye were not to be trusted, and could not stand against my eager eyes; seeking, as they did, for a lost heart in hers, and endeavouring to penetrate to her very soul.

More than once I took her hand. She struggled not *much* against the freedom. I pressed it once with my lips. She was not *very* angry. A frown indeed; but a frown that had more distress in it than indignation.

How came the dear soul (clothed as it is with such a silken vesture) by all its steadiness? Was it necessary that the active gloom of such a tyrant of a *father* should commix with such a passive sweetness of a will-less *mother*, to produce a constancy, an equanimity, a steadiness, in the *daughter,* which never woman before could boast of?

What *sensibilities*, said the divine creature, withdrawing her hand, must thou have suppressed! What a dreadful, what a judicial hardness of heart must thine be; who canst be capable of such emotions as sometimes thou hast shown; and of such sentiments as sometimes have flowed from thy lips; yet canst have so far overcome them all as to be able to act as thou hast acted, and that from settled purpose and premeditation; and this, as it is *said*, throughout the whole of thy life, from infancy to this time!

I told her that I had hoped from the generous concern she had expressed for me, when I was so suddenly and dangerously taken ill—(the ipecacuanha experiment, Jack!).

She interrupted me. Well have you rewarded me for the concern you speak of!

She paused. I besought her to proceed.

But let us break off discourse, resumed she. I have said too much. Nobody but Miss Howe, to whom, next to the Almighty, and my own mother, I wish to stand acquitted of wilful error, shall know the whole of what has passed.

We had gone but a few paces towards the house, when we were met by the impertinent women, with notice that breakfast was ready. I could only, with uplifted hands, beseech her to give me hope of a renewed conversation after breakfast.

No; she would go to church.

And into the house she went, and upstairs directly. Nor would she oblige me with her company at the tea-table.

Letter 250: MR LOVELACE TO JOHN BELFORD, ESQ.

Sunday afternoon
Oh Belford! what a hair's-breadth escape have I had! Such a one, that I tremble between terror and joy at the thoughts of what *might* have happened and did not.

What a perverse girl is this, to contend with her fate, yet has reason to think that her very stars fight against her! I am the luckiest of men! But my breath almost fails me when I reflect upon what a slender thread my destiny hung.

But not to keep thee in suspense; I have, within this half-hour, obtained possession of the expected letter from Miss Howe—and by *such* an accident! But here, with the former, I dispatch this; thy messenger waiting.

Letter 251: MR LOVELACE TO JOHN BELFORD, ESQ.

(In continuation)
Thus it was. My charmer accompanied Mrs Moore again to church this afternoon. I had been very earnest, in the *first* place, to obtain her company at dinner: but in vain. In the *next* place, I besought her to favour me after dinner with another garden walk. But she *would* again

go to church. And what reason have I to rejoice that she did!

ᐧMy worthy friend Mrs Bevis thought one sermon a day, *well*-observed, enough; so stayed at home to bear me company.

The lady and Mrs Moore had not been gone a quarter of an hour, when a young country fellow on horseback came to the door, and inquired for Mrs *Harriot Lucas*. The widow and I (undetermined how we were to entertain each other) were in the parlour next the door; and hearing the fellow's inquiry, Oh my dear Mrs Bevis, said I, I am undone, undone for ever, if you don't help me out! Since here, in all probability, is a messenger from that implacable Miss Howe with a letter; which, if delivered to Mrs Lovelace, may undo all we have been doing.

What, said she, would you have me do?

Call the maid in this moment, that I may give her her lesson; and if it be as I imagine, I'll tell you what you shall do.

WIDOW. Margaret! Margaret! come in this minute.

LOVEL[ACE]. My dearest widow, do you personate Mrs Lovelace—for Heaven's sake do you personate Mrs Lovelace!

WID[OW]. *I* personate Mrs Lovelace, sir! How can I do that? She is fair: I am a brown woman. She is slender: I am plump.

LOVEL. No matter, no matter. The fellow may be a new come servant: he is not in livery, I see. He may not know her person. You can but be bloated, and in a dropsy.

Now, my dear widow, lie along on the settee, and put your handkerchief over your face, that, if he *will* speak to you himself, he may not see your eyes and your hair—so—that's right. I'll step into the closet by you.

I did so.

PEGGY [MARGARET]. (returning) He won't deliver his business to me. He will speak to Mrs Harry Lucas her own self.

LOVEL. (holding the door in my hand) Tell him that this is Mrs Harriot Lucas; and let him come in. Whisper him, if he doubts, that she is bloated, dropsical, and not the woman she was.

Away went Margery.

In came the fellow, bowing and scraping, his hat poked out before him with both his hands.

WIDOW. What *is* thy business? I hope Miss Howe is well.

FELLOW. Yes, madam; pure well, I thank God. I wish you were so too.

WIDOW. My head aches so dreadfully, I cannot hold it up. I must beg of you to let me know your business.

FELLOW. Nay, and that be all, my business is soon known. It is but to give this letter into your own *partiklar* hands. Here it is.

Her lady mother must not know as how I came of this errand. But the letter, I suppose, will tell you all.

WIDOW. How shall I satisfy you for this kind trouble?

FELLOW. Nahow at all. What I do is for love of Miss Howe. She will satisfy me more than enough. But may-hap you can send no answer, you are so ill.

WIDOW. Was you ordered to wait for an answer?

FELLOW. No. I can't say I was. But I was bidden to observe how you looked, and how you was; and if you did write a line or so, to take care of it, and give it only to our young landlady, in secret.

WIDOW. You see I look strangely. Not so well as I used to do.

FELLOW. Nay, I don't know that I ever saw you but once before; and that was at a stile, where I met you and my young landlady; but knew better than to stare a gentlewoman in the face; especially at a stile.

He withdrew, bowing and scraping.

And so the shocking rascal went away: and glad at my heart was I when he was gone; for I feared nothing so much as that he would have stayed till they came from church.

Thus, Jack, got I my *heart's-ease*, the letter of Miss Howe; and through such a train of accidents, as make me say that the lady's stars fight against her.

They are all three just come in. I hasten to them.

Letter 252: MR LOVELACE TO JOHN BELFORD, ESQ.

By the enclosed thou wilt see that neither of the correspondents deserve mercy from me: and I am resolved to make the ending with one, the beginning with the other.

Here read the letter, if thou wilt. But thou art not my friend if thou offerest to plead for either of the saucy creatures, after thou *hast* read it.

to Mrs Harriot Lucas, at Mrs Moore's at Hampstead

Had the *villain* attempted to fire a city instead of a house, I should not have wondered at it. All that I am amazed at, is, that he (whose boast, as I am told it is, that no woman shall keep him out of her bedchamber, when he has made a resolution to be in it) did not discover *his* [cloven] *foot* before. And it is as strange to me that, having got you at such a shocking advantage, and in such an horrid house, you could, at the time, *escape dishonour*, and afterwards get from such a set of *infernals*.

Your thought of going abroad, and your reasons for so doing, most sensibly affect me. But, be comforted my dear; I hope you will not be under a necessity of quitting your native country. Were I sure that that must be the cruel case, I would abandon all my own better prospects, and soon be with you. And I would accompany you whithersoever you went, and share fortunes with you: for it is impossible that I should be happy if I knew that you were exposed not only to the perils of the sea, but to the attempts of other vile men; your personal graces attracting every eye, and exposing you to those hourly dangers which others, less distinguished by the gifts of nature, might avoid—All that I know, that beauty (so greatly coveted, and so greatly admired) is good for!

Sat. afternoon

I have just parted with Mrs Townsend. I thought you had once seen her with me: but she says she never had the honour to be personally known to you. She has a *manlike spirit*. She knows the world. And her two brothers being in town, she is sure she can engage them, in so good a cause and (if there should be occasion) *both their ships' crews,* in your service.

Give your consent, my dear; and the *horrid villain* shall be repaid with *broken bones, at least,* for all his vileness!

The misfortune is, Mrs Townsend cannot be with you till *Thursday next,* or *Wednesday at soonest.* Are you sure you can be safe where you are till then? I think you are too near London; and perhaps you had better be *in it.* If you remove, let me know *whither*, the very moment.

Mrs Townsend will in person attend you—she *hopes* on Wednesday. Her brothers, and some of their people, will scatteringly, and as if they knew nothing of you (so we have contrived), see you safe not only to London, but to her house at Deptford.

She has a kinswoman who will take your commands there, if she herself be obliged to leave you. And there you may stay till the wretch's fury on losing you, and his search, are over.

After a while, I can procure you a lodging in one of the neighbouring villages; where I may have the happiness to be your daily visitor. And if this Hickman be not silly and apish, and if my mother do not do unaccountable things, I may the sooner think of marrying, that I may without control receive and entertain the darling of my heart.

Many, very many, happy days, do I hope we shall yet see together: and as this is *my* hope, I expect that it will be *your* consolation.

I shall long to hear how you and Mrs Townsend order matters. I wish she could have been with you sooner. But I have lost no time in engaging her, as you will suppose. I refer to *her*, what I have further to say and advise. So shall conclude with my prayers that Heaven will direct, and protect, my dearest creature, and make your future days happy!

ANNA HOWE

And now, Jack, I will suppose that thou hast read this cursed letter.

Miss Howe will abandon her own better prospects, and

share fortunes with her were she to go abroad. Charming
romancer! I must set about this girl, Jack. I have always
had hopes of a woman whose passions carry her into
such altitudes! Had I attacked Miss Howe first, her passions (inflamed and guided as I could have managed
them) would have brought her to my lure in a fortnight.

But thinkest thou (and yet I think thou dost), that
there is anything in these high flights among the sex?
Verily, Jack, these vehement friendships are nothing but
chaff and stubble, liable to be blown away by the very
wind that raises them. Apes! mere apes of *us*! they think
the word *friendship* has a pretty sound with it; and it is
much talked of; a fashionable word: and so, truly, a single woman who thinks she has a soul, and knows that
she wants something, would be thought to have found a
fellow-soul for it in her own sex. But I repeat that the
word is a *mere* word, the thing a mere name with them;
a cork-bottomed shuttlecock, which they are fond of
striking to and fro, to make one another glow in the
frosty weather of a single state; but which, when a *man*
comes in between the pretended *inseparables*, is given up
like their music and other maidenly amusements; which,
nevertheless, may be necessary to keep the pretty rogues
out of more active mischief.

Thou hast a mind, perhaps, to make an exception for
these two ladies. With all my heart. My Clarissa has, if
woman has, a soul capable of friendship. Her flame is
bright and steady. But Miss Howe's, were it not kept up
by her mother's opposition, is too vehement to endure.
How often have I known opposition not only cement
friendship, but create love? I doubt not but poor Hickman would fare the better with this vixen, if her mother
were as heartily against him as she is for him.

Thus much indeed, as to these two ladies, I will grant
thee; that the active spirit of the one, and the meek
disposition of the other, may make their friendship more
durable than it would otherwise be; for this is certain,
that in every friendship, whether male or female, there
must be a man and a woman spirit (that is to say, one
of them a *forbearing* one) to make it permanent.

Miss Howe, Jack, is a charming girl. *She* has no reason
to quarrel with beauty! Didst ever see her? Too much

fire and spirit in her eye indeed, for a girl! But that's no
fault with a man that can lower that fire and spirit at
pleasure; and I know I am the man that can.

A sweet auburn beauty is Miss Howe. A first beauty
among beauties, when her sweeter friend (with such a
commixture of serene gracefulness, of natural elegance,
of native sweetness, yet conscious, though not arrogant,
dignity, every feature glowing with intelligence) is not
in company.

For my own part, when I was first introduced to this
lady, which was by my goddess, when she herself was a
visitor at Mrs Howe's; I had not been half an hour with
her, but I even hungered and thirsted after a romping
bout with the lively rogue; and in the second or third
visit was more deterred by the delicacy of her friend,
than by what I apprehended from her own. This charming creature's presence, thought I, awes us both. And I
wished her absence, though any other lady were present,
that I might try the difference in Miss Howe's behaviour
before her friend's face, or behind her back.

Delicate ladies make delicate ladies, as well as decent
men. With all Miss Howe's fire and spirit, it was easy to
see, by her very eye, that she watched for lessons, and
feared reproof from the penetrating eye of her milder-
dispositioned friend: and yet it was as easy to observe,
in the candour and sweet manners of the other, that the
fear which Miss Howe stood in of her was more owing
to her own generous apprehension, that she fell short of
her excellencies, than to Miss Harlowe's consciousness
of excellence over *her*.

As to the comparison between the two ladies, I will
expatiate more on that subject (for I like it) when I have
had them both—which this letter of the vixen girl's I
hope thou wilt allow warrants me to try for.

Letter 253: MR LOVELACE TO JOHN BELFORD, ESQ.

Sunday night—Monday morning
Should she fail in the trial; should I succeed; and should
she refuse to go on with me; and even to marry me;
which I can have no notion of—and should she disdain

to be obliged to me for the handsome provision I should
be proud to make for her, even to the *half of my estate*;
yet cannot she be altogether unhappy. Is she not entitled
to an independent fortune? Will not Colonel Morden,
as her trustee, put her in possession of it? And did she
not, in our former conference, point out the *way of life*
that she always preferred to the *married life*? To take
her good Norton for her directress and guide, and to
live upon her own estate in the manner her grandfather
desired she should live?

It is moreover to be considered that she cannot, according to her own notions, recover above *one half* of
her fame, were we now to intermarry; so much does she
think she has suffered by her going off with me. And
will she not be always repining and mourning for the
loss of the *other half*? And if she must live a life of such
uneasiness and regret for *half*, may she not as well repine and mourn for the *whole*?

Nor, let me tell thee, will her own scheme of penitence
in this case be half so perfect if she do *not* fall, as if she
does: for what a foolish penitent will she make, who has
nothing to repent of? She piques herself, thou knowest,
and makes it matter of reproach to me, that she went
not off with me by her own consent; but was tricked out
of herself.

Nor upbraid thou me upon the meditated breach of
vows so repeatedly made. She will not, thou seest, *permit*
me to fulfil them. And if she *would*, this I have to say,
that at the time I made the most solemn of them, I was
fully determined to keep them. But what prince thinks
himself obliged any longer to observe the articles of the
most sacredly sworn-to treaties, than suits with his interest or inclination; although the consequence of the infraction must be, as he knows, the destruction of
thousands?

And now, Belford, I set out upon business.

Letter 255: MR LOVELACE TO JOHN BELFORD, ESQ.

Well, but now my plots thicken; and my employment of
writing to thee on this subject will soon come to a con-

clusion. For now, having got the licence; and Mrs Townsend, with her tars [sailors], being to come to Hampstead
next Wednesday or Thursday; and another letter possibly, or message from Miss Howe, to inquire how Miss
Harlowe does, upon the rustic's report of her ill health,
and to express her wonder that she has not heard from
her in answer to hers on her escapes. I must soon blow
up the lady, or be blown up myself. And so I am preparing, with Lady Betty and my cousin Montague, to wait
upon my beloved with a coach and four, or a set.

Thou hast seen Lady Betty Lawrance several times—
hast thou not, Belford?

No, never in my life.

But thou hast; and lain with her too; or fame does
thee more credit than thou deservest. Why, Jack,
knowest thou not Lady Betty's other name?

Other name! Has she two?

She has. And what thinkest thou of Lady Bab Wallis?

Oh the devil!

Now thou hast it. Lady Barbara, thou knowest, lifted
up in circumstances and by pride, never appears or produces herself, but on occasions special—to pass to men
of quality or price for a duchess, or countess at least.
She has always been admired for a grandeur in her air
that few women of quality can come up to: and never
was supposed to be other than what she passed for;
though often and often a paramour for lords.

And who, thinkest thou, is my cousin Montague?

Nay, how should I know?

How indeed! Why, my little Johanetta Golding, a
lively, yet modest-looking girl, is my cousin Montague.

There, Belford, is an aunt! There's a cousin! Both
have wit at will. Both are accustomed to ape quality.
Both are genteelly descended. Mistresses of themselves;
and well educated—yet past pity. True *Spartan* dames;
ashamed of nothing but *detection*—always, therefore,
upon their guard against that. And in their own conceit,
when assuming top parts, the very quality they ape.

And how dost think I dress them out? I'll tell thee.

Lady Betty in a rich gold tissue, adorned with jewels
of high price.

My cousin Montague in a pale pink, standing end with

silver flowers of her own working. Charlotte, as well as my beloved, is admirable at her needle. Not quite so richly jewelled out as Lady Betty; but ear-rings and solitaire very valuable, and infinitely becoming.

Laces both, the richest that could be procured.

Thou canst not imagine what a sum the loan of the jewels cost me; though but for three days.

This sweet girl will half ruin me. But seest thou not by this time, that her reign is short? It must be so. And Mrs Sinclair has already prepared everything for her reception once more.

Letter 256: MR LOVELACE TO JOHN BELFORD, ESQ.

At Mrs Sinclair's, Monday afternoon

All's right as heart can wish! In spite of all objection—in spite of a reluctance next to fainting—in spite of all her foresight, vigilance, suspicion, once more is the charmer of my soul in her new lodgings!

Now throbs away every pulse! Now thump, thump, thumps my bounding heart for something!

My beloved is now directing some of her clothes to be packed up—never more to enter this house! Nor ever more will she, I dare say, when once again out of it!

Yet not so much as a condition of forgiveness! The Harlowe-spirited fair one will not *deserve* my mercy! She will wait for Miss Howe's next letter; and then, if she find a *difficulty in her new schemes* (thank her for nothing)—will—Will what? Why even *then* will take time to consider whether I am to be forgiven, or for ever rejected. An indifference that revives in my heart the remembrance of a thousand of the like nature. And yet Lady Betty and Miss Montague (one would be tempted to think, Jack, that they wish her to provoke my vengeance) declare that I ought to be satisfied with such a proud suspension!

They are entirely attached to her. Whatever she says *is, must be*, gospel! They are guarantees for her return to Hampstead this night. They are to go back with her. A supper bespoke by Lady Betty at Mrs Moore's. All the vacant apartments there, by my permission (for I had engaged them for a month certain), to be filled with them and their attendants, for a week at least, or till they can prevail upon the dear perverse, as they hope they shall, to restore me to her favour, and to accompany Lady Betty to Oxfordshire.

The dear creature has thus far condescended—that she will write to Miss Howe, and acquaint her with the present situation of things.

If she write, I shall see what she writes. But I believe she will have other employment soon.

Lady Betty is sure, she tells her, that she shall prevail upon her to forgive me; though she dares say, that I deserve not forgiveness. Lady Betty is too delicate to inquire strictly into the nature of my offence. But it must be an offence against herself, against Miss Montague, against the virtuous of the whole sex, or it could not be so highly resented. Yet she will not leave her till she forgive me, and till she see our nuptials privately celebrated. Meantime, as she approves of her *uncle's expedient*, she will address her as *already my wife, before strangers.*

Hard then if she had not obliged them with her company, in their coach and four, to and from their cousin Leeson's, who longed (as they themselves had done) to see a lady so justly celebrated!

'How will Lord M. be raptured when he sees her, and can salute her as his niece!

'How will Lady Sarah bless herself! She will now think her loss of the dear daughter she mourns for, happily supplied!'

Miss Montague dwells upon every word that falls from her lips. She perfectly adores her new cousin:

'What a happy family,' chorus we all, 'will ours be!'

In short, we are here, as at Hampstead, all joy and rapture: all of us, except my beloved, in whose sweet face (her almost fainting reluctance to re-enter these doors not overcome) reigns a kind of anxious serenity! But how will even *that* be changed in a few hours!

Methinks I begin to pity the half-apprehensive beauty! But avaunt, thou unseasonably-intruding pity! Thou hast more than once already well nigh undone me! And, adieu, reflection! Begone, consideration! and commiseration! I dismiss ye all, for at least a week to come! Be remembered her broken word! Her flight, when my fond soul was meditating mercy to her! Be remembered her treatment of me in her letter on her escape to Hampstead!—her Hampstead virulence!

Be her preference of the single life to *me* also remembered!—that she despises me!—that she even refuses to be my WIFE! A proud Lovelace to be denied a *wife*!—to be more proudly rejected by a daughter of the *Harlowes*!

Be the execrations of her vixen friend likewise remembered, poured out upon me from *her* representations, and thereby made her *own* execrations!

Is not *this* the crisis for which I have been long waiting?

Is not *this* the hour of her trial—and in *her,* of the trial of the virtue of her whole sex, so long premeditated, so long threatened? Whether her frost is frost indeed? Whether her virtue is principle? Whether, if *once subdued, she will not be always subdued?* And will she not want the very crown of her glory, the proof of her till now all-surpassing excellence, if I stop short of the ultimate trial?

Now is the end of purposes long over-awed, often suspended, at hand. And need I to throw the sins of her cursed family into the too weighty scale?

Abhorred be force!—be the thoughts of force! There's no triumph over the will in force! This I know I have said. But would I not have avoided it if I could? Have I not tried every other method? And have I any other recourse left me? Can she resent the *last outrage* more than she has resented a *fainter effort*? And if her resentments run ever so high, cannot I repair by matrimony? She will not refuse me, I know, Jack; the haughty beauty will not refuse me, when her pride of being corporally inviolate is brought down; when she can tell no tales, but when (be her resistance what it will) even her own sex will suspect a yielding in resistance; and when that modesty, which may fill her bosom with resentment, will lock up her speech.

But how know I that I have not made my own difficulties? Is she not a woman? What redress lies for a

perpetrated evil? Must she not *live*? Her piety will secure her life. And will not *time* be my friend? What, in
a word, will be her behaviour afterwards? She cannot
fly me! She must forgive me. And, as I have often said,
once forgiven, will be for ever forgiven.

Why then should this enervating pity unsteel my foolish heart?

It shall not. All these things will I remember; and
think of nothing else, in order to keep up a resolution
which the women about me will have it I shall be still
unable to hold.

I'll teach the dear charming creature to emulate me
in contrivance! I'll teach her to weave webs and plots
against her conqueror! I'll show her that in her smug-
gling schemes she is but a spider compared to me, and
that she has all this time been spinning only a cobweb!

What shall we do now! We are immersed in the depth
of grief and apprehension! How ill do women bear disappointment! Set upon going to Hampstead, and upon
quitting for ever a house she re-entered with infinite reluctance; what things she intended to take with her ready
packed up; herself on tip-toe to be gone; and I prepared
to attend her thither; she begins to be afraid that she
shall not go this night; and, in grief and despair, has
flung herself into her old apartment; locked herself in;
and, through the key-hole, Dorcas sees her on her
knees—praying, I suppose, for a safe deliverance.

And from what? And wherefore these agonizing
apprehensions?

Why, here, this unkind Lady Betty, *with* the dear creature's knowledge, though to her concern, and this mad-
headed cousin Montague *without* it, while she was
employed in directing her package, have hurried away
in the coach to their own lodgings. Only, indeed, to put
up some night-clothes, and so forth, in order to attend
their sweet cousin to Hampstead; and, no less to my
surprise than hers, are not yet returned.

I have sent to know the meaning of it.

In a great hurry of spirits, she would have had me
gone myself. Hardly any pacifying her! The girl, God

bless her! is wild with her own idle apprehensions! What is she afraid of?

I curse them both for their delay. My tardy villain, how he stays! Devil fetch them! Let them send their coach, and we'll go without them. In her hearing, I bid the fellow tell them so. Perhaps he stays to bring the coach, if anything happens to hinder the ladies from attending my beloved this night.

Devil take them, again say I!
Oh! here's my aunt's servant, with a billet.

to Robert Lovelace, Esq.

Monday night

Excuse us, dear nephew, I beseech you, to my dearest kinswoman. One night cannot break squares. For here Miss Montague has been taken violently ill with three fainting fits, one after another. The hurry of her joy, I believe, to find your dear lady so much surpass all expectation (never did family-love, you know, reign so strong as among us), and the too eager desire she had to attend her, have occasioned it: for she has but weak spirits, poor girl! well as she looks.

If she be better, we will certainly go with you tomorrow morning, after we have breakfasted with her at your lodgings. But, whether she be, or not, I will do myself the pleasure to attend your lady to Hampstead; and will be with you, for that purpose, about nine in the morning. With due compliments to your most worthily beloved, I am

Yours affectionately,
ELIZAB. LAWRANCE

Faith and troth, Jack, I know not what to do with myself: for here, just now, having sent in the above note by Dorcas, out came my beloved with it in her hand: in a fit of frenzy! True, by my soul!

She had indeed complained of her head all the evening.

Dorcas ran to me, out of breath, to tell me that her lady was coming in some strange way: but she followed her so quick, that the frighted wench had not time to say in what way.

It seems, when she read the billet—Now indeed, said she, am I a lost creature! Oh the poor Clarissa Harlowe!

She tore off her head-clothes; inquired where I was: and in she came, her shining tresses flowing about her neck; her ruffles torn, and hanging in tatters about her snowy hands; with her arms spread out; her eyes wildly turned as if starting from their orbits. Down sunk she at my feet, as soon as she approached me; her charming bosom heaving to her uplifted face; and, clasping her arms about my knees, Dear Lovelace, said she, if ever— if ever—if ever—And, unable to speak another word, quitting her clasping hold, down prostrate on the floor sunk she, neither in a fit nor out of one.

I was quite astonished. All my purposes suspended for a few moments, I knew neither what to say, nor what to do. But, recollecting myself, am I *again*, thought I, in a way to be overcome and made a fool of! If I now recede, I am gone for ever.

I raised her: but down she sunk, as if quite disjointed; her limbs failing her—yet not in a fit neither. I never heard of, or saw, such a dear unaccountable: almost lifeless, and speechless too for a few moments! What must her apprehensions be at that moment! And for what? A high-notioned dear soul! Pretty ignorance! thought I.

Never having met with a repugnance so *greatly* repugnant, I was staggered. I was confounded. Yet how should I know that it would be so till I tried? And how, having proceeded thus far, could I stop, were I *not* to have had the women to goad me on, and to make light of circumstances which they pretended to be better judges of than me.

I lifted her, however, into a chair; and, in words of disordered passion, told her all her fears were needless: wondered at them: begged of her to be pacified: besought her reliance on my faith and honour: and revowed all my old vows, and poured forth new ones.

At last, with an heart-breaking sob, I see, I see, Mr Lovelace, in broken sentences she spoke—I see, I see—

that at last—at last—I am ruined!—ruined—if *your* pity—Let me implore *your* pity! And down on her bosom, like a half-broken-stalked lily, top-heavy with the overcharging dews of the morning, sunk her head with a sigh that went to my heart.

Lady Betty would think it very strange, I told her, if she were to know it was so disagreeable to her to stay one night, for *her* company, in a house where she had passed *so many*!

She called me names upon this. She had called me names before. I was patient.

Let her go to Lady Betty's lodgings, then; *directly* go; if the person I called Lady Betty was really Lady Betty.

If! my dear! Good Heaven! What a villain does that IF show you believe me to be!

I cannot help it. I beseech you once more, let me go to Mrs Leeson's, if *that* IF ought not to be said.

Then assuming a more resolute spirit—I will go! I will inquire my way! I will go by myself! And would have rushed by me.

I folded my arms about her to detain her; pleading the bad way I heard poor Charlotte was in; and what a farther concern her impatience, if she went, would give her.

She would believe nothing I said, unless I would instantly order a coach (since she was not to have Lady Betty's, nor was permitted to go to Mrs Leeson's), and let her go in it to Hampstead, late as it was; and all alone; so much the better: for in the house of *people,* of whom Lady Betty upon inquiry had heard a bad character *(dropped foolishly this, by my prating new relation, in order to do credit to herself by depreciating others);* everything, and every face, looking with so much meaning vileness, as well as *my own (thou art still too sensible, thought I, my charmer!),* she was resolved not to stay another night.

I was all her fear, I found; and this house her terror: for I saw plainly that she now believed that Lady Betty and Miss Montague were both impostors.

But her mistrust is a little of the latest to do her service.

Letter 257: MR LOVELACE TO JOHN BELFORD, ESQ.

Tuesday morn. June 13

And now, Belford, I can go no farther. The affair is over. Clarissa lives. And I am

Your humble servant,
R. LOVELACE

Letter 259: MR LOVELACE TO JOHN BELFORD, ESQ.

Thursday, June 15

Let me alone, you great dog, you! Let me alone!—have I heard a lesser boy, his coward arms held over his head and face, say to a bigger, who was pummelling him for having run away with his apple, his orange, or his gingerbread.

So say I to thee, on occasion of thy severity to thy poor friend, who, as thou ownest, has furnished thee (ungenerous as thou art!) with the weapons thou brandishest so fearfully against him. And to what purpose, when the mischief is done; when, of consequence, the affair is irretrievable? and when a Clarissa could not move me?

Well, but after all, I must own that there is something very singular in this lady's case: and at times I cannot help regretting that I ever attempted her; since not one power either of body or soul could be moved in my favour.

But people's extravagant notions of things alter not facts, Belford: and, when all's done, Miss Clarissa Harlowe has but run the fate of a thousand others of her sex—only that they did not set such a romantic value upon what they call their *honour*; that's all.

And yet I will allow thee this—That if a person sets a high value upon anything, be it ever such a trifle in itself, or in the eye of others, the robbing of that person of it is *not* a trifle to *him*. Take the matter in this light, I own I have done wrong, great wrong, to this admirable creature.

But have I not known twenty and twenty of the sex, who have seemed to carry their notions of virtue high;

yet, when brought to the test, have abated of their severity? And how should we be convinced that *any* of them are proof, till they are tried?

A thousand times have I said that I never yet met with such a woman as this. If I *had*, I hardly ever should have attempted Miss Clarissa Harlowe. Hitherto she is all angel: and was not that the point which at setting out I proposed to try? And was not *cohabitation* ever my darling view? And am I not now, at last, in the high road to it? It is true, that I have nothing to boast of as to her will. The very contrary. But now are we come to the test, whether she cannot be brought to make the best of an irreparable evil? If she exclaim (she has reason to exclaim, and I will sit down with patience by the hour together to hear her exclamations, till she is tired of them), she will then descend to expostulation perhaps. Expostulation will give me hope: expostulation will show that she hates me not. And if she hate me not, she will forgive: and if she *now* forgive; then will all be over; and she will be mine upon my own terms: and it shall then be the whole study of my future life to make her happy.

Thou seest, Jack, that I make no resolutions, however, against doing her, one time or other, the wished-for justice, even were I to succeed in my principal view, *cohabitation*. And of this I do assure thee, that, if I ever marry, it must, it shall, be Miss Clarissa Harlowe. Nor is her honour at all impaired with *me*, by what she has *so far* suffered: but the contrary. She must only take care that, if she be at last brought to forgive me, she show me that her Lovelace is the only man on earth whom she could have forgiven on the like occasion.

But, ah, Jack! what, in the meantime, shall I do with this admirable creature? At present—I am loath to say it—but, at present she is quite stupefied.

I had rather, methinks, she should have retained all her active powers, though I had suffered by her nails and her teeth, than that she should be sunk into such a state of absolute—insensibility (shall I call it?) as she has been in ever since Tuesday morning. Yet, as she begins a little to revive, and now and then to call names and to exclaim, I dread almost to engage with the anguish of a spirit that owes its extraordinary agitations to a niceness that has no example either in ancient or modern story.

But I will leave this subject, lest it should make me too grave.

I was yesterday at Hampstead, and discharged all obligations there, with no small applause. I told them that the lady was now as happy as myself: and that is no great untruth; for I am not altogether so when I allow myself to *think*.

Well, but, after all (how many *after-all's* have I?), I could be very grave, were I to give way to it. The devil take me for a fool! What's the matter with me, I wonder! I must breathe a fresher air for a few days.

But what shall I do with this admirable creature the while? Hang me, if I know! For, if I stir, the venomous spider of this habitation will want to set upon the charming fly, whose silken wings are already so entangled in my enormous web that she cannot move hand or foot: for so much has grief stupefied her, that she is at present as destitute of will, as she always seemed of desire. I must not therefore think of leaving her yet for two days together.

Letter 260: MR LOVELACE TO JOHN BELFORD, ESQ.

I have just now had a specimen of what this dear creature's resentment will be when quite recovered: an affecting one! For, entering her apartment after Dorcas; and endeavouring to soothe and pacify her disordered mind; in the midst of my blandishments, she held up to Heaven, in a speechless agony, the innocent [marriage] licence (which she has in her own power).

She seemed about to call down vengeance upon me; when, happily, the leaden god in pity to her trembling Lovelace waved over her half-drowned eyes his somniferous wand, and laid asleep the fair exclaimer before she could go half through with her intended imprecation.

Thou wilt guess, by what I have written, that some *little* art has been made use of; but it was with a *generous* design (if thou'lt allow me the word on such an occasion) in order to lessen the too quick sense she was likely to

have of what she was to suffer. A contrivance I never
had occasion for before, and had not thought of now if
Mrs Sinclair had not proposed it to me: to whom I left
the management of it: and I have done nothing but curse
her ever since, lest the quantity should have for ever
damped her charming intellects.

Hence my concern—for I think the poor lady ought
not to have been so treated. *Poor lady*, did I say? What
have I to do with thy creeping style? But have not I the
worst of it; since her insensibility has made me but a
thief to my own joys?

I did not intend to tell thee of this little *innocent* trick;
for such I designed it to be; but that I hate disingenuity:
to thee especially: and as I cannot help writing in a more
serious vein than usual, thou wouldst, perhaps, had I not
hinted the true cause, have imagined that I was sorry
for the fact itself: and this would have given *thee* a good
deal of trouble in scribbling dull persuasives to repair
by matrimony; and *me*, in reading thy crude nonsense.
Besides, one day or other, thou mightest, had I not confessed it, have heard of it in an aggravated manner; and
I know thou hast such an high opinion of this lady's
virtue, that thou wouldst be disappointed if thou hadst
reason to think that she was subdued by *her own* consent, or any the *least* yielding in her will. And so is she
beholden to me in some measure, that at the expense of
my honour she may so justly form a plea, which will
entirely salve *hers*.

And now is the whole secret out.

Can it be helped? And must I not now try to make
the best of it? And the rather do I enjoin thee this,
and inviolable secrecy; because I begin to think that my
punishment will be greater than the fault, were it to be
only from my own reflection.

Letter 261: MR LOVELACE TO JOHN BELFORD, ESQ.

Friday, June 16

Who the devil could have expected such strange effects
from a cause so common, and so slight?

But these high-souled and high-sensed girls, who had

set up for shining lights and examples to the rest of the sex (I now see that such there are!) are with such difficulty brought down to the common standard, that a wise man, who prefers his peace of mind to his glory in subduing one of that exalted class, would have nothing to say to them.

I would at first have persuaded her, and offered to call witnesses to the truth of it, that we were actually married. Though the licence was in her hands, I thought the assertion might go down in her disorder; and charming consequences I hoped would follow. But this would not do.

Last night, for the first time since Monday last, she got to her pen and ink: but she pursues her writing with such eagerness and hurry, as show too evidently her discomposure.

I hope, however, that this employment will help to calm her spirits.

Just now Dorcas tells me that what she writes she tears, and throws the paper in fragments under the table, either as not knowing what she does, or disliking it: then gets up, wrings her hands, weeps, and shifts her seat all round the room: then returns to her table, sits down, and writes again.

One odd letter, as I may call it, Dorcas has this moment given me from her. *Carry this,* said she, *to the vilest of men.* Dorcas, a toad! brought it, without any further direction, to *me.* I sat down, intending (though 'tis pretty long) to give thee a copy of it: but, for my life, I cannot; 'tis so extravagant. And the original is too much an original to let it go out of my hands.

But some of the scraps and fragments, as either torn through, or flung aside, I will copy for the novelty of the thing, and to show thee how her mind works now she is in this whimsical way. Yet I know I am still furnishing thee with new weapons against myself. But spare thy comments. My own reflections render them needless. Dorcas thinks her lady will ask for them: so wishes to have them to lay again under her table.

By the first thou'lt guess that I have told her that Miss

Howe is very ill, and can't write; that she may account the better for not having received the letter designed for her.

PAPER I
(Torn in two pieces)

My dearest Miss Howe!

Oh! What dreadful, dreadful things have I to tell you! But yet I cannot tell you neither. But say, are you really ill, as a vile, vile creature informs me you are?

But he never yet told me truth, and I hope has not in this: and yet, if it were not true, surely I should have heard from you before now! But what have I to do, to upbraid? You may well be tired of me! And if you are, I can forgive you; for I am tired of myself: and all my own relations were tired of me long before you were.

How good you have always been to me, mine own dear Anna Howe! But how I ramble!

I sat down to say a great deal—my heart was full—I did not know what to say first—and thought, and grief, and confusion, and (Oh my poor head!) I cannot tell what—And thought, and grief, and confusion came crowding so thick upon me; *one* would be first, *another* would be first, *all* would be first; so I can write nothing at all—only that, whatever they have done to me, I cannot tell; but I am no longer what I was in any one thing. In any one thing did I say? Yes, but I am; for I am still, and I ever will be,

Your true—

PAPER II
(Scratched through, and thrown under the table)

And can you, my dear honoured papa, resolve for ever to reprobate your poor child? But I am sure you would not, if you knew what she has suffered since her unhappy—And will nobody plead for your poor suffer-

ing girl? No one good body? Why, then, dearest sir, let
it be an act of your own innate goodness, which I have
so much experienced, and so much abused. I don't presume to think you should receive me—no, indeed—my
name is—I don't know what my name is! I never dare
to wish to come into your family again! But your heavy
curse, my papa. Yes, I *will* call you papa, and help yourself as you can—for you are my own dear papa, whether
you will or not. And though I am an unworthy child—
yet I *am* your child.

PAPER III

A lady took a great fancy to a young lion, or a bear,
I forget which—but a bear, or a tiger, I believe, it was.
It was made her a present of when a whelp. She fed it
with her own hand: she nursed up the wicked cub with
great tenderness; and would play with it, without fear or
apprehension of danger: and it was obedient to all her
commands: and its tameness, as she used to boast, increased with its growth; so that, like a lap-dog, it would
follow her all over the house. But mind what followed.
At last, somehow, neglecting to satisfy its hungry maw,
or having otherwise disobliged it on some occasion, it
resumed its nature; and on a sudden fell upon her, and
tore her in pieces. And who was most to blame, I pray?
The brute, or the lady? The lady, surely! For what *she*
did, was *out* of nature, *out* of character at least: what *it*
did, was *in* its own nature.

PAPER V

Rejoice not now, my Bella, my sister, my friend; but
pity the humbled creature, whose foolish heart you used
to say you beheld through the thin veil of humility,
which covered it.

It must have been so! My fall had not else been
permitted:

You penetrated my proud heart with the jealousy of
an elder sister's searching eye.

You knew me better than I knew myself.

Hence your upbraidings, and your chidings, when I began to totter.

But forgive now those vain triumphs of my heart.

I thought, poor proud wretch that I was, that what you said was owing to your envy.

I thought I could acquit my intention of any such vanity.

I was too secure in the knowledge I thought I had of my own heart.

My supposed advantages became a snare to me.

And what now is the end of all?

to Mr Lovelace

I never intended to write another line to you. I would not see you, if I could help it. Oh that I never had!

But tell me of a truth, is Miss Howe really and truly ill?—very ill?—and is not her illness poison? And don't *you* know who gave it her?

What you, or Mrs Sinclair, or somebody I cannot tell who, have done to my poor head, you best know: but I shall never be what I was. My head is gone. I have wept away all my brain, I believe; for I can weep no more. Indeed I have had my full share; so it is no matter.

But, good now, Lovelace, don't set Mrs Sinclair upon me again! I never did her any harm. She *so* affrights me when I see her! Ever since—when was it? I cannot tell. *You* can, I suppose. She may be a good woman, as far as I know. She was the wife of a man of honour—very likely!—though forced to let lodgings for her livelihood. Poor gentlewoman! Let her know I pity her: but don't let her come near me again—pray don't!

Yet she may be a very good woman—

What would I say! I forget what I was going to say.

Oh! Lovelace! if you could be sorry for yourself, I would be sorry too—but when all my doors are fast, and nothing but the key-hole open, and the key of late put into that, to be where you are, in a manner without opening any of them—Oh wretched, wretched Clarissa Harlowe!

For I never will be Lovelace—let my uncle take it as he pleases.

Well, but now I remember what I was going to say.
It is for *your* good—not *mine*—for nothing can do me
good now! Oh thou villainous man! thou hated
Lovelace!

But Mrs Sinclair may be a good woman. If you love
me—but that you don't—but don't let her bluster up
with her worse than mannish airs to me again! Oh she
is a frightful woman! If she *be* a woman! She needed
not to put on that *fearful mask* to scare me out of my
poor wits. But don't tell her what I say. I have no hatred
to her. It is only fright, and foolish fear, that's all. She
may not *be* a bad woman—but neither are all *men*, any
more than all *women*, alike—God forbid they should be
like you!

Alas! you have killed my head among you. I don't say
who did it. God forgive you all! But had it not been
better to have put me out of all your ways at once? You
might safely have done it! For nobody would require me
at your hands—no, not a soul—except, indeed, Miss
Howe would have said, when she should see you, what,
Lovelace, have you done with Clarissa Harlowe? And
then you could have given any slight gay answer. Sent
her beyond sea; or, she has run away from me as she
did from her parents. And this would have been easily
credited; for you know, Lovelace, she that could run
away from *them*, might very well run away from *you*.

But this is nothing to what I wanted to say. Now I
have it!

I have lost it again. This foolish wench comes teasing
me. For what purpose should I eat? For what end should
I wish to live? I tell thee, Dorcas, I will neither eat nor
drink. I cannot be worse than I am.

I will do as you'd have me. Good Dorcas, look not
upon me so fiercely. But thou canst not look so bad as
I have seen somebody look.

Mr Lovelace, now that I remember what I took pen
in hand to say, let me hurry off my thoughts, lest I lose
them again. Here I am sensible. And yet I am hardly
sensible neither. But I know my head is not as it should
be, for all that. Therefore let me propose one thing to
you: it is for *your* good—not *mine*: and this is it:

I must needs be both a trouble and an expense to you.

And here my uncle Harlowe, when he knows how I am, will never wish any man to have me: no, not even *you*, who have been the occasion of it—but I forget what I would say again—

Then this is it: I never shall be myself again: I have been a very wicked creature—a vain, proud, poor creature—full of secret pride—which I carried off under an humble guise, and deceived everybody. My sister says so—and now I am punished—so let me be carried out of this house, and out of your sight; and let me be put into that Bedlam privately, which once I saw: but it was a sad sight to me then! Little as I thought what I should come to *myself*! That is all I would say: this is all I have to wish for—then I shall be out of all your ways; and I shall be taken care of; and bread and water, without your tormentings, will be dainties; and my straw bed the easiest I have lain in—for—I cannot tell how long!

My clothes will sell for what will keep me there, perhaps, as long as I shall live. But, Lovelace, *dear* Lovelace I will call you; for you have cost me enough, I'm sure!—don't let me be made a show of, for my *family's* sake; nay, for your *own sake*, don't do that. For when I know all I have suffered, which yet I do not, and no matter if I never do—I may be apt to rave against you by name, and tell of all your baseness to a poor humbled creature, that once was as proud as anybody—but of what I can't tell—except of my own folly and vanity—but let that pass—since I am punished enough for it.

So, suppose, instead of Bedlam, it were a private madhouse where nobody comes! That will be better a great deal.

But, another thing, Lovelace: don't let them use me cruelly when I am there. *You* have used me cruelly enough, you know! Don't let them use me cruelly; for I will be very tractable; and do as anybody would have me do—except what you would have me do—for that I never will. Another thing, Lovelace: don't let this *good* woman; I was going to say *vile* woman; but don't tell her that—because she won't let you send me to this happy refuge perhaps, if she were to know it.

Another thing, Lovelace: and let me have pen, and ink, and paper, allowed me. It will be all my amusement.

But they need not send to anybody I shall write to, what I write, because it will but trouble them: and somebody may do you a mischief, maybe—I wish not that anybody do anybody a mischief upon my account.

You tell me that Lady Betty Lawrance and your cousin Montague were here to take leave of me; but that I was asleep, and could not be waked. So you told me at first, I was married, you know; and that you were my husband. Ah! Lovelace! look to what you say. But let not them (for they will sport with my misery), let not *that* Lady Betty, let not *that* Miss Montague, whatever the *real* ones may do; nor Mrs Sinclair neither, nor any of her lodgers, nor her nieces, come to see me in my place. *Real* ones, I say; for, Lovelace, I shall find out all your villainies in time—indeed I shall—so put me there as soon as you can. It is for *your* good. Then all will pass for ravings that I can say, as, I doubt not, many poor creatures' exclamations do pass, though there may be too much truth in them for all that—and you know *I began to be mad at Hampstead*—so you said. Ah! villainous man! what have you not to answer for!

The miserably abused
Clarissa Harlowe

I will not hear thy heavy preachments upon this plaguy letter. So, not a word of that sort!

Mrs Sinclair is a true heroine and, I think, shames us all. And she is a *woman* too! Thou'lt say the best things corrupted become the worst. But this is certain, that whatever the sex set their hearts upon, they make thorough work of it. And hence it is, that a mischief which would end in simple robbery among men-rogues, becomes murder if a woman be in it.

I know thou wilt blame me for having had recourse to *art.* But do not physicians prescribe opiates in acute cases, where the violence of the disorder would be apt to throw the patient into a fever or delirium? I aver that my motive for this expedient was *mercy*; nor could it be anything else. For a rape, thou knowest, to us rakes is far from being an undesirable thing.

But is not wine itself an opiate in degree? How many women have been taken advantage of by wine, and other still more intoxicating viands? Let me tell thee, Jack, that the *experience* of many of the *passive* sex, and the *consciences* of many more of the *active*, appealed to, will testify that thy Lovelace is not the worst of villains. Nor would I have *thee* put me upon clearing myself, by comparisons.

If she escape a settled delirium when my plots unravel, I think it is all I ought to be concerned about.

Will is just returned from an errand to Hampstead; and acquaints me that Mrs Townsend was yesterday at Mrs Moore's, accompanied by three or four rough fellows. She was strangely surprised at the news that my spouse and I are entirely reconciled; and that two fine ladies, my relations, came to visit her, and went to town with her: where she is very happy with me. *She* was sure we were not married, she said, unless it was while we were at Hampstead: and *they* were sure the ceremony was not performed there. But that the lady *is* happy and easy is unquestionable: and a fling was thrown out by Mrs Moore and Mrs Bevis at *mischief-makers,* as they knew Mrs Townsend to be acquainted with Miss Howe.

Now, since my fair one can neither receive nor send away letters, I am pretty easy as to this Mrs Townsend and her employer. And I fancy Miss Howe will be puzzled to know what to think of the matter, and afraid of sending by Wilson's conveyance; and perhaps suppose that her friend slights her; or has changed her mind in my favour, and is ashamed to own it; as she has not had an answer to what she wrote; and will believe that the rustic delivered her last letter into her own hand.

Letter 262: MR LOVELACE TO JOHN BELFORD, ESQ.

Sunday afternoon, 6 o'clock (June 18)
I went out early this morning, and returned not till just now; when I was informed that my beloved, in my absence, had taken it into her head to attempt to get away.

She tripped down with a parcel tied up in a handkerchief, her hood on; and was actually in the entry, when Mrs Sinclair saw her.

Pray, madam, whipping between her and the street door, be pleased to let me know whither you are going?

Who has a right to control me? was the word.

I have, madam, by order of your spouse: And, kemboing her arms, as she owned, I desire you will be pleased to walk up again.

She would have spoken; but could not: and bursting into tears, turned back and went up to her chamber: and Dorcas was taken to task for suffering her to be in the passage before she was seen.

This shows, as we hoped last night, that she is recovering her charming intellects.

I will endeavour to see her. It must be in her own chamber, I suppose; for she will hardly meet me in the dining-room. What advantage will the confidence of our sex give me over the modesty of hers, if she be recovered! *I*, the most confident of men: *she*, the most delicate of women. Sweet soul! methinks I have her before me: her face averted: speech lost in sighs—abashed—conscious. What a triumphant aspect will this give me, when I gaze in her downcast countenance!

Letter 263: MR LOVELACE TO JOHN BELFORD, ESQ.

Sunday night

Never blame me for giving way to have art used with this admirable creature. All the princes of the air, or beneath it, joining with me, could never have subdued her while she had her senses.

I will not anticipate—only to tell thee that I am too much awakened by her to think of sleep, were I to go to bed; and so shall have nothing to do, but to write an account of our odd conversation, while it is so strong upon my mind that I can think of nothing else.

She was dressed in a white damask night-gown, with less negligence than for some days past. I was sitting, with my pen in my fingers; and stood up when I first saw her, with great complaisance, as if the day were still her own. And so indeed it is.

She entered with such dignity in her manner, as struck

me with great awe, and prepared me for the poor figure
I made in the subsequent conversation.

She came up with quick steps, pretty close to me; a
white handkerchief in her hand; her eyes neither fierce
nor mild, but very earnest; and a fixed sedateness in her
whole aspect, which seemed to be the effect of deep
contemplation: and thus she accosted me, with an air
and action that I never saw equalled.

You see before you, sir, the wretch whose preference
of you to all your sex you have rewarded—as it indeed
deserved to be rewarded. My father's dreadful curse has
already operated upon me in the very letter of it as to
this life; and it seems to me too evident that it will not
be your fault that it is not entirely completed in the loss
of my soul, as well as of my honour—which you, villainous man! have robbed me of, with a baseness so unnatural, so inhuman, that it seems, you, even *you*, had not
the heart to attempt it, till my senses were made the
previous sacrifice.

Here I made an hesitating effort to speak, laying down
my pen—but she proceeded. Hear me out, guilty
wretch!—abandoned man! *Man* did I say? Yet what
name else can I? since the mortal worryings of the
fiercest beast would have been more natural, and infinitely more welcome, than what you have acted by me;
and that with a premeditation and contrivance worthy
only of that single heart, which now, *base* as well as
ungrateful as thou art, seems to quake within thee. And
well mayest thou quake; well mayest thou tremble and
falter; and hesitate as thou dost, when thou reflectest
upon what I have suffered for thy sake, and the returns
thou hast made me!

Let me therefore know whether I am to be controlled
in the future disposal of myself? Whether, in a country
of liberty as *this*, where the sovereign of it must not be
guilty of *your* wickedness; and where *you* neither durst
have attempted it, had I one friend or relation to look
upon me, I am to be kept here a prisoner, to sustain
fresh injuries?

After a pause; for I was still silent:

Can you not answer me this plain question? I quit all

claim, all expectation upon you—what right have you to detain me here?

I could not speak. What could I say to such a question?

And she insisted upon being at her own disposal for the remainder of her short life for indeed she abhorred me in every light; and more particularly in that in which I offered myself to her acceptance.

And saying this, she flung from me; leaving me absolutely shocked and confounded at her part of a conversation, which she began with such uncommon, however severe composure, and concluded with so much sincere and unaffected indignation.

Monday morn.

  past three

Letter 264: MR LOVELACE TO JOHN BELFORD, ESQ.

                Monday morn. 5 o'clock (June 19)

Now indeed do I from my heart wish that I had never known this lady. But who would have thought there had been such a woman in the world? Of all the sex I have hitherto known, or heard, or read of, it was *once subdued, and always subdued*. The *first* struggle was generally the *last*; or at least the subsequent struggles were so much fainter and fainter, that a man would rather have them than be without them. But how know I yet—

The sun has been illuminating, for several hours, everything about me: for that impartial orb shines upon mother Sinclair's house, as well as upon any other: but nothing within me can it illuminate.

At day-dawn I looked through the key-hole of my beloved's door. She had declared she would not put off her clothes any more in this house. There I beheld her in a sweet slumber, which I hope will prove refreshing to her disturbed senses; sitting in her elbow-chair, her apron over her head, and that supported by one sweet hand, the other hanging down upon her side, in a sleepy lifelessness; half of one pretty foot only visible.

See the difference in our cases, thought I! She, the

charming injured, can sweetly sleep, while the varlet injurer cannot close his eyes; and has been trying to no
purpose, the whole night, to divert his melancholy, and
to fly from himself!

Six o'clock

Just now Dorcas tells me that her lady is preparing
openly, and without disguise, to be gone. Very probable.
The humour she flew away from me in last night, has
given me expectation of such an enterprise.

But she has sent me a message by Dorcas that she
will meet me in the dining-room; and desires (odd
enough!) that the wench may be present at the conversation that shall pass between us. This message gives me
hope.

Nine o'clock

Confounded art, cunning, villainy! By my soul, she
had like to have slipped through my fingers. She meant
nothing by her message, but to get Dorcas out of the
way, and a clear coast. Is a fancied distress sufficient to
justify this lady for dispensing with her principles? Does
she not show me that she can wilfully deceive, as well
as I?

Had she been in the fore-house, and no passage to
go through to get at the street door, she had certainly
been gone. But her haste betrayed her: for Sally Martin
happening to be in the fore-parlour, and hearing a
swifter motion than usual, and a rustling of silks, as if
from somebody in a hurry, looked out; and seeing who
it was, stepped between her and the door, and set her
back against it.

You must not go, madam. Indeed you must not.

By what right?—and how dare you?—and such-like
imperious airs the dear creature gave herself—while
Sally called out for her aunt; and half a dozen voices
joined instantly in the cry for me to hasten down, to
hasten down, in a moment.

I was gravely instructing Dorcas abovestairs, and wondering what would be the subject of the conversation
which she was to be a witness to, when these outcries
reached my ears. And down I flew. In her soft rage the

dear soul repeating, I *will* go! Nobody has a right. I *will* go! If you kill me, women, I won't go up again!

As soon as she saw me, she stepped a pace or two towards me; Mr Lovelace, I *will* go! said she. Do you authorize these women—what right have they, or *you* either, to stop me?

Is this, my dear, preparative to the conversation you led me to expect in the dining-room? And do you think I can part with you thus? Do you think I will?

And am I, sir, to be thus beset? Surrounded thus? What have these women to do with me?

I desired them to leave us, all but Dorcas, who was down as soon as I. I then thought it right to assume an air of resolution, having found my tameness so greatly triumphed over. And now, my dear, said I (urging her reluctant feet), be pleased to walk into the fore-parlour. Here, since you will not go upstairs—here we may *hold our parley*: and Dorcas *be witness to it*. And now, madam, seating her, and sticking my hands in my sides, your pleasure!

Insolent villain! said the furious lady. And rising, ran to the window, and threw up the sash. (She knew not, I suppose, that there were iron rails before the windows.) And when she found she could not get out into the street, clasping her uplifted hands together—having dropped her parcel. For the love of God, good honest man! For the love of God, mistress—to two passers-by—a poor, poor creature, said she, ruined!

I clasped her in my arms, people beginning to gather about the window: and then she cried out, Murder! Help! Help!—and carried her up to the dining-room, in spite of her little plotting heart (as I may now call it), although she violently struggled, catching hold of the banisters here and there, as she could. I would have seated her there, but she sunk down half-motionless, pale as ashes. And a violent burst of tears happily relieved her.

Dorcas wept over her. The wench was actually moved for her!

Violent hysterics succeeded. I left her to Mabel, Dorcas, and Polly; the latter the most supportable to her of the sisterhood.

This attempt, so resolutely made, alarmed me not a little.

Mrs Sinclair and her nymphs are much more concerned; because of the reputation of their house, as they call it, having received some insults (broken windows threatened) to make them produce the young creature who cried out.

While the mobbish inquisitors were in the height of their office, the women came running up to me, to know what they should do; a constable being actually fetched.

Get the constable into the parlour, said I, with three or four of the forwardest of the mob, and produce one of the nymphs, onion-eyed, in a moment, with disordered head-dress and neck-kerchief, and let her own herself the person: the occasion, a female skirmish; but satisfied with the justice done her. Then give a dram or two to each fellow, and all will be well.

Eleven o'clock

Mrs Sinclair wishes she never had seen the face of so skittish a lady; and she and Sally are extremely pressing with me, to leave the perverse beauty to their *breaking*, as they call it, for four or five days. But I cursed them into silence; only ordering double precaution for the future.

I am confoundedly out of conceit with myself. If I give up my contrivances, my joy in stratagem, and plot, and invention, I shall be but a common man: such another dull heavy creature as thyself. Yet what does even my success in my machinations bring me, but disgrace, repentance, regret? But I am overmatched, egregiously overmatched, by this lady. What to do with her, or without her, I know not.

Letter 266: MR LOVELACE TO JOHN BELFORD, ESQ.

Monday afternoon, June 19

Pity me, Jack, for pity's sake; since, if thou dost not, nobody else will: and yet never was there a man of my genius and lively temper that wanted it more.

She began with me like a true woman (*she* in the fault,

I to be blamed) the moment I entered the dining-room. Not the least apology, not the least excuse, for the uproar she had made, and the trouble she had given me.

Dearest madam, interrupted I, give not way to so much violence. You must know that your detention is entirely owing to the desire I have to make you all the amends that is in my power to make you. And this, as well for *your* sake as *my own.* Surely there is still *one* way left to repair the wrongs you have suffered.

Canst thou blot out the past week? *Several* weeks past, I should say; ever since I have been with thee? Canst thou call back time? If thou canst—

Then, turning towards me, who knew neither what to say *to* her, nor *for* myself: I renounce thee for ever, Lovelace! Abhorred of my soul! for ever I renounce thee! Seek thy fortunes wheresoever thou wilt!—only now, that thou hast already ruined me—

Ruined you, madam. The world need not—I knew not what to say.

Ruined me in my *own* eyes, and that is the same to me, as if *all the world* knew it. Hinder me not from going whither my mysterious destiny shall lead me.

Why hesitate you, sir? What right have you to stop me, as you lately did; and to bring me up by force, my hands and arms bruised with your violence? What right have you to detain me here?

Yet, if you think yourself in my power, I would caution you, madam, not to make me desperate. For you *shall* be mine, or my life shall be the forfeit! Nor is life worth having without you!

Be *thine*! I be *thine*! said the passionate beauty. Oh how lovely in her violence!

Yes, madam, be *mine*! I repeat, you *shall* be mine!

And am I then (with a kind of frantic wildness) to be detained a prisoner in this horrid house? Am I, sir? Take care! Take care! holding up her hand, menacing, how you make me desperate! If I fall, though by my own hand, inquisition will be made for my blood: and be not out in thy plot, Lovelace, if it *should* be so. Make *sure* work, I charge thee: dig a hole deep enough to cram in and conceal this unhappy body: for, depend upon it, that some of those who will not stir to protect me living, will move heaven and earth to avenge me dead!

A horrid dear creature! She had need, indeed, to talk of *her* unhappiness, in falling into the hands of the only *man* in the world who could have used her as I have used her! She is the only *woman* in the world who could have shocked and disturbed me as she has done. So we are upon a foot in that respect. And I think I have the *worst* of it by much. Since very little has been my joy; very much my trouble: and *her* punishment, as she calls it, is *over*: but when *mine* will, or what it *may be*, who can tell?

What a devil ails me! I can neither think nor write!

Lie down, pen, for a moment!

Letter 267: MR LOVELACE TO JOHN BELFORD, ESQ.

The dear creature resumed the topic her heart was so firmly fixed upon; and insisted upon quitting the *odious house*, and that in very high terms.

I urged her to meet me the next day at the altar, in either of the two churches mentioned in the licence. And I besought her, whatever were her resolution, to let me debate this matter calmly with her.

If, she said, I would have her give what I desired the least moment's consideration, I must not hinder her from being her own mistress. To what purpose did I ask her *consent*, if she had not a power over either her own person or actions?

But still she insisted upon being a free agent; of seeing herself in other lodgings before she would give what I urged the *least* consideration. Nor would she promise me favour even then, or to permit my visits. How then, as I asked her, could I comply, without resolving to lose her for ever?

She put her hand to her forehead often as she talked; and at last, pleading disorder in her head, retired; neither of us satisfied with the other. But *she* ten times more dissatisfied with me, than I with her.

What now! What now!

Letter 268: MR LOVELACE TO JOHN BELFORD, ESQ.

But, with all this dear creature's resentment against me, I cannot for my heart think but she will get all over, and consent to enter the pale with me. Were she even to die tomorrow, and to know she should, would not a woman of her sense, of her punctilio, and in her situation, and of so proud a family, rather die married, than otherwise?

As much of my heart as I know of it myself will I tell thee. When I am *from* her, I cannot still help hesitating about marriage, and I even frequently resolve against it; and am resolved to press my favourite scheme for cohabitation. But when I am *with* her, I am ready to say, to swear, and to do, whatever I think will be most acceptable to her: and were a parson at hand, I should plunge at once, no doubt of it, into the state.

A wife at any time, I used to say. I had ever confidence and vanity enough to think that no woman breathing could deny her hand, when I held out mine. I am confoundedly mortified to find that this lady is able to hold me at bay, and to refuse all my *honest* vows.

At the present writing, however, the turn of the scale is in favour of matrimony—for I despair of carrying with her my favourite point.

The lady tells Dorcas that her heart is broken; and that she shall live but a little while. I think nothing of that, if we marry. In the first place, she knows not what a mind unapprehensive will do for her, in a state to which all the sex look forward with high satisfaction. A few months' heart's ease will give my charmer a quite different notion of things: and I dare say, as I have heretofore said, once married, and I am married for life.

And for what should her heart be broken? Her will is unviolated—at *present*, however, her will is unviolated.

What nonsense then to suppose that such a mere notional violation as she has suffered should be able to cut asunder the strings of life?

To be sure she ought to have forgot it by this time, except the charming, charming consequence happen, that still I am in hopes will happen, were I to proceed no further. And if she apprehend this herself, then has the dear over-nice soul some reason for taking it so much to heart: and yet would not, I think, refuse to legitimate.

Oh Jack! had I an imperial diadem, I swear to thee that I would give it up, even to my *enemy*, to have one charming boy by this lady. And should she *escape me*, and no such effect follow, my revenge on her family, and in *such* a case on herself, would be incomplete, and I should reproach myself as long as I lived.

Were I to be sure that this foundation is laid (and why may I not hope it is?), I should not doubt to have her still (should she withstand her day of grace) on my own conditions: nor should I, if it were so, question that *revived* affection in *her* which a woman seldom fails to have for the father of her first child, whether born in wedlock or out of it.

Letter 275: MR LOVELACE TO JOHN BELFORD, ESQ.

Wednesday night

I have been so happy as to receive, this moment, a third letter from my dear correspondent Miss Howe. A little severe devil! It would have broke the heart of my beloved had it fallen into her hands. I will enclose a copy of it. Read it here.

Tuesday, June 20

My dearest Miss Harlowe,

Again I venture to write to you (almost against inclination); and that by your former conveyance, little as I like it.

I know not how it is with you. It may be bad; and then it would be hard to upbraid you for a silence you may not be able to help. But if not, what shall I say severe enough, that you have not answered either of my last letters? The first of which (and I think it imported you too much to be silent upon it) you owned the receipt of. The other, which was delivered into your own hands, was so pressing for the favour of a line from you, that I am amazed I could not be obliged—and still *more*, that I have not heard from you since.

The fellow made so strange a story of the condition

he saw you in, and of your speech to him, that I know not what to conclude from it: only, that he is a simple, blundering, and yet conceited fellow, who aiming at description, and the rustic wonderful, gives an air of bumkinly romance to all he tells. That this is his character, you will believe, when you are informed that he described you in grief excessive, yet so improved in your person and features, and so *rosy*, that was his word, in your face, and so flush-coloured, and so plump in your arms, that one would conclude you were labouring under the operation of some malignant poison; and so much the rather, as he was introduced to you when you were upon a couch, from which you offered not to rise, or sit up.

Upon my word, Miss Harlowe, I am greatly distressed upon your account; for I must be so free as to say that, in your ready return with your deceiver, you have not at all answered my expectations, nor acted up to your own character: for Mrs Townsend tells me, from the women at Hampstead, how cheerfully you put yourself into his hands again: yet, at the time, it was impossible you should be married!

Lord, my dear, what pity it is that you took so much pains to get from the man! But you know best! Sometimes I think it could not be *you* to whom the rustic delivered my letter. But it must too: yet it is strange I could not have one line by him: not one—and you so soon well enough to go with him back again!

I am not sure that the letter I am now writing will come to your hands: so shall not say half that I have upon my mind to say. But if you think it *worth your while* to write to me, pray let me know what fine ladies, his relations, those were, who visited you at Hampstead, and carried you back again so joyfully to a place that I had so fully warned you—But I will say no more: at least till I *know* more: for I can do nothing but wonder, and stand amazed!

Notwithstanding all the man's baseness, 'tis plain there was more than a lurking love—Good God! But I have done! Yet I know not how to have done, neither! Yet I must—I *will*.

Only account to me, my dear, for what I cannot at all

account for: and inform me whether you are really married, or not. And then I shall know whether there *must*, or must *not*, be a period shorter than that of one of our lives, to a friendship which has hitherto been the pride and boast of

Your ANNA HOWE

Letter 276: MR LOVELACE TO JOHN BELFORD, ESQ.

Thursday noon, June 22

At my repeated requests, she met me at six this morning. She was ready dressed; for she has not had her clothes off ever since she declared that they never more should be off in this house.

It is easy for me, Mr Lovelace, to see that further violences are intended me if I comply not with your purposes, whatever they are. I will suppose them to be what you so solemnly profess they are. But I have told you as solemnly my mind, that I never *will*, that I never *can*, be yours; nor, if so, any man's upon earth. All vengeance, nevertheless, for the wrongs you have done me, I disclaim. I want but to slide into some obscure corner, to hide myself from you, and from everyone who once loved me. The desire lately so near my heart, of a reconciliation with my friends, is much abated. They shall not receive me *now*, if they *would*.

I know that I have not now a friend in the world. Even Miss Howe has given me up—or you are—but I would fain keep my temper! By your means I have lost them all—and you have been a barbarous enemy to me. You know you have.

She paused.

I could not speak.

At last, she broke silence. I have no patience, said she, to find myself a slave, a prisoner in a vile house. Tell me, sir, in so many words tell me, whether it be, or be not, your intention to permit me to quit it? To permit me the freedom which is my birthright as an English subject?

And saying this, away she flung, leaving me in a confusion so great that I knew not what to think, say, or do.

But Dorcas soon roused me. Do you know, sir, running in hastily, that my lady is gone downstairs!

No, sure! And down I flew, and found her once more at the street door, contending with Polly Horton to get out.

She rushed by me into the fore-parlour, and flew to the window, and attempted once more to throw up the sash. Good people! Good people! cried she.

I caught her in my arms, and lifted her from the window. But being afraid of hurting the charming creature (charming in her very rage), she slid through my arms on the floor. Let me die here! Let me die here! were her words; remaining jointless and immoveable till Sally and Mrs Sinclair hurried in.

She was visibly terrified at the sight of the old wretch; while I, sincerely affected, appealed, Bear witness, Mrs Sinclair! Bear witness, Miss Martin! Miss Horton! Everyone bear witness, that I offer not violence to this beloved creature!

She then found her feet. But let not that woman come into my presence—nor that Miss Horton neither, who would not have dared to control me, had she not been a base one!

Hoh, sir! Hoh, madam! vociferated the old creature, her arms kemboed, and flourishing with one foot to the extent of her petticoats. What ado's here about nothing! I never knew such work in my life, between a chicken of a gentleman, and a tiger of a lady!

All thy new expostulations in my beloved's behalf I will answer when I see thee.

Letter 277: MR LOVELACE TO JOHN BELFORD, ESQ.

Thursday night

Confoundedly out of humour with this perverse lady. Nor wilt thou blame me, if thou art my friend.

With great difficulty I prevailed upon her to favour me with her company for one half-hour this evening. The necessity I was under to go down to M. Hall was the subject I wanted to talk to her upon.

If I go not down to M. Hall, madam, you'll have no scruple to stay here, I suppose, till Thursday is over?

If I cannot help myself, I must. But I insist upon being permitted to go out of this house, whether you leave it, or not.

Well, madam, then I will comply with your commands. And I will go out this very evening, in quest of lodgings that you shall have no objection to.

I will have no lodgings of your providing, sir. I will go to Mrs Moore's at Hampstead.

Mrs Moore's, madam? I have no objection to Mrs Moore's. But will you give me your promise to admit me there to your presence?

As I do here—when I cannot help it.

My heart, madam, my soul is all yours at present. But you *must* give me hope that your promise, in your own construction, binds you, no *new cause* to the contrary, to be mine on Thursday. How else can I leave you?

Let me go to Hampstead; and trust to my favour.

May I trust to it? Say, only, *may* I trust to it?

How will you trust to it, if you extort an answer to this question?

I will only say, madam, that I refer myself to your generosity. My heart is not to be trusted at this instant. As a mark of my submission to your will, you shall, if you please, withdraw—but I will not go to M. Hall. Live or die my uncle, I will not go to M. Hall—but will attend the effect of your promise. Remember, madam, you have promised *to endeavour to make yourself easy, till you see the event of next Thursday*. Next Thursday, remember, your uncle comes up to see us married. *That's the event!*

Away flew the charmer, with this half permission, and no doubt thought that she had an escape, nor without reason.

Letter 278: MR LOVELACE TO JOHN BELFORD, ESQ.

June 23. Friday morning

I went out early this morning, on a design that I know not yet whether I shall or shall not pursue; and on my return found Simon Parsons, my lord's Berkshire bailiff (just before arrived), waiting for me with a message in form, sent by all the family, to press me to go down, and that at my lord's particular desire; who wants to see me before he dies.

Nothing will do, Jack! I can procure no favour from her, though she has obtained from me the point which she had set her heart upon.

I will give thee a brief account of what passed between us.

I first proposed instant marriage; and this in the most fervent manner: but was denied as fervently.

'Tis well, madam! But ask me anything I can do to oblige you; and I *will* oblige you, though in nothing will you oblige *me*.

Then I ask you, then I request of you, to let me go to Hampstead.

I paused—and at last—By my soul you shall—This very moment I will wait upon you, and see you fixed there, if you'll promise me your hand on Thursday, in presence of your uncle.

I want not *you* to see me fixed—I will promise nothing.

You know the condition, madam—next Thursday.

You dare not trust—

My infinite demerits tell me that I *ought* not— Nevertheless I *will* confide in your generosity. Tomorrow morning (no *new cause* arising to give reason to the contrary), as early as you please, you may go to Hampstead.

This seemed to oblige her. But yet she looked with a face of doubt.

I will go down to the women. And having no better judges at hand, will hear what they say upon my critical situation with this proud beauty, who has so insolently rejected a Lovelace kneeling at her feet, though making an earnest tender of himself for a husband, in spite of all his prejudices to the state of shackles.

Letter 280: MR LOVELACE TO JOHN BELFORD, ESQ.

She claimed the performance of my promise, the moment she saw me, of *permitting* her (haughtily she spoke the word) to go to Hampstead as soon as I were gone to Berkshire.

Most cheerfully I renewed it.

She desired me to give orders in her hearing.

I sent for Dorcas and Will. They came. Do you both take notice (but, perhaps, sir, I may take *you* with me), that your lady is to be obeyed in all her commands. She purposes to return to Hampstead as soon as I am gone. My dear, will you not have a servant to attend you?

I shall want no servant there.

Will you take Dorcas?

If I should want Dorcas, I can send for her.

Shall I, my dear, call up Mrs Sinclair, and give her orders to the same effect, in your hearing?

I desire not to see Mrs Sinclair; nor any that belong to her.

As you please, madam.

And then (the servants being withdrawn) I urged her again for the assurance that she would meet me at the altar on Thursday next. But to no purpose. May she not thank herself for all that may follow?

One favour, however, I would not be denied; to be admitted to pass the evening with her.

All sweetness and obsequiousness will I be on this occasion.

This, Jack, however, shall be her last trial; and if she behave as nobly *in* and *after* this *second* attempt *(all her senses about her),* as she has done after the *first,* she will come out an angel upon full proof, in spite of man, woman, and devil: then shall there be an end of all her sufferings. I will then renounce that vanquished devil, and reform. And if any vile machination start up, presuming to mislead me, I will sooner stab it in my heart as it rises, than give way to it.

A few hours will now decide all. But whatever be the event, I shall be too busy to write again, till I get to M. Hall.

Meantime I am in strange agitations. I must suppress them, if possible before I venture into her presence. My heart bounces my bosom from the table. I will lay down my pen, and wholly resign to its impulses.

Letter 281: MR LOVELACE TO JOHN BELFORD, ESQ.

Fri. night, or rather Sat. morn. 1 o'clock

I thought I should not have had either time or inclination to write another line before I got to M. Hall. But have the first; must find the last; since I can neither sleep, nor do anything but write, if I can do that. I am most *confoundedly* out of humour. The reason let it follow; if it will follow—no preparation for it, from me.

I tried by gentleness and love to soften—What? Marble. A heart incapable either of love or gentleness. Her past injuries for ever in her head. Ready to receive a favour; the permission to go to Hampstead; but neither to deserve it, nor return any. So my scheme of the gentle kind was soon given over.

I then wanted her to provoke me: like a coward boy who waits for the first blow before he can persuade himself to fight, I half challenged her to challenge or defy me: she seemed aware of her danger; and would not directly brave my resentment: but kept such a middle course that I neither could find a pretence to offend, nor reason to hope.

She was very uneasy, upon the whole, in my company: wanted often to break from me: yet so held me to my promise of permitting her to go to Hampstead, that I knew not how to get off of it; although it was impossible, in my precarious situation with her, to think of performing it.

In this situation; the women ready to assist; and, if I proceeded not, as ready to ridicule me; what had I left me but to pursue the concerted scheme, and seek a pretence to quarrel with her in order to revoke my promised permission; and to convince her that I would not be upbraided as the most brutal of ravishers for nothing?

I had agreed with the women, that if I could not find a pretence in her presence to begin my operations, the note should lie in my way, and I was to pick it up soon after her retiring from me. But I began to doubt at near ten o'clock (so earnest was she to leave me, suspecting my over-warm behaviour to her, and eager grasping of her hand two or three times, with eye-strings, as I felt, on the strain, while her eyes showed uneasiness and apprehension), that if she actually retired for the night, it might be a chance, whether it would be easy to come at her again. Loath therefore to run such a risk, I stepped out at a little after ten, with intent to alter the preconcerted disposition a little; saying I would attend her again instantly. But as I returned, I met her at the door, intending to withdraw for the night. I could not persuade her to go back: nor had I presence of mind (so full of complaisancy as I was to her just before) to stay her by force: so she slid through my hands into her own apartment.

She had hardly got into her chamber, but I found a little paper, as I was going into mine; which I took up; and, opening it (for it was carefully pinned in another paper), what should it be but a [planted] promissory note, given as a bribe, with a further promise of a diamond ring, to induce Dorcas to favour her mistress's escape?

How my temper changed in a moment! Ring, ring, ring, ring, my bell, with a violence enough to break the string, and as if the house were on fire.

Every devil frighted into active life: the whole house in an uproar.

Flash came out my sword immediately; for I had it ready on. Cursed, confounded, villainous, bribery and corruption!

Up ran two or three of the sisterhood: What's the matter! What's the matter!

The matter! (for still my beloved opened not her door; on the contrary, drew another bolt). This *abominable* Dorcas! (Call her aunt up! Let her see what a traitress she has placed about me! And let her bring the toad to answer for herself) has taken a bribe, a provision for life, to betray her trust; by that means to perpetuate a quarrel between a man and his wife, and frustrate for ever all hopes of reconciliation between us!

Up came the aunt puffing and blowing! As she hoped for mercy, she was not privy to it! She never knew such a plotting perverse lady in her life! Well might servants be at the pass they were, when such ladies as Mrs Lovelace made no conscience of corrupting them. For *her* part, she desired no mercy for the wretch: no niece of hers, if she were not faithful to her trust! But what was the proof?

She was shown the paper—

But too evident! Cursed, cursed toad, devil, jade, passed from each mouth—and the vileness of the *corrupted* and the unworthiness of the *corruptress* were inveighed against.

Up we all went, passing the lady's door into the dining-room, to proceed to trial.

Stamp, stamp, stamp up, each on her heels; rave, rave, rave, every tongue!

Bring up the creature before us all, this instant!

And would she have got out of the house, say you!

These the noises and the speeches, as we clattered by the door of the fair briberess.

Up was brought Dorcas (whimpering) between two, both bawling out. You must go! You shall go! 'Tis fit you should answer for yourself! You are a discredit to all worthy servants!—as they pulled and pushed her upstairs—she whining, I cannot see his honour! I cannot look so good and so generous a gentleman in the face! Oh how shall I bear my aunt's ravings!

Come up, and be damned. Bring her forward, her imperial judge! What a plague, it is the *detection*, not the *crime*, that confounds you. You could be quiet enough for days together, as I see by the date, under the villainy. Tell me, ungrateful devil, tell me, who made the first advances.

But suppose, sir, said Sally, you have my lady and the wench face to face? You see she cares not to confess.

Oh my *carelessness*! cried Dorcas. Don't let my poor lady suffer! Indeed if you all knew what I know, you would say her ladyship has been cruelly treated.

Your lady *won't*, she *dare* not come out to save you, cried Sally, though it is more his honour's mercy than your desert, if he does not cut your vile throat this instant.

Say, repeated Polly, was it your lady that made the first advances, or was it you, you creature?

If the lady has so much honour, bawled the mother,

excuse me, *so*—excuse me, sir—(confound the old wretch! she had like to have said *son*!) If the lady has so much honour, as we have supposed, she will appear to vindicate a poor servant, misled as she has been by such large promises! But I hope, sir, you will do them *both* justice; I *hope* you will! Justice I ever loved.

Just then, we heard the lady's door unbar, unlock, unbolt.

Now, Belford, see us all sitting in judgement, re-solved to punish the fair briberess—and hear her *un-bolt, unlock, unbar,* the door; then, as it proved afterwards, put the key into the lock on the outside, lock the door, and put it in her pocket; Will I knew below, who would give me notice if, while we were all above, she should mistake her way and go downstairs, instead of coming into the dining-room; the street doors also doubly secured, and every shutter to the windows round the house fastened, that no noise or screaming should be heard (such was the brutal preparation)—and then *hear* her step towards us, and instantly *see* her enter among us, confiding in her own innocence; and with a majesty in her person and man-ner that is *natural* to her; but which then shone out in all its glory! Every tongue silent, every eye awed, every heart quaking, mine, in a particular manner, sunk, throbless. She silent too, looking round her, first on me; then on the mother, as no longer fearing her; then on Sally, Polly; and the culprit Dorcas! Such the glori-ous power of innocence exerted at that awful moment!

She would have spoken, but could not, looking down my guilt into confusion: a mouse might have been heard passing over the floor, her own light feet and rustling silks could not have prevented it; for she seemed to tread air, and to be all soul. She passed to the door, and back towards me, two or three times, before speech could get the better of indignation, and at last, after twice or thrice hemming, to recover her articulate voice—Oh thou contemptible and abandoned Lovelace, thinkest thou that I see not through this poor villainous plot of thine, and of these thy wicked accomplices?

Thou woman, looking at the mother, once my terror!

always my dislike! but now my detestation! shouldst
once more (for thine perhaps was the preparation) have
provided for me intoxicating potions, to rob me of my
senses.

And then, *turning to me,* Thou, wretch, mightest more
securely have depended upon such a low contrivance
as this!

And ye, vile women, who perhaps have been the ruin,
body and soul, of hundreds of innocents (you show me
how, in full assembly), know that I am not married—
ruined as I am by your helps, I bless God, I am *not*
married to this miscreant. And I have friends that will
demand my honour at your hands! And to whose authority I will apply; for none has this man over me. Look
to it then, what further insults you offer me, or incite
him to offer me. I am a person, though thus vilely betrayed, of rank and fortune.

And as for thee, thou vile Dorcas!—thou *double*
deceiver!—whining out thy pretended love for me!—
begone, wretch! Nobody will hurt thee! Begone, I say!
Thou hast too well acted thy part to be blamed by *any*
here but myself. Thou art safe: thy guilt is thy security
in such a house as this! Steal away into darkness!

Madam, said I, let me tell you; and was advancing
towards her with a fierce aspect, most cursedly vexed
and ashamed too.

But she turned to me: Stop where thou art, Oh vilest
and most abandoned of men! Nor, with that determined
face, offer to touch me, if thou wouldst not that I should
be a corpse at thy feet!

To my astonishment, she held forth a penknife in her
hand, the point to her own bosom, grasping resolutely
the whole handle, so that there was no offering to take
it from her.

I offer not mischief to anybody but myself. You, sir,
and ye women, are safe from every violence of mine.
The LAW shall be all my resource: the LAW, and she
spoke the word with emphasis, that to such people car-
ries natural terror with it, and now struck a panic into
them.

The LAW only shall be my refuge!

The infamous mother whispered me that it were better to *make terms* with this *strange lady*, and let her go.

Sally, notwithstanding all her impudent bravery at other times, said: *If* Mr Lovelace had told *them* what was *not true* of her being his wife—

And Polly Horton: That she must *needs* say, the lady, if she were *not* my wife, had been very much injured; that was all.

That is not now a matter to be disputed, cried I: you and I know, madam—

We do so, said she; and I thank God, I am *not* thine. *Once more*, I thank God for it! I have no doubt of the further baseness that thou hadst intended me by this vile and low trick: but I have my SENSES, Lovelace: and from my heart I despise thee, thou very poor Lovelace! How canst thou stand in my presence! Thou, that—

Madam, madam, madam—these are insults not to be borne—and was approaching her. She withdrew to the door, and set her back against it, holding the pointed knife to her heaving bosom; while the women held me, beseeching me not to provoke the violent lady.

Approach me, Lovelace, with resentment, if thou wilt. I dare die. It is in defence of my honour. God will be merciful to my poor soul! I expect no mercy from thee! I have gained this distance, and two steps nearer me and thou shalt see what I dare do!

Leave me, women, to myself, and to my angel! They retired at a distance. Oh my beloved creature, how you terrify me! Say you will sheathe your knife in the injurer's, not the injured's, heart; and then will I indeed approach you, but not else.

Thank God! Thank God! said the angel. Delivered *for the present*; for the *present* delivered from myself. Keep, sir, keep that distance (looking down towards me, who was prostrate on the floor, my heart pierced as with an hundred daggers!): that distance has saved a life; to what reserved, the Almighty only knows!

To *be* happy, madam; and to *make* happy! And Oh let me but hope for your favour for tomorrow. I will put off my journey till then. And may God—

This I say, of this you may assure yourself, I never,

never *will* be yours. And let me hope that I may be entitled to the performance of your promise, to permit me to leave this *innocent* house, as one called it (but long have my ears been accustomed to such inversions of words), as soon as the day breaks.

Then, taking one of the lights, she turned from us; and away she went, unmolested. Not a soul was *able* to molest her.

Mabel saw her, tremblingly and in a hurry, take the key of her chamber door out of her pocket and unlock it; and, as soon as she entered, heard her double-lock, bar, and bolt it.

By her taking out her key, when she came out of her chamber to us, she no doubt suspected my design: which was to have carried her in my arms thither, if she made such force necessary, after I had intimidated her, and to have been her companion for that night.

She was to have had several bedchamber women to assist to undress her upon occasion: but, from the moment she entered the dining-room with so much intrepidity, it was absolutely impossible to think of prosecuting my villainous designs against her.

This, this, Belford, was the hand I made of a contrivance I expected so much from! And now am I ten times worse off than before!

But for the lady, by my soul I love her, I admire her, more than ever! I *must* have her. I *will* have her still. *With* honour, or *without*, as I have often vowed.

I will press her with letters for the Thursday. She shall yet be mine, legally mine. For, as to cohabitation, there is now no such thing to be thought of.

The captain shall give her away, as proxy for her uncle. My lord will die. My fortune will help my *will*, and set me above everything and everybody.

But here is the curse. She despises me, Jack! What man, as I have heretofore said, can bear to be despised especially by his wife? Oh Lord! Oh Lord! What a hand, what a cursed hand have I made of this plot! and here ends

The history of the Lady and the Penknife!!! The devil

take the penknife! It goes against me to say, God bless the lady.

Near 5, Sat. morn.

Letter 284: MR LOVELACE TO MISS CLARISSA HARLOWE

(Superscribed, To Mrs Lovelace)

M. Hall, Monday, June 26

There is no time to be lost. And I would not have next Thursday go over without being entitled to call you mine, for the world; and that as well for your sake as my own. Hitherto all that has passed is between you and me only; but, after Thursday, if my wishes are unanswered, the whole will be before the world.

My lord is extremely ill, and endures not to have me out of his sight for one half-hour.

My Lord M. but just now has told me how happy he should think himself to have an opportunity, before he dies, to salute you as his niece.

Do not, dearest creature, dissipate all these promising appearances, and, by refusing to save your own and your family's reputation in the eye of the world, use yourself worse than the ungratefullest wretch on earth has used you. For, if we are married, all the disgrace you imagine you have suffered while a single lady will be my own; and only known to ourselves.

Once more then, consider well the situation we are both in; and remember, my dearest life, that Thursday will be soon here; and that you have no time to lose.

In a letter sent by the messenger whom I dispatch with this, I have desired that my friend Mr Belford, who is your very great admirer and who knows all the secrets of my heart, will wait upon you to know what I am to depend upon, as to the chosen day.

One motive for the gentle restraint I have presumed to lay you under is to prevent the mischiefs that might ensue (as probably to the *more* innocent, as to the *less*) were you to write to anybody, while your passions were so much raised and inflamed against me. Having apprised you of my direction on this head, I wonder you should have endeavoured to send a letter to Miss Howe, although in a cover directed to that young lady's servant; as you must think it would be likely to fall into my hands.

The just sense of what I have deserved the contents *should be* leaves me no room to doubt what they *are*. Nevertheless, I return it you enclosed with the seal, as you will see, unbroken.

Your ever-affectionate and obliged
LOVELACE

Letter 292: MR MOWBRAY TO ROBERT LOVELACE, ESQ.

Wednesday, 12 o'clock

Dear Lovelace,

I have plaguy news to acquaint thee with. Miss Harlowe is gon off! Quite gon, by my soul! I have not time for particulars, your servant being going off. But iff I had, we are not yet come to the bottom of the matter. The ladies here are all blubbering like devils, accusing one another most confoundedly: whilst Belton and I damn them all together in thy name.

If thou shouldst hear that thy fellow Will is taken dead out of some horse-pond, and Dorcas cutt down from her bed's tester, from dangling in her own garters, be not surprised. Here's the devill to pay. Nobody serene but Jack Belford, who is taking minnutes of exxamminations, accusations, and confessions, with the signifficant air of a Middlesex Justice, and intends to write at large all particulars, I suppose.

I heartily condole with thee: so does Belton. But it may turn out for the best: for she is gone away with thy marks, I understand. A foolish little devill! Where will she mend herself? For nobody will look upon her. And they tell me that thou wouldst certainly have married her had she stayed—but I know thee better.

Dear Bobby, adieu. If thy uncle will die now, to comfort thee for this loss, what a *seasonable* exit would he make! Let's have a letter from thee: prithee do. Thou canst write devil-like to Belford, who shows us nothing at all.

Thine heartily,
RD. MOWBRAY

Letter 294: MR LOVELACE TO JOHN BELFORD, ESQ.

Friday, June 30
I am ruined, undone, blown-up, destroyed, and worse than annihilated, that's certain! But was not the news shocking enough, dost thou think, without thy throwing into the too weighty scale reproaches which thou couldst have had no opportunity to make, but for my own voluntary communications? At a time too, when, as it falls out, I have another very sensible disappointment to struggle with?

Though it answer thy unfriendly purpose to own it, I cannot forbear to own it, that I am stung to the very soul with this unhappy—*accident*, must I call it? Have I nobody, whose throat, either for carelessness or treachery, I ought to cut in order to pacify my vengeance!

Let me add that the lady's plot to escape appears to me no extraordinary one. There was much more luck than probability that it should do: since, to make it succeed, it was necessary that Dorcas and Will and Sinclair and her nymphs should be all deceived, or off their guard. It belongs to me, when I see them, to give them my hearty thanks that they were; and that their selfish care to provide for their own future security should induce them to leave their outward door upon their bolt-latch, and be cursed to them!

Mabel deserves a pitch-suit and a bonfire, rather than the lustring; and as her clothes are returned, let the lady's be put to her others, to be sent to her when it can be told whither. But not till I give the word, neither; for we must get the dear fugitive back again, if possible.

I suppose that my stupid villain [Will], who knew not such a goddess-shaped lady with a mien so noble from the awkward and bent-shouldered Mabel, has been at

Hampstead to see after her: and yet I hardly think she would go thither. He ought to go through every street where bills for lodgings are up, to inquire after a newcomer. The houses of such as deal in women's matters, and tea, coffee, and suchlike, are those to be inquired at for her. If some tidings be not quickly heard of her, I would not have either Dorcas, Will or Mabel, appear in my sight, whatever their superiors think fit to do.

But I have so used myself to write a great deal of late, that I know not how to help it. Yet I must add to its length, in order to explain myself on a hint I gave at the beginning of it, which was that I have another disappointment besides this of Miss Harlowe's escape, to bemoan.

And what dost think it is? Why, the old peer, *pox* of his tough constitution! (for that would have helped him on), has made shift by fire and brimstone, and the devil knows what, to force the gout to quit the counterscarp of his stomach, just as it had collected all its strength in order to storm the citadel of his heart. In short they have, by the mere force of stink-pots, hand-grenades, and pop-guns, drove the slow-working pioneer quite out of the trunk into the extremities; and there it lies nibbling and gnawing upon his great toe; when I had hoped a fair end both of the distemper, and the distempered.

But I, who could write to *thee* of laudanum and the wet cloth formerly [i.e., contemplated murder], yet let £8,000 a year slip through my fingers, when I had entered upon it more than in imagination (for I had begun to ask the stewards questions, and to hear them talk of fines and renewals, and such sort of stuff), *deserve* to be mortified.

Thou canst not imagine how differently the servants, and even my cousins, look upon me since yesterday, to what they did before. Neither the one nor the other bow and curtsy half so low. Nor am I a quarter so often *his honour,* and *your honour,* as I was within these few hours with the former: and as to the latter—it is *cousin Bobby* again, with the usual familiarity, instead of *sir,* and *sir,* and, *If you please, Mr Lovelace.* And now they have the insolence to congratulate me on the recovery

of the *best of uncles*, while I am forced to seem as much
delighted as they, when, would it do me good, I could
sit down and cry my eyes out.

But thus, Jack, is an observation of the old peer's verified, *that one misfortune seldom comes alone*: and so
concludes

Thy doubly-mortified
LOVELACE

Letter 295: MISS CLARISSA HARLOWE TO MISS HOWE

Wednesday night, June 28

Oh, my dearest Miss Howe!

Once more have I escaped—but, alas! *I*, my *best self*,
have not escaped! Oh! your poor Clarissa Harlowe! *You*
also will hate me, I fear! Yet you won't, when you
know all!

But no more of myself! my *lost* self. You that can rise
in a morning to be blessed and to bless; and go to rest
delighted with your own reflections, and in your unbroken, unstarting slumbers, conversing with saints and
angels, the former only more pure than yourself, as they
have shaken off the encumbrance of body; you shall be
my subject, as you have long, long, been my only pleasure. And let me, at awful distance, revere my beloved
Anna Howe, and in *her* reflect upon what her Clarissa
Harlowe once was!

Forgive, oh! forgive my rambling. My peace is destroyed. My intellects are touched. And what flighty nonsense must you read, if now you will vouchsafe to
correspond with me, as formerly!

Oh! my best, my dearest, my *only* friend! What a tale
have I to unfold! But still upon *self*, this vile, this hated
self! I will shake it off, if possible; and why should I not,
since I think, except one wretch, I hate nothing so much!
Self, then, be banished from *self* one moment (for I
doubt it *will* for no longer) to inquire after a *dearer*
object, my beloved Anna Howe!—whose mind, all robed
in spotless white, charms and irradiates—but what would
I say?

*   *   *

And how, my dearest friend, after this rhapsody, which, on re-perusal, I would not let go but to show you what a distracted mind dictates to my trembling pen; *how do you?* You have been very ill, it seems. That you are *recovered*, my dear, let me hear! That your mamma is well, pray let me hear, and hear quickly! This comfort, surely, is owing to me; for if life is no *worse* than chequer-work, I must now have a little white to come, having seen nothing but black, all unchequered dismal black, for a great, great while!

And what is all this wild incoherence for? It is only to beg to know how you have been, and how you now do, by a line directed for Mrs Rachel Clark, at Mr Smith's, a glove shop, in King Street, Covent Garden; which (although my abode is a secret to everybody else) will reach the hands of *your unhappy*—but that's not enough—

Your miserable
CLARISSA HARLOWE

Letter 296: MRS HOWE TO MISS CLARISSA HARLOWE

(Superscribed as directed in the preceding)

Friday, June 30

Miss Clarissa Harlowe,

You will wonder to receive a letter from me. I am sorry for the great distress you seem to be in. Such a hopeful young lady as you were! But see what comes of disobedience to parents!

For my part; although I pity you; yet I much more pity your poor father and mother. Such education as they gave you! such improvements as you made! and such delight as they took in you!—and all come to this!

Here, people cannot be unhappy by themselves, but they must involve their friends and acquaintance, whose discretion has kept them clear of their errors, into near as much unhappiness as if they had run into the like of their own heads. Thus my poor daughter is always in tears and grief. And she has postponed her own felicity truly, because *you* are unhappy!

If people who seek their own ruin could be the only sufferers by their headstrong doings, it were something: but, oh miss, miss, what have *you* to answer for, who have made as many grieved hearts as have known you? The whole sex is indeed wounded by you: for who but Miss Clarissa Harlowe was proposed by every father and mother for a pattern for their daughters?

I write a long letter where I proposed to say but a few words; and those to forbid you writing to my Nancy: and this as well because of the false step you have made, as because it will grieve her poor heart and do you no good. If you love her, therefore, write not to her. Your sad letter came into my hands, Nancy being abroad, and I shall not show it her: for there would be no comfort for her if she saw it, nor for me whose delight she is— as you once was to your parents.

I may say too much: only as I think it proper to bear that testimony against your rashness, which it behoves every careful parent to bear. And none more than

Your compassionating well-wisher,
ANNABELLA HOWE

Letter 310: MISS HOWE TO MISS CLARISSA HARLOWE

(Superscribed, For Mrs Rachel Clark, etc.)

Wednesday, July 5

My dear Clarissa,

I have at last heard from you from a quarter I little expected.

From my mamma.

She had for some time seen me uneasy and grieving; and justly supposed it was about you. And this morning dropped a hint, which made me conjecture that she must have heard something of you more than I knew. And when she found that this added to my uneasiness, she owned she had a letter in her hands of yours, dated the 29th of June, directed for me.

You may guess that this occasioned a little warmth that could not be wished for by either.

In short, *she* resented that I should disobey her: *I* was as much concerned that she should open and withhold from me *my* letters: and at last she was pleased to compromise the matter with me; by giving up the letter and permitting me to write to you *once* or *twice*; she to see the contents of what I wrote. For, besides the value she has for you, she could not but have a great curiosity to know the occasion of so sad a situation as your melancholy letter shows you to be in.

Need I to remind you, Miss Harlowe, of *three* letters I wrote to you, to none of which I had any answer; except to the *first*, and that a few lines only, promising a letter at large; though you were well enough the day after you received my *second* to go joyfully back again with him to the vile house? But more of these by and by. I must hasten to take notice of your letter of Wednesday last week; which you could *contrive* should fall into my mother's hands.

Let me tell you that that letter has almost broken my heart. Good God! what have you brought yourself to, Miss Clarissa Harlowe? Could I have believed that after you had escaped from the miscreant (with such mighty pains and earnestness escaped), and after such an attempt as he had made, you would have been prevailed upon, not only to forgive him, but (without being married too) to return with him to that horrid house! A house I had given you such an account of! Surprising! What an intoxicating thing is *this love*? I *always* feared, that you, even you, were not proof against it.

You your *best self* have not escaped! Indeed I see not how you could expect to escape.

What a tale have you to unfold! You need not unfold it, my dear: I would have engaged to prognosticate all that has happened, had you but told me that you would once more have put yourself into his power after you had taken such pains to get out of it.

Your peace is destroyed! I wonder not at it: since now you must reproach yourself for a credulity so ill-placed.

Your intellect is touched! I am sure my heart bleeds for you: but, excuse me, my dear, I doubt your intellect was touched before you left Hampstead; or you would never have let him find you out there; or, when he did, suffer him to prevail upon you to return to the horrid brothel.

I tell you I sent you *three letters*: the *first* of which, dated the 7th and 8th of June (for it was wrote at twice), came safe to your hands, as you sent me word by a few lines dated the ninth.

The *second*, dated June 10, was given into your own hand at Hampstead on Sunday the 11th, as you was lying upon a couch in a strange way, according to my messenger's account of you, bloated, and flush-coloured; I don't know how.

The *third* was dated the 20th of June. Having not heard one word from you since the promising billet of the 9th, I own I did not spare you in it. I ventured it by the usual conveyance, by that Wilson's, having no other: so cannot be sure you received it. Indeed I rather think you might not; because in yours, which fell into my mamma's hands, you make no mention of it: and if you had had it, I believe it would have touched you too much to have been passed by unnoticed.

You have heard that I have been ill, you say. I had a cold indeed; but it was so slight a one that it confined me not an hour. But I doubt not that strange things you have *heard,* and *been told,* to induce you to take the step you took.

My mother tells me she sent you an answer desiring you not to write to me, because it would grieve me. To be sure I *am* grieved; *exceedingly* grieved; and *disappointed* too, you must permit me to say. For I had always thought that there never was such a woman, at your years, in the world.

My love for you, and my concern for your honour, may possibly have made me a little of the severest: if you think so, place it to its proper account; to *that* love, and to *that* concern: which will but do justice, to

Your afflicted and faithful,
A. H.

Letter 311: MISS CLARISSA HARLOWE TO MISS HOWE

Thursday, July 6

Few young persons have been able to give more convincing proofs than myself, how little true happiness lies in the enjoyment of our own wishes.

To produce one instance only of the truth of this observation; what would I have given for weeks past for the favour of a letter from my dear Miss Howe, in whose friendship I placed all my remaining comfort? Little did I think that the next letter she would honour me with should be in such a style as should make me look more than once at the subscription, that I might be sure (the name not being written at length) that it was not signed by another A.H. For surely, thought I, this is my sister Arabella's style: surely Miss Howe (blame me as she pleases in other points) could never repeat so *sharply* upon her friend, words written in the bitterness of spirit, and in the disorder of head.

But what have *I*, sunk in my fortunes; my character forfeited; my honour lost (while *I* know it, I care not *who* knows it); destitute of friends, and even of hope; what have I to do to show a spirit of repining and expostulation to a dear friend, because she is not *more* kind than a sister?

I find, by the rising bitterness which will mingle with the gall in my ink, that I am not yet subdued enough to my condition: and so, begging your pardon that I should rather have formed my expectations of favour from the indulgence you *used* to show me, than from what I *now deserve* to have shown me, I will endeavour to give a particular answer to your letter; although it will take me up too much time to think of sending it by your messenger tomorrow. He can put off his journey, he says, till Saturday. I will endeavour to have the whole narrative ready for you by Saturday.

But how to defend myself in everything that has happened, I cannot tell: since in some part of the time in which my conduct appears to have been censurable, I was not myself; and to this hour know not all the methods taken to deceive and ruin me.

Alas, my dear! I was tricked, most vilely tricked back, as you shall hear in its place.

Without *knowing* the house was so very *vile* a house from your *intended* information, I disliked the people too much, ever *voluntarily* to have returned to it.

But your account of your messenger's delivering to me your second letter, and the description he gives of me as *lying upon a couch, in a strange way, bloated and flush-coloured, you don't know how,* absolutely puzzles and confounds me.

Lord have mercy upon the poor Clarissa Harlowe! What can this mean! *Who* was the messenger you sent? Was *he* one of Lovelace's creatures too! Could nobody come near me but that man's confederates, either *setting out so*, or *made so*? I know not what to make of any one syllable of this! Indeed I don't!

Let me see. You say this was *before* I went from Hampstead! My intellects had not then been touched! Nor had I ever been surprised by wine (strange if I had!): how then could I be found in such a *strange way, bloated, and flush-coloured; you don't know how!* Yet what a vile, what a hateful figure has your messenger represented me to have made!

But indeed, I know nothing of ANY messenger from you.

Believing myself secure at Hampstead, I stayed longer there than I would have done, in hopes of the letter promised me in your short one of the 9th, brought me by my own messenger, in which you undertake to send for and engage Mrs Townsend in my favour.

I wondered I heard not from you: and was told you were sick; and, at another time, that your mother and you had had words on my account, and that you had refused to admit Mr Hickman's visits upon it: so that I supposed at one time that you was not *able* to write; at another that your mother's prohibition had its *due* force with you. But now I have no doubt that the wicked man must have intercepted your letter; and I wish he found not means to *corrupt your messenger* to tell you so strange a story.

It was on Sunday June 11 you say, that the man gave

it me. I was at church twice that day with Mrs Moore. Mr Lovelace was at her house the while, where he boarded, and wanted to have lodged; but I would not permit that, though I could not help the other. In one of these spaces *it must be* that he had time to work upon the man. You'll easily, my dear, find that out by inquiring the time of his arrival at Mrs Moore's, and other circumstances of the *strange way* he pretended to see me in, *on a couch*, and the rest.

Had anybody seen me afterwards, when I was betrayed back to the vile house, struggling under the operation of wicked potions, and robbed *indeed* of my intellects (for this, as you shall hear, was my dreadful case!), I might then perhaps have appeared *bloated*, and *flush-coloured*, and *I know not how myself.* But were you to see your poor Clarissa *now* (or ever to have seen her at Hampstead, *before* she suffered the vilest of all outrages), you would not think her *bloated*, or *flush-coloured:* indeed you would not.

In a word, it could not be *me* your messenger saw; nor (if anybody) who it was can I divine.

I will now, as *briefly* as the subject will permit, enter into the darker part of my sad story: and yet I must be somewhat circumstantial, that you may not think me capable of *reserve* or *palliation*. The *latter* I am not conscious that I need. I should be utterly inexcusable, were I guilty of the *former* to you. And yet, if you knew how my heart sinks under the thoughts of a recollection so painful, you would pity me.

As I shall not be able, perhaps, to conclude what I have to write in even two or three letters, I will begin a new one with my story; and send the whole of it together, although written at different periods, as I am able.

Allow me a little pause, my dear, at this place; and to subscribe myself

Your ever-affectionate and obliged
CLARISSA HARLOWE

Letter 316: MISS HOWE TO MISS CLARISSA HARLOWE

Sunday, July 9

Another shocking detection, my dear! How have you been deluded! Very watchful I have thought you; very sagacious—but, alas! not watchful, not sagacious enough, for the horrid villain you have had to deal with!

The letter you sent me enclosed as mine, of the 7th of June, is a villainous forgery. The hand, indeed, is astonishingly like mine; and the cover, I see, is actually my cover: but yet the letter is not so exactly imitated but that (had you had any suspicions about his vileness at the time) you, who so well know my hand, might have detected it.

In short, this vile forged letter, though a long one, contains but a few extracts from mine. Mine was a *very* long one. He has omitted everything, I see, in it that could have shown you what a detestable house the house is. You will see this, and how he has turned Miss Lardner's information and my advices to you (execrable villain!) to his own horrid ends, by the rough draught of the genuine letter[s] which I shall enclose.

And when you have perused them, I will leave you to judge how much reason I had to be surprised that you wrote me not an answer to either of those letters; one of which you owned you had received (though it proved to be his forged one); the other delivered into your own hands, as I was assured; and both of them of so much concern to your honour; and still how much more surprised I must be when I received a letter from Mrs Townsend, dated June 15 from Hampstead, importing 'That Mr Lovelace, who had been with you several days, had, on the Monday before, brought his aunt and cousin, richly dressed, and in a coach and four, to visit you: who, with your own consent, had carried you to town with them—to your former lodgings; where you still were: that the Hampstead women believed you to be married; and reflected upon me as a fomenter of differences between man and wife.'

I own to you, my dear, that I was so much surprised and disgusted at these appearances, against a conduct till then unexceptionable, that I was resolved to make myself as easy as I could, and wait till you should think fit to write to me. But I could rein in my impatience but for a few days; and on the 20th of June I wrote a sharp letter to you; which I find you did not receive.

What a fatality, my dear, has appeared in your case, from the very beginning till this hour!

But, for the future, if you approve of it, I will send my letters by the usual hand (Collins's), to be left at the Saracen's Head on Snow Hill: whither you may send yours (as we both used to do, to Wilson's), except such as we shall think fit to transmit by the post: which I am afraid, after my next, must be directed to Mr Hickman as before: since my mother is for fixing a condition to our correspondence which, I doubt, you will not comply with, though I wish you would. This condition I shall acquaint you with by and by.

Meantime, begging excuse for all the harsh things in my last, I beseech you, my dearest creature, to believe me to be,

Your truly sympathizing,
and unalterable friend,
ANNA HOWE

Letter 318: MISS CLARISSA HARLOWE TO MISS HOWE

Tuesday, July 11

I approve, my dearest friend, of the method you prescribe for the conveyance of our letters; and have already caused the porter of the inn to be engaged to bring to me yours, the moment that Collins arrives with them: as the servant of the house where I am will be permitted to carry mine to Collins for you.

As you are so earnest to have all the particulars of my sad story before you, I will, if life and spirits be lent me, give you an ample account of all that has befallen me from the time you mention. But this, it is very probable, you will not see till after the close of my last scene: and as I shall write with a view to that, I hope no other voucher will be wanted for the veracity of the writer.

I am far from thinking myself out of the reach of this man's further violence. But what can I do? Whither can

I fly? Perhaps my bad state of health (which must grow worse, as recollection of the past evils, and reflections upon them, grow heavier and heavier upon me) may be my protection. Once, indeed, I thought of going abroad; and had I the prospect of many years before me, I would go. But, my dear, the blow is given. Nor have you reason, now, circumstanced as I am, to be concerned that it is. What a heart must I have if it be not broken! And, indeed, my *dear*, my *best*, I had almost said my *only* friend, I do so earnestly wish for the last closing scene, and with so much comfort find myself in a declining way, that I even sometimes ungratefully regret that naturally healthy constitution which used to double upon me all my enjoyments.

Adieu, my dearest friend! May *you* be happy! And then your Clarissa Harlowe cannot be wholly miserable!

Letter 319: MISS HOWE TO MISS CLARISSA HARLOWE

Wedn. night, July 12

I write, my dearest creature, I cannot *but* write, to express my concern on your dejection. Let me beseech you, my charming excellence, let me beseech you, not to give way to it.

Comfort yourself, on the contrary, in the triumphs of a virtue unsullied; a will wholly faultless. Who could have withstood the trials that you have surmounted? Your cousin Morden will soon come. He will see justice done you, I make no doubt, as well with regard to what concerns your person as your estate. And many happy days may you yet see; and much good may you still do, if you will not heighten unavoidable accidents into guilty despondency.

But why, my dear, this pining solicitude continued after a reconciliation with relations as unworthy as implacable; whose wills are governed by an all-grasping brother, who finds his account in keeping the breach open? On this over-solicitude, it is now plain to me that the vilest of men built all his schemes. He saw you had a thirst after it, beyond all reason for hope. The view, the hope, I own extremely desirable, had your family

been Christians; or even had they been pagans, who
had bowels.

I shall send this short letter (I am obliged to make it
a short one) by young Rogers, as we call him; the fellow
I sent to you to Hampstead; an innocent, though prag-
matical rustic. Admit him, I pray you, into your presence, that he may report to me how you look, and how
you are.

Mr Hickman should attend you; but I apprehend that
all his motions, and my own too, are watched by the
execrable wretch: as indeed his are by an agent of mine;
for I own that I am so apprehensive of his plots and
revenge, now I know that he has intercepted my vehement letters against him, that he is the subject of my
dreams, as well as of my waking fears.

My mother, at my earnest importunity, has just given
me leave to write, and to receive your letters—but fastened this condition upon the concession, that yours
must be under cover to Mr Hickman (this with a view,
I suppose, to give him consideration with me); and upon
this further condition, that she is to see all we write.
'When girls are set upon a point,' she told one, who told
me again, 'it is better for a mother, if possible, to make
herself of their party, rather than to oppose them; since
there will be then hopes that she will still hold the reins
in her own hands.'

Pray let me know what the people are with whom
you lodge? Shall I send Mrs Townsend to direct you to
lodgings, either more safe, or more convenient for you?

Adieu, my dearest creature. Comfort *yourself*, as you
would in the like unhappy circumstances comfort

Your own
ANNA HOWE

Letter 320: MISS CLARISSA HARLOWE TO MISS HOWE

Thursday, July 13

I think I cannot be more private than where I am. I
hope I am safe. All the risk I run is in going out and

returning from morning prayers; which I have two or three times ventured to do; once at Lincoln's Inn chapel, at eleven; once at St Dunstan's, Fleet Street, at seven in the morning, in a chair both times; and twice at six in the morning, at the neighbouring church in Covent Garden. The wicked wretches I have escaped from will not, I hope, come to church to look for me; especially at so early prayers; and I have fixed upon the privatest pew in the latter church to hide myself in; and perhaps I may lay out a little matter in an ordinary gown, by way of disguise; my face half hid by my mob. I am very careless, my dear, of my appearance now. Neat and clean takes up the whole of my attention.

The man's name, at whose house I lodge, is Smith—a glove-*maker*, as well as *seller*. His wife is the shopkeeper. A dealer also in stockings, ribands, snuff and perfumes. A matron-like woman, plain-hearted, and prudent. The husband an honest, industrious man. And they live in good understanding with each other.

Two neat rooms, with plain, but clean furniture, on the first floor, are mine; one they call the dining-room.

There is, up another pair of stairs, a very worthy widow lodger, Mrs Lovick by name; who, although of low fortunes, is much respected, as Mrs Smith assures me, by people of condition of her acquaintance, for her piety, prudence, and understanding. With her I propose to be well acquainted.

I thank you, my dear, for your kind, your seasonable advice and consolation. I hope I shall have more grace given me than to despond, in the *religious* sense of the word—especially as I can apply to myself the comfort you give me that neither my will nor my inconsiderateness has contributed to my calamity.

At present my head is much disordered. I have not indeed enjoyed it with any degree of clearness since the violence done to that, and to my heart too, by the wicked arts of the abandoned creatures I was cast among.

I must have more conflicts. At times I find myself not subdued enough to my condition. I will welcome those conflicts as they come, as *probationary* ones. But yet my father's malediction—yet I hope even *that* may be made of so much use to me as to cause me to *double my attention to render it ineffectual.*

All I will at present add are my thanks to your mother for her indulgence to us. Due compliments to Mr Hickman; and my request that you will believe me to be, to my last hour, and beyond it, if possible, my beloved friend, and my *dearer* self (for what is now my self?),

Your obliged and affectionate
CLARISSA HARLOWE

Letter 321: MR LOVELACE TO JOHN BELFORD, ESQ.

Friday, July 7

I have three of thy letters at once before me to answer; in each of which thou complainest of my silence; and in one of them tellest me that thou canst not live without I scribble to thee every day, or every other day at least.

Why then, die, Jack, if thou wilt. What heart, thinkest thou, can I have to write, when I have lost the only subject worth writing upon?

Help me again to my angel, to my Clarissa; and thou shalt have a letter from me, or writing at least, part of a letter, every hour. All that the charmer of my heart shall say, that will I put down: every motion, every air of her beloved person, every look, will I try to describe; and when she is silent, I will endeavour to tell thee her thoughts, either what they are, or what I'd have them to be—so that, having *her*, I shall never want a subject. Having lost her, my whole soul is a blank: the whole creation round me, the elements above, beneath, and everything I *behold* (for nothing can I *enjoy*) is a blank without her!

Well but, Jack, 'tis a surprising thing to me that the dear fugitive cannot be met with; cannot be heard of. She is so poor a plotter (for plotting is not her talent), that I am confident, had I been at liberty, I should have found her out before now; although the different emissaries I have employed about town, round the adjacent villages, and in Miss Howe's vicinage, have hitherto

failed of success. But my lord continues so weak and
low-spirited, that there is no getting from him. I would
not disoblige a man whom I think in danger still: for
would his gout, now it has got him down, but give him,
like a fair boxer, the rising blow, all would be over with
him. And here (Pox of his fondness for me! it happens
at a very bad time) he makes me sit hours together entertaining him with my rogueries (a pretty amusement
for a sick man!): and yet, whenever he has the gout, he
prays night and morning with his chaplain.

There, Jack!—wilt thou, or wilt thou not, take this for
a letter? And if thou canst think tolerably of such execrable stuff, I will soon send thee another.

Letter 327: MISS HOWE TO MISS CLARISSA HARLOWE

Thursday night, July 13
I am to acquaint you that I have been favoured with a
visit from Miss Montague and her sister, in Lord M.'s
chariot and six. My lord's gentleman rode here yesterday
with a request that I would receive a visit from the two
young ladies, on a *very particular occasion*; the greater
favour if it might be the next day.

As I had so little personal knowledge of either, I
doubted not but it must be in relation to the interests
of my dear friend; and so consulting with my mother, I
sent them an invitation to favour me (because of the
distance) with their company at dinner; which they
kindly accepted.

I hope, my dear, since things have been so *very* bad,
that their errand to me will be as agreeable to you as
anything that can now happen. They came in the name
of Lord M. and his two sisters, to desire my interest to
engage you to put yourself into the protection of Lady
Betty Lawrance; who will not part with you till she sees
all the justice done you that now can be done.

He [Lovelace] promises by them to make the best of
husbands; and my lord and his two sisters are both to be
guarantees that he will be so. Noble settlements, noble
presents, they talked of: they say they left Lord M. and
his two sisters talking of nothing else but of those pres-

ents and settlements, how most to do you honour, the
greater in proportion for the indignities you have suffered; and of changing of names by Act of Parliament,
preparative to the interest they will all join to make to
get the titles to go where the bulk of the estate must go
at my lord's death, which they apprehend to be nearer
than they wish. Nor doubt they of a thorough reformation in his morals from your example and influence
over him.

I made a great many objections for you—all, I believe, that you could have made yourself, had you been
present. But I have no doubt to advise you, my dear
(and so does my mother), instantly to put yourself into
Lady Betty's protection, with a resolution to take the
wretch for your husband: all his future grandeur (he
wants not pride) depends upon his sincerity to you; and
the young ladies vouch for the depth of his concern for
the wrongs he has done you.

Indeed, my dear, you must not hesitate: you *must*
oblige them: the alliance is splendid and honourable.
Very few will know anything of his brutal baseness to
you. All must end in a little while in a genteel reconciliation; and you will be able to resume your course of doing
the good to every deserving object, which procured you
blessings wherever you set your foot.

You have now happy prospects opening to you: a family, *already noble*, ready to receive and embrace you with
open arms and joyful hearts; and who, by their love to
you, will teach another family (who know not what an
excellence they have confederated to persecute) how to
value you.

Like a traveller who has been put out of his way by
the overflowing of some rapid stream, you have only had
the fore-right path you were in overwhelmed. A few
miles about, a day or two only lost, as I may say, and
you are in a way to recover it; and, by quickening your
speed, will get up the lost time. The hurry upon your
spirits, meantime, will be all your inconvenience; for it
was not your fault you were stopped in your progress.

I shall impatiently expect your next letter. The young
ladies proposed that you should put yourself, if in town,
or near it, into the Reading stage-coach, which inns

somewhere in Fleet Street: and if you give notice of the
day, you will be met on the road, and that pretty early
in your journey, by some of both sexes; one of whom
you won't be sorry to see.

Mr Hickman shall attend you at Slough; and Lady
Betty herself, and one of the Misses Montague, with
proper equipages, will be at Reading to receive you; and
carry you directly to the seat of the former: for I have
expressly stipulated that the wretch himself shall not
come into your presence till your nuptials are to be solemnized, unless you give leave.

Adieu, my dearest friend: be happy: and hundreds
will then be happy of consequence. Inexpressibly so, I
am sure, will then be

Your ever-affectionate
ANNA HOWE

Letter 329: MISS HOWE TO MISS CHARLOTTE MONTAGUE

Tuesday morning, July 18

Madam,

I take the liberty to write to you, by this special messenger: in the frenzy of my soul I write to you, to demand of you, and of any of your family who can tell,
news of my beloved friend; who, I doubt, has been spir-
ited away by the base arts of one of the blackest—Oh
help me to a name bad enough to call him by! Her piety
is proof against self-attempts: it must, it must be him,
the only him who could injure such an innocent; and
now—who knows what he has done with her!

If I have patience, I will give you the occasion of this
distracted vehemence.

I wrote to her the very moment you and your sister
left me. But being unable to procure a special messenger, as I intended, was forced to send by the post. I
urged her (you know, I promised, that I would), I urged
her with earnestness, to comply with the desires of all
your family. Having no answer, I wrote again on Sunday
night; and sent it by a particular hand, who travelled all
night; chiding her for keeping a heart so impatient as
mine in such cruel suspense upon a matter of so much

importance to her; and therefore to me. And very angry I was with her in my mind.

But, judge my astonishment, my distraction, when last night, the messenger, returning post-haste, brought me word that she had not been heard of since Friday morning! And that a letter lay for her at her lodgings, which came by the post; and must be mine.

She went out about six that morning; only intending, as they believe, to go to morning prayers at Covent Garden church, just by her lodgings, as she had done divers times before. Went on foot! Left word she should be back in an hour—Very poorly in health!

Lord, have mercy upon me! What shall I do! I was a distracted creature all last night!

Oh madam! You know not how I love her! She was my earthly saviour, as I may say! My own soul is not dearer to me than my Clarissa Harlowe! Nay, she is my soul!—for I now have none!—only a miserable one, however!—for she was the joy, the stay, the prop of my life! Never woman loved woman as we love one another! It is impossible to tell you half her excellencies. It was my glory and my pride that I was capable of so fervent a love of so pure and matchless a creature! But now! Who knows whether the dear injured has not all her woes, her undeserved woes! completed in death; or is not reserved for a worse fate! This I leave to your inquiry—for—your—(shall I call the man—your) relation, I understand, is still with you.

Surely, my good ladies, you were well authorized in the proposals you made me in presence of my mother! Surely he dare not abuse your confidence, and the confidence of your noble relations. I make no apology for giving you this trouble, nor for desiring you to favour with a line by this messenger

Your almost distracted
ANNA HOWE

Letter 330: MR LOVELACE TO JOHN BELFORD, ESQ.

M. Hall, Sat. night, July 15

All undone, undone, by Jupiter! Zounds, Jack, what

shall I do now! A curse upon all my plots and contrivances!

Thy assistance I bespeak: the moment thou receivest this, I bespeak thy assistance. This messenger rides for life and death!—and I hope he'll find you at your town lodgings; if he meet not with you at Edgware; where, being Sunday, he will call first.

This cursed, cursed woman [Mrs Sinclair] on Friday dispatched man and horse with the joyful news, as she thought it would be to me, in an exulting letter from Sally Martin, that she had found out my angel as on Wednesday last; and on Friday morning, after she had been at prayers at Covent Garden church—praying for my reformation, perhaps!—got her arrested by two sheriff's officers as she was returning to her lodgings, who put her into a chair they had in readiness, and carried her to one of the cursed fellows' houses.

She has arrested her for £150 pretendedly due for board and lodgings: a sum, besides the low villainy of the proceeding, which the dear soul could not possibly raise; all her clothes and effects, except what she had on and with her when she went away, being at the old devil's!

And here, for an aggravation, has the dear creature lain already two days; for I must be gallanting my two aunts and my two cousins, and giving Lord M. an airing after his lying-in: pox upon the whole family of us!—and returned not till within this hour: and now returned to my distraction, on receiving the cursed tidings, and the exulting letter.

Hasten, hasten, dear Jack; for the love of God, hasten to the injured charmer! My heart bleeds for her! She deserved not this! I dare not stir! It will be thought done by my contrivance—and if I am absent from this place, that will confirm the suspicion.

Damnation seize quick this accursed woman! Yet she thinks she has made no small merit with me! Unhappy, thrice unhappy circumstance! At a time too, when better prospects were opening for the sweet creature!

Hasten to her! Clear me of this cursed job. Most sincerely, by all that's sacred, I swear you may.

Set her free the moment you see her: without conditioning, free! On your knees, for me, beg her pardon: and assure her that, wherever she goes, I will not molest her: no, nor come near her without her leave: and be sure allow not any of the damned crew to go near her. Only, let her permit *you* to receive her commands from time to time: you have always been her friend and advocate. What would I now give, had I permitted you to have been a successful one!

Let her have all her clothes and effects sent her instantly, as a small proof of my sincerity. And force upon the dear creature, who must be moneyless, what sums you can get her to take. Let me know how she has been treated: if roughly, woe be to the guilty!

The great devil fly away with them all, one by one, through the roof of their own cursed house, and dash them to pieces against the tops of chimneys, as he flies; and let the lesser devils collect their scattered scraps, and bag them up, in order to put them together again in their allotted place, in the element of fire, with cements of molten lead.

A line! a line! a kingdom for a line! with tolerable news, the first moment thou canst write! This fellow waits to bring it.

Letter 333: MR BELFORD TO ROBERT LOVELACE, ESQ.

Sunday night, July 16

What a cursed piece of work hast thou made of it, with the most excellent of women! Thou mayest be in earnest, or in jest, as thou wilt; but the poor lady will not be long either thy sport, or the sport of fortune!

I will give thee an account of a scene that wants but her affecting pen to represent it justly; and it would wring all the black blood out of thy callous heart.

Thy villain [Will] it was, that set the poor lady, and had the impudence to appear and abet the sheriff's officers in the cursed transaction. He thought, no doubt, that he was doing the most acceptable service to his blessed master. They had got a chair; the head ready up, as soon as service was over. And as she came out of the church, at the door fronting Bedford Street, the officers stepping to her, whispered that they had an action against her.

She was terrified, trembled, and turned pale.

Action! said she. What is that? I have committed *no bad action*! Lord bless me! Men, what mean you?

That you are our prisoner, madam.

Prisoner, sirs! What—How—Why—What have I done?

You must go with us. Be pleased, madam, to step into this chair.

With *you*! With *men*! Must go with *men*! I am not used to go with *strange men*! Indeed you must excuse me!

We can't excuse you: we are sheriff's officers. We have a writ against you. You *must* go with us, and you shall know at whose suit.

Suit! said the charming innocent; I don't know what you mean. Pray, men, don't lay hands upon me! They offering to put her into the chair.

She then spied thy villain. Oh thou wretch, said she, where is thy vile master? Am I again to be *his prisoner*? Help, good people!

A crowd had before begun to gather.

The people were most of them struck with compassion. A fine young creature! A thousand pities! some—while some few threw out vile and shocking reflections: but a gentleman interposed, and demanded to see the fellows' authority.

They showed it. Is your name Clarissa Harlowe, madam? said he.

Yes, yes, indeed, ready to sink, my name *was* Clarissa Harlowe—but it is now *Wretchedness*! Lord, be merciful to me! what is to come next?

You *must* go with these men, madam, said the gentleman: they have authority for what they do. He pitied her, and retired.

Indeed you must, said one chairman.

Indeed you must, said the other.

Can nobody, joined in another gentleman, be applied to, who will see that so fine a creature is not ill used?

Thy villain answered, Orders were given particularly for that. She had rich relations. She need but ask and have. She would only be carried to the officer's house, till matters could be made up. The people she had lodged with, loved her: but she had left her lodgings privately.

Well, if I must go, I must! I cannot resist. But I will not be carried to the woman's! I will rather die at your feet, than be carried to the woman's!

You won't be carried there, madam, cried thy fellow.

Only to *my* house, madam, said one of the officers.

Where is that?

In High Holborn, madam.

I know not where High Holborn is: but anywhere, except to the woman's. But am I to go with *men* only?

Anywhere—anywhere, said she, but to that woman's! And stepping into the chair, threw herself on the seat, in the utmost distress and confusion. Carry me, carry me out of sight. Cover me. Cover me up—for ever! were her words.

Thy villain drew the curtains: she had not power; and they went away with her, through a vast crowd of people.

The unhappy lady fainted away when she was taken out of the chair at the officer's house.

Several people followed the chair to the very house, which is in a wretched court. Sally was there; and satisfied some of the inquirers that the young gentlewoman would be exceedingly well used: and they soon dispersed.

Dorcas was also there; but came not in her sight. Sally, as a favour, offered to carry her to her former lodgings: but she declared they should carry her thither a corpse, if they did.

She asked, What was meant by this usage of her? People told me, said she, that I *must* go with the men!—that they had authority to take me: so I submitted. But now, what is to be the end of this disgraceful violence?

The end, said the vile Sally Martin, is for honest people to come at their own.

Bless me! Have I taken away anything that belongs to those who have obtained this power over me? I have left very valuable things behind me; but have taken nothing away that is not my own.

And who do you think, *Miss Harlowe*, for I understand, said the cursed creature, you are not married; who
do you think is to pay for your board and your lodgings;
such handsome lodgings! for so long a time as you were
at Mrs Sinclair's? . . . One hundred and fifty guineas, or
pounds, is no small sum to lose—and by a young creature, who would have bilked her lodgings!

You amaze me, Miss Martin! What language do you
talk in? *Bilk my lodgings!* What is that?

She stood astonished and silent for a few moments.

Now, Lovelace! Now indeed do I think I *ought* to
forgive thee! But who shall forgive Clarissa Harlowe!
Oh my sister! Oh my brother! Tender mercies were your
cruelties to *this*!

She cast up her eyes to heaven, and was silent—and
went to the farthest corner of the room and, sitting
down, threw her handkerchief over her face.

Sally asked her several questions: but not answering
her, she told her she would wait upon her by and by,
when she had found her speech.

She ordered the people to press her to eat and drink.

I have ordered pen, ink and paper, to be brought you,
Miss Harlowe. There they are. I know you love writing.
You may write to whom you please. Your friend Miss
Howe will expect to hear from you.

I have no friend, said she. I deserve none.

Rowland, for that is the officer's name, told her, she
had friends enow to pay the debt, if she would write.

She would trouble nobody; she had no friends; was all
they could get from her, while Sally stayed: but yet spoken with a patience of spirit as if she enjoyed her griefs.

The insolent creature went away, ordering them in her
hearing to be very civil to her, and to let her want for
nothing. Now had she, she owned, the triumph of her
heart over this haughty beauty, who kept them all at
such a distance in their own house!

About six in the evening, Rowland's wife pressed her
to drink tea. She said she had rather have a glass of
water; for her tongue was ready to cleave to the roof of
her mouth.

About nine o'clock she asked if anybody were to be
her bedfellow?

Their maid, if she pleased; or, as she was so weak and
ill, the girl should sit up with her, if she chose she should.

She chose to be alone, both night and day, she said.
But might she not be trusted with the keys of the room
where she was to lie down; for she should not put off
her clothes?

That, they told her, could not be.

She was afraid not, she said. But indeed she would
not get away, if she could.

They told me that they had but one bed, besides that
they lay in themselves (which they would fain have had
her accept of), and besides *that* their maid lay in, in a
garret, which they called a hole of a garret: and that *that*
one bed was the prisoner's bed; which they made several
apologies to me about. I suppose it is shocking enough.

But the lady would not lie in theirs. Was she not a
prisoner, she said? Let her have the prisoner's room.

Yet they owned that she started when she was con-
ducted thither. But recovering herself, Very well, said
she—Why should not all be of a piece? Why should not
my wretchedness be complete?

She found fault that all the fastenings were on the outside, and none within; and said she could not trust herself
in a room where others could come in at their pleasure,
and she not go out. She had not *been used* to it!!!

They assured her that it was as much their duty to
protect her from other persons' insults, as from escaping herself.

Then they were people of more honour, she said, than
she had of late been used to!

She asked if they knew Mr Lovelace?

No, was their answer.

Have you heard of him?

No.

Well then, you may be good sort of folks in your way.

Next morning Sally and Polly both went to visit her.

Sir, said she, with high indignation to the officer, did
not you say last night that it was as much your business
to protect me from the insults of others, as from escaping? Cannot I be permitted to see whom I please; and
to refuse admittance to those I like not?

Your creditors, madam, will expect to see you.

Not if I declare I will not treat with them.

Then, madam, you will be sent to prison.

Prison, friend! What dost thou call thy house?

Not a prison, madam.

Why these iron-barred windows then? Why these double locks, and bolts all on the outside, none on the in?

And down she dropped into her chair, and they could not get another word from her. She threw her handkerchief over her face, as once before, which was soon wet with tears; and grievously, they own, she sobbed.

Sally then ordered a dinner, and said they would soon be back again, and see that she eat and drink as a good Christian should, comporting herself to her condition, and making the best of it.

'Tis twelve of the clock, Sunday night. I can think of nothing but of this excellent creature. Her distresses fill my head and my heart. I was drowsy for a quarter of an hour; but the fit is gone off. And I will continue the melancholy subject from the information of these wretches. Enough, I dare say, will arise in the visit I shall make, if admitted tomorrow, to send by thy servant, as to the way I am likely to find her in.

At twelve Saturday night, Rowland sent to tell them that she was so ill that he knew not what might be the issue; and wished her out of his house.

And this made them as heartily wish to hear from you. For their messenger, to their great surprise, was not then returned from M. Hall. And they were sure he must have reached that place by Friday night.

Early on Sunday morning, both devils went to see how she did. They had such an account of her weakness, lowness, and anguish, that they forbore, out of compassion, they said, finding their visits so disagreeable to her, to see her. But their apprehension of what might be the issue was, no doubt, their principal consideration: nothing else could have softened such flinty bosoms.

They sent for the apothecary Rowland had had to her, and gave him, and Rowland, and his wife, and maid, paradeful injunctions for the utmost care to be taken of her: no doubt with an Old Bailey forecast. And they sent up to let her know what orders they had given: but that, understanding she had taken something to compose herself, they would not disturb her.

It is three o'clock. I will close here; and take a little rest: what I have written will be a proper preparative for what shall offer by and by.

If I find any difficulty in seeing the lady, thy messenger shall post away with this. But, if I am admitted, thou shalt have *this* and the result of my audience both together. In the former case, thou mayest send another servant to wait the next advices, from

J. Belford

Letter 334: MR BELFORD TO ROBERT LOVELACE, ESQ.

Monday, July 17

About six this morning I went to Rowland's. Mrs Sinclair was to follow me, in order to dismiss the action; but not to come in sight.

Rowland, upon inquiry, told me that the lady was extremely ill; and that she had desired not to let anybody but his wife or maid come near her.

I said I *must* see her. I had told him my business overnight; and I *must* see her.

His wife went up: but returned presently, saying she could not get her to speak to her; yet that her eyelids moved; though she either would not, or could not, open them, to look up at her.

Oons, woman, said I, the lady may be in a fit: the lady may be dying. Let me go up. Show me the way.

A horrid hole of a house, in an alley they call a court; stairs wretchedly narrow, even to the first-floor rooms: and into a den they led me, with broken walls which had been papered, as I saw by a multitude of tacks, and some torn bits held on by the rusty heads.

The floor indeed was clean, but the ceiling was smoked with variety of figures, and initials of names, that had been the woeful employment of wretches who had no other way to amuse themselves.

A bed at one corner, with coarse curtains tacked up at the feet to the ceiling; because the curtain rings were

broken off; but a coverlid upon it with a cleanish look,
though plaguily in tatters, and the corners tied up in
tassels, that the rents in it might go no farther.

The windows dark and double-barred, the tops
boarded up to save mending; and only a little four-
paned eylet-hole of a casement to let in air; more, however, coming in at broken panes than could come in
at that.

Four old turkey-worked chairs, bursten-bottomed, the
stuffing staring out.

An old, tottering, worm-eaten table, that had more
nails bestowed in mending it to make it stand, than the
table cost fifty years ago when new.

To finish the shocking description, in a dark nook
stood an old, broken-bottomed cane couch, without a
squab or coverlid, sunk at one corner, and unmortised,
by the failing of one of its worm-eaten legs, which lay
in two pieces under the wretched piece of furniture it
could no longer support.

I had leisure to cast my eye on these things: for, going
up softly, the poor lady turned not about at our entrance
nor, till I spoke, moved her head.

She was kneeling in a corner of the room, near the
dismal window, against the table, on an old bolster (as
it seemed to be) of the cane couch, half-covered with
her handkerchief; her back to the door; which was only
shut to (no need of fastenings!); her arms crossed upon
the table, the fore-finger of her right hand in her Bible.
She had perhaps been reading in it, and could read no
longer. Paper, pens, ink, lay by her book on the table.
Her dress was white damask, exceeding neat; but her
stays seemed not tight-laced. I was told afterwards, that
her laces had been cut when she fainted away at her
entrance into this cursed place; and she had not been
solicitous enough about her dress to send for others. Her
headdress was a little discomposed; her charming hair,
in natural ringlets, as you have heretofore described it,
but a little tangled, as if not lately kembed, irregularly
shading one side of the loveliest neck in the world; as
her disordered, rumpled handkerchief did the other. Her
face (Oh how altered from what I had seen it! yet lovely
in spite of all her griefs and sufferings!) was reclined,

when we entered, upon her crossed arms; but so as not more than one side of it to be hid.

When I surveyed the room around, and the kneeling lady, sunk with majesty too in her white, flowing robes (for she had not on a hoop), spreading the dark, though not dirty, floor, and illuminating that horrid corner; her linen beyond imagination white, considering that she had not been undressed ever since she had been here; I thought my concern would have choked me. Something rose in my throat, I know not what, which made me for a moment guggle, as it were, for speech: which, at last, forcing its way, Con-Con-Confound you both, said I to the man and woman, is this an apartment for such a lady? And could the cursed devils of her own sex, who visited this suffering angel, see her, and leave her, in so damned a nook?

Sir, we would have had the lady to accept of our own bedchamber; but she refused it. We are poor people—and we expect nobody will stay with us longer than they can help it.

Up then raised the charming sufferer her lovely face; but with such a significance of woe overspreading it that I could not, for the soul of me, help being visibly affected.

She waved her hand two or three times towards the door, as if commanding me to withdraw; and displeased at my intrusion; but did not speak.

Permit me, madam. I will not approach one step farther without your leave—permit me, for one moment, the favour of your ear!

No—No—go, go; MAN, with an emphasis—and would have said more; but, as if struggling in vain for words, she seemed to give up speech for lost, and dropped her head down once more, with a deep sigh, upon her left arm; her right, as if she had not the use of it (numbed, I suppose), self-moved, dropping down on her side.

I dare not approach you, dearest lady, without your leave: but on my knees I beseech you to permit me to release you from this damned house, and out of the power of the accursed woman who was the occasion of your being here!

She lifted up her sweet face once more, and beheld me on my knees.

Are you not—are you not Mr Belford, sir? I think your name is Belford?

It is, madam, and I ever was a worshipper of your virtues, and an advocate for you; and I come to release you from the hands you are in.

And in whose to place me? Oh leave me, leave me! Let me never rise from this spot! Let me never, never more believe in man!

This moment, dearest lady, this very moment, if you please, you may depart whithersoever you think fit. You are absolutely free, and your own mistress.

I had now as lieve die here in this place, as anywhere. I will owe no obligation to any friend of *him* in whose company you have seen me. So, pray, sir, withdraw.

Then turning to the officer, Mr Rowland I think your name is? I am better reconciled to your house than I was at first. If you can but engage that I shall have nobody come near me but your wife; no *man*! and neither of those women who have sported with my calamities; I will die with you, and in this very corner. And you shall be well satisfied for the trouble you have had with me. I have value enough for that—for, see, I have a diamond ring; taking it out of her bosom; and I have friends will redeem it at a high price, when I am gone.

But for *you*, sir, looking at me, I beg you to withdraw. If you mean me well, God, I hope, will reward you for your good meaning; but to the friend of my *destroyer* will I not owe an obligation.

You will owe no obligation to me, nor to anybody. You have been detained for a debt you do not owe. The action is dismissed; and you will only be so good as to give me your hand into the coach which stands as near to this house as it could draw up. And I will either leave you at the coach-door, or attend you whithersoever you please, till I see you safe where you would wish to be.

Will you then, sir, *compel* me to be beholden to you?

You will inexpressibly oblige me, madam, to command me to do you either service or pleasure.

Why then, sir—looking at me—but why do you mock

me in that humble posture! Rise, sir! I cannot speak to
you else.

I arose.

Only, sir, take this ring. I have a sister who will be
glad to have it, at the price it shall be valued at, for the
former owner's sake! Out of the money she gives, let
this man be paid; handsomely paid: and I have a few
valuables more at my lodgings (Dorcas, or the MAN William, can tell where that is); let them, and my clothes at
the wicked woman's where you have seen me, be sold
for the payment of my lodging first, and next of your
friend's debts, that I have been arrested for; as far as
they will go; only reserving enough to put me into the
ground, anywhere, or anyhow, no matter. Tell your
friend I wish it may be enough to satisfy the whole demand; but if it be not, he must make it up himself; or,
if he think fit to draw for it on Miss Howe, she will
repay it, and with interest, if he insist upon it. If I want
to say anything more to you (you seem to be an humane
man), I will let you know—and so, sir, God bless you.

I approached her, and was going to speak.

Don't speak, sir: Here's the ring.

I stood off.

And won't you take it? Won't you do this last office
for me? I have no other person to ask it of; else, believe
me, I would not request it of *you*. But take it or not,
laying it upon the table—you must withdraw, sir: I am
very ill. I would fain get a little rest, if I could. I find I
am going to be bad again.

And here being obliged to give way to an indispensable avocation, I will make thee taste a little in thy turn
of the plague of suspense; and break off, without giving
thee the least hint of the issue of my further proceedings.
I know that those least bear disappointment who love
most to give it. In twenty instances hast thou afforded
me proof of the truth of this observation. And I matter
not thy raving.

Another letter, however, shall be ready, send for it as
soon as thou wilt. But, were it not, have I not written
enough to convince thee, that I am

Thy ready and obliging friend,
J. BELFORD?

Letter 336: MR BELFORD TO ROBERT LOVELACE, ESQ.

Monday night, July 17

On my return to Rowland's, I found that the apothecary was just gone up.

She was sitting on the side of the broken couch, extremely weak and low.

The lady looked displeased, as well at me as at Rowland, who followed me, and at the apothecary.

I besought her excuse; and winking for the apothecary to withdraw (which he did), told her that I had been at her new lodgings, to order everything to be got ready for her reception; presuming she would choose to go thither: that I had a chair at the door: that Mr Smith and his wife (I named their names, that she should not have room for the least fear of Sinclair's), had been full of apprehensions for her safety.

I besought her to think of quitting that wretched hole.

Where could she go, she asked, to be safe and uninterrupted for the short remainder of her life; and to avoid being again visited by the creatures who had insulted her before?

I gave her the solemnest assurances that she should not be invaded in her new lodgings by anybody; and said that I would particularly engage my honour that *the person who had most offended her should not come near her, without her own consent.*

I represented to her that she would be less free where she was, from visits she liked not, than at her own lodging. And I expressed my surprise, that she should be unwilling to quit such a place as this; when it was more than probable that some of her friends, when it was known how bad she was, would visit her.

She said the place, when she was first brought into it, was indeed very shocking to her: but that she had found herself so weak and ill, and her griefs had so sunk her, that she did not expect to have lived till now: that therefore all places had been alike to her; for to die in a prison was to die; and equally eligible as to die in a palace (Palaces, she said, could have no attractions for a dying person): but that, since she feared she was not so soon to be released as she had hoped; since she was so little mistress of herself *here*; and since she might, by removal, be in the way of her dear friend's letters; she would hope that she might depend upon the assurances I gave her of being at liberty to return to her last lodgings (otherwise she would provide herself with new ones, out of my knowledge, as well as out of yours); and that I was too much of a gentleman to be concerned in carrying her back to the house she had so much reason to abhor; and to which she had been once before most vilely betrayed, to her ruin.

I assured her in the strongest terms *(but swore not)* that you were resolved not to molest her: and, as a proof of the sincerity of my professions, besought her to give me directions (in pursuance of my friend's express desire) about sending all her apparel, and whatever belonged to her, to her new lodgings.

She seemed pleased; and gave me instantly out of her pocket her keys; asking me if Mrs Smith, whom I had named, might not attend me; and she would give *her* further directions? To which I cheerfully assented; and then she told me that she would accept of the chair I had offered her.

I withdrew; and took the opportunity to be civil to Rowland and his maid; for she found no fault with their behaviour, for what they *were*; and the fellow seems to be miserably poor.

I was resolved to lose no time in having everything which belonged to the lady at the cursed woman's sent her. Accordingly, I took coach to Smith's, and procured the lady (to whom I sent up my compliments, and inquiries how she bore her removal), ill as she sent me down word she was, to give proper directions to Mrs Smith: whom I took with me to Sinclair's; and who saw everything looked out and put into the trunks and boxes they were first brought in, and carried away in two coaches.

Letter 338: MR BELFORD TO ROBERT LOVELACE, ESQ.

Tuesday, July 18, afternoon

I renewed my inquiries after the lady's health, in the morning, by my servant: and, as soon as I had dined, I went myself.

I had but a poor account of it: yet sent up my compliments. She returned me thanks for all my good offices; and her excuses that they could not be *personal* just then, being very low and faint: but if I gave myself the trouble of coming about six this evening, she should be able, she hoped, to drink a dish of tea with me, and would then thank me herself.

I am very proud of this condescension; and think it looks not amiss for you, as I am your *avowed* friend. Methinks I want fully to remove from her mind all doubts of you in this last villainous action: and who knows then, what your noble relations may be able to do for you with her, if you hold your mind? For your servant acquainted me with their having actually engaged Miss Howe in their and your favour, before this cursed affair happened.

She has two handsome apartments, a bedchamber and dining-room, with light closets in each. She has already a nurse (the people of the house having but one maid); a woman whose care, diligence, and honesty, Mrs Smith highly commends. She has likewise the benefit of the voluntary attendance, and *love*, as it seems, of a widow gentlewoman, Mrs Lovick her name, who lodges over her apartment, and of whom she seems very fond, having found something in her, she thinks, resembling the qualities of her worthy Mrs Norton.

Mrs Lovick gratified me with an account of a letter she had written from the lady's mouth to Miss Howe; she being unable to write herself with steadiness.

Let not your flaming impatience destroy all; and make me look like a villain to a lady who has reason to suspect *every man she sees* to be so. Upon this condition, you may expect all the services that can flow from true friendship, and from

Your sincere well-wisher,
JOHN BELFORD

Letter 340: MR BELFORD TO ROBERT LOVELACE, ESQ.

Wednesday, July 19
Three o'clock, afternoon

I just now called again at Smith's; and am told she is somewhat better; which she attributed to the soothings of her doctor. She expressed herself highly pleased with both gentlemen; and said that their behaviour to her was perfectly *paternal*.

Paternal, poor lady! Never having been, till very lately, from under her parents' wings, and now abandoned by all her friends, she is for finding out something *paternal* and *maternal* in everyone (the latter qualities in Mrs Lovick and Mrs Smith), to supply to herself the father and mother her dutiful heart pants after!

Mrs Smith told me that after we were gone she gave the keys of her trunks and drawers to her and the widow Lovick, and desired them to take an inventory of them; which they did, in her presence.

They also informed me that she had requested them to find her a purchaser for two rich dressed suits; one never worn, the other not above once or twice.

This shocked me exceedingly: *perhaps it may thee a little!!!* Her reason for so doing, she told them, was that she should never live to wear them: that her sister, and other relations were above wearing them: that her mother would not endure in her sight anything that was hers: that she wanted the money: that she would not be obliged to anybody when she had effects by her, which she had no occasion for. And yet, said she, I expect not that they will fetch a price answerable to their value.

They were both very much concerned, as they owned; and asked my advice upon it: and the richness of her apparel having given them a still higher notion of her rank than they had before, they supposed she must be of quality; and again wanted to know her story.

I told them that she was indeed a lady of family and fortune: I still gave them room to suppose her married: but left it to her to tell them all in her own time and manner. All I would say was, that she had been very vilely treated; deserved it not; and was all innocence and purity.

You may suppose that they both expressed their astonishment that there could be a man in the world who could ill-treat so fine a creature.

As to disposing of the two suits of apparel, I told Mrs Smith that she should pretend that upon inquiry she had found a friend who would purchase the richest of them; but *(that she might not mistrust)* would stand upon a good bargain. And having twenty guineas about me, I left them with her in part of payment; and bid her *pretend* to get her to part with it for as little more as she could induce her to take.

Adieu!

Letter 343: MISS CLARISSA HARLOWE TO MISS HOWE

Thursday afternoon

You oppress me, my dearest Miss Howe, by your flaming, yet steady love. I will be very brief, because I am not well; yet a good deal better than I was; and because I am preparing an answer to yours of the 13th. But, beforehand, I must tell you, my dear, I will not have that man. Don't be angry with me. But indeed I won't. So let him be asked no questions about me, I beseech you.

I do *not* despond, my dear. I hope I may say, *I will* not despond. Is not my condition greatly mended? I thank Heaven it is!

I am no prisoner now in a vile house. I am not now in the power of that man's devices. I am not now obliged to hide myself in corners for fear of him. One of his intimate companions is become my warm friend, and engages to keep him from me, and that by his own consent. I am among honest people. I have all my clothes and effects restored me. The wretch himself bears testimony to my honour.

Indeed I am very weak and ill: but I have an excellent physician, Dr H., and as worthy an apothecary, Mr Goddard. Their treatment of me, my dear, is perfectly *paternal*! My mind too, I can find, begins to strengthen: and methinks at times I find myself superior to my calamities.

I shall have sinkings sometimes. I must expect such.

And my father's maledict—But you will chide me for introducing that, now I am enumerating my comforts.

If you would contribute to *my* happiness, give way, my dear, to *your own*; and to the cheerful prospects before you!

You will think very meanly of your Clarissa Harlowe, if you do not believe that the greatest pleasure she can receive in this life is in your prosperity and welfare. Think not of me, my only friend, but as we were in times past: and suppose me gone a great, great way off!—a long journey! How often are the dearest of friends, at their country's call, thus parted—with a *certainty* for years—with a *probability* for ever!

Love me still, however. But let it be with a weaning love. I am not what I was when we were *inseparable* lovers, as I may say. Our *views* must now be different. Resolve, my dear, to make a worthy man happy, because a worthy man must make you so. And so, my dearest love, for the present adieu! Adieu, my dearest love! But I shall soon write again, I hope!

Letter 346: MR LOVELACE TO JOHN BELFORD, ESQ.

M. Hall, Friday, July 21

Just returned from an interview with this Hickman: a precise fop of a fellow, as starched as his ruffles.

Thou knowest I love him not, Jack; and whom we love not, we cannot allow a merit to; perhaps not the merit they should be granted. However, I am in earnest when I say that he seems to me to be so set, so prim, so affected, so mincing, yet so clouterly in his person, that I dare engage for thy opinion if thou dost justice to him, and to thyself, that thou never beheldest such another, except in a pier-glass.

I'll tell thee how I played him off.

He came in his own chariot to Dormer's; and we took a turn in the garden, at his request. He was devilish ceremonious, and made a bushel of apologies for the freedom he was going to take; and, after half a hundred hums and haws, told me that he came—that he came—

to wait on me—at the request of *dear Miss Howe*, on the account—on the account—of Miss Harlowe.

Well, sir, speak on, said I: but give me leave to say, that if your book be as long as your preface, it will take up a week to read it.

He stroked his chin, and hardly knew what to say. At last, after parenthesis within parenthesis, apologizing for apologies, in imitation I suppose of Swift's Digressions in Praise of Digressions—I presume, I presume, sir, you were privy to the visit made to Miss Howe by the young ladies your cousins, in the name of Lord M. and Lady Sarah Sadleir, and Lady Betty Lawrance?

I *was*, sir: and Miss Howe had a letter afterwards, signed by his lordship and those ladies, and underwritten by myself. Have you seen it, sir?

I can't say but I have. It is the principal cause of this visit: for Miss Howe thinks your part of it is written with such an air of levity—pardon me, sir—that she knows not whether you are in earnest or not, in your address to *her* for her interest to her friend.

Will Miss Howe permit me to explain myself in person to her, Mr Hickman?

Oh sir, by no means: Miss Howe, I am sure, would not give you that trouble.

I should not think it a trouble. I will most readily attend you, sir, to Miss Howe, and satisfy her in all her scruples. Come, sir, I will wait upon you now. You have a chariot. Are alone. We can talk as we ride.

He hesitated, wriggled, winced, stroked his ruffles, set his wig, and pulled his neckcloth which was long enough for a bib. I am not going directly back to Miss Howe, sir. It will be as well, if you will be so good as to satisfy Miss Howe by me.

What is it she scruples, Mr Hickman?

I know from Miss Howe that she highly resents the injuries you own: insomuch that Miss Howe doubts that she shall ever prevail upon her to overlook them: and as your family are all desirous you should repair her wrongs, and likewise desire Miss Howe's interposition with her friend; Miss Howe fears from this part of your letter that you are too much in jest; and that your offer to do her justice is rather in compliment to your friends' entreaties, than proceeding from your own inclinations: and she desires to know your true sentiments on this occasion before she interposes further.

Do you think, Mr Hickman, that if I am capable of deceiving my own relations, I have so much obligation to Miss Howe, who has always treated me with great freedom, as to acknowledge to *her* what I don't to *them*?

Sir, I beg pardon—but Miss Howe thinks that, as you have written to her, she may ask you by me for an explanation of what you have written.

I should be extremely glad to be reconciled to Miss Harlowe; and should owe great obligations to Miss Howe if she could bring about so happy an event.

Well, sir, and you have no objections to marriage, I presume, as the terms of that reconciliation?

I never liked matrimony in my life. I must be plain with you, Mr Hickman.

I am sorry for it: I think it a very happy state.

I hope you will find it so, Mr Hickman.

I doubt not but I shall, sir. And I dare say, so would you, if you were to have Miss Harlowe.

If I could be happy in it with anybody, it would be with Miss Harlowe.

I am surprised, sir! Then, after all, you don't think of marrying Miss Harlowe!—after the hard usage.

What hard usage, Mr Hickman? I don't doubt but a lady of her niceness has represented what would appear trifles to any other, in a very strong light.

If what I have had hinted to me, sir—excuse me—has been offered to the lady, she has more than trifles to complain of.

Let me know what you have heard, Mr Hickman? I will very truly answer to the accusations.

Sir, you know best what you have done: you own the lady is the *most injured, as well as the most deserving, of her sex.*

I do, sir; and yet, I would be glad to know what you have *heard*; for on that, perhaps, depends my answer to the questions Miss Howe puts to me by you.

Why then, sir, since you ask it, you cannot be displeased if I answer you. In the first place, sir, you will acknowledge, I suppose, that you promised Miss Harlowe marriage, and all that?

Well, sir, and I suppose what you have to charge me with is that I was desirous to have *all that* without marriage.

Cot-so, sir, I know you are deemed to be a man of wit: but may I not ask if these things sit not too light upon you?

When a thing is done, and cannot be helped, 'tis right to make the best of it. I wish the lady would think so too.

I think, sir, ladies should not be deceived. I think a promise to a lady should be as binding as to any other person, at the least.

I *believe* you think so, Mr Hickman: and I believe you are a very honest good sort of a man.

I would always keep my word, sir, whether to man or woman.

You say well. And far be it from me to persuade you to do otherwise. But what have you farther heard?

Sir, this is no part of my present business.

But, Mr Hickman, 'tis part of mine. I hope you would not expect that I should answer *your* questions, at the same time that you refuse to answer *mine*. What, pray, have you farther heard?

Why then, sir, if I must say, I am told that Miss Harlowe was carried to a very bad house.

Why, indeed, the people did not prove so good as they should be. What farther have you heard?

I have heard, sir, that the lady had strange advantages taken of her, very *unfair* ones; but what I cannot say.

And *cannot* you say? Cannot you *guess*? Then I'll tell you, sir. Perhaps some liberty was taken with her, when she was asleep. Do you think no lady ever was taken at such an advantage? You know, Mr Hickman, that ladies are very shy of trusting themselves with the modestest of our sex, when they are disposed to sleep; and why so, if they did not *expect* that advantages would be taken of them at such times?

But, sir, had not the lady something given her to make her sleep?

Ay, Mr Hickman, that's the question: I want to know if the lady says she had?

I have not seen all she has written; but by what I have heard, it is a very black affair—excuse me, sir.

I do excuse you, Mr Hickman: but, supposing it were so, do you think a lady was never imposed upon by wine, or so? Do you think the most cautious woman in the world might not be cheated by a stronger liquor for a smaller, when she was thirsty, after a fatigue in this very warm weather? And do you think if she was thus thrown into a profound sleep, that she is the only lady that was ever taken at such advantage?

Even as you make it, Mr Lovelace, this matter is not a light one. But I fear it is a great deal heavier than as you put it.

What reasons have you to fear this, sir? What has the lady said? Pray, let me know. I have *reason* to be so earnest.

Why, sir, Miss Howe herself knows not the whole. The lady promises to give her all the particulars at a proper time, if she lives; but has said enough to make it out to be a very bad affair.

I am glad Miss Harlowe has not yet given all the particulars. And, since she has not, you may tell Miss Howe from me that neither she, nor any lady in the world, can be more virtuous than Miss Harlowe is to this hour, as to her own mind. Tell her that I hope she never *will* know the particulars; but that she has been unworthily used: tell her, that though I know not what she has said, yet I have such an opinion of her veracity that I would blindly subscribe to the truth of every tittle of it, though it make me ever so black. Will this, Mr Hickman, answer any part of the intention of this visit?

Why, sir, this is talking like a man of honour, I own.

No age, from the first to the present, ever produced, nor will the future to the end of the world, I dare aver, ever produce, a young blooming lady, tried as she has been tried, who has stood all trials as she has done. Let me tell you, sir, that you never saw, never knew, never heard of, such another lady as Miss Harlowe.

Far be it from me to question the lady. You have not heard me say a word, that could be so construed. I have the utmost honour for her. Miss Howe loves her, as she loves her own soul; and that she would not do if she were not sure she were as virtuous as herself.

As herself, sir! I have a high opinion of Miss Howe, sir—but, I dare say—

What, sir, dare you say of Miss Howe? I hope, sir, you will not presume to say anything to the disparagement of Miss Howe!

Presume, Mr Hickman! That is *presuming* language, let me tell you, Mr Hickman!

The *occasion* for it, Mr Lovelace, if designed, is *presuming,* if you please. I am not a man ready to take offence, sir—especially where I am employed as a mediator. But no man breathing shall say disparaging things of Miss Howe, in my hearing, without observation.

Well said, Mr Hickman. I dislike not your spirit, on such a *supposed* occasion. But what I was going to say is this, that there is not, in my opinion, a woman in the world who ought to compare herself with Miss Clarissa Harlowe, till she has stood *her* trials, and has behaved *under* them, and *after* them, as she has done. You see, sir, I speak against myself. You see I do. For, libertine as I am thought to be, I never will attempt to bring down the measures of right and wrong to the standard of my actions.

But you may gather from what I have *said,* that I prefer Miss Harlowe, and that upon the justest grounds, to all the women in the world. And I wonder that there should be any difficulty to believe, from what I have signed, and from what I have promised to my relations, and enabled them to promise for me, that I should be glad to marry that excellent lady upon her own terms. I acknowledge to you, Mr Hickman, that I have basely injured her. If she will honour me with her hand, I declare that it is my intention to make her the best of husbands. But nevertheless, I must say that, if she goes on appealing her case, and exposing us both, as she does, it is impossible to think the knot can be knit with reputation to either. And although, Mr Hickman, I have delivered my apprehensions under so ludicrous a figure, I am afraid that she will ruin her constitution; and by seeking death when she may shun him, will not be able to avoid him when she would be glad to do so.

This cool and honest speech let down his stiffened muscles into complacency. He was my very obedient and faithful humble servant several times over, as I waited on him to his chariot: and I was his almost as often.

And so *exit* Hickman.

Letter 351: MISS HOWE TO MISS ARABELLA HARLOWE

Thursday, July 20

Miss Harlowe,

I cannot help acquainting you, however it may be received as coming from *me*, that your poor sister is dangerously ill at the house of one Smith, who keeps a glover's and perfume shop, in King Street, Covent Garden. She knows not that I write. Some violent words, in the nature of an imprecation, from her father, afflict her greatly in her weak state. I presume not to direct to you what to do in this case. You are her sister. I therefore could not help writing to you, not only for her sake, but for your own.

I am, madam, Your humble servant,
ANNA HOWE

Letter 352: MISS ARABELLA HARLOWE TO MISS ANNA HOWE

Thursday, July 20

Miss Howe,

I have yours of this morning. All that has happened to the unhappy body you mention is what we foretold and expected. Let *him* for whose sake she abandoned us be her comfort. We are told he has remorse, and would marry her. We don't believe it, indeed. She *may* be very ill. Her disappointment may make her so, or ought. Yet is she the only one I know, who is disappointed.

I cannot say, miss, that the notification from you is the *more* welcome for the liberties you have been pleased to take with our whole family, for resenting a conduct that

it is a shame any young lady should justify. Excuse this
freedom, occasioned by greater.

> I am, miss, Your humble servant,
> ARABELLA HARLOWE

Letter 358: MISS HOWE TO MISS CLARISSA HARLOWE

Sat. July 22

My dearest friend,

We are busy in preparing for our little journey and
voyage but I will be ill, I will be very ill, if I cannot hear
you are better before I go.

Rogers greatly afflicted me by telling me the bad way
you are in. But now you have been able to hold a pen,
and as your sense is strong and clear, I hope that the
amusement you will receive from writing will make
you better.

I dispatch this by an extraordinary way, that it may
reach you time enough to move you to *consider well*
before you absolutely decide upon the contents of mine
of the 13th, on the subject of the two Misses Montague's
visit to me; since, according to what you write, must I
answer them.

In your last, you conclude very positively that you will
not be his. To be sure, he rather deserves an infamous
death than such a wife. But, as I really believe him innocent of the arrest, and as all his family are such earnest
pleaders, and will be guarantees for him, I think the
compliance with *their* entreaties, and *his own, will* be
now the best step you can take; your own family remaining implacable, as I *can assure you they do.* He is
a man of sense; and it is not impossible but he may
make you a good husband, and in time may become no
bad man.

My mother is entirely of my opinion: and on Friday,
pursuant to a hint I gave you in my last, Mr Hickman
had a conference with the strange wretch. And though
he liked not, by any means, his behaviour to himself;
nor, indeed, had reason to do so; yet he is of opinion
that he is sincerely determined to marry you, if you will
condescend to have him.

So, my dearest friend, I charge you, if you *can*, to get over your aversion to this vile man. You may yet live to see many happy days, and be once more the delight of all your friends, neighbours, and acquaintance, as well as a stay, a comfort, and a blessing, to your Anna Howe.

I long to have your answer to mine of the 13th. Pray keep the messenger till it be ready. If he return on Monday night, it will be time enough for his affairs, and to find me come back from Colonel Ambrose's; who gives a ball on the anniversary of Mrs Ambrose's birth and marriage, both in one.

My mother promised the colonel for me and herself, in my absence. I would fain have excused myself to her; and the rather, as I had exceptions on account of the day: but she is almost as young as her daughter; and thinking it not so well to go without me, she told me she could propose *nothing* that was agreeable to me. And having had a *few sparring blows* with each other very lately, I think I must comply.

Oh my dear, how many things happen in this life to give us displeasure! how few to give us joy! I am sure I shall have none on this occasion; since the true partner of my heart, the principal half of the *one soul* that, it used to be said, animated *the pair of friends,* as we were called; You, my dear (who used to irradiate every circle you set your foot into, and to give me *real* significance, in a *second* place to yourself), cannot be there! Adieu, my dear!

A. Howe

Letter 359: MISS CLARISSA HARLOWE TO MISS HOWE

Sunday, July 23

What pain, my dearest friend, does your kind solicitude for my welfare give me! How much more binding and tender are the ties of pure friendship, and the union of like minds, than the ties of nature!

You set before me your reasons, enforced by the opinion of your honoured mother, why I should think of Mr Lovelace for a husband.

And I have before me your letter of the 13th, containing the account of the visit and proposals, and kind interposition, of the two Misses Montague, in the names of the good Ladies Sarah Sadleir and Betty Lawrance, and that of Lord M.

And I have as well weighed the whole matter, and your arguments in support of your advice, as at present my head and my heart will let me weigh them.

I am, moreover, willing to believe, not only from your own opinion, but from the assurances of one of Mr Lovelace's friends, Mr Belford, a good-natured and humane man, who spares not to censure the author of my calamities (*I think,* with undissembled and undesigning sincerity), that that man is innocent of the disgraceful arrest:

And even, if you please, in sincere compliment to your opinion, and to that of Mr Hickman, that (over-persuaded by his friends, and ashamed of his unmerited baseness to me) he, in earnest, would marry *me* if I would have *him.*

'Well, and now, what is the result of all? It is this—that I must abide by what I have already declared—and that is (don't be angry at me, my best friend) that I have much more pleasure in thinking of death, than of such a husband. In short, as I declared in my last, that I cannot—forgive me, if I say I *will* not—ever be his.

'But you will expect my reasons: I know you will: and if I give them not, will conclude me either obstinate, or implacable, or both: and those would be sad imputations, if just, to be laid to the charge of a person who thinks and talks of *dying.* And yet, to say that resentment and disappointment have no part in my determination would be saying a thing hardly to be credited. For I own I *have* resentments, strong resentments, but not unreasonable ones, as you will be convinced if already you are not so, when you know all my story—if ever you do know it. For I begin to fear (so many things more necessary to be thought of, than either this man, or my own vindication, have I to do) that I shall not have time to compass what I have intended, and, in a manner, promised you.

'But now, my dear, for *your* satisfaction let me say,

that although I wish not for life, yet would I not like a poor coward desert my post, when I can maintain it, and when it is my *duty* to maintain it.

'Oh my dear, you know not what I suffered on that occasion! Nor .do I what I *escaped* at the time, if the wicked man had approached me to execute the horrid purposes of his vile heart. High resolution, a courage I never knew before; a settled, not a rash courage; and such a command of my passions—I can only say I know not how I came by such an uncommon elevation of mind, if it were not given me in answer to my earnest prayers to Heaven for such a command of myself, before I entered into the horrid company.'

When appetite serves, I will eat and drink what is sufficient to support nature. A very little, you know, will do for that. And whatever my physicians shall think fit to prescribe, I will take, though ever so disagreeable.

And now, my dearest friend, you know all my mind. And you will be pleased to write to the ladies of Mr Lovelace's family, that I think myself infinitely obliged to them for their good opinion of me; and that it has given me greater pleasure than I thought I had to come in this life, that upon the little knowledge they have of me, and that not personal, I was thought worthy (after the ill usage I have received) of an alliance with their honourable family: but that I can by no means think of their kinsman for a husband: and do you, my dear, extract from the above, such reasons as you think have any weight in them.

I should be glad to know when you set out on your journey; as also your little stages; and your time of stay at your aunt Harman's; that my prayers may locally attend you, whithersoever you go, and wherever you are.

CLARISSA HARLOWE

Letter 365: MR BELFORD TO ROBERT LOVELACE, ESQ.

Wednesday, July 26

About three o'clock I went again to Smith's. The lady was writing when I sent up my name; but admitted of my visit. I saw a visible alteration in her countenance for the worse; and Mrs Lovick respectfully accusing her of too great assiduity to her pen, early and late, and of her abstinence the day before. I took notice of the alteration; and told her that her physician had greater hopes of her than she had of herself; and I would take the liberty to say that despair of recovery allowed not room for cure.

She said she neither despaired nor hoped. Then stepping to the glass, with great composure, My countenance, says she, is indeed an honest picture of my heart. But the mind will run away with the body at any time.

Writing is all my diversion, continued she; and I have subjects that cannot be dispensed with. As to my hours, I have always been an early riser: but now rest is less in my power than ever: sleep has a long time ago quarrelled with me, and will not be friends, although I have made the first advances. What *will* be, *must.*

She then stepped to her closet, and brought to me a parcel sealed up with three seals. Be so kind, said she, as to give this to your friend. A very grateful present it ought to be to him: for, sir, this packet contains all his letters to me. Such letters they are, as, compared with his actions, would reflect dishonour upon all his sex, were they to fall into other hands.

As to my letters to him, they are not many. He may either keep or destroy them as he pleases.

I thought I ought not to forgo this opportunity to plead for you: I therefore, with the packet in my hand, urged all the arguments I could think of in your favour.

She heard me out with more attention than I could have promised myself, considering her determined resolution.

I would not interrupt you, Mr Belford, said she, though I am far from being pleased with the subject of your discourse. The motives for your pleas in his favour are generous. I love to see instances of generous friendship in either sex. But I have written my full mind on this subject to Miss Howe, who will communicate it to the ladies of his family. No more, therefore, I pray you, upon a topic that may lead to disagreeable recriminations.

Her apothecary came in. He advised her to the air,

and blamed her for so great an application as he was told she made to her pen; and he gave it as the doctor's opinion, as well as his own, that she would recover if she herself desired to recover, and would use the means.

The lady may indeed write too much for her health, perhaps; but I have observed on several occasions, that when the physical men are at a loss what to prescribe, they forbid their patients what they best like, and are most diverted with.

Mr Goddard took his leave; and I was going to do so too, when the maid came up and told her a gentleman was below, who very earnestly inquired after her health, and desired to see her: his name Hickman.

She was overjoyed; and bid the maid desire the gentleman to walk up.

I would have withdrawn; but I suppose she thought it was likely I should have met him upon the stairs, and so she forbid it.

She shot to the stairs-head to receive him, and, taking his hand, asked half a dozen questions (without waiting for any answer) in relation to Miss Howe's health; acknowledging, in high terms, her goodness in sending him to see her before she set out upon her little journey.

He gave her a letter from that young lady; which she put into her bosom, saying she would read it by and by.

Letter 367: MISS HOWE TO MISS CLARISSA HARLOWE

Tuesday, July 25

Your two affecting letters were brought to me (as I had directed any letter from you should be), to the colonel's, about an hour before we broke up. I could not forbear dipping into them there; and shedding more tears over them than I will tell you of; although I dried my eyes, as well as I could, that the company I was obliged to return to, and my mamma, should see as little of my concern as possible.

How can I bear the thoughts of losing so dear a friend! I will not so much as suppose it. Indeed I *cannot*! Such a mind as yours was not vested in humanity to be snatched away from us so soon. There must be still a

great deal for you to do, for the good of all who have
the happiness to know you.

Know then, my dear, that I accompanied my mother
to Colonel Ambrose's, on the occasion I mentioned to
you in my former. Many ladies and gentlemen were
there, whom you know; particularly Miss Kitty D'Oily,
Miss Lloyd, Miss Biddy D'Ollyffe, Miss Biddulph, and
their respective admirers, with the colonel's two nieces,
fine women both; besides many whom you know not;
for they were strangers to me, but by name. A splendid
company, and all pleased with one another, till Colonel
Ambrose introduced one, who the moment he was
brought into the great hall set the whole assembly into
a kind of agitation.

It was your villain.

I thought I should have sunk as soon as I set my eyes
upon him. My mother was also affected; and coming to
me, Nancy, whispered she, can you bear the sight of that
wretch without too much emotion? If not, withdraw into
the next apartment.

I could not remove. Everybody's eyes were glanced
from him to me. I sat down, and fanned myself, and was
forced to order a glass of water. Oh that I had the eye
the basilisk is reported to have, thought I, and that his
life were within the power of it—directly would I kill
him!

He entered with an air so hateful to me, but so agreeable to every other eye, that I could have looked him
dead for that too.

After the general salutations, he singled out Mr Hickman, and told him he had recollected some parts of his
behaviour to him when he saw him last, which had made
him think himself under obligation to his patience and
politeness.

And so, indeed, he was.

Miss D'Oily, upon his complimenting her among a
knot of ladies, asked him, in their hearing, how Miss
Clarissa Harlowe did?

He heard, he said, you were not so well as he wished
you to be, and as you deserved to be.

Oh Mr Lovelace, said she, what have you to answer

for on that young lady's account, if all be true that I have heard?

I have a great deal to answer for, said the unblushing villain: but that dear lady has so many excellencies, and so much delicacy, that little sins are great ones in her eye.

Little sins! replied the lady: Mr Lovelace's character is so well known that nobody believes he can commit *little* sins.

You are very good to me, Miss D'Oily.

Indeed I am not.

Then I am the only person to whom you are *not* very good: and so I am the less obliged to you.

I still kept my seat, and he either saw me not, or would not yet see me; and addressing himself to my mother, taking her unwilling hand with an air of high assurance, I am glad to see you here, madam: I hope Miss Howe is well. I have reason to complain greatly of her: but hope to owe to her the highest obligations that can be laid on man.

My daughter, sir, is accustomed to be too warm and too zealous in her friendships for either my tranquillity or her own.

We are not wholly, madam, to live for ourselves, said the vile hypocrite. It is not everyone who has a soul capable of friendship: and what a heart must that be, which can be insensible to the interests of a suffering friend?

This sentiment from Mr Lovelace's mouth, said my mother! Forgive me, sir; but you can have no end, surely, in endeavouring to make *me* think as well of you, as some innocent creatures have thought of you, to their cost.

She would have flung from him. But, detaining her hand—Less severe, dear madam, said he, be less severe in *this* place, I beseech you. You will allow that a very faulty person may see his errors; and when he does, and owns them, and repents, should he not be treated mercifully?

Your air, sir, seems not to be that of a penitent. But

the place may as properly excuse this subject, as what you call my severity.

But, dearest madam, permit me to say that I hope for your interest with your *charming* daughter (was his syco- phant word) to have it put into my power to convince all the world that there never was a truer penitent. And why, why this anger, dear madam (for she struggled to get her hand out of his); these violent airs, so *maidenly*! Impudent fellow! May I not ask if Miss Howe be here?

She would not have been here, replied my mother, had she known whom she had been to see.

And is she here, then? Thank Heaven! He disengaged her hand, and stepped forward into company.

Charming Miss Howe!

I was all in a flutter, you may suppose. He would have taken my hand. I refused it, all glowing with indignation: everybody's eyes upon us.

When the wretch saw how industriously I avoided him (shifting from one part of the hall to another), he at last boldly stepped up to me, as my mother and Mr Hickman were talking to me; and thus, before them, accosted me:

I beg your pardon, madam; but, by your mother's leave, I must have a few moments' conversation with you, either here or at your own house; and I beg you will give me the opportunity.

Nancy, said my mother, hear what he has to say to you. In my presence you may: and better in the adjoining apartment, if it must be, than to come to you at our own house.

I retired to one corner of the hall, my mother follow- ing me, and he, taking Mr Hickman under the arm, fol- lowing her. Well, sir, said I, what have you to say? Tell me *here.*

Lady Betty, and Lady Sarah, and my Lord M. are engaged for my honour. I know your power with the dear creature. My cousins told me you gave them hopes you would use it in my behalf. My Lord M. and his two sisters are impatiently expecting the fruits of it. You must have heard from her before now: I hope you have. And will you be so good as to tell me, if I may have any hopes?

If I must speak on this subject, let me tell you that you have broken her heart. You know not the value of the lady you have injured. You deserve her not. And she despises you as she ought.

Dear Miss Howe, mingle not passion with denunciations so severe. I must know my fate. I will go abroad once more, if I find her absolutely irreconcilable. But I hope she will give me leave to attend upon her, to know my doom from her own mouth.

It would be death immediate for her to see you. And what must *you* be, to be able to look her in the face?

He vindicated not any part of his conduct, but that of the arrest; and so solemnly protested his sorrow for his usage of you, accusing himself in the freest manner, and by *deserved* appellations, that I promised to lay before you this part of our conversation. And now you have it.

My mother, as well as Mr Hickman, believes, from what passed on this occasion, that he is touched in conscience for the wrongs he has done you: but, by his whole behaviour, I must own it seems to me that nothing can touch him for half an hour together. Yet I have no doubt that he would willingly marry you; and it piques his pride, I could see, that he should be denied: as it did mine, that such a wretch had dared to think it in his power to have such a woman whenever he pleased; and that it must be accounted a condescension, and matter of obligation (by all his own family at least), that he would vouchsafe to think of marriage.

Now, my dear, you have the reason before you why I suspend the decisive negative to the ladies of his family.

You will let Mr Hickman know your whole mind; and when he acquaints me with it, I will tell you all my own.

Meantime, may the news he will bring me of the state of your health be favourable! prays, with the utmost fervency,

Your ever-faithful and affectionate
ANNA HOWE

Letter 368: MISS CLARISSA HARLOWE TO MISS HOWE

Thursday, July 27

My dearest Miss Howe,

After I have thankfully acknowledged your favour in sending Mr Hickman to visit me before you set out upon your intended journey, I must chide you (in the sincerity of that faithful love, which could not be the love it is if it would not admit of that *cementing* freedom) for suspending the decisive negative, which, upon such full deliberation, I had entreated you to give to Mr Lovelace's relations.

I am sorry that I am obliged to *repeat* to you, my dear, who know me so well, that were I sure I should live *many years* I would not have Mr Lovelace: much less can I think of him, as it is probable I may not live *one*.

As to the *world,* and its *censures,* you know, my dear, that, however desirous I always was of a fair fame, yet I never thought it right to give more than a *second place* to the world's opinion. The challenges made to Mr Lovelace by Miss D'Oily in public company are a fresh proof that I have lost my reputation: and what advantage would it be to me, were it retrievable, and were I to live long, if I could not acquit myself to *myself*?

Your account of the gay, unconcerned behaviour of Mr Lovelace at the colonel's does not surprise me at all, after I am told that he had the intrepidity to go thither, knowing who were *invited* and *expected*. Only this, my dear, I really wonder at, that Miss Howe could imagine that I could have a thought of such a man for a husband.

Poor wretch! I pity him, to see him fluttering about; abusing talents that were given him for excellent purposes; taking courage for wit; and dancing, fearless of danger, on the edge of a precipice!

But, indeed, his threatening to see me most sensibly alarms and shocks me. I cannot but hope that I never, never more shall see him in this world.

I commend myself, my dearest Miss Howe, to your prayers; and conclude with repeated thanks for sending Mr Hickman to me; and with wishes for your health and happiness, and for the speedy celebration of your nuptials,

> Your ever-affectionate and obliged
> CLARISSA HARLOWE

Letter 370: MR LOVELACE TO JOHN BELFORD, ESQ.

Friday, July 28

Come, come, Belford, let people run away with notions as they will, I am *comparatively* a very innocent man. And if by these, and other like reasonings, I have quieted my own conscience, a great end is answered. What have I to do with the world?

I hope thy pleas in my favour, when she gave thee (so generously gave thee) for me, my letters, were urged with an honest energy. But I suspect thee much for being too ready to give up thy client.

Since then thy unhappy awkwardness destroys the force of thy arguments, I think thou hadst better (for the present, however) forbear to urge her on the subject of accepting the reparation I offer; lest the continual teasing of her to forgive me should but strengthen her in her denials of forgiveness; till, for *consistency* sake, she'll be forced to adhere to a resolution so often avowed. Whereas, if left to herself, a little time and better health, which will bring on better spirits, will give her quicker resentments; those quicker resentments will lead her into vehemence; that vehemence will subside, and turn into expostulation and parley: my friends will then interpose, and guarantee for me: and all our trouble on both sides will be over. Such is the natural course of things.

In short, I cannot bear the thought that a lady whom once I had bound to me in the silken cords of love, should slip through my fingers, and be able, while *my* heart flames out with a violent passion for her, to despise me, and to set both love and me at defiance. Thou canst not imagine how much I envy *thee*, and her *doctor*, and her *apothecary*, and everyone whom I hear of being admitted to her presence and conversation; and wish to be the *one* or the *other* in turn.

Wherefore, if nothing else will do, I will see her.

But, in whatever shape I shall choose to appear, of this thou mayest assure thyself, I will apprise thee beforehand of my determined-upon visit, that thou mayest contrive to be out of the way, and to know nothing of the matter. This will save *thy* word; and, as to *mine,* can she think worse of me than she does at present?

Letter 371: MR LOVELACE TO JOHN BELFORD, ESQ.

This cursed arrest, because of the ill effects the terror might have had upon her in that hoped-for circumstance, has concerned me more than on any other account. It would be the pride of my life to prove, in this charming frost-piece, the triumph of nature over principle, and to have a young Lovelace by such an angel: and then, for its sake, I am confident she will live, and will legitimate it. And what a meritorious little cherub would it be, that should lay an obligation upon both parents before it was born, which neither of them would be able to repay! Could I be sure it is so, I should be out of all pain for her recovery: *pain,* I say; since, were she to *die* (die! abominable word! how I hate it!) I verily think I should be the most miserable man in the world.

As for the earnestness she expresses for death, she has found the words ready to her hand in honest Job; else she would not have delivered herself with such strength and vehemence.

Her innate piety (as I have more than once observed) will not permit her to shorten her own life, either by violence or neglect. She has a mind too noble for that; and would have done it before now, had she designed any such thing.

Moreover, has she it not in her power to *disappoint,* as much as she has been *disappointed*? Revenge, Jack, has induced many a woman to cherish a life, which grief and despair would otherwise have put an end to.

And, after all, death is no such eligible thing as Job in his *calamities* makes it. And a death desired merely from worldly disappointment shows not a right mind, let me tell this lady, whatever she may think of it.

I find, by one of thy three letters, that my beloved had some account from Hickman of my interview with Miss Howe, at Colonel Ambrose's. I had a very agreeable time of it there; although severely rallied by several of the assembly. It concerns me, however, not a little, to find our affair so generally known among the *flippanti* of both sexes. It is all her own fault. There never, surely, was such an odd little soul as this. Not to keep her own secret, when the revealing of it could answer no possible good end; and when she wants not (one would think) to raise to herself either pity or friends, or to me enemies, by the proclamation! Why, Jack, must not all her own sex laugh in their sleeves at her weakness!

I am glad, however, that Miss Howe, as much as she hates me, kept her word with my cousins on their visit to her, and with me at the colonel's, to endeavour to persuade her friend to make up all matters by matrimony; which, no doubt, is the best, nay, the *only* method she can take for her own honour, and that of her family.

I had once thoughts of revenging myself on that little vixen, and particularly as thou mayst remember, had planned something to this purpose on the journey she is going to take, which had been talked of some time. But, I think—let me see—yes, I *think* I will let this Hickman have her safe and entire, as thou believest the fellow to be a tolerable sort of a mortal, and that I had made the worst of him: and I am glad, for his own sake, he has not launched out too virulently against me to thee.

And thus, if I pay thee not in quality, I do in quantity (and yet leave a multitude of things unobserved upon): for I begin not to know what to do with myself here. Tired with Lord M.—tired with my cousins Montague—tired with the country—tired of myself: longing for what I have not; I must go to town; and there have an interview with the charmer of my soul: for desperate diseases must have desperate remedies; and I only wait to know my doom from Miss Howe; and then, if it be rejection, I will try my fate, and receive my sentence at her feet. But I will apprise thee of it beforehand, as I told thee, that thou mayest keep thy parole with the lady in the best manner thou canst.

Letter 372: MISS HOWE TO MISS CLARISSA HARLOWE

Friday night, July 28

You put me in hope that, were I actually married and Mr Hickman to *desire* it, you would think of obliging me with a visit on the occasion; and that, perhaps, when with me, it would be difficult for you to remove far from me.

Lord, my dear, what a stress do you seem to lay upon Mr Hickman's *desiring* it! To be sure he does, and would of all things desire to have you *near* us, and *with* us, if we might be so favoured. Policy, as well as veneration for *you*, would undoubtedly make the man, if not a fool, *desire* this. But let me tell you that if Mr Hickman, after marriage, should pretend to dispute with me my friendships, as I hope I am not quite a fool, I should let him know how far his own quiet was concerned in such an impertinence; especially if they were such friendships as were contracted before I knew him.

I know I always differed from you on this subject; for you think more highly of a *husband's* prerogative, than most people do of the *royal* one. These notions, my dear, from a person of your sense and judgement are no-way advantageous to us; inasmuch as they justify that insolent sex in their assumptions; when hardly one out of ten of them, their opportunities considered, deserve any prerogative at all. Look through all the families we know; and we shall not find one third of them have half the sense of their wives. And yet these are to be vested with prerogatives! And a woman of twice their sense has nothing to do but hear, tremble, and obey—and for *conscience*-sake too, I warrant!

But Mr Hickman and I may perhaps have a little discourse upon these sort of subjects before I suffer him to talk of the day: and then I shall let him know what he has to trust to; as he will me, if he be a sincere man, what he pretends to expect from me. But let me tell you, my dear, that it is more in *your* power than perhaps you think it, to hasten the day so much pressed-for by my mother, as well as wished-for by you—for the very day that you can assure me that you are in a tolerable state of health, and have discharged your doctor and apothe-

cary at their own motions on that account—some day in
a month from that desirable news shall be it. So, my
dear, make haste and be well; and then this matter will
be brought to effect in a manner more agreeable to your
Anna Howe than it otherwise ever can.

You are, it seems (and that too much for your health),
employed in writing. I hope it is in penning down the
particulars of your tragical story. And my mother has
put me in mind to press you to it, with a view that one
day, if it might be published under feigned names, it
would be of as much use as honour to the sex. My
mother says she cannot help admiring you for the propriety of your resentment in your refusal of the wretch;
and she would be extremely glad to have her advice of
penning your sad story complied with. And then, she
says, your noble conduct throughout your trials and calamities will afford not only a shining example to your sex;
but, at the same time (those calamities befalling SUCH a
person), a fearful warning to the inconsiderate young
creatures of it.

On Monday we shall set out on our journey; and I
hope to be back in a fortnight, and on my return will
have one pull more with my mother for a London journey: and, if the *pretence must* be the buying of clothes,
the *principal motive* will be that of seeing once more my
dear friend, *while* I can say I have not finally given consent to the change of a visitor into a relation; and so can
call myself MY OWN, as well as

Your
ANNA HOWE

Letter 379: MISS CLARISSA HARLOWE TO MISS HOWE

Sunday, July 30

You have given me great pleasure, my dearest friend, by
your approbation of my reasonings, and of my resolution
founded upon them, never to have Mr Lovelace. This
approbation is so *right* a thing, give me leave to say,
from the nature of the case, and from the strict honour
and true dignity of mind which I always admired in my
Anna Howe, that I could hardly tell to what but to my

evil destiny, that of late would not let me please anybody, to attribute the advice you gave me to the
contrary.

But let not the ill state of my health, and what that
may naturally tend to, sadden you. I have told you that I
will not run away from life, nor avoid the means that
may continue it, if God see fit: and if he do *not*, who
shall repine at his will?

If it shall be found that I have not acted unworthy of
your love and of my own character in my greater trials,
that will be a happiness to both on reflection.

The shock which you so earnestly advise me to try to
get over, was a shock, the greatest that I could receive.
But, my dear, as it was not incurred by my *fault*, I hope
I am already got above it. I hope I am!

I am more grieved (at times however) for *others*, than
for *myself*. And so I *ought*. For as to *myself*, I cannot
but reflect that I have had an escape, rather than a loss,
in missing Mr Lovelace for a husband: even had he *not*
committed the vilest of all outrages.

Let anyone who knows my story collect his character
from his behaviour to *me, before* that outrage; and then
judge whether it was in the least probable for such a
man to make me happy. But to collect his character from
his principles with regard to the *sex in general,* and from
his enterprises upon many of them, and to consider the
cruelty of his nature and the sportiveness of his invention, together with the high opinion he has of himself,
it will not be doubted that a wife of his must have been
miserable; and more miserable if she loved him, than if
she could have been indifferent to him.

Have I not reason, these things considered, to think
myself happier without Mr Lovelace than with him? My
will too unviolated; and very little, nay, not anything as
to him, to reproach myself with?

If anything could give me a relish for life, after what
I have suffered, it would be the hopes of the continuance
of the more than sisterly love which has for years uninterruptedly bound us together as one mind.

I am glad you have sent my letter to Miss Montague.
I hope I shall hear no more of this unhappy man.

I had begun the particulars of my tragical story: but it is so painful a task, and I have so many more important things to do and as I apprehend so little time to do them in, that could I avoid it, I would go no farther in it.

Then, to this hour, I know not by what means several of his machinations to ruin me were brought about; so that some material parts of my sad story must be defective if I were to sit down to write it. But I have been thinking of a way that will answer the end wished for by your mother and you full as well; perhaps better.

Mr Lovelace, it seems, has communicated to his friend Mr Belford all that has passed between himself and me, as he went on. Mr Belford has not been able to deny it. So that (as we may observe by the way) a poor young creature whose indiscretion has given a libertine power over her, has a reason *she little thinks of* to regret her folly; since these wretches, who have no more honour in one point than in another, scruple not to make her weakness a part of their triumph to their brother libertines.

I have nothing to apprehend of this sort, if I have the justice done me in his letters which Mr Belford assures me that I have: and therefore the particulars of my story, and the base arts of this vile man will, I think, be best collected from those very letters of his (if Mr Belford can be prevailed upon to communicate them).

There is one way which may be fallen upon to induce Mr Belford to communicate these letters; since he seems to have (and declares he always had) a sincere abhorrence of his friend's baseness to me: but that, you'll say when you hear it, is a strange one. Nevertheless, I am very earnest upon it, at present.

It is no other than this:

I think to make Mr Belford the executor of my last will (don't be surprised!): and with this view I permit his visits with the less scruple: and every time I see him, from his concern for me am more and more inclined to do so. If I hold in the same mind, and if he accept the trust and will communicate the materials in his power, those, joined with what you can furnish, will answer the whole end.

Then he exceedingly presses for some occasion to

show his readiness to serve me: and he would be able to manage his violent friend, over whom he has more influence than any other person.

But, after all, I know not if it were not more eligible by far, that my story should be forgotten as soon as possible; and myself too. And of this I shall have the less doubt, if the character of my parents cannot be guarded (you will forgive me, my dear) from the unqualified bitterness which, from your affectionate zeal for me, has sometimes mingled with your ink.

My father has been so good as to take off from me the heavy malediction he laid me under. I must be now solicitous for a last blessing; and that is all I shall presume to ask.

If you set out tomorrow, this letter cannot reach you till you get to your aunt Harman's. I shall therefore direct it thither, as Mr Hickman instructed me.

I hope you will have met with no inconveniencies in your little journey and voyage; and that you will have found in good health all whom you wish to see well.

Let me recommend to you, my dear, that if your friends and relations in the little island join their solicitations with your mother's commands to have your nuptials celebrated before you leave them, you do not refuse to oblige them. How grateful will the notification that you have done so, be to

Your ever-faithful and affectionate
CLARISSA HARLOWE!

Letter 391: MR BELFORD TO ROBERT LOVELACE, ESQ.

Friday night, Aug. 4

The lady is extremely uneasy at the thoughts of your attempting to visit her. For Heaven's sake (your word being given), and for pity's sake (for she is really in a very weak and languishing way), let me beg of you not to think of it.

Yesterday afternoon she received a cruel letter, as Mrs Lovick supposes it to be by the effect it had upon her, from her sister, in answer to one written last Saturday entreating a blessing and forgiveness from her parents.

But what thinkest thou is the second request she had to make to me? No other than that I would be her *executor*! Her motives will appear before thee in proper time; and then, I dare answer for them, will be satisfactory.

You cannot imagine how proud I am of this trust. I am afraid I shall too soon come into the execution of it.

Saturday morning, Aug. 5

I am just returned from visiting the lady and thanking her in person for the honour she has done me; and assuring her, if called to the sacred trust, of the utmost fidelity and exactness. I found her very ill. I took notice of it. She said she had received a second hard-hearted letter from her sister; and she had been writing a letter (and that on her knees) directly to her mother; which before she had not the courage to do. It was for a last blessing and forgiveness. No wonder, she said, that I saw her affected. Now that I had accepted of the last charitable office for her (for which, as well as for complying with her other request, she thanked me), I should one day have all these letters before me: and could she have a kind one in return to that she had been now writing, to counterbalance the unkind one she had from her sister, she might be induced to show me both together.

I let her know that I was going out of town till Monday: she wished me pleasure; and said she should be glad to see me on my return.

Adieu!

Letter 395: MR LOVELACE TO JOHN BELFORD, ESQ.

Sat. Aug. 5

Thou runnest on with thy cursed nonsensical *reformado* rote, of dying, dying, dying! and, having once got the word by the end, canst not help foisting it in at every period! The devil take me, if I don't think thou wouldst give her poison with thy own hands, rather than she should recover and rob thee of the merit of being a conjurer!

But no more of thy cursed knell; thy changes upon

death's candlestick turned bottom-upwards: she'll live to
bury me; I see that: for, by my soul, I can neither eat,
drink, nor sleep; nor, what's still worse, love any woman
in the world but her. Nor care I to look upon a woman
now; on the contrary, I turn my head from every one I
meet; except by chance an eye, an air, a feature, strikes
me resembling hers in some glancing-by face; and then
I cannot forbear looking again; though the second look
recovers me; for there can be nobody like her.

I have one half of the house to myself; and that the
best; for the great enjoy that least, which costs them
most: *grandeur* and *use* are two things: the common part
is theirs; the state part is mine: and here I lord it, and
will lord it, as long as I please; while the two pursy
sisters, the old gouty brother, and the two musty nieces,
are stived up in the other half, and dare not stir for fear
of meeting me: whom (that's the jest of it) they have
forbidden coming into their apartments, as I have them
into mine. And so I have them all prisoners while I
range about as I please. Pretty dogs and doggesses, to
quarrel and bark at me, and yet, whenever I appear,
afraid to pop out of their kennels; or if out before they
see me, at the sight of me run growling in again, with
their flapped ears, their sweeping dewlaps, and their
quivering tails curling inwards.

And thou art a pretty fellow, art thou not? to engage
to transcribe for her some parts of my letters written to
thee in confidence? Letters that thou shouldst sooner
have parted with thy cursed tongue than have owned
thou ever hadst received such: yet these are now to be
communicated to *her*! But I charge thee, and woe be to
thee if it be too late! that thou do not oblige her with a
line of mine.

If thou *hast* done it, the least vengeance I will take is
to break through *my* honour given to thee not to visit
her, as thou wilt have broken through *thine* to me in
communicating letters written under the seal of
friendship.

I am now convinced, too sadly for my hopes, by her
letter to my cousin Charlotte, that she is determined
never to have me.

Unprecedented wickedness, she calls mine to her. But how does *she* know what the ardour of flaming love will stimulate?

But what a whirlwind does she raise in my soul by her proud contempts of me! Never, never, was mortal man's pride so mortified. How does she sink me, even in my own eyes!

She might have done this with some show of justice had the last intended violation been perpetrated—but to go away conqueress and triumphant in every light! Well may she despise me for suffering her to do so.

I will venture one more letter to her, however; and if that don't do, or procure me an answer, then will I endeavour to see her, let what *will* be the consequence. If she get out of my way, I will do some noble mischief to the vixen girl whom she most loves, and then quit the kingdom for ever.

And now, Jack, since thy hand is in at communicating the contents of private letters, tell her this if thou wilt. And add to it, that if SHE abandon me, GOD will; and it is no matter *then* what becomes of

Her
LOVELACE!

Letter 396: MR LOVELACE TO JOHN BELFORD, ESQ.

Monday, Aug. 7

And so you have actually delivered to the fair implacable extracts of letters written in the confidence of friendship! Take care—take care, Belford—I do indeed love you better than I love any man in the world: but this is a very delicate point. The matter is grown very serious to me. My heart is bent upon having her. And have her I will, though I marry her in the agonies of death.

She is very earnest, you say, that I will not offer to molest her. *That,* let me tell her, will absolutely depend upon herself and the answer she returns, whether by pen and ink, or the contemptuous one of silence which she bestowed upon my last four to her: and I will write it in such humble and in such reasonable terms, that if she is not a true Harlowe she *shall* forgive me. But as to the *executorship* she is for conferring upon thee—thou shalt not be her *executor*. Let me perish if thou shalt. Nor shall she die. Nobody shall be anything, nobody shall *dare* to be anything to her, but me. Thy happiness is already too great, to be admitted daily to her presence; to look upon her, to talk to her, to hear her talk, while I am forbid to come within view of her window. What a reprobation is this, of the man who was once more dear to her than all the men in the world! And now to be able to look down upon me, while her exalted head is hid from me among the stars, sometimes with low scorn, at other times with abject pity, I cannot bear it.

This I tell thee, that if I have not success in my effort by letter, I will overcome the creeping folly that has found its way to my heart, or I will tear it out in her presence and throw it at hers, that she may see how much more tender than her own that organ is, which she and you and everyone else have taken the liberty to call callous.

Letter 401: MISS CLARISSA HARLOWE TO ROBERT LOVELACE, ESQ.

Friday, Aug. 11

'Tis a cruel alternative to be either forced to see you or to write to you. But a will of my own has been long denied me; and to avoid a greater evil, nay, now I may say the greatest, I write.

Were I capable of disguising or concealing my real sentiments, I might safely I dare say give you the remote hope you request, and yet keep all my resolutions. But I must tell you, sir; it becomes my character to tell you; that were I to live more years than perhaps I may weeks, and there were not another man in the world, I could not, I would not, be yours.

There is no *merit* in performing a *duty*.

Religion enjoins me not only to forgive injuries, but to return good for evil. It is all my consolation, and I bless God for giving me that, that I am now in such a state of mind with regard to you, that I can cheerfully obey its dictates. And accordingly I tell you that wherever you go, I wish you happy.

And now having, with great reluctance I own, complied with one of your compulsatory alternatives, I expect the fruits of it.

CLARISSA HARLOWE

Letter 409: MISS CLARISSA HARLOWE TO MRS NORTON

Thursday, Aug. 17

You give me a kind caution, which seems to imply *more* than you express, when you advise me against countenancing of visitors that may discredit me. You should, in so tender a point, my dear Mrs Norton, have spoken quite out. Surely, I have had afflictions enow to make my mind fitted to bear anything. But I will not puzzle myself by *conjectural evils*. I *might*, if I had not enow that were *certain*. And I shall hear all when it is thought proper that I should. Meantime, let me say for *your* satisfaction, that I know not that I have anything criminal or disreputable to answer for either in word or deed, since the fatal 10th of April last.

You desire an account of what passes between me and my friends; and also particulars or brief heads of my sad story, in order to serve me as occasions shall offer. My dear good Mrs Norton, you shall have a whole packet of papers which I have sent to my Miss Howe, when she returns them; and you shall have, besides, another packet (and that with this letter), which I cannot at present think of sending to that dear friend, for the sake of my *own relations*; whom she is already but too eager to censure heavily. From these you will be able to collect a great deal of my story. But for what is previous to these papers, and which more particularly relates to what I have suffered from Mr Lovelace, you must have patience; for at present I have neither head nor heart for such subjects.

By the letters I have sent to Miss Howe, you will see when you have them before you, that Lord M. and the ladies of his family, jealous as they are of the honour of

their house (to express myself in their language), think
better of me than my own relations do.

Some of the letters in the same packet will also let
you into the knowledge of a strange step which I have
taken (strange you will think it); and, at the same time,
give you my reasons for it.

It must be expected that situations uncommonly difficult will make necessary some extraordinary steps, which
but for those situations would be hardly excusable. It
will be very happy indeed, and somewhat wonderful, if
all the measures I have been driven to take should be
right. A pure intention, void of all undutiful resentment,
is what must be my consolation, whatever others may
think of those measures when they come to know them:
which, however, will hardly be till it is out of my power
to justify them or to answer for myself.

I am glad to hear of my cousin Morden's safe arrival.
I should wish to see him methinks: but I am afraid that
he will sail with the stream; as it must be expected that
he will hear what they have to say first. But what I most
fear is that he will take upon himself to avenge me.
Rather than this should happen, I would have him look
upon me as a creature utterly unworthy of his concern;
at least of his *vindictive* concern.

How soothing to the wounded heart of your Clarissa,
how balmy, are the assurances of your continued love
and favour! Love me, my dear mamma Norton, continue
to love me to the end! I now think that I may, without
presumption, promise to *deserve* your love to the end.

And what is the space of time to look backward upon,
between an early departure and the longest survivance?
And what the consolation attending the sweet hope of
meeting again, never more to be separated, never more
to be pained, grieved, or aspersed! But mutually blessing, and being blessed, to all eternity!

In the contemplation of this happy state, in which I
hope in God's good time to rejoice with you, my beloved
Mrs Norton, and also with my dear relations, all reconciled to, and blessing, the child against whom they are
now so much incensed, I conclude myself

Your ever dutiful and affectionate
CLARISSA HARLOWE

Letter 414: MR BELFORD TO MISS CLARISSA HARLOWE

Sat. morn. Aug. 19

Madam,

I think myself obliged in honour to acquaint you that I am afraid Mr Lovelace will try his fate by an interview with you.

I wish to Heaven you could prevail upon yourself to receive his visit. All that is respectful, even to veneration, and all that is penitent, will you see in his behaviour, if you can admit of it. But as I am obliged to set out directly for Epsom (to perform, as I apprehend, the last friendly offices for poor Mr Belton, whom once you saw), and as I think it more likely that Mr Lovelace will *not* be prevailed upon, than that he *will*, I thought fit to give you this intimation, lest otherwise, if he should come, you should be too much surprised.

He flatters himself that you are not so ill as I represent you to be. When he sees you, he will be convinced that the most obliging things he can do will be as proper to be done for the sake of his own future peace of mind, as for your health-sake; and I dare say in fear of hurting the latter, he will forbear the thoughts of any further intrusion; at least while you are so much indisposed: so that *one half-hour's shock,* if it *will* be a shock to see the unhappy man (but just got up himself from a dangerous fever), will be all you will have occasion to stand.

I beg you will not too much hurry and discompose yourself. It is impossible he can be in town till Monday at soonest. And if he resolve to come, I hope to be at Mr Smith's before him.

I am, madam, with the profoundest veneration,

Your most faithful and most obedient servant,

J. BELFORD

Letter 415: MR LOVELACE TO JOHN BELFORD, ESQ.

Sunday, Aug. 20

What an unmerciful fellow art thou! A man has no need of a conscience who has such an impertinent monitor.

But get thee gone to Belton as soon as thou canst. Yet

whether thou goest or not, up I *must* go, and see what I can do with the sweet oddity myself. The moment these *prescribing* varlets will let me, depend upon it, I go. Nay, Lord M. thinks she ought to permit me one interview. His opinion has great authority with me—when it squares with my own: and I have assured him, and my two cousins, that I will behave with all the decency and respect that man can behave with to the person whom he *most* respects. And so I will. Of this, if thou choosest not to go to Belton meantime, thou shalt be witness.

Colonel Morden, thou hast heard me say, is a man of honour and bravery—but Colonel Morden has had his girls as well as you and I. And indeed, either openly or secretly, who has not? The devil always baits with a pretty wench when he angles for a man, be his age, rank, or degree, what it will.

I have often heard my beloved speak of the colonel with great distinction and esteem. I wish he could make matters a little easier, for her mind's sake, between the rest of the implacables and herself.

Methinks I am sorry for honest Belton. But a man cannot be ill or vapourish, but thou liftest up thy shriek-owl note and killest him immediately. None but a fellow who is fit for a drummer in death's forlorn-hope could take so much delight, as thou dost, in beating a dead-march with thy goose-quills.

I shall call thee seriously to account, when I see thee, for the extracts thou hast given the lady from my letters, notwithstanding what I said in my last; especially if she continue to refuse me. An hundred times have I known a woman deny, yet comply at last: but by these extracts, thou hast I doubt made her bar up the door of her heart, as she used to do her chamber-door, against me. This therefore is a disloyalty that friendship cannot bear, nor honour allow me to forgive.

Letter 416: MR LOVELACE TO JOHN BELFORD, ESQ.

London, Aug. 21. Monday

I believe I am bound to curse thee, Jack. Nevertheless I won't anticipate, but proceed to write thee a longer letter than thou hast had from me for some time past. So here goes.

That thou mightest have as little notice as possible of the time I was resolved to be in town, I set out in my lord's chariot and six yesterday as soon as I had dispatched my letter to thee, and arrived in town last night: for I knew I could have no dependence on thy friendship where Miss Harlowe's humour was concerned.

I had no other place so ready, and so was forced to go to my old lodgings, where also my wardrobe is; and there I poured out millions of curses upon the whole crew, and refused to see either Sally or Polly; and this not only for suffering the lady to escape; but for the villainous arrest, and for their insolence to her at the officer's house.

I dressed myself in a never worn suit, which I had intended for one of my wedding suits—and liked myself so well, that I began to think with thee that my outside was the best of me.

I took a chair to Smith's, my heart bounding in almost audible thumps to my throat, with the assured expectation of seeing my beloved. I clasped my fingers as I was danced along: I charged my eyes to languish and sparkle by turns: I talked to my knees, telling them how they must bend; and in the language of a charming describer acted my part in fancy, as well as spoke it to myself.

In this manner entertained I myself till I arrived at Smith's; and there the fellows set down their gay burden. Off went their hats; Will ready at hand in a new livery; up went the head; out rushed my honour; the woman behind the counter all in flutters—respect and fear giving due solemnity to her features; and her knees, I doubt not, knocking against the inside of her wainscot fence.

Your servant, madam. Will, let the fellows move to some distance and wait.

You have a young lady lodges here; Miss Harlowe, madam: is she above?

Sir, sir, and please your honour (the woman is struck with my figure, thinks I): Miss Harlowe, sir! There is, indeed, such a young lady lodges here—but, but—

But what, madam? I must see her. One pair of stairs;

is it not? Don't trouble yourself. I shall find her apartment. And was making towards the stairs.

Sir, sir, the lady, the lady is not at home—she is abroad—she is in the country.

In the country! Not at home! Impossible! You will not pass this story upon me, good woman. I *must* see her. I have business of life and death with her.

Indeed, sir, the lady is not at home! Indeed, sir, she is abroad.

She then rung a bell: John, cried she, pray step down! Indeed, sir, the lady is not at home.

Down came John, the good man of the house, when I expected one of his journeymen, by her saucy familiarity.

My dear, said she, the gentleman will not believe Miss Harlowe is abroad.

John bowed to my fine clothes. Your servant, sir. Indeed the lady is abroad. She went out of town this morning by six o'clock—into the country—by the doctor's advice.

Still I would not believe either John or his wife. I am sure, said I, she cannot be abroad. I heard she was very ill—she is not able to go out in a coach. Do you know Mr Belford, friend?

Yes, sir; I have the honour to know 'Squire Belford. He is gone into the country to visit a sick friend. He went on Saturday, sir.

Well, and Mr Belford wrote me word that she was exceeding ill. How then can she be gone out?

Oh sir, she is very ill; very ill, indeed—could hardly walk to the coach.

Where is her servant? Call her servant to me.

Her servant, sir, is her nurse: she has no other. And *she* is gone with her.

Well, friend, I must not believe you. You'll excuse me; but I must go upstairs myself. And was stepping up.

John hereupon put on a serious and a less respectful face. Sir, this house is mine; and—

And what, friend? not doubting then but she was above. I must and will see her. I have authority for it. I am a Justice of Peace. I have a search-warrant.

And up I went; they following me muttering, and in a plaguy flutter.

The first door I came to was locked. I tapped at it.

The lady, sir, has the key of her own apartment.

On the inside, I question not, my honest friend; tapping again. And being assured if she heard my voice that her timorous and soft temper would make her betray herself by some flutters to my listening ear. I said aloud, I am confident Miss Harlowe is here: dearest madam, open the door: admit me but for one moment to your presence.

But neither answer nor fluttering saluted my ear; and the people being very quiet, I led on to the next apartment; and the key being on the outside, I opened it and looked all round it, and into the closet.

The man said he never saw so uncivil a gentleman in his life.

Hark thee, friend, said I: Let me advise thee to be a little decent; or I shall teach thee a lesson thou never learnedst in all thy life.

Sir, said he, 'tis not like a gentleman, to affront a man in his own house.

Then prithee, man, replied I, don't crow upon thine own dunghill.

I stepped back to the locked door: My dear Miss Harlowe, I beg of you to open the door or I'll break it open—pushing hard against it, that it cracked again.

The man looked pale; and, trembling with his fright, made a plaguy long face; and called to one of his bodice-makers above, *Joseph, come down quickly.*

Joseph came down: a lion's-face grinning fellow; thick and short, and bushy-headed, like an old oak pollard. Then did master John put on a sturdier look. But I only hummed a tune, traversed all the other apartments, sounded the passages with my knuckles to find whether there were private doors, and walked up the next pair of stairs, singing all the way; John, and Joseph, and Mrs Smith, following me trembling.

I looked round me there, and went into two open-door bedchambers; searched the closets, the passages, and peeped through the keyhole of another: No Miss Harlowe, by Jupiter! What shall I do! What shall I do! Now will she be grieved that she is out of the way.

I said this on purpose to find out whether these people

knew the lady's story; and had the answer I expected
from Mrs Smith. I believe not, sir, said she.

Why so, Mrs Smith? Do you know who I am?

I can guess, sir.

Whom do you guess me to be?

Your name is Mr Lovelace, sir, I make no doubt.

The very same. But how came you to guess so well,
Dame Smith? You never saw me before—did you?

Here, Jack, I laid out for a compliment, and missed it.

'Tis easy to guess, sir; for there cannot be two such
gentlemen as you.

Well said, Dame Smith—but mean you *good* or *bad?*
Handsome was the least I thought she would have said.

I leave you to guess, sir.

Condemned, thinks I, by myself, on this appeal.

Why, Father Smith, thy wife is a wit, man! Didst thou
ever find that out before? But where is widow Lovick,
Dame Smith? My cousin John Belford says she is a very
good woman. Is she within? Or is *she* gone with Miss
Harlowe too?

She will be within by and by, sir. She is not with the
lady.

Well, but my good dear Mrs Smith, where is the lady
gone? And when will she return?

I can't tell, sir.

Well, Mrs Smith, with a grave air, I am heartily sorry
Miss Harlowe is abroad. You don't tell me where she is?

Indeed, sir, I cannot.

You *will* not, you mean. She could have no notion of
my coming. I came to town but last night—Have been
very ill. She has almost broke my heart by her cruelty.
You know my story, I doubt not. Tell her I must go out
of town tomorrow morning. But I will send my servant
to know if she will favour me with one half-hour's conversation; for, as soon as I get down, I shall set out for
Dover, in my way to France, if I have not a countermand
from her who has the sole disposal of my fate.

And away I was carried to White's, according to
direction.

As soon as I came thither, I ordered Will to go and
change his clothes, and to disguise himself by putting on
his black wig and keeping his mouth shut; and then to

dodge about Smith's to inform himself of the lady's motions.

I intend to regulate my motions by Will's intelligence; for see this dear creature I must and will. Yet I have promised Lord M. to be down in two or three days at farthest; for he is grown plaguy fond of me since I was ill.

I am in hopes that the word I left that I am to go out of town tomorrow morning will soon bring the lady back again.

Meantime, I thought I would write to divert thee, while thou art of such importance about the dying; and as thy servant it seems comes backward and forward every day, perhaps I may send thee another tomorrow, with the particulars of the interview between the dear lady and me; after which my soul thirsteth.

Letter 417: MR LOVELACE TO JOHN BELFORD, ESQ.

Thursday, Aug. 22

I must write on to divert myself: for I can get no rest; no refreshing rest. I awaked just now in a cursed fright. How a man may be affected by dreams!

'Methought I had an interview with my beloved. I found her all goodness, condescension, and forgiveness. She suffered herself to be overcome in my favour by the joint intercessions of Lord M., Lady Sarah, Lady Betty, and my two cousins Montague, who waited upon her in deep mourning; the ladies in long trains sweeping after them; Lord M. in a long black mantle trailing after *him*. They told her they came in these robes to express their sorrow for my sins against her, and to implore her to forgive me.

'I myself, I thought, was upon my knees and with a sword in my hand, offering either to put it up in the scabbard, or to thrust it into my heart, as she should command the one or the other.

'At that moment her cousin Morden, I thought, all of a sudden flashed in through a window, with his drawn sword. Die, Lovelace, said he! this instant die, and be damned, if in earnest thou repairest not by marriage my cousin's wrongs!

'I was rising to resent this insult, I thought, when Lord M. run between us with his great black mantle, and threw it over my face: and instantly, my charmer, with that sweet voice which has so often played upon my ravished ears, wrapped her arms round me, muffled as I was in my Lord M.'s mantle: Oh spare, spare my Lovelace! And spare, Oh Lovelace, my beloved cousin Morden! Let me not have my distresses augmented by the fall of either or both of those who are so dear to me.

'At this, charmed with her sweet mediation, I thought I would have clasped her in my arms: when immediately the most angelic form I had ever beheld, vested all in transparent white, descended from a ceiling, which, opening, discovered a ceiling above that, stuck round with golden cherubs and glittering seraphs, all exulting: Welcome, welcome, welcome! and, encircling my charmer, ascended with her to the region of seraphims; and instantly, the opening ceiling closing, I lost sight of *her*, and of the *bright form* together, and found wrapped in my arms her azure robe (all stuck thick with stars of embossed silver), which I had caught hold of in hopes of detaining her; but was all that was left me of my beloved Miss Harlowe. And then (horrid to relate!) the floor sinking under *me*, as the ceiling had opened for *her*, I dropped into a hole more frightful than that of Elden and tumbling over and over down it, without view of a bottom, I awaked in a panic; and was as effectually disordered for half an hour, as if my dream had been a reality.'

Wilt thou forgive me troubling thee with such visionary stuff? Thou wilt see by it only that, sleeping or waking, my Clarissa is always present with me.

But here this moment is Will come running hither to tell me that his lady actually returned to her lodgings last night between eleven and twelve, and is now there, though very ill.

I hasten to her. But that I may not add to her indisposition by any rough or boisterous behaviour, I will be as soft and gentle as the dove herself in my addresses to her.

The chair is come. I fly to my beloved.

Letter 418: MR LOVELACE TO JOHN BELFORD, ESQ.

Curse upon my stars! Disappointed again!

It was about eight when I arrived at Smith's. The woman was in the shop.

So, old acquaintance, how do you now? I know my love is above. Let her be acquainted that I am here, waiting for admission to her presence and can take no denial. Tell her that I will approach her with the most respectful duty and in whose company she pleases; and I will not touch the hem of her garment without her leave.

Indeed, sir, you're mistaken. The lady is not in this house, nor near it.

I'll see that—Will! beckoning him to me, and whispering, see if thou canst any way find out (without losing sight of the door, lest she should be below stairs) if she be in the neighbourhood, if not within.

Will bowed and went off. Up went I, without further ceremony; attended now only by the good woman.

I went into each apartment, except that which was locked before, and was now also locked: and I called to Miss Harlowe in the voice of love; but by the still silence was convinced she was not there. Yet, on the strength of my intelligence, I doubted not but she was in the house.

I then went up two pair of stairs, and looked round the first room: but no Miss Harlowe.

And who, pray, is in this room? stopping at the door of another.

A widow gentlewoman, sir. Mrs Lovick.

Oh my dear Mrs Lovick! said I, I am intimately acquainted with her character from my cousin John Belford. I must see Mrs Lovick by all means. Good Mrs Lovick, open the door.

She did.

Your servant, madam. Be so good as to excuse me. You have heard my story. You are an admirer of the most excellent woman in the world. Dear Mrs Lovick, tell me what is become of her?

The poor lady, sir, went out yesterday on purpose to avoid you.

How so? She knew not that I would be here.

She was afraid you would come when she heard you

were recovered from your illness. Ah! Sir, what pity it is that so fine a gentleman should make such ill returns for God's goodness to him!

You are an excellent woman, Mrs Lovick: I know that, by my cousin John Belford's account of you; and Miss Harlowe is an angel.

Miss Harlowe is indeed an angel, replied she; and soon will be company for angels.

No jesting with such a woman as this, Jack.

Tell me of a truth, good Mrs Lovick, where I may see this dear lady. Upon my soul, I will neither fright nor offend her. I will only beg of her to hear me speak for one half-quarter of an hour; and if she will have it so, I will never trouble her more.

Sir, said the widow, it would be death for her to see you. She was at home last night; I'll tell you truth: but fitter to be in bed all day. She came home, she said, to die; and if she could not avoid your visit, she was unable to fly from you; and believed she should die in your presence.

And yet go out again this morning early? How can that be, widow?

Why, sir, she rested not two hours, for fear of you. Her fear gave her strength, which she'll suffer for when that fear is over. And finding herself, the more she thought of it, the less able to stay to receive your visit, she took chair and is gone nobody knows whither. But I believe she intended to be carried to the water-side, in order to take boat; for she cannot bear a coach. It extremely incommoded her yesterday.

But before we talk any further, said I, if she be gone abroad, you can have no objection to my looking into every apartment above and below; because I am told she is actually in the house.

Indeed, sir, she is *not*. You may satisfy yourself, if you please: but Mrs Smith and I waited on her to her chair. We were forced to support her, she was so weak. She said, Where *can* I go, Mrs Lovick? Whither *can* I go, Mrs Smith? Cruel, cruel man! Tell him I called him so, if he come again! God give him that peace which he denies me!

Sweet creature! cried I, and looked down and took out my handkerchief.

The widow wept. I wish, said she, I had never known so excellent a lady, and so great a sufferer! I love her as my own child!

Mrs Smith wept.

I then gave over the hope of seeing her for this time. I was extremely chagrined at my disappointment, and at the account they gave of her ill health.

Letter 421: MR LOVELACE TO JOHN BELFORD, ESQ.

Wednesday morn. Aug. 23

All alive, dear Jack! and in ecstasy! Likely to be once more a happy man! For I have received a letter from my beloved Miss Harlowe; in consequence I suppose of advices that I mentioned in my last, from her sister. And I am setting out for Berkshire directly, to show the contents to my Lord M. and to receive the congratulations of all my kindred upon it.

I went last night, as I intended, to Smith's: but the dear creature was not returned at near ten o'clock. And lighting upon Tourville, I took him home with me, and made him sing me out of my megrims. I went to bed tolerably easy at two; had bright and pleasant dreams, not such a frightful one as that I gave thee an account of: and at eight this morning, as I was dressing to be in readiness against Will came back, whom I had sent to inquire after his lady's return, I had this letter brought me by a chairman.

to Robert Lovelace, Esq.

Tuesday night, 11 o'clock (Aug 22)

Sir,

I have good news to tell you. I am setting out with all diligence for my father's house. I am bid to hope that he will receive his poor penitent with a goodness peculiar to himself; for I am overjoyed with the assurance of a thorough reconciliation through the interposition of a dear blessed friend, whom I always loved and honoured. I am so taken up with my preparation for this joyful and long-wished-for journey, that I cannot spare one moment for any other business, having several matters of the last

importance to settle first. So, pray, sir, don't disturb or
interrupt me—I beseech you don't. You may in time,
possibly, see me at my father's, at least, if it be not your
own fault.

I will write a letter which shall be sent you when I am
got thither and received: till when, I am, etc.

CLARISSA HARLOWE

I dispatched instantly a letter to the dear creature,
assuring her with the most thankful joy, 'That I would
directly set out for Berkshire, and wait the issue of the
happy reconciliation, and the charming hopes she had
filled me with. I poured out upon her a thousand blessings. I declared that it should be the study of my whole
life to merit such transcendent goodness. And that there
was nothing which her father or friends should require
at my hands, that I would not for *her* sake comply with,
in order to promote and complete so desirable a
reconciliation.'

I hurried it away without taking a copy of it; and I
have ordered the chariot and six to be got ready; and
hey for M. Hall! Let me but know how Belton does. I
hope a letter from thee is on the road. And if the poor
fellow can spare thee, make haste, I advise thee, to attend this truly divine lady, or else thou mayest not see
her of months perhaps; at least, not while she is Miss
Harlowe. And favour me with one letter before she sets
out, if possible, confirming to me, and accounting for,
this generous change.

But what accounting for it is necessary? The dear
creature cannot receive consolation herself, but she must
communicate it to others. How noble! She would not
see me in her adversity: but no sooner does the sun of
prosperity begin to shine upon her, than she forgives me.

I know to whose mediation all this is owing. It is to
Colonel Morden's. She always, as she says, loved and
honoured him: and he loved her above all his relations.

I shall now be convinced that there is something in
dreams. The ceiling opening is the reconciliation in view.
The bright form, lifting her up through it to another
ceiling stuck round with golden Cherubims and Seraphims, indicates the charming little boys and girls that

will be the fruits of this happy reconciliation. The welcomes, thrice repeated, are those of her family, now no more to be deemed implacable. Yet are they a family too, that my soul cannot mingle with.

But then what is my tumbling over and over, through the floor, into a frightful hole (*descending* as she *ascends*)? Ho! only this; it alludes to my disrelish to matrimony: which is a bottomless pit, a gulf, and I know not what. And I suppose, had I not awoke (in such a plaguy fright) I had been soused into some river at the bottom of the hole, and then been carried (mundified or purified from my past iniquities) by the same bright form (waiting for me upon the mossy banks) to my beloved girl; and we should have gone on, cherubiming of it, and carolling, to the end of the chapter.

But what are the black sweeping mantles and robes of my Lord M. thrown over my face, and what are those of the ladies? Oh, Jack! I have these too: they indicate nothing in the world but that my lord will be so good as to die, and leave me all he has. So, rest to thy good-natured soul, honest Lord M.

As to Morden's flashing through the window, and crying, Die, Lovelace, and be damned, if thou wilt not repair my cousin's wrongs! That is only that he would have sent me a challenge had I not been disposed to do the lady justice.

All I dislike is this part of the dream: for, even in a dream, I would not be thought to be threatened into any measure, though I liked it ever so well.

And so much for my prophetic dream.

Dear charming creature! What a meeting will there be between her and her father and mother and uncles! What transports, what pleasure, will this happy, long-wished-for reconciliation give her dutiful heart! And indeed, now, methinks I am glad she *is* so dutiful to them; for her duty to parents is a conviction to me that she will be *as* dutiful to her husband: since duty upon principle is an uniform thing.

I shall long to see the promised letter too, when she is got thither, which I hope will give an account of the reception she will meet with.

There is a solemnity, however, I think, in the style of

her letter, which pleases and affects me at the same time.
But as it is evident she loves me still, and hopes soon
to see me at her father's; she could not help being a
little solemn and half-ashamed (dear blushing pretty
rogue!) to own her love, after my usage of her.

And then her subscription: *Till when, I am,* Clarissa
Harlowe: as much as to say, *after that* I shall be, if not
your own fault, Clarissa Lovelace!

Oh my best love! My ever generous and adorable
creature! How much does this thy forgiving goodness
exalt us both!

Letter 423: MR LOVELACE TO JOHN BELFORD, ESQ.

Although I have the highest opinion that man can have
of the generosity of my dear Miss Harlowe, yet I cannot
for the heart of me account for this agreeable change in
her temper but one way. Faith and troth, Belford, I verily believe, laying all circumstances together, that the
dear creature unexpectedly finds herself in the way I
have so ardently wished her to be in; and that this makes
her at last incline to favour me, that she may set the
better face upon her gestation when at her father's.

If this be the case, all her falling away and her fainting
fits are charmingly accounted for. Nor is it surprising
that such a sweet novice in these matters should not
know to what to attribute her frequent indispositions. If
this should be the case, how shall I laugh at *thee*! and
(when I am sure of her) at the dear novice *herself*, that
all her grievous distresses shall end in a man-child: which
I shall love better than all the Cherubims and Seraphims
that may come after; though there were to be as many
of them as I beheld in my dream; in which a vast ex-
panse of ceiling was stuck as full of them as it could
hold.

Letter 426: MR BELFORD TO ROBERT LOVELACE, ESQ.

Sat. Aug. 26

After I had given some particular orders about the preparations to be made for his [Belton's] funeral, I went to town; but having made it late before I got in on Thursday night, and being fatigued for want of rest several nights before, and low in my spirits (I could not help it, Lovelace!), I contented myself to send my compliments to the innocent sufferer, to inquire after her health.

My servant saw Mrs Smith, who told him she was very glad I was come to town; for that the lady was worse than she had yet been.

It is impossible to account for the contents of her letter to you; or to reconcile those contents to the facts I have to communicate.

I was at Smith's by seven yesterday (Friday) morning; and found that the lady was just gone in a chair to St Dunstan's to prayers; she was too ill to get out by six to Covent Garden Church; and was forced to be supported to her chair by Mrs Lovick. They would have persuaded her against going; but she said she knew not but it would be her last opportunity. Mrs Lovick, dreading that she would be taken worse at church, walked thither before her.

Mrs Smith told me she was so ill on Wednesday night, that she had desired to receive the Sacrament; and accordingly it was administered to her by the parson of the parish: whom she besought to take all opportunities of assisting her in her solemn preparation.

This the gentleman promised: and called in the morning to inquire after her health; and was admitted at the first word. He stayed with her about half an hour; and when he came down, with his face turned aside and a faltering accent, 'Mrs Smith, said he, you have an angel in your house. I will attend her again in the evening, as she desires, and as often as I think it will be agreeable to her.'

Her increased weakness she attributed to the fatigues she had undergone by your means; and to a letter she had received from her sister, which she answered the same day.

'She said it was hard she could not be permitted to die in peace: that her lot was a severe one: that she began to be afraid she should not forbear repining, and to think her punishment greater than her fault; but recalling herself immediately, she comforted herself that her life would be short, and with the assurance of a better.'

On Wednesday morning, when she received your letter in answer to hers, she said, Necessity may well be called the mother of invention. But calamity is the test of integrity. I hope I have not taken an inexcusable step—and there she stopped a minute or two, and then said, I shall now perhaps be allowed to die in peace.

A letter and packet were brought her by a man on horseback from Miss Howe, while we were talking. She retired upstairs to read it; and while I was in discourse with Mrs Smith and Mrs Lovick, the doctor and apothecary both came in together. They confirmed to me my fears as to the dangerous way she is in. They had both been apprised of the new instances of implacableness in her friends, and of your persecutions: and the doctor said, he would not for the world be either the unforgiving father of that lady, or the man who had brought her to this distress. Her heart's broke; she'll die, said he: there is no saving her.

When thou receivest this letter, thou wilt see what will soon be the end of all thy injuries to this divine lady. I say, *when thou receivest* it; for I will delay it for some little time, lest thou shouldst take it into thy head (under pretence of resenting the disappointment her letter must give thee) to molest her again.

This letter having detained me by its length, I shall not now set out for Epsom till tomorrow.

I should have mentioned, that the lady explained to me what the *one thing* was that she was afraid might happen to ruffle her. It was the apprehension of what may result from a visit which Colonel Morden, as she is informed, designs to make *you*.

Letter 439: MR LOVELACE TO JOHN BELFORD, ESQ.

Monday noon, Aug. 28

But what is the meaning I hear nothing from thee? And why dost thou not let me into the grounds of the sudden reconciliation between my beloved and her friends, and the cause of the generous invitation which she gives me of attending her at her father's some time hence?

Thou must certainly have been let into the secret by this time; and I can tell thee I shall be plaguy jealous if there be any one thing pass between my angel and thee that is to be concealed from me. For either I am a principal in this cause, or I am nothing.

But let me whisper a word or two in thy ear. I begin to be afraid, after all, that this letter was a stratagem to get me out of town, and for nothing else: for, in the first place, Tourville, in a letter I received this morning, tells me that the lady is actually very ill (I am sorry for it with all my soul!). This, thou'lt say, I may think a reason why she cannot *set out as yet*: but then I have heard on the other hand, but last night, that the family is as implacable as ever; and my lord and I expect this very afternoon a visit from Colonel Morden; who undertakes, it seems, to question me as to my intention with regard to his cousin.

This convinces me that if she *has* apprised them of my offers to her, they will not believe me to be in earnest till they are assured that I am so from my own mouth. And then I understand that the intended visit is an officiousness of Morden's own, without the desire of any of her friends.

Now, Jack, what can a man make of all this? My intelligence as to the continuance of her family's implacableness is not to be doubted; and yet when I read her letter, what can one say? Surely the dear little rogue will not lie!

I never knew her dispense with her word, but once: and that was when she promised to forgive me, after the dreadful fire that had like to have happened at our mother's, and yet would not see me next day, and afterwards made her escape to Hampstead in order to avoid forgiving me: and as she severely smarted for this depar-

ture from her honour given (for it is a sad thing for good
people to break their word when it is in their power to
keep it), one would not expect that she should set about
deceiving again; more especially by the *premeditation
of writing*.

In this lady therefore it would be as unpardonable to
tell a wilful untruth, as it would be strange if I kept my
word. In love-cases, I mean; for as to the rest, I am an
honest moral man, as all who know me can testify.

By my soul, Jack, if it were only that I should be
outwitted by such a novice at plotting, and that it would
make me look silly to my kinswomen here who know I
value myself upon my contrivances, it would vex me to
the heart; and I would instantly clap a featherbed into
a coach and six, and fetch her away, sick or well, and
marry her at my leisure.

But Colonel Morden is come and I must break off.

Letter 440: MR BELFORD TO ROBERT LOVELACE, ESQ.

Monday night, Aug. 28
I got to town in the evening, and went directly to
Smith's. I found Mrs Lovick and Mrs Smith in the back
shop, and I saw they had been both in tears. They rejoiced to see me, however, and told me that the doctor
and Mr Goddard were but just gone; as was also the
worthy clergyman who often comes to pray by her; and
all three were of opinion that she would hardly live to
see the entrance of another week. I was not so much
surprised as grieved; for I had feared as much when I
left her on Saturday.

I sent up my compliments; and she returned that she
would take it for a favour if I would call upon her in
the morning, by eight o'clock. Mrs Lovick told me that
she had fainted away on Saturday, while she was writing,
as she had done likewise the day before; and having
received benefit then by a little turn in a chair, she was
carried abroad again. She returned somewhat better; and
wrote till late; yet had a pretty good night; and went to
Covent Garden Church in the morning: but came home
so ill, that she was obliged to lie down.

When she arose, seeing how much grieved Mrs Lovick and Mrs Smith were for her, she made apologies for the trouble she gave them. You were happy, said she, before I came hither. It was a cruel thing in me to come among honest strangers, and to be sick, and die with you.

Pray for me, Mrs Lovick. Pray for me, Mrs Smith, that I may—I have great need of your prayers. This cruel man has discomposed me. What a step has he made me take to avoid him! And will not yet, I doubt, let me be at rest.

She said, that though this was so heavy a day with her, she was at other times within those few days past especially blessed with bright hours; and particularly, that she had now and then such joyful assurances (which she hoped were not presumptuous ones) that God would receive her to His mercy, that she could hardly contain herself and was ready to think herself above this earth while she was in it.

She had a pretty good night, it seems, and this morning went in a chair to St Dunstan's church.

The chairmen told Mrs Smith that after prayers (for she did not return till between nine and ten) they carried her to a house in Fleet Street, where they never waited on her before. And where dost think this was? Why, to an undertaker's! Good God! what a woman is this! She went into the back shop and talked with the master of it about half an hour, and came from him with great serenity; he waiting upon her to her chair with a respectful countenance, but full of curiosity and seriousness.

As soon as you can, sir, were her words to him as she got into the chair.

She was so ill in the afternoon, having got cold either at St Dunstan's or at chapel, that she sent for the clergyman to pray by her; and the women, unknown to her, sent both for Dr H. and Mr Goddard: who were just gone, as I told you, when I came to pay my respects to her this evening.

And thus I have recounted from the good women what passed to this night since my absence.

I long for tomorrow that I may see her: and yet 'tis such a melancholy longing as I never experienced, and know not how to describe.

Tuesday, Aug. 29

I was at Smith's at half an hour after seven.

She desired me to walk up, and invited Mr Smith and his wife, and Mrs Lovick also, to breakfast with her. I was better pleased with her liveliness than with her looks.

The good people retiring after breakfast, the following conversation passed between us.

Pray, sir, let me ask you, said she, if you think I may promise myself that I shall be no more molested by your friend?

I hesitated: for how could I answer for such a man?

What shall I do if he comes again? You see how I am. I cannot fly from him now. If he has any pity left for the poor creature whom he has thus reduced, let him not come. But have you heard from him lately? And will he come?

I hope not, madam; I have not heard from him since Thursday last, that he went out of town rejoicing in the hopes your letter gave him of a reconciliation between your friends and you, and that he might in good times see you at your father's; and he is gone down to give all his friends joy of the news, and is in high spirits upon it.

As soon as he discovers that that was only a stratagem to keep him away, he will come up; and who knows but even *now* he is upon the road? I thought I was so bad that I should have been out of his and everybody's way before now; for I expected not that this contrivance would serve me above two or three days; and by this time he must have found out that I am not so happy as to have any hope of a reconciliation with my family; and then he will come, if it be only in revenge for what he will think a deceit.

I believe I looked surprised to hear her confess that her letter was a stratagem only; for she said, You wonder, Mr Belford, I observe, that I could be guilty of such an artifice. I doubt it is not right. But how could I see a man who had so mortally injured me; yet, pretending sorrow for his crimes, and wanting to see me, could behave with so much shocking levity as he did to the honest people of the house? Yet, 'tis strange too, that neither you nor he found out my meaning on perusal of my letter. You have seen what I wrote, no doubt?

I have, madam. And then I began to account for it as an *innocent* artifice.

Thus far indeed, sir, it is *innocent*, that I meant him no hurt, and had a right to the effect I hoped for from it; and he had none to invade me. But have you, sir, that letter of his, in which he gives you (as I suppose he does) the copy of mine?

I have, madam. And pulled it out of my letter-case: but hesitating. Nay, sir, said she, be pleased to read my letter to yourself—I desire not to see *his*—and see if you can be longer a stranger to a meaning so obvious.

I read it to myself. Indeed, madam, I can find nothing but that you are going down to Harlowe Place to be reconciled to your father and other friends: and Mr Lovelace presumed that a letter from your sister, which he saw brought when he was at Mr Smith's, gave you the welcome news of it.

She then explained all to me, and that, as I may say, in six words. A *religious* meaning is couched under it, and that's the reason that neither you nor I could find it out.

Read but for my *father's house, Heaven*, said she; and for the interposition of my dear blessed friend, suppose the *mediation* of my *Saviour*; which I humbly rely upon; and all the rest of the letter will be accounted for.

I read it so, and stood astonished for a minute at her invention, her piety, her charity, and at thine and my own stupidity, to be thus taken in.

And then she expressed a deep concern for what might be the consequence of Colonel Morden's intended visit to you; and besought me that if now, or at any time hereafter, I had opportunity to prevent any further mischief, without detriment or danger to myself, I would do it.

I assured her of the most particular attention to this and to all her commands; and that in a manner so agreeable to her that she invoked a blessing upon me for my goodness, as she called it, to a desolate creature who suffered under the worst of orphanage; those were her words.

This conversation, I found, as well from the length as the nature of it, had fatigued her; and seeing her change colour once or twice, I made that my excuse, and took leave of her: desiring her permission to attend her in the evening; and as often as possible; for I could not help telling her that every time I saw her, I more and more considered her as a beatified spirit; and as one sent from heaven to draw me after her out of the miry gulf in which I had been so long immersed.

I shall dispatch my packet tomorrow morning early by my own servant, to make you amends for the suspense I must have kept you in: you'll thank me for that, I hope; but will not, I am sure, for sending your servant back without a letter.

I long for the particulars of the conversation between you and Mr Morden: the lady, as I have hinted, is full of apprehensions about it. Send me back this packet when perused, for I have not had either time or patience to take a copy of it. And I beseech you enable me to make good my engagements to the poor lady that you will not invade her again.

Letter 442: MR LOVELACE TO JOHN BELFORD, ESQ.

Tuesday morn. Aug. 29

Now, Jack, will I give thee an account of what passed on occasion of the visit made us by Colonel Morden.

He came on horseback, attended by one servant; and Lord M. received him as a relation of Miss Harlowe's, with the highest marks of civility and respect.

After some general talk of the times and of the weather, and such nonsense as Englishmen generally make their introductory topics to conversation, the colonel addressed himself to Lord M. and to me, as follows:

I need not, my lord, and Mr Lovelace, as you know the relation I bear to the Harlowe family, make any apology for entering upon a subject which, on account of that relation, you must think is the principal reason of the honour I have done myself in this visit.

Miss Harlowe, Miss Clarissa Harlowe's affair, said Lord M. with his usual forward bluntness. That, sir, is

what you mean. She is, by all accounts, the most excellent woman in the world.

The colonel then in a very manly strain set forth the
wickedness of attempting a woman of virtue and character. He said that men had generally too many advantages
over the weakness, credulity, and inexperience of the
fair sex, who were too apt to be hurried into acts of
precipitation by their reading inflaming novels, and idle
romances; that his cousin, however, he was sure, was
above the reach of common seduction, or to be influ-
enced to the rashness her parents accused her of, by
weaker motives than *their* violence, and the most solemn
promises on *my part*: but, nevertheless, *having* those motives, and her prudence (eminent as it was) being rather
the effect of *constitution* than *experience* (a fine advantage, however, he said, to ground an unblamable future
life upon), she might not be apprehensive of bad designs
in a man she loved: it was, therefore, a very heinous
thing to abuse the confidence of such a lady.

He was going on in this trite manner: but, interrupting
him, I said: These general observations, colonel, perhaps,
suit not this particular case.

I own to you then that I have acted very unworthily
by Miss Clarissa Harlowe; and I'll tell you further, that
I heartily repent of my ingratitude and baseness to her.
Nay, I will say *still* further, that I am so grossly culpable
as to her, that even to plead that the abuses and affronts
I daily received from her implacable relations were in
any manner a provocation to me to act vilely by her
would be a mean and low attempt to excuse myself—so
low and so mean, that it would doubly condemn me.

He looked upon Lord M. and then upon me, two or
three times.

Let me put this question to you, Mr Lovelace. Is it
true, as I have heard it is, that you would marry my
cousin, if she would have you?

I then told him of my sincere offers of marriage; 'I
made no difficulty, I said, to own my apprehensions that
my unhappy behaviour to her had greatly affected her:
but that it was the implacableness of her friends that
had thrown her into despair, and given her a contempt
for life.' I told him, 'That she had been so good as to

send me a letter to divert me from a visit my heart was set upon making her: a letter on which I built great hopes, because she assured me in it, that she was *going to her father's*; and that *I might see her there, when she was received, if it were not my own fault.*'

Lord M. proposed to enter into the proof of all this: he said in his phraseological way *that one story was good, till another was heard:* that the Harlowe family and I, 'twas true, had behaved like so many *Orsons* to one another; and that they had been very free with all our family besides: that nevertheless, for the lady's sake more than for theirs, or even for *mine* (he could tell me), he would do greater things for me than they could ask, if she could be brought to have me: and that this he *wanted* to declare, and would *sooner* have declared if he could have brought us sooner to patience and a good understanding.

The colonel made excuses for his warmth on the score of his affection to his cousin.

My regard for her made me readily admit them: and so a fresh bottle of Burgundy and another of Champagne being put upon the table, we sat down in good humour after all this blustering, in order to enter closer into the particulars of the case: which I undertook at both their desires to do.

But these things must be the subject of another letter which shall immediately follow this, if it do not accompany it.

Meantime you will observe that a bad cause gives a man great disadvantages: for I myself think that the interrogatories put to me with so much spirit by the colonel made me look cursedly mean; at the same time that it gave him a superiority which I know not how to allow to the best man in Europe.

Letter 448: MISS CLARISSA HARLOWE TO WM. MORDEN, ESQ.

Thursday, Aug. 31

I most heartily congratulate you, dear sir, on your return to your native country. I heard with much pleasure that you were come; but I was both afraid and ashamed, till you encouraged me by a first notice, to address myself to you.

How consoling is it to my wounded heart to find that you have not been carried away by that tide of resentment and displeasure with which I have been so unhappily overwhelmed. But that, while my still nearer relations have not thought fit to examine into the truth of vile reports raised against me, you have informed yourself (and generously *credited* the information) that my error was owing more to my misfortune than my fault.

I have not the least reason to doubt Mr Lovelace's sincerity in his offers of marriage: nor that all his relations are heartily desirous of ranking me among them. I have had noble instances of their esteem for me, on their apprehending that my father's displeasure must have subjected me to difficulties: and this after I had absolutely refused *their* pressing solicitations in their kinsman's favour, as well as *his own.*

Nor think me, my dear cousin, blamable for refusing him. I had given Mr Lovelace no reason to think me a weak creature. If I *had*, a man of his character might have thought himself warranted to endeavour to make ungenerous advantage of the weakness he had been able to inspire. The consciousness of *my own* weakness (in that case) might have brought me to a composition with *his* wickedness.

I can indeed forgive him. But that is because I think his crimes have set me above him. Can I be above the man, sir, to whom I shall give my hand and my vows; and with them a sanction to the most premeditated baseness? No, sir, let me say that your cousin Clarissa, were she likely to live many years and *that* (if she married not this man) in penury and want, despised and forsaken by all her friends, puts not so high a value upon the conveniencies of life, nor upon life itself, as to seek to re-obtain the one, or to preserve the other, by giving *such* a sanction: a sanction which *(were she to perform her duty)* would reward the violater.

One day, sir, you will perhaps know all my story. But, whenever it is known, I beg that the author of my calamities may not be vindictively sought after. He could not have been the author of them but for a strange concurrence of unhappy causes. As the law will not be able to reach him when I am gone, any other sort of vengeance terrifies me but to think of it: for, in such a case, should my friends be *safe*, what honour would his death bring to my memory? If any of them should come to misfortune, how would my fault be aggravated!

God long preserve you, my dearest cousin, and bless you but in *proportion* to the consolation you have given me in letting me know that you still love me; and that I have one near and dear relation who can pity and forgive me (and then will you be *greatly* blessed); is the prayer of

> Your ever-grateful and affectionate
> CLARISSA HARLOWE

Letter 449: MR LOVELACE TO JOHN BELFORD, ESQ.

Thursday, Aug. 31

I cannot but own that I am cut to the heart by *this* Miss Harlowe's interpretation of her letter. She ought never to be forgiven. *She*, a meek person, and a penitent, and innocent, and pious, and I know not what, who can deceive with a foot in the grave!

'Tis evident that she sat down to write this letter with a design to mislead and deceive. And if she be capable of that at such a crisis, she has much need of *God's* forgiveness, as I have of *hers*: and, with all her cant of *charity* and *charity*, if she be not more sure of it than I am of her *real pardon*; and if she take the thing in the light she ought to take it in; she will have a few darker moments yet to come than she seems to expect.

She is to send me a letter after she is in heaven, is she? The devil take such *allegories*; and the devil take thee for calling this absurdity an *innocent* artifice!

I insist upon it that if a woman of her character at such a critical time is to be justified in such a deception, a man in full health and vigour of body and mind, as I am, may be excused for all his stratagems and attempts against her. And, thank my stars, I can now sit me down with a quiet conscience on that score. By my soul, I can, Jack. Nor has anybody who can acquit *her*, a right to blame *me*. But with some, indeed, everything *she* does must be good, everything *I* do must be bad. And why? Because she has always taken care to coax the stupid misjudging world like a *woman*: while I have constantly defied and despised its censures, like a *man*.

But notwithstanding all, you may let her know from me that I will *not* molest her, since my visits would be so shocking to her: and I hope she will take this into her consideration as a piece of generosity that she could hardly expect, after the deception she has put upon me. And let her further know that if there be anything in my power that will contribute either to her ease or honour, I will obey her at the very first intimation, however disgraceful or detrimental to myself.

But who that has so many ludicrous images raised in his mind by thy awkward penitence, can forbear laughing at thee? Spare, I beseech thee, dear Belford, for the future, all thy own aspirations, if thou wouldst not dishonour those of an angel indeed.

When I came to that passage where thou sayest that thou considerest her as one sent from heaven to draw thee after her—for the heart of me, I could not for an hour put thee out of my head in the attitude of Dame Elizabeth Carteret on her monument in Westminster Abbey. If thou never observedst it, go thither on purpose; and there wilt thou see this dame in effigy, with uplifted head and hand, the latter taken hold of by a cupid every inch of stone, one clumsy foot lifted up also, aiming, as the sculptor designed it, to ascend; but so executed as would rather make one imagine that the figure (without shoe or stocking as it is, though the rest of the body is robed) was looking up to its corn-cutter: the other riveted to its native earth, bemired like thee (*immersed* thou callest it), beyond the possibility of unsticking itself. Both figures thou wilt find, seem to be in a contention, the bigger, whether it should pull down the lesser about its ears—the lesser (a chubby fat little varlet, of a fourth part of the other's bigness, with wings not much larger than those of a butterfly), whether it

should raise the larger to a heaven it points to, hardly
big enough to contain the great toes of either.

But now, to be serious once more, let me tell you,
Belford, that if the lady be really so ill as you write she
is, it will become you *(no Roman style here!)* in a case
so very affecting, to be a little less pointed and sarcastic
in your reflection.

But if the worst happen!—as by your continual knell-
ing I know not what to think of it!—then say not in so
many dreadful words what the event is—only that you
advise me to take a trip to Paris: and that will stab me
to the heart

Letter 450: MR BELFORD TO ROBERT LOVELACE, ESQ.

Thursday night, Aug. 31

When I concluded my last, I hoped that my next attendance upon this surprising lady would furnish me with
some particulars as agreeable as now could be hoped for
from the declining way she is in, by reason of the welcome letter she had received from her cousin Morden.
But it proved quite otherwise to *me*, though not to *herself*; for I think I never was more shocked in my life
than on the occasion I shall mention presently.

When I attended her about seven in the evening, she
told me that she had found herself since I went, in a
very petulant way. Strange, she said, that the pleasure
she had received from her cousin's letter should have
had such an effect upon her. But she had given way to
a *comparative* humour, as she might call it, and thought
it very hard that her nearer relations had not taken the
methods with her, which her cousin Morden had begun
with; by inquiring into her merit or demerit, and giving
her cause a fair audit before condemnation.

She had hardly said this, when she started, and a blush
overspread her face, on hearing, as I also did, a sort of
lumbering noise upon the stairs, as if a large trunk were
bringing up between two people: and looking upon me
with an eye of concern, Blunderers! said she, they have

brought in something two hours before the time. Don't
be surprised, sir: it is all to save *you* trouble.

Before I could speak, in came Mrs Smith: Oh madam,
said she, what have you done? Mrs Lovick, entering,
made the same exclamation. Lord have mercy upon me,
madam, cried I, what have you done! For, she stepping
at the instant to the door, the women told me it was
a coffin.

With an intrepidity of a piece with the preparation,
having directed them to carry it into her bedchamber,
she returned to us: They were not to have brought it in
till after dark, said she. Pray, excuse me, Mr Belford:
and don't you, Mrs Lovick, be concerned: nor you, Mrs
Smith. Why should you? There is nothing more in it
than the unusualness of the thing. Why may we not be
as reasonably shocked at going to the church where are
the monuments of our ancestors, with whose dust we
even *hope* our dust shall be one day mingled, as to be
moved at such a sight as this?

We all remaining silent, the women having their
aprons at their eyes—Why this concern for nothing at
all, said she? If I am to be blamed for anything, it is for
showing too much solicitude, as it may be thought, for
this earthly part. I love to do everything for myself that
I can do. I ever did. Every other material point is so far
done and taken care of, that I have had *leisure* for things
of lesser moment. Minutenesses may be observed, where
greater articles are not neglected for them. I might have
had this to order, perhaps, when less fit to order it. I
have no mother, no sister, no Mrs Norton, no Miss
Howe, near me. Some of you must have seen *this* in a
few days, if not now; perhaps have had the friendly trouble of directing it. And what is the difference of a few
days to *you*, when *I* am gratified rather than discomposed by it? I shall not die the sooner for such a preparation. Should not everybody make their will, that has
anything to bequeath? And who that makes a will,
should be afraid of a coffin? My dear friends (to the
women), I have considered these things; do not give me
reason to think *you* have not, with such an object before
you as you have had in *me*, for weeks.

We were all silent still, the women in grief, I in a

manner stunned. She would not ask *me*, she said; but would be glad, since it had thus earlier than she had intended been brought in, that her two good friends would walk in and look upon it. They would be less shocked when it was made more familiar to their eye, than while their thoughts ran large upon it.

I took my leave; telling her she had done wrong, very wrong; and ought not, by any means, to have such an object before her.

The women followed her in. 'Tis a strange sex! Nothing is too shocking for them to look upon, or see acted, that has but novelty and curiosity in it.

While I waited for a chair, Mrs Smith came down, and told me that there were devices and inscriptions upon the lid. Lord bless me! Is a coffin a proper subject to display fancy upon? But these great minds cannot avoid doing extraordinary things!

Letter 451: MR BELFORD TO ROBERT LOVELACE, ESQ.

Friday morn. Sept. 1

I really was ill and restless all night. Thou wert the subject of my execration, as she of my admiration, all the time I was quite awake: and when I dozed, I dreamt of nothing but of flying hour-glasses, death's-heads, spades, mattocks, and eternity; the hint of her devices (as given me by Mrs Smith) running in my head.

However, not being able to keep away from Smith's, I went thither about seven. The lady was just gone out: she had slept better, I found, than I, though her solemn repository was under her window not far from her bedside.

I was prevailed upon by Mrs Smith and her nurse Shelburne (Mrs Lovick being abroad with her) to go up and look at the devices. Mrs Lovick has since shown me a copy of the draft by which all was ordered. And I will give thee a sketch of the symbols.

The principal device, neatly etched on a plate of white metal, is a crowned serpent, with its tail in its mouth, forming a ring, the emblem of eternity, and in the circle made by it is this inscription:

CLARISSA HARLOWE.
APRIL X.
[Then the year]

AETAT. XIX.

For ornaments: at top, an hour-glass winged. At bottom, an urn.

Under the hour-glass, on another plate, this inscription:

> HERE the wicked cease from troubling: and HERE the weary be at rest. Job iii. 17.

Over the urn, near the bottom:

> Turn again unto thy rest, Oh my soul! For the Lord hath rewarded thee. And why? Thou hast delivered my soul from death; mine eyes from tears; and my feet from falling. Ps[alm] cxvi. 7, 8.

Over this text is the head of a white lily snapped short off, and just falling from the stalk; and this inscription over that, between the principal plate and the lily:

> The days of man are but as grass. For he flourisheth as a flower of the field: for, as soon as the wind goeth over it, it is gone; and the place thereof shall know it no more. Ps ciii. 15, 16.

She excused herself to the women, on the score of her youth, and being used to draw for her needleworks, for having shown more fancy than would perhaps be thought suitable on so solemn an occasion.

The date April 10 she accounted for, as not being able to tell what her closing-day would be; and as that was the fatal day of her leaving her father's house.

She discharged the undertaker's bill after I was gone, with as much cheerfulness as she could ever have paid for the clothes she sold to purchase this her *palace*: for such she called it; reflecting upon herself for the expensiveness of it, saying that they might observe in *her,* that

pride left not poor mortals to the last: but indeed she
did not know but her father would permit it, when furnished, to be carried down to be deposited with her ancestors; and in that case she ought not to discredit them
in her *last appearance.*

It is covered with fine black cloth, and lined with white
satin; soon she said to be tarnished by viler earth than
any it could be covered by.

The burial-dress was brought home with it. The
women had curiosity enough, I suppose, to see her open
that, if she did open it. And, perhaps, thou wouldst have
been glad to have been present to have admired it too!

Letter 454: MR BELFORD TO ROBERT LOVELACE, ESQ.

Sat. morning, Sept. 2
The lady is alive and serene, and calm, and has all her
noble intellects clear and strong. She says she will now
content herself with her closet duties and the visits of
the parish minister; and will not attempt to go out. Nor
indeed will she, I am afraid, ever walk up or down a
pair of stairs again.

What has contributed to her serenity, it seems, is that
taking the alarm her fits gave her, she has entirely finished, and signed and sealed her last will: which she had
deferred doing till this time, in hopes, as she said, of
some good news from Harlowe Place; which would have
occasioned the alterations of some passages in it.

Miss Howe's letter was not given her till four in the
afternoon, yesterday; at what time the messenger returned for an answer. She admitted him to her presence
in the dining-room, ill as she then was; and would have
written a few lines, as desired by Miss Howe; but not
being able to hold a pen, she bid the messenger tell her
that she hoped to be well enough to write a long letter
by the next day's post; and would not now detain him.

Saturday, six in the afternoon
I called just now, and found the lady writing to Miss
Howe. She made me a melancholy compliment, that she
showed me not Miss Howe's letter because I should soon

have that and all her papers before me. But she told
me that Miss Howe had very considerately obviated to
Colonel Morden several things which might have occasioned misapprehensions between him and me; and had
likewise put a lighter construction, for the sake of peace,
on some of your actions than they deserved.

She added that her cousin Morden was warmly engaged in her favour with her friends: and one good piece
of news Miss Howe's letter contained; that her father
would give up some matters, which (appertaining to her
of right) would make my executorship the easier in some
particulars that had given her a little pain.

Will says he shall reach you tonight. I shall send in
the morning; and if I find her not worse, will ride to
Edgware, and return in the afternoon.

Letter 455: MISS HOWE TO MISS CLARISSA HARLOWE

Tuesday, Aug. 29

My dearest friend,

I am at length returned to this place; and had intended
to wait on you in London: but my mamma is very ill.
Alas! my dear, she is very ill indeed. And you are likewise very ill. I see *that* by yours of the 25th. What shall
I do if I lose two such near, and dear, and tender
friends? She was taken ill yesterday at our last stage in
our return home—and has a violent surfeit and fever,
and the doctors are doubtful about her.

If she should die, how will all my pertnesses to her fly
in my face! Why, why, did I ever vex her? She says I
have been all duty and obedience! She kindly forgets all
my faults, and remembers everything I have been so
happy as to oblige her in. And this cuts me to the heart.

I see, I see, my dear, you are very bad—and I cannot
bear it. Do, my beloved Miss Harlowe, if you *can* be
better, do, for *my* sake, *be* better; and send me word of
it. Let the bearer bring me a line. Be sure you send me
a line. If I lose you, my more than sister, and lose my
mamma, I shall distrust my own conduct, and will not
marry. And why should I? Creeping, cringing in courtship: Oh my dear, these men are a vile race of *reptiles*

in *our day,* and mere *bears* in *their own.* See in Lovelace
all that was desirable in figure, in birth, and in fortune:
but in his heart a devil! See in Hickman—Indeed, my
dear, I cannot tell what anybody can see in Hickman, to
be always preaching in his favour. And is it to be expected that I, who could hardly bear control from a
mother, should take it from a husband?—from one too,
who has neither more wit, nor more understanding, than
myself? Yet he to be my instructor! So he will, I suppose; but more by the insolence of his will than by the
merit of his counsel. It is in vain to think of it. I cannot
be a wife to any man breathing whom I at present know.
This I the rather mention now, because on my mother's
danger I know you will be for pressing me the sooner
to throw myself into another sort of protection, should
I be deprived of her. But no more of this subject, or
indeed of any other; for I am obliged to attend my
mamma, who cannot bear me out of her sight.

Wednesday, Aug. 30

My mother, Heaven be praised! has had a fine night
and is much better. Her fever has yielded to medicine!
And now I can write once more with freedom and ease
to you, in hopes that you also are better. If this be
granted to my prayers, I shall again be happy. I write
with still the more alacrity, as I have an opportunity
given me to touch upon a subject in which you are
nearly concerned.

You must know then, my dear, that your cousin Morden has been here with me. He told me of an interview
he had on Monday at Lord M.'s with Lovelace; and
asked me abundance of questions about you, and about
that villainous man.

I could have raised a fine flame between them if I
would: but, observing that he is a man of very lively
passions, and believing you would be miserable if anything should happen to him from a quarrel with a man
who is known to have so many advantages at his sword,
I made not the worst of the subjects we talked of. But,
as I could not tell untruths in his favour, you must think
I said enough to make him curse the wretch.

I don't find, well as they all used to respect Colonel

Morden, that he has influence enough upon them to
bring them to any terms of reconciliation.

What can they mean by it! But your brother is come
home, it seems: so, the honour of the house—the reputation of the family, is all the cry!

The colonel is exceedingly out of humour with them
all. Yet has he not hitherto, it seems, seen your brutal
brother. I told him how ill you were, and communicated
to him some of the contents of your letter. He admired
you, cursed *Lovelace*, and raved against all your *family*.

He says that none of your friends think you so ill as
you are; nor will believe it. He is sure they all love you,
and that dearly too.

The colonel (as one of your trustees) is resolved to
see you put into possession of your estate: and in the
meantime he has actually engaged them to remit to him,
for you, the produce of it accrued since your grandfather's death (a very considerable sum); and proposes
himself to attend you with it. But by a hint he dropped,
I find you had disappointed some people's littleness by
not writing to them for money and supplies; since they
were determined to distress you, and to put you at
defiance.

Like all the rest! I hope I may say that without
offence.

I am obliged to leave off here. But having a good deal
still to write, and my mother better, I will pursue the
subject in another letter, although I send both together.
I need not say how much I am, and will ever be,

> Your affectionate, etc.
> ANNA HOWE

Letter 456: MISS HOWE TO MISS CLARISSA HARLOWE

Thursday, Aug. 31

The colonel thought fit once to speak it to the praise of
Lovelace's *generosity*, that *(as a man of honour ought)*
he took to himself all the blame and acquitted you of
the consequences of the precipitate step you had taken;
since, he said, as you loved him, and was in his power,
he *must* have had advantages which he would *not* have

had if you had continued at your father's, or at any friend's.

Mighty generous, I said (were it as he supposed) in such insolent reflectors, the best of them; who pretend to *clear* reputations which never had been *sullied,* but by falling into their dirty acquaintance! But in this case, I added, that there was no need of anything but the strictest truth, to demonstrate Lovelace to be the blackest of villains, you the brightest of innocents.

This he catched at; and swore that could he find that there were anything uncommon or barbarous in the seduction, as one of your letters had indeed seemed to imply (that is to say, my dear, anything *worse* than perjury, breach of faith, and abuse of a generous confidence!—sorry fellows!), he would avenge his cousin to the utmost.

Upon the whole I find that Mr Morden has a very slender notion of women's virtue in particular cases: for which reason I put him down, though your favourite, as one who is not entitled *to cast the first stone.*

He even hinted (as from your relations indeed) that it is impossible but there must be some *will* where there is much *love.* These sort of reflections are enough to make a woman who has at heart her own honour and the honour of her sex, to look about her and consider what she is doing when she enters into an intimacy with these wretches; since it is plain that whenever she throws herself into the power of a man, and leaves for him her parents or guardians, everybody will believe it to be owing more to her good luck than to her discretion if there be not an end of her virtue: and let the man be ever such a villain to her, she must take into her own bosom a share of his guilty baseness.

I find he is willing to hope that a marriage between you may still take place; which he says will heal up all breaches.

I would have written much more—But am obliged to leave off to attend my two cousins Spilsworth, and my cousin Herbert, who are come to visit us on account of my mother's illness. I will therefore dispatch these by Rogers; and if my mother gets well soon (as I hope she will) I am resolved to see you in town, and tell you everything that now is upon my mind: and particularly, mingling my soul with yours, how much I am, and will ever be, my dearest dear friend,

> Your affectionate
> ANNA HOWE

Letter 457: MR BELFORD TO ROBERT LOVELACE, ESQ.

Sunday evening, Sept. 3

I wonder not at the impatience your servant tells me you express to hear from me. I was designing to write you a long letter, and was just returned from Smith's for that purpose; but since you are so urgent, you must be contented with a short one.

I attended the lady this morning, just before I set out for Edgware. She was so ill overnight, that she was obliged to leave her letter to Miss Howe unfinished: but early this morning she made an end of it, and had just sealed it up as I came. She was so fatigued with writing, that she told me she would lie down after I was gone, and endeavour to recruit her spirits.

They had sent for Mr Goddard when she was so ill last night; and not being able to see him out of her own chamber, he for the first time saw her *house*, as she calls it. He was extremely shocked and concerned at it; and chid Mrs Smith and Mrs Lovick for not persuading her to have such an object removed from her bedchamber: and when they excused themselves on the *little authority* it was reasonable to suppose they must have with a lady so much their superior, he reflected warmly on those who had *more* authority, and who left her to proceed in such a shocking and solemn whimsy, as he called it.

It is placed near the window like a harpsichord, though covered over to the ground: and when she is so ill that she cannot well go to her closet, she writes and reads upon it, as others would upon a desk or table. But (only as she was so ill last night) she chooses not to see anybody in that apartment.

I went to Edgware; and returning in the evening, attended her again.

She had spent great part of the day in intense devotions; and tomorrow morning she is to have with her the same clergyman who has often attended her; from whose hands she will again receive the Sacrament.

Thou seest, Lovelace, that all is preparing, that all will be ready; and I am to attend her tomorrow afternoon to take some instructions from her in relation to my part in the office to be performed for her.

I shall dispatch Harry tomorrow morning early with her letter to Miss Howe: an offer she took very kindly; as she is extremely solicitous to lessen that young lady's apprehensions for her on not hearing from her by Saturday's post: and yet, to write the truth, how can her apprehensions be lessened?

Letter 458: MISS CLARISSA HARLOWE TO MISS HOWE

Saturday, Sept. 2

I write, my beloved Miss Howe, though very ill still: but I could not by the return of your messenger; for I was then unable to hold a pen.

What, I wonder, has again happened between you and Mr Hickman? Although I know it not, I dare say it is owing to some pretty petulance, to some half-ungenerous advantage taken of his obligingness and assiduity. Will you never, my dear, give the weight you and all our sex ought to give to the qualities of sobriety and regularity of life and manners in that sex? Must bold creatures and forward spirits, for ever, and by the best and wisest of us, as well as by the indiscreetest, be the most kindly used?

I must lay down my pen. I am very ill. I believe I shall be better by and by. The bad writing would betray me, although I had a mind to keep from you what the event must soon—

Now I resume my trembling pen. Excuse the unsteady writing. It *will* be so—

I have wanted no money: so don't be angry about such a trifle as money. Yet am I glad of what you incline me to hope, that my friends will give up the produce of my grandfather's estate since it has been in their hands: because, knowing it to be my right and that *they* could not want it, I had already disposed of a good part of it: and could only hope they would be willing to give it up at my last request. And now how rich shall I think myself in this my last stage! And yet I did not want before—indeed I did not—for who, that has many *superfluities*, can be said to want?

Do not, my dear friend, be concerned that I call it my *last stage*; for what is even the long life which in high health we wish for? And at last, when arrived at the old age we covet, one heavy loss or deprivation having succeeded another, we see ourselves stripped, as I may say, of everyone we loved; and find ourselves exposed as uncompanionable poor creatures, to the slights, to the contempts, of jostling youth, who want to push us off the stage, in hopes to possess what we have—and, superadded to all, our own infirmities every day increasing: of themselves enough to make the life we wished for the greatest disease of all!

In the disposition of what belongs to me, I have endeavoured to do everything in the justest and best manner I could think of; putting myself in my relations' places, and in the greater points ordering my matters as if no misunderstanding had happened.

I hope they will not think much of some bequests where wanted, and where due from my gratitude: but if they should, what is done, is done; and I cannot now help it. For I would not, on any account, have it thought that, in my last disposition, anything undaughterly, unsisterly, or unlike a kinswoman, should have had place in a mind that is *so* truly free (as I will presume to say) from all resentment that it now overflows with gratitude and blessings for the good I *have* received, although it be not all that my heart wished to receive. Were it even an *hardship* that I was not favoured with more, what is it but an hardship of half a year, against the *most* indulgent goodness of eighteen years and an half that ever was shown to a daughter?

My cousin, you tell me, thinks I was off my guard, and that I was taken at some advantage. Indeed, my dear, I was not. Indeed I gave no room for advantage to be taken of me. I hope, one day, that will be seen, if

I have the justice done me which Mr Belford assures me of.

I should hope that my cousin has not taken the liberties which you, by an observation (not unjust), seem to charge him with. For it is sad to think that the generality of that sex should make so light of crimes which they justly hold so unpardonable in their own most intimate relations of ours—Yet cannot commit them without doing such injuries to other families and individuals as they think themselves obliged to resent unto death, when offered to their own families.

I am very glad you gave my cous—

Sunday morning (Sept. 3) six o'clock

Hither I had written, and was forced to quit my pen. And so much weaker and worse I grew, that had I resumed it to have closed here, it must have been with such trembling unsteadiness that it would have given you more concern for me, than the delay of sending it away by last night's post can do: so I deferred it, to see how it would please God to deal with me. And I find myself after a better night than I expected, lively and clear; and hope to give you a proof that I do, in the continuation of my letter, which I will pursue as currently as if I had not left off.

I am glad you so considerately gave my cousin Morden favourable impressions of Mr Belford; since, otherwise, some misunderstanding might have happened between *them*: for although I hope this gentleman is an altered man, and in time will be a reformed one, yet is he one of those high spirits that has been accustomed to resent *imaginary indignities* to *himself*, when I believe he has not been studious to avoid giving *real offences* to *others*; men of this cast acting as if they thought all the world was made to bear with them, and they with nobody in it.

All my apprehension is what may happen when I am gone; lest then my cousin, or any other of my family, should endeavour to avenge me and risk their own more precious lives on that account.

Yet one comfort it is in your power to give me; and

that is, let me know, and very speedily it must be if you wish to oblige me, that all matters are made up between you and Mr Hickman; to whom, I see, you are resolved with your bravery of spirit to owe a multitude of obligations for his patience with your flightiness.

May you, my dear Miss Howe, have no discomforts but what you make to yourself! Those, as it will be in your own power to lessen them, ought to be your own punishment if you do not. As there is no such thing as *perfect happiness* here, since the busy mind will *make* to itself evils were it to *find* none, you will pardon this limited wish, strange as it may appear till you consider it: for to wish you no infelicities, either within or without you, were to wish you what can never happen in this world; and what perhaps ought not to be wished for, if by a wish one *could* give one's friend such an exemption; since we are not to live here always.

I *must* conclude—

God for ever bless you, and all you love and honour, and reward you here and hereafter for your kindness to

Your ever obliged and affectionate

CLARISSA HARLOWE!

Letter 460: MR BELFORD TO ROBERT LOVELACE, ESQ.

Monday, Sept. 4

When I was admitted to her presence, I have received, said she, a long and not very pleasing letter from my dear Mrs Norton: it will soon be in your hands. I am advised aginst appointing you to the office you have so kindly accepted; but you must resent nothing of these things. My choice will have an odd appearance to them; but it is now too late to alter it, if I would.

Mrs Smith, as well as Mrs Lovick, was with her. They were both in tears; nor had I, any more than they, power to say a word in answer: yet she spoke all this, as well as what follows, with a surprising composure of mind and countenance.

But, Mr Belford, said she, assuming a still spritelier air and accent, let me talk a little to you while I am thus able to say what I have to say.

Mrs Lovick, don't leave us; for the women were rising to go. Pray sit down; and do you, Mrs Smith, sit down too. Dame Shelburne, take this key and open that upper drawer. I will move to it.

She did, with trembling knees. Here, Mr Belford, is my will. It is witnessed by three persons of Mr Smith's acquaintance.

I dare to hope that my cousin Morden will give you assistance, if you request it of him. My cousin Morden continues his affection for me: but as I have not seen *him*, I leave all the trouble upon *you*, Mr Belford.

She then took up a parcel of letters enclosed in one cover, sealed with three seals of black wax: this, said she, I sealed up last night. The cover, sir, will let you know what is to be done with what it encloses. This is the superscription (holding it close to her eyes, and rubbing them): *As soon as I am certainly dead, this to be broke open by Mr Belford.* Here, sir, I put it (placing it by the will). These folded papers are letters and copies of letters, disposed according to their dates. Miss Howe will do with those as you and she shall think fit. If I receive any more, or more come when I cannot receive them, they may be put into this drawer (pulling out and pushing in the looking-glass drawer), you'll be so kind as to observe that, Mrs Lovick and Dame Shelburne, to be given to Mr Belford be they from whom they will.

Here, sir, proceeded she, I put the keys of my apparel (putting them into the drawers with her papers). All is in order, and the inventory upon them, and an account of what I have disposed of: so that nobody need to ask Mrs Smith any questions.

There will be no immediate need to open or inspect the trunks which contain my wearing apparel. Mrs Norton will open them, or order somebody to do it for her, in your presence, Mrs Lovick; for so I have directed in my will. They may be sealed up now: I shall never more have occasion to open them.

After this, she locked the drawer where were her papers; first taking out her book of *Meditations*, as she called it; saying she should perhaps have use for that; and then desired me to take the key of that drawer; for she should have no further occasion for that neither.

All this in so composed and cheerful a manner, that we were equally surprised and affected with it.

I shall leave the world in perfect charity, proceeded she. And turning towards the women, Don't be so much concerned for me, my good friends. This is all but needful preparation; and I shall be very happy.

Then again rubbing her eyes, which she said were misty, and looking more intently round upon each, particularly on me—God bless you all, said she! how kindly are you concerned for me! Who says I am friendless? Who says I am abandoned and among strangers? Good Mr Belford, don't be so *generously* humane. Indeed (putting her handkerchief to her charming eyes) you will make me less happy than I am sure you wish me to be.

Will engages to reach you with this (late as it will be) before you go to rest. It is just half an hour after ten.

J. BELFORD

Letter 466: MR LOVELACE TO JOHN BELFORD, ESQ.

Wed. morn. Sept. 6, half an hour after three

I am *not* the savage which you and my worst enemies think me.

I could quarrel with all the world; with thee as well as the rest; obliging as thou supposest thyself for writing to me hourly. How daredst thou (though unknown to her) to presume to take an apartment under the same roof with her? I cannot bear to think that thou shouldst be seen at all hours passing to and repassing from her apartments, while *I*, who have so much reason to call her mine, and once was preferred by her to all the world, am forced to keep aloof and hardly dare to enter the *city* where she is!

I can neither eat, drink, nor sleep. I am sick of all the world.

Surely it will be better when *all is over*—when I know the *worst* the Fates can do against me. Yet how shall I bear that *worst*? Oh Belford, Belford! write it not to me; but if it *must* happen, get somebody else to write; for I shall curse the pen, the hand, the head, and the heart, employed in communicating to me the fatal tidings. But what is this saying, when already I curse the whole world except her—myself most?

Thy LOVELACE

Letter 472: MR LOVELACE TO JOHN BELFORD, ESQ.

Kensington, Wednesday noon

Will neither vows nor prayers save her? I never prayed in my life, put all the years of it together, as I have done for this fortnight past: and I have most sincerely repented of all my baseness to her. And will nothing do?

But after all, if she recover not, this reflection must be my comfort; and it is *truth*; that her departure will be owing rather to wilfulness, to downright female wilfulness, than to any other cause.

It is difficult for people who pursue the dictates of a violent resentment to stop where first they designed to stop.

To bring these illustrations home; this lady, I suppose, in her resentment intended only at first to vex and plague me; and finding she could do it to purpose, her desire of revenge became stronger in her than the desire of life; and now she is willing to die as an event which she supposes will cut my heart-strings asunder. And still the more to be revenged puts on the Christian, and forgives me.

But I'll have none of her forgiveness! My own heart tells me I do not deserve it; and I cannot bear it!—And what is it but a mere *verbal* forgiveness, as ostentatiously as cruelly given with a view to magnify herself, and wound me deeper? A little, dear, specious—but let me stop—lest I blaspheme!

Reading over the above, I am ashamed of my ramblings: but what wouldst have me do? Seest thou not that I am but seeking to run out of myself in hope to lose myself; yet, that I am unable to do either?

If *ever* thou lovedst but half so fervently as I love— but of that thy heavy soul is not capable.

Send me word by thy next, I conjure thee, in the names of all her kindred saints and angels, that she is living, and likely to live! If thou sendest ill news; thou

wilt be answerable for the consequence, whether it be
fatal to the messenger or to

						Thy LOVELACE

Letter 473: MR BELFORD TO ROBERT LOVELACE, ESQ.

						Wednesday, 11 o'clock
This moment a man is come from Miss Howe with a
letter. Perhaps I shall be able to send you the contents.

Miss Howe to Miss Clarissa Harlowe
						Tuesday, Sept. 5
	Oh my dearest friend!
	What will become of your poor Anna Howe! I see by
your writing, as well as read by your own account
(which, were you not very, *very* ill, you would have
touched more tenderly), how it is with you! Why have
I thus long delayed to attend you! Could I think that
the comfortings of a faithful friend were as nothing to a
gentle mind in distress, that I could be prevailed upon
to forbear visiting you so much as *once* in all this time!
I, as well as everybody else, to desert and abandon my
dear creature to strangers! What will become of me if
you be as bad as my apprehensions make you!
	I will set out this moment, little as the encouragement
is that you give me to do so! My mother is willing I
should! Why, oh why, was she not *before* willing!
	Yet she persuades me too (lest I should be fatally
affected were I to find my fears too well justified) to
wait the return of this messenger, who rides our swiftest
horse. God speed him with good news to me—else—but,
oh! my dearest, dearest friend, what else! One line from
your hand by him! Send me but *one* line to bid me
attend you! I will set out the moment, the very moment,
I receive it. I am now actually ready to do so! And if
you love me, as I love you, the sight of me will revive
you to my hopes. But why, why, when I can think this,
did I not go up sooner?
	Blessed Heaven! deny not to my prayers, my friend,
my monitress, my adviser, at a time so critical to myself!
	But methinks your style and sentiments are too well

connected, too full of life and vigour to give cause for
so much despair as the staggering pen seems to threaten.

I am sorry I was not at home (I *must* add thus much
though the servant is ready mounted at the door) when
Mr Belford's servant came with your affecting letter. I
was at Miss Lloyd's. My mamma sent it to me; and I
came home that instant. But he was gone. He would not
stay, it seems. Yet I wanted to ask him an hundred thousand questions. But why delay I thus my messenger? I
have a multitude of things to say to you. To advise with
you about! You shall direct me in everything. I will obey
the holding up of your finger. But, if *you* leave me—
what is the world, or anything in it, to

Your ANNA HOWE?

The effect this letter had on the lady, who is so near
the end which the fair writer so much apprehends and
deplores, obliged Mrs Lovick to make many breaks in
reading it, and many changes of voice.

This *is* a friend, said the divine lady (taking the letter
in her hand, and kissing it), worth wishing to live for.
Oh my dear Anna Howe! How uninterruptedly sweet
and noble has been our friendship! But we shall one
day, I hope (and that must comfort us both), meet, never
to part again! Then, divested of the shades of body, shall
we be all light and all mind. Then how unalloyed, how
perfect, will be our friendship! Our love then will have
one and the same adorable object, and we shall enjoy it
and each other to all eternity!

She said her dear friend was so earnest for a line or
two, that she would fain write if she could: and she tried;
but to no purpose. She could dictate, however, she believed, and desired Mrs Lovick would take pen and
paper. Which she did, and then she dictated to *her*. I
would have withdrawn; but at her desire stayed.

She wandered a good deal at first. She took notice
that she did. And when she got into a little train, not
pleasing herself, she apologized to Mrs Lovick for making her begin again and again; and said that third time
should go, let it be as it would.

She dictated the farewell part, without hesitation; and
when she came to the blessing and subscription, she took

the pen, and dropping on her knees, supported by Mrs
Lovick, wrote the conclusion; but Mrs Lovick was forced
to guide her hand.

Letter 476: MR BELFORD

(In continuation)
The lady has been giving orders with great presence
of mind about her body: directing her nurse and the
maid of the house to put her into her coffin as soon
as she was cold. Mr Belford, she said, would know the
rest by her will.

She has just now given from her bosom, where she
always wore it, a miniature picture set in gold of Miss
Howe: she gave it to Mrs Lovick, desiring her to fold
it up in white paper, and direct it *To Charles Hickman,
Esq.*; and to give it to me, when she was departed, for
that gentleman.

She looked upon the picture before she gave it her.
*Sweet and ever-amiable friend—companion—sister—
lover!* said she, and kissed it four several times, once
at each tender appellation.

Thursday afternoon, 4 o'clock

Letter 479: MR BELFORD TO ROBERT LOVELACE, ESQ.

Seven o'clock, Thursday even. Sept. 7
I have only to say at present—Thou wilt do well to take a
tour to Paris; or wherever else thy destiny shall lead thee!!!
JOHN BELFORD

Letter 481: MR BELFORD TO ROBERT LOVELACE, ESQ.

Thursday night
I may as well try to write; since, were I to go to bed, I
shall not sleep. I never had such a weight of grief upon

my mind in my life, as upon the demise of this admirable woman; whose soul is now rejoicing in the regions of light.

You may be glad to know the particulars of her happy exit. I will try to proceed; for all is hush and still; the family retired; but not one of them, and least of all her poor cousin, I dare say, to rest.

At four o'clock, as I mentioned in my last, I was sent for down; and as thou usedst to like my descriptions, I will give thee the woeful scene that presented itself to me, as I approached the bed.

The colonel was the first that took my attention, kneeling on the side of the bed, the lady's right hand in both his, which his face covered, bathing it with his tears; although she had been comforting him, as the women since told him, in elevated strains but broken accents.

On the other side of the bed sat the good widow; her face overwhelmed with tears, leaning her head against the bed's head in a most disconsolate manner; and turning her face to me, as soon as she saw me: Oh Mr Belford, cried she, with folded hands—the dear lady—a heavy sob not permitting her to say more.

Mrs Smith, with clasped fingers and uplifted eyes, as if imploring help from the only Power which could give it, was kneeling down at the bed's feet, tears in large drops trickling down her cheeks.

The lady had been silent a few minutes, and speechless as they thought, moving her lips without uttering a word; one hand, as I said, in her cousin's. But when Mrs Lovick on my approach pronounced my name, Oh! Mr Belford, said she in broken periods; and with a faint inward voice, but very distinct nevertheless. Now! Now! (I bless God for His mercies to his poor creature) will all soon be over. A few—a very few moments—will end this strife—and I shall be happy!

My dearest cousin, said she, be comforted. What is dying but the common lot? The mortal frame may *seem* to labour—but that is all! It is not so hard to die, as I believed it to be! The preparation is the difficulty. I bless God, I have had time for that—the rest is worse to beholders than to me! I am all blessed hope—hope itself.

She was silent for a few moments, lifting up her eyes
and the hand her cousin held not between his. Then, *Oh
death!* said she, *where is thy sting!*

Then turning her head towards me—Do *you*, sir, tell
your friend that I forgive him! And I pray to God to
forgive him! Let him know how happily I die—And that
such as my own, I wish to be his last hour.

After a short silence, in a more broken and faint
accent—And you, Mr Belford, pressing my hand, may
God preserve you and make you sensible of all your
errors.

And she spoke faltering and inwardly: Bless—bless—
bless—you all—and now—and now (holding up her almost lifeless hands for the last time)—come—Oh
come—blessed Lord—JESUS!

Oh Lovelace! But I can write no more!

Letter 486: MR BELFORD TO ROBERT LOVELACE, ESQ.

                              Friday night, Sept. 8, past ten
I unlocked the drawer in which (as I mentioned in a
former) she had deposited her papers. I accused myself
for having not done it overnight. But really I was then
incapable of anything.

I broke it open accordingly, and found in it no less
than eleven letters, each sealed with her own seal and
black wax, one of which was directed to me.

The other letters are directed to her father, to her
mother, one to her two uncles, to her brother, to her
sister, to her aunt Hervey, to her cousin Morden, to Miss
Howe, to Mrs Norton, and lastly one to you, in performance of her promise *that a letter should be sent you
when she arrived at her Father's house!* I will withhold
this last till I can be assured that you will be fitter to
receive it than Tourville tells me you are at present.

Copies of all these are sealed up and entitled, *Copies
of my ten posthumous letters, for* J. Belford, *Esq.;* and
put in among the bundle of papers left to my direction,
which I have not yet had leisure to open.

No wonder, while able, that she was always writing,

since thus only of late could she employ that time which heretofore, from the long days she made, caused so many beautiful works to spring from her fingers. It is my opinion that there never was a lady so young, who wrote so much and with such celerity. Her thoughts keeping pace, as I have seen, with her pen, she hardly ever stopped or hesitated; and very seldom blotted out, or altered. It was a natural talent she was mistress of, among many other extraordinary ones.

I gave the colonel his letter, and ordered Harry instantly to get ready to carry the others.

Meantime (retiring into the next apartment) we opened the will. We were both so much affected in perusing it, that at one time the colonel, breaking off, gave it to me to read on; at another, I gave it back to him to proceed with; neither of us being able to read it through without such tokens of sensibility as affected the voices of each.

The colonel and I have bespoke mourning for our selves and servants.

Letter 497: MR LOVELACE TO JOHN BELFORD, ESQ.

Uxbridge, Sat. Sept. 9

Jack,

I think it absolutely right that my ever-dear and beloved lady should be opened and embalmed. It must be done out of hand—this very afternoon. Your acquaintance Tomkins and old Anderson of this place, whom I will bring with me, shall be the surgeons. I have talked to the latter about it.

I will see everything done with that decorum which the case, and the sacred person of my beloved require.

Everything that can be done to preserve the charmer from decay shall also be done. And when she *will* descend to her original dust, or cannot be kept longer, I will then have her laid in my family vault between my own father and mother. Myself, as I am in my soul, so in person, chief mourner. But her heart, to which I have such unquestionable pretensions, in which once I had so large a share, and which I will prize above my own, I *will* have. I will keep it in spirits. It shall never be out of my sight.

Surely nobody will dispute my right to her. Whose was she living? Whose is she dead, but mine? Her cursed parents, whose barbarity to her no doubt was the *true* cause of her death, have long since renounced her. She left *them* for *me*. She chose *me* therefore: and I was her husband. What though I treated her like a villain? Do I not pay for it now? Would she not have been mine had I not? Nobody will dispute but she would. And has she not forgiven me? Whose then can she be but mine?

I will free you from your executorship and all your cares.

Take notice, Belford, that I do hereby actually discharge you, and everybody, from all cares and troubles relating to her. And as to her last testament I will execute it myself.

Her bowels, if her friends are very solicitous about them, and very humble and sorrowful (and none have they of their own), shall be sent down to them—to be laid with *her* ancestors—unless she has ordered otherwise. For, except that she shall not be committed to the unworthy earth so long as she can be kept out of it, her will shall be performed in everything.

I charge you stir not in any part of her will, but by my express direction. I will order everything myself. For am I not her husband? And being forgiven by her, am I not the chosen of her heart? What else signifies her forgiveness?

What I write to you for is:

1. To forbid you intermeddling with anything relating to her. To forbid Morden intermeddling also. If I remember right, he has threatened me, and cursed me, and used me ill. And let him be gone from her if he would avoid my resentments.
2. To send me a lock of her hair instantly by the bearer.
3. To engage Tomkins to have everything ready for the opening and embalming. I shall bring Anderson with me.

4. To get her will and everything ready for my perusal and consideration.

I will have possession of her dear heart this very night;
and let Tomkins provide a proper receptacle and spirits,
till I can get a golden one made for it.

I will take her papers. And as no one can do her
memory justice equal to myself, and I will not spare
myself, who can better show the world what she was,
and what a villain he that could use her ill? And the
world shall also see, what implacable and unworthy parents she had.

Although her will may in some respects cross mine,
yet I expect to be observed. I will be the interpreter
of hers.

Next to mine, hers shall be observed, for she is my
wife; and shall be to all eternity. I will never have
another.

Adieu, Jack. I am preparing to be with you. I charge
you, as you value my life or your own, do not oppose
me in anything relating to my Clarissa Lovelace.

R. LOVELACE

Letter 500: COLONEL MORDEN TO JOHN BELFORD, ESQ.

Sunday night, Sept. 10

Dear sir,

According to my promise, I send you an account of
matters here.

When we were within five miles of Harlowe Place, I
put on a hand-gallop. I ordered the hearse to proceed
more slowly still, the cross-road we were in being rough,
and having more time before us than I wanted; for I
wished not the hearse to be in till near dusk.

I got to my cousin's about 4 o'clock. You may believe
I found a mournful house.

At my entrance into the court, they were all in motion.
Every servant whom I saw had swelled eyes, and looked
with so much concern that at first I apprehended some
new disaster had happened in the family.

They all helped on one another's grief, as they had before each other's hardness of heart.

My cousin James met me at the entrance of the hall. His countenance expressed a fixed concern; and he desired me to excuse his behaviour the last time I was there.

My cousin Arabella came to me full of tears and grief. Oh cousin! said she, hanging upon my arm, I dare not ask you any questions! About the approach of the hearse, I suppose she meant.

I myself was full of grief; and without going farther or speaking, sat down in the hall, in the first chair.

The brother sat down on one hand of me, the sister on the other. Both were silent. The latter in tears.

My cousin Harlowe, the dear creature's father, as soon as he saw me said, Oh cousin, cousin, of all our family you are the only one who have nothing to reproach yourself with! You are a happy man!

The poor mother bowing her head to me in speechless grief sat with her handkerchief held to her eyes with one hand.

Miss Arabella followed her uncle Antony as he walked in before me; and seemed as if she would have spoken to the pierced mother some words of comfort. But she was unable to utter them, and got behind her mother's chair; and inclining her face over it on the unhappy lady's shoulder, seemed to claim the consolation that indulgent parent used, but then was unable to afford her.

Young Mr Harlowe with all his vehemence of spirit was now subdued. His self-reproaching conscience, no doubt, was the cause of it.

As I was the only person (grieved as I was myself) from whom any of them at that instant could derive comfort: Let us not, said I, my dear cousin, approaching the inconsolable mother, give way to a grief which however just can now avail us nothing. We hurt ourselves, and cannot recall the dear creature for whom we mourn. Nor would you wish it, if you knew with what assurances of eternal happiness she left the world. She is happy, madam! Depend upon it, she is happy! And comfort yourselves with that assurance.

One in the morning

About six o'clock the hearse came to the outward gate. The parish church is at some distance; but the wind sitting fair, the afflicted family were struck, just before it came, into a fresh fit of grief on hearing the funeral bell tolled in a very solemn manner. A respect as it proved, and as they all guessed, paid to the memory of the dear deceased out of officious love, as the hearse passed near the church.

Judge, when their grief was so great in expectation of it, what it must be when it arrived.

A servant came in to acquaint us with what its lumbering heavy noise up the paved inner court-yard apprised us of before.

He spoke not. He could not speak. He looked, bowed, and withdrew.

I stepped out. No one else could then stir. Her brother, however, soon followed me.

When I came to the door, I beheld a sight very affecting.

You have heard, sir, how universally my dear cousin was beloved. By the poor and middling sort especially, no young lady was ever so much beloved. And with reason: she was the common patroness of all the honest poor in her neighbourhood.

These, when the coffin was taken out of the hearse, crowding about it, hindered for a few moments its being carried in; the young people struggling who should bear it; and yet with respectful *whisperings* rather than clamorous *contention*. A mark of veneration I had never before seen paid, upon any occasion in all my travels, from the under-bred many, from whom noise is generally inseparable in all their emulations. At last six maidens were permitted to carry it in by the six handles.

The corpse was thus borne, with the most solemn respect, into the hall, and placed for the present upon two stools there. The plates, and emblems, and inscription, set every one gazing upon the lid, and admiring. The more, when they were told that all was of her own ordering: They wished to be permitted a sight of the corpse; but rather mentioned this as their wish than their hope. When they had all satisfied their curiosity, and remarked upon the emblems, they dispersed, with blessings upon her memory, and with tears and lamentations; pronouncing her to be happy; and inferring that were *she* not so, what would become of them?

Your faithful and obedient servant,
WM. MORDEN

Letter 515: MR LOVELACE TO JOHN BELFORD, ESQ.

Tuesday, Sept. 26

Your solicitude to get me out of this heavy changeable climate exactly tallies with everybody's here. They all believe that travelling will establish me. Yet I think I am quite well.

But wilt thou write often when I am gone? Wilt thou then piece the thread where thou brokest it off? Wilt thou give me the particulars of *their* distress, who were my *auxiliaries* in bringing on the event that affects me? Nay, *principals* rather: since, say what thou wilt, what did I do worth a woman's breaking her heart for?

Faith and troth, Jack, I have had very hard usage, as I have often said—to have such a plaguy ill name given me, pointed at, screamed out upon, run away from, as a mad dog would be; all my own friends ready to renounce me!

Yet I think I deserve it all: for have I not been as ready to give up myself, as others are to condemn me?

What madness, what folly, this! Who will take the part of a man that condemns himself? Who can? Out upon me for an impolitic wretch! I have not the art of the least artful of any of our Christian princes; who every day are guilty of ten times worse breaches of faith; and yet, issuing out a manifesto, they wipe their mouths, and go on from infraction to infraction, from robbery to robbery; commit devastation upon devastation; and destroy—for their *glory*! And are rewarded with the names of *conquerors*, and are dubbed *Le Grand*; praised, and even deified by orators and poets, for their butcheries and depredations.

While I, a poor, single, harmless prowler; at least *comparatively* harmless; in order to satisfy my hunger, steal but one poor lamb; and every mouth is opened, every hand is lifted up against me.

Nay, as I have just now heard, I am to be *manifested* against, though no prince: for Miss Howe threatens to have the case published to the whole world.

Upon the whole, Jack, had not the lady died, would there have been half so much said of it as there is? Was I the cause of her death? or could I help it? And have there not been, in a million of cases like this, nine hundred and ninety-nine thousand that have not ended as this has ended? How hard, then, is my fate! Upon my soul, I won't bear it as I have done; but, instead of taking guilt to myself, claim pity. And this (since yesterday cannot be recalled) is the only course I can pursue to make myself easy. Proceed anon.

Letter 517: MR BELFORD TO COLONEL MORDEN

Thursday, Sept. 21

Give me leave, dear sir, to address myself to you in a very serious and solemn manner on a subject that I must not, cannot dispense with; as I promised the divine lady that I would do everything in my power to prevent that further mischief which she was so very apprehensive of.

I will not content myself with distant hints. It is with very great concern that I have just now heard of a declaration which you are said to have made to your relations at Harlowe Place, that you will not rest till you have avenged your cousin's wrongs upon Mr Lovelace.

Far be it from me to offer to defend the unhappy man, or even *unduly* to extenuate his crime: but yet I must say, that the family, by their persecutions of the dear lady at first, and by their implacableness afterwards, ought *at least* to *share* the blame with him. There is even great reason to believe that a lady of such a religious turn, her virtue neither to be surprised nor corrupted, her will inviolate, would have got over a *mere personal* injury; especially as he would have done all that was in his power to repair it; and as, from the application of all his family in his favour, and other circumstances attending his sincere and voluntary offer, the lady might have condescended, with greater glory to herself than if he had never offended.

When I have the pleasure of seeing you next, I will acquaint you, sir, with all the circumstances of this melancholy story; from which you will see that Mr Lovelace was extremely ill-treated at first by the whole family, this admirable lady excepted. This exception, I know, heightens his crime: but as his principal intention was but to try her virtue; and that he became so earnest a suppliant to her for marriage; and as he has suffered so deplorably in the loss of his reason for not having it in his power to repair her wrongs; I presume to hope that much is to be pleaded against such a resolution as you are said to have made.

My dear Colonel Morden, the highest injury was to *her*: her family all have a share in the *cause*: she forgives it: why should we not endeavour to imitate what we admire?

You asked me, sir, when in town, if a brave man could be a premeditatedly base one? Generally speaking, I believe bravery and baseness are incompatible. But Mr Lovelace's character, in the instance before us, affords a proof of the truth of the common observation that there is no general rule but has its exceptions: for England, I believe, as gallant a nation as it is deemed to be, has not in it a braver spirit than his; nor a man who has greater skill at his weapons; nor more *calmness* with his skill.

Excuse me, sir, for the sake of my executorial duty and promise, keeping in eye the dear lady's *personal injunctions* as well as *written will*, enforced by *letters posthumous.* Every article of which (solicitous as we *both* are to see it duly performed) she would have dispensed with, rather than farther mischief should happen on her account. I am,

Dear sir, Your affectionate and faithful servant,
JOHN BELFORD

Letter 519: COLONEL MORDEN TO JOHN BELFORD, ESQ.

Sat. Sept. 23

Dear sir,

I have indeed expressed myself with vehemence upon the occasion. Who could forbear to do so? But it is not my way to resolve in matters of moment till opportunity brings the execution of my purposes within my reach. We shall see what manner of spirit this young man will be acted by, on his recovery. If he continue to brave and defy a family which he has so irreparably injured—if— But resolutions depending upon future contingencies are best left to future determination, as I just now hinted.

As to your arguments; I hope you will believe me when I assure you as I now do, that your opinion and your reasonings have, and will always have, great and deserved weight with me: and that I respect you still more than I did, if possible, for your expostulations in favour of the end of my cousin's pious injunctions to me. They come from *you*, sir, with the greatest propriety, as her executor and representative; and likewise as you are a man of humanity, and a well-wisher to both parties.

I am not exempt from violent passions, sir, any more than your friend; but then I hope they are only capable of being raised by other people's insolence, and not by my own arrogance.

You, sir, who know more of the barbarous machinations and practices of this strange man can help me to still more inflaming reasons, were they needed, why a man *not perfect* may stand excused to the generality of the world, if he should pursue his vengeance.

I intend to wait upon Miss Howe in person with the diamond ring, and such other of the effects bequeathed to her as are here. I am, sir,

Your most faithful and obliged servant,
WM. MORDEN

Letter 520: COLONEL MORDEN TO JOHN BELFORD, ESQ.

Tuesday, Sept. 26

Dear sir,

I waited upon Miss Howe myself, as I told you I
would, with what was bequeathed to her and her mother.
If I make a few observations with regard to that young
lady, so dear to my beloved cousin, you will not be displeased perhaps, as you have not a personal acquaintance with her.

There never was a firmer and nobler friendship in
women than that which the wretched man has put an
end to between my dear cousin and Miss Howe.

Friendship, generally speaking, Mr Belford, is too fervent a flame for female minds to manage: a light that
but in few of their hands burns steady, and often hurries
the sex into flight and absurdity. Like other extremes, it
is hardly ever durable. Marriage, which is the highest
state of friendship, generally absorbs the most vehement
friendships of female to female; and that whether the
wedlock be happy or not.

What female mind is capable of two fervent friendships at the same time?

This I mention as a *general observation:* but the friendship that subsisted between these two ladies affords a
remarkable exception to it: which I account for from
those qualities and attainments in *both*, which, were they
more common, would furnish more exceptions still in
favour of the sex. Both had an *enlarged*, and even a
liberal education: both had minds thirsting after virtuous
knowledge. Great readers both: great writers (and *early
familiar writing* I take to be one of the greatest openers
and improvers of the mind that man or woman can be
employed in). Both generous. High in fortune; therefore
above that dependence each on the other that frequently
destroys the familiarity which is the cement of friendship. Both excelling in *different ways*, in which neither
sought to emulate the other. Both blessed with clear and
distinguishing faculties; with solid sense; and from their
first intimacy (I have many of my lights, sir, from Mrs
Norton) each seeing something in the other to *fear*, as
well as *love*; yet making it an indispensable condition of

their friendship each to tell the other of her failings; and
to be thankful for the freedom taken. One by nature
gentle; the other *made so* by her *love* and *admiration*
of her exalted friend—impossible that there could be a
friendship better calculated for duration.

I must however take the liberty to blame Miss Howe
for her behaviour to Mr Hickman. And I infer from it,
that even women of sense are not to be trusted with
power.

By the way, I am sure I need not desire you not to
communicate to this fervent young lady the liberties I
take with her character.

I dare say my cousin could not approve of Miss
Howe's behaviour to this gentleman: a behaviour which
is talked of by as many as know Mr Hickman and her.
Can a *wise* young lady be easy under such censure? She
must know it.

Mr Hickman is really a very worthy man. Everybody
speaks well of him. But he is gentle-dispositioned, and
he adores Miss Howe; and love admits not of an air of
even due dignity to the object of it. Yet will he hardly
ever get back the reins he has yielded up; unless she, by
carrying too far the power she seems at present too sensible of, should, when she has no favours to confer which
he has not a right to demand, provoke him to throw off
the too heavy yoke. And should he do so, and then treat
her with negligence, Miss Howe of all the women I know
will be the least able to support herself under it. She
will then be *more* unhappy than she ever made him: for
a man who is uneasy at home can divert himself abroad;
which a woman cannot so easily do without scandal.

Permit me to take further notice as to Miss Howe,
that it is very obvious to me that she has, by her haughty
behaviour to this worthy man, involved herself in one
difficulty from which she knows not how to extricate
herself with that grace which accompanies all her actions. She intends to have Mr Hickman. I believe she
does not dislike him. And it will cost her no small pains
to descend from the elevation she has climbed to.

Another inconveniency, she will suffer from her having taught everybody (for she is above disguise) to think
by her treatment of Mr Hickman much more meanly of

him than he deserves to be thought of. And must *she* not suffer dishonour in *his* dishonour?

Mrs Howe is much disturbed at her daughter's behaviour to the gentleman. He is very deservedly a favourite of hers. But (*another* failing in Miss Howe!) her mother has not all the authority with her that her daughter's good sense ought to permit her to have. It is very difficult, Mr Belford, for people of *different* or *contrary* dispositions (though no bad people neither) to mingle REVERENCE with their *love* for each other; even where *nature* has called for *love* in the relationship.

Miss Howe is *open, generous, noble.* The mother has not any of these fine qualities. Parents, in order to preserve their children's veneration for them, should take great care not to let them see anything in their conduct or behaviour, or principles, which they themselves would not approve of in others.

But, after all, I see that there is something so charmingly brilliant and frank in Miss Howe's disposition, although at present visibly overclouded by grief, that it is impossible not to love her even for her failings. She *may*, and I hope she *will*, make Mr Hickman an obliging wife. And if she do, she will have an additional merit with me; since she cannot be apprehensive of check or control; and may therefore by her *generosity* and *prudence* lay an obligation upon her husband by the performance of what is no more than her *duty.*

Her mother both *loves* and *fears* her.

Yet once she praised her daughter to me for the generosity of her spirit, with so much *warmth* that had I not known the old lady's character, I should have thought her generous *herself.* And yet I have always observed that people even of narrow tempers are ready to praise generous ones—and thus have I accounted for it, that such persons generally find it to their purpose, that all the world should be open-minded but themselves.

The old lady applied herself to me to urge to the young one the contents of the will, in order to hasten her to fix a day for her marriage: but desired that I would not let Miss Howe know that she did.

I took the liberty upon it to tell the young lady that I hoped that *her* part of a will, so soon and so punctually in almost all its other articles fulfilled, would not be the only one that would be slighted.

Her answer was she would consider of it: and made me a curtsy with such an air as showed me that she thought me more out of my sphere than I could allow her to think me had I been permitted to argue the point with her.

I found both Miss Howe and her own servant-maid in deep mourning. This, it seems, had occasioned a great debate at first between her mother and her. Her mother had the words of the will on her side; and Mr Hickman's interest in her view; as her daughter had said that she would wear it for six months at least. But the young lady carried her point—'Strange, said she, if I who shall mourn the heavy, the irreparable loss to the last hour of my life should not show my concern to the world for a few months.'

Mr Hickman for his part was so far from uttering an opposing word on this occasion, that on the very day that Miss Howe put on hers, he waited on her in a new suit of mourning as for a near relation. His servants and equipage made the same respectful appearance.

Whether the mother was consulted by him in it, I cannot say; but the daughter knew nothing of it till she saw him in it. She looked at him with surprise, and asked him for whom he mourned?

The dear, and ever-dear Miss Harlowe, he said.

She was at a loss, it seems. At last—All the world ought to mourn for my Clarissa, said she; but who, man (that was her address to him), thinkest thou to oblige by this appearance?

It is more than *appearance,* madam. I love not my own sister, worthy as she is, better than I loved Miss Clarissa Harlowe. I oblige *myself* by it. And if I disoblige not you, that is all I have to wish.

But let me add, Mr Belford, that if this compliment of Mr Hickman (or this *more* than compliment as I may well call it, since the worthy man speaks not of my dear cousin without emotion) does not produce a short day, I shall think Miss Howe has less generosity in her temper than I am willing to allow her.

You will excuse me, Mr Belford, I dare say, for the particularities which you have invited and encouraged.

I hope soon to pay my respects to you in town. Meantime, I am, with great respect, dear sir,

Your faithful and affectionate humble servant,
WM. MORDEN

Letter 521: MR BELFORD TO MISS HOWE

Thursday, Sept. 28

Madam,

I do myself the honour to send you with this, according to my promise, copies of the posthumous letters written by your exalted friend.

These will be accompanied with other letters.

One of the letters of Colonel Morden's which I enclose, you will observe, madam, is only a copy. The true reason for which, as I will ingenuously acknowledge is some free but respectful observations which the colonel has made upon you, madam, for declining to carry into execution your part of your dear friend's last requests. I have therefore, in respect to that worthy gentleman (having a caution from him on that head) omitted those parts.

Will you allow me, madam, however, to tell you that I myself could not have believed that my inimitable testatrix's own Miss Howe would have been the most backward in performing such a part of her dear friend's last will as is entirely in her own power to perform—especially when that performance would make one of the most deserving men in England happy; and whom, I presume, she proposes to honour with her hand?

Excuse me, madam. I have a most sincere veneration for you; and would not disoblige you for the world.

I am, madam, with the greatest respect and gratitude,
Your most obliged and faithful humble servant,
J. BELFORD

Letter 523: MISS HOWE TO JOHN BELFORD, ESQ.

Monday, Oct. 2

When you question me, sir, as you do and on a subject so affecting to me, in the character of the representative

of my best-beloved friend, and have in every particular
hitherto acted up to that character, you are entitled to
my regard: especially as in your questioning of me you
are joined by a gentleman whom I look upon as the
dearest and nearest (because worthiest) relation of my
dear friend: and who, it seems, has been so severe a
censurer of my conduct, that your politeness will not
permit you to send me his letter, with others of his; but
a copy only, in which the passages reflecting upon me
are omitted.

I presume, however, that what is meant by this
alarming freedom of the colonel's is no more than what
you both have already hinted to me; as if you thought I
were not inclined to pay so much regard to my beloved
creature's last will in my own case, as I would have others pay to it. A charge that I ought not to be quite
silent under.

You have observed, no doubt, that I have seemed to
value myself upon the freedom I take in declaring my
sentiments without reserve upon every subject that I pretend to touch upon: and I can hardly question that I
have, or shall, in your opinion, by my unceremonious
treatment of you upon so short an acquaintance, run
into the error of those who, wanting to be thought above
hypocrisy and flattery, fall into rusticity, if not ill-
manners; a common fault with such who, not caring to
correct constitutional failings, seek to gloss them over
by some *nominal* virtue; when all the time perhaps it is
native arrogance; or at least a contracted rust, that they
will not, because it would give them pain, submit to have
filed off.

You see, sir, that I can, however, be as free with myself as with you: and, by what I am going to write, you
will find me still more free: and yet I am aware that such
of my sex as will not assume some little dignity, and
exact respect from yours, will render themselves cheap;
and perhaps, for their modesty and diffidence, be repaid
with scorn and insult.

But the scorn I will endeavour not to deserve; and the
insult I will not bear.

In some of the dear creature's papers, which you have
had in your possession, and must again have for tran-

scription, you will find several friendly but severe reprehensions of me, on account of a natural, or at least an *habitual*, warmth of temper which she was pleased to impute to me.

I was thinking to give you her charge against me in her own words, from one of her letters delivered to *me* with her own hands, on taking leave of me, on the last visit she honoured me with. But I will supply that charge by confession of more than it imports; to wit, 'That I am haughty, uncontrollable, and violent in my temper'; *this I say:* 'Impatient of contradiction,' *was my beloved's charge* (from anybody but her dear self, she should have said); 'and aim not at that affability, that gentleness next to meekness, which in the letter I was going to communicate she tells me are the peculiar and indispensable characteristics of a real fine lady; who, she is pleased to say, should appear to be gall-less as a dove; and never should know what warmth or high spirit is, but in the cause of religion or virtue; or in cases where her own honour, the honour of a friend, or that of an innocent person, is concerned.'

Now, sir, as I must needs plead guilty to this indictment, do you think I ought not to resolve upon a single life? I, who have such an opinion of your sex, that I think there is not one man in an hundred whom a woman of sense and spirit can either *honour* or *obey*, though you make us promise *both*, in that solemn form of words which unites or rather *binds* us to you in marriage?

When I look round upon all the married people of my acquaintance, and see how *they* live, and what *they* bear, who live *best*, I am confirmed in my dislike to the state.

Well do your sex contrive to bring us up fools and idiots in order to make us bear the yoke you lay upon our shoulders; and that we may not despise you from our hearts (as we certainly should if we were brought up as you are) for your ignorance, as much as you often make us do (as it is) for your insolence.

These, sir, are some of my notions. And, with these notions, let me repeat my question, *Do you think I ought to marry at all?*

Long did I stand out against all the offers made me, and against all the persuasions of my mother; and, to tell

you the truth, the *longer* and with the *more* obstinacy, as
the person my choice would have at first fallen upon was
neither approved by my mother, nor by my dear friend.
This riveted me to my pride, and to my opposition: for
although I was convinced after a while that my choice
would neither have been prudent nor happy; and that
the specious wretch was not what he had made me believe he was; yet could I not easily think of any other
man: and indeed from the detection of him took a settled aversion to the whole sex.

At last Mr Hickman offered himself; a man worthy of
a better choice. He had the good fortune (he thinks it
so) to be agreeable (and to make his proposals agreeable) to my mother.

As to myself; I own that were I to have chosen a
brother, Mr Hickman should have been the man; virtuous, sober, sincere, friendly, as he is. But I wished not
to marry: nor knew I the man in the world whom I could
think deserving of my beloved friend. But neither of our
parents would let us live single.

The accursed Lovelace was proposed warmly to *her*
at one time; and, while she was yet but indifferent to
him, they by ungenerous usage of him (for then, sir, he
was not known to be Beelzebub himself) and by endeavouring to force her inclinations in favour first of one
worthless man, then of another, in antipathy to him,
through her foolish brother's caprice, turned that indifference (from the natural generosity of her soul) into a
regard which she never otherwise would have had for a
man of his character.

Mr Hickman was proposed to me. I refused him again
and again. He persisted: my mother his advocate. My
mother made my beloved friend his advocate too. I told
him my aversion to all men: to him: to matrimony. Still
he persisted. I used him with tyranny: led indeed partly
by my temper, partly by design; hoping thereby to get rid
of him; till the poor man (his character unexceptionably
uniform) still persisting, made himself a merit with me
by his patience. This brought down my pride (I never,
sir, was accounted very ungenerous, nor quite ungrateful) and gave me, at one time, an inferiority in my own
opinion to him; which lasted just long enough for my

friends to prevail upon me to promise him encouragement; and to receive his addresses.

Having so done, when the weather-glass of my pride got up again, I found I had gone too far to recede. My mother and my friend both held me to it. Yet I tried him; I vexed him an hundred ways; and not so much neither with design to vex him, as to make him hate me and decline his suit.

While my dear friend was in her unhappy uncertainty, I could not think of marriage: and now, what encouragement have I? She, my monitress, my guide, my counsel, gone, for ever gone!—by whose advice and instructions I hoped to acquit myself tolerably in the state into which I could not avoid entering. For, sir, my mother is so partially Mr Hickman's friend, that I am sure, should any difference arise, she would always censure me, and acquit him; even were he ungenerous enough to remember me in his day.

This, sir, being my situation, consider how difficult it is for me to think of marriage.

And yet, engaged to enter into that state as I am, how can I help myself? My mother presses me; my friend, my beloved friend, writing as from the dead, presses me; and you and Mr Morden, as executors of her will, remind me; the man is not afraid of me (I am sure were I *the* man, I should not have half his courage); and I think I ought to conclude to punish him (the only effectual way I have to do it) for his perverse adherence and persecution, as many other persons are punished, with the grant of his own wishes.

Let me then assure you, sir, that when I can find in the words of my charming friend in her will, writing of her cousin Hervey, that my grief for her is *mellowed by time into a remembrance more sweet than painful,* that I may not be utterly unworthy of the passion a man of some merit has for me, I will answer the request of my dear friend, so often repeated, and so earnestly pressed; and Mr Hickman shall find, if he continue to deserve my gratitude, that my endeavours shall not be wanting to make him amends for the patience he has had, and must still for a little while longer have, with me: and then will it be his own fault (I hope not mine) if our marriage answer not those happy *prognostics, which filled her* generous *presaging mind,* upon this view, as she once for *my* encouragement, and to induce me to encourage *him*, told me.

Thus, sir, have I, in a very free manner accounted to you, as to the executor of my beloved friend, for all that relates to you, as such, to know; and even for more than I needed to do, against myself: only that you will find as much against me in some of *her* letters; and so, *losing* nothing, I *gain* the character of *ingenuity* with you.

And now let me remind you of one great article relating to yourself, while you are admonishing me on this subject: it is furnished me by her posthumous letter to you. I hope you will not forget that the most benevolent of her sex expresses herself as earnestly concerned for your thorough reformation, as she does for my marrying. You'll see to it then that her wishes are as completely answered in that particular, as you are desirous they should be in all others.

I have, I own, disobeyed the dear creature in one article; and that is where she desires that I will not put myself into mourning. I could not help it.

Your obliged servant,
A. HOWE

Letter 525: LORD M. TO JOHN BELFORD, ESQ.

M. Hall, Friday, Sept. 29

Dear sir,

My kinsman Lovelace is now setting out for London; proposing to see you, and then to go to Dover and so embark. God send him well out of the kingdom!

On Monday he will be with you, I believe. Pray let me be favoured with an account of all your conversations; for Mr Mowbray and Mr Tourville are to be there too; and whether you think he is grown quite his own man again. What I mostly write for, is to wish you to keep Colonel Morden and him asunder, and so to give you notice of his going to town. I should be very loath there should be any mischief between them, as you gave me notice that the colonel threatened my nephew. But my kinsman would not bear that; so nobody let him know that he did. But I hope there is no fear: for the colonel does not, as I hear, threaten now. For his own sake, I am glad of that; for there is not such a man in the world as my kinsman is said to be, at all the weapons—as well he was not; he would not be so daring.

We shall all here miss the wild fellow. To be sure there is no man better company when he pleases.

Pray, do you never travel thirty or forty mile? I should be glad to see you here at M. Hall. It will be charity, when my kinsman is gone; for we suppose you will be his chief correspondent: although he has promised to write to my nieces often. But he is very apt to forget his promises; to us his relations particularly. God preserve us all; Amen! prays

Your very humble servant,
M.

Letter 526: MR BELFORD TO LORD M.

London, Tuesday night, Oct. 3

My lord,

I obey your lordship's commands with great pleasure.

Yesterday in the afternoon Mr Lovelace made me a visit at my lodgings. As I was in expectation of one from Colonel Morden about the same time, I thought proper to carry him to a tavern which neither of us frequented (on pretence of an half-appointment); ordering notice to be sent me thither, if the colonel came: And Mr Lovelace sent to Mowbray, and Tourville, and Mr Doleman of Uxbridge (who came to town to take leave of him), to let them know where to find us.

Mr Lovelace is *too well* recovered, I was going to say. I never saw him more gay, lively, and handsome. We had a good deal of bluster about some parts of the trust I have engaged in; and upon freedoms I had treated him with; in which, he would have it, that I had exceeded our agreed-on limits: but on the arrival of our three old companions, and a nephew of Mr Doleman's (who had a good while been desirous to pass an hour with Mr Lovelace), it blew off for the present.

I can deal tolerably with him at my pen; but in conversation he has no equal. In short, it was his day. He was glad, he said, to find himself alive; and his two friends clapping and rubbing their hands twenty times in an hour, declared, that now once more he was all himself; the charmingest fellow in the world; and they would follow him to the furthest part of the globe.

Mr Doleman and his nephew took leave of us by twelve. Mowbray and Tourville grew very noisy by one; and were carried off by two.

The clock struck three before I could get him into any serious or attentive way—so natural to him is gaiety of heart; and such strong hold had the liveliness of the evening taken of him. His conversation you know, my lord, when his heart is free, runs off to the bottom without any dregs.

But after that hour, and when we thought of parting, he became a little more serious: and then he told me his designs, and gave me a plan of his intended tour; wishing heartily that I could have accompanied him.

We parted about four; he not a little dissatisfied with me; for we had some talk about subjects which, he said, he loved not to think of; to wit, Miss Harlowe's will; my executorship; papers I had in confidence communicated to that admirable lady (with no unfriendly design, I assure your lordship); and he insisting upon, and I refusing, the return of the letters he had written to me from the time that he had made his first addresses to her.

He would see me once again, he said; and it would be upon very ill terms if I complied not with his request. Which I bid him not expect. But, that I might not deny him everything, I told him that I would give him a copy of the will; though I was sure, I said, when he read it, he would wish he had never seen it.

I had a message from him about eleven this morning, desiring me to name a place at which to dine with him, and Mowbray, and Tourville, for the last time: and soon after another from Colonel Morden, inviting me to pass the evening with him at the Bedford Head in Covent Garden. And, that I might keep them at distance from one another, I appointed Mr Lovelace at the Eagle in Suffolk Street.

There I met him, and the two others. We began where we left off at our last parting; and were very high with each other. But, at last, all was made up, and he offered to forget and forgive everything, on condition that I would correspond with him while abroad, and continue the series which had been broken through by his illness; and particularly give him, as I had offered, a copy of the lady's will.

I promised him: and he then fell to rallying me on my gravity, and on my reformation schemes, as he called them.

In our conversation at dinner, he was balancing whether he should set out the next morning, or the morning after. But finding he had nothing to do, and Colonel Morden being in town (which, however, I told him not of), I turned the scale; and he agreed upon setting out tomorrow morning; they to see him embark; and I promised to accompany them for a morning's ride (as they proposed their horses); but said that I must return in the afternoon.

With much reluctance they let me go to my evening's appointment: they little thought with whom.

I found the colonel in a very solemn way. We had a good deal of discourse upon the subject of letters which had passed between us in relation to Miss Harlowe's will, and to her family.

He has some accounts to settle with his banker; which, he says, will be adjusted tomorrow; and on Thursday he proposes to go down again to take leave of his friends; and then intends to set out directly for Italy.

I wish Mr Lovelace could have been prevailed upon to take any other tour than that of France and Italy. I did propose Madrid to him: but he laughed at me, and told me that the proposal was in character from a mule; and from one who was become as grave as a Spaniard of the old cut, at ninety.

I expressed to the colonel my apprehensions that his cousin's dying injunctions would not have the force upon him that were to be wished.

They have great force upon me, Mr Belford, said he; or one world would not have held Mr Lovelace and me thus long. But my intention is to go to Florence; not to lay my bones there, as upon my cousin's death I told you I thought to do; but to settle all my affairs in those parts, and then to come over and reside upon a little paternal estate in Kent, which is strangely gone to ruin in my absence. Indeed, were I to meet Mr Lovelace, either here or abroad, I might not be answerable for the consequence.

He would have engaged me for tomorrow. But having promised to attend Mr Lovelace on his journey, as I have mentioned, I said I was obliged to go out of town, and was uncertain as to the time of my return in the evening.

I will do myself the honour to write again to your lordship tomorrow night. Meantime, I am, my lord,

Your lordship's, etc.

Letter 527: MR BELFORD TO LORD M.

Wed. night, Oct. 4

My lord,

I am just returned from attending Mr Lovelace as far as Gads Hill near Rochester. He was exceeding gay all the way. Mowbray and Tourville are gone on with him. They will see him embark, and under sail; and promise to follow him in a month or two; for they say, there is no living without him, now he is once more himself.

He and I parted with great and even solemn tokens of affection; but yet not without gay intermixtures, as I will acquaint your lordship.

Taking me aside, and clasping his arms about me, 'Adieu, dear Belford! said he: may you proceed in the course you have entered upon! Whatever airs I give myself, this charming creature has fast hold of me *here* (clapping his hand upon his heart); and I must either appear what you see me, or be what I so lately was.

'But if I live to come to England, and you remain fixed in your present way and can give me encouragement, I hope rather to follow your example than to ridicule you for it. This will (for I had given him a copy of it) I will make the companion of my solitary hours. You have told me part of its melancholy contents; and that, and her posthumous letter, shall be my study; and they will prepare me for being your disciple, if you hold on.

'*You*, Jack, may marry, continued he; and I have a wife in my eye for you. Only thou'rt such an awkward mortal.

'And for *me*, I never *will*, I never *can*, marry. That I will not take a few liberties, and that I will not try to start some of my former game, I won't promise. Habits are not easily shaken off. But they shall be by way of weaning. So *return* and *reform* shall go together.

'And now, thou sorrowful monkey, what aileth thee?' I do love him, my lord.

'Adieu! And once more adieu!—embracing me. And when thou thinkest thou hast made thyself an interest *out yonder* (looking up) then put in a word for thy Lovelace.'

Joining company, he recommended to me to write often; and promised to let me quickly hear from him; and that he would write to your lordship, and to all his family round; for he said that you had all been more kind to him than he had deserved.

And so we parted.

Your most faithful and obedient servant,
J. BELFORD

Letter 533: MR BELFORD TO ROBERT LOVELACE, ESQ.

London, October 26
I cannot think, my dear Lovelace, that Colonel Morden has either threatened you in those gross terms mentioned by the vile, hypocritical, and ignorant Joseph Leman, or intends to follow you. They are the words of people of that fellow's class; and not of a gentleman: not of Colonel Morden, I am sure. You'll observe that Joseph pretends not to say that he heard him speak them.

I have been very solicitous to sound the colonel, for your sake and for his own, and for the sake of the injunctions of the excellent lady to me, as well as to him, on that subject. But, in so many words, he assured me that he had not taken any resolutions; nor had he declared himself to the family in such a way as should bind him to resent: on the contrary, he has owned that his cousin's injunctions have hitherto had the force upon him which I could wish they should have.

He went abroad in a week after you. When he took his leave of me, he told me that his design was to go to Florence; and that he would settle his affairs there; and then return to England, and here pass the remainder of his days.

I have, as you required, been very candid and sincere with you. I have not aimed at palliation. If you seek not Colonel Morden, it is my opinion he will not seek you: for he is a man of principle. But if you seek him, I believe he will not shun you.

Adieu therefore! Mayest thou repent of the past: and may no new violences add to thy heavy reflections, and overwhelm thy future hopes, is the wish of

Thy true friend,
JOHN BELFORD

Letter 534: MR LOVELACE TO JOHN BELFORD, ESQ.

Munich, Nov. 11–22

And so you own that he has threatened me; but not in gross and ungentlemanly terms, you say. If he has threatened me like a gentleman, I will resent his threats like a gentleman. But he has not done as a man of honour, if he has threatened me at all behind my back. I would scorn to threaten any man to whom I *knew* how to address myself either personally or by pen and ink.

He had not taken any resolutions, you say, when you saw him. He *must* and *will* take resolutions, one way or other, very quickly; for I wrote to him yesterday, without waiting for this your answer to my last. I could not avoid it. I could not (as I told you in that) live in suspense. I have directed my letter to Florence. Nor could I suffer my friends to live in suspense as to my safety or otherwise. But I have couched it in such moderate terms, that he has fairly his option. He will be the challenger, if he take it in the sense in which he may so handsomely avoid taking it. Yet, if we are to meet (for I know what *my* option would be, in *his* case, on *such a letter,* com-

plaisant as it is), I wish *he* had a worse, *I* a better cause.
It would be sweet revenge to him, were I to fall by his
hand. But what should I be the better for killing him?

On reperusing yours in a cooler moment, I cannot but
thank you for your friendly love and good intentions. My
value for you, from the first hour of our acquaintance till
now, I have never found misplaced; regarding at least
your *intention*: thou must, however, own a good deal of
blunder of the over-do and under-do kind, with respect
to the part thou actedst between me and the beloved of
my heart. But thou art really an honest fellow, and a
sincere and warm friend. I could almost wish I had not
written to Florence till I had received thy letter now
before me. But it is gone. Let it go. If he wish peace,
and to avoid violence, he will have a fair opportunity to
embrace the one and shun the other. If not—he must
take his fate.

Wholly yours,
LOVELACE

Letter 536: MR LOVELACE TO JOHN BELFORD, ESQ.

Trent, Dec. 3–14

Tomorrow is to be the Day, that will in all probability
send either one or two ghosts to attend the *manes* [spirit]
of my Clarissa.

I arrived here yesterday; and inquiring for an English
gentleman of the name of Morden, soon found out the
colonel's lodgings. He had been in town two days; and
left his name at every probable place.

He was gone to ride out; and I left *my* name, and
where to be found: and in the evening he made me a
visit.

He was plaguy gloomy. That was not I. But yet he
told me that I had acted like a man of true spirit in my
first letter; and with honour, in giving him so readily this
meeting. He wished I had in other respects; and then we
might have seen each other upon better terms than now
we did.

I said there was no recalling what was passed; and

that I wished some things had not been done, as well
as he.

To recriminate now, he said, would be as exasperating
as unavailable. And as I had so cheerfully given him this
opportunity, words should give place to business. *Your*
choice, Mr Lovelace, of time, of place, of weapon, shall
be *my* choice.

The two latter be yours, Mr Morden. The time tomorrow, or next day, as you please.

Next day, then, Mr Lovelace; and we'll ride out tomorrow, to fix the place.

Agreed, sir.

We parted with a solemn sort of ceremonious civility:
and this day I called upon him; and we rode out together
to fix upon the place: and both being of one mind, and
hating to put off for the morrow what could be done
today, would have decided it then: but De la Tour, and
the colonel's valet, who attended us, being unavoidably
let into the secret, joined to beg we would have with us
a surgeon from Brixen, whom La Tour had fallen in with
there, and who had told him he was to ride next morning
to bleed a person in a fever, at a lone cottage which, by
the surgeon's description, was not far from the place
where we then were, if it were not that very cottage
within sight of us.

They undertook so to manage it, that the surgeon
should know nothing of the matter till his assistance was
called in. And La Tour being, as I assured the colonel,
a ready-contriving fellow (whom I ordered to obey him
as myself were the chance to be in *his* favour), we both
agreed to defer the decision till tomorrow, and to leave
the whole about the surgeon to the management of our
two valets; enjoining them absolute secrecy: and so rode
back again by different ways.

We fixed upon a little lone valley for the spot—ten
tomorrow morning the time—and single rapier the word.
Yet I repeatedly told him that I value myself so much
upon my skill in that weapon, that I would wish him to
choose any other.

He said it was a gentleman's weapon; and he who
understood it not, wanted a qualification that he ought
to suffer for not having: but that, as to him, one weapon

was as good as another throughout all the instruments of offence.

So, Jack, you see I take no advantage of him: but my devil must deceive me, if he take not his life, or his death, at my hands, before eleven tomorrow morning.

We are to ride thither, and to dismount when at the place; and his footman and mine are to wait at an appointed distance, with a chaise to carry off to the borders of the Venetian territories the survivor, if one drop; or to assist either or both, as occasion may demand.

And thus, Belford, is the matter settled.

A shower of rain has left me nothing else to do: and therefore I write this letter; though I might as well have deferred it till tomorrow twelve o'clock, when I doubt not to be able to write again, to assure you how much I am

Yours, etc.
LOVELACE

Letter 537: F. J. DE LA TOUR TO JOHN BELFORD, ESQ., NEAR SOHO SQUARE, LONDON

(Translation)

Trent, December 18. N.S.

Sir,

I have melancholy news to inform you of, by order of the Chevalier Lovelace. He showed me his letter to you before he sealed it; signifying that he was to meet the Chevalier Morden on the 15th. Wherefore, as the occasion of the meeting is so well known to you, I shall say nothing of it here.

The two chevaliers came exactly at their time: they were attended by Monsieur Margate (the colonel's gentleman) and myself. They had given orders overnight, and now repeated them in each other's presence, that we should observe a strict impartiality between them: and that, if one fell, each of us should look upon himself, as to any needful help, or retreat, as the servant of the survivor, and take his commands accordingly.

After a few compliments, both the gentlemen, with

the greatest presence of mind that I ever beheld in men, stripped to their shirts, and drew.

They parried with equal judgement several passes. My chevalier drew the first blood, making a desperate push, which by a sudden turn of his antagonist missed going clear through him, and wounded him on the fleshy part of the ribs of his right side; which part the sword tore out, being on the extremity of the body: but, before he could recover himself, his adversary, in return, pushed him into the inside of the left arm, near the shoulder: and the sword, by raking his breast as it passed, being followed by a great effusion of blood, the colonel said, sir, I believe you have enough.

My chevalier swore by G-d, he was not hurt: 'twas a pin's point: and so made another pass at his antagonist; which he, with a surprising dexterity, received under his arm, and run my dear chevalier into the body: who immediately fell; saying, The luck is yours, sir. Oh my beloved Clarissa! Now art thou—Inwardly he spoke three or four words more. His sword dropped from his hand. Mr Morden threw his down, and ran to him, saying in French—Ah monsieur, you are a dead man! Call to God for mercy!

We gave the signal agreed upon to the footmen; and they to the surgeons; who instantly came up.

Colonel Morden, I found, was too well used to the bloody work; for he was as cool as if nothing so extraordinary had happened, assisting the surgeons, though his own wound bled much. But my dear chevalier fainted away two or three times running, and vomited blood besides.

However, they stopped the bleeding for the present; and we helped him into the voiture; and then the colonel suffered his own wound to be dressed.

The colonel, against the surgeons' advice, would mount on horseback to pass into the Venetian territories; and generously gave me a purse of gold to pay the surgeons; desiring me to make a present to the footman; and to accept of the remainder, as a mark of his satisfaction in my conduct; and in my care and tenderness of my master.

The surgeons told him, that my chevalier could not live over the day.

When the colonel took leave of him, Mr Lovelace said in French, You have well revenged the dear creature.

I have, sir, said Mr Morden, in the same language: and perhaps shall be sorry that you called upon me to this work, while I was balancing whether to obey, or disobey, the dear angel.

There is a fate in it! replied my chevalier—a cursed fate!—or this could not have been! But be ye all witnesses, that I have provoked my destiny, and acknowledge that I fall by a man of honour.

Sir, said the colonel, with the piety of a confessor (wringing Mr Lovelace's hand), snatch these few fleeting moments, and commend yourself to God.

And so he rode off.

The voiture proceeded slowly with my chevalier; yet the motion set both his wounds bleeding afresh; and it was with difficulty they again stopped the blood.

We brought him alive to the first cottage; and he gave orders to me to dispatch to you the packet I herewith send sealed up; and bid me write to you the particulars of this most unhappy affair, and to give you thanks, in his name, for all your favours and friendship to him.

Contrary to all expectation, he lived over the night: but suffered much, as well from his impatience and disappointment, as from his wounds; for he seemed very unwilling to die.

He was delirious, at times, in the two last hours; and then several times cried out, Take her away! Take her away! but named nobody. And sometimes praised some lady (that Clarissa, I suppose, whom he had called upon when he received his death's wound) calling her, Sweet Excellence! Divine Creature! Fair Sufferer! And once he said, Look down, blessed Spirit, look down! And there stopped—his lips however moving.

At nine in the morning, he was seized with convulsions, and fainted away; and it was a quarter of an hour before he came out of them.

His few last words I must not omit, as they show an ultimate composure; which may administer some consolation to his honourable friends.

Blessed—said he, addressing himself no doubt to Heaven; for his dying eyes were lifted up—a strong convulsion prevented him for a few moments saying more. But recovering, he again with great fervour (lifting up his eyes, and his spread hands) pronounced the word *Blessed*. Then, in a seeming ejaculation, he spoke inwardly so as not to be understood: at last, he distinctly pronounced these three words,

LET THIS EXPIATE!

And then, his head sinking on his pillow, he expired; at about half an hour after ten.

He little thought, poor gentleman! his end so near: so had given no direction about his body. I have caused it to be embowelled, and deposited in a vault, till I have orders from England.

This is a favour that was procured with difficulty; and would have been refused, had he not been an Englishman of rank: a nation with reason respected in every Austrian government—for he had refused ghostly attendance, and the Sacraments in the Catholic way. May his soul be happy, I pray God!

I have had some trouble also on account of the manner of his death, from the Magistracy here: who have taken the requisite informations in the affair. And it has cost me some money. Of which, and of my dear Chevalier's effects, I will give you a faithful account in my next. And so, waiting at this place your commands, I am, sir,

Your most faithful and obedient servant,
F. J. De la Tour

Selected Bibliography

Babb, Howard S. "Richardson's Narrative Mode in *Clarissa*." *Studies in English Literature* 16 (1976): 451–60.

Ball, Donald L. *Samuel Richardson's Theory of Fiction*. The Hague: Mouton, 1971.

Bartolomeo, Joseph F. *Matched Pairs: Gender and Intertextual Dialogue in Eighteenth-Century Fiction*. Associated University Presses, 2002.

Blewett, David, ed. *Passion and Virtue: Essays on the Novels of Samuel Richardson*. Toronto: University of Toronto Press, 2001.

Bloom, Harold, ed. *Samuel Richardson: Modern Critical Views*. New York: Chelsea House, 1987.

Braudy, Leo. "Penetration and Impenetrability in *Clarissa*." In *New Approaches to Eighteenth-Century Literature*. Ed. Phillip Harth. New York: Columbia University Press, 1974. 177–206.

Brissenden, R. F. *Virtue in Distress: Studies in the Novel of Sentiment from Richardson to Sade*. London: Macmillan, 1974.

Brophy, Elizabeth Bergen. *Samuel Richardson: The Triumph of Craft*. Knoxville: University of Tennessee Press, 1974.

——. *Samuel Richardson*. Boston: Twayne, 1987.

Brown, Murray L., ed. "Editor's Comment: Richardson Discovers the Modern Imagination." *Studies in the Literary Imagination* 28 (Spring 1955): *Refiguring Richardson's Clarissa*.

Brownstein, Rachel Mayer. " 'An Exemplar to Her Sex': Richardson's Clarissa." *Yale Review* 66 (1977): 30–47.

Bueler, Lois E. *Clarissa's Plots*. Newark: University of Delaware Press, 1994.

Butler, Janet. "The Garden: Early Symbol of Clarissa's Complicity." *Studies in English Literature* 24 (1984): 527–44.

Carroll, John. "Lovelace as Tragic Hero." *University of Toronto Quarterly* 42 (1972): 14–25.

Carroll, John, ed. *Samuel Richardson: A Collection of Critical Essays.* Englewood Cliffs, NJ: Prentice-Hall, 1969.

Castle, Terry. *Clarissa's Ciphers: Meaning and Disruption in Richardson's "Clarissa."* Ithaca, NY: Cornell University Press, 1982.

———. "Lovelace's Dream." *Studies in Eighteenth-Century Culture* 13 (1984): 29–42.

Coetzee, J. M. *Stranger Shores: Literary Essays, 1986–1999.* New York: Viking, 2001.

Cohan, Steven M. "Clarissa and the Individuation of Character." *ELH* 43 (1976): 163–83.

Cook, Elizabeth Heckendorn. *Epistolary Bodies: Gender and Genre in the Eighteenth-Century Republic of Letters.* Stanford, CA: Stanford University Press, 1996.

Day, Robert Adams. *Told in Letters: Epistolary Fiction before Richardson.* Ann Arbor: University of Michigan Press, 1966.

Doederlein, Sue Warwick. "Clarissa in the Hands of the Critics." *Eighteenth-Century Studies* 16 (1983): 401–14.

Doody, Margaret Anne. "Disguise and Personality in Richardson's *Clarissa.*" *Eighteenth-Century Life* 12 (1988): 18–39.

———. *A Natural Passion: A Study of the Novels of Samuel Richardson.* Oxford: Clarendon Press, 1974.

———. "Samuel Richardson: Fiction and Knowledge." In *Cambridge Companion to the Eighteenth-Century Novel.* Ed. John Richetti. Cambridge: Cambridge University Press, 1996. 90–119.

Doody, Margaret Anne, and Peter Sabor, eds. *Samuel Richardson: Tercentenary Essays.* Cambridge: Cambridge University Press, 1989.

Doody, Margaret Anne, and Florian Stuber. "*Clarissa* Censored." *Modern Language Studies* 18 (1988): 74–88.

———. "The Clarissa Project and *Clarissa*'s Reception." *Text: An Interdisciplinary Journal* 12 (1999): 123–41.

Downs, Brian W. *Richardson.* London: Routledge, 1928.

Dussinger, John A. "Conscience and the Pattern of Christian Perfection in *Clarissa.*" *PMLA* 81 (1966): 236–45.

Duyfhuizen, Bernard. "Epistolary Narratives of Transmission and Transgression." *Comparative Literature* 37 (1985): 1–26.

Eagleton, Terry. *The Rape of Clarissa: Writing, Sexuality and Class Struggle in Samuel Richardson.* Oxford: Blackwell, 1982.

Eaves, T. C. Duncan, and Ben D. Kimpel. "The Composition of *Clarissa* and Its Revision before Publication." *PMLA* 83 (1968): 416–28.

——. *Samuel Richardson: A Biography.* Oxford: Clarendon Press, 1971.

Farrell, William J. "The Style and the Action in *Clarissa.*" *Studies in English Literature* 3 (1963): 365–75.

Ferguson, Frances. "Rape and the Rise of the Novel." *Representations* 20 (1987): 88–112.

Flynn, Carol Houlihan. *Samuel Richardson: A Man of Letters.* Princeton, NJ: Princeton University Press, 1982.

Flynn, Carol Houlihan, and Edward Copeland, eds. *Clarissa and Her Readers: New Essays for The Clarissa Project.* Brooklyn, NY: AMS, 1999.

Frega, Donnalee. *Speaking in Hunger: Gender, Discourse, and Consumption in "Clarissa."* Columbia: University of South Carolina Press, 1998.

Gillis, Christina Marsden. *The Paradox of Privacy: Epistolary Form in "Clarissa."* Gainesville: University Presses of Florida, 1984.

Goldberg, Rita. *Sex and Enlightenment: Women in Richardson and Diderot.* Cambridge: Cambridge University Press, 1984.

Golden, Morris. *Richardson's Characters.* Ann Arbor: University of Michigan Press, 1963.

——. "Richardson's Repetitions." *PMLA* 82 (1967): 64–67.

Gopnik, Irwin. *A Theory of Style and Richardson's "Clarissa."* The Hague: Mouton, 1970.

Gordon, Scott Paul. "Disinterested Selves: *Clarissa* and the Tactics of Sentiment." *ELH* 64 (1997): 473–502.

Gunn, Daniel P. "Is *Clarissa* Bourgeois Art?" *Eighteenth-Century Fiction* 10 (1997): 1–14.

Gwilliam, Tassie. *Samuel Richardson's Fictions of Gender.* Stanford, CA: Stanford University Press, 1993.

Hannaford, Richard Gordon. *Samuel Richardson: An Annotated Bibliography of Critical Studies.* New York: Garland, 1980.

Harris, Jocelyn. "Protean Lovelace." *Eighteenth-Century Fiction* 2 (1990): 327–46.

——. *Samuel Richardson.* Cambridge: Cambridge University Press, 1987.

Hill, Christopher. "Clarissa Harlowe and Her Times." *Essays in Criticism* 5 (1955): 315–40.

Hinton, Laura. "The Heroine's Subjection: Clarissa, Sadomasochism, and Natural Law." *Eighteenth-Century Studies* 32 (1999): 293–308.

How, James. "Clarissa's Cyberspace: The Development of Epistolary Space in Richardson's *Clarissa.*" *Eighteenth-Century Novel* 1 (2001): 37-69.

Hudson, Nicholas. "Arts of Seduction and the Rhetoric of *Clarissa.*" *Modern Language Quarterly* 51 (1990): 25–43.

Kaplan, Fred. " 'Our Short Story': The Narrative Devices of *Clarissa.*" *Studies in English Literature* 11 (1971): 549–62.

Karl, Frederick. *A Reader's Guide to the Eighteenth-Century English Novel.* New York: Noonday, 1974.

Karpuk, Susan Price. *Samuel Richardson's "Clarissa": An Index Analyzing the Characters, Subjects, and Place Names.* Brooklyn, NY: AMS, 2000.

Kearney, Anthony M. "*Clarissa* and the Epistolary Form." *Essays in Criticism* 16 (1966): 44–56.

——. *Samuel Richardson.* London: Routledge and Kegan Paul, 1968.

——. *Samuel Richardson, Clarissa.* London: Edward Arnold, 1975.

Keymer, Tom. *Richardson's "Clarissa" and the Eighteenth-Century Reader.* Cambridge: Cambridge University Press, 1992.

Kinkead-Weekes, Mark. "*Clarissa* Restored." *Review of English Studies* 10 (1959): 156–71.

——. *Samuel Richardson: Dramatic Novelist.* Ithaca, NY: Cornell University Press, 1973.

Koehler, Martha J. "Epistolary Closure and Triangular Return in Richardson's *Clarissa.*" *Journal of Narrative Technique* 24 (1994): 153–72.

Konigsberg, Ira. *Samuel Richardson and the Dramatic Novel.* Lexington: University of Kentucky Press, 1968.

Lams, Victor J. *Clarissa's Narrators.* New York: Peter Lang, 2001.

Lee, Joy Kyunghae. "The Commodification of Virtue: Chastity and the Virginal Body in Richardson's *Clarissa.*" *The Eighteenth Century: Theory and Interpretation* 36 (1995): 38–54.

MacCarthy, B. G. *The Female Pen: Women Writers and Novelists, 1621–1818;* with a preface by Janet Todd. New York: New York University Press, 1994.

Martin, Mary Patricia. "Reading Reform in Richardson's *Clarissa.*" *Studies in English Literature* 37 (1997): 595–614.

McCrea, Brian. "Clarissa's Pregnancy and the Fate of Patriarchal Power." *Eighteenth-Century Fiction* 9 42 (1997): 125–48.

McKeon, Michael. *The Origins of the English Novel, 1600–1740.* Baltimore: Johns Hopkins University Press, 1987.

McKillop, Alan Dugald. *The Early Masters of English Fiction.* Lawrence: University of Kansas Press, 1956.

——. *Samuel Richardson: Printer and Novelist.* Chapel Hill: University of North Carolina Press, 1936.

Myer, Valerie Grosvenor, ed. *Samuel Richardson: Passion and Prudence.* London: Vision Press, 1986.

Napier, Elizabeth R. " 'Tremble and Reform': The Inversion of Power in Richardson's *Clarissa.*" *ELH* 42 (1975): 214–23.

Ostovich, Helen M. " 'Our Views Must Now Be Different': Imprisonment and Friendship in *Clarissa.*" *Modern Language Quarterly* 52 (1991): 153–69.

Park, William. "*Clarissa* as Tragedy." *Studies in English Literature* 16 (1976): 461–71.

Pascoe, Judith. "Before I Read *Clarissa* I Was Nobody: Aspirational Reading and Samuel Richardson's Great Novel." *Hudson Review* 56 (2003): 239–54.

Preston, John. *The Created Self: The Reader's Role in Eighteenth-Century Fiction.* London: Heinemann, 1970.

Price, Martin. "Clarissa and Lovelace." In *To the Palace of Wisdom: Studies in Order and Energy from Dryden to Blake.* New York: Doubleday, 1964.

Rabkin, Norman. "*Clarissa:* A Study in the Nature of Convention." *ELH* 23 (1956): 204–17.

Richardson, Samuel. *Clarissa or The History of a Young Lady.* Ed. Florian Stuber. Brooklyn, NY: AMS Press, 1990. [Facsimile; third edition].

——. *Clarissa or the History of a Young Lady.* Ed. Angus Ross. Harmondsworth, England: Penguin, 1985.

——. *Clarissa or the History of a Young Lady.* Ed. Philip Stevick. San Francisco: Rinehart Press, 1971.

——. *Clarissa or the History of a Young Lady.* Ed. George Sherburn. Boston: Houghton Mifflin, 1962.

——. *Clarissa or the History of a Young Lady.* Ed. John Butt. New York: E. P. Dutton & Co., Inc., 1932.

——. *The Richardson-Stinstra Correspondence and Stinstra's Prefaces to "Clarissa."* Ed. William C. Slattery. Carbondale: Southern Illinois University Press, 1969.

——. *Samuel Richardson's Published Commentary on "Clarissa," 1747–65*; introduction by Jocelyn Harris; texts edited with headnotes by Thomas Keymer. London: Pickering and Chatto, 1998.

Richetti, John J. *The English Novel in History, 1700–1780.* London: Routledge, 1998.

——. *Popular Fiction before Richardson: Narrative Patterns, 1700–1739.* Oxford: Clarendon Press, 1969.

Rivero, Albert J., ed. *New Essays on Samuel Richardson.* New York: St. Martin's Press, 1996.

Rogers, Katharine M. *Feminism in Eighteenth-Century England.* Urbana: University of Illinois Press, 1982.

Roussel, Roy. *The Conversation of the Sexes: Seduction and Equality in Selected Seventeenth- and Eighteenth-Century Texts.* New York: Oxford University Press, 1986.

Sale, William Merritt Jr. "From *Pamela* to *Clarissa*." In *The Age of Johnson: Essays Presented to Chauncey Brewster Tinker*. New Haven, CT: Yale University Press, 1949. 127–38.

——. *Samuel Richardson: A Bibliographical Record of His Literary Career*. New Haven, CT: Yale University Press, 1936.

——. *Samuel Richardson, Master Printer*. Ithaca, NY: Cornell University Press, 1950.

Sherbo, Arthur. "Time and Place in Richardson's *Clarissa*." *Boston University Studies in English* 3 (1957): 139–46.

Smith, Sarah W. R. *Samuel Richardson: A Reference Guide*. Boston: G.K. Hall, 1984.

Spacks, Patricia Ann Meyer. *Desire and Truth: Functions of Plot in Eighteenth-Century English Novels*. Chicago: University of Chicago Press, 1990.

Stephanson, Raymond. "Richardson's 'Nerves': The Philosophy of Sensibility in *Clarissa*." *Journal of the History of Ideas* 49 (1988): 267–85.

Stewart, Keith. "Towards Defining an Aesthetic for the Familiar Letter in Eighteenth-Century England." *Prose Studies* 5 (1982): 179–92.

Stuber, Florian. "On Fathers and Authority in *Clarissa*." *Studies in English Literature* 25 (1985), 557–74.

——. "On Original and Final Intentions, or Can There Be an Authoritative *Clarissa*?" *Text: Transactions of the Society for Textual Scholarship* 2 (1985): 229–44.

Todd, Janet M. *Sensibility: An Introduction*. London: Methuen, 1986.

——. *Women's Friendship in Literature*. New York: Columbia University Press, 1980.

Traugott, John. "*Clarissa*'s Richardson: An Essay to Find the Reader." In *English Literature in the Age of Disguise*. Ed. Maximillian E. Novak. Berkeley: University of California Press, 1977.

——. "Molesting *Clarissa*." *Novel* 15 (1982): 163–70.

Turner, James Grantham. "Richardson and His Circle." In *Columbia History of the British Novel*. Ed. John Richetti. New York: Columbia University Press, 1994. 73–101.

Van Ghent, Dorothy. *The English Novel: Form and Function.* New York: Rinehart, 1953.

Vermillion, Mary. "Clarissa and the Marriage Act." *Eighteenth-Century Fiction* 9.4 (1997): 395–412.

Warner, William Beatty. "Proposal and Habitation: The Temporality and Authority of Interpretation in and about a Scene of Richardson's *Clarissa*." *Boundary 2: A Journal of Postmodern Literature and Culture* 7 (1979): 169–200.

——. *Reading "Clarissa": The Struggles of Interpretation.* New Haven, CT: Yale University Press, 1979.

Watt, Ian. *The Rise of the Novel: Studies in Defoe, Richardson and Fielding.* London: Chatto and Windus, 1957.

Wehrs, Donald R. "Irony, Storytelling and the Conflict of Interpretation in *Clarissa*." *ELH* 53 (1986): 759–78.

Wendt, Alan. "Clarissa's Coffin." *Philological Quarterly* 39 (1960): 481–95.

Wilt, Judith. "He Could Go No Farther. A Modest Proposal about Lovelace and Clarissa." *PMLA* 92 (1977): 19–32.

Wolff, Cynthia Griffin. *Samuel Richardson and the Eighteenth-Century Puritan Character.* Hamden, CT: Archon Books, 1972.

Signet Classics proudly brings you the most compelling heroines in the Western Canon.

JANE EYRE Charlotte Brontë   526554

With this book, Brontë invented the romantic novel of passion and created one of the most unforgettable heroines of all time. Jane is a governess, an orphan, penniless and plain, but full of courage and spirit. Her employer, Mr. Rochester, is a brooding, melancholic figure, given to outbursts of temper. Their unconventional love is at the heart of this stormy and introspective novel.

WUTHERING HEIGHTS Emily Brontë   529251

There are few more convincing, less sentimental accounts of passionate love than this book. It is a novel filled with the raw beauty of the moors and an uncanny understanding of the truths about men and women.

ANNA KARENINA Leo Tolstoy   528611

Sensual, rebellious Anna renounces respectable marriage and fine position for a passionate involvement which offers a taste of freedom and a trap of destruction.

MADAME BOVARY Gustave Flaubert   528204

Dissatisfied with her lot as a simple country pharmacist's wife, Mme. Bovary longs for the thrilling world she has read about in the popular novels of her day. "Whatever thought I didn't give to pure art, to the craft itself, I have put into Mme. Bovary; and the heart I studied was my own." —Gustave Flaubert

Available wherever books are sold or at
signetclassics.com

"The greatest writer that has ever written."

—George Eliot

Jane Austen

SENSE AND SENSIBILITY   525892
Two sisters of opposing temperament share the pangs of tragic love in this dramatically human narrative. Elinor, practical and conventional, is the perfection of sense. Marianne, emotional and sentimental, is the embodiment of sensibility. To both comes the sorrow of unhappy love. Will sense give way to sensibility? Will sensibility give way to sense? Will love triumph in the end?

PRIDE AND PREJUDICE   525884
The romantic clash of two opinionated, head-strong individuals provides the plot line for this entertaining novel of matrimonial rites and rivalries. Timeless in its hilarity and honesty, it nevertheless creates a vivid portrait of the class conscious 19th century English family, with a cast of characters who live a truth beyond time.

EMMA   526279
"Emma Woodhouse, handsome, clever, and rich, with a comfortable home and happy disposition, seemed to unite some of the best blessings of existence, and had lived nearly twenty-one years in the world with very little to distress or vex her." Thus Jane Austen describes her most unforgettable character—a woman seeking her true nature and finding true love in the process.

ALSO AVAILABLE:
MANSFIELD PARK   526295
NORTHANGER ABBEY   526368
PERSUASION   526384

Available wherever books are sold or at
penguin.com